<u>Thank you all!</u>

As my first departure from the science fiction genre, I didn't get here all on my own. I had a lot of helpful people getting me to this point, and I wish to thank them for all their help in bringing my vision of Talon to life.

To my wife Theresa, thanks for being my sounding board on this one. Always supportive, and your criticisms were always constructive, and never anything but. All my love, now and forever.

To my friends Willie LoScuito & Noe Wagonner, thanks for all those late night phone calls & Skype calls. Your talents on the covers that brought my visions to life was, and is, greatly appreciated. It is truly magnificent work.

Also on the covers, many thanks to my model Aaliyah Browder, and her photographer Casey O'Neill Sweetman, for making 'Lucinda' a reality. All those conversations trying to get it just right... and you nailed most of it on the first shot. It was a pleasure indeed. When perfection happens, you don't mess with it. Thanks to all of you for being ever so much so.

I'd also like to thank all the helpful ladies at 'Junkee' Clothing. Trying to outfit a model thousands of miles away was tough enough, but you made it nearly painless. After shopping several other 'hole in the wall' shops and getting rather unhelpful attitudes to match, I expected yours to be no better. I was pleasantly surprised to find a large store, and super helpful staff. It was my first visit to your store and, that day, it was my last stop. For the future, you will be my first stop for any of my 'modeling needs'. Thanks for helping a crazy guy with a crazy request, and making a first time customer a life-long one.

Mike S? Joy M? I know you're waiting for the end of my other series, and I promise I will get it to you in time. Thanks however, regardless of series, for being some of my best fans and biggest champions.

A big thanks as always to freedigitalphotos.com for having everything I needed, exactly when I needed it. Also, to Officer Aaron Glass. Your original art was great, but unfortunately couldn't survive the special effects process. It did however provide all I worked with a 'model' for which to go by. Seeing as how I couldn't use your excellent artwork, I hope you'll find being a character in a the book a fitting substitute.

A huge thank you to Phil, and Sterlings Steakhouse, for letting me use his name and that of his restaurant in my book. Never... not once... have I ever had a bad experience in your fine establishment. This was my way of thanking you for many years of treasured memories. You will be missed Phil, but I wish you all the best on your retirement. I have no doubt that those who will follow in your footsteps, will do as fine a job as you have.

To my sister Eileen. Now you can say I based a character on you, for this time I truly did. I mixed fiction with real life and portrayed you as I have always seen you. May the fictional memories in the book, that mirrored our own, make you smile.

Lastly, to all my fans, and residents of 'Planet 51'... thank you oh so much for getting me this far.

You can see my other works... "Seven Ghosts: The BirdOfPrey Chronicles"... exclusively on Amazon. Or you can join us at www.facebook.com/BirdandLone

Talon Grayson:
Lucinda Adair, And The Making Of I.C.E
By Brian T.L. Strauss

Chapter 1

"A Will..... And A Willpower"

"You expect 'us'.... to fix THAT!?" Grant told Talon in disbelief as he pointed to the wreck in front of them.

"Why not? Best contractor west of the Mississippi... isn't that what it says on your business card?" Talon kindly taunted his younger brother.

"Listen bro, this thing doesn't need a contractor... it needs a wrecking ball... and a team of bulldozers with guys in haz-mat suits."

Talon looked up at the behemoth wreck with faraway eyes, and told Grant honestly, "To tell the truth, I forgot how big this place was."

"I don't remember it at all. I also don't mind telling you I'm glad I don't. Jesus... this thing gives me the creeps. No wonder Eileen wouldn't come here."

Talon joked, "No shit!" He then imitated his sister saying, "Talon, don't do it that way!"

Grant laughed lightly and joined him.

"Grant you're doing it wrong!"

Talon quipped back, "Well sis, why don't you come over here and show us how then!?"

Grant finished the teasing with, "That's what you guys are for."

Talon calmed his laughing some saying, "Yeah sis was always quick to tell you how wrong you were doing it. She wouldn't do the manual work herself mind you..."

Grant chuckled saying, "Haha... yeah... just quick to tell us how wrong we were doing it."

The Eileen they were referring to was the oldest of 3 siblings. She was the oldest by three years. Talon was the middle child making Grant the baby by two more years after Talon. Being close in age they were typical children with each other growing up. Not so much with other children though. Those 3 were home schooled till they were 15 each. At that age, 'Papa Joe' insisted each of the children needed the contact of other kids their age and off to public school they went. Thanks to mom Diane, by the time those 3 hit school age, the only knowledge they needed was exactly what dad was sending them there for. Mom was a strong woman, but not headstrong. However, much to the children's chagrin... mom and dad were die-hard hippies. 'Electricity' along with certain other factors of life were seen as the enemy, or simply a necessary evil. As such, instead of following in mom and dad's footsteps as they had hoped... each one became the exact opposite.

Eileen was the organizer. So much so that, at 18, she left, got her own place, and took a job in the city as an office clerk. She skipped college, learned all she could... and became more than a little good at it. Now she lives on the opposite end of the country and runs her own company, going into others where payroll and HR are in shambles... fixes and trains the office staff... and moves on to the next office disaster. She also helps small businesses become bigger ones, correctly, and with little or no mistakes. It was she who set Talon up as his own boss... and Grant several years after Talon. That work was also not restricted to the USA. As such, Eileen is what most would call, well traveled.

Talon was the non ginger of the 3. Grant's hair had gone darker as he got older, but Eileen's stayed the original flame red. Talon just turned 25 a few months ago but had been silver gray since he was 21. It pissed him off at first... till he saw how much the ladies liked it. The latter was never a problem for Talon. He was close with both of his siblings but Eileen was his 'partner in crime'. She would teach him things about girls that most men never figure out... and he was only 13. By 17, he was the class hottie. He used to chuckle when the other guys would try to be what he called satellites. Those were the 'friends' who would hang near him to get girls. Talon was smart though, and never tolerated them for long.

Only one girl though ever caught his eye with any real interest. He caught hers as well. Of the three, he was the only one to marry so far. He was 21 when he did. It was Eileen who pulled him back from the brink of despair when Talon's wife, and squad, got hit by an I-E-D on her second tour. She was a field medic. Tough and brave, but kind to those around her. Smart as hell, and able to take care of herself. Both of Talon's siblings liked her, and her them. She was close with Eileen and the latter claimed her as the sister she never had. Now, sadly, Talon was a widower and he wasn't even 23 at the time.

Talon was what one would call charismatic. He and Grant were the builders in the family. Talon made his money though dismantling things. Companies who'd gone under were his stock and trade. Eileen fixed broken ones. Talon however broke down and sold off companies that went belly up. All of them were comfortably 'well off' and by their own hand as well... but Talon was the most so. By the time he was 22 he had made his first million. Then he did something that shocked even Eileen. She was the master investor of the 3. So, Talon gave her that million to invest for him. She however, turned it into 5 in two and a half years. Grant didn't have as much money as Talon but he had a bit from his own business. He would follow Talon anywhere and always looked up to him so, what was good enough for Talon was good enough for him. Eileen tripled his investment in a little over a year. Talon was also the one who financed his sister and brother when they started up their own companies. He had only two conditions in doing so... that they were keenly aware he would only do this once... and that they were NOT to pay him back.

Now, with mom's recent passing from ovarian cancer, that left all 3 alone once again. 'Papa Joe' had passed some years earlier, and while the siblings were close with each other, they were kind of estranged from their parents. All 3 grew up on a small ranch in the hills just outside of Carson and Virginia City in Nevada. They literally lived off the land as much as they could. All 3 hated it and while they understood their parents motivations, it wasn't a life for them. Now, as they got older, they were all looking back with kinder eyes and fonder memories.

That left Grant. He was a contractor by trade but, he was the guy you called in when the first guy did a shitty or dangerous job. If you had a mansion however, and needed that quality of work... the only phone that rang was Grant's. When he and Talon got together, as the saying goes... shit happened. He even called Talon in a few times on some of his tougher jobs saying there was no one else in the world he trusted more than him. Talon liked working with him too and they always got along. Talon's forte' was more street smart engineering and overall construction. Grant was the master craftsman but had the same engineering sense as his brother. Talon built it, Grant came in behind him and put in the finishing touches. He was a certified master metal worker, but could do any of the trades. Talon could as well but he was the carpenter. Also, because of what he did, he always knew where, or how, to get the parts no one else would or could. Talon once had an entire warehouse dismantled, brick by brick, so Grant could build a house for a client using 'authentic period piece bricks'. Grant laughed as he was even able to charge more for them too. In the end though, Grant delivered on his boasts and seeing that... got 7 more jobs from friends of the owners.

Of the three, Grant had the most contact with his mother.

"Ya know," he said at his mother's wake a few weeks ago, "We all bitched about growing up. Everyone cranks about school and stuff but, I'll say this... I'm glad now for how mom and dad taught us."

Both Talon and Eileen raised and clinked their glasses with Grant's saying "Yeah, me too," and "You'll get no argument from me," as they all had a drink together after mom's wake.

"I actually couldn't wait to go to school," Grant told them. "Then... I got there... and I thought I'd go out of my mind. Unlike you brother, history was not my best subject. But mom would make it fun and tell a story to make you learn. The teachers in high school however, holy shit, droll mother-fuckers just spitting out facts. Bitch all ya want about how mom and dad taught us but... because of that... I swear I knew more than the teachers did!"

"And manners! Oh don't EVEN get me started on those!" Eileen said in an exasperated tone. "Most of those skanky whores didn't even know the meaning of the word... no less have some."

Talon joked "I'll assume when you say 'skanky whores' you're not referring to just the girls?"

Eileen smirked, and answered snidely "Why dear brother... you know how much I like to be fair."

Talon just laughed.

Grant was serious and chimed in with "Yeah, we all bitched about how we were raised." He walked over to his mother's casket, raised his drink, and with a kind smile said "But looking back on it with the wisdom of age... I'm ever so glad you did."

Talon and Eileen flanked him and did the same.

"I have to admit mom... little brother here is right... thanks," Talon said.

"For what it's worth mom, I'm with them. You always said we'd be glad about it when we were older. Guess you were right on that one huh?" Eileen replied kindly.

Ten days later they were in the lawyers office for the reading of mom's will. Talon had been busy at his old home during those ten days doing what he does best... getting rid of a lifetime of junk. All the personal stuff was split up amicably but he and Grant were hoping Eileen would get the house. Talon had his own 10 acres in the area between Carson and Reno with a picture perfect view of Slide Mountain and Mt. Rose. Grant was on the California side of Tahoe but Eileen only had a nice sized apartment in upstate New York. Having sis possibly move in so close was sitting all sorts of okay with him. Teasingly, but lovingly, Grant said if she would move home, and Talon helped, they would build her a house befitting her 'beauty and stature'. Eileen didn't say she would... but Talon knew better because... she didn't say she wouldn't either.

"And to my three children equally," the lawyer started, "I leave the family home and property."

Talon and Grant were on it in a shot asking if he could help do the legal stuff and that each one would gladly give Eileen their share. He said it would take more time than effort but could easily be done. Eileen thanked them both with a silent nod. What came next would shock Talon and send his life on a path he couldn't fathom in a hundred lifetimes.

"And lastly, I leave to you my dearest Talon," the lawyer continued, "The old boarding house and property your father and I bought. We never did get to turn it into the bed and breakfast we planned on. I know how much you love history. So I leave it to you my dear son, to do what your father and I never got around to."

"Holy shit!" Talon blurted out. "I forgot about that place!"

"I wish I had," Eileen said with a hint of terror in her voice. "I only went there a few times. Gave me the creeps that place did."

"Uh... little help here for the baby brother perhaps?" Grant extolled.

"Sorry Grant. You were little... really little. To my knowledge you were only there once and the place really freaked me and Eileen out as kids. Mom and dad kindly never took us back there again seeing that. As I recall, last we were there, I was around 5. You were but a baby and even you didn't like the place, but you sure loved the house. Man... I totally forgot about this till just now."

"Forgot about what exactly?"

Talon thought back to an even worse memory than his childhood upbringing and told Grant "You weren't freaked out by it... but you sure freaked mom out though. You were in a stroller and in front of the place. Mom left you there for a bit to go get something from the car. Eileen and I hated that place but you... you were different. You were looking in wonder. You kept smiling, laughing, and waving... to only one upper window. We all looked and saw nothing... except you. I never saw mom scared of anything... but I did that day. She hustled us into the car, you first, and she bolted down the driveway like her life depended on it. More like all of our lives did. You were maybe 2 or 3, and mom NOR dad ever took us there again."

The lawyer pulled out the deed. He was a born and raised local. Seeing the name on the place, his face went white and he hustled the papers back into the folder he was reading from.

Now, 2 able bodied men were staring at a partially burned out hulk of a monstrosity as the Nevada wind and heat beat down on them. They had a shitload of talent, two pickup trucks, each with an arsenal of tools... and no clue where to start.

“Grant... mom and dad were 'green' before anyone knew what the term meant... fair to say?”

Grant looked at the monumental project before them and answered “Yeah, I'd say that's a fair assessment. What of it?”

“Look little brother, one of the reasons I was so successful was because of that. None of us kids were like mom and dad... and yet all of us are just like them. Any company I parted out, I always found a way to make everyone around benefit in some way. Contractors get raw materials. Classic corbels and moldings went to specialty suppliers... shit like that. I guess what I'm saying is, I made a life out of tearing stuff down. For a change, I'd like to build something up... or in this case, back up. I got enough money and contacts that I can become semi-retired.”

“Try fully retired,” Grant snorted.

“Yeah well, oh hell I dunno, creepy as this place is, I just can't bring myself to going with 'your plan'. I can afford to take the time off I'll need AND hire the best contractor around. I'd like to restore the place to her former glory.”

“Best contractor west of the Mississippi!” Grant smarted.

Talon smarted right back saying “Or... so the business card says.”

“Okay my crazy brother, say we fix her back up... THEN what?” Grant asked thinking the Nevada sun had fried his brother a little more than he'd admit.

“Well little brother... ya hafta admit... it would make a cool office.”

Grant thought a moment, then told Talon “Okay brother, I'll help you, but on one condition.”

“And that would be?”

Grant looked the place over as he spoke.

“Look at the place! You're the history buff. A place like this? This large? Way the fuck out here!? No Tal, I'm pretty damn sure this place has some history to it. If we're going to do this... and I'm going to be crazy enough to help you... then I wanna do it right. Research this place. Let's get the details and the accents just right. Let's do this for mom and dad, and you, and make this 'the' project we tell our kids about, wadda ya say?”

Talon looked kindly on his brother and told him “Mom willed it to me. I say with our combined 'willpower'... and talents... what's to stop us?”

Two men walked into a place that had been vacant for over a century... possibly more. When they'd emerge, they would start on a path that would change one brother, and a whole lot of other lives, forever.

Chapter 2

"Just What The Hell Have I Gotten Myself Into?"

"So big brother... which window was it?" Grant asked as he started unloading his truck.

Talon was doing the same and stopped a moment.

"That one up there... the one all by itself."

"Figures," Grant said with some annoyance, "The creepiest one of all." Grant looked puzzled and told his brother "Okay this is bugging me. Even dilapidated as it is... I can't help but think I've seen this place somewhere before."

"You did," Talon chuckled, "When you were two."

"No dickhead I mean recently."

Talon sneered "I'll overlook the snide comment but how about this? You've worked on a lot of old homes, and got a lot more requests to work on even more. Many of these houses were all very similar during that age. Any chance you're just merging them all together and just 'thinking' you've seen it?"

"Normally I'd agree with you, but not this time. I mean just look at it! I'm no history scholar like you are but I've seen enough old homes to know NONE of them looked like this! No Talon, this one is unique but I just can't place it."

"Heh heh, good thing for you I can," Talon boasted.

He took out his cell phone and took a picture of the front. Then he brought up one of his work programs.

"Grant check this out. You know of facial recognition software right?"

"Yeah?"

"Well, this program does the same thing but with architecture."

"Dude... I'm lucky if I can send a picture and a text at the same time," Grant chuckled as he watched his brother work his magic. "I'll say this much about ya brother... you always were good at the tech." Grant looked over his brother's shoulder and asked "So, this doo-hickey helps us how?"

Talon chuckled at his brother and explained.

"We're right about how a lot of buildings of certain periods are the same.

When I would get one to take down I used this program. It uses the same type of software, but to find matching buildings all over the states. I would contact the owners of the ones it found and ask them if they were interested in any of the features or fixtures of the one I had."

"And?"

"And... I made my first million before I was 23. Most of them were a LOT interested. I had no idea there was such a market for stuff like that... nor how much they were willing to pay for it too! I dealt fairly and was price and cost effective. Not only that, but now I got people calling me for parts I don't even have. I had wish lists a mile long pretty soon, so getting stuff sold off was never an issue. Re-builders, recyclers, or antique dealers and suppliers, I got tons of them. Trust me little brother, if it's parts we need, or period piece supplies, I either already have it in one of my warehouses, or I know where I can get it."

The program stopped scanning and said it found a match.

"That's it! THAT'S where I recognize this place from... it's Halcyon Hall!" Grant exclaimed with a touch of vindication. He looked at Talon and told him "That place was a wreck, and I mean a wreck. It was an old hotel in New York not far from where Eileen is now. It failed as a hotel and was sold to a rich lady who turned it into a college for women. It went bust in the 70's and closed it's doors. For some damn reason, they never turned the water off. Bad winter, no heat, super cold... pipes burst... I think you can figure out the rest."

Talon looked at the result on his phone and said "You're right. How'd you know about this?"

"It was bought and sold a few times over the decades. Last owners called me to see what I could do with the place and if a restoration was even feasible." Grant told his brother seriously "Bro listen, I wanted that job real bad. I low balled the bid big time just to get it. Restore that behemoth, and do you know what that would do for my reputation!?"

Seeing and hearing his brother's wisdom, Talon told him "I do indeed brother. I take it you didn't get it? The bid I mean."

"Nah, the guy in charge called me personally though. Seems I was the lowest bid but even mine was too high. Shame too, I saw pictures of it in its heyday and I would have spent months if not years on it. Truly classic and beautiful it was. What a waste that was... truly sad."

Talon was looking over the results, and the history, and came up with a conclusion. It was also one he wasn't happy about.

"Okay Grant, it says here this hall was built in 1893."

"Yeah so?"

"Soooo... that means when it opened its doors. Back in those days, a construction of this magnitude would have taken nearly a decade. That puts us 10 years earlier on a good day. I agree this place, big as it is, is a smaller version of that one. What are you willing to bet the same guy who designed this," Talon said pointing to his phone, "... also designed this!?" and he pointed to the house.

Grant had a light bulb moment and said "Okay I get ya now. This architect ain't gonna get a job like Halcyon unless he already has some street cred. That means 'our' place was a major undertaking at the time and was the jumping point to get him the bigger version... right?"

Talon replied "Yep. Now, this place isn't far from the Comstock. Now, if I time this right, then we got a bit of a mystery on our hands."

Grant chuckled and asked nicely "A little help for the historically challenged please?"

"Well, you know what the Comstock was right?"

Grant was a little insulted and said "Big silver mine... put this place on the map... duuuuh."

Talon continued "Right. Now... gold rush in California was 1849. Silver here comes into play 10 years later in 1859. It lasted till around 1874 in the boom days, and until the 1920's on a small scale thereafter. That means trouble."

"How come?"

"Pre civil war. Info is hard to come by from that era, well, accurate info anyway. That also means this house has a fixed window of construction. Now, you have everyone from the hob knobs to the panhandlers floating about. Boarding houses would have been built in Virginia City or really close by." Talon turned to his brother and said "You're the master contractor. Look at this place and imagine it in its prime. Think anyone is gonna wanna board out here? Even in a place as fine as that? Even if they did it would take some serious bank to do it. Back in the day it would've been a one hour ride at least to VC from out here and that was in good weather."

Grant was still a tad clueless so Talon laid it out for him.

"Bro think. Super fine mini fortress on the outskirts of the locals prying eyes and gossiping tongues. Not to mention, out of reach of the long arm of the law... where, shall we say... refined gentlemen of the day could find a certain 'entertainment'." Talon looked down at his brother from the back of his truck asking "And... you're smiling why?"

"So... it's a whore house! Actually? That's pretty cool. Helps us out too!"

"How do you figure?"

"Well..." Grant began, "... if it was this super fine mega-mansion back in the day, then there HAS to be some history on it."

"History that was covered up or buried... and spoken of only in hushed whispers," Talon reminded. "We'll get stats on the place very likely. Unlikely however we'll get any real truth or history."

Grant laughed and said "I believe you meant to 'you will'... not 'we will'... you're doing the history part remember?"

"Yeah yeah. Tell ya what, head inside and start running the extension cords. I'll get the generator setup out here while you do."

Grant hoisted some cables over his shoulder and called back "Yeah... I'm already on it!"

Talon laughed and said "Try not to fall into the hole in the floor... you know... like you did before?"

"Brother?... Bite me," and Grant headed inside.

He was laying cords about when a breeze crossed his bare neck.

"...... 'Brothel' ginjuh chyld... naht 'hawhouse'," a whispering voice said softly in a kind but corrective manner.

That voice not only had a Cajun accent... it was also female.

Grant bolted outside and hollered at Talon "So, this is how it's gonna be!? This place is creepy enough without your stupid jokes!"

Talon stood up utterly clueless.

"I have no idea what the fuck you're talking about bro."

Grant was still a tad pissed and said "Yeah... whatever!" and walked back inside.

He looked up to the ceiling suddenly as he could have swore he heard a soft giggle... right before he heard an upstairs door shut.

Talon looked up at the house as he fired up the generator. The window Grant so loved as a child was the only one left intact. It had a curtain pulled back on either side. He looked away for a moment as he sneezed from the blowing dust. When he looked back... the curtain was shut.

Talon took in the whole of it, shook his head, and said to himself "Sweet Jesus... what the hell have I gotten myself into?" and walked inside to get started with Grant.

Halfway across the country, in a no name town just outside of Nashville, a young woman woke from a nap in near terror. She was all alone in a nondescript 1 bedroom rental house, set back from a road that barely saw traffic once a week... and that was just the way she wanted it.

She pulled herself into a fetal ball, crying hysterically, and began to rock saying in a mild panic "Not again... dear God please... not again!"

It took a few moments but she finally calmed herself. When she did, she felt drawn to a western facing window. She just stared out it but was truly staring to some far off place. The stray dog she took in for company came up and nuzzled her seeing her upset. That broke her concentration.

She leaned down and pet him kindly saying "They have no idea what they've woken up buddy... whoever 'they' are that is. Sadly, I do..." and she stared out the window once more, "... all too well," she finished as she headed off to the kitchen.

The dog was still hovering around her as she sat down with a fresh cup of herbal tea.

"At least THIS time," she said as she spoke to the dog, "The gray haired one is kinda handsome."

Chapter 3

"Documentation"

"Oh Jesus Christ... this is hopeless!" Grant complained. "Face it Tal, the only way we're going to get this right is obviously not the way we've been doing it."

"Dammit! You know how much I hate admitting defeat but, I agree." Talon leaned back a moment, then said "I need a drink... and a re-think. C'mon baby brother let's get out of this hole before we become ghosts in this place ourselves."

"Now THAT'S a plan I'm down with!" Grant agreed.

Both men crawled and climbed out of the half stone basement and got back up to the front by the trucks. Talon grabbed a beer from a cooler and tossed it to his brother. Grabbing one himself he began to think aloud.

"Okay, first things first... we need a better plan."

"Agreed," Grant told him. "We have to shore up that stone foundation. I know it, and you know it. We can't do anything topside till we take care of that first. If we don't, and that section collapses... it's game over."

Talon looked at it in the setting sun and said "Yeah, you're right. By my general calculation... if that goes... the whole house will flat pack itself tighter than a box from Ikea."

"No shit. They likely used mule teams or teams of horses to put those boulders in place. They had the benefit of open ground and sky, but we have the whole side of the house to contend with that they didn't. That leaning wall is beyond dangerous but all our temporary beams won't hold the weight."

Talon was annoyed and blurted "Those were 80 ton jack posts! NO WAY they should have fallen down! Yet time after time not one held. It was more like someone knocked them over." Talon chuckled and teased Grant saying "Hey I know... maybe it was your ghost lady friend! Maybe if we ask her real nice she won't..."

"Bro?... Fuck off."

Talon just laughed.

Grant looked at the house and muttered to himself "I'll say this much... ghost lady had one hell of a sexy voice."

Both men drank in silence for a bit with each man deep in thought. Talon was about six foot two, and about 195 pounds. Grant was six foot even and a little stockier at around 215. Both men felt, at first, they had enough bulk to get the shoring beams in so they could fix the stone basement walls. Both were wrong. Talon was right in one respect though. Three days of work on just this one item, and each time they came back, the support poles were laying on the ground as if someone had deliberately knocked them over.

Like the real Halcyon Hall, this house was set half upon a high dirt hill. The other half had a stone foundation that butted up to the hill, keeping the house supported and level. Two of the three walls though were leaning not only dangerously, but, in opposite directions.

"C'mon," Talon told Grant as he headed inside. He stopped just inside the double door entrance and called out "Okay house listen up! Me and my brother here will fix you up to your former glory. Work with us, and you will be glorious again. Fight us however... and I swear to God... I will finish the job mother nature never seemed to do!" and Talon walked out of the house with his brother on his heels laughing at his audacious older sibling.

"Feel better?" Grant laughed.

With a grand and sinister smile, Talon told him "I do indeed."

"Okay Grant, here's the deal. You tease me. What's your favorite reminder... 'more money than God' I believe?"

Grant chuckled and said "Yeah, that's the one. Look Tal, I'm only giving ya shit. You know I'm happy for ya if you could pull that off... right?"

"Oh I know. Thing is though, I think it's time I use it. I agree we need more muscle than just you and me... so I'm gonna get it. Let's pack up here for now. Give me a day or two to make some calls... and about 2 weeks to get in some resources."

"Okay, and then what?" Grant asked as he started up his truck.

Talon was getting in his and said "Then, I'm gonna deliver on my promise. HEY GHOST LADY!" Talon called out leaning out of his open window. "Try not to wreck the place till I get back!"

Teasing his brother, Grant pretended to hear something.

"Ha ha ha... she says... 'or'?"

Talon looked up at what the 2 men now refer to as 'the window', and got downright evil.

"Or... you'll see how well I keep my word," and both men drove off.

"Aww, don't be sad buddy," the dark chestnut haired young woman said to the sad dog laying on the floor. "I'm sure someone will take over here and play with you lots and lots," She told him as she finished packing up.

She had a high sitting backpack that she was zippering up. It was the serious kind that hard core hikers use. She kept her life light and, to a degree, ready to go at a moment's notice. All set to go, she hoisted the pack on her back, and looked over her shoulder at her 4 legged friend on the floor.

"It's been fun pal. Now.... be a good doggy, okay?"

The dog looked up from the floor, wagged his tail, and woofed. She checked her straps and looked back to the floor. She smiled slightly.

"That's a good boy," she said kindly.

She said that because... there was nothing but bare floor... as she walked out the door leaving the keys in the mailbox.

The setting sun saw a nice looking dark brunette lady sticking her thumb out as she walked backwards along the side of the westbound road.

"Thanks Mike. What do you think... 5 days?" Talon asked the guy on the phone. "Okay great, that'll give me time to do my usual investigation," He said as he paced about his place. "What? Oh yeah... but this one is different... I'm keeping this one. Thing is, this monstrosity seems to have a bit of local history to it. Anyway, call me when you're a few hours out and I'll make sure I keep the front door open for ya!" Talon chuckled. "Okay buddy thanks again... see ya then!" and he hung up the phone. Talon smirked at the phone in his hand and finished quoting an old song saying "Sakes alive, looks like we got us a convoy!"

Talon walked into his office, and set about solving a riddle wrapped in an enigma. He had a huge wall he used like the police use when solving a murder. It was loaded with pictures and stat sheets from different jobs both old and new. He ripped it all down and started fresh. What Talon didn't know now was... a murder was exactly what he was going to solve... and get assistance he couldn't imagine to help him do it.

"Okay, lets start from the air. Google!? Here I come!"

He brought up a satellite image of his legacy on the computer. Something caught his eye, and he set his printer to poster mode. He had a picture printed of the house that took a whole ream of paper. It was the house in the center, and 3 miles in any direction and it was 7 feet tall by ten wide.

He sat back in his chair and stared at it once he put the last piece in place. He was staring at it when something caught his eye yet again.

"What the fuck!?" he exclaimed as he grabbed a magnifying glass.

He got close and looked at the front of the house where he and Grant usually park their trucks.

"Okay... where the hell did you come from?" he asked himself honestly.

What Talon saw was the front of the house. Under the magnifying glass, he saw an old stagecoach sitting 10 feet from the front door. Thing was though... it was in pristine condition. No horses either, just the stagecoach. What he didn't notice however, was that the stagecoach was on the picture on the wall... but not the one on the computer.

Talon promised his brother he would research this place. This was something that he did for any job he took. Talon loved the history of it. History was a serious passion of his. He loved figuring out what things were like back when his 'job' was built. Part of that love of history extended to transportation as well. His dream cars were a '71 Dodge Hemi Cuda... and a 1979 Lamborghini Countach LP500S... and he had 1 of each in his garage. The Cuda was dad's, and Talon spent 30 grand having it restored. He never even blinked when he signed the check and paid the shop that restored it. The 'Lambo' as he called it, was an auction baby. He was damn proud of himself too for paying only a third of its worth at the time. For vacation he would take the Cuda, and travel the old Route 66. He would spend a week or two just driving, checking out some of the local forgotten history, and just de-stress.

"Dude... what do you got against Disneyland?" Grant would tease him.

Eileen got her license first. She would take Talon in dad's car and they would spend many an afternoon just getting lost on purpose. Talon treasured those times and memories. When he got the Lambo... Eileen was the first person he called AND... he refused to take it out till she could fly in on vacation and give him the chance to return the favor. She was thrilled when he even let her drive it.

"Talon... this thing costs more than I make in 3 years. What if something happens?" she asked nervously.

He couldn't have cared less and teased "Well then... I suggest you don't let anything 'happen'."

"Oh yeah... YOU'RE a big help!"

Talon just laughed.

Now Talon was looking for two things. He wanted the topological because the house had no power. He needed to find the closest power poles, then calculate how much cable he'd need to tap into it, and get it over to the house. He laughed at the 'estimate' the power company gave him for the job.

"That's okay I'll run it myself," he snorted, "How much just to tie it in?"

The price for that was far more to his liking.

"If those overpriced morons think they're going to clutter up my landscape with their ugly ass poles, they got another thing coming," Talon said to the now dead phone call.

Second thing he was looking for was the 'what am I not seeing?' factor. Every job he took had history. Modern housing and streets and such often weren't around when his jobs were built. Knowing the layout of 'then', more times than not, helped him in the 'now'. Talon absolutely loved being a history detective, and took that role very seriously. When a show by the same name came on PBS... he recorded every episode.

"Okay... what do we have here?" Talon mused as he looked over the aerial layout.

Talon took a highlighter marker and dotted what he found.

"No way that's natural... not all of it anyway. So the question is... what are you for?"

It was a warm early May day. This time of year it was nicely warm, not the brutal hot that was to come in the next two months. As such, Talon had his windows open. In the distance, almost on cue, came a train whistle. That one noise set the discoveries coming like a flood.

"Oh no way!" he exclaimed with glee. "Damn, Ghost lady..." he said as he plopped into his chair, "...that must have been some operation you had there!"

He turned to his computer, and shifted the view he was looking at a mile or two over... and smiled.

"No way you had one of those for just the locals. No wonder this place was over the top. Okay, but you still would have catered to those too... sooooo... let's see, where did they come in?"

Talon smiled, and pulled the marker out again. When he was done, there was a layout on paper that, in real life, hadn't been seen in centuries. Talon got his phone out and called Mike again.

"Hey Mike? It's Talon again. Yeah, I'm gonna need a couple of extra things," and he told him what he wanted from his warehouses. "Oh and one last thing... I want Al in the lead on this one. Only one I trust with this is Al."

Mike told him he'd get it done. Minutes later, an old Dodge muscle car was cruising north and on its way to the next stop in the puzzle. Back on the wall in the house, the picture still showed the stagecoach out front. Difference now was... its doors were open.

The brown haired girl was never 'well off'. Her life was more like 'unwell off'. Money for her was always limited but she was never wasteful with it when she had it. That now was evident as she stowed her backpack in the overhead rack of a Greyhound bus bound for Denver.

"Mayke haste chyyyld... mayke haste!" the southern accented voice whispered to her.

"I would if I could. Ya know, instead of bitching at me for it, why don't you help!? Oh waaaait... that's right.... you can't. Trust me lady," she told the voice with a high degree of annoyance, "You're lucky I'm going at all."

The lady in front of her asked "I'm sorry dear, were you talking to me?"

Kindly the brown haired girl said "No ma'am sorry, I was just talking to myself." She looked out the window, muttered to herself, and added "Myself... and the ghosts of Christmas past that is."

Talon ran into brick wall after brick wall. More like stonewall. He was a fairly prominent citizen but he never bothered with that. He was always getting requests from the Democratic society or the Republican party to either run for office, or support someone who was. Politics was not Talon's forte and he avoided it wherever and whenever he could. What had Talon very curious was his house... there were no records. Like, none at all. Add to that, he noticed how he was being treated. He went to two different historical societies. One in Reno and the other in Carson. He knew from experience people like them don't get a lot of attention. As such, when someone shows an actual interest, that person usually gets a plethora of information. Talon noticed however, these people seemed to be walking a fine line around him. They appeared to be trying to be helpful and polite to a prominent citizen... but as Talon put it... still not tell him shit. Even his own research turned up nothing. It was as if whatever this house was or did, some person... or persons... removed those records deliberately.

"Well Mr. Grayson," Talon chuckled to himself, "Like they always say... if ya can't go through the front door... ya go sneak around the back!" He further laughed and mused to himself as he fired up the throaty dual exhausts, "Always wondered who 'they' were anyway."

Within minutes, he had CCR cranked up on the stereo... the same one he listened to with Eileen when they would 'get lost'... and cruised the Cuda southbound for Virginia City.

VC was always an interesting place for Talon. Many places would replicate the old west. This city actually was. It was Talon's favorite place growing up. Even today, the people who dress up for the tourists, do so in authentic, centuries old, clothing. Not to mention no one gets out of hand, as all the six-shooters floating around are loaded... and just as real as the costumes.

"Mister Grayson! My Lord look at you! All grown up I see," the elderly lady said as she handed him a ticket. "Shame about your mother. All my condolences... she was a fine woman."

"Thank you Miss Betsy. Yeah, it has been awhile huh?" he told the white haired lady at the train station.

"And your wife. My condolences for her as well. If ya still speak to her family, tell them I said thanks for her service... and sacrifice."

Talon hadn't seen this woman for about 6 or 7 years, and was a bit shocked to still see her here. How she knew of his family though, was no shock at all... and it made him smile. It was the very reason he came here.

"I do on occasion. I'll give them your thanks for sure next time I do."

"And what of you? Never re-married?" Betsy asked kindly.

"Oh now Miss Betsy... you know I'm waiting for you to become available," Talon teased kindly.

"Oh you," she laughed. "Still the smooth talking, good looking, tall drink of water you are. Aaaaaahhhhh... If only I were about 150 years younger," she chuckled.

"Oh now... what's a century or two between friends hmm?"

"Ha ha ha... get out of here ya silver haired flirt before I adopt you or something," Betsy laughed calling him on it. "Mr. Grayson?"

"Oh Betsy... I will always be Talon to you... and yes?"

"Enjoy your ride... and don't be such a stranger... okay?"

"I will my dear... on both counts."

Talon took his ticket and turned to go, but stopped and turned around.

"Hey Betsy, do you know the mansion my mom and dad bought years ago? It's about ten miles east of here."

Betsy told him "Yeah I know it."

"Anything you can tell me about it?"

Betsy answered "Rumors really. You're a big boy now, so I can tell you it was said it was a house of ill repute."

"Yeah I already figured out that much. Anything 'else' you can tell me about it perhaps?" Talon asked in a tone that implied he knew she could.

Betsy looked like bringing up that info was a tad hard due to the lapses of age.

"Rumor has it, it wasn't just a whore house... it was THE whorehouse. Seems it catered to the well to do. Back then Talon women didn't own property. Not that they couldn't... it's just that few did. Rumors tell this one was owned AND run by a rather fancy one. More than that I don't know."

"Oh Betsy, I'm not a young man anymore... nor a little boy. You and I both know that isn't true. I know for a fact you won the blue ribbon for gossip 5 years running. What is it you're NOT telling me?"

Betsy looked around a few times, closed the door behind the counter, and waved Talon over.

"Just rumor and conjecture mind you but... back in the day... I told you it was 'the' social house. I'm talking like senators, congressmen, rumor even has it some men of the cloth as well."

"Keep going," Talon almost commanded.

"Well... seems she was not only feared... but honestly loved and respected too. One day she was found in her room, and horribly burned. It was thought a jealous lover had done it. It was said, for the day, her death was investigated no less than the President's would be. It was even rumored the very same visited her once or twice. It was rumored a local prominent... and married... doctor did it. It ruined him and his reputation never recovered. Years later he was found dead under what was described as mysterious circumstances. Turns out, you're not the only one who's asked me about that old place."

"Oh?" Talon said with honest surprise.

"Mm hmm... seems his great great grandson lives in town. Doctor too. I got the impression from him he didn't believe his great grandfather did it... and was trying to clear his name." Betsy crossed her arms over her chest, and leaned back saying "Or... so I heard tell."

Talon took her hand and kissed the back of it.

"Thank you," he said softly. "Why yes ma'am! I will enjoy my ride! Thank you!" Talon said loudly and with a wink as Betsy opened the door again.

He grabbed a map that showed the rail lines from back in Virginia City's heyday, paid for it with a smile, and got on the train.

Talon had taken this ride over 100 times in his youth. He was in the caboose. He knew this ride like the back of his hand, and walked outside at just the right time.

"Jeez, first Betsy, and now you Jim? Does this place ever change?" Talon asked jovially when he saw the tail of the train wasn't as empty as he'd hoped.

"Talon my boy! Its been ages!" Jim told him. "Well young man, ya can't have a city about history, without a bit of history to run it now can ya!?"

"No I suppose not. Good to see you too Jim."

Jim pushed him to the side and away from the door.

"Now you know you're not supposed to be back here. Seeing as how it's you and all though... wellll... just don't let the rest of the folk see ya okay?"

With a kind smile, Talon said "See what?"

With a wink, Jim said "Exactly." He checked the train car quick then asked "What are ya do'in back here anyway?"

"Just here to take a few pictures if you don't mind."

"Oh sure... I don't mind. What do ya want pictures of old steam rails for anyway?" Jim asked not fathoming why anyone would.

"Just a project I'm working on. Tell me Jim, this train still make the mock water stop?"

"Sure does, why?"

"And does the next train still come by an hour later?" Talon asked with a sly and sneaky tone.

"Yep."

"And can I assume you'll be in the same spot when it does?"

"Sure will be," Jim said warily.

"So Jim, if someone was to say, get off there and explore then, hop back on the next train..." and Talon handed him a $20 as he spoke and finished with "... might it be said you wouldn't notice it?"

Jim smiled but kept his hand out. Talon laughed and handed him another $20. Jim smiled, put it away in his pocket, and handed Talon a canteen of water.

"Notice what exactly?" Jim said with a wink... then headed inside.

Jim kept his word, and Talon hopped off as he planned. He ducked around and hid behind a small mound and waited for the train to leave. It was an authentic old steam train for tourists. What had Talon riding it today was... it still used original tracks.

Nevada, like many western states, had an open carry law. Talon used to work in the city as a summer job. He had hopped off at this spot before. Back in high school, it was his little spot for stealing a kiss... or more... with the girlfriend of the day. One time though, his fun got ruined suddenly by a visit from a copper-head. He spent his whole next paycheck on a holster and a wheel gun to put in it. He kept the .45 at home under lock and key and never wore it... except when he came here. The train was a good distance away when Jim heard a single shot ring out.

"Ha ha ha ha! Still not a fan of them snakes are ya sonny!?" the old man bellowed to the open air.

Talon was not only tech savvy, he was a smart man in general. He knew enough to turn the geo-tagger option on his phone off. Now, out here in the middle of nowhere, he turned it back on. Now, every picture he took had a latitude and longitude on it.

"Well... if I can't get any real documentation on the place... heh heh, a picture is worth a thousand words right?"

He climbed a hill and got cell service. Then he brought up the maps of where he was in relation to the mansion.

"Okay then, we need to get from here to there. So, that means... if I'm right... there should be a switch around there somewhere," he said looking at a spot on the map.

Talon took a swig from the canteen, capped it, and headed down the tracks taking pictures as he went.

He got about a mile and a half down the track and got pissed off. No switch anywhere.

"Dammit, I thought for SURE you'd be around here somewhere!"

Suddenly, something spooked him from the corner of his eye. He turned and saw nothing but swore someone had just walked past him about ten feet away and... right on the tracks.

"Jesus... now you're getting spooked!" he said reprimanding himself.

Then he laughed and decided to play along.

"Okay ghost lady... what am I missing?"

A super soft breeze blew past the back of his neck. Talon then got truly spooked when a soft Creole voice said something even softer in his ear. Talon recoiled... spooked... and looked around hard.

The voice said only one word.

"........ Syze......" said the southern accent.

Talon never believed in ghosts. He didn't disbelieve in the them either. He really had no opinion either way. Now however, he was questioning a lot of things and, in a hurry. His mother was the one into the mystical and 'spiritual energies', not him. He always laughed at her and called her a hippie.

Mom would just smile, or curtsy playfully, and say "And damn proud of it too!"

Now he was thinking how he wished he'd maybe paid a little more attention.

Talon composed himself finally and decided he was okay so... let's see what's up.

"Okay ghost lady... we'll play it your way. I swear though, you EVER spook me like that again, and the next shot won't be for the snake... you understand me lady!?"

He got no answer.

"Thank you," he told the open air.

He also said it... putting his gun back in his holster.

Talon looked around and said "Well, a promise is a promise. Now, what size?"

He looked at the mounds on the sides. He looked down, then up the tracks, but nothing caught his eye.

That's when he figured "Oh what the hell." He looked around and said "Okay lady... a lil help here?"

Talon laughed at himself. Next he jumped out of reflex and fear. He heard the unmistakable sound of a train track switch... shifting. He jumped to the side of the tracks pulling his feet high as he did. Then he realized... he was on a straight piece of track.

"WHAT did I tell you!?" he shouted clearly spooked and more than a tad pissed off.

Then he heard the switch again.

"Alright lady, I will NOT be beaten. What are you trying to tell me?" Talon said playing along for now.

He looked around and spoke to himself.

"Okay... switch... and size... what the hell are you..." and Talon hung his head. "Oh I'm such an idiot!" and he ran up the hill behind him.

He looked down the track, then up.

"Hmm, lets see.... 4....5... okay, up the track all the same size sections." then he looked the opposite way and said "Same in the opposite direction. All the same size... all except heeeeere," Talon said with a triumphant grin. "25 foot sections up and down," and Talon looked down the hill saying "All but you my friend. You're maybe 15 feet tops!"

Talon could see from the top of the hill, that the one section of straight track he was standing by was once something else... and replaced. Talon took a few pictures, then heard the train whistle. He ran fast to get to a curve in the track where he knew the train would slow down enough for him to hop back on.

"Well son, did ya get what ya needed?" Jim asked as Talon hopped back on the caboose.

"Nope... but I did get more than I bargained for."

Talon looked back, and threw a sincere but friendly salute to his mysterious assistant.

Chapter 4

"A House Call... A Politician... And A Printer"

Talon did not sleep well that night. Not well at all. He finally gave up and made himself a coffee.

"STOP it you asshole! What the fuck are you doing!?" he said chastising himself. "It wasn't real... it COULDN'T be real...............……........ could it?"

He was chastising himself because, he'd caught himself talking to 'ghost lady'. He had perhaps the best history puzzle yet, and took to talking to the mysterious lady more and more, and had no idea why. One thing he avoided though... flat out avoided... was the poster he had on his office wall. He had enough of a spook fest for one day. That poster though had his imagination on overdrive, and not in a good way. He was also doing something else he never did before, ever. He was walking around his own house... with his holster on his hip or over his shoulder.

"Great... just greeeeeaaaaatttt," Talon scorned seeing the sun come up as he drank his coffee.

Two hours later, he was back at the mansion. Grant hadn't arrived yet. He was waiting on him when he saw the dust come over the hill.

"Okaaaaaayyyy... you're not Grant," Talon said softly and curiously seeing a car, not a truck, pull up and park by his.

"Good morning!" the gentleman said getting out. "Would you be Talon Grayson?" the man asked.

"A little early for a house call ain't it Doc?" Talon chuckled from the front covered porch.

"How'd you know I was a doctor? Have we met somewhere before?"

Talon motioned, cup in hand, to the man's car and chuckled saying "Says so on your plates."

"Heh heh, yeah okay, ya got me there," the doctor said walking up and sticking out his hand. "Doc Holliday, Mr. Grayson... pleased to meet you."

Talon shook his back but never got out of his chair.

"You're joking right?"

"What, about the name?"

"No Doc, the two wheel drive BMW over there in a 4 wheel drive front yard... YES the name," Talon smarted.

The young man told him "Actually no. My mother divorced my father when I was very little. He was an ass, so I took my mother's maiden name. The patients love it and, well, with a name like that, it's kind of fun."

"Hmm, I guess. Well doc, ya got a first name? And I warn you... if you say John Henry... and that you're a dentist.... I WILL laugh at you," Talon joked.

"A student of history I see?" the doc said pleasantly surprised. "And no. The name is Cody. As for the doctor bit, I'm a general practitioner for now but I used to be a surgeon."

"Doc, you're roughly my age. Surgeon? What... did you start medical school when you were like 12 or something?" Talon asked.

"Thank you," Cody said cheerily at the young reference. "Baby face. Runs in the family. To answer your question, I'm actually 35."

"Nice genes ya got there doc," Talon chuckled as he sipped his coffee.

"Yeah well, aside from the girls in high school not wanting to date 'some kid'... it's had its advantages."

Talon sized Cody up. He was about an inch shorter than he was and about the same weight. He was in good shape and Talon could tell this guy went to the gym like most people went to church. Dirty blond hair and brown eyes framed a face that seemed to be hiding something.

"Well Doc, you likely trashed that fancy suspension of yours getting out here. Gotta be a reason. Care to share?" Talon queried.

"My reasons are personal. Suffice to say, county records show you to be the new owner. Mind if I ask what you plan to do with it?"

"Not at all. I plan on knocking this eyesore down and putting up a strip mall. Tell ya what, seeing as how you were all friendly and such, heh heh, I'll save you the space on the end."

Talon was only teasing but Doc didn't know that. That news also didn't sit well with him.

"Well then, if that's the case... care to sell it?"

"What does an old saw bones like you want with a wreck like this?"

"Like I said, it's personal. Suffice to say I would seriously make it worth you're while."

"Sorry Doc, she's not for sale. Tell me something. What kind of personal are we talk'in about here? This is where I lost my virginity kind of personal?" Talon then stared straight in his face and asked "Or clear my family name kind of personal?"

Cody was still friendly but got just as serious as Talon.

"Looks like I'm not the only one doing a little research huh?"

"Doctor Holliday? Let's just say recent events have caused me to do a little more than I first planned on."

Cody was still thinking Talon was going to raze the place.

"Mind if I call you Talon?"

"Sure thing Doc," Talon said with a true friendly tone.

"If you know why I'm here then you know why I want to buy the place. Mind at least, telling me, why you won't sell?"

"Ha ha ha... chill Doc... I was only teasing about knocking her down. My brother and I are planning on restoring the place."

Cody felt a year's worth of anxiety just drain out of his body.

Talon asked him "You got history on this place don't you?"

"On it... and with it. Sadly though, neither of which is in large quantities."

Then Doc said something that threw Talon a bit off.

"Tell me something Talon... do you believe in ghosts?"

Talon told him "I'm not a believer nor disbeliever. Recent events however have been causing me to re-think that."

"Things going bump in the night are they?" Doc teased.

"More like falling down, when it should take a crane the size of this house just to budge them."

"You mind?" Doc asked pulling out a pipe.

Talon waved a hand and replied "Spark it up Doc, I don't mind at all."

Cody got serious and walked to the open front door.

"Likely?... You're about to."

He walked up to the open front door, and blew a huge puff of smoke into the parlor beyond. Talon got up out of his chair in a hurry when he saw the smoke stop at the threshold and go no further. Talon had a reaction Cody didn't expect. He loved it, he just didn't expect it.

"Dammit ghost lady!! These little parlor tricks of yours aren't scaring me... NOT anymore. Now? They're just PISSING ME OFF!!" Talon hollered in anger.

Doc had a touch of sadness in his tone and said "If that pisses you off, imagine being me... and having this happen."

Cody walked to the front door... and it acted as if it was slammed shut from the inside.

"See?" Cody said in a tone that implied he was used to that and, had seen it happen before.

Talon was near livid now. Broad daylight and now this was twice in just as many days.

"Doc? Back up please. I wanna try something."

Cody backed away and Talon walked in like nothing was wrong.

"Let's see if this shit works on phantoms like it does vampires. Doc? My

name is Talon Grayson... LEGAL title holder of this not so fine establishment."
With anger in his tone, though not at the Doc, Talon stuck out his arm and said
"I hereby welcome you to MY home." He looked toward the ceiling and
hollered upward "WITH MY PERMISSION!... You may enter at any time and
stay as long as you like."

Talon had no idea why he did that. He only knew it made him feel better.
He was truly and utterly tired of having his chained yanked. If he was only
going to get whispers and vague hints, then he was going to at least show who
was in charge.

Cody expected only the same. He ended up getting nothing of what he
expected. Talon neither. Cody walked in again only this time... the door never
moved. Cody was beaming at the fact he was standing inside... actually inside...
for the first time since he started his quest.

"Huh, would ya look at that!" Talon said in happy shock.

Cody said in the most sincerest of tones "Thank you."

He blew another puff of smoke... and all hell broke loose.

"What the...?" Talon said as he watched.

The smoke blew outward like it should have. As it did though it
coalesced into two outstretched arms... heading right for Doc. It formed into an
upper torso of a man in an old rancher or duster like coat. Old west hat and face
all blurred, 'he' howled in anger and disgust.

"nnnnnNOT YOU... and NOT HERE!!!" the ghostly voiced wailed as
Cody and Talon got nearly thrown out the front door.

Tossed like a couple of drunks in an old west movie, both men saw the
door slam shut again. Talon felt cold, and felt like he'd never forget that voice as
long as he lived. To him, it was part man, part cement mixer, and just a touch of
reverb.

Talon was getting up and heading back for the door. Now he was done...
fully and utterly.

"Talon wait. It's me they don't like. You just... got in the way."

"DOC!?? You're awful fucking calm for someone who just got
steamrolled out a door by a FUCKING PUFF OF SMOKE!" Talon seethed.

Calmly, Cody said "Perhaps because I've had a longer time to get used to
it. You see Talon, truth is, this isn't the first time I've been here."

"Naw... YA THINK!??"

Talon was on the porch, looked at the door, then walked out into the
open by his truck.

"I warned you not to mess with me!" he hollered up to 'the window'.
"Now you're going to find out why! I swear I will dig this place up... turn it
upside down... and expose EVERY Godddd daaaaamn secret you have! I'm

done with you... YOU HEAR ME!??.... DONE!!!"

Talon then pulled out his phone.

"Yo bro... change of plans. Where are you?"

"About to turn off the main road, why, what's up?" Grant told him.

"Head for my house. Don't ask why... just go. I'll meet you there in 30 minutes or so."

"On it!" Grant called out as he swung his truck around. "You okay Tal?"

"Not even close but... for the moment... undamaged. See you there," and Talon just hung up the call.

Next he made another call.

"AL!! Good to hear you're voice!" Cody heard Talon say. "When do you think you'll get here?" Talon paused and said "Two days? Around noon? Perfect! Thanks Al see ya then!" and Talon hung up that call as well.

Cody was sitting on the ground and Talon held out his arm and hauled the Doc up.

"I will be back in two days... TWO! Batter up lady... it's hardball time!" Talon yelled to the window. "Doc? If you had any plans today they just got canceled. My place, follow me. You're gonna tell me everything you know or so help me God I will toss you back into the arms of that shadow myself!"

Doc fired up his car, and calmly said "Lead the way."

Talon pulled out with a BMW in his rear-view mirror.

He had the radio on as he drove away. Suddenly, it went nuts. The digital display went up and down frantically like it was searching for something. It paused at different times, but Talon got the message.

"It.......(static)....... wasn't....(garble)...... me," was the message made up of different voices. Different female voices that is.

"Ghost lady? I don't fucking care.............. you got two days," and Talon and Cody turned onto the main road.

Over a thousand miles away... on a westbound bus... a young woman woke up from a nap in a sweat.

"Well Mr. gray hair, ya got balls I'll grant ya that." She looked to the empty seat next to her, and in a rather annoyed tone, said "Jesus lady, what hell are you getting me into!?"

A half burned apparition that only she could see told her in a soft and lady like southern drawl "Ah wish I knew dah'lin........... ah wish ah knew."

The brunette rubbed her eyes as she woke up and when she finished, the seat next to her was empty once more. She shifted over into that window seat, gazed out the window, and almost smiled.

"Talon Grayson huh? So... Mr. gray hair has a name after all." Now she was smiling as she finished with "Actually? I think it's kinda sexy."

Talon walked into his home with Cody on his heels. Grant was already there.

"Bro? What's going on. Are you okay?" Grant asked with a friendly hug.

"No, I'm not. Grant? Meet Doc Holliday."

"Look'in pretty svelte for a dead guy there Doc," Grant teased as he shook his hand.

"Meh... I've heard worse. A pleasure to meet you Grant," Cody replied.

"Gentlemen? My office if you please."

Grant waved a hand to Cody and said "This way Doc."

Talon told Grant everything. The train ride, the stonewalling of the town folk, the smoke monster... all of it. Talon could see Grant was not taking it very well but he was also not believing either.

"Listen little brother, I doubt I'd believe me either if I were you. So, try this one on for size. Google map the mansion on my computer."

"Listen Talon, you know I'd..."

"JUST... do it.... please."

Grant huffed but did as asked.

"Okay... same as the big one behind me... so?"

"Not exactly," Talon told him as he handed him the magnifying glass.

"HOLY SHIT!" Grant extolled as he backed up quickly.

"Told you," Talon said sadly.

Cody picked up the magnifier, and calmly asked "Okay even I'm a little spooked by this."

Talon smarted "A puff of smoke tosses you around like a rag doll... and this spooks you?"

"Hmm, point taken. Still, I wonder who those men are?"

"What men you talking bout Doc?"

Cody just smirked and handed Talon the magnifier.

"Oh THIS just keeps getting better and better!" Talon exclaimed in a clearly agitated tone.

Days ago he saw only the coach. Now he saw it, with the doors open, and 3 men in bowler hats and proper suits were heading for the front door. Each had guns on but they were high on the hip, and not the usual 'down low' gunslinger style.

"My question is... who are they?" Cody asked.

"Part of the story obviously," Talon said leaning back as he thought about it.

"Obviously," Cody retorted.

Now Talon thought out loud.

"Okay, wadda we know. Later 1800's and... waaaaait a second," and Talon looked at the men again. "Well check this out! They're heading for the front of the house... notice anything?"

Grant and Cody both looked but neither said they did.

"Look again," Talon smirked. "This is a picture... a SATELLITE picture. At most it's like 10 years old. As such the house should be the partially burned up falling down wreck we see today... but it ain't. It's burned some, but it looks like it just happened yesterday."

"You're right!" Cody said as he looked again.

"Now, they're not wearing uniforms, not military ones anyway. Federal Marshals were cowboys with a badge. Most never wore a suit as it would make them an instant target anywhere they traveled. Like now, when they did wear fancy clothes, it was usually dark suits like the feds wear to this day. Those are more like business suits. Only one group I know of that dressed like that in the western Utah territories."

"Western Utah?" Cody asked.

"Yeah Doc. Nevada wasn't a state yet and all this was considered western Utah."

"Okay Talon... so who are they?" Grant asked clearly unsettled by the morning's revelations.

"Boys? I'll bet a week's pay... those are Pinkerton men."

Cody looked at Talon and said "All I know of them is what I've seen in old westerns. Care to enlighten me with knowledge that I'm betting you just might have?"

Grant chuckled at the comment, and Talon granted the Doc's request.

"Pinkerton was the guy who built a security empire. There was nothing they wouldn't do and nowhere they wouldn't go to get their man. Take a boat to China to elude capture? I mean like literally sail to China... and those guys would be on the next boat chasing you... or on the one before you and be waiting on the dock for you to arrive. They were also the high tech outfit of the day. Kind of like a private version of the FBI. Thing was, they had an amazing track record but they didn't work cheap. If those really are Pinkerton men, then someone with deep pockets wanted to know what happened."

"So... kind of like expensive pit-bulls with badges?" Cody asked.

"More like German Shepherds but, pretty much," Talon confirmed.

Grant kicked in now, and threw out some thoughts for debate.

"Tal, let's say you're right. Didn't Betsy tell you our place was a super high end whorehouse?"

"Careful little brother... that's 'brothel'. Ha ha ha... don't want ghost lady getting pissed off at you again now do we?" Talon scolded playfully.

"Yeah yeah," Grant smirked. "Still, consider this. Ya got all the powerful men of the day coming and going. What if Pinkerton wasn't hired to find out who did it? What if they were hired to find the books I'm sure a woman like her had... and see to their removal or destruction?"

"Hmm, possible," Talon mused. "Betsy said though that she was loved by everyone too. Add to that Pinkerton's men were considered the noble guardians of the day. I get the impression she was the glue that held it all together. If she was killed in that fire, or simply out of business, the good times were over. If you're a super powerful mine owner, senator or train baron... you're not gonna stop having a good time but finding another safe haven isn't easy either. No Grant, while I can't say you're wrong, I'll bet I'm right."

"How about both?" Cody interjected.

Talon turned to Cody and said "Okay Doc. I throw a historical ghost story at you... and you don't even blink. Most people would be running away screaming by now just from the mural alone. Add to that, a puff of smoke comes to life and tosses you about the place, and aside from being caught off guard, you act like your dinner reservations got canceled. I've told you my story, Grant hasn't had but a minor brush with our house, but even he told us his story as well. I think it's time Doc, that we heard yours."

Talon sat down, Cody nodded, and told his tale.

"I was about 15 or so... and I looked like I was 10. As you can imagine, I didn't have a lot of real friends at the time. Three things always fascinated me, anatomy, science and history. I had no friends as I said and found myself with a lot of time on my hands. I was born and raised in a more affluent neighborhood of Chicago, but I was never a city boy."

"Same here," Talon said in agreement about being a city boy.

"Me too," Grant chimed in with. "Talon and I were never fans of 'how' we were raised... but we always loved 'where' we were raised."

Talon raised his glass to his brother and Grant raised his right back.

"Indeed," Cody continued. "Thing is, so did I. Every summer I would get sent to my grandparents. They actually live not far from here. Anyway, most kids that age would dread coming here for a whole summer."

Talon cut in with "Let me guess, you couldn't wait eh?"

"Each and every year," Doc confirmed. "As I was saying, I was about 15. No friends here or back east, grandma took pity on me and did her best to keep me occupied. She had a ton of shit in her attic and, well, loving history, I suggested we go through it. Most of it was just that... shit. We cleared out likely

70% of it and dove into sorting the remaining 30. That's when I found it. It was a box of old letters and some photos and things from HER grandfather. He was a doctor like me. He was almost 72 when he was diagnosed with terminal cancer. As such, he wrote down all he could about his life and gave it to his son. That child only had a daughter... my grandmother... and she took it when he died."

Cody leaned back and impersonated his grandmother.

"Oh Cody, I forgot about all this. Quite frankly when we cleaned out my father's place I always meant to go through it and see what was what. Something always came up though and, well, to be honest I forgot about it."

Grant asked "So Doc, what did ya find?"

"More than I bargained for. His letters told of his childhood. Seems his mother doted on him but was a bit overbearing as well. I got the impression she was more concerned about status and appearances, than actually being a mother. 'He' had to succeed and make something of his life. One line he wrote was that his mother said his father had made a shambles of his life, and she wouldn't let him make the same mistake. So, now with something to do, I set about finding out what happened. I was almost 17 when I met your mother," Cody told Talon.

"You met my mother? Oh THIS should be good."

"Hardly. Death already didn't bother me as it did others. One reason I became a doctor I guess. In my profession, sadly, you see more than your fair share. I think that's why the house always fascinated me, but never bothered me."

"Makes sense so far," Talon told him.

"In my career, I've lost a few patients. A lot of my colleagues have too. To me it always seemed so clinical. 'Bag em and tag em' as we say, then move on to the next person. A good and wise teacher of mine once told me 'Cody? Ya can't help the dead... only the living'. When I went to the house the first time I reacted much like you did today. I went back several times over the years. One of those times I met your mother as she caught me snooping around."

"Knowing mom she would have offered you herbal tea or some shit like that," Grant chuckled.

"Ginger... to be exact. By the way gentlemen, I know you own the place now Talon but can I assume it was an inheritance?"

"You assume correct," Talon told him.

"Then you have my true condolences. I only met her that once but she was an amazing lady. She asked me why I was there and I told her. Honestly guys... she acted more like a shaman than a hippie. No insult intended."

"Yep," Talon said with a kind smile, "That was mom alright."

"So, what did mom do?" Grant asked truly wanting to know.

"She said a spirit in pain, living or dead, is still a spirit in pain. I told her I was studying to be a doctor. She said she wouldn't call 'the fuzz' on me. I laughed at that term as I had no idea what it meant, but I got the reference. She told me she felt there were two spirits in the house... one lost... and one angry. She was there to see if she could help either of them. Or, so she said."

Cody took a sip of his coffee Talon got him, and continued.

"She said something to me I never forgot. She said if I did become a doctor, I would see just as much death as I did life. That house, to her, already had inhabitants. She told me 'Understand young man that in life and death, there are some lines you just don't cross. That said... with death already inhabiting the house, if I sorted that, perhaps it would help me later when I became a doctor'."

Recalling a fond memory, Talon told Cody "I used to tease her. I would call her the high priestess of hippie-dom. She actually relished that title." Talon set down his drink and asked "So, mom caught you. I now know why you were there but... why was she?"

Cody told him "I asked her that actually. She said she may have been a hippie, but she was a mom first and foremost. She said she recently took you kids there, but felt like the house was enticing her family somehow. She didn't say how and I didn't ask. She did say however, that she neither liked it nor trusted it, and would check the house from time to time just to be safe."

Talon told him "Doc? Thanks. That means more than you know."

The Greyhound bus pulled into Omaha. The elderly lady had made friends with the strange but nice brunette girl. They parted ways and the younger was walking away from the elder to catch the next bus to Denver. As she was walking away though, she just couldn't leave her. She dropped her shoulders, rolled her head... and turned around.

"Gloria... wait!"

"Yes dear?" the elderly lady asked as she stopped and turned back.

The brunette let out a huff, and said "Charlie asked me to give you a message. He said you have it backwards. You're worrying over nothing about which dress to wear for your birthday, and thinking the pain in your side is just old age. He said just wear the red one... and see a doctor soon."

The old lady was rattled and asked "How did you... I mean I never told you about..."

The younger lady said "I'm sorry if I upset you. It usually does which is why I rarely 'do that'. As for how, trust me, ya don't wanna know. If you did... you'd likely wish you hadn't."

The older lady just smiled, looked around, and took the young girl's hand in hers.

"Bless you child and... thank you. As for my departed husband, welllll, he always did like me in red." Gloria winked at the young lady and walked away saying "He always said it made me look sexy! Ha ha ha ha! Safe journey my dear!" and Gloria turned a corner and was gone.

The brunette shifted her backpack, and headed for her own bus. For a change, she was smiling when she did.

"Senator! Thank you for returning my call!" Talon said as he picked up his land line office phone.

"Is this line secure?" came a concerned voice.

"This one is," Talon said just as seriously. "Encrypted and digitally scrambled AND... setup by yours truly."

A much more at ease voice said "Well then, good to talk to you. What's it been... two years now?"

"Three," Talon replied as he waved Cody and Grant out of the room.

"A senator?" Cody queried.

"C'mon Doc, I'll tell you in the kitchen," Grant said as he politely hustled him out of the room.

"So, what can I do for you TG?" the senator asked.

He always called him that. Talon never knew why, nor cared.

"Listen Bob, I need to call in that favor you promised me."

A cautious "As long as it's within reason... say what you need."

"Have no fear Bob. You know me, it will be."

"I'm listening," the senator told him.

"Bob, I inherited a house. More of an old dilapidated mansion. A mansion that seems to not only have a history... but a history that's been, shall we say, 'redacted'. I'll be calling you in a day or two with a name. All I ask is that you ask your friends and see what you find. I have no doubt one of your colleagues... or their bosses... know of some file or files somewhere that will give me the history I need."

"And just what is this 'need' of yours?"

"Simple, I plan to restore to original. Any photos or drawings or any shit of that nature will help with that. My brother's company will get the feather in its cap, and I can put some ghosts that won't leave us alone to rest."

Talon chuckled at the truth of that last bit... and how the senator would have no clue.

"Can I assume you will treat it the same way as you did 3 years ago? Assuming there's anything to find mind you."

"Oh I think you'll find my talents at editing the truth are as good today as they were back then," Talon proclaimed slyly. "The public will get all that they need... and none of what they don't. Just like at the mill."

"Do that, and I'll honor your request. I have several re-election dinners and luncheons over the next month. Get me whatever you can and I'll spread the word. Tell you what. Call me when it's finished and I'll come tour the place. You give me some good PR... and I'll see to it some nice folk hear of your brother's talents."

"Ha ha ha ha... some things never change huh Bob? Senator? Ya got yourself a deal!"

Pleasant goodbyes on both ends and that call was done.

While Talon was on the phone, Grant was explaining in the kitchen.

"Listen Doc, I probably shouldn't be telling you this but, here goes. Do you know what Talon does for a living?"

"Sorry, can't say that I do."

"Well, he's a salvager basically. Folk don't like the old eyesore of a factory or mansion and such in their town. They also don't like seeing it demolished either. Talon made a name for himself by dismantling those buildings and selling off the parts. The building comes down but the town is happy their piece of history will live on somewhere."

"I've never heard of that but it's noble and makes sense. So, the senator? How does he fit in?"

Grant explained "Doc, Talon is a multimillionaire from doing that. Get into that class and you start getting the attention of those on the lower rungs of the social ladder, who are looking to climb up. Talon's star was on the rise and this job was gonna put him on the national map. There was a 100 year old mill in Kentucky owned by a prominent family."

"Let me guess... the senator's?"

"Bingo. His great grandfather had a thing for young men. He was in his 40's when the newspaper at the time reported him missing."

Doc asked "And that's relevant why?"

Grant told him "I'm getting to that. Senator Bob Harrison was a newly elected senator and this project was going to make him shine. He built his campaign on rejuvenating the rundown southern side of the city. He struck a deal with my brother... each one helps show off the other."

"And?"

"It was working. Everything was going smooth. Around 1910 or so the mill had a concrete floor poured in its basement... a rarity for buildings back then. Stone foundation, and pretty soon that's all that was left."

Doc laughed lightly saying "This isn't going to end well is it?"

"No... and yes. The local university wanted to come in and do an archaeological study to teach the students. Talon said sure and so did senator Harrison. Both thought it would be good PR for them. Talon gave them 3 days and no more. They hit the floor with ground penetrating radar... when they came across two skeletons... two male skeletons... buried under the floor."

Cody chuckled saying "There's the 'no' part."

"Indeed. Talon however took off like a shot. Ya see, the mill was still owned by the senator's family and by taking it down, he thought he'd show the townspeople not even his prominent family would get in the way of progress. Now, being the historian, and good looking brother that he is, Talon schmoozes some chick at the courthouse to let him look at records... arrest records. Talon 'accidentally' took the files... then returned them a few days later when the reporters came up empty and stopped looking. He said he accidentally mixed them up with his files. There was a big media splash and they were looking for a scandal. Talon however took the limelight... and the heat... and confidently told them even if it was Bob's missing grandfather, it was ancient history and nothing but. He also told them, if it had been a cover-up, why would either of them let them look in the first place?"

Doc asked "Kinda risky don't ya think?"

"Perhaps but Talon told me other than family ties, and ancient ones at that, the senator had nothing to do with that. The coroner told him they both died from blunt force trauma. His grandfather was found draped over the body of the younger one. Whether he crawled to him prior to death, or they were just dumped that way no one knows. That pose however, as you can imagine, got a lot of folk talking. In the end, Talon told Bob what he did, got the town re-focused on the project and current times, told them to enjoy the story but that it was only that... a story... and saved Bob's career along with his own."

"Pretty ballsy. I doubt I would have done something like that."

Grant concluded "Yeah well, Talon hates bullies. He was the guy in high school that would pounce on them in support of the one being picked on. He hates reporters and the media and sees them as nothing more than lying bullies with cameras. Ever since the mill incident he's never gone that high profile again. Before we left, Bob told Talon if he ever needed a favor to let him know. It looks like he just did."

Doc looked kindly on Grant and said "While I appreciate you trusting me with that, let me ask you something... why tell me?"

Grant laughed and told him "Doc? You don't know my brother. He's a fantastic judge of character. He's had to be with the jobs he's done. This home you're standing in? Yeah... this is his private haven. No one gets through that front door unless you're family or part of the inner sanctum of friends. Trust me Doc, if you're standing in THIS house?... Ha ha ha ha... you just got adopted!"

Doc wasn't sure what to make of that but asked "And just how big is this 'inner sanctum' of his?"

"Mr. Holliday... right now?"

"Yeah."

"One."

Both men headed back to the office hearing Talon was now off the phone. Cody though would indeed spend the rest of his life calling the brothers Grayson close and dear friends.

Back in the office, Talon went back to problem solving.

"Well Doc, how about you fill in more of those pieces of your story?"

"Wadda ya wanna know?" Cody asked.

"Your family history would be nice. How about that part where I hear tell a young doctor is going around town asking about 'my' house... but trying to clear 'his' family name?"

"Certainly," and Cody began his tale again.

He told them of how he found the letters. He said most of them had vague, yet constant reminders, of 'what happened' and how he wasn't to make the same mistake. Seems he was an only child and, to Doc anyway, a bit of a mamma's boy. He told the brothers how he hooked up with a genealogist to get more info, but ran into the same stonewalling Talon did. Past a certain point, that information was just simply gone. The genealogist was a bit of a flake he said, but more than a little talented at his job. When he passed away from old age, Cody enlisted his grandson.

"Doc..." the grandson said as he ran into the same information hole his grandfather had. "... problem with real life is one thing always touches another. History is only past tense real life. Cut a hole in a piece of paper... and you still have the rest of the paper. The trick isn't to try and find the missing piece, it's to start at the edges and fill it back in."

Talon smirked and said "I like his thinking. Do ya think you could introduce me to him?"

Doc frowned saying "Doubt it. Last I heard he was 'off the grid' as the term goes."

"Jesus Doc, just what kind of history does this house have!?" Grant exclaimed loudly. "Not for nuth'in but... it makes a genealogist go underground!?"

"Oh no no no, nothing like that," Cody answered him. "If you were to trace your roots, do you know where the Mecca of such things is?"

Talon cut in saying "I do. Salt Lake City. The Mormons are beyond anal about stuff like that."

"Mm hmm. And do you know anything about the Mormons?

"Heh heh heh... I know that I'm NOT one... 'bout it."

"Indeed," Doc said. "Ya see, his family was Orthodox Mormon."

"Okay, so?" Grant asked.

"So... one day he showed up to a family dinner... with a new bride. A new 'Jewish' bride... from a wedding no one knew of nor got invited to."

"Oh," was the out loud affirmation from both Grayson boys.

"He was ostracized. Last I heard he was in San Francisco somewhere. No one in the family will even talk about him no less help me find him."

Talon just smiled and pulled out his phone.

"Hi Marie? Yeah it's me."

Doc looked at Grant and asked "Who's Marie?"

Grant smiled knowing what Talon was up to and said "His secretary. I told you Doc this is his sanctuary. He keeps an office in Idaho. Nothing of his business life touches this one. That's his security as well."

"Ah... got it."

Talon kicked in with "Marie? I need you to do something for me. I want you to flood the personals in every paper in San Fran. Write this down... 'Man with house that doesn't exist seeks Orthodox genealogist to fill in hole in piece of paper. If you're not him but think you know him... show him this ad'. Put the office number on it and call me with any legit responses okay?" Talon waited a moment then said "Okay thanks sweetie," and hung up the phone.

Cody chuckled and looked at Grant and asked "He always do shit like that?"

Grant smirked and answered "Doc... you have no idea."

"So, meanwhile, back on Doc's history... wouldn't happen to have any photos would ya?" Talon said smoothly getting right back on track.

Doc pulled out his phone and told him "Only one. I'm told this was the grandfather in question... along with his German bride."

Grant asked "German?"

"Indeed. I've looked at this picture thousands of times and, well, not wishing to speak ill of my own family, I can't help but think it was a marriage of convenience. This was taken in front of the fireplace in my house."

"Your house? What... you got ghosts too!?" Talon joked. He got serious and asked "Let me guess, the house stayed in the family?"

"Yep. When my grandmother's father died, she didn't want it. I was old enough to live on my own when I was 18... so grandma held it for me. I couldn't wait to leave Chicago and took it over when I was 19. I started fixing it up when I was 21. I moved into it full time only 3 years ago."

Talon was thinking again and said aloud "So, it's the late 1800's. Most of Europe's aristocracy is dwindling and 'the colonies' are flush with money from silver and gold. The Europeans are looking to hang onto their status, but are out of cash. The Americans are full of cash but no status. It was quite common for them to merge families with each one giving the other what each one lacked. I have to agree Doc, it's likely a marriage of convenience. Sorry but, she looks a bit brutish to me so... yeeeaaaah... I'm going with your theory."

Grant took a look and declared "I know I wouldn't wanna meet her on a bad day."

"All I know about her was that she was his nurse... and from the letters I read from her to her son... was all about family in a major way. It was nearly pathological to her. On her, that's all I got as I lost my genealogist by then, not to mention medical school kinda took a priority at the time."

"Doc would you mind sharing any of that history?" Talon asked nicely.

"I would. I never let the originals out of my possession. If you're okay with copies however... those I have no problem sharing. With your obvious talent at history, who knows, maybe you'll see something I didn't."

"That Doc, is more than acceptable... thanks."

Now Talon shifted gears and said "Well little brother, get a good night's rest. I got Ahern coming bright and early tomorrow."

That actually got Grant excited.

"This Ahern a what or a who?" Cody asked.

Grant was like a little kid and had a smile a mile wide and told him "It's a what. Rental place but... biiiiiiig equipment. What are you up to 'big brother'?"

"Heh heh... I know how much you love the big boy toys," Talon smarted. "Al is coming and I..."

"Wait... AL IS COMING!?"

"Heh heh... yep."

Grant was beaming and said "Oh THIS just gets better and better!"

"I'm sure Al will be happy to see you too," Talon smirked. "Anyway, look at the mural." Grant did and Talon pointed saying "I got a pair of 3 yard bucket loaders, one for each of us. Al is showing up with 5 loads. By end of tomorrow, you and I need to clear from here..." And Talon traced a path on the mural with his finger "... to here... and you're gonna help me get it done. IF I read my geography right, this was the original 'driveway' in. You and I are gonna clear 150 plus years of overgrowth and give Al a place to park."

"Oh HELL YEAH!!!" Grant beamed.

"Oh and one other thing... I ordered 'Big Mack' as well," Talon said in an enticing tone.

Grant teased back in kind saying "Stop it... you're giving me a woody."

Doc said sneakily "Sounds like you got a fun day planned. Perhaps I should tag along... you know... in case someone gets hurt."

Talon smirked and said "Doc... the dozers arrive at 7... be there at 6."

"Wouldn't miss it. Sounds like this Al guy is someone to meet."

Both brothers laughed and Grant told him "Doc? One doesn't meet Al... uh... one 'experiences' Al."

Cody sneered at that thought and told them "I'll bring the coffee."

It was night time and Talon wasn't sleeping well again. He went into his office and stared at the mural. The men outside the coach were now walking away from the house... not into it. Talon gave up and just dove in head first.

"Okay guys tell me this... were you there to cover it up? Or find the truth? I truly don't care which... I just want to know."

Talon stared a moment, then, laughed at himself and his desperation for answers. He was about to walk away, when he heard his printer fire up. There were only 2 words on the paper that came out.

'FIND TRUTH'

Talon was shaking some... then asked... "So, did you?"

Once more the printer fired up.

'NO'

Talon was starting to question a lot of things lately. Beliefs mostly. Still, he couldn't argue with what he's seen and heard in the last few days. That's when he decided, like in poker, that he was going 'all in'. That choice... that one choice... would influence the rest of his life.

"Well then gentlemen, I'll make you a deal. I don't like being pushed around in my own home. I'll do my best to solve what you couldn't. In return, you help me where and when you can. Do we have a deal?"

Silence.

"Ya know gentlemen, my mother used to say spirits here were trapped due to unfinished business. I'm sure this wasn't Pinkerton's only failure but I'm betting it was a pretty big one. I'd call that unfinished business wouldn't you? This is a one time offer so I'll ask you only once more... DO WE... have a deal?"

It was almost a minute, but the printer came to life one final time.

'WE'LL BE WATCHING'

"That gentlemen, is good enough for me," and Talon dropped the sheets in the shredder telling himself "Eh... no one would believe me anyway."

He went back to his room, and for the first time in days, slept like a rock.

Chapter 5

"Special Delivery"

Talon and Grant were watching the sun come up at the side of the main road when they saw Cody pull up... in a Jeep.

"Aw... and I liked the Beemer," Talon joked as Doc handed out 3 coffees and a few bagels with eggs.

"Yeah well, when the mechanic asked "Which one of you is the tank commander?", I knew it was time to bring something a little more appropriate."

Talon and Grant laughed but thanked Doc for the breakfast.

"So, I get you want better access to the house. I also get you want to restore her both inside AND out. My question is, why focus on this now when there's so much more to do on the house first?" Cody asked truly wanting to understand the game plan.

"Doc, I can't do shit in that house with just the tools Grant and I have. Being the owner of a salvage company has its perks. We get this driveway clear, and you'll see why tomorrow."

Grant kicked in asking "The driveway I ain't worried about but do ya think we'll get the trench done for the power lines?"

"Nope," Talon told him. "Not even gonna try either. We'll be okay for awhile with the generators. I plan to use Big Mack for that when we're ready."

Cody asked "Who is this big mack anyway?"

"Like my brother said yesterday," Talon began, "Not who... what. It's a 10 yard capacity backhoe on treads like a tank. Grant said he told you what I do for a living yes?"

"Mm hmm."

"Well Doc, a lot of those buildings and such have old timber in them. Some of them in the tons and tens of feet long. Got too expensive renting equipment on each job, so I just bought one at auction. I get most of my big equipment that way. I've gone all over the world getting stuff you wouldn't believe, at rock bottom prices. My sister is the financial whiz and she helps me write it off on the company. I show up... onsite... AND with my own crew and tools... and people take notice. Sometimes, just the impression you make is half the battle. That thing has a 30 ton load capacity and we use it to haul out stuff. I always give the locals first dibs on things before I sell it on the auction market."

"There's a market for such things?" Cody asked truly impressed.

"Doc, I had over a thousand followers before anyone knew what Facebook was. Not all old buildings are in sad shape but getting parts for them is near impossible. Most of them are on historical registers so someone like me and Grant have to get approval for anything going in or out. I made my life easier by making their lives easier... and got rich doing it," Talon said with a hint of pride.

Before Doc could comment, 2 delivery trucks showed up right on time.

Talon signed for them and the delivery guys got them off the flat beds and down onto the road. The Grayson brothers hopped in, one each, and started working. They cleared about 20 feet in then got out of the way so the delivery guys didn't have to make a 6 mile round trip just to turn around. The delivery guys thanked them, turned around, and headed out leaving the two brothers to work in earnest. At 30 feet in, Grant heard a rather nasty 'clang' and shut down the dozer.

"What do you think it is... an old piece of track?" Grant asked aloud.

Talon looked it over and hollered back "Hey Doc? Back of my truck there's a hefty piece of rope. Mind getting it for me?"

"On it!" Doc hollered as he went to grab it.

This was history he didn't have and was stoked to find anything. That's why he wanted to buy the place. To him, the mansion was the biggest historical dig of his life. All 3 men cleared some more of the exposed iron and saw what appeared to be a curve.

"Don't know Grant but, wadda ya say we find out?" and Talon backed up his machine.

He gently scraped about 18 inches of dirt off the whole area while Cody and Grant tied off the rope to the iron. When Talon was done, they tied off the other end to a few teeth on the bucket. Talon raised it, and put it in reverse.

"Well... son... of... a... bitch," Cody said as the moniker was raised from the past.

As Talon backed up in the dozer... a wrought iron sign came to life. The arid climate and soil of the high Nevada desert preserved it in near pristine condition. It was two sides with a high arch connecting them. Some of the fanciest scroll work either brother had ever seen graced the arch.

Talon said "Excuse me guys... I need to make a phone call," and he walked off behind the bucket loader. "Senator? I have that name for ya," Talon told him in near disbelief as he stared at the metal artwork.

What they raised up was a ranch sign. Highest quality any of the men had ever seen. Across the arch in big bold letters were two words.
"ADAIR HOUSE"

Talon came back from his call and said "Okay, as big as this is, it wasn't built with Al in mind. Let's get a few more ropes and set it to the side. We can mount it later but if we rig it now, Al will never get under it.”

"Agreed brother. Some bitch, do you believe this thing!?” Grant asked.

Talon AND Cody were both snapping pictures. Talon fired up the dozer and with the help of Grant and Cody... worked the iron banner off to the side.

With near menace as he went back to work, Talon said “Told you I'd open up all your secrets ghost lady... or should I say... 'Miss Adair'?”

Talon went back to work with a huge smile on his face.

Another 20 feet in and Grant hit something else. This time it was a big rock. Then, working the left side of the 'driveway', Talon hit one too. They were big but all 3 men noticed, they were quarried, not natural.

"Looks like we found the border!” Grant shouted over the radio.

These boulders were 4 feet long, 3 feet high and 3 feet deep.

"Looks like it! This entrance is the worst down here, and gets easier the closer we get to the house. Careful bro but let's expose them... not move them.”

"You got it Tal!”

Cody was riding with Talon and was loving the work... and each new discovery... and was only hoping for more. Doc actually got excited when Talon let him drive it and taught him as they went.

"Hey Grant?” Talon called over the walkie-talkie.

"Yeah?”

"Maybe not but, I'm betting there's a good chance there's cobblestone under all this dirt. Just in case there is, watch how deep you dig okay?”

"Sounds good,” Grant called back over the roar of twin diesel engines.

Talon was right, but it would take another 2 weeks to get to that job, thousands of gallons of water, and 4 pressure washers to expose them.

Talon and Grant got the driveway cleared. It was 4:30pm and the delivery guys were coming back at 5. The brothers started the trench for the power-line so the bigger backhoe could maneuver into place and finish the job, then brought the two dozers back to the road to be picked up.

"My BMW thanks you,” Cody said jokingly as he looked back towards the house and the now flattened, cleared, and marked path to it.

Talon got in his truck, told the men to stay behind, and drove up to the house.

"Tomorrow.......... Miss Adair,” he said menacingly out the window.

He drove back down, stopped by the two men and said “I'm going home to take a shower. Pizza and beer is on me, who's down?”

Both men laughed but... each one followed Talon.

It was nearly noon the next day. All 3 men were on the porch eagerly awaiting a delivery. Roughly 25 minutes later, Talon smiled, and the men waited no longer. Five huge semi-trucks pulled into, then lined the driveway. The first one had 'Big Mack' written on the front edge of the hood of the truck. Behind it was a flatbed with the biggest backhoe on it Cody had ever seen in real life. Another flatbed behind that one had the biggest timbers he ever saw as well. The remaining 3 were regular semi's but long... really long.

"Mista G and little G! HOW my two most favuhriet men in tha whole world be liv'in?!" came a booming and very animated... female voice.

Talon smiled kindly and hollered out from the porch "Liv'in large Al... ha ha... liv'in large!"

The slightly tall slightly hefty black woman pointed behind her at the 5 trucks saying "Well iffin you weren't... Ya are now! HAAAAAA ha ha ha ha! Come on down here and give Althea some shugah!"

Cody was laughing and said "Al... is Althea!?"

All 3 men walked over and Althea gave Grant a hug that lifted him off the ground.

"And just who is this tall hunk o'man you brought for me?" Al asked Talon all playful like.

Talon was smiling and said "Doc? Allow me to introduce you to Althea James... truck driver and pilot extraordinaire!" Talon turned saying "Al? Allow me to introduce you to Doc Holliday."

Doc was stunned, but pleasantly so, and asked "You fly!?"

"Yeah why? Don't think a woman like me can do it? Doc let me tell ya somethin'... if it rolls on the ground, or flies through the air..."

The brothers finished her motto for her in her same flair saying "...Althea James will get you there!"

"And don't y'all forget it neethuh!" Al laughed. She looked at Cody and teased "So, you're a Doc eh? Maybe you can help me with some'thin. Seems I got this pain in mah ass. Doc's back home tell me I got Talon Grayson syndrome and it ain't treatable. Think you might wanna take a look?"

Doc laughed as he mock bowed and kissed the back of her hand.

"I'll see about getting you an appointment."

Al smiled, then playfully admonished the two brothers like the adopted mother she made herself to be.

"Hmmf... bout time you two started hang'in out with maw 'refined' characters."

Doc liked Al and realized the brothers were right, one experiences her. He felt her accent was a mix of slight southern drawl, and south Detroit. He would actually be right on both counts.

Althea wound down some and looked at the house saying "So, this is what you needed good ole Althea for eh Mista G? And from the looks of it not a moment too soon neethuh." Althea had a look of familiarity on her face, then asked "Mista G? What you do'in with a Naw'Lins ho house in the middle o' nowhere?"

"Careful Althea... ha ha ha... the 'lady of the house' prefers the term brothel," Talon answered Al, but gave a wink to Grant.

"Hmmf! I'll bet she duz," Althea said in a 'I don't give a shit what you want' tone of voice. "I'm tell'in ya," and she pointed over her shoulder saying "Sho as my name is Althea James... THAT is a bayou ho house... out here in the middle of tumble weeds and tuh-rantchulaz!"

Talon whispered seriously to Doc and said "Tough demeanor, and larger than life personality aside... don't let her fool you. Al is ANY thing but stupid. You wanna find out more about this house? Then shut up and listen."

Cody said he would and Talon called Althea on her boast.

"Well then my dear Al... if you think you know so much... prove it!"

"Awrite fine then! You been inside yet?"

"Grant and I have explored some... yes," Talon told her.

"Well it's obvious I ain't. Here's what I know... walk in that fancy door right there and you walk into a parlor. Off to the left is a hall with a door to tha outside and racks to put up coats an hats an such. Go to tha right and it's a large living room... real large. Got a bar in it too. Stairs would be just to tha left but set back from tha main door. Under that staircase is a hidden door to a private meeting room downstairs AND... it's tha only door in or out. Upstairs is a main hall go'in tha entire length o'da place, but all tha rooms are on the back side an not one o'them got a winduh. See tha winduh up there!? Thah one belong to tha pimp or madam. Only room on that floor too and got a real long hallway go'in to it. Have ya noticed the odd holes in tha see'lin of each room? THAT is so tha boss can peer in and check that things doen get outta hand. Gotta keep tha men folk happy an not ornery so kitchen is on tha 2nd floor too but all tha way to that side. Can't put it in tha basement as tha moisture would ruin tha food... and there'd be a food elevatuh on that side that doubles as a laundry chute. THAT would be in tha basement. Tell me Mista G... Howz Althea do'in so far?"

Talon said nothing, he merely smiled, and applauded.

Talon told her "You only missed one thing... heh heh... you forgot about the ghosts."

"Ghosts?"

"Mm hmm. Al? Do me a favor and walk through the front door please."

Al did but exclaimed loudly and unhappily "If you or your brother got somethin' rigged to make me scream I swear I will whoop BOTH yo asses!"

She walked in, stopped a moment then walked out.

"Okay... so?"

"So... watch this." Talon looked and saw the other drivers were nowhere nearby, then asked "Doc... would you mind showing her?"

Doc asked kindly "You sure about this?"

"Trust me... I know Al," Talon said with confidence.

Althea was standing on the ragged porch and to the side as Cody walked up. Right on cue, the smoke got stopped at the door.

Al jumped and strutted off the porch saying "Oh HEEEELLLLLLL no!" She looked at Talon asking in near disbelief "You got yo'self a Naw'Lins ho house AND it's haunted!? Lawd in heaven I swear, if there was a white elephant from Mars, Mista G would either have it or know where it was. Haunted ho house in tha middle o'the desert... OF COURSE he'd be tha one tuh have it!"

Cody was stunned and asked "You mean you're not afraid?"

With utter confidence in herself, Al told him "Doc? I was born in Naw'Lins an lived there till I was 15. That's how I know bout this house. We lived two blocks from that area and my blessed momma kept us all with a roof over our heads be'in a cook to them people when poppa done run off. I used tuh help her out when I got old enough... till God gave me these fine curves you see here. Momma stopped bringing me around by then. Ain't been a John or a hoochie-mama alive OR dead that's eeevvver got the better of Althea James... and they aint gonna start now! Moved to the Motor City and went straight into tha army right outta high school. I spent 25 years runn'in supplies to some of the worst hell holes on Earth. Did 2 tours in Bosnia and Kosovo. Last tour was the first Iraq war with papa Bush. I seen stuff Doc that would make even you puke. No Doc... I ain't stupid... but I ain't scared neethuh."

Doc was just open mouthed and stunned.

Grant walked by him saying "I told you Doc that one 'experiences' Al."

"Ha HAAAAAAAA... Is THAT what you told him!? LAWD ain't that tha truth!!?" Althea shrieked with glee and pride.

Suddenly Talon was a tad shocked. A 14 year old girl came walking up. She was also, thankfully, what Talon called a techno-zombie. Buried in her phone she had no clue what was going on around her. Talon and Grant weren't hiding the fact that the place was haunted. They also knew who they could tell and who they shouldn't.

"Granmomma gonna stick that phone somewhere you'll need the good doctor here to remove if you don't put it away this instant," Althea scorned. "What did I tell you about that thang? Yo momma an daddy may let you act like that. Around here and these folk tho... you gonna show granmomma taught you some manners!"

That ended that.

"Yes ma'am," the young girl said as the phone quickly went away.

"Gentlemen, this is ma granddaughter. School is out back home... and back home is nowhere for a pretty young thing like my grandbaby to be by herself."

"No........ it's not," Talon said in extreme agreement. Then Talon teased some and said "So, does this pretty young thing have a name?... And I only say that as being Althea's granddaughter how could you be anything but?"

Althea teased right back saying "Mista G? I been married fo nearly 30 years now. Say the word and I'll move in and get a divorce... cute as you are," and she winked at him.

The young girl stuck her hand out "I do Sir... it's Lashonda. Pleased to meet you."

Talon shook it back and said "That sucked Lashonda. Take it from me, if you're gonna shake someone's hand... grab it and shake it. Grandma is right, you are a pretty girl. That handshake though says I could walk all over you in 5 minutes."

"Sorry Sir."

"Nothing to be sorry for my dear. Grandma is a very dear friend of mine. I'm just looking after one of hers the way I know she'd look after one of mine."

"Yes Sir."

Talon introduced Grant and Cody and this time, Lashonda got it right.

With a kind smile, Grant told her "There ya go," referring to her improved handshake.

Talon called the other drivers over and had them help him unchain Big Mack. It got its name because it was big, and built by the Mack truck company. Talon hopped in, fired it up, and put the bucket down onto the ground. Using its shear strength, Talon used the bucket to pop the cab off the flatbed. A swing to the side and Big Mack was off the flatbed, on its treads, and ready for business.

"Lashonda?"

"Yes Sir?"

"Do you know that nickname grandma calls me? The one that she thinks I don't know about?"

She shrunk a little and said "Yes Sir."

Talon smiled and said "You're about to see why she calls me that." He looked past the young girl and said "Doc? I'd like to show you why too. How about you go stand by the door hmm?"

"Uh... okay," and Cody stood right by the closed door.

"Um... Doc? Ya might wanna move over a lil bit."

Cody did and without a word, Talon fired up the bucket.

"TALON WAIT! THOSE DOORS ARE OVER 150 YEARS... (crash!)... old," Grant hollered to no avail.

"Jesus Christ!" Cody hollered as he recoiled back hard.

Talon had level armed the boom... and put the bucket right through the front door with ramming speed.

He left it running, hopped down, and walked along the boom and into the new front opening.

"MY HOUSE!... NOT YOURS!" he hollered.

"We'll see about that," the shadow voice said menacingly in only Talon's ears.

"No... we won't," Talon said just as menacingly as he walked back to the cabin of Big Mack and backed the bucket out of the doorway.

He shut off the machine, hopped out, and stared up at 'the window'.

"I told you Miss Adair! Now!?? Your two days are up!!"

"Whoa! That was cool!" Lashonda exclaimed as only a 14 year old could.

Grant leaned down to her and asked "And just what is this nickname grandma has for my brother?"

Lashonda shrank some again and worried she'd get in trouble.

"Crazy ass white boy...... Sir."

Grant laughed hard and imitated Al.

"LAWD ain't that tha truth!!?" and just kept on laughing.

Talon hopped down and said "Doc? I know why you've been tagging along. You have my permission to search anywhere... GO anywhere... and any time you please on one condition... anything you find you share with Grant and me. Now at least they can't slam the door in your face but, how about... no smoking 'in' the house... wadda ya say?"

Cody was still a bit stunned and only said "Yeah.......... deal."

Al was uncharacteristically quiet.

"There a problem Al?" Talon asked.

"You said 'Miss Adair'... would that be Lucinda Adair?"

"I don't know," Talon told her. "We found a ranch sign that said Adair House on it. Al? We got less than nothing on this house. You've been with me long enough to know that ain't possible... and yet it is. So, not sure if that was her name or just the name of the house, that's what I've taken to calling her."

"Her 'who'?"

Talon was kind and asked "Ya really wanna know?"

"Sweet Jesus Mista G... when do I EVUH wanna know?"

"Heh heh, how about... always?"

Al was still unsettled and exclaimed "Heaven knows one of these days my nosiness is gonna get tha bettuh of me. Now who is this 'lady'?"

Talon told her about the voices. That alone rattled her, so he left out the part about the mural, and what he and Doc had taken to calling 'Shadow Man'.

"Now it all makes sense," Al said with a touch of revelation.

"Al I got nothing on this place except stories, rumors, and vague whispers. If you got anything, some story or even a hypothesis, ANY thing at all then trust me... no matter how 'out there'... I wanna hear it," Talon nearly commanded.

Talon was truly a good friend of hers. He helped her out when he could have turned his back. So, she told her story only now, he was her friend, not her boss.

"Mista G... I toeld ya I lived near tha French Quawtuh. There was an old legend among tha locals, well known too. Aside from tha fact that it's a replica of tha one's back east, I truly don't know a thing about tha house itself. But... I may know how it got here."

Talon just said "I'm listening."

Al pulled Talon off to the side and told her tale.

"Legend has it, there was a real powerful voodoo priestess named Arella Adair. She was known to all tha locals but, not one tha tourists or tha histry shows evuh heard 'bout. The story goes she lost her husband at sea and was left to raise their only child... a daughter... alone."

"Let me guess... Lucinda?" Talon asked remembering Al from before.

Al continued "Mm hmm. Now, Arella was what you would call a white witch. She was planning on having her daughter follow in her footsteps. That daughter howevuh grew up liking tha finer things in life. Tha parties, tha modern times, and most importantly, tha modern men. The story goes, she was such a beauty that she became desired by that life as well, and had more than a few fight'in over her. Desiring no man... she desired them all. Her mother caught her one day but Lucinda stood up tuh her. Lucinda called it old wives tales and such and thought her mother a flake and a relic of the past. Worse... she toeld her so. Arella saw her as her heir and was furious. So, legend tells, she put a curse on Lucinda that if she didn't change her ways, and settle down, that she would nevuh know love, and one day leave Naw'Lins only nevuh to return. She laughed at her mother, boarded a steamship with her rich boyfriend at tha time to take a vacation........ but nevuh returned."

Talon was about to say something. Another voice beat him to it. It was a voice he heard but, this time, so did Althea.

"A fanciful tale," was the soft southern whisper. "Sadly... it's not entirelee untrue."

Al looked up in shock at Talon. He just had an annoyed look on his face that seemed to say 'Yeah, that's her'.

"And the gray haired gentleman is correct... I prefer brothel. I swear woman, if yaw go'in to act like a boisterous man, y'all could at least enunciate like one."

Al was scared for a moment. That moment was short lived.

"You listen to me carefully witch... no 'whore' is gonna tell me what ta do. Nevuh did... nevuh will! You WILL stay away from me AND my grandbaby... you hear me woman!??" Al declared looking around.

" (giggle) Or you will...?"

"OR!... I will find a way to come over there and whoop yo ass mahself! I still know people back home... who know 'other people'. Your mothuh may not have taught you her craft... but that doen mean she didn't teach it to another. That legacy exists to this day and I know where tuh find 'em. You get mah mean'in witch!?"

A soft breeze was followed by another giggle.

"Witch? I thought that was mah mothuh... I was thah whore remember?" the soft voice taunted.

Then, Talon heard something meant for only him.

".... Come and see me sometime, 'Mista G'," the southern voice teased, ".... but leave thah guttersnipe owtsiiide when ya do."

Another light bit of laughter and the voice was gone. Talon looked to 'the window'...... and saw the ragged curtains flutter to a stop when he did.

Althea stomped away all pissed off and exclaimed "Only you Mista G... I swear.... only you!"

Several states away, in a bunker that didn't exist on any map nor show up on any government roster, a printer fired up with a 'special request' order. That printer was in a buried vault over 5 city blocks long and housing secrets and 'evidence' dating back hundreds of years.

"Huh, this is odd," the one man said to the other.

"What is?"

"This authorization code."

"Yeah? What of it?"

The man gazed a moment and told his partner "This one hasn't been used since before the civil war."

"Meh, wouldn't be the first time someone used an alias to cover his tracks. Not even this week. Check the transport codes... are they legit?"

The man ran it under a laser scanner and told the other guy "Yeah... comes up legit."

"Well then, fill the requisition and get it in the out-box. Pickup comes in one hour."

The man did. He got the old box, put all its contents in a chemically treated spy-proof envelope, and sent it out for 'special delivery'. That method of delivery however, was not the same kind the Post Office uses.

The monster that was his mansion faced north. The whole east side was the part that had the stone foundation. Talon and Grant spent a day getting iron beams and chains down into the tiny entrance they made. They did that because, due to all the damage, going in through the house would've been suicide. Next morning the whole crew was far frostier than they were the day before, thanks to a good night's sleep. Althea was there and sassier than ever but, only to 'the house'.

Talon fired up Big Mack and took it to the outside wall on the east side. Grant fed him some chains through a center hole, and Talon hooked them to the massive bucket. Once rigged Grant gave the all clear, and hopped out from the basement. Talon then let out a deep breath, and spoke to the past.

"Listen to me very closely Lucinda. This stone wall is the tipping point. I will bring this house back to its former glory like I said... or I will let it collapse and take the house with it and build something new. God as my witness I will haul off every last bit of this mystery and start from scratch. THAT my dear will leave you lost forever and only haunting a garbage dump somewhere. I back this machine up, and the netting of chains and iron bars on the inside will straighten the wall and we can begin. This lever here however, swings the boom forward. Do that, and the wall goes inward and your once precious home collapses like a house of cards."

Talon crossed him arms over his chest and leaned back in his seat.

"Give me a sign, SOME thing but, your call from here. IF we save it though... no more lies and no more secrets... choose."

Grant saw his brother and hollered "Yo Tal! We gonna do some work today or what!?"

Althea saw the look on his face however and told Grant kindly "Leave him be hun... leave him be."

Talon refused to move. It took 2 whole minutes but, he got his answer. Suddenly, the mighty diesel engine roared to life. The gear shifter on the floor moved back 3 notches... to reverse... and the engine shut down. Talon still had his arms across his chest when it did.

"Madame? And I use that term correctly... you and I are about to get allll sorts of friendly," and Talon fired up Big Mack.

Talon waved Grant over and pointed to the chains. Grant ran over, checked them one last time, then gave his brother the thumbs up as he backpedaled away. Talon did as he said he would. The wall did as he said it would as well. Fifteen Minutes later, two stone walls were upright again for the first time in decades. The restoration of a lifetime.... several lifetimes actually... had finally begun in earnest.

The whole day was spent putting in hard setting, high strength, mortar and concrete to keep the foundation solid for another 100 years. Talon was exhausted and was driving home when his phone rang.

"Grayson Industries... this is Talon speaking."

An electronic and distorted voice was what greeted him. It was the kind one would hear in some sort of spy movie.

"Special delivery Mister Grayson."

"I'm listening."

"When you get home, you may want to look in your fancy sports car," the voice told him. "We have a message for you regarding the senator."

"And that is?"

"You're even," and the call hung up.

Talon drastically sped up his slow ride home.

'Mista G' was pissed when he pulled into his driveway. He knew the package he was told about would be right where the voice said it would be. What pissed him off was how easily 'these guys' got around his security. He had a total of 25 cameras around his home and property. The front gate had biometric controls on it as well. The moment the gates opened, the driveway lit up along the edges. After dark, high intensity lamps would light up from the street to the garage, making the entrance to said garage, look like a runway for NASA. Not to mention, two high speed cameras were focused on the driveway at all times and hooked to military grade heat and motion sensors.

Grant teased him the first time he saw it and asked "Paranoid much?"

Talon told him "Dude I got one car in there worth three mil and another worth almost one. Every day they stay in their current condition, those values only go up. If you were me what would you do?"

Granted teased no more.

Talon parked the truck in its end spot and went immediately to the Lambo. There, as told, was a nearly overstuffed white plastic like envelope sitting on his drivers seat. He opened the door, picked it up, and sat down.

"Place both thumbs in markers above... remove ALL contents within 60 seconds... then place envelope in or on fireproof container," Talon said with a chuckle as he read the instructions on the back aloud.

Talon was a lover of tech. Not a geek but, more like someone who could truly appreciate its usefulness. He had gone to several trade shows and had seen some pretty mind-blowing stuff. As such, knowing who likely sent him this and what type of tech they would have... he took the instructions seriously.

Talon got out of the car and closed the door. He had a red fireproof garbage can that he kept his oily rags in. He laid the envelope on a workbench, grabbed the can, and dumped its contents on the floor. Then... he followed the instructions. He put both thumbs where it said to, and what looked like a circuit out of the Tron movie glowed from side to side. Then, a strip across the seal just melted away opening the envelope.

"Uh oh," Talon said in earnest as he saw something else.

Numbers glowed from what looked like inside the material of the envelope. They started at '59' and were counting down. Talon quickly poured the contents onto the bench... checked twice, quickly, to ensure it was empty... then dumped it in the can. He sealed the lid, knocked it on its side, and rolled it out of his garage. He saw a muted flash of light from around the top seal then... smoke poured out for a whole two minutes.

"Okay Senator, I have to admit," Talon joked out loud to no one, "That was COOL!"

When the smoke in the can finally died off, Talon laughed and spoke to the rags on the floor.

"Looks like I gotta get you guys a new home."

Talon checked the can to make sure it was cool, then took it and tossed it in the recycle bin. The can had been warped and blistered from the heat and was no longer viable.

Talon brought the contents into his office, and made a phone call.

"Senator? Is this line secure?" Talon said in a serious tone.

"When last checked. What can I do for you 'old friend'?"

"Accept my thanks. My... shall we say, 'request'... arrived today."

The senator was not happy and Talon could hear it.

"That's not exactly good news my friend."

"And why not?" Talon asked suddenly not liking Bob's tone.

"I haven't mentioned it to anyone yet. Haven't had a chance to."

Talon just sighed.

"I swear Bob, when this mystery of mine is all over, I'm gonna write a best seller out of this one. Have your tech guys do a security sweep but... don't be surprised if they come up empty. Give my best to the family," and the call hung up abruptly from the other end.

Talon got up and walked to the mural. This time, there was only one 'Pinkerton Man' outside the coach. He was also older, a lot older. The house also looked more like it does today

"This was you... wasn't it?" Talon said in a more comfortable tone.

Offhandedly, he looked to his printer with a small grin on his face. This time however, nothing happened. He was actually a little let down, then laughed at himself for it.

"Okay then, my old science teacher taught us that you'll never get the right answers, or any answers for that matter, if you don't ask the right questions." Talon looked at the printer and said aloud "Think man... think. Okay then, tell me this," he said as he turned back to the mural to see only the coach once more. Talon looked and said "Where do I start?"

He was staring at the mural, when he heard a sound behind him. In the envelope's contents was something that looked like a diary. It was wrapped with an old leather strap the size of a shoelace. The sound Talon heard was that of a book falling to the floor. He never even turned around.

"I know that," he said with utter confidence, "THAT is not what I meant and you know it. Tell me gentlemen... where do I start?"

Talon stood defiant and just stared. Suddenly, he heard the whinny of horses and the coach faded away. He heard it again and this time Talon was really impressed. What reappeared, about 150 yards away from the house, was Big Mack. It was where Talon marked out where he thought the train tracks were that circled the house.

"Gentlemen?" Talon said as he started walking away, "Its been a pleasure doing business with you."

He smiled as he saw the book that fell, was still actually sitting on the desk right where he left it. He turned off the lights, activated the alarm system, and headed off to bed.

Chapter 6

"Investing In The Future...
And The First Set Of Clues"

After the debacle at the mill years ago, Talon bought his own ground penetrating radar unit. Never, he swore, would he be caught off guard like that again. He also had a second unit that looked almost identical, but that one was a metal detector. Unlike the one's people use on the beach, and as such, this thing had 10 times the range and 5 times the accuracy.

Now, he was out in the hot sun with both.

"And jes what are you expecting ta find Mista G?" Althea asked.

"Another piece of the puzzle Al," Talon answered her sweetly.

It didn't take long for the metal detector to beep wildly. Al was running that one. Talon swung over immediately, and called out to Lashonda where to put the markers. Lashonda was with them today and wouldn't let Al out of her sight.

Seems that, as any 14 year old would be, she thought she was as tough and fearless as 'granmomma'. Reality however, as it always is, can be a harsh teacher. She was exploring the house grandma told her not to go into without her. Being a typical young teen, she didn't listen and was exploring the rooms on the second floor. Also typical was how quickly she discovered how right granmomma was. Lucinda saw to it a few creaky doors, and a few shadows in the corner of her eye, spooked her enough to get her out of where she felt a 'child' didn't belong. Al didn't say a word at her behavior. She knew. She also had a 'I don't care serves you right' tone in her voice the whole rest of the day.

"Hey Eileen... how's my favorite sister!?" Talon said all cheerily as he answered his phone.

"I'm your only sister ya dingbat," she chuckled back at him.

"Yeah yeah. So, what can I do for you?"

"Set me up on a blind date? I hear tell you got a doctor in your little circle of friends now," Eileen nearly giggled. "So, is he single?"

"Dunno," Talon teased, "Should I ask him if he likes redheads?"

"Nah... heh heh... but I might!" Eileen calmed down and asked "So, what are ya up to? Having fun with the haunted house?"

In a serious but kind tone, Talon told her "Sis... you have no idea."

"Speaking of dates... blind or otherwise... how about you? Any new girl of consequence I should know about?"

Talon called her on it and said "Actually yeah. She's an older woman though... like, reeeeeeeeeaaalll old. Real pretty I'm told but she has this odd habit of staring out third floor windows."

"Ha haaaaa. Ya know Tal, you can't stay buried in your work forever."

Talon changed tones saying "Don't start. Was there a reason you called? I'm kinda in the middle of..." and he winked at Althea and finished with "... tumbleweeds and tarantulas right now."

"Actually there is. I wanted to let you know I'll be back out in 3 weeks. I also want to talk to you when I get there. Nothing bad but definitely serious."

"I'll have dinner reservations ready at Sterling's," Talon told her.

"Sterling's huh? Wellllll... throw in a ride in that fancy car of yours... and maybe I'll make it there in two!" Eileen taunted playfully.

With a kind tone, and an equally kind smile to back it up, Talon taunted right back.

"I'll have the tanks topped off by the time you land."

"Love ya bro... I'll let you know when I have flight details. See ya then!" and the call ended.

Eileen wouldn't have to worry about Talon's love life for long. That was actually only a few days away. The second oldest Grayson had no clue... but it was coming all the same.

Althea sat in the truck for a bit to cool off. While she did, Talon decided to talk with Lashonda.

"So... 14 eh? Ya know, when I was your age, I had no clue what I wanted to be. Tell me, got any plans? Career, college... anything?"

"Not really sir," she answered as she placed marker flags in the ground. "I know I don't wanna be like my granmomma that's fo sho."

Talon was a tad insulted for Althea and admonished "That's 'for' 'sure' young lady. Your grandma may not be a head of state or anything, but she is a mighty fine woman."

Lashonda quickly added "Oh no Mista G, I know she is. I didn't mean it like that. My granmomma is a strong woman. I know it and I respect that. I just meant that, I'd rather do what you do than what she does... for a liv'in I mean."

Talon backed off and said "Well then, fair enough. For the record, your grandma may be doing what's considered a man's job... but she does it better than any man I know."

"Can I tell ya somethin' Mista G?" Lashonda asked in a meek tone.

"Sure."

"Grandma treats me like a little kid. Now, I know I'm not a grownup like you or her, and I'm not saying I am. But grandma, well, she treats me more like a 5 year old than ma actual age."

Talon now acted like the cool older brother.

"Well, ya hafta understand something. Your grandmother was in the army. Without giving away details she may not want you knowing, I can tell you she was in some really bad places."

"Okay sir... so?"

"So Lashonda, she was in not one but two different war zones. She saw stuff no one should have to. You see shit like that and, well, when you have babies of your own some day you'll understand what the word protection really means. I have no doubt she's just keeping you from seeing and experiencing things I'm sure even she wishes she hadn't. Add to that, your great grandmother brought her up under not so great circumstances. Grandma Al hasn't always had it so good in her life. Part of that protection is keeping them safe yes, but it's also a desire to see them do better than you did. That hard life taught grandma that being a techno-zombie, um, isn't the way to go. Sometimes when you are your age, ya get babied... and sometimes you get exactly what you give... know what I'm say'in?"

"No disrespect Sir, but there's protecting your babies... and then there's treat'in 'em like one when they ain't."

"Well then, perhaps it's time a young woman, and NOT a child absorbed in teenage texting drama, told her that and... in a tone and manner befitting one," Talon said supportively.

"Mista G?"

"Yeah?"

"Thanks sir," Lashonda said in a thankful tone.

"So Lashonda, I believe you said you wanted to be like me. Okay then, in what way?"

The young girl replied "I don't know if I'd want to run my own business, but I like the idea of running yours."

"Ha ha ha, mine? Trust me, there are days even I can't manage it."

"Yeah well, (chuckle) I like organizing. I mean, I really like it. I like finding better ways of doing things too. Back home my room is neat and organized. Then every week or so I tear it all apart, just so I can have something to set back up," Lashonda said making sure she 'spoke properly' like grandma said to do.

"Hmm, I have an idea," Talon told her. "YO AL! I'm taking your grandbaby up the hill... be back in a few okay!?"

"Yeah awright Mista G!" Althea hollered back.

Talon took Lashonda up the hill they were behind. At the summit they could see the house but more importantly, the trucks in the driveway.

"Okay Lashonda, consider this a job interview," he told her.

"Mista G sir... I'm only 14," she said slightly reserved.

"I don't care. Treat it like one."

"Yes sir."

"Now, see those trucks? I brought out everything I had in stock that I thought I would need. You know what I do for a living right?"

Again, only a "Yes sir."

"Well then. Big part of that job is seeing it first. Then I need to know what I will need but most importantly, in what order. Get that wrong and we lose days of work on a job. Tell me, how would YOU organize..." and Talon pointed to the distance, "...that?"

Now Lashonda's eyes lit up. With pride, she gave Talon exactly what he asked for.

"First I'd get the supplies sorted, but ya need a big and flat place to put them first."

Then she said how she'd arrange them in piles but far enough apart to get a truck or even Big Mack in between them. With extreme pride in herself, she explained how it did no good to stack them up only to find out what you need is buried. She spent 5 minutes giving Talon a rundown. In the end, Talon was impressed, and called his sister back.

"Back so soon?" Eileen joked.

"Hey Ei, you know Al right?"

"Althea? Of course I do, what about her?"

"She has her granddaughter with her on this trip. She seems to have a certain knack for organizing and improving. Wouldn't happen to have an internship available would ya?"

"For Al? Hell, I'll make one if I have to. How old is she?"

Talon said "14."

"Can't do it bro... too young. However, she could volunteer and I could offer her school a recommendation for some form of credit perhaps. Legally I can't pay her if she does that but, let's just say there may be a top of the line cell phone in it for her when school starts again."

"I'll talk to Al. How long you staying for when you come?" Talon asked.

"Only a week this time then I have to get back."

"Ya might have a traveling companion when ya do," Talon said slyly.

"Tell Al I can put her up in my guest room. Anything else?"

"Nah that's it."

Eileen's voice was bright and said "Well then, assuming Al approves, I look forward to meeting my new shadow!"

Talon got back down and got him and Lashonda in the truck, then drove back to the house. He got out and made a grand announcement.

"Alright people listen up," Talon called out to the drivers. "You all know Al here. This is her granddaughter Lashonda, though I'm sure you know that too. What you don't know is, as of 5 minutes ago, I'm putting her in charge of off-loading and organizing! I don't care how young she is nor what parts God put between her legs. She says something goes somewhere? Then that's where it goes. She says arrange it 'this way'? Then that is how you arrange it. I want this equipment and supplies down and organized by dinner tomorrow AND!... You do it her way. Once your truck is empty, get it outta here and head on back for home. We all clear on that!?"

Everyone gave a nod or something to indicate they were. No one bitched about it either because they all knew Talon. He was a good boss but they knew he liked to give good people a chance. Half of them had jobs because of that philosophy, including Al, so they all knew he was just doing that to the young lady as well.

"Well young lady, you want to be a grown up? Here's your chance. I'll tell you same as I told grandma when I hired her. I expect no mistakes. If you make one however, I expect you to own up to it AND correct it. Understood?"

A hefty and happy "Yes sir!" was his answer.

She immediately got out her phone and brought up an aerial shot of the house.

"I won't treat you mean if you don't treat me like a kid," she told them. "I need to know what you got and if I don't know it I want you to explain it to me." She then imitated grandma by saying "Okay y'all, 'baby Al' says let's get this done! Dinner comes up quick and we got work to do!"

She smiled back at Talon and grandma, then headed off to her task.

"Mista G?"

"Yeah Al?"

"Thanks for that," Althea said in the kindest of tones.

"You're welcome. C'mon Al, we have 'Lashonda business' to discuss."

Al laughed and said "Sho thang Mista G... ha HAAAAAAAA! Just as lawng as it ain't inside thaht house!"

Both headed off to discuss Lashonda's future.

About two hours later, Lashonda asked to speak to Talon and grandma. Those two both smiled because they were going to ask her the same.

"Come have a seat baby," Al said sweetly to her granddaughter. Lashonda sat down on the porch with the 2 grownups and Al told her "Me an Mista G wanna talk to you... 'bout your future."

"Yes ma'am," was her polite response.

"Mista G here tells me you be look'in tuh spread ya wings a bit, that true?"

Again, Lashonda only said "Yes ma'am."

"He also tells me you feel like I ain't treat'in you right. That so?"

Lashonda remembered Talon's advice, and put it to work.

"Granmomma, I think it's sweet when ya call me 'baby'. Not so much when ya treat me like one."

"Hmm... let me tell ya some'thin. I had ta grow up way soonah than I should have. Not ta mention when I did... I had ta do most of it on mah own. Baby, you should be laughing with ya friends and having sleepovers. Ya should be plann'in yer wedding and what man you gonna marry like all girls your age do. You should NOT have ta worry about where your next meal will be come'in from. You should also not have ta be work'in at your age neitha, just ta make sure you an yours even have a meal. Baby girl, I went inta tha army not cuz I wanted to... but because I had ta. I got ma diploma chyld, and then some, because o'that. Some'thin I would NEV'A had the opportunity to do, the way I was go'in."

"Granmomma, like I told Mista G, you're a strong woman and I respect that. I know ya just want me ta have better than you did and trust me, I do love ya for it. But I ain't you, and I don't have your life."

"Baby girl, I ain't wish'in ill on nobody but... one bad turn in life... and you just might."

Lashonda held her ground but, politely and with logic.

"I know that granmomma. And if it did turn bad, I would do my best to step up to the challenge." She smiled kindly and said "Just like my granmomma did. Answer me this though... wouldn't it make more sense to teach me what you know... rather than protect me from it?"

Althea smiled, looked at Talon, and joked "She gets her good looks AND her smarts from her granmomma ya know." She got serious again and said "I just want ya to know, I only wanted you to have the thangs I didn't have... and ta not know tha life I did."

"I know granmomma. But you had to do those things... I don't. You HAD to learn as you went... I don't. What I'm saying is, in your life things had to get done, with no time to learn. I am not like you were so, while we have it, take the time to teach me. I'm not a little kid anymore granmomma, but I ain't a grownup either. Ya know what I'd really love?"

Althea was proud of her granddaughter and asked "Wha's that baby girl?"

Lashonda told her seriously, and with pride, "To be Mista G's age, or even yours, and look back with a smile and be able ta say honestly... that my granmomma taught me all I know."

Althea was near tears and hugged Lashonda.

"I'd like that too baby girl."

Now it was Talon's turn. He had a plan of his own. Just like the buildings he found, he was investing in the future.

"Lashonda, I can't argue with your logic. Here's the thing, I am a grownup and as such, I know your plan has some serious holes in it. You said you wanted to run a company like mine. Okay then, ever make payroll?"

"Um... no sir."

"Ever make the physical work line up with the financing?"

A meeker "No sir," was his answer.

"Cost delays and overruns. Even know what those are?"

"No sir," she answered shrinking into her chair.

"In my job... the physical and the financial always go hand in hand. I don't even look at a job until I figure out the money. How much will the property cost? How much will it cost to get in equipment? Will I even make a profit? No one so much as even takes a picture of the place till I get that figured out. I've turned many a job down, just because it just wasn't financially sound. Now, how you even gonna know if it is or not if you don't understand the money? I'm not yelling at you but, I do want an answer."

Lashonda smirked saying "You do remember the part about me saying I'm only 14... right?"

"Heh heh heh, trust me, I do. That's where I come in. You wanna grow up, then I have a plan to do it. My sister is the money girl. I'm very good with money, but she's a wizard compared to me. She's accepted to take you into her home, and let you shadow her for a few weeks. She owns a company showing other companies how to manage, or manage better, their money. Maybe you wanna do her job later in life, maybe you don't. IF however, you wanna do MY job?... You need to know hers first. You following me?"

"I am sir."

"Good," Talon continued. "My sister will mentor you for 1 to 2 weeks. My general manager Mike will be starting up a new project right after that. Granmomma is heading up the transport team. You shadow my sister, and learn all you can. Then you do the same to Mike."

Althea kicked in and told her "You'll be with me for that. I'll teach you how to drive a truck. Not actual driving but, Mista G hires me. I have ta figger out how much fuel will cost... plus my time and expenses. If I'm too expensive, well then, Mista G and others like him hire someone else."

Lashonda asked "So, not meaning ta be rude but, what's in it for me?"

Talon told her "My sister will test you. So will I. Those tests will be fair but not easy either. The results will be turned over to your school for verification. Once they verify it was an honest test, they've agreed to give you 3 points credit towards graduation. Assuming you pass, you may wanna go to college one day. ANY college will want a letter of recommendation. My sister and I have agreed to give you one each."

With reservation, Lashonda asked "Do I even get a say in the matter?"

Grandma had that one covered.

"Of course ya do baby girl. It's all up ta you but, trust me, this is a mighty fine deal and you'd be foolish ta pass it up. I tawked ta momma and daddy. They agree with me on that but they said tha same thang... it's up ta you."

Lashonda was all smiles at that. She wasn't stupid enough to pass up the deal, not even at her age. She was just hoping to be asked, and not forced, like any teenager would.

"Granmomma?"

"Yes baby girl?"

"You just watch how proud I make you," and she hugged Al.

"I know ya will baby girl... I know ya will," Al told her smiling as she hugged her back.

"So Lashonda, you wanted to talk to us?" Talon sorta reminded.

"I did," she said and laid out her plan.

Like any teenager trying to be a grownup, she went a little overboard. Thankfully not much so, but did all the same. She thought if she proved to Talon that she was, she might get some recognition or something. Even if she just proved to Al she wasn't a baby that would be worth it.

"Mista G, can I see that layout pictcha ya got of this place?"

Talon pulled it out and showed it to her.

"Now, this is where we were marking right?"

"Mm hmm."

"Okay. You said there was a circle around this place. For a train right?"

Talon told her "Or so I believe... yes."

"Well, I can't do what ya asked me to. You ordered a lot of stuff Mista G... a LOT o'stuff. Problem is no place ta put it all. If you can get this cleared by today... from here to here... I can have all the trucks out of here in two days tops. All I need is my granmomma for tha afternoon, 500 dollars, and your trust. Remember when you told me I was on a job interview?"

Talon smirked at the audacious teenager.

"I do."

"Well, consider this my application."

Talon mused a moment, then said "200 and no more. I'll give the other 300 to Al. If, and ONLY if, she thinks it's required... you go through her for the rest. Deal?"

"Deal!" a smiling Lashonda said sticking out her hand. "I think you'll like what I came up with. I only need one last thing. I need to show you something inside the house."

Al was NOT happy about that but Lashonda said she'd be with Mista G and she only needed to go into the front parlor area. Al relented and all 3 left the porch and went inside.

"Okay Mista G. These boards on the walls are everywhere. Most are burned up or rotted but, what are they for?"

Talon told her "Back in the day, the walls were made of plaster. These are called lath boards. They would put these up then slap the plaster over them. The plaster would squeeze between them and harden, holding the plaster in place. Why do ask?"

"All that old stuff ya want me to sort... is it because ya gonna put the house back tha way it was?"

"That's the plan yes," Talon told her in a 'what are you up to?' tone.

"Then I think ya really gonna like what I came up with." Before he could say anything, Lashonda smiled big and said "I'd like ta go shopping now if ya wouldn't mind?" and held her hand out flat.

Talon just laughed and pulled out a credit card. He laughed harder as he snapped it back... then handed it to Al instead.

"I think we'll let grandma hold on to that."

Lashonda smirked, then grabbed Al and nearly dragged her out of the house saying "C'mon grandma!"

Al just laughed but headed off with Lashonda.

"What was that all about?" Cody asked Talon as he and Grant walked in.

With a faraway gaze, Talon just said "With any luck? I just invested in my future."

Cody told him "Well, you ready to tour the place? Now that we know the house won't collapse on us that is." Then he chuckled and said "I thought you'd like to know... I left my pipe in the jeep."

"Smart move Doc... smart move," Grant said honestly.

Talon and Grant barely went in the house as it spooked them to think it might collapse at any minute just from their weight alone. Talon had a 4 prop drone he bought online that he used to get the upper floor layouts. It wasn't fancy nor lasted for long. It didn't have to. Now, the 3 men were off to tour the house themselves, now that they knew the basement wouldn't cave in on them.

"Well, it don't take an arson investigator to know where this fire started," Talon said confidently.

Grant looked and said "No it doesn't. Also don't take a rocket scientist to know it WAS arson. Look here. See how the wall and floor right here is blistered?"

Cody stated "Even I can figure out that must have been an accelerant."

Talon told them "Likely from an oil lamp popular at the time."

A whisper greeted them all in a slightly harsh manner.

"I doen allow men folk in here."

This time... it was Grant who was pissed.

"Tough shit lady! What part of 'this isn't your house anymore' do you not understand!?"

"I liked yue bettah when y'all had mannahs ginger chyld," the same whisper admonished.

"And I liked you better when you were a campfire story! Talk to me, or us, like that again!? Forget my brother... 'I' will turn this three story mansion into a TWO story one by the end of the week!"

Cody and Talon were staring at him, and barely containing their amusement.

"WHAT!?" he barked at both of them.

Now both men let out a chuckle.

Grant had calmed down some now. Talking to a ghost still spooked him some whereas the other two had become more used to it. It seems, when talking to a ghost, acceptance is the first thing. Like his brother, it was usually preceded by an angry outburst. Far calmer now, he now treated her with the same 'I don't care anymore' attitude as did the Doc and his brother.

"So lady, it ain't hard to figure out this was your room wasn't it?" Grant asked rather than hollered.

"Still is," the whisper told him.

"Don't start with me lady! Now, if this was your room, we know the fire started here. That only means two things... and one thing," Grant assured the open air.

"Enlighten me ginger chyld."

Talon was a tad pissed now and exclaimed "No longer a child Lucinda," letting the ghost know just who's side he was on.

"I am listening................. ginger man."

"Thank you," Grant said offering a slight bow to the empty room. "This room was the start. That means either someone set the fire, or caused you to. Either way, that takes care of the 2 things I mentioned. The 1 thing is, you were the target."

".........Explain ginger man......."

"AHEM!" Cody barked.

".............. please," said the southern whisper.

"What he's saying is, whether someone set the fire, or caused you to set it, you were specifically targeted," Talon said calmly. "And that means only one thing," he said ominously.

"Whaht are ya say'in 'Mista G'," Lucinda's voice asked. "I assure ya I was in thah finest of health... an I hahd no reason ta kill mahself. I loved this house and mah girls."

Cody kicked in saying "I believe you. Still, even in your time madam, you knew of certain drugs to make one, shall we say, woozy?"

"..................... Ah dooo........"

"Bottom line Lucinda, whether you were attacked, or drugged in some way to make it look like you did it or look like an accident," and Talon told her in no uncertain terms "You were murdered."

Every door in the house open and shut violently for about 15 seconds. Then, as quickly as it came... everything fell silent again.

"Feel better Lucinda?" Talon almost joked.

"........ Get out gray man ahn take yor friends with you.... NOW!... hurry gray man HURRY!..........."

"Lucinda, remember the part about us getting friendly? Oh yeah, and no more spooking me... ya remember that part?"

Lucinda's voice wasn't angry, it was worried.

"........MAYKE HASTE!!...."

"Jeez, take it easy there dead girl," Grant joked.

With extreme concern and worry, that same dead girl told them "............... Thaht wasn't me............."

Now, 3 men heeded some friendly advice.

All 3 men turned to head out. They were going down the long hallway when the door at the far end closed. Now, another voice was among them. It was also one only 2 of them had heard before.

"Now, you can die too and join your little whore friend!" the voice cackled.

Suddenly... the hallway was in flames.

Cody joined in the mix saying "I doubt that," and walked right through the flames.

"COME NO CLOSER!!" the shadow hollered.

"Kiss my ass," Cody told him. "Do you know how many camping trips I went on as a child?"

Wherever Cody walked the flames literally backed off. It was like he had a shield around him of some kind.

"I care not!" Shadow barked.

"Lots actually. Do you know what wood is the hardest to light?" Cody stopped face to face with the Shadow Man now and finished with "Wood that's already been burned....... grandpa."

"rrrrrrrrrrrrRRRRRRRAAAAAARRRRGGGHHHH!!!" Shadow bellowed in extreme frustration as the flames, and him, just went away like the illusion they were.

Talon was easing off his recoil and looking around.

"Pretty ballsy move there Doc," Talon said as pure compliment.

"It's bad enough a member of my family may have done this. One life however... is one too many. Adding 3 more is unthinkable." Cody sighed and said sadly "Looks like the stories are true."

"How did you know Doc?" Grant asked with a tone that belied 'I don't believe what just happened'.

Cody let out a deep breath.

"I didn't..." and looking at the spot where Shadow Man once was, finished with "... till now."

Just inside the Utah border, a dark brunette was pissed off, and impressed, at the same time.

"You iiiiiiidiots! You have no idea what you've woken up!" she complained. "Still, lesser men would have shit their pants by now. Not bad guys... not bad at all."

"I tayke it you saw?" Lucinda asked the girl.

The brunette noticed something. Lucinda's 'life force' was a whole lot stronger now... a LOT stronger. Brunette girl noticed it immediately but knew something else. If Lucinda's was stronger... then so was the Shadow Man's.

"Then you know y'all need tah hurry chyld... hurry. I kan keep them safe for now but, naht for lawng."

"I'll be there by dinner tomorrow," the brunette told her in a voice dripping with resignation at the fact that she was about to relive, yet again, a painful childhood memory.

"Iel doo whut I kan till then," Lucinda's voice told her.

Grant was looking around and asked his brother a question.

"Fair to assume the fire wasn't as bad as it could've been due to the plaster and heavy timbers?"

"You assume correct little brother."

Doc was shaken a little. He didn't think before, he just acted. Now, in hindsight, he was a tad disturbed.

"More your fields than mine. Care to clue me in?"

Talon told him "Even with the oil Doc, all it lit up was the soft stuff. This place truly was built like a fortress. The beams in here are one foot square in some places. The heavier the timber..."

Cody cut him off saying "I gotcha, the harder it is to lite it up."

"You got it. The fire did do some damage, but mostly to the upper floors. The smoke from it, the water used to put it out... and mother nature and father time did the rest."

"Speaking of, hey Lucinda?"

Grant chuckled saying "Only you would talk to a dead lady like it was no big deal."

Talon laughed too and said "Yeah... welllllll...."

All 3 men just laughed.

"......... Ah lyke thah sound of thaht......" the southern voice said in a rather happy tone.

"Sound of what?" Cody asked.

"....... Lafftah....... its been far too lawng since that was heard in heeyuh."

Kindly, Grant told her "Get used to it lady... with me and my brother working together trust me... there's more to come."

Talon went back to his original question.

"Lucinda, just the hallway alone shows huge amounts of gray in the wood. THAT means it was hit by water, a lot of it. What kind of bucket brigade did you have here anyway?"

Lucinda's voice now had pride in it when she answered.

"..... Leave 'Mista G'..... then...... stop by tha daw......"

Talon shrugged, then got up and did as asked.

"Aaaaaaaand........ your point?"

"..... thah bottom panel on thah wawl... remove it please...."

Talon looked at the wainscot panels that lined the hall. He was happily surprised when the one at the doorway did as he was told it would.

"HA HA HA HA!! Oh Grant you have GOT to see this!" Talon bellowed with extreme delight.

Grant and Cody walked over to the end of the hall by Talon.

"Sonuvabitch!.... A PUMP!!??"

Talon playfully chastised his brother in a poor southern accent.

"Ginger chyld... watch yaw language! Y'all are in thah presence of a laydee!"

Grant faced the door to Lucinda's room, gave a grin and a mock bow, and followed his brother's lead.

"Apologeees fo cuss'in madam," Grant said openly.

".......Thank ya ginger chyld......." was the kind yet ghostly response.

"He he... but I'm still calling it a whore house," and he gave a wink to the door.

Talon spoke to the air "So, what about these Lady Adair?"

"........ I used ta say...... fyre was owuh worst enemy. Putting it out was as easy as 1-2-3......"

"One two three?" Talon questioned.

"..... Ah loved mah girlz...... an I loved this house.... one day evree two weeks we practiced.... thayuh is thah one, two behlow, an three on thah main flawuh....."

Talon was impressed... highly impressed. So were Grant and Cody. All three said so.

"One two three... ooh Lucinda you clever girl you!"

"...... Thank ya kindly...... (giggle).... 'Mista G'....."

"With thinking like this!? YOU lady.... call me Talon!"

"....... I will....."

Talon then had a thought, and promptly marched back into Lucinda's room. He was looking for something when he did.

"Okay Lucinda... this is the part where I talk and you listen. Back in your day, photographs didn't exist yet. Even if they did, the fire would'a trashed them. What you DID have though was paintings. One would have needed status class or money to afford one... and you had all three. Tell me true Lucinda, were you really the driving force behind this place?"

"....... from tha day tha first stone was laid......."

"Then I know you would have had one somewhere. Okay lady... where is it?"

Grant was clueless and asked "What are you looking for bro?"

Talon looked at him and said "A portrait."

There was no voice this time... just the slow creaking of a closet door opening. Talon walked into it, and for the day, it was opulent. It was a walk in closet. That, and the pump in the hallway, cemented in his mind that Lucinda was waaaay ahead of her time. He walked to a back wall and there it was. It was rectangular and hung horizontally. It was about 5 feet wide and 3 feet tall... and charred coal black.

"Oh well, that 'was' a nice idea for like... 30 seconds," Grant chuckled.

"Bro?.... It still is," Talon said smiling sadistically as he took it down.

"............. Mah Henry painted thah......." Lucinda told them.

All 3 men though noticed her voice was getting weaker.

"NOT YOUR HENRY!!" a husky voice shouted in anger.

Shadow Man was back and furious. The remnants of the clothes were now flung about like a tornado.

It died down, but Talon stood tall and proud... and sporting a sneer.

"Shadow? You just fucked up, and I caught you!"

Tall and proud he left the closet. Clinging to the charred painting, he headed out with 2 men on his heels.

"Lucinda?"

"....... yes Talon?........."

"I think I would like to take you up on your invitation. I'll be back tomorrow." He smiled from the doorway at the far end of the hall and asked "Would you mind entertaining a gentleman caller?"

".......... Ied bee deh-lited......"

Talon saw Lucinda's door slowly close. He smiled, picked up the old painting, and headed down the stairs after his brother and Cody.

"I'll see you then," he hollered back.

Chapter 7

"Looking Towards The Future...
And At A Photo From The Past"

Talon went to the back of his truck and pulled out a new roll of plastic. He shrouded the painting in it, then made a phone call.

"Marie? Hey........ look in my contacts for me. Find me the info for Viking ArtWorks will ya?" Talon paused a moment, then told her "Yeah that's it. Put me through to that sweetie and text me his info please okay?" Another pause and "Yeah that's it thanks."

A moment later and Talon heard "Viking ArtWorks... this is Erik."

"I thought Erik the viking was a redhead, not gray like me?"

"TALON GRAYSON! How are ya buddy!?" Erik said cheerily

"Doing well Erik. How's business?"

"Also doing well thanks to you. West Coasters like you got a lil pissy at the delays so I opened a shop near you... in Boise. Thanks to you, I had the business to even open a second office. So, what can I do for you?"

"I got a linen job for ya but... this one is personal to me. I'll pay you extra if need be but, I need this done asap. I'm doing a restore this time not a tear down. Ya might say it was a family heirloom."

"You!? A restore!? That's new. Eh, regardless, I wouldn't even be in business if it wasn't for you. I'm actually in that location now. What is it, burned? Water damage? What?"

"Burn job."

"Get it up to me, and I'll do it personally," Erik told him.

"I can't stay but I'll catch an early flight tomorrow. Listen, I can wait for the repro, but I need the scan like yesterday. I'll get it printed locally till you get the original cleaned up and shipped back, okay?"

"No problem," Erik confirmed. "How big?"

"About 3 foot by 5."

"Get it to me before lunch, and if there's anything to be had, I'll have the scan in your inbox by nightfall. That work for you?"

"Nicely," Talon said smiling.

"Okay then... see ya tomorrow."

A doctor and a brother were staring and had no clue.

Talon saw their stares and began to explain.

"Okay guys, listen. A little tech and a little history... ya ready?"

Both men nodded and Talon told of his plan.

"That portrait was very common back in Lucinda's day. It's called a linen portrait. True canvas was rarer than rare out 'this far'. It was used in industry and precious little to go around. So, to fight that, many western artists painted on linen. Follow me so far?"

"I'm with ya," Cody said as Grant nodded as well.

"Okay then. Paints of the day weren't like they are today. Paint on linen and a lot of colors bleed badly. The better artists put the canvas on a wood backing to help combat that."

"Okay, I'm following you," Grant told him.

"Fine. Now, fast forward to only a few years ago. I was at a trade show and saw something amazing. I had no idea why it wasn't more popular but this poor guy got no love from the patrons. 'That guy' was Erik I just called. I guessed at the time that the muscle heads just didn't get the tech... but I did."

Grant chuckled and teased "You? Tech!?.... Naaaaah."

Cody asked "So, this Erik guy. He fits into this how?"

Talon resumed, "Doc, most of the houses and buildings we work on are landmarks and in the historical registers. Those people don't care that we use new materials, or reproductions... they only care that the look and feel are historically accurate once finished. Many of these buildings I get have prints or art on the walls that's long gone. That's where Erik comes in. He told me he was going to be a doctor and minor in art. Life however reversed those two. Cody, you know what a mass spectrometer is right?"

"Of course. We have one in the lab."

"Well, Erik took his love of art, and his knowledge of medicine, and combined them. He uses an array of laser scanners, high res high depth cameras, and the mass spec, to pull up images everyone thought lost."

Talon had flights up for the next day and held up a moment while he booked a round-trip flight.

"Okay, got my flights. Now, where was I?" Talon asked.

"Mass spec," Grant reminded.

"Ah yes. So this guy has a booth setup. I felt sorry for him being ignored so I took a few moments. He had me paint something on a piece of glass, fabric, and wood. The trick was I couldn't let him see. I'm no artist, so I wrote my first and last name, one on each, and my initials on the third. I laughed when the guy took the wood one and ran it through a planer. He wiped the glass with bleach, and literally torched the surface of the fabric."

Cody chuckled saying "Sounds interesting so far."

"Oh it gets better... and it's why I'm going to Boise," Talon confirmed. "Using the cameras alone, he brought back what I put on the canvas. Using the laser scanners and the mass spec, he brought back the images on the wood and the glass."

Grant was in slight disbelief and asked "How'd he do that?"

"Simple really," Talon answered. "Paint on wood or glass and you stain the wood or even the glass. Hard as they are they are actually porous on a microscopic level. Wood fibers are more like a basket weave. Paint on either and even hundred year old paint or stain, gets picked up because the original colors or stains get trapped in the material. The mass spec reads what the lasers burn off, translates it into pigments and colors, then feeds it into a computer. That brings up an image of what was once on the material. Once he has a clean image, he can then reprint it on any material, and make a reproduction of an original piece of art. I'm betting that this burned up frame was once a portrait of Lucinda. Paint on linen and some of those colors would bleed into the wood. What I'm hoping for... is enough for Erik to pull up an image and in a sense, bring her back to life." Talon got annoyed and told Grant "I don't know about you, but I'm tired of talking to a blank."

Cody asked with a smile at this possible new clue, "What's a blank?"

Grant was smiling too and said "It's 'Talon slang' Doc. Talk to someone over the phone, or text for a really long time. After awhile you wanna know who you're talking to and not a...?"

"Blank. I got ya now," Cody said as he now realized.

Talon told them how he took some pictures and portraits that had been ruined, and shipped them off to Erik for recovery. The locals, especially the local historians and such, were thrilled at the finds. Talon would always factor those into the job. The locals were appeased, and a nice man got his business off the ground. Every one he did, he gave Erik's name along with his 'gift'.

"We rediscover AND reproduce history. The local tight-asses are happy because though a reproduction it may be, it's historically accurate... so they can't, and don't, bitch," Talon finished.

"Okay but I have a question," Grant said. "Ghost lady said 'my Henry' painted it. Well Doc... what was great grandpa's name again?" he asked with a laugh knowing what the answer would be.

"Doctor Holliday. And yes Grant... Doctor 'Henry' Holliday," Cody told him.

"Okay that figures," Grant chuckled.

With a smile of discovery, Talon told him "Not exactly."

"Uh oh... HERE he goes!" Grant playfully chastised.

"Indeed," Talon started with pride. "Shadow Man said 'Not your Henry' but he didn't say 'I am not'... there was no personal on it. Assume for a moment Lucinda was delusional, and imagined a love that really wasn't. Mom told us ghosts are just people with unfinished business here in the living right?"

"Jesus.... alllll the damn time," Grant agreed in a slightly annoyed tone.

"Well then, Lucinda has her business. I haven't figured it out exactly yet but I will. Now, we all assumed Shadow Man is here because he's the murderer. Think about this. If it WAS Doc's great great granddad, why would he not say 'I am'? Whoever Shadow Man is, I think it's safe to say a few things here. First, I highly doubt Lucinda was delusional. Therefore, I'm comfy in saying her love for the old Doc was likely mutual. Agreed?"

"Totally," Grant said.

"Second, if he's painting her, it's likely there was an intimate attraction."

Cody answered this time saying "Also agreed."

"Lastly," Talon told them, "Shadow Man said 'Not your'. That tells me Lucinda had an admirer she wasn't aware of who didn't like Doc Cody's lineage getting in the way."

Cody was loving this and said "So like what... if I can't have her no one can? That sorta thing?"

"Exactly Cody. I think it's fair to say Shadow Man exists... but he ain't family. Well, not yours anyway."

Doc Holliday felt like a world's worth of vindication was just handed to him on a silver platter.

"What's that Al? You're breaking up," Talon said as he was yet again on his phone. "Okay that's better. An hour? Okay we'll be ready!"

Talon put it away and got a plan in motion.

"Okay bro, Al is on her way back she said. We need to get 200 feet of old train track cleared. I got Big Mack, you take the tractor with the bucket. Watch how deep you dig but I'll bust up the big stuff... you haul it away."

"Let's do it bro!" was Grant's gung ho response.

Cody said he had to get back as he had some patients to see. He wished Talon a safe flight and said he'd be back in a couple of days.

Talon fired up the big diesel and asked "Doc? A moment if you please."

Cody climbed up into the cabin asking "What's up?"

"Don't ask but... ya know that history you and I couldn't find locally?"

"Yeah, what about it?"

"Ya might say I got a special delivery the other day. Anyway, I held off going over it till I got your stuff to go with it. Full picture and all that. Think you could get those copies to me like you promised?"

"I got patients today and tomorrow. Day after that though... drop them by the house? That be okay?”

"Perfect."

Doc chuckled and asked "Maybe before you dig into them we could go for a drive... say... in that Lamborghini of yours?"

"Ha ha ha ha ha... who are you... my sister!?"

Doc chuckled back and said he'd see him in two days. He hopped out and Talon went to clear some dirt... with Grant right on his tail.

Al showed up right on time. Talon and Grant took another 15 minutes but got the area cleared Lashonda asked for. They rode back to the front of the house and Talon was baffled.

"Lawd I swear Mista G, we been evreeware from Susanville down ta Minden and back!" Al said slightly annoyed.

"Okay, don't mind me but... what the fuck is this?" Talon asked, unsure and unhappy about Al's cargo.

She had the big flatbed that Big Mack was on. Now it was loaded with stacks and stacks... of used pallets.

Lashonda had a fake annoyed attitude in her voice when she said "Whatzamatta Mista G... you don't like ma plan or somethin'?" Then she laughed at all the clueless grownups and said sweetly "Don't worry... you will soon."

"Alright little girl... I'll bite... let's hear this plan of yours? Talon said looking over the truck.

"Hey! Do these curves look like a little girl to you Mista G!?" Lashonda said waving her hands down her sides and getting insulted as only a teenage girl would or could.

Suddenly her face went forward as Al planted a hard slap on the back of her head.

"And you don't need ta be point'in them out neither! There's enough hoochie-mamas in that house... we doent need none out here. You hear me baby girl?"

"Ow granmomma! I was just teas'in!"

"Yeah? Well... I wasn't," Althea said in a 'don't mess with me' tone of voice.

"Okay Lashonda, let's hear this plan of yours... ha ha... before granmomma makes you part of the landscape."

She looked at Talon with pride, and told him her plan.

"Look Mista G, you ain't do'in nothin' but stand'in there, and you're already sweat'in. You got a lot of metal in these trucks. Sinks and lights and stuff. How hot you think that's gonna get?"

"I concede your point... keep going."

"Aside from lunch and gas... I used the money to buy tarps. Really big ones. See all these wood things?"

"Um... nope," Talon teased.

"Yeah well, places be giv'in 'em away. Half o'them from one place alone. If you stack them up, you can put the tarps over them. Mark 'em wood or electric or whatever. Two stacks of them things, then the tarp over top. Put the supplies inside and y'all got a storage tent. Keeps 'em shaded, gives us folk some shade, and you can pick your supplies like y'all go'in to a flea market. Spread them out and you can get your trucks and such in there. Remember those lath thingies ya showed me?"

Talon was grinning now at the clever teenager and just said "Yup."

"Well, the wood things were free so... break 'em apart and cut 'em up and you got free wood to fix tha walls an ceil'ins."

Talon got very serious now and said "Lashonda?" in a not so happy tone.

"Yes Sir?"

"How much of my money did you spend on this idea of yours?"

Her voice was meek now and said "Four hundred of it."

"Al?.... My card if you please," Talon commanded.

Talon took it back and put it in his wallet. Then, he pulled out 2 fifty dollar bills... and smiled.

"Nice work there kiddo. Tell ya what," and he handed Lashonda the two fifty's saying, "How about you keep the change hmm?"

Lashonda was stunned and stared at Al as if to ask if it was okay. Al had a stern look on her face, that just seemed to say 'did you forget something?'.

Lashonda looked back and said "Yes sir... thank you sir."

Al hugged her now with pride and a smile saying "Ha HAAAAAAA!! Now THAT'S tha baby girl I helped raise!"

Talon sweetened the deal and told her "Your plan... you're riding with me," and he fired up Big Mack.

The drivers got the pallets unloaded. A day ago Grant got the area around the house opened up so the trucks could pull out. Al was the first one around. Empty and facing out, she unhitched the trailer and left it out back as she drove her bobtail down the driveway.

Lashonda showed Talon her vision and Talon moved the bucket. The drivers loaded a bunch of pallets in the bucket, and Talon swung them in place. Grant and another driver on the ground stacked them, then threw the tarp over the top and anchored them with big rocks. The first makeshift tent was built at the end of the clearing and the first truck got unloaded. Working their way towards the house, they repeated the process. It was a fine assembly line and after 3 hours, the last truck was emptied and the last 'tent' was in place.

Al pushed Lashonda gently saying "Well? What do you got ta say for yo'self baby girl?"

"Mista G sir?"

"Yes Lashonda?"

"Thanks faw giv'in me a chance."

Talon smiled at the sweet kid and asked "Ya remember when I said you were on a job interview?"

"Uh... yes sir?"

Talon walked off to his truck to call it a night and said "You're hired."

Lashonda was beaming knowing she did good. Behind her... so was Al.

Early the next morning, Talon was in a cab and on his way to the airport. He called Erik from the plane letting him know he was on his way.

"I'll meet you there gray guy," Erik teased.

"I only got a 1 hour layover before the next flight ya damn viking," Talon teased right back.

"Ha ha ha.... yeah no worries I'll be there."

"See ya soon," and Talon shut off his phone as the plane pulled away from the gate. An hour later Talon was earthbound again.

"Yes..... it's Kona," Erik said with a playful smile as he greeted his friend in the downstairs concourse.

Erik handed him a cup of coffee.

"Is there any other kind?" Talon said just as playfully as he gave the big gray Norwegian a friendly hug.

"So, that it?" Erik said pointing to the plastic wrapped frame.

"It is," Talon told him as Erik peeled back a corner.

"Actually, it's not as bad as I thought. The frame might be savable too." Erik thought a moment and said "Hey I have something for ya. I had some tech kid tweak the scanners. We think we can now even pull a print off of it, but have yet to test it out. Mind if we try?"

"Just as long as it don't ruin the image... sure!" Talon said happily.

"Trust me, it won't," Erik said as he hugged his friend goodbye.

"Sorry I couldn't stay Erik... and thanks for the coffee!" Talon hollered back as he headed back upstairs and out of sight.

Talon was back in Reno/Tahoe airport an hour later. Back in home territory, he was pleased with his trip... and it wasn't even lunchtime.

"Y'all take care o' yoself now Mista G!" Althea said as she dropped him off at the mansion.

She and Lashonda had picked him up from the airport.

"I will Al. You and Lashonda have a safe trip now. Enjoy your family but don't forget..."

"I know I know. We'll be back in 2 weeks or so for when Miss Eileen comes in. We'll only be 2 hours away ovuh tha border in California. Thaht ho momma gives you ANY trouble you just let Althea know... and I'll be back heeyuh light'nin quick ta give her what for... ha HAAAAAAA!"

Talon smiled and laughed, gave each of them a hug, and waved as she pulled away.

"Muss she be so loud?" the southern whisper in Talon's ear complained.

Talon just laughed at Lucinda's dislike of Al's trademark ear-piercing laugh, and headed down the area for the tracks.

Talon was where Big Mack was shown on his mural. The area for the tracks went quite a bit out from the house. It also circled it. Talon was now at the farthest point from the house on that circle. The mansion faced north but was going east to west. Talon was now due east of the house and about a hundred or so yards away.

"Alright gentlemen... I'm where you pointed me to. Now how about a little help, and show me, why you brought me here?"

Talon got no response. He went around the circle some, then doubled back. He was back in his original spot, then started heading back for the tents. That's when he heard it... the unmistakable sound... of a slow moving steam locomotive. It was also behind him. He turned around and the closer he got the louder the sound became. Finally, he heard it stop and let out a blast of steam... right where he was standing. He heard a soft murmur of men talking. Just loud enough to hear, but not loud enough to make out what they were saying. He smiled when he realized, he didn't have to. The voices were going away from him, and sounded as if they walked right into the dirt mound he was staring at.

"Gentlemen? Thank you," he said kindly.

He picked up some small boulders the size of bowling balls and marked the ground with a circle.

"I'm not ready for this yet but trust me... I'll be back when I am."

Talon heard the train ring its bell twice, then sound like it was leaving. It faded to nothing seconds later.

Talon got a measuring tape and a rope from Grant's truck. He tossed them in the cabin, and fired up Big Mack.

"Miss Adair? I think it's time we put you back on the map," Talon said nicely.

He didn't get an answer, nor needed one. He drove around back and put the big backhoe on its trailer.

"Nice work baby brother!" Talon said honestly at seeing Grant's progress on the front parlor.

"Lashonda had a real good idea with those pallets. I got all 4 walls redone and only used 5 pallets," Grant exclaimed with pride in the little girl.

He was re-plastering the walls. There was still a big hole in the floor but both men were busy on separate jobs, and the new floor joists that were needed was a 2 man job. Talon smiled and was truly happy with each little progress.

"Hey Grant, why don't you take a break, and come give me a hand?"

"Yeah sure," and both men headed out back.

Talon took the end of the rope, and climbed up on Big Mack's boom. Grant marked the other end at ground level, and Talon climbed back down.

"Okay so, we got 14 feet 7 inches. I say let's go 17 feet and call it a day."

Grant was confused and asked "Call what a day?"

Talon told him "I wanna put up some iron... care to help?"

Grant smiled saying "Get out of that dreary and spooky house? Hell yeah I am allllll over that!"

"Heh heh, thought you might be."

Two men stacked the back of Grant's truck with bags of concrete. They headed down to the end of the driveway and started gathering rocks... big ones. Grant dug a deep hole on one side of the driveway while Talon did the same on the other side. Each one then got filled with rocks and concrete and each man built up a rock piling 5 foot tall each while leaving the centers hollow.

Talon declared "Let's let the concrete harden for a day or two, then we'll come back and mount the iron," he said as he took some final measurements.

Talon looked over the 2 pilings while Grant checked for level and alignment. Both men were satisfied, and Talon helped Grant clean up.

"I have to come back in a few hours and check the walls. Make sure no air bubbles surface and make sure there's no sagging," Grant told his brother.

"Hey you've been hard at work... I'll get this one. Why don't you drop me off, go home, get cleaned up, and see about making me an uncle sometime soon why don't ya?"

"Yeah okay... I'll get right on that," Grant teased. "Truth is dude, they're either silly little girls, or self absorbed in their careers. I've been trying though, Lord knows, I've been trying."

Talon didn't tease back, but honestly said "Yeah... they don't make 'em like mom anymore, do they?"

Grant took off his cap and covered his heart like they do at the beginning of a baseball game. Then he hung his head in a moment of silence.

He put it back on and said kindly "No they don't big brother." He stowed the last of the supplies then called out "C'mon... let's call it a day."

"Sounds good," Talon agreed.

For one brother it truly was the end of a long day. For the other, it was about to get a bit longer.

"Ladies and gentlemen I'd like to thank you all for riding Greyhound. I thought you'd like to know we'll be in Reno in 1 hour. That will also be this bus's last stop. One hour to Reno and once again, thank you for riding Greyhound," the driver's voice called over the intercom.

The brunette looked to the empty seat next to her and asked "Care to give me a clue where to go from there?"

She got no answer... none at all.

"Figures," she said in annoyance and went back to watching the sunset color the mountains purple.

Grant dropped Talon off. He showered quick, then got dressed. This was no ordinary dress up. For the first time in a long time, he put on his Virginia City outfit he used to wear for the tourists. Complete with sidearm. He grabbed the keys to the Cuda, set the house alarm, and headed for a date.

The moment he left the driveway, a lovely brunette girl was grabbing her gear from under a bus. She was feeling 'off' when she did. Not in a good way, and not in a bay way either... just... 'off'.

"Hey sweetheart where you go'in? You need a ride?" the greasy dark-haired man asked her.

She took one look at him, half grinned, and told him "Listen guy, I may be new here... but I am not new. Let's just say 'no thanks', and leave it at that shall we?"

He grabbed her arm saying "Oh now why you gotta be like that?"

She didn't answer him, but he did lose his grip on her arm. Even with the backpack on she was fast, real fast. The arm that was holding her, was now firmly pinned behind his back. The right side of his face however was being pressed into the mailbox... hard.

"The guys in the psych ward were twice your size... and it took a minimum of 4 of them JUST to get me to sit still. Tell me me something you half-assed tweaker, does the name Wanda mean anything to you? Cause right now? She's nearly screaming in my ear. Touch me again... ever... and the local police will get some interesting info on her 'supposed' overdose. By the way, she wants to know why you left her in the tub?"

"Y... y... you're fuck'in crazy bitch!" he hollered as he backpedaled away in true fear.

"Dude? You don't know the half of it," was all she said as she made her way south.

It was nightfall now and Talon parked the Cuda in front of the house. He shut it off, then turned the generators on. The moment he breached the door, he was being watched.

"What the hell!?" the brunette exclaimed in true shock.

Seems she could, under the right circumstances, see SFTP's. It's what she referred to as her visions, or rather, 'Scenes From The Past'. They were intense at times but, always that, the past. This vision however was new and it concerned her heavily. This vision she realized... was live.

"What are you up to Mister Grayson?" she mused. "Nice outfit by the way," she said a little more honestly than she would have liked.

She shook her head and the street scene returned as the vision went away.

"Get a grip on yourself girl!" she chastised herself. "No getting involved... you know the rules!"

She sighed heavily and let out a few demons of her own. The personal kind, and not the kind that require an exorcist.

"He wouldn't want anything to do with a piece of work like you anyway. Just get in, get out... do what ya gotta do... and you can get back to your quiet little life and shut that southern lady up once and for all."

That plan wouldn't work out exactly as she thought.

A few questions later and she got on a bus that would take her as far south as possible. It went to a mall way downtown. She had very little money left and knew she'd need a taxi. She didn't know why, she just knew south was the way to go. She also noticed something else. The closer she got, the stronger... and more frequent... the real-time visions became.

Talon walked in, and played his part. He checked the walls first, then announced himself like it was done in years past.

"Talon Grayson, Miss Adair," he said as he tipped his hat, "I believe I was invited."

He didn't know what to expect. What he got was totally unexpected.

"How pleasant ta heeya maanuh's... (giggle)... and ta see ya dint bring tha loud one," the southern voice told him kindly, but with flair.

"Yes well, a gentleman always honors the request of a lady when he can," Talon replied with a grin. "I also know, it's not polite for a lady to keep a gentleman caller waiting," Talon told her in a tone that reeked of 'don't screw with me lady'.

"Now... you wouldn't dehnyyy a lady her grand entrance now wuud you?"

He chuckled and replied "Why no ma'am I would not," then added, "As long as that arrival is sometime today."

"Thahs guud... because, you see... I do soooo love ta make an entrance," the southern voice teased him.

Talon was in the newly cleaned up front parlor. Open the doors and a massive fireplace on the far wall greeted a visitor's gaze. The long and open stairway was set back and to the left, just like Althea described. Talon was standing in the parlor, fireplace to his right, and facing that staircase. Suddenly, the stairway had a small glow in it. It was as if a flame from a candle came down the stairs, but without an actual candle attached to it. It came down the stairs slowly, but moved like it had a mind of its own. Talon didn't know if he should piss his pants... or ask it out on a date.

It came almost to him. About 10 feet away it grew, and as it grew, it took shape.

"Mistuh Grayson I presume?" the slightly distorted image asked in a most well mannered way.

Talon was blown away, utterly and truly. History he NEVER thought he'd ever experience... was a mere 3 feet away.

He actually bowed politely and said "You presume correctly, lady Adair."

The image walked around Talon as if she was examining him.

"Trust me good suh... I may run this here fiiiine establishment but I ahshaw you... I'm no lady."

"Why my dear Lucinda... ha ha ha... are you flirting with me?"

"Welllll... maybee jes a little."

Talon was staring at a blurred image. It was a woman for sure, just not a clear one.

"Oh... my... God," a stunned and disbelieving brunette said as a vision returned. "Watch what you say gray guy... watch what you say."

She turned sideways, and hopped into a taxi.

"Where to, miss?"

She threw a $20 into the front seat and said "South and east."

"Okay but... where to exactly?"

"I'm not sure yet but, I'll let you know when we get there."

The driver just shrugged and said "Your dime. Okay, south and east it is," and he pulled away from the curb.

"By the way... I'd like to do it quickly."

Talon had a favorite music video. It was 'Take On Me' by A-Ha. The song wasn't bad either but he liked the effect they used. It's called rotoscope. It was a way of stripping a cartoon like image, and merging it with real life. That was what Talon appeared to be seeing. It was as if he had a blurred view into the past, but only of Lucinda. Seeing that, he suddenly didn't feel afraid.

He saw a woman in a cobalt blue velvet dress that was sliced high up her left leg to nearly her hip. A slight smile came to his lips as he saw Lucinda stop and stand, but looked more like a pose, as she exposed her bare feet and long legs through the side slit of the dress. What appeared to be white lace 'highlighted' her chest and shoulders by forming a slight U shape. The same lace trimmed the edges of some rather short sleeves. Well, short for the day anyway. This was a custom job though, and only close to the fashion of the day. Long dark wavy hair, and truly perfect makeup finished out the look.

"Oh now Lucinda, no need to be bashful around me," Talon hinted regarding her blurred image.

"Oh now hush. A lady nevuh reveals awl her secrets when first meet'in a gentleman cawlluh now does she?" Lucinda countered.

Talon just smiled.

"I wouldn't know, I wasn't around back then. Around now however, well, you'd be surprised what secrets we can reveal."

Talon proudly pulled out a rolled up paper from inside his ¾ coat.

"Oh?" Lucinda said sweetly. "Doo tell."

"Not tell, Lucinda... show."

Lucinda was truly clueless and asked "Why, whutevuh doo you mean?"

Talon grabbed a few finishing nails and took the rolled paper over to the fireplace, and explained.

"You wanna make a dramatic entrance? Okay, two can play at that game."

Talon unrolled only a little of the right edge. He used the nails like tacks and put one each in both corners.

"Ya see Lucinda, I stopped on the way here and had something printed. I don't mind if you want to be bashful becaaaaaaaaaauuuuuussssssssseee..." and he unrolled the paper and pinned the left side when he got to it.

It was a photograph, but of a painting. Not quite as big as the original but roughly two thirds the size.

Talon had a huge 'gotcha' grin on and finished with "... I already know what you look like."

"Oh my!"

Talon unrolled the printout of the image Erik sent him. He got a mostly perfect print. He told Talon in an email it was indeed canvas not linen. However, it wasn't treated. The fire destroyed the canvas but actually locked in the image into the wood for the most part. The overall image had some issues here and there where Erik's computers had to 'guess', but considering the original was a burnt piece of wood, Talon was still highly impressed at the final result.

Talon was staring at a truly stunning woman. Long black wavy hair, and a 'come hither' look on her face. Talon likened it to a combination of old west styling, meets 1940's pinup. Talon noticed mulatto skin, with chiseled yet feminine features. High cheekbones and a well defined jawline... with dark yet sensual eyes. The photo showed a couch popular for the era. Light blue and all the scroll work on the frame one would expect for back in the day. In the background was Lucinda's bedroom showing only a section of the twin windows framing her floor to ceiling fireplace. On the couch, was a nearly naked woman laying on her right side, facing the painter. It was one of those paintings that spooked most people because her eyes seemed to follow you wherever you went. Her left arm laid comfortably along her fine curves, while her right arm appeared to hold her up slightly, yet effortlessly. The expression on her face is what caught Talon's attention. It was an expression of both caring, and confidence. He could tell this woman was not only comfortable in her femininity... she relished it. Her ample breasts had what looked like blue satin material draped over them, but with just the right amount of cleavage peaking out. That material almost touched the floor before curving back up and over her pelvic patch and part of her hips. Her ankles were crossed and hanging over the edge with her toes pointed. Curves and beauty to die for, and aside from what the blue satin covered... there was nothing else left to the imagination. Talon decided that, to him, the original, was once sensual artistry at its finest.

"In my humble opinion madam... *you*... were stunning."

"Go up there!? I don't think so," the taxi driver said getting a metal rod handy.

He thought he was about to be robbed... or worse.

"This is as far as I go, and your $20 is up... get out."

He was about a 20 yards from the entrance to the mansion on the main road. He let out a sigh of relief when the brunette did just that. He saw her hustling up the road in his rear view mirror as he pulled away.

Lucinda was near tears at the sight of it, and all the memories it brought back. She touched it lovingly and was actually choked up.

"Mah Henry painted thaht."

"Oh look... the whore is being modest," came an evil tone.

"I figured it wouldn't be long before you crashed the party," Talon told the new voice in a tone that belied he wasn't afraid.

Shadow Man had arrived.

The evil spirit wasn't outright angry this time like he'd been in the past. Now he was taunting.

"Show him whore... go on... SHOW him!"

"Why doo you purvey such evil upon me!?" Lucinda half cried and half shouted in anger. "Were you some rancher I spurned? A lawyer or perhaps some train baron? WHY do you haunt me!!??"

Shadow Man nearly floated to Talon with sadistic glee.

"Do you know why she hides from you, gray one? Hmm?"

Shadow Man flung his arm, at Lucinda, and basically made her come into focus.

"THIS is why! HA HA HA HA HA!! Tell me you silly man... what do you think of her stunning beauty now!?"

Lucinda was indeed in focus now. In focus... and nothing like the photo on the wall. Talon saw a female frame. He called it that because that's all it really was. Female... and horribly burned. Only a wisp or two of hair, and skin mangled blistered and distorted. A horror movie couldn't have done a better job.

Lucinda looked at Talon, then at her hands and body, broke out in tears, and ran off. She faded away as she did.

Now it was playtime. Shadow Man was incensed and was ready to let loose. A gray haired man's courage surprised him however.

"There's that picture on the wall... and the horror you showed me," Talon said staring down the smoky image. "As for showing true images... HAH!... You're one to talk. As for the lady of the house, I know both images are real. I can handle the first one. It's obvious to me you couldn't. Still can't. Worse still, for you anyway, I can handle the second one too. You were a coward then, and clearly still are. Don't bother threatening me or even trying to scare me... cowards never do."

"We'll see about that..." and the doors that had been open the whole time slammed shut.

Talon put them back in personally and now was a tad miffed that he had. Next, Lucinda's painting burst into flames. Shadow Man tried to light the walls with it, but got frustrated instead, and flung Talon to the floor.

"wwwwwWWWWWHAT!!??"

Talon got up and said as he dusted himself off, "Go ahead, try it... for all the good it'll do you. Consider that a little chemical magic from this century. It's called a flame retardant you asshole. THAT trick," Talon challenged "Will only work once."

"I killed her... now I shall you as well!" Shadow Man threatened angrily.

"Let's test that theory shall we?" Talon said as he grabbed a handful of ashes from the fireplace and hurled it right in Shadow Man's face. "Just as I thought," Talon said triumphantly as Shadow curled away coughing hard, "My mother knew a thing or two about shitheads like you... JUST like Lucinda's did. She said anything like you comes into this realm to play? Yeah... you're affected by the same laws of physics we are."

Talon tried bolting for the door, but Shadow Man flung him away. Suddenly, the room rocked like there was a sudden earthquake. The walls rippled some then... chunks of plaster came flying off the walls... and headed straight for Talon. He blocked them but more kept coming. He was getting hammered pretty hard and knew he was in deep shit. He made another attempt for the door but caught a large chunk to his back and down he went. He got the wind knocked out of him and hard as he tried, he just couldn't fight back. He laid on the ground in near agony and was just shy of passing out... when the doors opened back up... hard.

"BACK OFF, asshole!" a gorgeous brunette hollered as she burst in.

The moment she crossed the threshold, there seemed to be a wind around her that blocked most of the small to medium stuff.

"Take it easy there Mister Grayson, I'm gonna get you outta here," she said in the kindest and caring of tones.

Talon was on his back and on the floor. The brunette was acting like she was shielding him, and trying to get more weight than she could lift off the floor. He was facing the fireplace and she was facing the door. A large chunk she didn't see coming was about to take her out. Just shy of passing out, Talon pulled her down on top of him with his right arm... and fired a single round with his left. The chunk of plaster heading straight for them was a threat no more. Now this strange new girl was angry. She wanted to care for this gray haired guy... and had no clue why. She stood up, spread her feet a little, and put her arms at her side. She curled two fists, looked down, and hollered.

"I said......... back..........OFF!!!!"

She looked up hard on that last word. Her words almost echoed in Talon's head but, in an instant... every chunk fell to the floor and the room was quiet once more. She got Talon to his feet, sort of, and helped him out of the house as quick as she could.

"Are you okay?" she asked.

"I (cough cough) will be... as soon as I can catch my breath. Are (cough cough cough)... are you?"

"Not really," she said weakly... just before passing out.

Talon tried to catch her, and did actually. His own strength was not quite back yet though and and only managed to cushion her fall.

"Thanks... 'Mista G'," said a lady with the most sparkling pair of violet eyes Talon ever saw.

They looked up at him in total kindness... right before they closed.

He put his hand on her neck, and his ear to her mouth.

"Pulse, check. Breathing, check. And for the record, mysterious one... thank you."

Talon now turned his attention to the house. His attention, and his anger.

"I will NOT be kicked out of my own house!!!! NOR be run off!" Talon hollered as he stumbled to his feet. "Still not dead though, so I'm calling this first round just that... round 1! I'll be back you piece of shit."

He saw a backpack on the driveway behind the car. It looked like it was left there in a hurry. He politely searched it looking for a clue.

"Great. No ID, no key card to a hotel or motel... just a big fat load o'nothin."

Talon wasn't moving real fast or real well, but managed to put the backpack in the trunk.

"Well lady... whoever you are... I guess the least I could do is offer you a good night's sleep," he said looking down at the girl on the ground.

It took a bit and, while polite, it certainly wasn't graceful... but he got the lovely girl into his car.

"I'll be back, you sonuvabitch... and when I do... it'll be in force!!" Talon hollered as pure truth and even purer warning.

"You don't scare me gray man," Shadow told him.

"Nor you I," Talon replied confidently.

The Cuda took off down the driveway and headed back for home.

Chapter 8

"Purple Haze"

Talon had no idea where to take this girl. The police option was out.

"Yeah officer, I was being attacked by a ghost and this lady came in outta nowhere and sent it back to wherever it came from," Talon teased aloud to the open air as he drove along. "Yeah, I can see nothing but good things coming from that," he mused snidely.

No key card so no hotel or motel to drop her off at. He and Grant had gotten passed-out drunk in the past. This girl didn't seem drunk, but had the same type of passed out.

"Hiya Doc... sorry to call you so late but uh... I got a problem."

"What's wrong?"

Talon gave him a brief rundown, and how he had company this time.

"I'll meet you at the house," Cody said all concerned.

"Doc?... I sure would appreciate that," Talon said kindly.

Talon got home and carried the pretty girl to his couch. Five minutes later, Doc was pinging his intercom. Talon opened the gates for him and Doc was checking them both out a minute later.

"You got some nasty bruises and a few scrapes, but nothing more serious. She however concerns me," Cody diagnosed.

"Why's that?"

"Physically there's nothing wrong with her. Yet, every major vital sign is very low. Corny as this may sound, it's almost as if her 'life energy' was badly drained," Doc said perplexed at even his diagnosis.

Talon sneered and told him, "Life energy, eh? Pity mom ain't around anymore huh?"

Cody told him "Honestly? She'd likely do more good right now than I would based on her readings. Listen, that bruise between your shoulder blades is a real nasty one. No work at all till you can move without feeling like there's a rock in your back... or you could do some real damage."

"10-4 Doc. I'm not big on doctors, or rather going to one. I am however all about not hurting myself. Trust me Cody, I'll heed your advice."

"Good. Talon?"

"Yeah?"

"I'm glad you called me."

In a brotherly and kind tone, Talon replied "Doc? I'm glad ya came."

"Get some rest and I'll come by later today with those copies and check in on you both."

"Yeah okay Doc. She'll be fine there for now. Least I can do is give her a place to sleep for the night, for what she did."

Cody heard the words, but the intent was what caught his attention. Talon wasn't being kind... he was being tender. He also thought it nice and didn't mention a thing. He merely picked up his bag, and saw himself out.

The lovely girl slept like a rock. For the first time since she could remember, she slept soundly. Even the drugs 'they' used to give her, didn't do that. She was used to waking up several times a night, sometimes violently, from all the messages she received. Now, there was nothing but silence. That alone made her smile. It was still dark out when she briefly woke up. She saw she was on a nice couch in a nice room yet... still had all her clothes on. A quick look about the room and she saw her backpack, seemingly untouched, right beside her on the floor. Ten feet away, was her gallant, gray-haired knight. Asleep on a reclining chair was Talon. He was in only his pants and shirt but he was still wearing his boots. The bulge under the blanket he wore told her... he was still wearing the gun too.

"Aw... my protector," she said softly and liking the sound of that... and so wanting to believe it.

She smelled the fresh scent of her blanket. It was also the warmest and softest she ever felt. Still drained, she smiled and fell back to sleep. There was another first for her when she did. For the first time, she felt............ safe.

She finally woke up for good and now the sun was up. Looking about, she saw a kitchen next to the seemingly obvious living room she was in. Talon was still where he was when she last looked... and still asleep. Gray guy took off her sneakers but, nothing more. It made her smile knowing that's all he took off. She decided she'd be nice and make some coffee. Walking softly to the kitchen, she stopped, smiled, and backed up. That's when she decided to steal something. She leaned down, and gave Talon a soft kiss on his cheek. That kiss though, was the only thing she stole.

Walking away she said quietly and, in a rather feminine way "And how is my big brave protector this morning?"

She got truly spooked next, and that wasn't something that happened to her anymore.

"Still alive... thanks to you," Talon said in a kind but grumbling tone.

Her heart about jumped out of her chest. The coffee also spewed out of the bag she was holding as well.

"You'll find your stuff is intact and right beside you. The only person who 'checked you out' was a doctor friend of mine... and there's no nasty pics of you on the internet." Talon chuckled and said "Not from me anyway."

She was now pissed at herself. She wanted to be sweet and most importantly, feminine. The latter now more than ever. Years of living on the run, in the shadows, and under the radar however... left her not knowing how.

"You're very welcome," was all she could manage.

"I'd get up and help you but, sorry, I'm a little lame at the moment," Talon said with a wince of pain.

She had no idea why but, all she wanted to do was care for him. The Florence Nightingale effect was in full swing... and she was truly stumped as to why. Most of the guys she knew were sleazy at best. This guy however was different... way different... and she was almost compelled to him.

"So purple girl... how bout we start with a name?" Talon politely commanded.

"Purple girl?" she queried.

Talon swung around in his chair. He stared straight at her and waved his finger back and forth at his eyes.

"Ah... right. Listen, I want to thank you for letting me stay the night. I promise I won't be a bother and I'll be out of your hair shortly," she evaded.

"A name..... I won't ask again."

Damn that natural confidence of his she thought.

"Violet.... Violet Hayes," she answered meekly.

She had given many names in the past, and not one of them real. She was telling this stranger her real name and was not liking the effect he had on her.

"Violet? Clever I'll give you that. I'm guessing mom or dad or both were Hendrix fans?"

Now she nearly giggled.

"This is the part where most people play the air guitar."

"I wouldn't be so crass," Talon sneered.

The moment her back was turned, Talon did indeed play the air guitar and silently mouthed 'SCUSE ME!... While I kiss the sky!'.

Another giggle and she proudly proclaimed "Uh... you do know I can see you, right?"

She was looking away from Talon but, saw him anyway.

"Okay, sorry," he chuckled. "Still, a fitting name. And a pretty one too... just like the lady in my kitchen."

Talon was flirting now too and was also asking himself why. He hadn't behaved like this since he first met his departed wife in high school.

"Why, Mistuh Grayson," Violet playfully teased in Lucinda's accent, "Would you all be flirt'in with me?"

"HA ha ha... ya know... I think I am," Talon said with a devil may care attitude. "And it's "Y'all" by the way... not 'You all'."

Talon tried to get up, but winced in pain and sat right back down again.

"Easy there Mister Grayson," Violet said nearly running over. "Where does it hurt?"

"OW!..... Shoulder blades," Talon gruffly replied.

Violet gently ran her fingers over the area, and Talon sucked wind at the mere touch.

"Okay, take off your shirt and let me look."

Talon gave her a look. Violet held her ground though and gave him a look right back that just seemed to say 'Really? Is that how you're going to be?'.

Talon laughed slightly at her reply and said "I'm not being modest... it's just that I can barely move my arms ha ha ha ha... ow!"

She swung around and straddled his lap. Next she grinned.

"I'm impressed... most guys usually stare a little lower."

With awe and wonder in his voice, Talon remarked "They truly are stunning ya know," referring to her purple eyes.

Violet didn't know what to say again.

"Thank you," yet again was all she could manage.

She unbuttoned Talon's shirt as gingerly as she could. A powerful chest and firm upper body had her thinking a whole different set of thoughts right about now. Talon didn't have a body builder's torso... but it was highly toned.

"Okay now, niiiiiiice and easy," Violet said as she carefully peeled off the shirt one arm at a time.

She was being kind and Talon knew it. She was also being tender and caring... and Talon knew that too. She could be some psychopath or something, but Talon didn't seem to think so. All the clues so far pointed to a likely hard life perhaps, but she didn't strike him as crazy.

She gently leaned him forward and proclaimed "That's bad." Then she sat up and in an authoritative tone ordered "Towels... bath kind... where do you keep them?"

"Mmff.... closet in the bathroom, around the corner," Talon grunted.

Just the look on his face made her want to hold him. She got what she asked for instead.

Kindly, and jokingly, she told him "Now don't do anything I wouldn't do while I'm away."

"After last night? I doubt I could do ANY thing you could do."

Violet smiled sweetly, then ran off to get the towel. She came back with a nice thick one, and headed for the kitchen. She soaked it in the sink, wrung it out, and popped it in the microwave. A minute later she took it out and folded it up and went back to Talon.

"Okay there big guy... nice and gentle like, let's get you onto my bed," Violet said referring to the couch. "Okay... that soooooooo didn't come out like I meant it," she said slightly embarrassed.

She helped him over to the couch, laid him face down on it, and put the hot towel between his shoulders.

"Crafty one aren't you, Violet?" Talon said honestly as he felt the heat.

"More than you know Mister Grayson," she said in an avoiding tone.

"Speaking of... two things. First... call me Talon."

"Alright... 'Talon'... and second?"

"Second is... we're going to play a game. It's called the truth. I tell some, then you do. The trick is, to tell it no matter what."

"Not so sure I like this game," Violet said in a dreading tone.

"Tough. Now, I'll go first." He smirked and started with, "I reeeeaalllyy want a cup of coffee."

Violet giggled but went to make the coffee she got interrupted from earlier.

"White with the lady on it? Or Red with the gold seal?" she asked sweetly holding two different bags of coffee.

"First, the fact that you knew where that was is just a tad scary," Talon said with his face half buried in the couch. "And second... the red one... it's ALWAYS the red one. I only keep that white shit for my sister who, apparently, doesn't know her ass from her elbow when it comes to the dark elixir."

Violet looked at the bag and asked "Kona? What is it?"

"The only true coffee on God's green earth aside from Jamaica Blue Mountain. All the rest is nothing more than black acid in bean or powder form," Talon said truly believing every word.

Violet shrugged, and made the red bag. Right now, Talon would get anything he asked for, though she wouldn't admit it.

She came back with the coffee and now the two had switched positions. Talon was now on the couch and enjoying the relief the hot towel was providing. Violet pulled her knees up as she sat in the chair Talon slept on and, to Talon, just looked sexy as hell.

"I could spend a week in this house and never come out," Violet said with sweetness and awe. "It's so quiet and peaceful."

"Yeah, not a lot out here except the birds," Talon told her.

"That's not what I meant," she said with some dread. "Okay look, you wanna play this truth thingy? Fine, here it is then. This house is more than a little quiet... it's more like a sanctuary. At least to me anyway. Did you build it?"

"A good portion of it. It was a wedding present for my wife."

Violet's heart about sank.

"And... uh... where is she?"

"Why don't you tell me?" Talon said trying to probe a little.

Violet was clueless and just cocked her head.

"She's in Crest Hill in Virginia where her family is."

"Oh I'm sorry. Divorced?"

Now Talon smiled a little and probed further.

"Now, what makes you say that?"

"Didn't notice a ring," Violet said meekly.

"Ha ha ha ha!.... Ow. Why Miss Hayes, were you checking me out?"

"Truth huh?" she asked uncomfortably.

"That's the rules," Talon playfully confirmed.

"Well... maybe a little."

Talon saw how uncomfortable she was, but decided not to tease.

"Thank you... I'm flattered," Talon said kindly. "And no not divorced. More like... separated.... permanently." Violet still didn't get it so Talon told her "Crest Hill is a military cemetery. I have my memories, and a few mementos. She wasn't a slab of stone... not to me anyway. She was very close to her parents and them to her. I know it's what she would have wanted so, I left her to rest with them. The only sad thing, to me that is, is that she never got to see this house. Not finished anyway."

Violet was squirming now. Talon was being kind. That alone made her want to hold him. That also was very sexy to her. Talon was pretty much winning her heart, and he wasn't even trying to.

"So... you mentioned it's quiet here. I heard the tone in your voice though. Why do I get the feeling that my definition of quiet, and yours, aren't exactly the same?"

Violet decided to play the truth game. Not all of it mind you, just let out enough to see what reaction she'd get. She wanted to make sure her 'new man' was all she was imagining, and hoping, him to be.

"There is a very feminine 'vibe' here. Some woman loved you very much. Fair to say you have an idea what I am, or at least, can do?" she asked cautiously.

"Fair to say," Talon eluded not wanting to tip his hand either.

Violet was truly surprised but for a change, in a nice way.

"And that doesn't freak you out?"

"If you knew my upbringing Violet, you'd know why it doesn't."

"If you knew mine... you'd have thrown me out by now," she said sadly.

Now Talon just wanted to hold her. Like the lovely brunette, he also had no idea why.

"True your 'talents' are not exactly what you'd call normal. Still, you came all the way from Tennessee to help a stranger. I figure the least I could do is be open minded about it and hear you out."

The paranoia was back now and Violet asked "How'd you know about that?"

"Some girl comes blowing in and saves my ass. Then, said girl collapses on me and goes into a near coma. I politely checked your pack for ID or a motel key or something. All I found were some bus receipts."

Violet calmed back down and thought about it. She also thought, if she were him, she'd likely do no different.

"I believe you were about to tell me about the 'quiet'?" Talon reminded.

"Okay fine then. Ever been to New York City? Or any other like it?"

"I have actually... heh heh... and there is no other place like it in the world."

"Well then, you know the hustle and bustle of the street right?"

"I do."

"Imagine living in the middle of fifth avenue then, 24 hours a day, every day, without a single day off or change of scenery. That... sadly... is my life. I 'hear' and see all that's around me. If you actually walked that street, you learn to accept it but, to a degree, your brain tunes it out. Me? I get rude reminders from time to time but... the 'noise' never goes away... ever. Not till here anyway. This place, right here right now, is the first time in my life I've ever known 'quiet'. I'm sorry for your loss, I truly am. This quiet though isn't from her, or because of her. It's a woman for sure who was responsible for this, I can feel it. It was also... someone... whoooo..." and Violet had a realization and asked Talon, "It was your mother wasn't it?"

Talon was surprised for a moment but, only a moment. He was smiling because at least it was a pleasant surprise.

"My mom and dad were your classic hippies. I'm talking commune loving live off the land fight 'the man' protest everything die-hard hippies. Mom always fancied herself to be some sort of shaman. When the house was finally built, she came over and blessed it in her own unique way. I didn't care and thought it was nice. I didn't believe it but hey... heh heh... who am I to turn down free good karma ya know?" Talon chuckled.

"Either mom got reeeeeaallly lucky, or she knew way more than you gave her credit for. Only a lot of love... and pure love at that... could create something like this. I've heard of things like this, but never in my life experienced it till now."

"Ya know, now that you mention it... mom did say something. I was only half paying attention at the time, but she said only love, peace, and noble spirits would know the inside of these walls or walk these grounds for all my days. I just thought she was being a silly hippie so I kinda blew it off. Mom mentioned one day, I'd know what she meant. My wife was gone by that time and mom was sick again. She told me that was her gift to me, and a lasting love from her for when she was gone." Talon was slightly lost in a dream and finished with "The last thing she said before she left was, when that day came, I would understand now... what I couldn't then."

"She sounds like an amazing woman. I would have loved to have met her. Anyone who could do what she did would be someone worth meeting indeed."

Talon struggled to his feet. Violet immediately went to him but he shrugged her off.

"I gotta stretch anyway," he told her slightly grimacing.

God, she just wanted to hold him so bad. Talon walked to a hallway and took a picture off the wall. He came back and handed it to Violet.

"Violet? Mom. Mom? Violet. There... now you have."

She took the picture and saw a young couple obviously in love. It was Talon's mother and father. It was a side shot and the lovely lady with the long brown hair was staring into the man's eyes. He was staring back at hers. Suddenly, Violet broke into tears and gently pet the picture frame. What she saw was the woman in the picture... turn and smile at her.

"You okay Violet? It's not THAT sentimental," Talon said seeing the tears.

The woman in the photo gave one last smile, and turned back to the original pose.

Violet handed it back saying softly and kindly, "It is to me." She dried her tears, said honestly "It was a pleasure meeting you Mister and Mrs Grayson," and handed Talon the photo.

Talon went to put it back. While his back was turned, she looked to the ceiling. She silently, and sincerely, said 'thank you', and waited for Talon to return.

A soft whisper and even kinder 'presence' suddenly appeared and told Violet "Care for him, and protect my baby as only you can... and one day he will do the same for you. The peace of this house I left for both of you. I brought you together............ the rest is up to you," and the whisper, and the presence, was gone.

Now... Violet's tears returned.

"So, for a stranger, you seem to know a lot about me." Talon chuckled and said "Ya even met the family!" He calmed back down and got serious and practically commanded "Mind telling me about yours? Not to mention how you found me... and why?"

"Truth?" Violet asked not wanting to tell it.

"Nothing but."

" I had visions of you. A red headed guy too. Your brother I presume?"

"Younger. His name is Grant."

"There was another guy too, not often but he was there. Can I tell you something?"

"Anything you'd like," Talon assured her as she put the re-heated towel back between his shoulders.

Violet took a deep breath, and told a stranger something no one but her grandmother knew.

"First of all, you have to understand, these 'visions' as most people call them... more times than not they're representational."

She waited to see how Talon would react. She didn't get the one she was used to.

"I'll take your word for it. Care to clarify a little?"

Violet was floored and just silent.

"Yo, ghost girl... snap out of it. You were saying?" Talon sort of barked.

"Well, one time I was looking for a safe place to stay for awhile. All I kept seeing was a bear in a pond. I was also looking at him and could see the sunrise."

"Um... okay, so... you were facing east. That means you were on the west side of the bear."

Yet again, Violet only had stunned silence.

Kindly, Talon told her "Mom used to make us analyze our dreams."

"Indeed," Violet finally said picking back up her story. "I got a map of the area at a truck stop. Turns out, 20 miles north of where I was there was a summer vacation spot called Bear Lake. There were also closed up cabins on the west side."

"Bear... west... got it," Talon told her affirming he indeed got it. "So what does that have to do with the third guy you mentioned?" Talon said trying to test her.

"Like I said, it's not always like I'm looking at an instant replay. Sometimes it is, but most times it isn't. When it is, I still have to sort out what's real and what isn't. That third guy... every time I saw him I would always see that actor guy Val Kilmer. Still haven't sorted that one out."

"Ha ha ha... he looks nothing like Val," Talon laughed.

"It's NOT funny!" Violet said rather sadly.

"Seems your vision was right after all. That was the doctor I told you about. He's coming back later to check on us by the way."

"So... you hang out with Hollywood actors do you?" Violet said snidely and defensively.

"Violet, his name is Cody Holliday... as in 'Doc Holliday'. Val Kilmer played him in the movies." Talon said in a 'calm your ass down' kind of tone.

Violet dropped the attitude in an instant, and meekly said "Oh."

"So, westerly bears in ponds?... Hiding out? Visions of me , and looking for a safe place to stay? Jesus Violet Hayes, just what kind of life did you lead?"

"Sadly, not a good one... and one I'd rather not tell."

Talon wanted to hear it anyway.

"Violet, I got a mansion that's haunted apparently. People in my life lately seem to show up out of nowhere, yet be exactly what I need and when I need them. One of those people just happens to be related to the ghosts we ran into. Shit like that doesn't happen by chance Violet. Life has seen fit to throw me into a cold case murder mystery. And all because I wanted to restore an old house. It's as if this is all some cosmic play that I'm suddenly in, and the 'powers that be' don't like the odds stacked against me so they're leveling the playing field. So trust me... if you travel halfway across the country to lend your talents to a total stranger... and manage to somehow kick Shadow Man's ass!?... Then you best believe I wanna know everything there is to know. I got enough questions without answers, I don't need any more," Talon nearly ranted in frustration.

Violet wouldn't look at Talon. She was painfully sad, and told her story. A story only her grandmother knew.

"I lost my mother when I was 8. But that wasn't my problem. My problem was, I didn't realize it till I was 10."

Violet waited for some sort of response. When none came she was surprised, but continued.

"I had no idea why we had to move into grandma's house. My grandmother is like me but even she said not to my level. You know how children have imaginary friends? Well, mine weren't imaginary."

"I really am sorry about your mother Violet. Please, continue."

She still wouldn't look at him, but did as he asked.

"I was 12 when the horrors started."

"The horrors?" Talon queried.

"It's what I call the really bad traumas. You look at a plane crash or a murder on TV and think 'oh isn't that terrible'? Imagine being me... and living it. Every gory detail, every sight and every sound."

Talon truly never did think of it that way. Now that he had, he really felt sorry for Violet.

"Okay so, your 12... what then?"

"A girl, same age as me, appeared. Every time she did I couldn't breathe. She practically begged me to help her. She had blood between her legs and I had no idea why at the time. Turns out her dad was a high powered lawyer. He raped his own daughter. When she went to tell her mother what he did, he choked her to death to keep his secret. The cops already had him in their sights but there was no evidence."

Talon interjected "Till a little purple eyed girl pointed them to some."

"And wanted to know how I knew. Needless to say, when the evidence I told them about actually turned up... well, they reeeally wanted to know how I knew. The father knew he was caught, and tried to make a run for it. That asshole was actually pissed that he was caught. Given no other choice, and now cornered by the police, he did the blaze of glory thing."

Talon said kindly "I'd ask you why you're crying but, yeah, I think I won't."

Violet was indeed crying and shouted "I was twelve Talon... TWELVE! No kid should have to go through that. Grandma taught me what she could but told me I had to hide what I was and what I could do. I did but, I was a good girl. Still am. But this was murder! Surely I shouldn't lie about this, right?"

Violet was sniffling now and in a fetal ball on the chair.

"I was only twelve."

Talon was pissed now. All he wanted to do was hold her, but the bruise on his back made that impossible.

"You would think that the end of the story but OH NO!... It gets worse."

Talon just listened.

"One officer saw my potential. He tried to use me like a hound dog. Right about then... asshole started harassing me. He tried to rape me too. He was beyond angry I caused him so much trouble. Finally, one night he came and tried raping me again. This time though I had had enough, and did what I did last night. I didn't know how I did it at the time but, his daughter showed up then as well. Between my outburst, and her asking him why he hurt her, I was finally rid of both of them. That's when the horrors started. Suddenly I was flooded by more than I could handle. I would see 'them'... and not the car as I was crossing the street. Grandma couldn't protect me anymore and I was put in an asylum. The doctors were convinced I was somehow creating these visions. I was 'medicated' and 'tested' for 3 years. Grandma died while I was in the hospital and the bastards wouldn't even let me go to her funeral. I decided then and there I would get out and never go back in... ever. It took me a month but I got out. One of the orderlies was a perv and would have sex with the patients. I tempted him in finally, knocked him out, took his access card... and have been laying low ever since. I have been dealing with the visions, and looking over my shoulder... since I was 16. That, was 5 years ago. Technically, I'm still an escapee from a mental hospital."

Violet was rocking back and forth now and holding her knees to her chest.

"I avoided large crowds and stuff like that. Staying low key reduced the visions to a manageable level. I would take waitress jobs or do Tarot readings to make money for food and rent and such.

Talon didn't know what to say. Finally he did.

"And... what brought you to me exactly?"

"I haven't had a vision like that girl since then. Hers were THE most intense to date. I managed to, as I put it, quiet the noise. Then, you and your brother walked into that house, and a lady with a southern accent started talking to me. Yours however, by far, were even more intense then that little girl's were. Even her piece of shit dad wasn't as strong. I sensed two things, that you desperately needed help... and that I somehow belonged here. The closer I got, the more frequent the visions got. Talon?"

"Yeah?"

"You scared me. I couldn't fight your visions nor control them like I had others. What scared me the most was, I have only seen the past. With you though, I saw what was going on... live... by the time I got out of the taxi."

"I don't mean this in a bad way but... I … I truly don't know what to say."

"Well then, here's one last piece of truth for you," Violet answered him. "All those visions I had, somebody always wanted something. Tell my wife this or, tell my husband that. Most practically ordered me to help them, like it was my duty or something. All of them except you. If you must know... that is why I came."

Talon stared at her for a moment, then gave an order.

"Pick up your pack and go..."

"I understand. Would you mind if I at least got changed first? I've been wearing these clothes for 2 days now," Violet interrupted knowing all to well this conversation.

"Can I finish now?"

"Fine," Violet huffed.

"Pick up your pack and go... down the hall. First door on the left past the bathroom. It's the guest room. Laundry is the closet doors just outside the bedroom if you need it."

"Wait... you're NOT kicking me out?" Violet said totally not getting it.

"You gonna go all psycho on me?"

"Not likely."

"Well... there ya go then. Hit the shower too if you want."

"Sooooo..... I can stay?"

"For now. I'm sure at least a couple days rest couldn't hurt. You have a fine frame Violet but even that looks like you could do with a sandwich or two. Tell you what, you nurse me back to health in exchange for room and board. There... now it's an honorable arrangement. Tell me Violet Hayes, wadda ya think of that?"

With a bit of kindness, and a bit of unbelievability, Violet said "I think it sounds heavenly. One condition though."

"What's that?" Talon asked.

"We still telling the truth?"

"Last bit," Talon told her. "Go for it."

She smiled at him and said "The flirting stays. I kinda liked it when you did that."

Just as sweetly, Talon told her "Me too. Deal."

Violet grabbed her stuff, and did as she was told.

Chapter 9

"The Return Of Talon Grayson"

"Ya know, quiet thing aside, this truly is a beautiful house," Violet said coming out wrapped in a towel. She was drying her hair with another, and asked "Which one is your room?"

Talon chuckled having no idea why she wanted to know, but played along anyway.

"That hallway... last door on the left. Why?"

With a playful smile, she just said "You'll see." A disembodied voice called out "Jesus Christ... I've stayed in motel rooms smaller than this closet!"

Talon just chuckled.

She came back out barefoot, with some really long and lovely legs, and wearing one of his silk dress shirts.

"Okay, go back to that truth thing for a moment. Tell me, who does this look better on... me or you?" Violet asked in the sexiest of grins.

"Truth?"

"Mm hmm."

"Ha ha, that's not flirting... that's downright teasing," Talon said with a huge grin of approval.

Violet got sad and plopped down in the chair.

"Is it really?" she said sad that she got it wrong. "I didn't exactly have a lot of boyfriends 'being me'. Sorry, I thought it was a good idea."

Talon was supportive and said "Oh trust me, it's an excellent idea... heh heh heh... it just isn't flirting."

Violet beamed, then sashayed into the kitchen.

"How's your back feeling?"

"Like Doc implanted a bowling ball on my spine. Hurts like hell but thanks to you, 'Florence Nightingale'... I got a good bit of mobility back."

Talon got up and sat at his kitchen counter. Two hours ago that was impossible, so while still painful, he was ecstatic for the progress.

"Speaking of boyfriends, how many were there exactly?" Talon asked still trying to find out about his new house guest.

"Truth?"

"Mm hmm,"

Violet was a bit shy now and asked as she cooked "Am I allowed to count the ghosts?"

"Nope," Talon said with a light laugh.

A rather sad "None," was his answer.

Talon was about to tell her how sorry he was for her. He decided to get cocky instead.

"Well... lucky for me then eh!?"

Violet giggled a little and hid behind her hair some.

With a smile on her face, and in her voice, she told him "If you say so Mister Grayson."

"HA HA HA! Okay... now THAT was flirting!"

Violet had a smile on her face as she went back to cooking breakfast.

Violet left his breakfast in front of him and went off to change. She came back in jeans and a T-shirt but, to keep the flirting going some, she remained barefoot.

"Aw... I liked the other outfit better," Talon jokingly teased like a 4 year old boy.

She smiled knowing someone 'real' actually liked her, but went to check his injuries.

"Well, most of the swelling has gone down. Still a real nasty bruise though. Suffice to say you'll be uncomfortable for awhile, but I doubt it will be more than that," was Violet's prognosis.

"So ghost lady... what about you? Seems grandma was a cool lady but what about mom and dad?... any brothers or sisters?"

"Dad and mom got divorced when I was little. Mom said he basically ran off with some college girl. I got sick in my mother's eyes, and she couldn't handle it, and basically drank herself to death. My grandmother was indeed a cool lady, but I was an only child so me and her were the only family we knew."

"Jeez Violet, is there anything in your life that isn't bad... worse... hide out... and more lousy?" Talon asked her with true sympathy.

"Sorry Mr. Grayson... afraid not," she said sadly as she woofed down her food.

"Talon."

"Sorry no. My life may have been hard, but I told you I'm a good girl in spite of all of it. 'Talon' is personal. As long as I'm taking care of you in return for room and board, then I'm working. As long as I am, that makes you the boss so... Mr. Grayson it is," she told him playfully but meaning her words.

"Careful there, Miss Hayes," Talon playfully taunted, "I think you'll find out I like being the boss," and he gave her a wink.

She got him right back in the same tone and said "Careful yourself there gray guy... I think you'll find out I like that kind of man," and she winked back.

"Well if that's the case then... hey wait a second..." he shifted tones and exclaimed " Awwww... does that mean no more flirting?" Talon teased with a grin that made Violet shuffle in her seat.

"Well... I wouldn't say that exactly," she responded with a playful smile.

"Heh heh... good to know."

Violet cleaned up the dishes, and asked "So tell me, what makes you tick?"

"Wadda ya mean?"

"I pull you out of a maelstrom of a ghostly temper tantrum, and you're pissed. Don't lie I can tell."

"Yeah okay.... so?"

"So? SO!?" Violet asked not believing what she was hearing. "So 'Mista G'... most people are cowering wrecks by now. They also don't come anywhere near me, no less offer me a job." then she got playfully snotty and continued with "But oh no, not you. You tell the unseen to go fuck themselves. Oh yeah... and for the record?... That thing on your hip is really loud."

"Let's just say I don't like people... seen or unseen... telling me what I can and can't do in my own house." Talon already had a plan in his head and asked "So... how does this ghost thing work anyway? I get the impression it's not exactly like it is in the movies."

"Yeah..." Violet chuckled, "... um... not exactly." She looked at Talon in almost disbelief and asked "You really wanna know don't you?"

"I actually do," Talon said with conviction.

"Wow... this is new for me. No one ever asked to be taught before. Okay, here goes. Mind you, all of what I'm about to tell you is only based on me and my own experiences... okay?"

"Fair enough."

"Well, they need energy same as we do. We get it through food and rest. They get it from the things around them or other people... living or otherwise."

"Okay then, if that's so, why does Lucinda show up more often than Shadow Man does?"

Violet explained, "Go and run right now, Mister G. Do that, and you suddenly need far more energy than if you just walked. Also, when you're done running, you're way more out of gas than you would be if you just walked."

"Okay let me take a stab at this then, see if I got it."

"Go for it," Violet said smiling and totally not believing this conversation.

She was loving it, she just wasn't believing it.

"So Shadow Man is angry. Lucinda seems confused sometimes but very calm usually. So like what, Shadow only shows up now and then because he has to build up more steam?"

"Exactly. Also, these ghosts are in a realm where time doesn't exist. Coming into our world most often throws them off. That's why Lucinda seems to be very 'with it'... and other times seems to be 'out there'. She's different though. Most are really 'out there' but not her though and not Shadow Man. Those two are far more lucid of current times than any I've ever met. More powerful too."

"Hmm," was all the deep in thought Talon said.

Just then, Talon's phone rang. Talon answered it and put it on speaker-phone.

"Mr. Grayson's phone... Florence Nightingale speaking," Violet playfully answered cutting off Talon.

"Uh....... who?" said the confused voice.

"Oh hello, you must be Grant Grayson, Talon's brother."

"Uh, yeah, is um........ my brother there?"

Violet giggled and Talon just chuckled at her.

"Yeah bro... what's up?"

"Well for starters, ya mind telling me why there's a bullet hole in my new wall? Kinda looks like it came from your gun too."

Talon laughed and told him "Dude, the entire room gets trashed and you're worried about one little hole?"

"Uh you okay over there bro? Aside from your little target practice I need to patch, the walls are perfect. I'm getting ready for the final coat now and we can paint by tomorrow."

"Grant, don't fuck with me... are you sure?" Talon said with a stare to Violet.

She was as stunned as Talon was.

Talon wanted to see and said "Grant, hang up and vid call me... I wanna see this."

"See what, weren't you here last night?"

"JUST!... Do it... and don't argue with me," and Talon hung up the phone.

His phone rang back and a good looking red head was on the screen.

"Here... see for yourself," Grant said as he flipped cameras.

He panned back and forth and he was right. Aside from an obvious patch job on the right side of the fireplace... the room was intact.

"Bro, we need to talk. Finish the patch job then... nothing but outside work today. Till I can sort out what happened, I don't want you in that house alone."

"Bro, is everything okay?"

"I had a rather nasty run-in with Mister Shadow last night. Suffice to say," and Talon turned around so Grant could see his back, "I won't be coming into work today."

"Holy shit! Yeah, ya know, it is a rather nice day outside. I just got one last question for you?"

"What's that?" Talon asked as he saw Grant's camera swing around.

"Who is THAT!??" Grant said with true glee.

Talon smiled and teased, "Why ginjuh chyld... doen y'all recognize yaw favorite winduh laydee?"

"Figures," Grant said all let down. "First smokin' hot woman I find in ages... and she's been dead for over a century. My brother gets Florence Nightingale... and I get stuck with Nightmare Adair. I swear I have no luck."

Violet giggled, but Grant heard it.

"Uh... bro?"

Talon knew what he meant. So did Violet. She decided to end his misery and came in over Talon's shoulder... smiled... and waved.

"Florence I assume?" Grant asked.

"Hi Grant... the name is Violet actually."

"Dayum! TWO hotties in one day and I miss them both. My life sucks." Grant said "Okay brother, take care of yourself and I'll see you for dinner."

"Grab some pizzas on the way, Doc will be here too."

"You got it bro... later!" and the call went dead.

Talon sneered at the phone but spoke to Violet.

"Ten bucks says my sister calls within the hour."

Across the country, a slightly lonely, slightly nerdy, dirty blond was researching her family tree. She was adopted and as a gift for her 21st birthday, her adopted parents gave her all they had on her adoption and what little they were given of her true family. That same birthday was also, only a month ago. They loved her and she loved them. She promised them she would always be their daughter, and they supported her search. She was using the computers in the New Hampshire Public Library, and hit a snag.

Lucinda always liked Grant. She thought him the most adorable baby and his cuteness at the time just touched her heart. There wasn't a woman alive back in the day Lucinda would take crap from. Men however were her weakness. 'Back then' Lucinda was the type that if a man said jump, she'd ask how high. Having only been raised by a mother, modern folk would say Lucinda had a bit of a father figure issue.

For his compliment over her beauty, and just because he grew up so well, Lucinda decided to lend her adopted 'ginjuh chyld' a hand. Being a mother, or rather, NOT getting to ever be one, affected her psyche as well. Next, she lent a hand to an adopted blond one.

"Two pages bahk honey chyld," was the whisper the blond heard.

It was the kind you don't acknowledge... you just follow. Next thing she knew, she was turning the pages backwards, not forwards.

Talon was now deep in thought... and not a happy camper.

"Okay ghost girl, start talking." Talon was pissed and said "What... now the ghosts have ghosts!??"

She was still stunned and said "I call it a reflection."

"No dear, reflections are what you see in a mirror or in a pond. They make you go 'Oh look, I need to comb my hair'. They don't make you go 'LOOK OUT!!' and shoot at WALLS!!!!!" and Talon backhanded his coffee mug across the kitchen.

Violet jumped and shrank back when it smashed.

"Sorry dear. I am indeed angry... but not at you."

Violet wouldn't move though.

"Actually... uh... ya might be soon," she said in a slight panic.

Talon's attitude changed. More like, 'shifted'.

"I'm not gonna like this am I?" he asked staring directly at her.

That alone made her shrink a little more.

"Wellllll...."

Talon took a deep breath and let it out.

"Tell me. I promise you I won't hurt you."

"Says the man with the big loud gun," Violet stated.

"Huh? Oh, heh heh," Talon said as he forgot he was still wearing it.

He took a moment and took it off. Then he put it on the counter and slid it out of reach.

"Better?" he asked.

Violet let out her breath some and began to explain.

"They can't always communicate like Lucinda does. Ghosts like her are extremely rare. Mostly they show you things as a way to communicate. I told you I was in a mental hospital. The reason for that was I lost my grip and didn't notice it. I got distracted and saw a building on fire. There was only the fire chief on scene at that point. I thought for sure it was an illusion... or what I call a reflection. Looks real. Sounds and feels real too. Thing is... it ain't. If I know it's an illusion, I can reorient my mind and see it for what it is. I ran into that building thinking it merely a reflection. I was trying to figure out the message. I was about 30 yards in and started suffering. I thought I lost my focus and got involved in the illusion. Turns out..."

Talon finished her sentence saying "It wasn't an illusion was it?"

"No it wasn't. The fire chief told the cops what I did. Child services came and took me away thinking I was a danger to myself. It wasn't the first 'mistake' I made and that was the last thing they needed to take me away."

Violet seemed lost in a memory and finished her story.

"My grandma literally spent her last years trying to get me out. When she died, she came to me before 'moving on' as you would call it. She taught me something I never forgot, and use to this day."

Talon was sweet and as non-threatening as he could be.

"And what was that?" he asked.

"Well, up till then, I either ran or tried to hide from them. Mostly the latter. Grandma told me it was time I stopped running, and started fighting back. She told me to stop being afraid, and to start using them just like they used me. It was like an epiphany. I truly believe to this day grandma knew how I felt and that's why she moved on, knowing now I could take care of myself and no longer needed her."

"Smart lady," Talon said kindly.

"She was indeed," Violet said just as kindly.

Talon was still 'gathering intel'.

"Okay but, this is what doesn't make any sense. You saw it too."

"I did," Violet said shyly.

"Care to explain that one?"

"Not...... really?" was her impish reply.

Talon just stared at her the way a father does an errant child.

"Fine. Things like Shadow Man can't actually do those things in real life. At least I haven't encountered one who could. The energy it would take to do what he did is enormous and beyond even them. They can do small things but then all their energy gets used up or seriously drained. In order to fight a reflection, you have to believe beyond anything rational that it is just that, an illusion. The energy it takes to make your mind see things however is far smaller. Shadow Man likely used up all his energy when he threw you the first time. You must have thought, even for a short time, that you were in true danger. Shadow Man took that feeling and used it against you."

"Okay but that leaves two things. First: he actually moved that stuff around then... put it back. Based on what you just said, that's near impossible so... not likely. Second: he fooled you too. You're right, I did know I was in trouble. Felt like it too. I wasn't scared but I was worried about how to fight back. I wanted to, I just didn't know how against something like that. So question is, why did you see.... it... too................ oh no. Violet? You were distracted too weren't you?"

"Look, that experience was enough to freak out any....."

"VIOLET!!..... weren't you?" Talon said staring her down.

Violet got sad at what she was sure would be the loss of 'her man', then hollered in anger because of it.

"Oh alright!! YES! YES I WAS!! There... ya happy!?"

"Yeah but, given your obvious talents, what was there but an old house to distract someone like you?"

"Oh sweet Lord you are dense aren't you? It wasn't the house that distracted me."

In a rare moment, Talon truly was being dense.

"Okay... what then?" he asked truly not getting it.

"IT WAS YOU, YOU IDIOT!! I saw you in trouble and I wasn't going to stand for you getting hurt." Violet broke down and said through her sniffles, "I was shown you, and your brother. I saw you stand up to what even I run from sometimes. You hadn't met me but I had you. I saw a strong and handsome man and... well..." and through her tears asked "... do I really need to tell you the rest?"

She wasn't looking at him. She had her back to him and just closed her eyes and waited for what she knew would come. What she knew would come... and what actually did... were two totally different things. To her true surprise, a pair of strong arms held her arms at her side, and gave her a gentle hug from behind.

"No you don't," was all the owner of those arms said.

Violet couldn't believe it. She thought for sure she'd be called names, laughed at, and told to go. Instead, the made up hero in her head, turned out to be everything she imagined. Now, she just let loose and nuzzled into his shoulder.

Now, Violet was worried.

"You're going back in that house aren't you?"

"Back... and 'en mass'."

Violet was confused and asked "On who?"

Talon laughed some and said "It means 'in force'." He pulled her back to the kitchen and tickled her the whole way saying "Okay you... no sadness allowed! Heh heh... so says the boss!"

She giggled and shrieked but Talon stopped and sat her on the stool.

"Okay, seriously now, I need one last thing. How come I can hear her, or more often, than the others. Like, just everyday people, why do some hear it and some don't?"

Violet straightened herself out, then straightened herself up with pride at being a teacher again.

"That one is easy. My grandma gave me this analogy. Think of an

AM/FM radio."

"Um... sure," Talon said having no clue.

"Okay, people like you? AM. People like Lucinda?... FM. They have the ability to transmit on AM but it takes a lot of power. Power that most of the FM folk don't have. Every once in awhile, someone like you comes a long who's both AM aaaaand FM. Usually that ability is passed down from someone like your mother. Thing is, when someone like you does come along, your FM side is usually only tuned to get one or two stations."

"Fair analogy. So, what about you then?"

"Even rarer still is me. I get all the stations and... I can transmit."

"Gotcha."

Talon had a heavy night and even heavier morning so far. That morning was now turning into lunch. Talon did the tickle thing because he truly didn't know how else to get out of an awkward situation. When his wife died, he truly felt like he lost his soul mate. He never even looked at another woman, nor had any desire to... until now. He knew two things right now. He knew to watch himself because this girl could be a complete bullshit artist. Second was, if she wasn't... then he was seriously out of practice.

"Okay... I don't care if I'm a HAM radio that can talk to Mars. Do you want to know, what I know for a fact, I'm not?"

Violet hid a smile behind her hair again and only said "Hmm?"

"Heh heh... you're flirting again."

"Am not," Violet said in a rare display of confidence.

She had tons of confidence in her abilities. In just Violet? Not so much.

"Well... okay... maybe just a little," she finished in a shy and sexy tone. She snapped out of it and said "Okay Mister 'I'm too bad-ass for you ghosts' guy... what is it that your not?"

"Heh heh... I'm not a vampire. Care to go for a walk outside?"

"I'd love to."

Talon opened the slider to his back patio and stepped out to a crisp but warm mountain day. Violet did not.

"Soooo... I'm obviously not a vampire but, uh, I'm guessing you are?" Talon said jokingly seeing Violet hang back in the doorway.

She was truly nervous and said "Kind of. I walk out there... and the FM radio comes back. You really ready for that?"

Talon gave her a grin that had her shuffling again.

He held out his hand and said "Let's find out shall we?"

Violet wasn't afraid of 'them'. She was having a glorious day for the first time in her life. She just didn't want it ruined. She stepped out and took Talon's hand and... the silence remained.

Politely, she looked around and said in the kindest of tones "Oh Mrs.

Grayson... 'mom'... you're gooooooood."

Violet was in heaven but said the contraction of 'you are', instead of 'you were' and she said it that way... deliberately.

Talon was walking off the bruises. He swore that now knowing what they were, they were healing even that much faster.

"So Violet tell me this. If that was an illusion, how come I can still feel the bruises?"

"Your mind thought you were actually being hit by plaster. As such, it reacted the way it should. Your mind created in real life, what it didn't know was a reflection."

"Speaking of, you keep calling it that, and not an illusion. Why?" Talon asked knowing he was missing something.

"I don't know much about video games. Certainly don't own one. However, ya ever see the one's where you're view is from the end of the gun?"

"They're called first-person-shooters. I hate them. That viewpoint not only annoys me... it makes me nauseous."

"Yeah well, when it's a strong one... most of it I see through their eyes, not mine. They usually stop at a mirror or something. It's a very common theme and it's their way of showing me who they are or were."

"Reflection. I get ya now."

Talon then laughed. He did so because his phone rang. He looked at the time on the phone, and added a devilish grin to his laughter as he looked at Violet.

"57 minutes. Ha ha ha... she must have been in a meeting or something."

In a tone that dripped of 'I know why you're calling', Talon answered "Why hellooooo sister of mine. Something I can do for youuuu?"

Eileen laughed and said "Yeah yeah cut the crap bro. Who is she? How'd you meet? What are your plans!? C'mon now... I want details details details!" Eileen playfully admonished.

Violet was walking beside him and was in shear bliss just doing that 'ghost free'. She was truly hoping to stick around for awhile. This new phone call made her suddenly nervous. What if this sister of his didn't like her?

Eileen's tone changed from playful, to kind, and full of sisterly love for a close brother.

"Tell me this though... are you happy?"

Talon smiled quickly at Violet, then answered "So far."

"Well, if this one sticks around... bring her to Sterling's. NO one gets near my brother that isn't worthy of my approval first ya know," Eileen jested.

"Yes ma'am, of course ma'am... anything you say ma'am," Talon joked right back.

"Yeah yeah... check your e-mail slacker... I sent you my itinerary. I touch down in 9 days."

"Would you like a limo... the Cuda... or...?" Talon said with a grin that just implied he already knew the answer.

"Oh... I'll take the 'or'... if you don't mind."

"Ha ha ….. how'd I know?"

"See ya then. Tal?"

"Yes my dear?"

"Even if she doesn't stick around... I'm happy you're looking again."

"Love you too sis... call me from the plane."

"Will do... love ya!" and the call was over.

Nervously, Violet asked "What did she say?"

"Violet my lovely new friend... wouldn't happen to have an evening dress in that pack of yours would ya? Perhaps a pair of heels?"

Violet was feeling something new in Talon's presence. For the first time since her grandmother, she was feeling comfortable with another human being... and a live one at that.

"Pfff... are you kidding me? I have the whole spring collection from Saks neatly tucked away in there."

"Well good. Violet my dear, how would you like to accompany me on a dinner date to one of the best 5 star steakhouses around?" Talon said with a teasing air of authority.

"Did... did you just ask me out on a date?"

"Um... yep."

"No seriously... don't tease me. Did 'you'... just ask 'me'... on a date?"

"Yes I did. You know, if you're gonna be sticking around, we should really work on that self confidence of yours."

"Good luck with that," Violet replied. "Yes I would love to. Sorry for my reaction but, I've never been asked out on a date before. Well, not a real one anyway. You were kidding about the dress and the shoes though right?"

"Uh...... yeeeeeaaaahhhh......... no."

"That then, uh, could be a problem," Violet said sadly knowing her date was likely over before it even began.

"Look purple girl. My sister comes into town in 9 days. I make reservations for us at our favorite restaurant. Some people come in dressed like you but, well, we Grayson's... uh... don't. Look, my sister stays with me when she's in town. She also likes to shop. She keeps clothes in the closet in the room I gave you. Most of her stuff still has the price tag on it. Why not just pick one of those? I doubt highly she'd notice."

Violet giggled at him and said "Go to meet your sister, in one of her own dresses? Why not just write 'street urchin' on my forehead while you're at it?"

Talon snickered at himself. Violet was right. The snicker was for him as he just realized how truly out of practice he really was.

"Okay then. How about we start simple. Lunch tomorrow... the food court at the mall... my treat of course." He winked at her saying "Current mode of dress will be perfectly acceptable."

Violet bounced a quick and playful curtsy. The smile on her face when she did melted Talon's heart.

"Whah I doo deh-clare... ah find yaw offuh most acceptable Mista Grayson sir!" Violet teased imitating Lucinda as best she could.

Talon gave her a smile and a mock bow that had Violet looking very much forward to tomorrow.

"Alright, one last thing," Talon started as they walked back into the house. "You said people like Lucinda get their energy from things and such around them. So, also fair to say, you can tune into her in ways we can't. Think you could tell me just where she gets it from?"

"Oh that house for sure," Violet said with absolute certainty.

"I was hoping you'd say that," Talon confirmed. "So, is it fair to say, just like you said with me running... choke the food, choke the energy?"

"Pretty much," Violet agreed. "Are you trying to get rid of her? Because if you are, fixing up that house will do the exact opposite... you know that right?"

"Know it?... I'm counting on it," Talon said with true menace.

Violet didn't say a word. Hearing his tone, she was afraid to. Once back in the house, Talon got a text. He answered it and put his phone away.

He grabbed his holster to put that away too and said "Heh heh... 'Val Kilmer' is on his way over," and he locked the gun away in the safe.

"Doc Holliday, at your service m'lady," Cody cheerfully said as he introduced himself. "Nice to see you recovered so nicely."

"Indeed it is," the lovely brunette told him. "Violet Hayes, doctor, a pleasure to meet you." Violet giggled slightly and told Cody, "Feel free to play the air guitar at anytime."

"Sorry... I'd do that why exactly?" Cody asked having truly no clue.

"Yo Doc... violet?... Purple?.... Hayes?... Haze? Purple Haze? Oh Doc yer kill'in me here... Jimi Hendrix!??" Talon laughed as Cody still had no clue, but did recognize the name.

"Sorry... more of an old school R&B and Motown man myself."

"Eh... not my style, but respectable," Talon relented. Then he laughed saying "A rich upper class white boy from Chicago?... Yeah... I bet you blended right in at a Stevie Wonder concert huh?"

Even Violet giggled at that.

"Well, musical tastes aside... how are you doing my new friend?"

Talon had been walking around the house without a shirt all day, and for three reasons. First, it was his house and he could. Second, it still sorta hurt to move his arms and put one on. Third... he saw how much Violet liked it.

Talon answered him saying "Still a bit sore but, thanks to my new nurse here... not as bad as it was. Technically, I shouldn't be hurt at all. Grant is coming over in an hour or so with pizza and such. I'll tell you why when he arrives."

"Fair enough. How about you let me check your vitals just to be safe?"

"You're the Doc!" Talon exclaimed.

"Yes... I am," Cody answered seeing a whole different Talon than what he was recently used to.

Seeing Violet, and how she acted around him, and how Talon acted around her, told him all he needed to know.

"So, is she pretty? Nerdy? C'mon Grant this is Talon we're talking about here. Ya gotta give me something!" Eileen protested to her youngest brother.

Grant was on his way down the mansion's driveway when she called.

"Like I don't know that, sis?"

"Look baby G, no one should have to be a widower, but it happens. To happen when you're 22 though!? We all loved Sarah and she us. But she's gone now. That really affected him and you know it. Jesus, I thought he'd become a monk or something after she died. He doesn't even notice a woman then BAM!... This chick shows up."

"Look sis, I know you're just looking out for him like you always do. Just remember though... so am I."

"Oh Grant I know you are. Look, you can't deny that as far as men go, Talon is a hell of a catch. All I want to make sure of is that she's deserving of his gold... and not digging for it."

"Big catch... gold... jeez sis what am I chopped liver!?" Grant said half teasing and half serious."

"You a barely legal widower with millions in the bank, a Lambo in your garage, and not even looked at a woman in 3 years?"

"Point taken. Listen, I know you care, we all do. All I'm saying is don't talk to me like you're the only one."

"Sorry lil bro. I'm not really, I'm just happy for him... and worried for him... at the same time."

Grant chuckled and asked "Let's say she checks out... then what?"

"If that happens, then us girls are gonna start planning a wedding!"

Grant was still chuckling at his sister and asked "And if she don't?"

"If she don't..." Eileen stated with a total tone change, "... I will find every scrap of paper that girl came across since she was born, and turn her life to shreds."

"Ha ha ha ha... sis?... Remind me not to piss you off," Grant teased. "Speaking of looking out for your sibling... when are YOU gonna make me 'Uncle' Grant hmm?"

"Actually, I'd love to. If you saw what was floating around the dating pool however... you'd lock me away in a nunnery somewhere. These flaming locks of mine don't make it easy either. It's like a beacon for every barracuda, shark and piranha out there."

Eileen realized she was doting on Talon, but at Grant's expense. So she ended the call on a positive note.

"I just wanna find a guy like my brothers... BOTH of them... is that so bad?"

Eileen shifted gears, as Grant shifted directions.

"Okay let's forget about the new girl for a moment. What can you tell me about this new doctor friend!?"

"Actually, I'm on my way to meet both right now. I'll let you know anything you need to in a day or so. As for the Doc? Heh heh... ya know come to think of it... 'Eileen Holliday' does have a nice ring to it!" Grant joked shaking his head as he got on the highway.

"Wait... his name is Holliday? As in DOC Holliday? You're joking right?"

"Ha ha ha ha ha........ nope."

With a feminine, and mischievous tone in her voice, Eileen just said "Tell me everything."

Grant kind of shuffled into Talon's front door, carrying two pizza pies and a six pack. Grant and Eileen were the only two souls other than Talon who could open his gate.

"HEY OLD PEOPLE!! BABY BROTHER'S IN DA HOOOOUUUSSE! STOP HAVING SEX THIS INSTANT AND COME GET SOME PIZZA AND BREWSKIS!!" Grant hollered as he entered.

It was a standard rule the brothers had. Neither knocked going into the other's home. The brothers had a 'mi casa su casa' understanding but... in case the other was in the middle of something... they always announced themselves.

Good thing he did too because the next thing he heard, was coming from behind the guest room door.

"Oh Talon! YES! YES!... Oh yes riiiight THERE! OH GOD!"

Grant turned suddenly when a voice he didn't expect spooked him.

"Hey bro... I see you brought the pizza... c'mon in."

What spooked Grant was Talon, coming in from his side. Violet sort of giggled and almost skipped in behind him, fully dressed, and grabbing the pizzas from him.

"But you were... I heard... okay not funny bro, NOT funny." Grant said as he pointed back and forth.

"Next time lil brother... watch who you call old," Talon said with a sneer as he high fived Violet for her part in the prank.

"You're lucky," Cody teased, "I suggested a medically induced coma."

Violet came back from the kitchen and was a lady this time.

"Sorry for the joke but, with an entrance like that... (giggle) I couldn't resist. Violet Hayes," she said extending her hand, "A pleasure to meet you."

Grant went for a little payback as he shook her hand.

"And you. Let me know the moment my 'elder' brother slips up... and I'll be by in a flash to steal you away." Grant walked past Talon and snickered "I didn't say old!"

A low key, but fun dinner was had. Violet was in heaven as she only saw scenes like this on TV, but never had the pleasure of being in one.

"Okay gentlemen," Talon began, "Miss Hayes here has some info to get you up to speed on."

Talon was now in battle-mode and this was just the first salvo. Violet however was in a panic.

"I... uh... I do?"

"Trust me purple eyes. Tell these guys how you met us, then... how we met. Tell them about the AM/FM thing... and the first-person shooter thing."

"Do I have to?" she said dreading it already.

"Yes please. I can if you'd rather but, I think it would be better coming from you. For now though, these two fine gentlemen only. YOU two guys... never heard a thing. Tell ANY one," and Talon stared right at Grant, "ESPECIALLY Eileen... and I will make it my personal mission for the next 6 months to make your lives as miserable as I can make them." Talon saw how nervous Violet was and told her "Not all of it, just the basics so they can get up to speed."

Grant stood up and said "Wait a second. Before you do, and... just so I'm clear... how is it my brother thinks you fit into our little rehab project?"

Violet shot a look to Talon. He just smiled kindly and nodded.

"Doc? Let me just say that was one brave stunt you pulled on Shadow

Man the other day."

Grant's face was stunned but, like his card playing namesake, Doc was poker faced.

"And just what are you referring to exactly?"

"Let's just say the jeep was the wiser choice... and putting out fire is 'as easy as 1-2-3.'"

"Impressive."

Sadly, she told Cody "You'd be only the third person to think so."

She told them how she woke up in a sweat back in Tennessee... and told of her time-line to present company. She also told them, along the way, what Talon asked her to.

"Soooo... what... like you've been spying on us or something?" Grant asked unsure what to make of her story.

"More like being forced to watch instant replays of you three against my will."

Talon then told them of his date with Lucinda. So did Violet. They told the story in tandem with each one telling their side of events.

Talon finished with... "And that's when I called you Doc."

Grant was shaking his hands saying "Okay hold up a second. Let's say I believe all this. If that's true, then that puts us in a whole other league. If that's the case then.... wait a second... the impromptu pizza dinner... the back story," and Grant looked at his brother and just finished with "Oh noooo."

Talon nearly beamed and answered "Oh yes."

Cody looked on the two men and asked "Someone mind filling me in?"

"Yeah, me too while you're at it," Violet said now just as concerned as Cody was.

"Do you wanna tell them, lil brother, or should I? You did say you wanted this to be 'the' story we told our kids as I recall."

Grant changed expressions, and now sported a 'ya know what?... yeah... let's do this' sort of look now.

He clinked his beer with Talon's and said "Doc?... Violet?... My brother has declared war. Gear up folks, this roller-coaster just crested the top and we're about to pick up speed."

Cody was actually getting pumped over this.

"Mind enlightening the rest of the group? Cody teased but truly wanting to know.

Grant told him "Doc? There was a job in Indiana a few years back. It was supposed to be a routine in and out. Then the town and the local sheriff made it damn near impossible. Even got the notice of a politician or two. They really went out of their way to make Talon out to be the bad guy. My brother tried to be nice and got more and more fucked for it. Finally, they pushed him over the edge with a frivolous lawsuit. No grounds for it but the publicity would have tarnished his growing reputation. Talon had enough and went all out. He called in the best lawyers... out of state lawyers that is. That job was the only one my sister was ever onsite for. He went to the state and secured an injunction. He was given 3 days to take it down. That was their exact wording... take it down. The locals thought him screwed as there was no way we could dismantle it in a month no less 3 days. Wanna know what Talon said?"

Talon was almost snickering at his brother's tale.

"Now mind you," Grant continued, "My brother gave them all kinds of concessions but it still wasn't enough. They had no plan to fix it up either. Those stupid yokels just wouldn't let go of their little bubble. Talon looked me straight in the eyes and said 'Grant? If it's a war they want... then it's a war they're gonna get!'. I still remember that like it was yesterday."

"So... what did you do?" Violet asked like a little kid being told a bedtime story.

"I called in a demolition crew, paid double their fee to get a rush job... and had the place imploded. I didn't say a word... and had it blown at 2 in the morning just to piss off the locals. The sheriff was dirty and I knew it. I had only half the lawyers working on my behalf. The other half were digging up dirt on him. When he showed up he tried to arrest me. He never did as I had Federal Marshals waiting for him. I then used every contact I had to make their little piss-ant town a professional-grade black hole. Just like the lawyers, I hired out of town help and dragged the whole thing to the local dump and turned my back on the bastards. That job cost me money but... Grayson Industries was officially on the map. Ha ha ha, Eileen even managed to write off 80% of the whole job as an advertisement expense. When last I looked, a town of 5,000 was down to less than 100."

Violet joked and said "Remind me not to piss you off."

"Violet?"

"Yes 'Mista G'?" Violet teased.

Talon half grinned and said, "Don't piss me off."

She chuckled and said, "Duly noted, Mister Grayson sir!"

Talon grinned and told her "Oooooh... I like it when you call me that."

Violet winked at him but said under her breath "I wouldn't mind calling you a whole lot more than that."

Grant sat back and told his brother proudly "Tal? I was by your side then... and I'll be by your side now. So 'General'... what's the battle plan?"

"It starts with a phone call," he said as he picked up his phone and made a call.

"Talon! What can I do for you? Something wrong with the scan?"

"No Erik that was top notch... just like always. Listen I got a question. Can you tell me stains and such or just paintings and prints?"

"As in...?"

"As in... can you come to the house I'm working on, and take scans or samples from the site. I wanna know what color this wood was, or what print was on this fabric... shit like that. I wanna know, in detail, what this place looked like when it was new."

"The scans can be done. Your problem might be time. As in, I'm gonna need a lot of it to get you a 3D rendering."

Talon thought a moment.

"Hey Erik, how about a floor by floor? You get me all the scans you can but just the first floor. Then while we work on that, you come back and scan the second while we work on the first. Would that work?"

Erik's voice was cheery and said, "Like a charm. When do you need me to start?"

"Erik, I want you to know... I'm hiring you for this job... not your crew. I want you onsite or it's no deal. As for when? How does yesterday sound?"

"I'll have my crew assembled and be down there in 2 days. Sound good?"

"Perfect. I'll have Marie wire you a retainer to get you started."

Talon was on fire and Violet found herself getting very turned on.

"See you in 2 days my friend," and Erik hung up.

Next, Talon turned to Grant.

"You buddy... take two days off. Come 2 days from now the war party starts. Take those two days and get the best crews you know. I want framers, roofers, gardeners... the works! First things first though... get the electricians. Two days from now, you and I are digging a trench and we Grayson boys are gonna get Lucinda 'juiced'."

"Ooh... this is gonna be fun."

"Indeed. I'm sick of dicking around and if that house is Lucinda's energy... then I'm gonna light up her world."

Cody asked "And where do I fit into all this?"

"Doc? I'm about to hook you up. You love history just as much as I do. Not to mention you got a personal stake in that history. Only we 4 know this is technically an active crime scene. Far as I know, one of the oldest laws we got is that there is no statute of limitations on murder. I want you going over Lucinda's room. Go over the downstairs too. Check the doorways and such for any fibers... blood... anything."

"Yeah okay but, I'd have to send anything I find to the lab for analysis.

Gonna be a little hard to describe why I'm sending in samples when I can't tell them why."

Talon smiled saying, "That's the hook you up part I mentioned. I want this house rebuilt and I want this mystery solved... period. You tell me what you need Doc... and I'll go shopping. Fuck them, I'll set you up with your own damn lab!"

Cody was smiling and said, "Well, can't say I don't like the sound of that."

Talon told Cody, "Doc I know of auctions all over the world. You get me a list, and I'll get you some tools. They may be last years model, or slightly scratched but... know of anyone else with their own lab?"

"No I certainly do not," Doc said nicely as he raised his beer to Talon.

Violet asked "Um... do I fit into this little war of yours anywhere?"

"You my dear have just been hired by Grayson Industries as a security consultant."

"Security!?" Violet nearly barked thinking Talon was crazy.

"Yep. Listen Vi... you can run from the Lucinda's... or you can fight back. Keep an eye out for Shadow Man or anything else we can't see or hear. Keep us safe and if you can't... warn us. Also, I think it's time to start being your own business woman."

"Wait... what?"

"You heard me. These 'spirits' or whatever. You've been doing a lot of work for free. They want something? Now... so do you. They wanna get a message across, well, I think it's time you started making them pay for it. Doc is gonna be looking for a needle in a haystack. I want you to find the haystack... and make them show you where it is."

Violet had a pleasant look of surprise on her face.

"Ya know... I actually like the sound of that... heh heh... 'boss'."

"Aw... I liked sir better," Talon teased.

Talon had one last order.

"Listen you 3. My sister comes here in 9 days. We keep everyone in the dark about what really lurks in that house... ESPECIALLY Eileen. That house freaked her out as a kid. I have no desire to do the same to her as an adult."

"She finds out we lied to her, she's gonna be pissed," Grant warned him.

"Shadow fooled me, and I still ended up with this," Talon said pointing to his back. "Illusion or no, I'd be dead if it wasn't for Violet. ANY thing comes after Eileen?... I will burn that God-damned place to the ground!... we clear?" Talon said with a tone of pure venom.

"Crystal," Grant confirmed.

"Speaking of lying to my sister... I sort of did that today Doc," Grant said with a cheeky grin.

"Remind me to tell your mommy on you," Cody teased. "My question is, why tell me?"

"Well, seems my sister... my SINGLE sister... found out my brother had a new doctor friend. I sorta told her you were a slightly balding, kinda short forty year old with a bit of a paunch."

"HA HA........ that wasn't very nice," Cody bemused.

"Yeah well, you don't know her... yet. She gets her sights on something and she don't let go. Trust me on this Doc, I think... so far anyway... you're an okay guy. If you and her hit it off or not, that's your business. When she finds out the truth it'll be a pleasant surprise. IF however you hurt her... forget me..." and Grant pointed right at Talon and finished with "... you'll have to deal with him. When he's done with you... I'll see to it that what's left of you finds it way into the concrete mix on my next job."

Talon teased by wiping fake tears away and spoke like he was crying.

"I'm proud of you baby G."

Doc sneered and spoke in his own defense.

"An interesting proposition. I assure you however, your concrete will have no need of any additives."

Talon asked Cody "Doc, think I can work tomorrow?"

"No. A half day though I think would be alright but... no lifting or bending of any kind."

"How about working Big Mack?"

"That should be okay."

"Good. Grant?"

"Yeah bro?"

"Get Big Mack going tomorrow morning. Forget the 2 day thing, I want this done asap. I'll come by later and finish up. I wanna get that main power line trenched AND connected by the weekend. Oh and... one other thing."

"Heh heh... yeah?"

"If you happen to 'see' Lucinda... Tell her I said to prepare for the return of Talon Grayson," he said with utmost conviction.

"Gladly," Grant said in a 'you're so fucked' kind of tone.

That tone was also... not for anyone at the table.

Cody left and came back with some papers for Talon. Talon called him into his room for a private conference. Sitting at the table, Violet was getting nervous again.

"Grant... are Talon and your sister really that close?"

"Heh heh... close? Ask him to tell you about the Argentine Tango. That'll tell you all you need to know."

"Is there anything you can tell me?" she asked still slightly nervous.

"Look, I was never excluded, but those two? They've been each other's protectors for as long as I can remember. Hurt Talon, and Eileen will shred you in ways you couldn't imagine. Talon is the same with her. I know this because... I've seen them do it. They're both shrewd judges of character. Tell me, are you asking me this because you're planning on sticking around?"

"Honestly? I'd like to but then, that's really up to him."

"Then why are you so nervous?"

"He asked me out on a date," she said shyly.

"Talon did!??"

"Shhh keep your voice down," Violet chastised. "He's taking your sister to a steak place. I think he wants her to meet me. What if she doesn't approve?"

"Sterling's!?" Grant said with a laugh.

"Yeah... that's the place. What are you laughing at?"

"Sterling's, huh? Well... yeah okay... you can be a little nervous heh heh."

"Gee, you're a big help," Violet said as she went back to imagining monsters.

"Grant tell me, you know what I am, or at least can do. Doesn't that freak you out even a little?"

"If I, or Talon, or even Eileen were anyone else... I'm sure it would. Did Talon tell you about mom?"

"Promise not to freak out?" Violet asked very carefully.

"About?"

"Uh... I met her... sort of."

Grant changed tones on a dime.

"Listen stranger, I'm gonna be as polite as I can about this but... I'm warning you... watch what you say next."

Kindly Violet said "Oh no nothing like that. Ya know that silence I mentioned?"

"Yeah?" Grant said still with a 'watch it' tone in his voice.

"She made it. Talon showed me a picture of your parents. The moment I touched it I heard her voice. She said she made it for Talon... and me. In 'ghostly' terms... you could say it was a recording. At first when I got visions of you and your brother, I thought it was Lucinda asking for help. After today though, I'm not so sure." Grant was staring warily and Violet told him "Grant look, believe me or not, that's up to you. What I can tell you is, only someone extremely powerful could leave a message like that. Do so, and a bit of your energy gets left with it. Sort of tells me what kind of person they were. For what it's worth... I think she was an amazing woman and I'm truly sorry for your loss. I would have loved to have met her. I also got the impression she loved you all a lot more than you knew. I know you don't know me, and certainly don't owe me any favors but... please don't tell Talon what I just told you. The loss of your mother hurt him more than he lets on. I told him your mother created the peace of this place... but not about the photo. I didn't know how he would react but, I didn't want it to hurt him."

Grant was dumbfounded. He didn't know whether to laugh in her face, or kiss her hand in thanks. He actually decided to just do both.

While Grant and Violet were having their conversation in the kitchen, Talon was talking to Cody.

"Doc can you take a look at my bruises?"

"Sure," and Cody did. "Same as I said earlier... no heavy work just yet."

"So, being that you checked me out, I guess that makes me your patient right?"

"I guess it does... why?"

"Well then, this falls under doctor patient confidentiality."

Cody laughed and said "Damn that was slick. Okay your grayness... what's up?"

Talon was serious and said "Doc, it's about Violet. She said she was in a mental hospital for 3 years due to her 'condition'. I need to know I'm not being scammed or something, Doc. You yourself have faced down Shadow Man and won where I only lost. I feel if anyone can look at her record with an objective eye, it would be you. If what she said is true, I don't care."

"And if it's not?" Cody asked warily.

"Then... I wanna know that too. Look Doc, I'm not out to judge nor to go on a witch hunt."

"But...?"

"But," Talon said clearly unhappy with the current scenario in his head, "If she is some sort of one, then I wanna know that too... now."

Cody was about to say something. Another voice beat him to it.

"Rock Ridge Rehabilitation Hospital. It's in upstate New York. Consider that my way of shortening your search, and giving you your first haystack Doc."

Both men looked to see Violet standing in the door holding Talon's shirt.

"I was doing laundry and was coming to return this," Violet said feeling like Camelot was over.

"Violet I..."

"No, you're right. If I'm to be hired, someone like you would certainly do a background check anyway. Better I come clean now."

She was sad and it was breaking Talon's heart. Cody's too.

"Would you like me to leave?"

"Truth?" Talon grinned.

"Yes please," Violet said still sad.

"No, I would not."

"Thank you. I used the last of my money for the bus and taxi here. Per our agreement, I'll check on you one last time before you go to bed. Sorry to have intruded gentlemen."

Violet laid the shirt down by the door and left with tears running down her cheeks.

"Shit," Talon said in frustration and annoyance.

Cody told Talon "I'll see myself out. We can do a pow-wow over those papers, and yours, another time. I'll grab Grant when I do."

"Doc... you're an okay guy. You know I'm a widower right?"

"I do."

"Well, I'm not some teenager hiding a crush. I'm sure you've noticed I've taken a fancy to the Elizabeth Taylor lookalike."

"And her to you it would seem."

Talon said "Yeah well, I never fool myself Doc. I loved my ex wife dearly. I haven't even looked at other women since she died. Kinda hard to when ya lose a soul mate, ya know?"

"I don't actually, but I can imagine," Cody said kindly.

"Trust me Doc, without going through it yourself... ya can't. Anyway, I wasn't looking to find anyone but, it would seem, someone found me. I can't say I don't like how I feel but... like I said I don't fool or lie to myself either. If her story is true then I truly don't care. If it's not... well... one guy to another, I don't think my heart could take another blow like that."

"Tell me Talon, is this sister of yours as protective as you and Grant claim?"

"Heh heh... every bit and more. If I know her, she's combing through every record and document she can find right now."

"Well then, here's hoping I beat her to the haystack."

Cody left and Talon felt worlds better.

Two hours later, Talon was stoking a fire in his fireplace. Nevada nights in the high desert usually got as cold as the days were hot. He and Grant would often remark how, around this place, even a blind man would know when the sun went down. Violet had dried her tears by now. She was more confused now than anything. She was sad Talon didn't trust her. She was living in some fairytale princess dream, and was actually more upset at deluding herself. Of course they would think that of her... why wouldn't they? It took her awhile but she finally realized, she was still there. She also knew the truth of it was, if she were Talon, she'd likely do no different. At least he did it with some concern, and discretion.

It was an hour ago while she was thinking all this. Suddenly, her bad thoughts were broken by a shuffle at the door. She got up and looked. Slid under the door... was a man's long sleeve shirt. That made her smile. To her, it was a sign there was still some hope. She wasn't trying to seduce Talon but, right now, anything that pleased him pleased her. She never cared for anyone like this and had no idea how to. She knew it was his way of saying he was sorry. At least, that's how she took it. So, for now, if it made Talon happy... that was good enough for her.

The peace and love of this house was almost overwhelming to her at times. Never had she known this level of calm. She also liked something else, and sought to keep it going as long as they, or rather 'he', would let her. What she liked, was that she felt like she found someplace where she belonged.

"Whoa!... Oowwwww... sorry Violet, I thought you went to bed," Talon told her.

Talon was spooked by her. He was laying in front of the fire and didn't hear her walk up.

"I didn't think you'd wear that," Talon said kindly.

"Yeah, well, suffice to say I'm not upset anymore. I realized I would likely do the same if I were you. I do wish to thank you though for at least being discreet about it. Even that is more than I'm used to."

"I won't lie to you, Violet. You may have known me longer than I have you but... I'm careful... I have to be. I have no problem letting someone in, as long as it's the right person and for the right reason. Tell me true purple girl, is Doc gonna find out anything I wouldn't wanna know?"

"Oh lots. Any lies however... no... those he won't find. There are 'gaps' in my memories due to some of the med's they had me on. Of what I recall though, I have told you the truth."

Violet was checking his bruises, and rubbing some sore muscles.

"And the shirt? Tell me Vi, why did you really wear it?"

"I know it makes you happy. Also, I've never been thought of as sexy before. You could have kicked me out, but you kept your word. I know you think I might be some crazy psycho, and I'm not mad that you do. It only shows you care enough to protect yourself and those around you, and that you're wise. You also showed fairness and held up your end of the deal, because, I'm still here. That tells me you're willing to believe I might be telling the truth too. I really was sad at first. Then I started thinking, I'm glad you did. I want to prove to you I am as messed up as I said I was, but that I'm not a danger to either myself or anyone else." Violet looked at him with loving eyes and said

"Especially to you."

"And... if Doc finds out otherwise?"

With true conviction, Violet told him "You won't have to kick me out. If Doc did find something bad... I would leave on my own."

Talon smiled up at her, slid over, and patted the floor next to him.

Violet scrunched her face and said "Tempting as that is, I don't think that's a good idea right now."

Talon grinned and Violet had to stop herself from ripping his clothes off.

He put up both hands in surrender and told her "I promise I'll be a good boy. Well... at least till the Doc gets me a report."

Violet glared at him.

"Ha ha ha … PROMISE!"

Violet relented, and laid down beside him. Talon kept his word and soon, sleep claimed them both.

Doc would indeed get a report... and he would indeed show it to Talon. When he did, it would change Talon... and Violet... forever.

Chapter 10

"A Trip To The Mall... And A Declaration Of War"

Talon woke up in the middle of the night. He was cold and realized the fire had died down. He put a few more logs on the fire, stoked it good, and laid back down. Violet was still asleep. Talon saw her laying there and thought how nice that was. Since his wife passed, he didn't mind being alone. Lately though, he was thinking how nice it was that he wasn't. Talon pulled a blanket off the couch, draped it over himself and Violet's lovely frame, and went back to sleep.

Talon woke up alone. Now the blanket was on only him. The sun was up, and the fire was nearly out.

"I don't mind telling you, I'm no gourmet chef... but ya won't starve either. (giggle) G'mornin, 'Mista G'," came a sweet voice from the kitchen.

Talon smiled... she was still wearing his shirt.

"Okay Violet, I got a couple questions for ya," Talon said as he sat down gingerly at the kitchen counter. "First, you caught me playing the air guitar. You had your back to me so...?"

Violet just smiled, and tapped the glass on the oven door.

"I've had to, for obvious reasons, live my life always looking over my shoulder. Not a fun way to live I know but, it's become more habit now than anything else. Trust me on this... it's not a good thing to get spooked in some diner somewhere by something only you can see."

Talon told her "That's gotta suck, always looking over your shoulder like that."

Violet shrugged and said "Eh... better than the alternative."

"Hmm... I guess."

"Hey boss... can I tell you something?"

"Heh heh... still like sir better," Talon teased.

"Yes sirrrrrrrrrrrrrrr," Violet teased right back. "Anyway. I just wanted to say... I like telling you things."

"Why's that?" Talon asked nicely.

"Well, many nights I had no one to talk to. I lived alone... always on the run... always being careful NOT to be noticed. It gets lonely. Then one day I realized, no one knew I existed. That's when I thought, if I joined the FM side, who would notice that I was gone?”

"Sorry, purple girl. I imagine it wasn't easy. When my late wife died, I felt alone like I never have in my life. Even then though, I had a loving family to help me. I honestly don't know what I would have done without them." Talon looked at her and said, "I hear a lot of doubt and insecurity in your voice. Trust me, that's probably the greatest illusion of all. NO one could do what you have done, and not be strong. Trouble with you is, you don't believe that you are. Remember that date of ours today?”

Violet was unsure how to react. No one really praised her before aside from grandma. She decided to just answer the question for now.

"Yes..." Violet said. Then she winked and playfully added "...Sir?”

Talon smiled back and continued.

"New game today, Vi... today is the 'let's trust Talon today' game.”

"Hmm," Violet said not sure she was liking this game. "And how do we play this one?”

"Easy," Talon said with utter confidence. "First, we start by you... going into your room... and bringing me those bus receipts.”

Violet looked at him oddly, but did as she was told. Talon took them when she returned, and added them up.

"I'll be right back," he said as he walked into his room. He came back with a hundred, a fifty, and a twenty... and handed them to Violet.

"Being that you came to help me out, Grayson Industries will pay your travel expenses. If you have any other receipts, let me have them and I'll reimburse you for those too.”

Violet was a tad stunned and said "I didn't get any for food and stuff. The taxi thought I was going to kill him or something when he saw your driveway.”

Talon grinned playfully, and told Violet "Well, let's say that... and your food... will another hundred do?”

"More than do... what are you up to?” Violet asked warily.

"Teaching you how the business world works. Okay, so no receipts for those... looks like I'll have to make an investment then. Hmm, okay, new plan. Go into your room and empty your pack. Lay everything on the bed and use the floor if you run out of space.”

Violet cocked her head at him.

"Go ahead," Talon told her nicely. "Call me when you're done.”

It took Violet 20 minutes but she accomplished her task and told Talon she was ready.

Talon came in and saw her dressed in the same clothes she was in yesterday. When he entered the room, he was holding a large plastic bag. He looked at her clothes laid out in organized piles, and inspected them. He opened her wallet, looked a bit, and tossed it off to the side. Some photos and mementos were nicely put to the side. Everything else, from socks to bras, had seen better days. Now Talon knew why she was wearing the same clothes. They were likely the only ones not torn, tattered, or both.

Next he looked over her backpack. Once it was a serious piece of camping equipment. Now, according to Talon... it was a serious piece of shit.

"This Violet... this is your life?" Talon asked.

"Sad isn't it?" she said meekly.

"Very much so. Okay then, here's the thing... when was the last time you did this?"

"What, lay it out like this?" Talon nodded and Violet told him "How about, never."

"What a shocker," Talon said snottily. "Tell me this, and be brutally honest." Talon waved his hand about and asked "Do you like what you see?"

Violet had never stopped to assess her life like this. Now that she had, she realized Talon was right.

Sadly she told him "It may not be much... but it's mine."

"Not anymore. When my wife died, I went into a bit of a funk. I finally realized my life sucked because I was holding onto old sad yesterdays so much... I couldn't see the new tomorrows. Violet Hayes? Do you trust me?"

"No."

"Heh heh... fair enough but... you will. I'm going to do something now. I am however reserving the right to tell you something when our date is over."

Talon then took all her stuff and put it in the plastic bag.

"HEY! That stuff is all clean! What are you doing!?"

With the utter confidence Violet has come to find attractive, Talon told her "Ending your sadness. Someone did it for me once. Now... it's my turn to pay it forward."

Talon took her stuff out back and tossed the bag, and the backpack, in a barrel. It wouldn't be the first time someone did that, and she figured she'd just get it later. Violet screamed at him when he doused it with lighter fluid. She almost freaked when he tossed a lit pack of matches in as well.

"You arrogant bastard! That was all I have in this world!" Violet half yelled half cried.

"Incorrect... had... past tense," Talon said as he walked back into the house. "Give me a minute to get dressed. Once I have, you and I are going on that date I promised you."

Without another word, he walked into his room and closed the door.

Talon came out in crisp gray slacks and a blood red nicely pressed collared shirt. Sporting a bolo tie, and a vest that matched the slacks, Talon was making Violet squirm again. Dark black spit shine boots, and a gambler flat top hat that matched the boots completed the look.

"Hey!... Now what!?" Violet barked as Talon dragged her across the living room.

He stood behind her in the mirror and remarked "See this?" Talon said as he waved his hand up and down her frame. "Say goodbye to it... because this is the last time you're going to see her. I want to see Violet Hayes," and with a touch of annoyance in his voice, Talon finished with "And not that street urchin you mentioned." He told her "Don't move," as he set his alarm system. He set it and hustled him and her out into the garage.

"Oh you have GOT to be kidding me!"

Talon was ahead of her and heading for the truck. He knew what she meant and got playful.

"About?"

"THAT!" Violet said pointing sideways. "You own a Ferrari!??"

"Nope."

"Then mind telling what that is doing parked there?"

"By my best estimation... about 0 miles an hour," Talon smarted.

"Ha haaa, Mister smartass. I've never even seen a real one."

Talon kept toying with her and said, "And your not seeing one now."

Violet said "Sure looks real to me. I thought the Plymouth was a sweet ride..."

"That's because it is," Talon said quickly.

"Yeah... but... THAT... is a Ferrari!"

"No it's not."

"Okay mister, 'I have so much money I don't even know what I have in my garage'... enlighten me!"

Talon smirked "Oh look... we're finally asking the right questions. It's not a Ferrari because it isn't. It's a Lamborghini."

"A Lama who what?"

"Lam... bore... gee... nee."

"Okay... what's the difference?"

"About 1.2 mil," Talon said flippantly. "Violet? Ferrari's are nice cars but, Lamborghinis are what Ferraris become when they grow up."

"ONE POINT TWO MILLION!!?" Violet said in shock.

"Heh heh... would you like to go in that instead?"

"HELL no! At that price, I'm not even going to look at it!"

Talon just laughed and opened the garage door, along with the passenger door to the truck.

Talon was always practical with his money. Now was no exception. So the first stop was the chain stores. Seven was the number of the day. Talon insisted she get all new underwear, socks, and something new for Violet... stockings. Talon insisted she get one for each day of the week. That way it would pack small and travel well but she'd always have enough.

Talon laughed when Violet asked for a bra in a 34C and the lady snorted at her.

"Sweetheart, you'll choke yourself in one of those. 36D... easy," the lady told her.

What made Talon laugh was Violet's reaction when she found out the underwear lady was right. Jeans were next and Violet was starting to enjoy something. Having no money most of the time, she was always frugal. She felt uncomfortable spending this much money on just clothes. What she was liking though, was how it was making 'her man' smile. Tops were next. Some T's and some nice but casual blouses went in the basket with the rest. Around the corner to shoes was the last stop. She got two pairs of nice but comfy sneakers, but at Talon's insistence, a pair of hiking shoes as well. One thing Violet did however, without even realizing it, was make sure that everything she bought... would fit in a backpack.

Talon paid for it and waited for Violet to come out of the bathroom. She emerged, and did a playful 'wadda ya think?' twirl. Talon said nothing. He just leaned back, smiled, and applauded slowly. Violet was over the moon at that reaction.

"How are you holding up?" Talon asked.

"A little hungry actually but otherwise I'm fine."

"And all the ghouls and goblins?"

"Actually? I felt them return the moment we got out of your fancy gates. Oddly enough, nowhere near what it used to be. It's almost like 'ghost town' actually became one. Does that make sense?"

"It does. Violet, I'm not you but, if I had to guess, I'd say you're recharged."

"In what way?" Violet asked looking for a bit of insight.

"Well," Talon started as he drove towards the mall, "In your days and ways, you were constantly moving. Never a day of rest. Like you said about me and the running thing. Honestly Vi, I believe they were so bad, because you never had a break... and were getting hammered simply because you were worn out."

"Well I told you Grandma was like me but far less 'sensitive'. She taught me what she could but that wasn't much. Mostly she gave me wisdoms to help me figure stuff out when I was on my own. All the rest I learned on my own but, it's not like there's a school for this. What you say makes sense, and I can't say I don't feel more rested than I ever have... on the inside as well as the outside. I've figured out a lot of stuff but, doesn't mean I did correctly. I like your theory. Tell ya what, let's go with that for now?"

"Deal," Talon said nicely as he pulled in the parking lot.

"Aaaaaand we're at a tack shop why exactly?" Violet asked.

Then, just to get him back for the Lamborghini stunt, she acted like a little teenage girl with a crush. Aside from the womanly curves that so caught the gray guy's attention, the rest wasn't much of a stretch.

"Ooh ooh I know! We're here to get kinky sex stuff right!?" Talon gave her an annoyed 'really?' look and Violet beamed saying "I knew IT! Oh you would look soooooo hot in leather!"

Talon was still annoyed, but played right back.

"I'm going in here to get something. Tell you what, if I find a nice harness of some kind... I'll consider it."

Violet was giggling and, just to embarrass him some, hollered after him "Don't forget... 36D!... I know that cuz the lady at the store said so!"

Talon shot her an annoyed look that made her giggle even more, and Talon headed inside. He was only inside 10 minutes or so when he came back with a bag.

"Aw... no harness?" Violet teased.

"I asked but they were all out of your size."

Violet chuckled and asked "Okay... what did ya get?"

"See for yourself," Talon said confidently as he backed up.

Violet looked in the bag. There was only one thing in it... a cattle prod.

"Okaaaay... uh... you do know I was only kidding about the kinky sex thing right?"

"No you weren't," Talon said quickly.

"Yeah well.... HEY!... You... you.... OOOoooh that wasn't funny."

Now Talon was laughing and said "Actually... it was hilarious!" He looked at her reassuringly and told her, "Suffice to say that is for someone... it just isn't you."

Talon said that as he pulled into the mall parking lot.

The two of them headed to the food court and got something to eat.

"So, how is this date thing going so far?" Violet asked holding onto his arm as they walked along the shops on the upper level.

"Dunno... why don't you tell me?" Talon commanded politely.

"I dunno either. Never had one before remember?"

Talon asked "Well, are ya having a good time so far?"

Smiling, Violet said "I am."

Talon smirked and asked "And the guy you went with... how was he?"

Violet was getting used to his dry sense of humor by now, got cocky, and played along.

"Eh, he wasn't bad. I've had better though."

"Thought you hadn't had any?"

"Oh yeah... that's right," Violet giggled. "Honestly though, so far, I'm having a great time."

"Violet?... Me too," Talon stated with conviction.

Violet beamed and just hugged his arm a little tighter.

Grant had a bit of trouble at first. He was following the GPS on Big Mack. The problem was, he hit a huge granite shelf 5 feet down and for the first 75 feet. Digging through that wasn't easy so, when he finally stopped for lunch, he wasn't as far in as he had hoped. He shut down Big Mack and started walking back to his truck. On his way, he saw a blond girl, dirty blond, in old clothes. She was soaked but then Grant realized, it was more like soaked with sweat. She smiled at Grant, then bent over. She reached under her simple ankle length dress, and seemed to have grabbed something from inside it. The dirty blond stood up... cradling a baby. One more smile, and she turned and walked behind a hill.

"Of course not!" Grant extolled in annoyance as he ran over to find no one there. "Yep, no doubt about it... this place just keeps getting weirder and weirder," he said as he resumed his walk.

He finished his lunch, then drove back to Big Mack. Grant had a tank in the back of his truck and it was filled with diesel fuel. He pulled up alongside the behemoth and pumped the tank. He was about to fill Big Mack, when something caught his eye. About 30 feet away, the blond girl returned holding the baby. She was holding it lovingly and staring at it. Then she slowly lifted her gaze to Grant. She smiled, but yet again, said nothing. She did something that confused Grant however. She pointed to the baby... then to him... then faded away.

Grant wasn't spooked... just confused... and hollered out "Do I at least get to know your name!??" He got no answer, and just said "Figures."

He started fueling Big Mack when he heard a drawn out whisper. It was faint... but he heard it.

"Aaaaaabbbbiiiiiigggaaaaaaaiiiiilllll," said the whisper... and nothing more.

Grant just laughed.

"Trust me 'Abigail'... ha ha ha ha... that baby ain't mine!"

One more whisper of "Noooootttttttt...... yyyyeeetttttt," and Grant was alone once more.

"A hundred and fifty dollars... for a dress!!??" Violet barked thinking that was a ridiculous amount of money.

Talon calmly said "You're right... that is a tad lame." He looked at the girl helping him saying "My friend appears to be insulted by the prices. Could you show us the more expensive ones please?"

The girl smirked, said "Certainly," and did as she was asked.

Violet glared at Talon and he just chuckled back at her.

"How did... no offense but... 'a guy'... learn about stuff like this?" Violet asked as they looked about the store.

"Eileen actually. Do you really wanna know?"

Violet said "Ya know... I would."

"Okay. Eileen was teaching me how to impress girls. She told me, she believed girls don't just dress up to look pretty, or sexy, for just themselves. She believed that while some do, they mostly do it to impress someone. It may be a man, or woman, in their life. Sometimes there isn't one but hey, ya never know who you might meet, right? Anyway, most men bitch about coming to a shop like this. Some won't even come in. But, a confident guy who will, and knows what he likes... well... that would get me the effect I was after. 'Talon?' she said... 'You could be the hottest looking guy but confidence will win every time'. Girls also love dressing up for their man she said. Ha ha ha ha... this I never forgot. She said, find something I like that's classy, but never trashy, and they'll not only wanna show off but... it'll likely come off later."

"That's one smart sister you got there, sir," the shop girl said slyly.

"Careful," Violet said, "He kinda likes the whole 'sir' thing."

"Yes sir," she said with a coy smile to Talon.

The look on Violet's face when she said that made Talon laugh.

Violet tried not to show it on her face but... she was thinking how right his sister was. She felt odd thinking 'her secret' was not only out... but that Talon knew it all along. In the end, she and Talon agreed on two, and she went to try them on. She felt odd trying on 2 dresses that cost around $750... but Talon liked them so, try them on she did.

"They both fit very well, and I can't decide." Violet told him when she returned from the dressing room.

Talon casually grabbed both of them, said "Then don't," and handed them to the shop girl.

"You 'sir'... are insane," Violet said in shock.

Another shop for a sexy pair of heels. Those were easy as both of their eyes were drawn to the same pair at the same time. She was a tad wobbly in them but, Violet actually loved them. Talon suggested she leave them on to get used to them. Not to mention they made Violet look hot as hell in Talon's mind. A few more bags for the back seat and the shopping date had only one more stop. Talon left the mall and headed to a camping store he knew of. Violet got sad when she saw why. Talon picked out a replacement for her backpack. To Violet, it was a stark reminder that, that life might return, and that Camelot might end. Neither thought pleased her right now. Still, she chose one and the shopping date was over.

"Violet, I want you to know something," Talon said as he started the truck.

"Hmm?" she said staring out the window, unable to look at him.

"Look Vi, I'm neither an optimist nor a pessimist. I'm a realist. I trashed your trashy life and with good reason... because it was trash. Maybe Doc shows me something I can't live with. Maybe you decide to leave on your own. Either way your life was shitty and your stuff reflected that. This was my gift to you that someone once gave to me. Now, if you do leave and go back to your old life... well... maybe you'll do things a little different, or a little better. Just having nicer stuff is sometimes the only thing you need. If however your old life returns, you'll at least have a fresh start... and a few nice things added to the pile. If you do leave though, promise me something?"

"What's that?" Violet asked with a slightly quivering voice.

"Promise me that you'll look at that stuff, realize its time to try something different, and remember that there still are a few nice folk left in the world."

Violet had tears running down her cheeks.

"I promise," was all she said as she went back to staring out the window.

Talon's radio stopped playing tunes and started ringing.

"Hey Doc," Talon said over the speaker-phone.

"I got your text. I'm on my way to the mansion now."

"So are we."

"We?" Cody queried.

"Heh heh... I got Jimi Hendrix with me."

"Aah, gotcha. Well I just wanted to let you know I'm on my way. Be there in 10."

"Doc I need two things please. First, you'll beat us there so save me a phone call and let Grant know I'm coming to relieve him, will ya?"

"Will do, and second?"

"Meet us in the parlor and, uh... bring your pipe."

"This sounds almost fun. See ya there!" and the music returned.

Talon and Violet pulled up and Cody and Grant were waiting for them. Talon got out and took off his shirt vest and tie. He reached into his toolbox in the back and pulled out, and put on, a work shirt. Next he took off his boots then dropped his pants. He had on boxers... the tight kind not the loose one's.

Grant teased "Uh... Violet?"

"Shhh... a lil busy right now," she answered not looking at him, but definitely looking at Talon.

"Heh heh... I can see that."

Talon put on some work jeans then strapped on some steel toed boots. He took his nice clothes and laid them in the truck. He put on a plaid shirt but kept it unbuttoned except for the cuffs. Last he went back to the toolbox again. He pulled out a bullet proof vest that said 'Detroit Police' on it and put it on.

Cody cocked an eyebrow at him.

"Still a little bruised, Cody, and my doctor told me to watch it."

"Good advice that doctor gave you but... heh heh... a police vest?"

Talon smirked and told him "I got it at an auction. It was only, uh..." and Talon pointed to a single bullet hole saying "... 'slightly' used... heh heh heh."

Talon walked into the house and had 3 people on his heels when he did.

"Doc? Spark it up please," Talon told him.

Cody did and a nice smoky cherry aroma filled the air.

"Ya know something? Lucinda was an unbelievable beauty," Talon told the others loudly as he stared at the photo on the wall. "I mean... really... no woman of the day would stand a chance against something like that. It would take a hell of a man to even consider trying for a woman like her."

"Why thank ya kindly, Mista Grayson," was the sweet yet ghostly response.

Violet however was starting to tingle and... not in a good way.

"Ah look, the beauuuuuuuutiful lady of the house has come to join us," Talon stated being very grand and animated.

"Careful there, gray guy," Violet warned softly.

"Trust me, purple... I am." Talon went back to his plan and asked "Tell me Lucinda, just how many suitors did you have back in your time?"

"Too many tuh count," the voice almost giggled.

Violet called out warningly, "You sir, are about to be torpedoed... nine o'clock," and she started coming out from behind the men.

"Heh heh, thanks for the heads up," Talon said as he turned left. "Doc?

I'll take a little of how we first met right about now."

"You sure about this?"

"Very."

"Don't say I didn't warn you," and Cody blew a puff of smoke.

As it did once before, the smoke coalesced. This time though, it went to Cody.

"You soil your very name by being here," Shadow Man seethed.

"I have nothing to say to you," Cody stated boldly and honestly.

"Hey... smoke dude... remember me?" Talon challenged.

The smoke turned and floated to Talon and got right in his face.

"Heh heh heh..." and Talon was hurled back hard against the fireplace, "... I do indeed. The braggart and his whore," Shadow Man taunted.

"I... am NOT.... a whore, you piece of shit," Violet challenged right back.

"If it talks like a whore... and walks about in such tight clothing..." but Shadow Man never finished his line.

It got interrupted by Talon's laughter.

"Jeez Shadow... you crack me up. Here's another bit of last century's technology for ya... HAHAHAHAHA!... It's called Kevlar," Talon said getting back up off the wall seemingly undamaged.

He walked over to Shadow and challenged him as he walked.

"You, ya fucktard, are likely out of gas," Talon stated.

"I'll agree with that statement," Violet confirmed in a rather nasty tone.

A tone that was directed at the puff of semi-solid smoke.

"Thank you, my dear," Talon said sweetly and totally ignoring Shadow. He turned back to the blurred ghostly form and said, "That leaves you with nothing but illusion. Now that I know that's all it is, save your effort."

Talon paced back and forth a little, mostly to walk off the shot to the wall, and laid out his plan to the ghostly pair.

"Ya see, a little birdie told me you all need energy to appear like you do. Your energy, Shadow, comes from Lucinda's fear. Well, I'd guess just fear in general. I hereby declare war on you Shadow Man. You, are a pathetic piece of shit who couldn't measure up in real life, and took out Lucinda in nothing more than a jealous rage. Oh, by the way..." and Talon dropped a bomb on him by saying "... we know you're not the Doc's great granddad. His name is already being cleared as we speak."

Shadow Man taunted right back saying, "Your mother thought herself special. I'll take great delight in showing you the same as I did her... that your not!" and Shadow's arms reached out and choked Talon.

"TALON!" Violet hollered.

He waved a hand outward, and spoke gruffly.

"Yeah... mmff... I know... this   one   is   mmmf   real." Talon stared his tormentor dead on and said, "I got   two   words for   you."

Talon slipped the cattle prod out from his sleeve, stuck it into Shadow Man's form... and turned it on.

"AAAARRRGGGGHHHH" Shadow wailed in true pain as he dissipated and faded away.

Talon stood firm and finished his sentence stoked that his idea worked.

"Piss off."

"Why, Mista Grayson... I ain't nevuh seen such brayvuhree." Lucinda said with wonder in her tone. "Ya mean tuh tell me all this time, and it wasn't mah Henry!?"

"Nope. Not sure who... yet... but it wasn't the Doc's grandfather."

"Are yuh shawuh?"

"Positive. You've been fearing Shadow all these years thinking him the wrong man."

Lucinda turned away, not that they could see but she did all the same. Then... she had anger in her voice.

"Oh ah feel like such a fool!" she hollered in frustration.

"Lucinda, I need to know something," Cody said. "Did you truly love him? Henry I mean."

"With awl mah harht. And befaw yuh ask... yes... he loved me jus tha same," Lucinda answered in her typical drawl.

"Thank you," Cody said kindly and honestly.

"Maw than welcome, young man."

Now it was Talon's turn.

"Lucinda, now I need to know something. Were you the one who called Violet to help us?"

"No dahlin' ah didn't. I felt sumthin like hope, far off in tha distance. Once ah did, ah reeched out to it. Howevuh, I neither called it, naw woke it up."

"Woke it up?" Talon asked

"Indeed Mista Grayson. It felt like, well, woke it up is tha bess way ah kin put it." Lucinda softly went to Violet and told her "Y'all are an amaezin chyld. I want tuh thank ya for come'in ta help but, it wasn't me who made yuh aware of Mista Grayson... I only asked for ya help once ah noticed yuh had."

Talon was processing this new info, but Grant was already on the move.

"Lucinda... have you ever seen this woman?" Grant asked showing his phone to Lucinda.

Violet giggled... but pointed him in the opposite direction.

"Heh heh, thanks," and Grant turned around.

He had a video on his phone of his mother. It was old film stock he had converted to digital.

"Gingjuh Chyld! What an uhMAZEzin muhsheen!" Lucinda said heartily. "And yes... I hahv. She would come heeyuh from time tuh time. Always tawked ta me but she nevuh seemed tuh hear me. She took somethin' of mine. Sumthin' I would lyke back iffin ya doen mind."

"What's that?" Talon asked seeing this could be a new clue.

"I had a wooden box I hid in tha hall outside mah boudoir. It had tha only links ta Henry I had."

Violet said aloud, "Lucinda," then under her breath said "I can't believe I'm doing this," then aloud again "Uh... can you show it to me?"

Lucinda did, Violet was a tad thrown off but recovered easily. Violet was looking at Lucinda putting it away many years ago.

"Wood... dark... ebony I think," Violet said as she appeared to be staring into space. "About the size of those boxes you keep silverware in. Fancy scroll work on all 4 sides."

Grant said "Not me, I didn't take anything like that."

"I cleaned out the house and grounds," Talon said. "I never saw anything like that, no less took it. I know Eileen didn't take it either." He turned to Lucinda and said "I will look for it and, if I find it, I will honor the request of a lady."

"Thank ya kindly, Mista Grayson."

Talon finished up his business before getting to work.

"SHADOW! This... isn't over. Every day I get closer to finding out who you are. One day... I will."

"No, Talon," Cody supportively interjected, "We all will."

Talon nodded a thanks and hollered "Yeah! What he said!" Then he turned to Lucinda and said "Lady, I have an army of workers arriving in two days tops. We are gonna restore this place to her former glory I swear it. Violet tells me this house is the source of, well, 'you'. I can only imagine the nicer it gets, the stronger you become. I will... no... WE will fix this place up, but I need something from you."

"Name yaw price, Mista Grayson."

"I need you to help keep them safe, and warn one of us if you can't."

"Mista Grayson, sir... y'all got yawself a deal," and Lucinda was gone now too.

Talon turned and said, "Well, war has been officially declared... and the proverbial gauntlet has been thrown down. Wadda ya say we go finish getting 'our girl' all juiced up eh?"

Four people walked out... and 'Talon's War' as it will jokingly come to be called... had begun.

Chapter 11

"The Green Pentagon, The Spotted Football... And The Yellow Star"

Violet was last out of the house. Talon was heading for Big Mack. Doc was too. Cody never really did this kind of work in his life. He was finding himself liking it though... a lot. He wasn't a pro at it like the brothers were, but he was helping and absorbing and learning what he could.

Violet though, touched Grant on the shoulder softly, then nodded off to the side.

"Give me a second will ya?" she asked Grant.

Grant teased and hollered after his brother.

"Yo Talon... I'll catch up to ya in a minute. I'm uh, gonna try and steal your girlfriend away from you okay?"

Talon never turned around, but hollered back "Not my girlfriend buddy but... give it a try... let me know how that works out for ya!?"

"Yeah yeah..." Grant laughed, "... arrogant prick."

"Why ginjuh chyld... y'all have tha sharpest tongue!" Talon retorted.

Grant laughed, Violet giggled.... and so did Lucinda.

"So, what did you want to talk to me about?" Grant asked.

Violet told him, "Ya know how if you sit around a campfire... you walk away smelling of smoke?"

"Yeah?"

"Ghosts can be kind of like that. They leave a sort of residual energy... like the smoke. Since I've met you and your brother, you've had none, till now. Mind telling me about it?"

Grant actually smiled at the thought.

"She said her name was Abigail," Grant said sweetly at the memory.

"Tell me everything."

Grant playfully challenged and asked "Why?"

Violet was all business though and told him, "Well, as the new head of ghostly security, it's my job." Then, she got even more serious and said, "These 'hauntings' you guys have found yourself in. Trust me, they're not always nice. Some are just downright evil... but will trick you at first into thinking they are anything but."

"Fair enough," Grant acknowledged, and told her of his encounter.

Violet listened then gave her assessment.

"Seems okay for now, but I can tell you that you misread her."

"In what way?" Grant asked.

"She wasn't telling you the baby was yours."

"What then?"

Violet smiled kindly and told him "She wasn't saying the baby was yours... she was saying it was FOR you."

"HUH!?"

"Yeah, I'm not sure either but... it's what she meant all the same."

Talon was working Big Mack. Another 10 feet past the shelf Grant ran into, and it was back to easy dirt and rocks. Grant was back at Lashonda's tent city and getting the cable spools ready. Talon had a lot of it in storage but no spool was long enough on its own to do the whole run. Grant brought the tractor out and got the big terminal box moved into the back yard and close to the house. It was the big dual door metal box kind, like you see on a street corner somewhere. He had poured a small concrete pad for it yesterday and ran plastic piping in to run the cable through. Talon had tons of 2 inch PVC pipe and insisted that with that much juice running across the property, it would be shielded in plastic and not conductive metal.

Violet even helped. She was no stranger to hard work, and was feeling proud of herself for how she held it together in the house. She was also seeking to keep that feeling going. So, after Grant hooked up the main box, he drove slow along the trench while Violet helped Grant roll out the wire along the ground. When it ran out, she started running the plastic piping down it. Grant showed her how to glue the sections together and that was that. Grant got another roll on the back of the truck, took 15 minutes to splice the dual thick wires, and the process started anew.

Talon took two hours but, finally got to the open area by the telephone poles. He turned and made a diagonal run to the pole the power company said to. The bucket on Big Mack was capable of digging a 5 foot deep trench in one pass. It was also 3 and a half feet wide. Talon insisted with all the seismic activity in northern Nevada, it would be that deep to protect the main power line from frost and any possible ground shift. He was done long before Grant and Violet were so, he and Doc went back to assist. By dinner time, the inspector for the county signed off on it, and now all they had to do was wait for tomorrow for the power company to hook it to the pole and install the meter.

"I got the electricians coming in tomorrow," Grant told the group as they sat in the parlor and dug into some Chinese takeout. "Erik's gang will be here too but his crew is small and neither should get in the other's way."

Violet was given center stage by Grant and Cody, who, wanted to hear all about the date she had. She had them laughing, and they were all having a good time. Lucinda said nothing and didn't disturb them. With the shot Shadow Man took, he wasn't bothering anyone for quite awhile. So, the 4 of them had a fun time just laughing, telling stories, and all while sitting on some buckets. Lucinda's power was the house. With the sound of life ringing throughout the halls and rooms once more, and with Talon's revelation that Shadow wasn't her Henry, the grand Dame of Adair House was getting stronger and stronger.

"Listen you two," Talon said speaking to Grant and Cody, "We got 5 days till Eileen comes in. I want you to come to dinner with us. Al and Lashonda will be there and I see no reason you shouldn't come too."

"I look forward to it," and "Sounds like fun, count me in," were the 2 men's replies.

"Good... heh heh... cuz I already made reservations for 7. Saturday night guys, and reservations are for 6pm."

Grant teased Violet slightly saying "Nervous?"

"Very," was her honest reply.

Cody smiled and said "Well, nervousness aside, if the imaginary monsters I see on your face do come to life... at least you'll look good!"

"HERE HERE!" the Grayson brothers cheered in unison as they raised their beers high.

The power company was onsite around 9am the next morning. Doc was seeing patients so it was just Talon and Grant and their 'spiritual bodyguard'. By 10:30am, Lucinda had something she'd never known... electricity.

Grant, prior to finishing the plastering, had run some wiring in the walls and up to the ceiling. The ceiling was still unfinished but now, thanks to some new and heavy bracing, the parlor had a 100 year old crystal chandelier in it.

"And jus whaht is thaht Mista Grayson?" Lucinda's voice spoke.

"Lucinda? It's called a switch. Up is on and down is off. I would be honored if... you were the one to flip it," Talon told her.

"I'll try," Lucinda said.

She wasn't used to moving solid objects like Shadow Man was. It took her a few tries but, she finally figured it out. Three adults watched as a light switch went on, seemingly all by itself. Those same three adults cheered and applauded both Lucinda... and the new illumination.

"Why... thaht is beautiful beyond enny thang I evuh saw," Lucinda said with true pleasure, shock and awe.

"I'm glad you like it Lucinda. In one hour, they'll be 20 men here running wiring all over this floor," Grant told her in a rather proud tone.

Lucinda giggled and told him "Ginjuh chyld, there were sometimes as many as a hundred men here at any one time. Ah think Ah kahn handul 20."

Just then, Grant heard the giggling sound of a happy baby.
"Yo ghost girl, what was that?" Grant asked.
"What was what?" Violet asked having truly no clue.
"That baby laughing."
Violet was now quite concerned. She truly heard nothing.
"Okay, that's not good. Sorry red... I truly didn't hear a thing."
Then Grant heard a soft whisper... and a rather loving one at that.
"My baby................ is only for you ginger man."
Grant was not happy. He gave Violet a look that said 'Okay, did ya hear that?'. She gave him only a slight shake of her head.
Now Grant looked about and asked "Lucinda?"
"Yes Ginjuh chyld?"
"Not a child anymore, remember? My brother asked you for a date. If you wouldn't mind, I would like one now. Would it be okay if I came calling after dinner tomorrow night?"
"I look foewahd to it..." then to show her intent, Lucinda finished with "... Mista Grayson."
"Not so sure I like this idea, bro," Talon said with heavy concern.
He grinned at his brother and told him "Have no fear big brother. Me and the Caribbean black suit will be just fine."
"See that you are," Talon instructed with brotherly love.
"I'll get Talon to bring me up here, just call and let me know when you're leaving," Violet told him.
"Sorry, sweetheart... but I got this."
Now Violet politely warned him.
"That better be some suit."
"Trust me... it is," and Grant said nothing more on the subject.

The next day came, and Adair House was seeing a flurry of activity. Erik was onsite with a 3 man crew, and doing what he does best. Talon told the electricians the 1st floor was safe but not the upper ones. He, however, was pleased with their work, and promised them all they'd be the only ones he called when the 2nd and 3rd floors were secured. They had strict orders not to make the outlets garish. They were to also hide them as best they could so as to keep with the overall feel of the house. Needless to say, they delivered. They also, with the help of the small backhoe on the tractor, got power run down to the pylons that hold the iron sign. Talon and Grant were doing that project today so as to stay out of the workers' hair. When it was up, Violet took a picture of the two brothers standing under it.
Violet was also made the documentarian. In order to keep an eye out for

Shadow Man... all were told that she was taking video and pictures to document the work being done on the house. All the workers were okay with it and she never got in their way either. Two jobs now taken care of and no one but 3 men were the wiser as to her 'other job'.

Grant left early and headed home. His house was about 45 minutes away. He got dressed up nice but, as underwear, he wore the black suit he promised his brother he would. Once cleaned up, he headed out. Talon may have been the Cuda man... but Grant was more of a Dukes Of Hazard fan. A 1969 Dodge Charger was his choice... painted gloss black and silver. It was a near wreck when he got it but, Grant fixed it back up and now, that car gets noticed anywhere he goes. Right now however, it was going eastbound on US50 and heading straight for Adair House.

Grant arrived just after sunset. He checked his 'underwear' quickly, then headed into the house. He was, dressed as sharply as his brother was only a few days earlier. Unlike Talon however, his clothes, though nice, were a tad more modern in design.

"Lucinda Adair! My name is Grant Grayson... heh heh, but you might know me as 'Ginjuh Chyld'. If it wouldn't be too much of a bother, would you do me the honor of gracing me with your radiant beauty?"

Grant remembered what Talon told him. As such, that request was made looking up the stairs. He got a reply... it just wasn't the one he was expecting.

"I apologize young Mister Grayson, but the madam of the house is a bit busy at the moment. She asked me to see to your needs in her place."

That voice came from behind him... way behind him. It was coming from a table in the massive living room to the right of the parlor. There was no electric in that room yet. Not live electric anyway. Yet, there was light coming from the room. There was a single candle in a fine, but very antique glass holder, sitting in the middle of the table. It was the only light in the room. At that same table, sat a single 'soul'.

"A pleasure to meet you finally... Abigail."

"The pleasure is all mine (giggle) 'Ginger Child'."

Grant smiled, stared up the staircase, and tipped his hat.

"Mind if I join you?" Grant asked the nice looking blond at the table.

"I'd be delighted if you would Mista Grayson."

"As would I but, if you wouldn't mind, I'd like to get some business out of the way first."

"As you wish sir," Abigail said sweetly.

Grant, still in the parlor, turned in a slow circle and said aloud "C'mon...

I know you're there. Let's get your visit out of the way first shall we?"

Grant got no answer or reaction.

"Hmm... should I get a pipe? That tobacco really does have a lovely aroma, don't ya think?" Grant taunted.

Suddenly, a coil of 12/2 wire the electricians left came to life. It unraveled some and the top part began to whip about like a cobra going for a strike. It acted like a whip and struck Grant from his right hip to his left shoulder. Grant however surprised Abigail. He barely budged, and never flinched once. The wire came in for another strike but Grant caught it in his right hand.

"Are you through yet?" Grant asked in an uncharacteristically cold tone. "You died before all this technology came into existence Shadow Man. Shall I teach you a little bit about the science of it?"

He got no answer, but he did get a response. He started getting whipped again but now, from the other end of the coil.

"Fine then," Grant said calmly as he was repeatedly lashed. "My brother had two words for you. I however, have three."

Grant pulled out a contact stun gun from his pocket and, putting the two points on the wires on the end he was holding, turned it on.

"Metal.... is conductive."

The wire flailed wildly then, just dropped to the floor like the inanimate object that it was.

"Idiot," Grant stated in an annoyed tone.

Grant walked into the living room now only to find it empty.

"If you ruined my date you asshole... you're gonna find out the younger Grayson can get JUST as pissed off as the older one!" Then, just to amuse himself, Grant threw in "And don't let my normally calm demeanor fool you. I assure you... push me... and you'll find I'm just as lethal as he is!"

13 miles away, a purple-eyed girl smiled.

"Way ta go little brother," she said sweetly. She looked at Talon and said "He'll be be okay now," with a kind and tender smile.

"Are you sure?"

"Positive," Violet said honestly.

"Okay then but... thanks Vi," Talon said with gratitude in his voice as he fired up the Lambo.

He had it parked outside his gate, and ready to go at a moment's notice. Talon wanted to let Grant do this on his own. He wasn't however, going to leave him on his own. With Violet's confident tone in his ears, he fired up the engine and took them, and the car, back inside the gates.

Grant walked in and gave his 'date' a moment.

"That was mighty brave of you Mister Grayson. You must be very strong to have endured such a lashing as you did," Abigail said coming from behind him and nearly purring her comment.

"Oh I'm strong alright but... heh heh... I had a little help."

Abigail cocked her head and Grant opened his shirt to reveal his black underwear.

"It's made of a new fabric called carbon fiber. Stronger than steel. It was built to withstand a shark attack."

"A what?"

Grant smiled at the cooing blond, pulled out his phone... and did a quick search.

"The madam was right... that is an amazing machine!"

"Perhaps but... this... is a shark."

Grant showed her a scene from the movie Jaws. Abigail recoiled hard.

"What a horrid beast!" she said looking away quick.

Baby G did indeed have a shark suit. He had it custom made too. He wanted to go swimming when he took a Caribbean vacation once. The 'horrid beasts' Abigail wouldn't look at scared the shit out of him though. Likely the only thing that did. So, Grant had a full body scuba suit built with carbon fiber mesh and padding in all the key places. He looked cool enough, and no one was the wiser that it was actually body armor. He figured if the nasty creatures did show up... he'd have a surprise for them.

When Grant showed it to Talon, he teased his younger brother saying "Grayson... Grant Grayson."

Grant noticed that Abigail was 'playing' with him in a manner as if it was still the 1860's, and she was still working. He didn't mind, and played along for the moment. He wanted answers and if this was how he would get them, then so be it. He also remembered what Violet said. How they seem 'with it' at times, not so much at others.

"I have to say my dear, you look a lot finer than when I last saw you," Grant said with a sincere smile.

"Well, Lucinda runs the finest house to be found anywhere. When she asks you to entertain a gentleman, well, (giggle) one likes to impress."

Grant took her hand and kissed it. He noticed right away how ice cold it was. He ignored it... but he noticed it.

"With beauty like yours... consider me... impressed."

Abigail curtsied and said "Thank you kindly sir."

"Mister Grayson, I must leave shortly. I can see by the look on your face, that you have questions. While there's still time, ask me what you wish."

"Baby," Grant half stated, half asked.

Abigail's face changed. It went sad but, honored Grant's request.

"Miss Lucinda ran the finest house. Not just for the men, but for us ladies as well. She had the local doctor check us twice a week like clockwork. We were more a group of sisters rather than 'soiled doves'. Holidays, time off, we had it all. Part of that care, was children. If we had any, they were raised here until such an age as it would no longer be proper. Lucinda helped many of her girls. We learned proper manners... and got just as proper of an education."

"Okay, I follow you so far," Grant said.

"Miss Lucinda helped some of the ladies who became mothers. She set them up as proper ladies in hat shops or something similar. A way to be a proper woman, and provide for our children. Miss Lucinda loved children dearly, but had a strict rule that this was no place for them to be. When one of us found love, she was actually supportive."

"And I'm guessing you did?" Grant asked.

"Aaahhhh, My Michael was the most handsome man in all the world. We had such plans. I became pregnant with his child, and we planned to marry. He was a miner. He asked Miss Lucinda for my hand all proper like too."

"Let me guess, he didn't show up?"

"There was an accident before our baby was born. I went to see but the men treated me horribly. Miss Lucinda too. That's when she reminded them, the same man they called boss... she called dear friend. I was heartbroken. Miss Lucinda though had the mine owner do an investigation."

Grant queried "Miss Lucinda must have wielded some fierce power back in the day huh?"

"More than I'm sure many would have cared for. Still, she never abused it and helped those in need more so than turned her back."

"So," Grant started getting back on track, "The baby?"

He knew he was getting priceless information. Maybe not on Lucinda herself but, any intel was good intel.

"I was heartsick my love was gone. I barely ate or drank. The mine owner said the ground shook, and some timbers that held things up gave way... if you can believe such nonsense. The baby came two weeks later and, to my own shame, I was too weak to deliver her. She took all I had and sadly, my baby survived but... I did not. Since then, my bloodline has not known peace Mister Grayson sir."

Abigail was starting to fade now. Grant saw it and asked his final questions.

"Abigail, while you have my sympathies for what happened to you, your baby is long since dead. There's no way I could look after her."

Abigail smiled as she faded away. Her voice also went back to a whisper. "Not yet Mister Grayson...... not...... yet......" and Abigail was gone.

Grant tipped his hat to where she had been, and left the table.

"Violet says you need energy to do what you do," Grant said looking up at the photo over the fireplace. "You gave her some of yours didn't you?"

"Ah hahv awlways looked aftuh mah girls," was the weak but kind voice in his ears.

"Lucinda, I would help if I could. Sadly... your little drama was long before I was born." Then Grant gave Lucinda the smile she so loved and said "Thank you though for doing that... it was very kind of you. Sadly, I can't help Abigail, nor her baby."

"Some yes, ginjuh chyld... an some no. Ah told you I looked aftuh mah girls. In a way, I still am... and you dear boy."

Grant bowed to a proper lady and said "I thank you for a lovely, and interesting, evening.... and wish you a peaceful goodnight."

Without another word, Grant turned for the door, shut off the lights, and locked the mansion up as he left.

"Hey bro... I'm out. Suffice to say, all's well that ends well," Grant said over the phone as the 440ci engine roared to life. "Also, fair to say, Mister Shadow now knows he has two Grayson's to deal with... not one."

Talon's voice told him "I had your back by the way. I'm truly glad however I wasn't needed. Bro? I'm proud of you."

"Thanks Tal," Grant said as the peek-a-boo lights lit up the driveway.

"My place... lunch tomorrow. We're going over what I got, and what Doc brought over."

"Count me in. I got a little intel myself this evening to add to the mix."

Talon asked "You good? Or do you wanna stay here?"

"Ya know what?... Yeah... have a cold 1 or 5 ready for me."

Kindly, Talon told him "Already chilled bud... see ya when you get here."

Grant hung up the phone, and drove the monster ground-pounding Mopar off into the night.

Grant woke up to a heavenly smell. Being a single guy, his diet sort of reflected that. He cooked for himself but... he also had 5 different takeout restaurants on his speed dial. Every one of them had at least one girl that worked there. Each one of them were hoping the hot redhead would take them for a ride in that slick black and silver car. Each one of them, also, was hoping for a little more.

Grant was what one would call, a romantic. He told Talon AND Eileen, many times, that he was waiting for a girl to wow him. He liked those girls in the food places... it's just that none of them wowed him.

"What is that smell!? No... no wait," Grant said stopping in his tracks with a playful grin. "Don't tell me... (sniff sniff)... why... I do believe they call it... breakfast perhaps?"

Talon wished him good morning as Grant sat down beside him.

Violet giggled saying "Yeah well, I love to cook. This kitchen... sheesh... don't even get me started. I've only ever seen one like this in a magazine."

Grant looked at Violet and changed to a very serious tone.

"Answer me this purple eyes... and don't even think about lying to me."

Violet was a little taken aback by his attitude. Suddenly Grant's face changed to puppy dog eyes and he practically pleaded.

"PLEASE tell me you have a sister? Cousin? SOME thing?"

Violet didn't know how to handle the praise. She just wasn't used to it.

She just managed to shrug and "Sorry... only child," was all she could think of to say. She did however imitate Lucinda by saying "But I thank ya for yaw kind words Mista Grayson sir," and popped a mock curtsy.

Grant buried his face in his forearms and in a defeated tone said "Man... this sucks."

Talon half hugged him saying "Cheer up buddy... there's always Abigail!"

"Bro?... Fuck off."

Talon just laughed.

All 3 ate breakfast and were having a pleasant time, when Talon's phone rang. He didn't recognize the number and did something rare for him... he answered it.

"Grayson Industries... Talon Grayson speaking."

"I believe sir... you were looking for me?"

"Was I?"

"Interesting ad you ran."

Talon wasn't sure and said "I run a lot of those. Care to pick one?"

The head of Grayson Industries was having a rather unusual life these days. As such, he decided to play along.

"Let's just say, I'm the guy who can fill in the hole from the edge of a piece of paper."

"Well then young man... you have my attention. Got a name?"

"Several actually. Before I tell you, how do I know you're not a member of my family? Wouldn't be the first time they've tried something like this to get me 'de-programmed' and come back to the flock."

"Fair enough," Talon said in a '2 can play that game' tone of voice. "I happen to have what you might call a psychic in my employ. I'm going to tell you of your life to come over the next hour, and I won't even need her for it. I'm going to give you a name. You're going to research it... but come up nearly empty. Actually? Make that 2 names. Those names are Lucinda Adair, and Adair House in Nevada. The latter is just east of the Comstock Mine. You're going to be quite intrigued by what you find... and what you don't. So much so, that I'll expect to hear back from you within the hour.”

“Pretty cocky there, aren't you Mr. Grayson?”

“I prefer the term, passionately confident. You have an hour. Your talents come highly recommended but, I'm sure you're not the only talented one out there. One hour mystery man,” and Talon hung up the phone.

“Who was that?” Grant asked.

“With any luck? The genealogist.”

“Pretty ballsy move there bro. Why were you talking like an agent in some sort of cheesy spy movie?”

“He thinks we're family trying to get him back for de-programming.”

“Okay then. Weird but... okay. Think you should have challenged him like that?”

“Bro? That's exactly what I should have done. People like him are naturally curious. He doesn't give a shit about Lucinda, only me. Right now he's curious AND paranoid but trust me... he's looking.”

“And if he don't call back?” Violet asked.

“Then I'll show him how right I was.”

Talon laughed slightly at the other two. He was truly carefree for the moment. Grant and Violet however, kept looking at his phone but, pretending not to look. About 35 minutes later it rang again.

“I suppose you're looking to impress me by bouncing your internet phone through a New Orleans switch. Clever,” Talon stated with utter confidence.

“Nice to see I'll be working for a smart man for a change. Let me tell you something Mister Grayson. My grandfather was a brilliant man. I however make him look like an idiot. For the record... two things.”

“First?” Talon asked flippantly.

“It's Zachariah Jameson... but I go by Zack.”

“Nice to meet you. And second?”

In the same tone Talon took earlier, Zack said “Second... there is no better than me. If there was, you wouldn't be advertising.”

“Nice to know the person I hire is a smart man as well. When can we meet?”

In a more friendly tone than before, Zack said “Have no fear Mister Grayson. To show you just how good I am... I'll find you... and I'll do it at the house that doesn't exist."

"See ya then... 'Zack'," and Talon hung up the phone.

Doc showed up around an hour later. He was also extremely uncomfortable when he did.

"Yo Doc Holliday... you okay?" Talon asked seeing his expression.

"To be honest, I'm not sure. Remember what you asked me to 'look into'? Well, it appears to have arrived," Cody said producing a manila envelope.

"Sorry Doc but, if yours needs a fire-proof container... I'm fresh out," Talon joked.

"Huh?"

"Never mind," Talon said with a laugh. Next, he got serious again, and asked "Have you looked at it yet?"

"Actually, seeing how friendly you and Miss Hayes have become, I left that honor for you."

Violet was nervous now. Talon saw that, and kindly asked her "All of us see it? Or would you prefer just me?"

Violet straightened up and stated "I told you it wouldn't be pretty. I also told you... I had nothing to hide. Nothing I'm aware of anyway. As such, I say it's all or nothing."

Talon was kind right now knowing how this affected Violet.

"Well then... everyone?... My office. Let's start sorting this out, and start getting some answers."

Slowly, everyone made their way to Talon's office.

Violet hadn't seen this room yet. The mural impressed her. Just from looking at that, and some accompanying sheets of other info, she could tell how Talon's mind worked.

"It looks like those walls you see in those cop shows on TV," she remarked.

"It's been an interesting source of... um... 'inspiration'... to say the least," Talon told her.

Doc opened the envelope. Inside was a file folder, and a CD.

"What's on it?" Grant asked as Talon scanned it first.

"A few text files and... hello... what do we have here?"

Violet nervously asked "What is it? What did you find?"

Talon said in a curious tone "One of the files... is a video."

He looked at Violet with a questioning look.

Violet took a deep breath, let it out, and said "Play it."

Talon did.

"Wait... pause it a moment please," Violet asked. She looked at the men and said "For your own knowledge, understand this. What you're seeing is my room. See this office? My room was about the same size. To avoid any escape or self harm, the walls were ten feet high. There were cameras behind domes mounted in the upper corner where the two walls and the ceiling met. That's where this footage came from. I just wanted you 3 to have a point of reference."

All of them nodded and Talon resumed the video. It showed Violet on a sparse bed. She also appeared to be semi comatose. A male nurse wheeled in a tray, and gave her some medicines. Then he left. There was a time-stamp running in in the bottom right corner the whole time. Violet just laid there for about 2 minutes. Right about the 2 minute mark, 3 grown and sizable men almost jumped out of their chairs. Violet thrashed about, suddenly, and violently. Next... she was gone. Then, just as suddenly, and just as violently, she reappeared... 6 inches from the camera. She had the most evil sneer on her face. The last thing the video showed was Violet ripping the camera off the wall before the video went to static.

"Tell me this Violet. Was there anything in the room that you could have climbed to get up there?" Talon asked not even looking at her.

Violet was crying softly and just said "...................... nothing."

Still not looking at her, Talon just said "I didn't think so."

In Violet's mind, that video, along with Talon's attitude, told her one thing. Right now? Camelot, was over.

"Bro, I don't... I mean I... Talon listen, I..."

"Gentlemen? And lady... if you wouldn't mind, I'd like to be alone right about now," Talon said to the group coldly.

He never even turned around. He just stared at the monitor.

Violet ran out without a word. She was sobbing when she did. She ran into the room Talon gave her and locked the door. Cody, for all he's seen and done in the medical profession, was as stunned as Grant was.

"Doc? You're the medical guy. What the FUCK was THAT!?"

Still in shock, Cody said "I wish I knew."

Talon was not a happy camper right now. He paced around his office and tried to absorb this new information. He thought it faked somehow, but even going frame by frame, the time-stamp didn't lie. Now he was both angry and sad. He wasn't angry at, or even with, Violet. He was angry because he found himself truly starting to care for her. That video however showed her to be nothing more than a ticking time bomb. He was desperate for some sort of idea, or angle... but nothing came. He was about to rejoin the others when a little divine intervention came his way. It was his printer... and it was printing.

'forgery'

Talon wouldn't even look at the mural. He just shredded the paper in utter sadness.

"Let me tell you a little something gentlemen," Talon said with his back still to the mural. "This technology is..." and the printer fired up again.

'FORGERY!'

The printer spat that out again. Talon just crumpled it up and threw it in the trash can. When he turned around... it was flattened out... and laying on his desk by the monitor.

"I'm telling you gentlemen, it would be near impossible to..." and the printer went wild.

It spit out 30 sheets all with the same message. It was as if even the printer itself was mad at Talon.

"FINE THEN!" Talon shouted in anger. "If you've got something to explain all this... I am MORE than willing to accept any help you're willing to offer!"

The printer was quiet for a moment. That only made Talon even angrier.

"I didn't think so," he nearly seethed.

That's when... he heard the horses... and a stagecoach come to a stop. The printer then fired up one final time.

'Look into the eyes of the past... then into hers... turn around'

Talon huffed, but he did turn around.

He stared at the mural, and damn near shit his pants. There was one man, a young man, standing beside the coach by the front porch. What caught Talon's attention was this time, though still small, he saw it without the magnifier. Then, the image grew and grew and took over that whole area of the mural. The Pinkerton man... was Talon. Older by a few years, and with a Colonel Sanders style beard and mustache... but it was his face. Talon was frozen as he stared at the image. The agent tipped his hat to Talon with a slight grin. Then, he pointed two of his fingers at his own eyes... then pointed to the computer monitor. Another tip of his hat... and the image faded back to the original mural. Once it had, the printer fired up one last time.

'We shall meet but once more... when the time is right'

Talon took the papers littering his floor, collected them, and tossed them in the trash.

Violet was in tears. She looked at the dresses hanging on the wall, and only cried harder as she packed them last. She hoisted her new backpack on her shoulders, tightened the straps, and took a last look around.

"I'm sorry Mrs. Grayson... I really am. I won't hurt him though and, I think you know that."

Violet turned, and left the room. She looked from the hallway's edge to see Grant and Cody sitting in the kitchen. As a lucky break, they had their backs to her. With a sad last look, she snuck out the back patio behind them. Neither man saw, nor heard, a thing.

"Where's Violet!?" Talon said quite happily as he burst from his office.

"She went into the guest room. Haven't seen her since she closed the door," Grant told him in a tone that implied he was still a bit freaked out.

"Oh, you mean the open one right there?" Talon said pointing to an open door he was just told was closed.

"Shit! I swear bro, I didn't see her! Maybe she used some of that magic of hers on us to slip away!"

Talon was now annoyed.

"Magic? Next you'll be saying that goblins and unicorns are real."

Now Grant was annoyed and said "Well how the hell else do you explain that!?"

"I know it ain't witchcraft," Talon said admonishingly.

"Says the man who talks to a dead whore," Grant challenged right back.

"Ya know... if you ruin my rhododendrons... I'm gonna be a tad pissed," was the voice Violet heard behind her.

She knew about the driveway and tried to hop over the main fencing instead. She was still crying, and spoke without turning around.

"Please, if you care for me even a little... don't make this harder than it has to be."

"Mind telling me why you're leaving?" Talon asked almost flippantly.

"You know why!" she practically shouted. "I told you there were 'gaps' in my memories. I also told you I wouldn't hurt you. Please... just... let me go."

"No," Talon said with all the confidence in the world.

"Talon... I can't take the chance I might hurt you. What if that happens again? What if...?"

"I can't say for certain it won't... but I'm betting it won't."

Violet hung her shoulders, but still wouldn't turn around.

"Talon... I..."

Suddenly Violet was wrapped in the same arms of the very man she was trying to protect.

"Shhh. I'll tell you what. Come back in, and see what I discovered. Then, if you still want... I'll open the gates for you myself."

Violet was sobbing hard and said "But... but... I'm scared."

"I know my dear. C'mon, come see. Besides, if you do leave, this isn't how I want to remember you."

Violet couldn't believe this crazy gray-haired man. What made her sadder than sad was, for the first time in her life, she was not only in love... but she admitted it. True it was only to herself but even for Violet, that was huge. Now, she was hoping with all her heart he truly found something, ANY thing, that would allow her to stay. With full surrender, she swung around and hugged him hard.

"Remember when you asked me if I trusted you?"

Talon smirked and replied "As I recall, you told me no."

She looked up at him with loving eyes and said "Talon?"

"Mm?"

Sweetly, and drying her tears, Violet told him "I do now."

Grant and Cody were in the office, per Talon's request. He brought Violet back in the way she left. He asked the men to wait in the office because you couldn't see the patio door from in there. Talon just wanted to give Violet any dignity he could. Grant and Cody also promised they wouldn't say a thing.

"Okay gentlemen... watch and learn!" Talon boasted as he came in with Violet and restarted the video.

He played it in its entirety and still not one of them saw or figured it out.

"Okay, let me spell it out for you. You're spooked, I get it. I was too, till I saw the whole video."

"There's more?" Cody asked.

"No, that's all of it," Talon said with not a care in the world.

"Then what are we missing? We all saw the same thing," Grant protested.

"Yes and no," Talon said as he backed up to the beginning. "First, while a tad freakish, you did indeed see the whole video. What you're missing is your focus. You all focused on the last few seconds. Sadly, so did I. That's why I didn't see it at first and!... Neither did any of you."

Talon went back to the beginning and paused the video.

"First, Violet was given some drugs. Anyone here know what? Cuz I sure don't. Can't really see it on the video. Now, watch this. The orderly dude leaves but... does anyone actually see him do it? No... because the door is out of the camera angle. For all we know, that rolling tray, AND him, are just off camera. Now, and this one still bugs me out... here comes the creepy part," and Talon froze it on Violet's face seconds before the end.

"Okay... show me!" Cody said getting pumped.

In his mind, Talon was right, they were so focused on the end they never considered anything else.

"Tell me, oh wise and noble beings," Talon joked, "What are you NOT seeing?"

Grant looked but couldn't see anything different.

"Well, I'd play the air guitar right about now but... according to the video... I'd have no reason to," Talon told the group.

"Holy shit!" Violet blurted out. "My eyes... they're brown!!!"

Talon sat back on his desk, smiled, and just said "Mm hmm."

"That! Okay THAT, is NOT possible!" Cody blurted out nearly in anger.

Talon grinned and stated "A puff of smoke comes to life... and that's possible... but a 15-year-old girl's eyes change color and you're freak'in?"

Doc Holliday was bugging out because he was always a man of science first, faith second. He was feeling now as if the former, had betrayed him.

"Listen people, you 3 don't know how sensitive, and how intricate, the eye really is. In the 1960's, there was a trial to inject a dye to change a person's eye color. It was in two parts. Half were dye's, and the other half were chemicals to effectively bleach the eye color."

"End result?" Grant asked.

"Half the subjects reverted back to their original color as their bodies treated it like a foreign invader."

"And the other half?" Talon asked in a tone like he already knew it was going to be bad news.

"They became legally blind. In the end, the eye colors changed, but never to anything we would consider 'normal'. So you see, changing a color from one to another...without using contacts that is... isn't medically possible."

Talon was still thinking. He truly believed her eyes changed color. Now all he had to do was figure out how. Violet thought she knew, and was shaking at the thought.

"Well, if the local medical community is baffled... howzabout we hear from the in-house ghost society?" Talon teased lightly.

Violet was nervous and had her fist to her mouth and was chewing on her fingernail.

"There's no proper term for it that I'm aware of. I call it habitation. My grandmother warned me about it. Warned me never to let it happen that is. You would likely be more familiar with the movie and biblical term however," she told them in a somewhat frightened voice.

"And that would be 'possession'?" Talon asked.

"Bingo."

Violet took a deep breath, exhaled, and began to explain.

"Grandma told me, the one thing I could never do, is lose all control. Even when I sleep, I'm the same as you. You know, in the sense that if your nightmare becomes too powerful, you wake yourself up as protection."

"Okay, with ya so far," Grant said still a little nervous of Violet.

"Grandma said that if I got too weak, certain powerful entities might take advantage... and take over. In a sense, use me to temporarily 'come back'. Grandma was afraid though that if I lost control like that, even once, they could take over anytime they wanted. I would lose control and... according to her... likely never get it back."

Grant joked and told Talon "Well Captain my Captain... where do we go from here?"

Talon was thinking hard. He had a few things and figured he'd start with that and hope the rest would come.

"Okay, first... Violet here, has put a lot of trust in me. Time for me to return some of it. First... I believe grandma was right... and she was wrong. Violet, since I've met you, I never once saw you do what you're dearly afraid of. You saved my life, rather than let Shadow Man take over. Grant?"

"Yeah?"

"When you went on your date last night, she was beside me the whole time but... 'keeping an eye' on you. Violet? It's quite clear you've become fond of my home." Talon smiled kindly at her and said "For the record, it's become rather fond of you too. So, for the time being, your job is still secure, and unless you choose to... you ain't going anywhere." Talon politely, but firmly, stared at Cody and Grant and asked "Anyone got a problem with that?"

Grant looked at Violet. He liked her as much as Talon did. He also liked Talon far more.

"For the record, if my crazy brother is willing to trust you, then I will respect that and follow his lead." Then he got serious and told her "If however," and he pointed to the video and finished with "You EVER turn into psycho bitch though... I'm gonna find something particularly nasty looking in Doc's bag... and take your ass down. Deal?"

Before she could answer, Cody chimed in with "I will also go with Talon's assessment. If however, like the younger version said, you 'lapse' on us... I'll make sure there's something in my bag for him to find. Deal?"

Violet was stunned. She hugged Talon. The gray-haired guy couldn't have said more perfect words to her right then if he tried. Then she addressed Cody and Grant.

"Gentlemen, I know I haven't known you long, nor you me. That said though, I've come to not only like you two, but find you to be two fine and capable men. It would mean a great deal to me to be able to call you my friends. As a friend, we help each other out right?"

"I suppose," Cody said.

"Well then, know that... IF I ever go crazy like that again... it won't be me doing it. Not the real me anyway. As such, I'll be counting on your claims... to bring the 'real me' back. Deal?"

Cody and Grant both smiled, and hands shook all around.

"OH WAIT! HOLD THAT THOUGHT!" Doc barked happily. "I got an idea! Give me a minute I got to get something out of my car!" and he bolted out the front door.

He came back in with 3 really thick books.

"Violet, we couldn't see the drugs they gave you on the video. But we DO know they gave you some. These books have every known drug in them, their uses, and their interactions. Is there ANY thing you remember about them? Anything at all?"

"Sure," she said easily. "I remember it was the same ones every time. A green pentagon, a spotted football, and a yellow star."

Talon laughed "The what and a who?"

Cody was already drilling through the books though.

Violet said matter of factly "I don't know what they were, as they never told us. But when I tried to break out, I started only making it look like I was taking them. I don't know why but, I remember their shapes. It was always in that order too. The first one looked like the Pentagon in DC, and it was green. That one made me real woozy and it made me feel like I was out of control of my own thoughts. The spotted football was white with blue spots and had the number 315 stamped on it. I remembered that because they gave it to me once at 3:15 pm one day, and it kinda stuck."

"What the fuck!?" Cody said with annoyed realization. He turned the book around and asked Violet "Is this the green Pentagon?"

"Sure looks like it."

Cody flipped to a page his finger was marking and asked "And this one?"

"Hey! That's the spotted football!" Violet said in slight wonder.

"The yellow star I need no book for. That one I know." Cody looked at the men and said "Keratotomine, Myacyn and Philagrin. Gentlemen, this is not good."

"Well Doc? What are they!?" Grant said getting impatient.

"Gentlemen, insanity is based on brain chemicals misfiring, or portions of the brain being either hyperactive or dead. Bottom line, the brain is, in non technical terms... malfunctioning. When you are deemed insane, its been found in many patients, sedatives have an opposite effect. You would think someone like how Violet was behaving would calm down when given a sedative. Many patients though, the opposite is true. Now, Violet seems quite normal to all of us correct?"

"Damn straight!" Violet said heartily.

"So, those drugs are extremely powerful in inducing psychotic episodes if given to a normal person. It would appear they weren't trying to calm her down... they were trying to power her up." Cody thought a moment and stated "Ya know what? Forget 'they'. Those drugs are HIGHLY regulated and can only be prescribed by an attending physician."

"Doctor Barnes," Violet said in a tone that implied if he was in the room right now, she'd strangle him with her bare hands.

Talon thought a moment then came up with a plan.

"Violet, remember how you said you trusted me?"

"Mm hmm."

"Do it now. Doc? You're with me. Violet? Go with my brother. Grant, check the work on the mansion, then take Violet food shopping. My fridge is getting a little empty. I say, if Violet likes to cook, I'm willing to let her. Dinner here tonight. Let's see what I have, what Cody brought, and this new info on Violet... and see how it all fits together." Talon chuckled and asked "Anyone up for a home cooked meal... and a murder mystery!??"

Grant beamed like a little kid on purpose and waved his hand in the air.

"OOH OOH... pick me pick me!!" and all 4 just laughed.

Grant and Violet left, and Talon turned to Cody.

"Doc... I'm no sawbones like you but... I get the feeling this doctor Barnes guy was after something."

"Only thing I can think of was either he knew what Violet's 'talents' were, or suspected. Either way, you thinking what I'm thinking?"

"Doc, if my dad were here right now he'd claim this was a classic government conspiracy. I don't know that it's a government one, but I do indeed smell a conspiracy. I feel with all my heart this guy tried to use her for some purpose. I intend to make sure he never does it again... and I'm gonna need your help to do it."

"Since becoming a doctor, nothing has disgusted me more than one of my own abusing that power AND that trust." Cody got ice cold and told Talon "Count me in... and say what you need."

While Grant and Violet were off running errands... Talon was planning on protecting the woman he was now claiming as 'his gal'.

"Marie? Yeah it's Talon. Listen sweetie when you get in tomorrow, I need you to round up the Kansas gang for me. Tell them I have a new dilemma that requires the utmost care... and their unique talents."

Talon thanked her, then hung up the phone.

Chapter 12

"Digging Into The Past... And Digging It Up"

"BOO!!" Violet yelled coming up behind Grant in the supermarket.

"JESUS! Quit doing that already will ya!? Okay okay I get it... point made."

Violet giggled and said "Stop being such an easy target then."

She saw how he was still nervous around her. Instead of being sad though, she believed them when they told her they'd 'yank her back to reality'. That actually made her feel comfortable, not sad. So, seeing Grant still a tad nervous... she couldn't help but tease him a little.

"Ya know Violet," Grant started kindly, "You've only been around a week or so. I have to say though... spooky video aside... you make it feel like you've been around us forever."

"Ya sure I'm not just bewitching you into thinking that?" Violet smarted with a sly smile.

"Listen you, I'm spooked enough as it is. How about if we go back to acting like adults again hmm?"

Violet smiled, gave him a friendly hug, and agreed.

"Thank you though Grant... for your comment I mean. I never knew people like you in my life. I suppose growing up you tease your siblings some, help them some, and stand by them all the other times. I never knew that so, you'll have to excuse me if you find me making up for lost time."

Grant was friendly now and spoke as they shopped.

"Honestly though Violet, doesn't that video freak you out even a little?"

"Don't get me wrong Grant, it freaks me out a lot. Ya know why I'm not though?"

"Tell me."

Violet was kind and said "Because for the first time since my grandmother, I have friends who promised to look out for me. They know who I am... and what I am... and accepted both. I know your brother is rich and all but, just having you 3 is more gold than I'll ever need." Violet smiled and said "Talon played a truth game with me when I first arrived. How about you and I play it now?"

"Hmm... this game got rules?" Grant asked warily.

"Yep. I ask questions, and you tell the truth no matter how awkward. You promise not to make your answers hurtful, and I promise not to take them that way if they seem so."

Grant was confident now and boldly stated "Okay then... ladies first!"

Violet was equally as confident. She was finding the Grayson gang to be truly honorable men. As such, she believed them when they said something. This was a new feeling for Violet and, even if it was an illusion as it had been in the past... this was at least a nice one... and she sought to keep it going. She knew her insecurities were pissing off Talon at times. So, if she was going to stick around, then those were the first thing to go. She also realized that if Talon turned out to be a dud... she could still do with losing quite a few of those anyway. She truly believed Talon when he said shitty stuff reflects a shitty life, and only perpetuates more of the same. She was determined that if she did return to the road, she would indeed do things differently next time.

Now Violet asked her first question.

"Do you think I'm a gold digger?"

"Truth huh?"

"Mm hmm," Violet confirmed.

"I was afraid you might be at first. I have no doubt Eileen is making sure you're not. Otherwise, to answer your question, yes I did but... not anymore."

"Grant, he spent more on me in one day than I usually make in months. I felt bad but, he wanted to do it. Normally, I'm the type to hoard the gold, not spend it recklessly. Look at me, even now, I'm making the money he gave me go as far as I can make it. Coupons... buying $3 steak instead of $5 steak... and all because I know, with my talents, I can make it taste like a $5 steak. I truly don't blame you for thinking what you did. I just wanted to make you know I'm not 'that girl'... and that I would likely have done no different if I were you."

Violet picked out a small bag of dog food next, and 2 small cans of the same.

Grant chuckled saying "Uh... you do know we don't have a dog right?"

Violet just smiled and answered "Oh... I know."

Now it was Violet's turn to ask a question again.

"Talon, and his departed wife... that I understand. Tell me, why is a nice guy like you walking around without a woman of your own?"

Grant told her "I'm looking for a certain something in a woman. She could be a princess or a commoner, I don't care... I'm just looking for a certain spark... ya know?"

"Not really," Violet said as they finished shopping.

"Violet, I can't really define it. Just a certain 'something' to her. I've only known 4 women like that in my life. One was my mother, the other is my sister. Another still, has been dead for 150 years or so..."

"And the fourth?" Violet asked as she loaded her groceries onto the counter.

"The fourth has fallen in love with my brother," Grant stated, but with a caring smile.

Violet was thrown a bit by that one. A compliment, and someone else noticing what she thought was hidden.

She gave Grant a look but he called her on it saying "Eh eh ehhhh... truth remember?"

Violet gave in and gave him a kiss on the cheek.

"THAT... was for the compliment." Then she warily asked "That noticeable is it?"

"It is to me," Grant said nicely.

"Okay, my turn again. How do you feel about my sister coming?" Grant asked as he took the bags of groceries and started heading out.

Violet was a tad nervous and said "She scares me on two fronts."

"Oh now THIS I gotta hear!" Grant said with a chuckle.

"I'm afraid she won't approve... and I'm afraid of what will happen if she does. Let me tell you something," Violet said as she walked alongside him. "Give me a ghost or something, and I'm right at home. Sad as that sounds, it's familiar to me. I know who I am... who and what they are... and I know how to behave accordingly. I never knew people like you, your brother, and Doc. Give me a 'reflection' and I'm fine. It's the real life I have a bit of trouble with."

She stopped him outside and took the dog food from him.

"As for you, I see a good man who appears to be looking for a bit of quality for himself... and I see nothing wrong with that. I also think you should hold out for that quality. Do that, and I have no doubt that one day, if you don't find it... it will find you," Violet said in a tender and caring tone.

Grant had no idea how right Violet would be in time... and how that plan was already in motion.

Without another word, she turned and walked to the edge of the parking lot. A homeless man was there begging for food, or money to buy some. He didn't look too shabby to Violet... but the loyal dog whimpering from hunger at his side did. It backed away from her but Violet's approach was soft and kind.

"Here ya go buddy... I know... you gotta eat too right?" Violet said kindly petting the dog.

He tore into the food, but stopped, and licked Violet's face in appreciation. Violet pet him back and giggled.

"You're very welcome young man," she said to the dog as she got up to return to the truck, and Grant.

"Bless you miss for your kindness," the homeless man told her.

Grant saw it all and, softly,... and to no one... he stated "Oh I think Eileen will like you just fine."

Violet wasn't a gourmet chef. True to her word though, what she did make was delicious. Not only that, all 3 men said so. It was Grant who declared that, not knowing what they'd find in the papers Talon had, dinner conversation was to be about anything but. Talon agreed and, so it became. Grant told them how the house was at the 'early' stage but coming along nicely.

"Early stage?" Cody queried.

"Yeah Doc," Talon answered, "It's the part in the beginning of the project. It's where you put in a week's worth of work... but it looks like nothing was done." Talon looked at Grant and told him "Erik has finished the first floor and said he'll have a rendering for us by mid next week. Preliminary so far but, as you'd expect, a lot of rich browns and earth tones."

"Yeah, pretty standard. What about the walls?"

Talon told Grant "It would seem our gal was a fan of pastels. Soft blues and pale pinks and yellows and creams."

Grant smiled "A little bit masculine, a little bit feminine... heh heh... whorehouse madam AND interior decorator! Damn she was good eh?"

Talon grinned and confirmed "Indeed she was."

Violet was feeling more and more comfortable around these men. As such, she playfully turned on Cody.

"Ya know Doc, Eileen may be making sure Talon hasn't consorted with some 'loose woman' but, let's not forget, she also has her eye on a certain doctor. Heh heh... a doctor who, just happens to be, not so old nor bald nor fat as once described."

Cody calmly stood and put his empty plate in the sink.

"Perhaps but... unlike you... 'I' have already passed the brother test," Doc said in a 'nice try lady' sort of tone.

"Oh?... Is that so?"

That response was Talon... AND Grant... in unison. Even Doc laughed at that one.

Dinner was done, and all 3 headed back into Talon's office. Talon split up everything he had between the 4 of them. Violet, got the string sealed book.

"Hmm..." and she read the first page aloud as the other men sorted their piles. "If found, please return to Lucian R. Garrison, at the Pinkerton office in... HEY! What was that for!?" Violet barked as Talon practically ripped it from her hands.

Grant was standing now and stated "No way!"

Talon stared at it the way one would stare at a note from God. It was part reverence, and part disbelief. Grant was the same way and right over his shoulder.

"Well... sonuvabitch," Talon said low.

"Care to fill us in?" Cody asked referring to him and Violet.

He was staring at the page but gave Cody his answer.

"Garrison... was our mother's maiden name. We were told an uncle, that Grant and I never met, was named Lucian. We were also told he was named after some great grandfather who just happened to be a Pinkerton agent back in the day."

Cody knew the implications of that, and immediately went to the mural.

"Talon? Uh, you may wanna come see this," Cody said.

Grant and Talon did look.

"Fucking figures! I swear brother... when this little mystery adventure of ours is over... I'm not stepping in this room again," Grant extolled in a highly aggravated manner.

What all 3 men saw was the coach... it was gone.

"Uh... what am I missing here?" Violet asked all confused.

"Exactly," was all Talon said.

Grant pulled out an old paper. He read it and as soon as he did, the answers Talon so wanted, would start flowing.

"Wow, I've never seen a real one of these," Grant stated in wonder.

"What is it?" Violet asked.

"It's a very old version of a C.O."

"A what?"

Talon told her with a grand smile "Certificate of Occupancy. Build a new house, or rebuild one, and the town or county needs to issue one before the house can be lived in."

"Okay makes sense but, you're beaming like a Cheshire cat why?"

"Because my dear, it gives us a build date," Talon told her happily.

"Indeed," Grant said beaming as well. "Damn bro, your good."

Talon fanned himself jokingly and said "Why ah dooo dehclare ginger chyld... you doo flattuh me so."

"Bro? Ha ha ha ha … fuck off."

"Well?" Talon asked.

"July 4th........ 1859."

Talon smirked.

"Oh Lucinda, you shrewd lady you."

Cody asked "Not that I disbelieve you but, care to tell me why you suddenly think so?"

"Doc, a mansion like hers would've taken years to construct. Silver here wasn't discovered till that year. So you tell me, why build a mansion like that in literally the middle of nowhere?"

Doc had an 'I get it now' tone and answered "Unless you knew something the locals didn't. Niiiice. And how would she know of that unless she had the privilege of some VERY inside information."

"Oh I get it," Violet kicked in. "She wants to setup shop. Let me give you some insight. You may have noticed her personality is a tad large. What I can do for this little pow-wow... is confirm it. She's the kind of woman who would have wanted to out-do everyone else in the region. She didn't want to just be a madam... she wanted to be a madam like no other."

"That leaves us with only two scenarios then," Talon kicked back in. "Tell me this, are we all agreed that a mansion like that... back then... would have taken a serious fortune to build?"

All did agree.

"Okay then this is how I see it. Lucinda knows silver is coming. She also wants to set herself up as THE destination in all the western territories. She has access to San Francisco, and all the money that resides there at the time. Most of that money was banking and trains. The latter had tons of cheap Chinese labor imported to help lay tracks. Now, if you're a train baron, you can lay tracks anywhere you damn please. Most of the tracks through the pass are original, but laid far later. No, trains back then, would have come through Carson. The mountains over there were easier to get through at the time. Making Virginia City a mud hole of a last stop. The train barons get over the mountains and, get access to Lucinda. She sets up as a legitimate hotel, because men like that wouldn't stay at no flop house. No one is the wiser, and the rich boys get their playground setup, all at the same time."

Grant chimed in with "Don't forget, a woman they trust keeping an eye on things out here for when the Comstock opens for business. Wow, part madam... part business partner. Our gal was bad-ass indeed... at least for the times."

Talon said "Indeed Grant. Nearby money, power, and cheap labor. She sets up shop far enough away that high society of the day keeps an entire city from gossiping. Knowing silver was coming, Lucinda was literally, in the right place at the right time. No wonder she had such power. She had secret information long before she even setup shop."

Talon mused a moment then had more.

"Okay then, here's the scenarios I mentioned. Let's say 5 years to build the mansion. That puts us back in the middle of the gold rush. We know she came from Al's neck of the woods so, what was she doing out here prior? Scenario one is, using her stunning and exotic looks, she charms the high class gentlemen. Scenario one is she made her fortune out here, then parlayed that into getting some loans from the rich guys. Having a person like her in charge, and someone they can trust, then Lucinda gets her wish... and they get the nicest playground anywhere. Everybody wins."

Cody was loving this. He was getting farther in just a few weeks than he had on his own in over a decade.

"Okay then, plausible so far. And scenario number two?"

"Scenario two is... she came out here with her fortune already intact. If that was the case... then where, and how, did she get it?"

Everyone was deep in thought when Grant broke the silence.

"Looks like we're gonna need that genealogist. We track Lucinda, we can build a time-line of events."

Talon looked at Cody and asked "Doc, seriously, is he truly that good?"

"Ya know the Mayflower right?"

"Duh."

"He could tell you how many rats were onboard," Doc said with utter confidence. "Thing is though, he had some seriously high tech gear. He was beyond amazing at tracking records but... he couldn't tell a CD from a gigabyte. I could tell his brother was the source of that. If you can get him the high tech, he can get you the rest."

Talon had his chin in his fist and stated "I'm no slouch when it comes to the tech. If however you're talking about the kind of tech I'm thinking of, that kind of high end stuff is a tad out of my field."

"Well, I'm sure we'll get something setup," Cody said.

"Yeah well, I can always hire someone if that's the case."

Talon wouldn't have to... because Grant would. He didn't know it, but a blond and a black-haired lady did.

Talon now redirected the focus for a moment.

"Okay I want to point something else out. I plan on bringing the cobblestone driveway up all the way to the porch. I also plan on adding a patio area out back. Part of that back yard includes some new trees, and flowers."

"Sounds pretty," Violet stated. "How does that fit into this stuff though?"

Talon told them "Well, we're all focused on Lucinda right? Primarily, what we **don't** know about her. Just like Violet's video though, we're overlooking what's right in front of our faces."

Cody smirked "Oh this should be good."

Talon offered a playful bow to the Doc, and continued.

"I get these plant catalogs in the mail all the time. I like roses and such as much as the next guy. What I like though, is having some kind of rose no one else has. Or a tree you wouldn't find locally. I got trees and flowers and such just like any of my neighbors do. Difference with me is, I have a variety you've never seen or heard of."

"Okay but... your point?" Violet asked knowing he was going somewhere with this insight into his personal tastes.

Talon tapped some keys and brought up the image of Lucinda Erik sent him.

"Like the end of Violet's video, Lucinda's beauty distracts you from seeing other things. Now I mentioned the flower catalogs for a reason. I've grown up here all my life and never seen one anywhere around here. The catalog said this flower was 'new' and available only for the first time this year."

"What was it?" Cody asked.

"Edelweiss."

"Huh?" Violet asked having no clue.

Talon smiled and told her.

"It's a wildflower common to the Alps of Austria and... Germany."

Cody's faced just totally changed.

Violet asked "Sounds cool. What does it look like?"

Talon smirked... and pointed to the white star shaped flower... in Lucinda's hair.

"Ohhhhhh," Violet said slowly now getting it.

"Lucinda said 'my Henry'. In heart perhaps but, I'm guessing the official Mrs. Henry Holliday was none too happy about that. While it wasn't uncommon for the era for men like him to have trysts, this went way beyond that. Violet, you haven't seen this part of the house yet but, ya see this background here?"

Violet asked "Yeah, what about it?"

Talon told her "There's only one place in the whole house with a fireplace like that. It's in Lucinda's bedroom."

"I got ya now," Violet confirmed.

"The part we all overlooked, was that Lucinda was actually committing adultery... and so was Henry. Get a mail order bride, and I have no doubt she would have brought something of the old country with her. So think of this, how did Lucinda get a flower that I've never even seen in real life?... No less around here." Talon then smirked and told the gang "For the record... heh heh... I ordered two dozen of them."

Cody was nearly beaming. He was getting answers now he thought he might never get. True, many of them were educated guesses but, they were good ones. Now he threw a few things out for discussion.

"Okay my turn now. It's in the papers I gave you but essentially, Henry was described as being 'despondent' over Lucinda. What you and I today would call depressed. Seems my great great whatever grandmother gave him a sort of 'serves you right' attitude for it as well. Seems that, and Lucinda, was what brought down his name, fortune, and reputation. In the letters she doesn't mention it in detail, but, I get the feeling she felt trapped. Henry and her had their son about a year before it all went bad. That son also wrote that 'mom' didn't like him getting friendly with his own father. He described it as almost a competition between his parents. He said she wanted to move but Henry forbid it. Some years later, Henry died, and she left and ended up in Chicago."

Doc had a thought just then and it nearly made him giggle.

"Ya know.. how funny is this? Henry gets embroiled in a love affair great grandma's not very keen on. She takes her family away for a fresh start... only to have that same family end up right back here."

Violet was mulling all this over and said "In a way, I can actually relate to her."

Cody was a bit shocked and asked "You? How do you figure?"

Violet answered "Well think about it. I'm a stranger here and know no one. Say I married one of you 3 tomorrow, well I'd still be a stranger. I know nothing about this place, nor the local customs and such. Those same locals don't know me either. Add to that, there's not a town anywhere on this planet that likes strangers. Trust me... I would know. Now say, I was suddenly on my own again but, under bad circumstances. I'd be an un-liked stranger in a strange land, with the whole town against me AND, for something I didn't do. So tell me, am I really so different from her?"

"Well... you are strange I'll grant you that," Talon teased.

Violet got playfully annoyed and said "Yo gray guy... ya like that shirt of yours?"

Talon chuckled and knew where this was going.

"Yes dear."

"Yeah well... ya wanna see it again?"

"No dear... uh, I mean yes dear... whatever you say dear," Talon mocked in a rather henpecked tone.

"Asshole," Violet said with a giggle. Then she barked at Grant saying "Yeah yeah... laugh it up, carrot top! See how soon YOU get another home cooked meal!" Violet said still giggling.

Grant bolted to his feet and teased his brother.

"Why Mistuh Grayson sir... ah doo emplore you tuh mind yaw mannuhs!" he teased at the potential loss of future dinners.

Everyone just laughed then got back to the business at hand.

Grant had gone with Cody to his house. It was late and Grant wanted to get an early start. Cody offered to let him sleep at his place. Being that it was only 15 minutes from the mansion, Grant kindly accepted.

Talon was in his office alone. He was reading through Lucian's book like it was a best seller. Violet tried sneaking up on him. She only laughed when she got about a foot away.

"You'll have to do a better job than that if you're trying to spook me."

"Ha ha ha... party pooper. How'd you know?"

Talon just smiled and tapped the black monitor for his computer.

"A little trick this girl I knew taught me once," Talon smarted.

Violet however, decided to match wits with him.

"Oh? This girl you mention... was she pretty?"

"Gorgeous,"

"Hmm," Violet played along with fake annoyance. "More gorgeous-er than me?" she asked nearly laughing at her made up word.

"Oh for sure... way more 'gorgeous-er' than you. A tad crazy though," Talon taunted.

"Ooooh better watch it there Mister Grayson 'sir'... those crazy ones can be big trouble."

"Well... coming from you and all... I'll take it under advisement."

Talon stopped teasing, and switched to kind curiosity.

"I thought you weren't going to wear that anymore?"

He said that because, Violet was wearing his shirt again.

Without missing a beat she told him "Yeah well, someone promised me a harness, but it's on backorder or something. Sorry but, till it comes in, I guess your stuck with this."

Talon smirked, closed the book and tossed it on the desk, and pulled Violet over his shoulder and onto his lap. She giggled the whole way.

"Well... give me that guy's name and I'll see to his immediate removal in the morning."

"Oh I wouldn't mess with him if I were you," she said. "He's like, rich I think. I know that because he drives a lamb or genie."

"One of those eh? He's probably one of those guys with good looks, brains, class... and charm just oozing out from everywhere. Oh... and confidence... can't forget confidence. The kind the ladies really like. I'll bet he has a big house too. Yeah, you're right, probably best to steer clear of that guy."

"Yeah that's him! You know him?" Violet exclaimed.

"Nope... can't say that I do."

Violet had her legs draped over the side of the chair, and sporting a pair of pink socks. Talon had all he could do to not throw her on the floor and 'do her' right there and then. She leaned into his shoulder and gave him a soft hug as she did. When she did, Talon was sporting a hard-on the size of the truck in his garage.

"So, anything interesting in there?" she nearly cooed.

Talon had to literally force himself to focus.

"Well, seems great uncle Lucian was made the lead investigator on the case. Seems Grant was right, and so was Cody. I only got about a third the way in before this smoking hot lady interrupted me."

"Thank ya kindly good sir," Violet teased, but meant her words. "So, what were they right about?"

"Seems the elite didn't want any of their secrets to get out. They had them gather the books and bury Lucinda not only in the ground, but from history as well. They did it to protect themselves but, they wanted this done 'in house'. Seems those same elite truly did love Lucinda. She was their friend and they really wanted to know who did it. They not only wanted the investigation done in house but, they planned on serving up justice the same way. 'Uncle Lucian' was starting to have doubts though."

"(Yawwwwn) About?" Violet asked but, more like mumbled.

"He was starting to figure out what we already know... that Lucinda's killer wasn't Henry. Seems there was a private investigator who got hired by Henry's wife. Lucian thought he may have fallen for Lucinda and saw the Doc as a threat. He 'acquired' a letter from him to Mrs. Holliday. He nearly defended Henry and had a rather odd tone to his writing. He was fired shortly after that letter arrived but witnesses saw him at the mansion long after. Those same witnesses also saw him trying to get to Lucinda. Being that every red blooded male at the time tried as well, no one thought anything of it."

Talon looked down to see Violet had fallen asleep. As softly as he could, he stood up, cradled her in his arms... and carried her off to her bed. He laid her down and put the blanket on her. All he wanted to do was join her but, not like that. Either she would come to him, or he would ask... but it wasn't going to be like this. In Talon's mind, a stunt like that was what college guys did... not him. He sighed, but closed the door as he left. He had a California King bed but, lately, the alpaca blanket on the floor by the fire was the place for him. He set the alarm, then turned off the light. He got the fire roaring, then drifted off to sleep himself.

Seeing the lights in the house go off, a shadowy figure outside the driveway gates merely got back in his car and drove off. This figure was indeed shadowy but, unlike the one at the mansion, this one was very real.

Violet woke up, and pounded the pillow.

"Dammit!" she said chastising herself.

She had planned on 'not' sleeping alone. She never really enticed someone like that before, but knew that falling asleep wasn't the way to do it. She stayed mad at herself for a minute more, then managed a soft smile. She was in her bed and, exactly as she was the night before. She didn't get 'her man' as she planned... but at least that same man didn't do anything sleazy either.

Talon was already up. Coffee in hand, he was right back where Violet had left him hours earlier. To get Violet a little flustered though this time... no shirt. He was going over papers when she walked in.

"Good morning. Jeez, you don't stop when you get your claws in something do you?"

"Good morning to you too. And to answer your question... no... not usually." Talon had a thought and asked "Vi? Can I ask a small favor?"

"Sure what's up?"

"I need your talents."

"Um... okay?" Violet sort of asked.

"The mural here... can you touch it... and tell me if you get anything off of it?"

"Ooooookaaaayyyy," Violet answered warily.

She did as requested, and got wave after wave... of nothing.

"And I did that why exactly?"

Talon was a tad let down but, actually expected that.

"Meh, just looking for an edge is all. Don't worry about it but, thanks."

Violet was still in 'take care of my man' mode, and told Talon "C'mon, put that stuff away for now and I'll make you something to eat."

Talon did a cheesy Marlon Brando accent and stated "Now there's an offer I can't refuse."

Violet chuckled and pulled Talon to the kitchen. Violet didn't notice it, and Talon was ignoring it but, if anyone were to look at those two right now they'd say the sexual tension between them could be cut with a knife.

"So, Eileen comes in tomorrow. Are ya excited?" Violet asked Talon as she cooked.

"Shouldn't I be asking you that?" Talon questioned.

"Well, I got two things on that," Violet began. "First, I'll admit I was a tad petrified over it. Lately though, not so much. I mean I'm excited to meet her sure... just not nervous about it though."

Talon smiled kindly, and honestly said "I'm glad. And the second thing?"

Violet was nervous about how Talon would take this news.

"I want to sleep at Grant's tonight. I already asked him and he said sure."

Talon wasn't sure why, but he wasn't liking that idea.

"Any particular reason?" Talon said, not realizing, in an 'I'm not happy about that' tone of voice.

"Well gray guy... I... um..."

"Spit it out Violet."

"Oh fine! I just wanted to look nice. For myself and.... well... for you. I just wanted to surprise you is all, seeing me all dolled up. I know how close you and Eileen are, and I didn't want meeting me to get in the way of that. This way, you get time with her, and I'll see you later for dinner."

Now... Talon was happy again.

Talon smiled and said "That's fine... on one condition."

"Hmm?"

"If my brother tries to steal you from me... keep in mind I'll be stealing you back."

Violet grinned from behind her hair coquettishly.

"Promise?"

It was about an hour later, and Talon and Violet were just starting to head into the back roads that they took to the mansion. Violet knew how to work a computer but didn't own one. Talon gave her a nice, but slightly older digital camera he had. She was drawn to it and didn't know why. Talon's computer in his office was strictly off limits, so he gave her a tablet he had. She used the tablet to research the camera. Talon was laughing a little to himself as Violet spat out facts and minutia about the camera as they drove along. She found it all on the internet and was now, nearly, giving a book report no one asked for. They were about 10 minutes out and Talon had a nice thought that he shared with her.

"Ya know Violet, ghost hunting aside, you could do with a real life profession. Would you care for an observation?"

"Just don't be mean okay?" Violet said a little too impishly for Talon's liking.

"Fine but... make that two observations. First, how did you ever survive what you did being such a scared little rabbit?"

"I wasn't actually," Violet began. "I was more of what you would call battle hardened. I was truly a kick ass woman. In my own defense though, I have noticed it too... the rabbit thing. You have to understand something though. For me, it was like being in the middle of a battle everyday. Suddenly, the war is over and quite honestly, well, ya might say I'm having a hard time adjusting to civilian life. I never really knew a life like I've had with you 3 guys. It truly is a complete 180 from what I've known. I would watch TV and see these family shows and think 'oh wouldn't that be nice if I had that?'. I used to imagine that if I did, 'I would do this'... or 'I would do it that way'. Now I feel like I'm actually in that TV show, but it's a whole lot different being in one, than watching one. I find myself not knowing how to act most of the time, or what to say. It annoys you... the scared rabbit... doesn't it?"

"A bit yes... but mostly because I know it's based on fear, and I get the feeling you're capable of much more. Now... second observation."

"Go for it."

"You said in the past, you did Tarot readings or waitressing to get by, am I correct?"

"Mm hmm."

Talon stated with confidence "Well, why not photographer? Honestly Violet, the shots you took of me were goofy at best. The sunrise shots you took from the backyard however were truly beautiful. I'm no expert but if I had to guess, I'd say you would make an excellent landscape photographer. We live everyday knowing, by need or by choice, your life on the road could return at anytime. Even if it was kid portraits in a mall somewhere, tell me, would that be so bad?"

Violet was checking the camera Talon gave her to use and said "No, I can't say that it would be."

Talon was sweet and said "I don't care for the scared rabbit thing. I can't really say I'm a fan of 'Miss Rambo' either. How about, somewhere in the middle? Tell ya what. Get good with the camera. Ya seem to like it so that shouldn't be too hard. If you do, I'll take you to a real camera shop, and get you some accessories, then see how you do. 'IF' that goes well too, then there are some fine community colleges here that offer all sorts of courses. I'll invest in you... and you pay me back when you have your first gallery showing... wadda ya say?"

Violet was pleasantly amazed and asked "Why are you being so nice to me?" Violet looked at Talon as they pulled into the mansion's driveway and said "Look at me... no rabbit right now, and no hard-ass soldier bitch... just me, Violet... tell me, why?"

Talon shut off the truck, and stared into her eyes saying "You told me you were a good girl. I firmly believe that. I just think it's time you became a good woman... and left the girl part behind. It's clear to me, due to your life, you don't know how. I won't lie to you Violet... I'm becoming very fond of you and I truly enjoy having you around. You could do as I've said on your own but, I just wanna help and, I think it would be fun if we kind of did it together."

Violet smiled, gave him a quick kiss, then said "I do too," as she got out of the truck.

She was on cloud nine when she did. So was Talon.

Talon and Violet emerged to a flurry of activity. The roofers were busy stripping the roof shingles. The were getting the whole roof... all of it... ready for a gut job. Grant had Big Mack pointing skyward. It was offering safety support for them. Two of them had the tablesaw on overload running the old timbers Talon had shipped in. Once cut, they sent them up to the 3rd floor, and the guys on the roof made new trusses out of them. Only a small section near Lucinda's bedroom was burned away. The rest of the damage was from decay and years of neglect. The roof tiles were slate gotten from on the property. Half a dozen were sent to a local mason company, along with a few tons of matching boulders from the property. They would use them as templates to make new one's out of the boulders. Making and installing them was easy. The time it took to do it though was immense. Hand-shaved stone went in by hand, not by nail gun. As such the masons said they would make daily shipments with what they had so far, so as to keep them and the roofers working.

Violet found Talon inside going over plans with the plumbers. Talon was telling them anything exposed had to be period specific. Inside the walls however, he wanted nothing but the PVC stuff. Lucinda's bedroom was going to become his, but only when he didn't want to go home. As such, he was putting in a master bathroom. The plumbers were working on plans to tie those in to the mains below that they were running today. Talon had removed all the pumps Lucinda showed him. He decided a good idea then was a good idea now. As such, he sent them out to be rebuilt and powder coated. The well that fed them was to be re-drilled early next week. The original one had clogged over time and when given the price to fix it, Talon decided it was just better to drill a whole new line.

Violet kept touring... and scanning. So far, all things 'ghostly' were well at bey... so she took pictures and just moved on. Knowing those ghosts can be pesky at times, she checked every picture she took, just to make sure there were no other worldly photo bombs. Everything so far was just as normal as it should be so, she headed back outside.

Talon was outside now and Violet told him all was well. Suddenly, the ground shook. It wasn't very hard, and it didn't last long, but shake it did. Violet thought it felt like when Big Mack was rolling and one was standing nearby. Except, Big Mack was shut off.

"What the hell was that?" She said with extreme curiosity.

"Earthquake," Talon said in a 'no big deal' tone. "Probably about a 3 or a 3.5 by my guess."

Before Violet could say a thing, Talon was running at top speed for Big Mack. He did so because of the loud crash behind him... and the man screaming. Talon raced up the boom and called for Grant as he did. He laid down at the top to balance his weight, and not fall off himself.

"YOU OKAY BUDDY!!?" Talon hollered to the man dangling beneath the bucket.

The earthquake shook loose a small pile of roof tiles and sent the man tumbling into one of the holes in the roof. Thankfully though, the safety line did its job.

"I'm okay, Mr. Talon, thanks. More surprised than hurt thankfully. Good thing for this safety line huh?"

"Indeed. I'm glad you're not hurt. Hang in there and we'll get you out."

The roofer guy hollered back "Don't bother. I can let loose the line and drop to the floor... it's not that far."

"Perhaps but, your dead weight may send you through the floor if you did that... leaving you nothing but actually dead. Sorry pal, not gonna happen on my job site."

"The floor looks solid enough but, yeah, I see your point." Suddenly that same man just said "What the...??" at the sight he saw.

What he saw, was an old chair against the wall... slide over and stop... right under his feet.

"Did... did... did you see that!!!??" the man nearly hollered.

Talon played dumb and said "See what? Oh hey nice, you managed to pull a chair over. Okay, try it now."

The man reached as far as he could then let the safety line go. He fell only a foot or so... but no further. The man stood a moment in stunned silence. When nothing further happened, he smiled to the room.

"Thanks," he told it honestly.

Grant was now in Big Mack and fired it up. Ever so gently, and slowly, he lowered the boom to the roof line, then shut it off again. Cody was onsite today and came running up with a rope. Now Big Mack had 3 men on the boom as Talon lowered the rope Grant fed him.

"Alright pal..." Talon called down "...that floor isn't safe yet. You're okay there but, no way out so... we take you out the way you went in."

"Got it, Mister Grayson!"

Talon lowered him the rope and he tied it off to his lanyard. Talon gave a wave, and three men on the boom pulled a fourth to the safety of Big Mack's bucket. Grant fired it up again and gently lowered the man back earthbound once more. When he hopped out of it unharmed, applause broke out all around.

Pats on the back and grateful handshakes from a saved man, and this incident was over. Talon then walked inside and stared up at a photo over a fireplace.

"I know those roof tiles wasn't you but... chalk one up for the good guys." He tossed a soft and playful salute and told the photo "Thanks for the help lady."

"Maw than welcome Mista Grayson sir," was the sweet whisper in his ears as he walked outside.

From that moment on, Lucinda became a sort of good luck charm. All the workers onsite would now talk to 'her' or give her photo a friendly pat for good luck. For the first time in over a century and a half, Lucinda was adored once more by throngs of men. Also, the more she was, the stronger she became.

"Don't act so pleased with yourself, 'whore'," was the angry voice of Shadow Man.

Lucinda though, was feeling more like her old self with each passing day, and gave Shadow guy 'what for'.

"Iel act anyway ah please. Ah buhleev Mista G. Purrhaps, it's you who should watch yaw back faw a change."

"We'll see about that, whore."

Lucinda's ghost looked out the dual front doors to see Violet giving Talon a huge kiss for his bravery.

With pure confidence, and a smile, Lucinda's voice replied as she watched her champions, "This time, you horrid beast... I buhleev you may be right," and two lost souls drifted back to the ether.

Talon took Big Mack along the train track area while the roofers took lunch. He had some earth to dig up but, while the small tractor could clean it up quick enough, busting it up however would be hours with the smaller bucket. So that's what he did. He used the monster bucket to clear the equivalent of an acre's worth of land, then brought the behemoth back to the roofers and switched to the more maneuverable tractor.

Violet wanted to try her hand at driving the tractor. Talon chuckled but taught her how. She did far better with the backhoe than the bucket, but for a first time, she did fairly well. That's what Talon liked most about Violet, she was an all around kind of girl. The kind who could get down and dirty in a garden, or in this case drive a tractor, then shower and throw on a dress and some heels. What really attracted Talon was, insecurities aside, she could truly handle either. It's what also attracted him once to his wife. Mom was a very capable woman, and so is Eileen. Talon married his wife because he felt she was 'cut from the same cloth' as the saying goes. Now, here, was Violet. Not only working the tractor AND getting the hang of it, but liking it too. Add to that, she was telling Talon how she was looking forward to getting 'all dolled up' while she worked it.

"Aaaaand... since when does dirt go 'clang'?" Violet asked with strange curiosity as she backed the tractor away.

"I was about to ask that myself," Talon said offhandedly as he looked at what Violet hit. "Get the shovels off the back please will ya?"

Violet brought both over, handed one to Talon, but kept one for herself.

Talon just cocked an eyebrow at her and smirked.

"What? Think I can't handle it?" Violet nicely challenged.

"Not at all," Talon said with an amused smile. "It's just nice to see you not shy away from it."

"Yeah well, let me tell ya something. If it's work I can do... then I'm gonna do it. I'm not your typical girlie girl by any stretch of the imagination."

Talon laughed and imitated the great Althea.

"lllllLLLLLAWD! Ain't dat da truth!!" Talon snickered and said "That was my imitation of Al by the way."

"Uh... okay. Who's he?" Violet asked as they both dug the side of the hill.

Talon winked and said "Someone you'll meet tomorrow night."

Violet dug into the ground and hit another clang. Without asking, she grabbed the broom off the back of the tractor. She started sweeping the area while Talon skimmed the dirt off.

"How did you know something would be here?" Violet asked as they both cleared the ground.

"One of my first introductions into the world of AM/FM. Lucian showed it to me when I asked him for a place to start. Thing was though, he used Big Mack to point it out, not the coach."

"Ya know," Violet started, "Being me, well, I kinda got used to the whole ghost thing. It's as normal to me as living here is to you. Having someone else like me, even a little bit, that is what freaks me out sometimes."

"Well, you said the 'sensitivity to things'... you said it runs in families yes?" Talon asked.

"Usually yes. I mean, from what I've learned, you could be a totally normal couple, but have a child like me. Usually though, it runs in families."

"Yeah ya see, my mom and dad were die-hard hippies. Mom was into that stuff but I just thought it one of my mother's quirks. One thing I always thought, however, was that mom was hiding something."

"Like?" Violet asked.

"Well, like she was an MIT professor who didn't want anyone to know how smart she really was, so she played dumb... or worse, silly... just to throw everyone off. Knowing you, and seeing what you can do... well... it kind of makes me think I should have followed my gut and have mom tell me more about it." Talon had a thought and said "All 3 of us kids were home schooled. Mom made it lots of fun but us kids were always a year ahead usually. When she died, we toasted her and gave her our thanks for it. Looking back on it now, I can't help but feel like she was preparing us kids, rather than teaching us. It might be nothing but, to me anyway, there always seemed like there was a purpose to her teaching us that was more than just educating her kids."

"I struggled with that. Honestly Talon, if I wasn't living in the digital age, I wouldn't know a thing. One thing I found right away was that I needed my GED at the very least. Once or twice I felt like I may have stayed somewhere too long just so I could pass a class or two." Violet put the broom to the side and asked "So, ya think mom may have had a plan all along? Like she had some plan or, at least, if HER plan failed... you kids would be educated enough to stay safe in her absence?"

Talon confirmed "I never thought of it like that. All my life I felt like mom had some agenda we were being kept in the dark about. Just a sense or a feeling mind you, but it was there all the same. Lately, however, and given recent events... I've begun revisiting some old theories."

They had cleared away enough dirt to see something odd. There was an iron track that ran along the ground sideways. It was about 10 feet wide. Talon could see a groove with gear teeth running the entire width inside it. Leaning back on a 45 degree angle was two troughs running on the vertical. A little more digging and Talon uncovered an identical rail across the top.

"Okay, mister building guy... what the hell is it?" Violet questioned.

Talon mused a moment.

"Good question. These rails at top and bottom," Talon pointed, "They're geared so that means, whatever these vertical troughs are, they were designed to move back... aaaaand... fooooorth.....I got an idea!" Talon blurted having had an epiphany. "Okay, when I say to, push that one by you away from me, and I'll do the same on this one."

Violet braced herself and so did Talon.

"Okay... PUSH!" Talon shouted.

There were two sounds. The scraping of metal that hadn't moved in ages that one would expect. The other one was a similar sound but... sounded like it came from inside the hill they were digging at.

"Oh Lucinda, you clever, clever girl you!" Talon sweetly boasted to no one.

Talon fired up the tractor and put the backhoe on the rear to work. He dug carefully in between the troughs. Within 3 or 4 passes, the small bucket no longer met with resistance.

"A cave?" Violet asked in a bit of slight confusion.

"Not a cave," Talon said as he shut off, then hopped off, the tractor. "It's a tunnel! The train tracks ran right here. Train pulls in, stops, and whatever guests you don't want being seen... never are. Lucinda had a secret entrance into the mansion. As protected, and connected, as she was... the law likely wouldn't touch her. Still, in her profession one can't take any chances. This was a way to get the elite in unseen... or, if all hell broke loose when they were here... it could be used to get them out the same way."

"Okay, even I'm impressed," Violet said honestly.

Then she spooked like someone snuck up behind her and grabbed her. "Jesus! Warn a person next time will ya!?"

"Sorry to have startled you ma'am but this is a restricted area and I'm afraid I'm going to have to ask you to leave."

The man that said that was wearing a dark suit. A very old suit.

"Don't look at me," Talon told Violet who had a very annoyed look on her face. "I don't see shit."

"GREAT! I get involved with the Grayson and Garrison gang for only a few weeks, and now I'm out of practice!!??"

The serious gentleman asked Violet "Garrison? Any relation to Lucian Garrison?"

Violet got sweet and said "Why it is indeed..." then she winked at Talon and told the new guy "... he's soon to be my uncle-in-law."

"I served under his command in the cavalry. A fine man he is and you're marrying into a fine family. It was a pleasure to meet you ma'am but, I'm afraid I must insist. You need to go... now." The man turned and spoke to someone even Violet couldn't see and said "Stay with the stovepipe. I'm going ahead to make sure the way in is secure."

He looked back at Violet, tipped his hat, then... walked into the partially opened entrance... and disappeared.

Violet looked at Talon and asked "Who is stovepipe?"

Talon chuckled and said "In case you were wondering... it's a 'what' not a 'who'. You know... big black tube thing?"

"Okay, mister smart-ass, tell me this then. Why would someone tell someone else to stay with one?" Violet said still clearly annoyed.

"To stay warm I guess. Violet I told you the truth, I didn't see nor hear a thing. It's obvious you just did. Tell me, what did you see?" Violet told him and Talon said "Whoa hold up. Describe this guy again."

Violet did.

"Dark suit, looked like wool. From the look of it, I'd say from the era this mansion was originally in operation. Gun on his hip and another inside his coat. Some sort of yellow rope going around his hat. He said he was in the cavalry and from the old westerns I've seen, I'd say that sorta fit."

Talon had a look on his face like he knew what she just told him, but couldn't place it. Then Violet gave him the key that opened up a whirlwind of information.

"Also, he had spurs on. Not the pointy kind though. These jangled a bit but didn't spin. They looked like eagles."

"SONUVABITCH!!" Talon hollered in true surprise.

Page 180

Violet teased and asked "Did I do good, Mister Grayson sir?"

Talon was still stunned and told her "I'll overlook the snide comment Miss GED. You just described a cavalry elite guard."

"Yeah okay but I already told you that," Violet stated with a huff.

"No you didn't. You said he served under Garrison IN the cavalry. This guy was still in it. Only one's that wore eagle spurs were the cavalry elite. They were THE best of the best. Ya know what they did?"

"Enlighten me," Violet said still with a bit of attitude.

"They protected visiting heads of state... and our own. They were the precursor to the secret service. In this case, it would appear, the president himself. All presidents have a secret name given to them. Stovepipe refers to President Lincoln." Talon got a tad nervous, something Violet never saw him do, and he told her "You don't mention ANY of this to Grant... or ANYONE!"

"Talon you're scaring me," a slightly nervous Violet told him.

"Good! If Lincoln was here, well, THAT is some seriously deep shit. You saw all the info I had. What you don't know is what I had to do to get it. It was buried deeper than deep. Now I sorta know why. I didn't tell you how I got it... and I'm not going to either. That's to keep you safe."

Talon got very serious now and told her "Okay Violet... time to earn your paycheck. Call him."

"Uh... call who?"

"Santa Claus... you know who!"

"It's not like I can command them at will ya know!"

"Why not? You said you were different because you could transmit. Well Miss Hayes... start broadcasting."

"And if it works?" Violet asked back in her previously unhappy attitude.

"I need a date. Get me a month and a year and... do it quick."

Violet felt silly but, gave it a try. To her shock, it worked.

"Yoo hoo! Mister guard, sir?"

Externally nothing seemed different on Violet. Internally, she felt like a dynamo on steroids.

"I will escort you out of here myself madam if you don't leave at once!" the guard guy said angrily coming back out of the hill.

"I assure you, good sir, I am on my way. I just ask one small favor if you would... and I promise you will see me no more. Could you please tell me the date? My fiancé and I play this game and... well... it would take ages to explain."

"July 19th 1864. Now, are you going to leave on your own? Or am I going to have to carry you out?"

"Thank you sir... consider me a bother no more. I'll just leave you to your business," and Violet started walking away.

"Let that be the last I see of you!" the man hollered.

Once more he turned and disappeared back into the hill. Vanished, would be a better word for it.

Violet got about 20 feet away, felt her insides calm down, and with a last look at the hill, returned to Talon.

"Okay, Mr. history book... July 19th 1864... now start talking," Violet commanded with a small huff.

"Violet? Look around you... what do you see?"

"Dirt and rock, and too damn much of it."

"True but, what else?"

"I don't know," Violet said getting exasperated. "Rock... sand... some bushes and..."

"Those bushes, as you call them, are sagebrush. Old growth sages can get as tall as me. These troughs? They're planters. Look Violet... do you see how many of them, seem to grow in clusters?"

"Yeah... so?" Then Violet changed attitudes on a dime and stated "I get it! Sagebrush, old iron planters on rails... they covered the entrance!"

"Indeed. Anyone poking around out here would be none the wiser. Human nature is to walk the tracks to see where they will take you to... not take you past. Anyone out here that shouldn't be, well, they'd likely never even notice. Lucinda's little hidden entrance goes unnoticed, and that buys her time to get any trespassers off her property."

"Okay, ya gotta admit, that is slick."

Talon said cheerily "I doth agree."

"Two of these, closed together, hell you'd walk right by that thinking it no different than any other clump. This hill is tall so you can't see over it, and possibly figure out there's a tunnel right to the mansion... heh heh... or is it the bat cave?" Violet joked.

"Batman was a pussy. No bat caves in my mansion... sorry," Talon scorned as he hated anything 'Batman'.

Talon and Violet dug out the opening a little more. They got it cleared just enough for Talon to get in. He saw timbers, and something that really impressed him... cobblestones. This place at one time was a secret, but grand, entrance. It looked like a mining tunnel but something caught Talon's eye. He was standing upright and easily at that. He also noticed the timbers were not upright. There were stone walls on left and right, going up just above his knees. Then on top of that was the timbers but they were carefully mitered. He took a few pictures then got back out.

"Well... what did you see?" Violet asked highly curious.

"At first, I thought it was dug out by the miners. Then I realized, this wasn't dug out... it was created. They trenched to the mansion, then, timber framed over it, then covered it over. The beams still appear to be holding, but whatever was between them is long gone. Now that I know it's here, we'll come back to it. I'm going back to my truck and getting the drone. Nothing goes in there but that thing. I'll get some pictures and video, then we'll see what it'll take to rebuild it."

"Cool!" Violet teased. "The Lambo can be the bat mobile!"

Talon got her right back saying "Spiderman... Iron Man. On the ladies side there was Storm and Wonder Woman. All these truly cool superheroes... and you pick the pansy."

Violet giggled and said "Actually... Mister Incredible is my favorite."

Now Talon smiled, and played along.

In a slightly high pitched, and accented voice, he said "Edna... Mode..."

Violet laughed and finished with "... And guest."

Talon laughed too as he and Violet took the tractor back to the mansion.

Chapter 13

"Three Argentine Tangos... One Song"

Grant was stoked when he saw the remote footage from the drone. Talon told him what he found, but not how... well... not all of it anyway. Grant's mind however was ablaze with ideas.

"Talon, how about you let me handle this one hmm? Oh you are gonna so love what I've come up with, just from seeing this footage alone."

"No," Talon said flatly. "We do this together or not at all. However, as long as I'm left with a functional hidden entrance when it's all done... then you can do whatever you wish little brother. WE do this together, but I'll let you call the shots... deal?"

Grant smiled, shook Talon's hand and said "Deal."

Talon then thought of something.

"Ya know baby G, the whole point of having a secret entrance is... well, you know... that it's secret. We work on this with all the workers around and that whole idea is blown out the window."

Grant mused "So like, me and you... and that's it?"

"Doc and Violet too but, yeah, pretty much."

Grant thought a moment, then smiled big.

"I have been waiting for a project like this to try out some new toys, and talents, I've come across." Grant stared at his brother and said "Okay then, us 4 it is. However, I reserve the right to bring in any power tools I need."

"Little brother? I await your inspiration in completed form," Talon said kindly but, with true anticipation. "Just remember though, before we go destroying any possible evidence... we give Cody first crack at this place."

"I have no problem with that but, do you think it's safe enough?"

Talon said "I wasn't sure at first but, if it hasn't caved in in over a century, I doubt it will in the next few days."

Grant and Talon got back in the truck and traced the trail for the rail lines. Grant shifted his truck into 4WD when they hit the area Talon hadn't gotten to yet. Both men were stoked to actually find some tracks still in place on about 60% of the entire loop.

Talon arranged a meeting with the family of the train baron of the day. They were suspicious and immediately went to close ranks. Talon just laughed and said he did indeed have proof of some 'ancient philandering'. He also told them if he wanted to hurt them, he wouldn't be on the phone with them now. He basically explained he needed some tracks laid, and how he would see to it they'd get some good press out of it. As luck would have it, the family still owned a sizable cargo rail line. Talon also made them aware, if they thought this was some sort of trap... he knew a senator that could vouch for him. That call hung up. An hour later, it called back. Some assistant called to say Talon was invited... to the family estate... for lunch.

"She doesn't seem to be doing anything special. She actually appears to be helping restore some old wreck of a house," a nondescript man said on the phone from his even more nondescript car.

It was parked on the road that went passed the length of Talon's property, and another mile or two beyond.

"Yeah, I heard you the first hundred times. No sir, no one has seen me."

"See that it stays that way," the man's voice on the phone told him.

The man in the car shuffled some photo's of Violet on his passenger seat, and reported "She seems to have gotten close to some gray-haired guy. Local big shot who likes to keep himself under the radar."

"Keep an eye on her but, for now, track her movements and nothing more. I'll be coming out that way in 2 weeks or so. More than that you don't need to know. Keep me apprised of anything important, otherwise... don't call me again," and the call was over.

The evening sun watched as the nondescript car started up and took off down the road and headed out.

"Miss Adair? Would you do us the honor of gracing us with your presence?" Talon hollered from the living room to the right of the parlor.

Grant half smiled, and followed with "And you, Miss Abigail."

The two Grayson's were sitting at the bar on freshly refurbished, by the mansion's new owner, bar stools. The doctor and the ghost hunter were at a table. That same table was the first to be rebuilt and refinished. Talon did that one too. It was nearing dinnertime and Talon called a halt to the work early today, and sent everyone home to get an early start on their weekends.

"Ah buleev you requested tha lady of tha house?" Lucinda's voice teased playfully.

Grant crossed his arms over his chest and huffed jokingly.

"Hmmf... stood up... and by a ghost no less!"

"Now how could I let such a fine gentleman be by himself?" Abigail cooed as she dragged her fingertips across Grant's chest as she walked past.

Talon raised a questioning eyebrow to Violet. No words from either of them. She took a quick look around, and nodded the 'all clear'. Now Talon laid out his surprise.

"Lucinda, my dear, I have yet another surprise for you," Talon stated with pride and confidence. "Several of them come to think of it."

Grant went over and flipped the switch on the wall... and the grand living room was awash in light. He had made wrought iron sconces for the walls and set them up everywhere around the room.

"I'm working on chandelier-sized ones, but they won't be ready for another week or two," Grant said proudly.

"Miss Lucinda, ain't this grand! Candles that light themselves!" Abigail stated with pleasant wonder.

"Why chyld, it is grand indeed," Lucinda said in the same tone as Abigail.

Talon headed across the floor. Cody smiled mischievously, and tossed Talon his phone as he passed. Talon had rigged a temporary setup so he could show off for Lucinda. Doc tossed him his phone because Cody liked classical music and Talon didn't. As such, only Doc's phone had that type of music on it. Talon plugged a wire into the earpiece, and showed it to Lucinda.

"Tell me madam, do you recognize this machine?" Talon asked with a boyish grin.

"Is that tha way of tha times now? Tell me, do y'all have such amazing mahsheens?" Lucinda asked not imagining one 'machine', no less everyone having one.

Grant flashed his, so did Violet, and Talon pointed to his hip.

"Why ah doo dehclare!"

Talon declared "You saw motion pictures the other night Abigail. These devices not only play moving pictures but, they can be an entire orchestra."

"Oh Mister Grayson, (giggle), I think you'd need a little more room than that small box to fit an entire band in there," Abigail said in a tone like she knew she was being teased.

Talon was dead-pan and said "I didn't say band... I said orchestra," and he pushed play.

Talon had rigged a small amplifier. He was showing off the new speakers he ordered buried in the ceiling... and the twin 12-inch sub-woofers at either end of the same. Two ghostly images were absolutely stunned and looked around for a 'band' they couldn't see. The living room, for the first time since the mansion was boarded up, had music ringing throughout the grand room. Talon chose Fur Elis.

He winked at Violet, then told the ghost ladies "I considered a little Hendrix but, heh heh, I was out voted."

Lucinda was positively beaming, and sweetly took Abigail into her arms. They waltzed around the room. They disappeared, then reappeared, then disappeared again... all around the room. Talon turned it down then off, then tossed the phone back to Cody.

"Pretty amazing huh?" Talon asked kindly.

"Ah swear, Mista G, y'all nevuh cease to amaze me," Lucinda told them all with true honesty and praise. "Ah could ownlee have dreemd of such gloriously played music in my day."

"Yeah well, in your day, labor was cheap. Even then, a mansion of this size must have taken a considerable amount of money just to maintain it."

"You'd be correct sir," Lucinda stated shifting back into business mode.

"And in today's money, it would cost a fortune I don't have. To help pay for this place, I intend to rent it out for parties, weddings, and formal affairs. Only half of this floor can be saved. Grant and I will re-lay the floor around the edges, leaving a big hole in the center. That I intend to have tiled by some very nice craftsmen I just happen to know. That will be a beautiful showpiece... and double as a dance floor."

Lucinda was truly amazed and said "Ah find it maw than pleas'in how evree day my home comes back to its formah glawree."

"I believe you meant to say 'my house'," Talon politely but firmly reminded.

Lucinda curtsied slightly to him and said "Indeed sir but... tah bee fair... it was mine first," with a sneaky smile. "I will say this much... it will bee nice ta heeyuh tha sounds of joy an celebration once again..." and she stared at Talon as she faded out and finished with "... in 'this' fine home."

Talon tipped an imaginary hat to her and bowed slightly to the fading apparition.

"It was nice to see you again, Abigail," Grant said as he got up to leave.

Abigail however was already gone.

"Oh well," Grant said.

He turned around to see her blocking his path... and holding a baby.

"Have no fear Mister Grayson sir... you'll see me again... and sooner than you imagined."

Grant spooked just a bit but only from her surprising him. Once again however, only he saw her. He just shook his head and walked out with all the others.

Talon was home alone. He was there alone long before Lucinda, and long before Violet. Now, for the first time since he built it, he was lonely in his own house. He stared at the mural, but got nothing for his efforts. Violet had been around only a couple of weeks. Talon however felt now, the same way Grant explained it to Violet... like she'd been around forever. When his wife died, he didn't feel lonely in his own home because she never lived there. Now, without Violet around, Talon found himself without a clue what to do.

He fed himself but, it was on leftovers from Violet's cooking. He figured he had to occupy his time somehow, so he dove in earnestly to the papers he had, but mostly, Uncle Lucian's book. He started to read it when his phone rang. He went for it all excited thinking it would be Violet. He was acting like he did once or twice, in high school. His mood changed in a heartbeat when he saw what number was ringing. It was on one of his private business lines that Violet didn't know or have. It was also one of the encrypted ones.

"This is Talon," he said in a rather business-like tone.

"Good evening Mr. Grayson, this is Mr. Smith."

"Mister Smith, I hope you are well?" Talon said playing along.

"Very thank you. I wanted you to know your secretary called us with a job you wanted doing."

"Indeed. Tell me, Mr. Smith, are you from the legal division... or the investigatory department?"

"Oh, the latter for sure."

Talon was a bit concerned and asked "Not like your department to call me directly. Trouble?"

"Sadly... a lot of it.," Mr. Smith confirmed. "I wanted you to know personally... my team and I are doing this one for free. We see this as not only good business, but the right thing to do."

"You have my utmost attention," Talon said, now heavily concerned.

"I want you to know you are safe. The reason for my contacting you like this is because once we started digging, even those in my employ were sickened by what we found. I have sent a courier to your home. Not your office in Idaho mind you but... the home you're sitting in this very moment. He has strict instructions to give this information to you and you alone. When you see its contents, you'll know why I did this."

"Mr. Smith, you and your department served me well in the past. You also gained my trust. If you feel this course of action necessary, then I'll abide by your decision."

"Thank you sir. Two last things. First, 'she' is being watched by a hired local. Second, should you run across what's in the parcel I'm sending you... know that I and my team will be happy to assist with, or facilitate, any necessary 'removal services' you may require. Anywhere, anytime."

Talon was nearly nervous and asked "Is it really as bad as that?"

Mr. Smith told him calmly "Let's just say... 'she' is not... but she was very wise to run."

Then the voice on the phone asked an odd question.

"You have siblings, don't you sir?"

"Your point?" Talon said nearly threateningly.

"I do as well. I have no doubt you care for yours as much as I care for mine. When you read what I've sent, you'll know why I asked... and why there is no charge for this job. Know this however, if you don't end this on your own... I can't guarantee you that we won't. Keep 'her' safe, and have a pleasant rest of your evening," and Mr. Smith hung up without waiting for a reply.

Talon knew who that was. To shield Grant all that he could back then, Grant was told only part of the truth. Talon did indeed hire outside lawyers. They weren't from Kansas though... they were from New York. They also, for the right clients of course, employed a security team on occasion. That team was actually out of New Jersey. Ex Army Rangers and Navy Seals that formed a private security firm. For people like Talon though, they did investigations as well. Those 'private investigations' however, were part military exercise, and part mission impossible. Still, for the fee they charged, they more than delivered on the results. When Talon got the results on the corrupt sheriff, he asked how they could get such information. He was politely told he shouldn't ask, so... he never did. Now Talon was concerned. If these guys found something that bothered them that badly, he knew he was somehow in some seriously deep shit.

"Well senator... ha ha ha... looks like that best seller I told you about just got an interesting new chapter added to it," Talon joked to no one but the open air of his office.

Talon went back to Lucian's book. Poured into it was more like it. Talon discovered the first half was a well laid out, and meticulous, note book of everything he found out. The second half was more like a diary. He never did solve it. He thought he was onto some things. He also thought he had some solid leads, not to mention suspects. Talon could read the frustration in his words as they either became dead ends, or red herrings. Talon was about 10 pages from the end, and realized Lucian wrote no more. His last entry he read aloud to no one, but he somehow felt it the right thing to do all the same.

"November 1st, 1885. It has been 20 years to the day that my failure began. I have no desire to set upon any man my convictions of guilt, lest it be true. Sadly, on this somber and slightly macabre anniversary, I am no closer to solving this mystery. As it was in my youth, I still carry the fire in my soul to see justice done. Sadly, I feel I will meet my maker before I see that day come to pass. I, Lucian Garrison, wish with all my heart to see my desire come true... and not my prediction.

I have been both praised and ridiculed by my peers for my tenacity in this matter. This has consumed me like nothing else in my life. Now, in my waning years, I have accepted my defeat. This will be my last entry. If I write more, it will only be to tell of my victory in seeing justice done. If not, then I leave it to those who may follow in my footsteps. May God see fit to grace you, whoever you may be, with more luck than He apportioned me."

Talon was choked with pride, and sadness, for an uncle he never knew till now. There was one last line on the page. It was only a partial one. It said "And the rock cried out..." and nothing more. Talon decided he'd sort that out another day. With reverence, he closed the book, and laid it on his desk. He then got up, turned off the light, and spoke to the mural.

"You were a good man, Uncle Lucian... and I'm glad I got to meet you."

Talon turned and headed off to bed.

The winds were up today. A storm front was blowing in from California. As per usual, Talon's side of the Sierras only got the wind out of the deal. That was a problem as he had to leave in an hour to pick up Eileen from the airport in Reno. The problem Talon had was he had to go up an old road that he and Grant refer to as the Washoe Wind Tunnel. The only road north or south was already closed to 'high profile' vehicles. He texted Eileen to let her know when she got to her layover in Denver.

"Fucking figures," she said when she called to check in. "Tell the Storm King I said if I toss my cookies on approach, I'm going up there to kick his ass!"

"Heh heh... I'll be sure to text him as soon as I get off the phone with you," Talon joked.

"Ha ha ha... see that you do. Gotta go. Love ya bro, see ya in a couple of hours."

"Love ya too. Stay safe and I'll see ya then," and Talon hung up.

The 'Storm King' Eileen referred to was a mythical character that resided in the mountains. He was said to cause all the storms up there. All 3 Grayson's blamed any foul weather on him. Right now, Talon was worried he may not be able to take the Lambo. The highway was put in, and finished only a year ago. That was literally cut into the side of the mountains. Beautiful ride on a good day... deadly when it wasn't. So he was stuck with the old road that paralleled it. That was not much better.

He checked in with Grant and updated him. Grant thanked him and teased him telling him what a wonderful breakfast he missed. Grant told him he'd have Violet at Sterling's on time, and that he was stopping by Cody's place along the way. Talon hung up with him and his phone rang again. Talon smiled and answered it.

"Liv'in large Al... liv'in large!"

"Ha HAAAAAAA. How is Eileen, Mista G?"

"So far so good, Al. She just called to say she's boarding at Denver and will be here shortly. I was just about to head out when you called."

"Well I hope she stays safe. I only called ta let ya know I'm heading out mahself, and me an tha grandbaby will see ya tonight."

"Watch it over the pass, Al. Winds are horrid up there. See ya tonight," Talon said kindly as he hung up the call.

He went into the office and opened the safe. The keys to the Cuda, and the Italian hot rod, were kept in there. He was about to grab the Cuda keys.

"Oh screw it," he said as he looked out the window one last time.

He closed up the safe, set the alarm, and headed out to the garage. When he did, the safe still had the keys to the Mopar muscle in it.

He was cruising north, and once or twice, almost turned around. He had some happy and upbeat tunes on the stereo as he did. The stares, honks, and waves he got as he passed traffic, finally let him relax and just enjoy the ride. He slowed down and paced one SUV along the way. The looks from the teenage girls in the back made him chuckle and he decided to let them stare and enjoy. The look on the lady driving them however, made him laugh hard. He put down the passenger window, tipped his hat to the lady driver with the sexy smile... put the window back up... and blasted out of sight.

"The Storm King sends his regards," Talon laughed seeing Eileen appear around the corner.

A huge hug and "I'll bet he does," was Eileen's reply as she chuckled heartily.

Talon was waiting for her in the baggage claim. Her bags came off the plane shortly thereafter. Talon grabbed them from the carousel, and the two of them headed to the parking garage.

"Well... hello gorgeous," Eileen said seeing Talon brought her requested mode of transportation. "So, I'm driving right?" Eileen taunted standing by the driver's door, and holding her hand out.

Talon lifted the hood, put her bags in and closed it as he chirped the alarm and opened the doors. Next, he walked right past her.

"Your chair, m'lady... is on that side," Talon smirked pointing to the passenger seat.

"Hmmf. As the oldest... I could order you, ya know."

Talon laughed saying "As the owner... I could tell you to go to hell."

Eileen walked around, got in, and closed the door.

"Well, if I don't get to drive, there had better be some CCR and a bit of 'In n Out' in it for me at least."

"That..." Talon said kindly, "... I can do."

The sign on the store clock said 1:30pm when he hit the southbound ramp.

"Doot doot doooooo look'in OUT MY back doooorrrr," the siblings sang on the way to the requested burger shop.

Song over, and another memory secured, Eileen laced into Talon with questions she'd been waiting to ask.

"So... new girl... tell me about her."

"Not much to tell really," Talon said calmly. "Convicted ax murderess with a narcissistic streak. Daughter of a mob boss... nothing special."

"You're as bad as Grant," Eileen chastised.

"No... heh heh... I'm worse."

Talon didn't like the crowded parking lot as he pulled in, so he went to the drive-thru instead. There was a small line so he got stopped by the large side windows. Typical for him when he drove the car, faces got pressed against the glass. Two of those faces were some fine looking ladies about 21 years old each. Talon put down the window, smiled, and nodded to them. They actually flirted with him.

"Oh puleez," said Eileen.

The girls in the window waved coyly to the sexy driver. Eileen decided to have a little fun. From their point of view, the girls couldn't see her. Before Talon could respond, she smiled big... leaned across Talon's chest... and waved back for him. She laughed as she sat back in her chair, and two girls at a window made themselves scarce. Talon laughed as well, kept the window down, and pulled up to the window to get his food.

"Spill any of that... and I'm sending you the cleaning bill," Talon said to Eileen meaning every word.

Back on the highway again, and there was nothing but CCR, and good times, all the way to his garage.

Eileen was happily munching at the kitchen table along with her brother.

"Ya know, brother... she doesn't exist. Did you know that?"

Talon smirked and just shook his head.

"Eileen look, why are you asking me questions you obviously already know the answers to?"

"Bro, this girl shows up out of nowhere. Now, you give her a room here...HERE! Of all places! Don't think for a second I don't know what 'that', and this place, means to you." Eileen let go of some frustrations and said "After 16 or so, she disappeared. Look Tal, you know I love you. I was the one who pulled you out of your funk when Sarah died. She was a special lady, and I envied the couple you two made. Now you're single again, but my brother forgets women even exist. Suddenly, a girl whose last known address was an insane asylum, wins my brother's cold heart... and 'wows' BOTH of my brothers! Oh excuuuuse me for being a tad protective."

Talon got up to throw his food away. He smiled and gave Eileen a sweet kiss on the cheek as he did.

"Thanks for caring, sis."

Before Eileen could bark some more, the door bell rang. Talon brought up the camera to the gate and asked "May I help you?"

"I have a special, and personal, delivery for Talon Grayson."

"From?"

"Mister Smith."

The man heard a buzz... just before the gates opened. He walked up to the front door and was greeted by a gray haired man.

"I was given specific instructions I was to ask for identification," the courier told him.

Without a fuss, Talon pulled out and showed him his license. The man looked it over, unlocked the handcuffs on his wrist, and handed Talon a small briefcase.

"Tell Mister Smith his services are greatly appreciated. Also tell him... if need be... I'll be in touch," Talon said flatly.

"I will. Have a nice day sir," the courier said as he left.

A few moments later, the gates were closed, and it was just Talon and Eileen once more.

"Why don't you go relax, and take a shower if you wish. I have to look this over," Talon told Eileen.

Without another word, Talon walked into his office, and locked the door.

Softly, and warningly, Eileen told the closed door "Mr. Smith eh? Watch your ass, little brother. Just remember, I was there. I know who... and what... he is," and Eileen headed to her room to unpack.

Talon opened the case. The files inside it did two things. They impressed him, and disgusted him, at the same time. He was impressed by their level of detail. This wasn't the public stuff that Eileen would be able to find. Talon thought to himself that even the CIA couldn't have gotten better intel. What those files told him though, and the history they revealed... that is what disgusted him. He went to put them away having seen enough. There was only one mystery in the whole case. It was a thumb drive with a note attached.

It read [These are copies of originals. Heavily encrypted and we were unable to break it in the time we had. Good luck but you'll need a serious hacker for this one. 'Mr. Smith']

Talon scrunched his face, then put the contents in his safe as he made a call.

"Yo Grant... anything to report?" Talon said slightly coldly.

"Checking up on your purple haze eh?" Grant teased.

"No jokes this time, brother. Listen to me very carefully. Is she okay?"

Grant changed tones and stated "She's in my guest room doing her hair. You okay, Tal? Given your tone of voice, is she? Hell... am I!?"

"The Kansas team reported in."

"Uh oh."

"Indeed. You're safe but... you likely got a local PI spying on you. More like on Violet." Talon got ice cold and told Grant "I would greatly appreciate it if you would see to it that when you leave for dinner... you two do so alone."

"Ha ha... you remember Tommy in high school?"

Talon had a devilish smile at the memory and said "That will do nicely."

"Okay bud, I'm on it... see ya later," and Grant hung up.

Talon went to shower, while his brother went to work.

"Hey Violet?" Grant called out as he rifled through a small toolbox.

"You call me!?" Grant heard from behind a closed door as a hairdryer shut off.

"Yeah. I'm going outside to secure the garbage cans. I don't want the critters getting into them after we leave. I just wanted to let you know. I'll be back in a few minutes."

"Okay thanks!" and the hairdryer went on again.

Grant smirked, grabbed a pair of pliers, and headed outside.

Grant's place was 3 acres of heavily wooded bliss. His home was more of a mountain retreat, whereas Talon's was more in the 60's modernistic style. It was a condemned house due to a forest fire some 15 years earlier. Grant jumped at it when he found it. Talon sent him a crew for a week and they dismantled all they could. Every brick, and every piece of lumber that could be saved... was. Grant demolished the rest and built a home from scratch that blended into its surroundings, rather than contrasted it. Everything he saved however found its way into the new house. When it was done, it not only made the cover of the local magazine... it was his showcase to show clients who wanted work done.

A small and private road went along the property, and that of his neighbors. Just big enough for two cars to pass and that was it. Grant snuck through his property, then his neighbors, and came out behind a parked car that shouldn't have been there. Slowly, he crept up on it from behind. Once certain that he wasn't spotted by the guy in the driver's seat... he slid on his back and underneath by the bumper. A minute or two later, he did the whole sneaking around thing... in reverse.

"Grant... that you!?"

"Yeah, all good to go," he hollered back with the most devilish of grins.

Grant was dressed and waiting on Violet. When she emerged, Grant was floored.

"Well... how do I look?" Violet asked nervously.

With frustration in his voice, Grant said "Ya know... it's moments like this that I really hate my brother sometimes."

Violet was elated.

"Why 'ginger chyld'... I'll take that as a compliment," she said sweetly.

Grant grinned saying "Wouldn't mean it any other way. Well then, shall we be off?"

Violet nicely grabbed his arm, and told him "Lead the way."

Grant locked up his house, and minutes later, a Dodge ground-pounder was heading off to an evening that would be talked about looong into the future. Grant saw headlights come on as soon as he turned left out of his driveway. They followed him only for a short bit... before coming to a complete and utter stop. Grant went a little farther and the lights in his rear-view mirror were seen no more.

"Heh heh... yep... that trick still works," he said snidely.

"What? You say something?" Violet asked.

"Not a thing, my dear," and Grant headed for Cody's house.

Talon finished getting dressed. Eileen came out looking as lovely, as Talon did dashing. Black dress with an angled bottom hem and slight silver trims. Her long flowing amber hair had tons of waves in it. She had heels on that basically went up to her shoulder blades. Eileen didn't wear heels like those very often but when she did, she 'owned it', and walked with all the grace and poise of an extremely confident woman.

Talon had 3 'looks'. Work, business casual... and downright hot. Right now he had the latter going on for sure. Black slacks with spit shine dress boots. Those actually had spurs on them. Smaller dress style ones but, spurs none the less. Black suspenders went over a satin silver shirt, sporting real silver cuff links. Jet black satin narrow tie held in place with a silver tie clip, and a black suit jacket with dark gray piping finished out the look. Eileen straightened out his handkerchief, and Talon put a rose from his garden in Eileen's hair.

"Shall we, my dear?" Talon asked joyously as he hooked his arm in hers.

"Why, my dear Mr. Grayson... I believe we shall," Eileen chuckled.

Shortly thereafter, his gates closed, and the Cuda was winding its way through the back streets and heading for the northbound lanes.

Sterling's Steakhouse was an elegant place. By no means the only steakhouse in town but, to the Grayson's... it might as well be. Lots of dark oak and walnut paneling and trims everywhere. Upon walking in, the diner was greeted by a wine rack that covered the wall all the way to the ceiling. Tables in the center, and booths along the edges. The latter also had curtains that could be drawn to give the diners an extra bit of privacy. It was on a side hall just down from the lobby of the Silver Legacy hotel and casino. That lobby alone was almost the size of Talon's house.

The Grayson's had been coming here since they were kids. It was a special treat from mom and dad usually. Big events like high school graduations and such were celebrated here. Those were special times in all 3 of the Grayson's minds, as it was the only time mom and dad left the ranch. Phil was the manager, and occasional host...and a school friend of dad's. As the children got older though, they thought coming here was such good times when they were younger, they merely kept the tradition going. Eileen and Talon were now waiting outside for everyone to arrive.

"Lose a few people?" Eileen joked seeing Grant walk up alone.

"Nah... they're bringing up the rear. Looking stunning as ever there, sis," Grant said kindly.

"Thank you. Look at you!" Eileen winked at him and said "Not looking too shabby there yourself, baby G."

He hugged Eileen heartily, and she did the same in return.

"Give us a second will ya?" Grant asked as he pulled Talon off to the side.

He took Talon to a garbage can nearby, pulled out a set of pliers, and tossed them in.

"Mission accomplished," Grant said with a grin of pure delight as he tossed the pliers away.

"Thank youuuuu," Talon jested as he and Grant returned to their sister.

"Ha HAAAAAAAA! Lady G how you be liv'in!?" came a new booming voice from behind.

"Ha ha ha ha... liv'in large and walk'in tall Al!" Eileen said as she hugged the finely-dressed Althea. Eileen looked down and said "And this lovely young lady must be Lashonda?"

"I am. Nice to meet you, Miss Grayson."

Eileen smirked saying "Oh pfff... call me Eileen. I can't wait to hear all about you and... um..." and she gave Althea a sly grin and finished with "... tell you stories I'm sure grandma doesn't want you to hear ha ha ha."

Lashonda was dressed nicely, but also age appropriate as well. She barked a bit at some of grandma's choices. Al barked at some of hers. In the end though, they found a nice dress and some shoes to match that both could agree on. Her long satin black hair was pulled back, and Talon thought with a few more years on her, she would make a very beautiful woman one day.

"So, all we need now is Cody and Violet," Talon remarked.

Grant chuckled saying "Doc is with her. She went to the bathroom first."

Eileen sneered mischievously and asked "Last chance to puke from the nerves?"

Grant was still chuckling and said "Likely."

Almost on cue, Mr Holliday arrived. At his side was a stunning woman that made a chill run down Talon's spine.

"Okay... now THAT guy is hot!" Eileen said low and in Talon's ear.

Talon just beamed at his sister's discomfort as he said "Doc Holliday! Nice of you to join us! May I present my sister Eileen?"

Eileen had no clue who he was, and gave Grant a rather nasty look.

"NOT funny, baby G."

Grant was beaming and said "Actually?.... It was hilarious! The look on your face... ha ha ha... oh man, too funny."

Eileen shot a sharp look to Talon.

He was laughing slightly too and said "Sorry, sis... I'm with him."

Cody walked up with a slight smile, and took Eileen's hand, and kissed the back of it.

"Doctor Cody Holliday at your service, Eileen. A pleasure to meet you finally. I've heard so much about you. I must say however, even the kind descriptions your brothers gave, do not do the live version justice."

Cody knew the joke played on Eileen. He decided to play along for a bit, and it's why he put such a flourish on his intro.

Eileen was caught off guard for a moment. True to herself, it was only a moment.

"A pleasure to meet you as well. Sibling pranks aside, I look forward to meeting the real you."

Cody smiled and told her "As do I."

Talon was staring the whole time at Violet. He was also thankful he chose the looser fitting pants right about now, and not the tighter slacks that was his first choice. She was amazing looking. Long flowing hair, that was perfectly wavy, framed her face. Strapless dress that had a corset style top, and a more flowing dress like bottom. Dark dusty red on top, dull black satin below. Talon thought, if Lucinda was brought into the modern age, this would be a dress she'd wear. Violet had a clutch bag that matched the dress, the heels, and those eyes.... damn... those eyes were just sparkling right now.

With extreme pride, Talon walked over to her, gave her a slight bow, and held out his arm. With a smile, she took it, and Talon walked with all the poise in the world... right over to his sister.

"Eileen? I'd like to introduce you to Miss Violet Hayes. One of the latest employees of Grayson Industries... and my date for this evening."

Violet was nervous as hell but, managed to hold it together. From the squeezing on his arm, Talon knew how nervous she was too.

"A pleasure to meet the sister I've heard so much about," Violet said holding out her hand.

Eileen smiled back, shook Violet's extended hand, and said "A pleasure to meet you as well. I look forward to hearing about the woman that 'I' have heard so little about."

"I'd be happy to tell you anything you'd like to know."

With polite sisterly menace, Eileen said "And I'd be happy to hear it."

"And you must be the great Althea I was told of?" Violet said desperate for an escape.

"Lawd chyld look at you," Al said all impressed at the sight before her. Althea leaned into Lashonda and teased "Baby girl, did I not tell ya Mista G got some good taste or what?"

Violet smiled, and stated "From what I see before me, I would have to agree with that statement."

Al beamed and let loose her trademark cackle.

"Ha HAAAAAAAA! Mista G? Y'all have ma full puhmission ta keep this one!" She leaned into Violet and said "Just you remember, don't you buhleev everything this crazy ass white boy toeld you 'bout me." She winked at Talon and told Violet "Well... maybe one aw two things."

Violet giggled and Al introduced Lashonda. The latter was almost in awe of the beautiful woman in front of her. Even said as much.

"Thank you my dear," Violet said kindly. "From what I can see, grandma is going to need a small platoon for you... and in the very near future."

Violet thought the whole night could go to shit but, if Talon was pleased, then she was happy. Seeing his reaction to her, gave her self esteem a serious boost. That's when she decided to pull a bold move. Part to get rid of those doubtful demons, and part because she liked how having confidence felt.

"Well Talon, it seems I have Al's approval," she told him gazing into his eyes. Without missing a beat she turned to Eileen and said "Perhaps by the end of the night... I'll have yours as well."

"Time will tell," Eileen said with a polite nod.

Talon was impressed Violet pulled such a move, and Eileen was cautiously optimistic. She was expecting far worse. Hell, from the little info she got from her brothers, she actually didn't know what to expect.

"Aah the Grayson children. Lovely to see you all, as always. Also, as always, I see you have lovely guests with you this evening," Phil came out saying in a very friendly manner.

Sterling's had a lovely woman hostess named Christina that would seat you at your table. Talon always found her gracious and charming, and one of those types of women that never seemed to age. For the Grayson's however... Phil saw to them personally.

"Thank you Phil. Good to see you as well. You know my brother and sister... this here is Doctor Cody Holliday. Beside him, Althea James and her granddaughter, Lashonda."

Phil shook their hands and made nice with a huge smile all around.

"And this ravishing beauty on my arm is Miss Violet Hayes," Talon said with a touch of pride.

Phil looked at Talon and said "Sarah was a wonderful woman. The kind a man finds once in a lifetime. You're a lucky man to have done it twice," he said finishing with a polite grin to Violet.

Violet wasn't used to this... AT all. The attention, the dressing up... all the manners... none of it. She felt oddly comfortable, and heinously out of place, and both at the same time.

"Thank you, Phil. I'll do all I can to live up to your kind observation," Violet told him.

She felt like she was in a movie. They hadn't even gone in yet and already this night was way beyond what she expected... and hoped for.

"I have no doubt of that. WELL... if you'd all like to follow me? I have your table all ready for you," and Phil led them all inside.

He sat them all in a large corner booth. It was also in a closed off section so Talon's party would have a bit more privacy.

"A Reisling to start perhaps, Mr Grayson?" Phil asked.

"Wise choice, yes, thank you, Phil."

Then he asked Al "Mr. Grayson told me you're from New Orleans, am I right?"

"Originally," Al answered.

"Well, the tablet here has our wine list and our menu on it. For you however... if you choose... I have our fine chef ready to cook Cajun style blackened catfish."

Al was impressed and said "Thank you, sir. Ya know... I just may have to try out the talents of that chef of yours."

He nodded and headed off saying "I hand picked your waiter myself. He'll be around to take your orders momentarily. Enjoy your evening," and Phil was gone.

"Gary! Pleasure to see you again," Talon said as he stood up and gave Phil's right hand man a hearty handshake. "Phil overworking you I hope?" Talon joked.

"Always!" Gary joked back. "Actually Mr. Grayson, I came to tell you, as I thought you would want to know... Phil is retiring this year," Gary told him in a hushed tone.

Talon was happy for Phil, but not happy at the loss of some dear memories, and said "Thanks for the heads up. When is his last day?"

"December 31st."

"Ladies and gentlemen? I'll be back in a moment," and Talon went out to the front desk.

"Hi Mister Grayson how can I help you?" Christina asked sweetly.

"I need reservations for 15. You might say, I just discovered what I'll be doing for New Years Eve."

With an understanding smile, Christina just said "You're all set."

Talon tipped his hat and rejoined his guests.

"Problem?" Grant queried.

"Just making some New Years Eve reservations."

"Dude, it's not even July yet," Grant laughed.

"Phil is retiring."

Grant said seriously "Bro? If there isn't a seat for me... I will hurt you."

Talon just chuckled at his brother, and dove back into his evening.

Talon's party was all set now. With orders taken, Talon dove into business.

"So Eileen, we're here because you're here. You're here because you have something to tell me. Ladies first, ya know."

"Alright then. Nothing present company can't hear as well. I wanted to let you know I've decided to take you up on yours and Grant's offer."

"Which one? The one about the house?"

Eileen smiled and said "Mm hmm. You know my assistants... Tom and

Christen?"

"I do... what about them?"

"They got married 3 weeks ago. I got a year and a half left on my lease. Quite frankly, I'm losing interest in my own business. They're looking to secure their future. I've decided to sell it to them. Winters back east are getting worse and worse. Two weeks ago I was stuck in my apartment for two days because of the snow for Christ's sake. With dad gone... and now mom... well, living out here again is looking far more appealing than it did 10 years ago when I left."

Talon was thrilled, but cautious.

"Not that I'm against this but, what will you do for money?"

Eileen told the table "I'll make profit enough from the sale. I wanted to take some time off then, perhaps start my own business out here. Small scale mind you, and only taking occasional clients. I also plan to invest some of that profit and do for me, what I did for you and Grant."

Talon smiled and raised his glass.

"However early it may be... welcome home, sis."

Grant was next to Eileen.

He hugged her sweetly and said "Whenever you're ready... Tal and I will make sure your house is finer than fine."

With sisterly love, she hugged him back saying "Thanks, baby brother."

Eileen turned to Lashonda and asked "So, you ready for a working vacation back east?"

"Yes ma'am," was the smiling response.

"Trust me when I tell you, I'll be putting you to work. I expect you to learn, but I won't make you a pack mule either."

"I won't let you down, Eileen. Thanks for giving me a chance. Mom and dad trust granmomma... and she trusts you. If it's good enough for them, it's good enough for me."

Violet wasn't the only one feeling out of place... and minding her manners because of it.

Eileen smiled and said "Well then, I look forward to it."

The only female Grayson left, was having a hard time not staring at the handsome doctor. She was truly pleased the same was true in reverse. Doc went for the dark look. All black from shoes to tie. Only his jacket was gray pinstripe. That look suited Eileen juuuuust fine.

"So... 'Doc Holliday'... I'll bet that gets a chuckle or two," Eileen jested.

More like flirted.

"It makes for a fun day at the office," Cody replied. "The sad thing is, the older patients get it. The younger one's are like 'who'?"

"Don't even get me started on the education system in this country,"

Grant extolled with huge aggravation.

"Nor me," Eileen stated in agreement.

She was actually a little annoyed at Grant for interrupting her beautiful daydream.

"Well then, Doc... seeing as how you're neither bald nor fat... is there any other lies my brothers may have told me that you'd like to dispel?"

Cody grinned and answered "Not much to tell really. Half-crazed World War One vet who just happens to be an opium addict. On weekends I help out at the local chapter of the Aryan Nation Brotherhood. Not too fond of green veggies either. Pretty dull actually."

Eileen gave a scornful look to Talon and snidely admonished "Is this some sort of guy thing I'm not aware of?"

Talon laughed knowing she was referring to his earlier description of Violet, and mocked "Why, my dear sister... whatever do you mean?"

"Yeah yeah," she growled at Talon. She turned and stared at Cody and asked "Answer me this Doc... are you a fan of strong women?"

"Truth?"

"It would be preferred," Eileen answered sharply.

"I don't know... I've never had one before," Cody answered truthfully and, just a touch sadly.

"Well then...how about a date? One with, shall we say, a little less company? There's a place by Grant I like to go to when I'm in town. My treat... wadda ya say?"

Talon chuckled saying "Careful there Doc, or you might find yourself in..."

"I accept!" Cody interrupted.

Grant just shook his head and chuckled. So did Talon. Violet was back to being nervous again. Seems Talon was right, Eileen truly was a force to be reckoned with.

Eileen grinned at Lashonda's open-mouthed stare of disbelief and told her "Welcome aboard, kid. Let that be your first lesson in how I get things done."

"Y...y... yes ma'am!" Lashonda said all smiles at seeing true girl power in action.

Althea joked "Oh Lawd what have I got ma baby into!?"

The whole table laughed including Eileen.

Now Eileen turned her attention elsewhere. When she wasn't staring at Cody, she was keeping an eye on the new girl... AND her brother. Recon would be a more accurate term.

"How about you Violet?"

"Uh... how about me what?"

"A date. We can go do some shopping, and get to know each other. Girlie stuff... just you and me... wadda ya say?"

"I... I'd like that," Violet stammered nervously. "If you'll excuse me though... I, uh... I'd like to freshen up."

Talon stood and let her out. Eileen however grabbed her purse and bolted out as well.

"Sounds like a good idea... I'll join you!"

Violet smiled, but was nervous as hell. Both women left and Talon sat back down.

Grant smirked and teased "Oh.............. to be a fly on the wall right about now. Ha ha... think she'll survive?"

Talon was looking at the ladies departing and warned in a low voice "She had better."

"Ha ha ha... which one?" Grant jested.

"How about either," was the low toned warning.

That warning however... was from Cody. Grant just laughed and dove back into his dinner.

Eileen followed Violet in, and wasted no time.

"Okay new girl, what's your game plan?" Eileen asked sharply.

Violet was caught off guard a bit and asked "Excuse me?"

"Play coy with my brother all you want, but don't even think of messing with me. You're hiding something. Whatever it is, you got my brother doing it too. You're 21 years old, soon to be 22. After 16... and a stint in the loony bin... you've been off the grid till recently. Tell me 'Violet'... if that's even your real name... what do you think of the protective sister now? You know, the one I'm sure you've been warned about."

This... is exactly what Violet was afraid of. Still, she played nice for now.

"I find her exactly as described."

"Fair warning, Violet," Eileen said nastily, "If you have eyes on my brother for ANY thing other than him... I will put you back in that asylum and bury you so fucking deep no one will ever find you again."

Now, the 'old' Violet was back... and she was pissed.

"You... you clueless carrot head... don't EVER threaten me like that again. Trust me when I tell you, if you even TRY and make good on a threat like that... it won't be you burying me in an asylum... it'll be me burying YOU!... Period."

Eileen smirked and told her "Wellll... ghost girl has a backbone after all. Let me tell YOU something. Until either I, or my brothers, have a daughter... I

Page 203

am the last of a long line of Grayson women. We have been strong, kick ass women in our own right, for over 7 generations. IF! And that's a big 'if'... if you become one someday, it'll be nice to know my brother didn't choose some slacker."

Violet did a hard 180.

"Wait... you were testing me?"

"If you were me, wouldn't you?" Eileen backed off, but asked seriously, "Now, 'Violet Hayes'... tell me in your own words... who the hell are you?"

Violet now decided, if Eileen was gonna play the part of the tough bitch, so would she. Violet was, for the first time since arriving, thinking long term. The Grayson women were tough ladies? Well then, Violet decided then and there that she was going to announce her application for membership.

"Interesting you call me ghost lady. Can I assume it's because of my seemingly non-existent past?"

"Ooh... smart too," Eileen taunted.

"Listen, Eileen, you have noooo clue. Tell me, who did you know named Thomas?"

Eileen had a 'huh?' look on her face suddenly and said "I don't know anyone by that name."

Violet got bold and said "I didn't say 'know', I said 'knew'... past tense." Then Violet got even bolder and said "Never mind, I'll tell you. He was a college boy you became close to... very close. He also died in a car crash of an overdose. Or... so everyone thought. He was a football player. Quarterback by the looks of it. He wants you to know something. He didn't OD. He blew out his knee but never told anyone. He had half a season to go to make pro he says."

Violet nearly got in Eileen's face, and kept going.

"He was taking steroids. Injections. That's what the puncture marks were from, that they found on his leg. It was an under the table kind of deal though. Seems he got a bad batch of it. He shot himself with it, had an allergic reaction, and began suffering from a heart attack. He wants you to know he didn't suffer but... he saw the impact with the bridge before he died." Violet nearly sneered and she asked "Tell me, what do you think of 'ghost lady' now, hmm?"

Eileen was almost shocked. Then, she laughed at herself.

"Nice trick. Okay, I get it. You figure I'm coming out here. You also know how close me and Talon are. You likely heard, or figured out, I'd be checking up on you. So, you did the same to me. Gotta say Violet, ya almost had me fooled there for a moment."

Violet was still in kick ass mode and calmly said "Almost? Hmm, okay, try this one on for size then. Let's say you're correct, and that I did get all that from public records." Violet smiled slightly and told Eileen "Milky white skin, and fire red hair. It's why he called you his candlestick. Tell me this Eileen, would that be in any public record?"

Now Eileen was the one who was nervous... and finally shocked.

Violet headed out, but, kindly told her "You wanted to know who I was? Well, now you know. And for the record, I have truly fallen in love with your brother. I can only hope that one day, that love is returned. I came here by a request you couldn't begin to fathom. You may have been, and I know still are, his protector. The night I arrived however... I was. I want you to know I truly hope that one day, we can be friends, and share that duty together."

Violet said that kindly, and meaning every word, as she left Eileen to pause and wonder.

Alone now, Eileen had tears running down her cheeks as she said "Oh Thomas... I'm soooo sorry."

A smile she couldn't see, and one she didn't know was shadowing her since that night........ was happy as he simply faded away.

Eileen emerged from the bathroom to find Violet waiting for her.

Violet asked with true kindness "Are you okay? I thought I should wait for you. I didn't want our party to think anything seeing me return alone."

With pure curiosity, Eileen asked "Just who the hell are you Violet. No wait, screw that, WHAT are you?"

Violet was enjoying this new feeling of relief. For over a week, Eileen had been an imaginary monster made up by Violet's insecure imagination. Now, with the proverbial dragon tamed, she was feeling like she was on top of the world. Also, now knowing what kind of women the Grayson's were, she was even happier knowing she had a path she could follow. Simply having a direction made her smile.

"Let's just say, I'm nowhere near the threat you perceived me to be. Let's also say that Talon, Grant and Cody know what you now know... but in far greater detail. Althea however does not and, it's your brother's wish to keep it that way for now. Those details however, I'll be more than happy to get you up to speed on. Say... on our shopping trip?"

Eileen, a lot nicer now, said "I look forward to it... 'ghost lady'."

Violet actually smiled at that and said "So do I, heh heh... 'candlestick'."

Both ladies giggled at the other as they headed back for the table.

"You 'sir', are a lucky man," Violet told Talon as she sat back down.

"And you say that why exactly?" Talon probed politely.

"Why, to have a sister such as Eileen of course," Violet said with a wink.

Talon was thinking now, how he wished he was the fly on the wall his brother mentioned. Two women left moments ago. In his mind, two different ones returned.

Eileen joked and spoke in a posh tone like a queen and stated "Why thank you my dear. Talon? I'm with Althea... you have my permission to keep this one... heh heh... for now."

Violet rolled her eyes playfully and giggled.

Grant whispered to Cody saying "That must be one magical bathroom."

Cody smiled at Eileen, but patted Grant on the back in agreement.

The rest of dinner was all that Talon had hoped for. Althea, Eileen and Lashonda made plans for Lashonda's trip back with Eileen. Cody even tried his hand at flirting some. He wasn't very good at it, but Eileen ignored it and just thought it was nice that he even would. She was liking the handsome doctor, and made plans with him as well for their date.

Cody thought Eileen was a stunning beauty. He'd never had a woman like her before. True, he'd had some of course but, none like her. Now he was trying his best to be a nice guy, and not a creepy one.

Talon paid the bill. The tip he left let the wait staff know how happy he was with their service. Handshakes all around from Phil, and wishes for a speedy return, and the Grayson party moved across the hall to the lounge area.

They were all sitting in chairs and small couches around a circular table. Talon being Talon, the bartender told him he'd overlook Lashonda's age, if he promised him she'd get no alcohol. Talon thanked him for his discretion, and easily gave the bartender his wish. Talon paid him for the drinks, and the non alcoholic Pina Colada, and rejoined the group.

Now that Violet wasn't afraid of Eileen anymore... she truly wanted to be her friend.

"Eileen?"

"Hmm?" Eileen asked as she sipped on her Manhattan.

"I won't lie and say your coming here didn't make me a tad nervous. I know you and him are close. Mind if I ask a question?"

Talon laughed at the new and improved Violet and asked "Who are you... and what did you do with my girl?"

Eileen chuckled and told him "Oh hush, you." She looked at Violet and asked "What's your question?"

Violet was feeling more comfortable around other people than she ever had in her life. More confident too. A combination of both those factors, made her snuggle into Talon's shoulder.

She sipped her wine and said "Well, I asked Grant to tell me about it, but he said ask Talon. Talon wouldn't tell me. Grant told me to ask about something called an Argentine Tango." Violet joked "Seeing as how these two sadistic bastards took great delight in making me squirm in my nervousness... how about if you tell me?"

Talon jested "Well... I wouldn't say sadistic exactly."

Grant laughed into his drink and stated "I would."

Eileen smirked and said "So, my brother didn't tell you about that eh? Well, wadda ya wanna know?"

Violet chuckled and said "How about... everything?"

Talon told Eileen offhandedly "I had to leave something for you two to talk about. Besides, you tell it better anyway."

"Modesty? From Talon Grayson!?? Why Lucinda, you have woven such a spell on my brother. Wait, who's Lucinda and why did I even say that name? Sorry, I meant Violet. Wow that was weird, I have no idea where that name even came from," Eileen said totally confused.

The look on all the other faces... except Violet's... gave Eileen cause for concern.

"Okay guys... what am I missing here?"

Talon nervously said "Viiiiioleeeetttt?"

She just snuggled and smiled.

"Just someone's way of introducing themselves. Totally harmless. Tell you what, Eileen... you tell me about this tango thing... and when we go shopping, I'll tell you all I can about Lucinda. Deal?"

Eileen was looking at all the suddenly nervous people go back to being not nervous... slowly. Including Lashonda.

Cody chimed in nicely with "I'd like to hear this as well."

"Ooooookaaaaayyy then," Eileen said warily, and began to tell her tale.

"Violet, were you told of my brother's and my upbringing?"

"Yes I was, but not in great detail."

"Well then," and Eileen continued. "Mom and dad saw how miserable we were. They had hoped we would become like them, but we didn't. So, our parents decided that, when we each hit 14, we would be allowed a hobby. It had conditions though. They had to approve, and it had to be something that would benefit us in some way. I chose dance. When Talon got old enough, he chose self defense. Grant was like my father. I swear that man could build or fix anything. Grant took up every shop class he could get into."

Eileen sipped her drink, then continued.

"Anyway, I got quite good. Talon didn't care for it much, but he was always in the stands cheering me on. I guess you could say, he learned by association. One day, we had a competition. I was one of two finalists. The other guy was an arrogant dickhead though. Each couple picked a choice from a jar. The judges picked one of those two, and it was the Argentine tango. We each had to do a side by side."

Violet asked "Side by side?"

Talon told her "Both couples on the floor at the same time. Judges decision is final."

"Ah... gotcha."

Eileen told them "So the big day comes. I was almost 19... Talon just turned 16. As always, my biggest champion was in the stands. Now, the Argentine is a Latin dance, and a rather sultry one at that. The other couple were slated to win as Latin was his strong suit... but I had a lot of people in my corner cheering on the underdog. Me, and my partner at the time, were actually starting to show the other couple up. I had on a dress with spaghetti straps. We did a spin, and the other couple cut across us. Suddenly, my strap got undone. That wasn't possible as it was the kind you pull over your head, not the kind you tie."

"Oh damn... what happened then?" Violet asked getting totally into this story.

"Heh heh, well, I wasn't about to flash my tits to a crowd of hundreds, so we stopped, and went to the judges. They were about to tell us, essentially, tough shit. That's when Talon showed up."

"Ha HAAAAAAA! Oh this just gets betta an betta! How come you nevah told little ole me this story, Mista G!?" Al bellowed.

"Just like in the military, Al... don't ask, don't tell," Talon told her.

Eileen smirked at Talon's uncomfortable expression. So did Violet.

"So, what did he do?" Althea asked.

"Heh heh... he decked the other guy... hard. The guy was down and wailing, and I was mortified. Then, Talon grabbed him by the wrist, and dragged him over to the equally mortified judges. Talon said nothing, he just pulled out his fingers, and showed the judges the tiny sharp pointed blade under his ring. In an effort to win, he cut my strap. Talon saw it though from up in the stands."

Althea sat back with a slight huff saying "Uhhh HUH! Yep, that be Mista G awlrite!"

That made even Lashonda giggle.

"So, what did the judges do?" Lashonda asked.

She was enthralled by this story as only a 14 year-old girl could be.

"Talon essentially gave them no choice. They were about to declare us the winners by default. I however had just as much fire as Talon did back then. I wanted to win but, not like that. The judges then asked me what I thought was fair. I told them I wanted a rematch. My partner, however, was a pussy and couldn't stand conflict. He told me flat out if there was to be a rematch, he was out. Talon told him just one word... heh heh... 'leave'. You had to see it. Looking back on it now it's hilarious to think of all these grownups being petrified of a 16 year-old boy. Yet, they were. I swear Talon could've asked for the moon and they would've given it to him."

Violet smiled up at Talon lovingly and said "My kind of man."

Eileen kicked back in with "The judges wanted out of this situation, but Talon had them in a corner, and in front of hundreds of people no less. They told me that without a partner, it was take the win or forfeit. Talon put his coat over me, stared them down, and told them I would have one. The judges gave me two weeks, and I'd have my rematch." Eileen looked at Talon and reminded "Ya know, you never did tell me what you said to that dickhead, right before we left the floor."

Talon told her "I told him to stay down... there was more where that came from if he didn't... and that I'd be sleeping with his partner later."

Eileen laughed and Althea teased "Mista G!? Oh no you didunt?"

Talon had a slight grin and raised his drink to her saying "Heh heh... Oh yes I did! More than once too!"

Althea let loose her ear piercing cackle and said "Mista G, y'all are incorrigible... funny... but incorrigible!"

"Damn," Cody said in awe. "I wish I knew you all back then. I remember something about a big dance in a gymnasium once, but it wasn't my thing at the time. Shit, if I had only known."

Violet giggled "Well!? Don't stop now!"

"Okay so, Talon... school hottie at the time... I think you get the picture. He rallies the whole damn school to my cause. Problem is, I don't have a partner. Talon stepped up yet again, and got me one."

"Who!?" Lashonda nearly barked.

"Me," Talon said, still clearly uncomfortable at the memory.

"YOU!?" Lashonda barked in disbelief.

"Mm hmm," Eileen confirmed. "Talon had watched me for years. Typical for him, he saw only a problem to be solved. He asked me to fine tune him, and he worked like a madman perfecting every little detail and nuance. Now, here's the cool part. I'm freaking out because it's 4 hours to showtime... and mom, dad AND Talon have my dress and shoes half apart. Calm as ever, and with a very sneaky smile on his face, he and mom assured me it'll be perfect and ready on time. True to his word, it was."

Smiling, and proud of 'her man', Violet asked "And then?"

"Then, I got nervous. I walked in and the place was standing room only. This challenge was all over town thanks to my brother. There had to be 3 or 4 thousand people in the stands. Anyway, I sucked it up, and walked out with Talon when our names were called. The applause we got was deafening, which only made me more nervous. The only thing that calmed me down was Talon. He wasn't nervous at all." Eileen chuckled at them all saying "And we danced and that was it," teasingly cutting the story off short.

"HEYYYYYY" Lashonda barked yet again.

Eileen laughed when Cody said "Yeah... what she said!"

"Okay okay. So, we start the dance. The music kicks in, and Talon warned me."

"Of?" Althea asked.

"That I was to think of him only as my dance partner... not my brother. I did, and it worked. We take off, and Talon was amazing. He was playing his part to perfection. We made it still sultry, without making it creepy. This other guy though, oh my God I had to laugh, the crowd was treating him like Hitler. Talon took me in for another close pass. This idiot actually tried the same trick twice, but on my zipper this time. Talon just smiled at him as we just passed him by... and nothing happened. The look of shock on his face was priceless. That's why Talon and mom had my dress and shoes apart."

"Sorry, not getting it here," Cody scorned.

Talon told him "I had mom sew in 200 pound test fishing line into her straps. Dad had her heels filled with a steel rod, and used industrial strength glue on them. Mom re-sewed the zipper using piano wire, the kind you hang pictures with. Heh heh, to be a tad crude AND... to quote my mother of all people... not even prom night would get that dress off or ruined when we were done with it."

Cody said nothing. He just beamed, reached over, and high five'd Talon.

Eileen finished with "The event got so blown up, the judges bowed out in favor of unbiased out of town judges from a rival school. They judged fairly, and I won fairly. Mom and dad were proud of him but no one more so than me. That night was the first night we came here. Needless to say, we've been coming here ever since." Eileen looked at Violet with sisterly eyes and told her "That's why Grant mentioned that. So you would understand what Talon would do, and has done, for me... and I him. Tell me, that answer your question?"

Violet was smiling large and said "Thank you... it does indeed."

Lashonda had a 'wow' kind of glazed look on her face.

"That must have been amazing. I wish I could have seen it."

Cody smiled and honestly said "Me too."

Violet quickly chimed in with "Me three!"

Eileen waved her hand saying "Thank you but, I haven't danced like that in ages."

Talon went from being uncomfortable, to wanting to show off for Violet.

"The great Eileen Grayson? Back away from a challenge!? Hmmf, not the sister I remember."

Eileen was a tad shocked and said "You hated dancing with me, well, dancing in general really. You only did it to support me."

"Meh, I still remember most of it. I can wing the rest if I had to," Talon stated confidently and flippantly.

Now, Eileen's fire was back.

"Well then brother, I'm game if you are. Let's see if your feet can match what your mouth is dishing out," Eileen challenged.

Talon huffed slightly, and sat Violet up.

"Grant? Cody? A little assistance if you please?" Talon said over his shoulder as he headed for the bar. Talon pulled out his phone, pulled up his playlist, and asked the bartender to hook it into the sound system.

While he did, Grant happily said "C'mon Doc, gimme a hand!" and he and Cody moved some empty tables out of the way.

Talon took off his coat and threw it over his shoulder as the music started. He swaggered back to the group as the music kicked in. Luckily for Cody, it was a song he knew too.

'BrrrrrrrrrrrrAMP amp amp amp amp!' the music echoed as it started. It was 'Santa Maria' by Gotan Project. The ghostly female voice sang out, and no more perfect a song there ever was for an Argentine Tango.

Talon threw his jacket to the side, as he stared purposely at Eileen. She slowly extended her hand. Talon took it, and snapped her up to him, staring into her face. Eileen played her part, and stared right back.

The music kicked in in earnest, and Eileen snapped her heel through Talon's legs. He threw his around her side, and spun her for the open area.

"Hay milonga de amor... Hay temlbor de Gotan.......este tango es para vos!" the haunting voice sang.

Talon grabbed her from the small of her back and lifted her up in a half spin. Eileen bent her knees, crossed AND twirled her ankles in what looked like an impossible full 360 degrees. She came back down and crossed her arms over her chest as she did a rolling spin inside Talon's arms. He grabbed her coming out of the spin and jolted her to a stop. Eileen extended from it... stopping inches from Cody's face. She slowly took the arm that wasn't being held, and ran her fingers under his chin. Cody leaned forward, and nearly fell forward, as Eileen teasingly snapped away.

Lashonda was open mouthed and said "Okay.... THAT... was hot!"

Althea was a bit stunned too and answered "Baby girl? You got that right."

That was it for Cody. He knew this song and he also knew it was six minutes long. Around halfway, he got up, and took off his jacket too. No one in the Grayson party noticed, they had a crowd now outside the open area lounge.

Talon went for another spin and stopped halfway as his face nearly ran into Cody's. Neither man however, broke character. They circled each other then, with tons of machismo, Cody stuck his hand out... and found it filled shortly thereafter. He looked deep into Eileen's eyes, and took up where Talon left off. He threw Eileen over his shoulder. She curled over the other one and came down in a straight arm spin, never once breaking the flow. Talon and Cody each played the rival, and Eileen was loving it, and played her part to the hilt.

"De la cantina...................... Buenos Aries!" the male voice chirped sharply, pausing shortly between musical hits.

Knee bends, ankle flips, and Eileen getting thrown around like a rag doll. Everything a good Argentine Tango should be. It ended with Eileen hugging Talon but... staring at Cody... and holding his hand. The now fully packed hallway erupted with applause, cheers and whistles. So did the lounge. Talon just smiled and spun his sister into a curtsy like they did at tournaments. The gray-haired Grayson walked back to his date. Cody and Eileen walked back too but, holding hands. Talon gave Cody a raised eyebrow as he sat down.

"Rich kid, remember? Piano and dance lessons kinda went without saying," Cody told him answering Talon's unasked question. "Besides, with a baby face like mine, it was the only way I could get even close to a girl."

Eileen was pleasantly surprised... VERY pleasantly.

"Well, perhaps I should take up dancing again?" She nearly cooed staring at Cody.

"Well if you do..." Cody said confidently, "... THIS dance partner won't chicken out on you."

Eileen nearly beamed at Talon, raised her drink to him, and stated "Brother? Tonight's choice of entertainment was a very good choice indeed!"

Talon grinned, and raised his back. Grant chuckled slightly seeing his brother, and now his sister, both snuggled into someone.

"Man, I have got to get me one of those," Grant said to himself, and in response to his having no one to do that with.

"Don't lose hahrt ginger chyld... yaw day is com'in soon," the Cajun whisper said in his ear.

Grant just sighed and said softly "If you say so lady... if you say so."

Talon invited everyone back to his house for drinks. Althea thanked him but bowed out saying she and Lashonda had to get up early and head back to California. Everyone else took Talon up on his offer.

Talon got the fireplace going strong, pulled out a bottle of wine, and enjoyed good company for the next few hours.

Eileen laughed hearing of Talon's 'first date' and said "Ha ha ha ha ha!

You took her shopping!?? Who are you... Richard Gere? Why didn't you just give her one of my dresses? It's not like I don't have a ton to choose from."

Talon just smirked at Violet, and semi-pointed to Eileen as if to say 'See? I told you.'

Violet just squirmed a bit, but said nothing.

The girls had ditched the heels, and the dresses, for socks and comfy clothes. In an attempt to show off a little... Eileen's were a tad tighter than Violet's. Off in the back room though, Eileen gave Violet something she didn't expect.

"Listen, new girl. Straight up, no bullshit... if you hurt him... I WILL find a way to bury you. That said however, if you can make him happy, well then, do so. We understand each other?"

Permission? From Eileen!? Oh Violet understood quite well.

"I promise you here and now, I won't hurt him. Not on purpose anyway. And for what it's worth... thank you. I've known a lot of scummy men in my life, but none like him. Know that, for him, I would fight even you if I had to. I truly hope however... I never have to."

Eileen chuckled, but showed support by saying "Oh, you've had dates like that too eh?"

Violet giggled slightly, but meant her words when she said "I have no brothers or sisters. I see how you look at Cody. I also saw how he looked at you. Like a sister would, well, I want you to know I'll help you with that in any way that I can."

Both girls smiled, hugged, and headed back out to the waiting men.

Talon was elated Eileen gave, at least for now, her stamp of approval. Now, he felt it was his turn to give her his.

"Okay everyone... Violet here is a great cook. If she doesn't mind... breakfast is here tomorrow." Talon looked to his side and said "Doc? That includes you." Talon got playful, winked at Eileen, and said "Stand up my sister... and you and her brother are gonna have words. As my mother used to say... you dig?"

Cody answered Talon, but smiled at Eileen and said "Wouldn't miss it for the world."

Violet smiled at Talon, both for what he did for Eileen, and the confidence he proudly pronounced in her.

"Looks like a date!" Violet said cheerfully.

An hour later and Grant was leaving. Cody was too. Suddenly, so was Eileen. She came out with a small overnight bag.

"And you're going where exactly?" Talon asked curiously.

"I'm staying at Grant's till Monday or so. I'm always staying here and I hardly ever see him when I come out. Me and baby G are gonna catch up is all," Eileen explained weakly. Before Talon could respond, she hugged Violet and said "It was nice to meet you and I had a great time. See you in the morning."

Violet was a little unsure, but hugged her back. Out of Talon's sight, Eileen winked at Violet.

"Remember... happy," Eileen warned but kindly.

She gave Talon a kiss and whispered in his ear sweetly.

"Thanks for the start, bro... I'll take it from here," and she headed out with the men.

An hour after that, and Talon was stoking the fire one last time before heading to bed. Violet, however, was heading straight back for the nervousness that plagued her when she first arrived.

"Talon?"

"Yeah?"

Violet gulped, and said "I have a question for you."

"Any you'd like," he answered nicely.

"To quote you... you stated... 'who are you and what did you do with my girl'. Question is, did you mean it? The 'my girl' part I mean."

Talon changed attitudes on a dime.

"I had a wonderful time tonight. More so than I've had in a long long time. YOU looked amazing. I would, very much so, like it if... it were to happen again. So yeah, I guess so. If you'll have me, I'd be more than proud to call you mine."

Violet was crying softly now. No man, no real man that is, had ever wanted her before, no less told her so.

"Even though, to a man like you, I'd be considered damaged goods?" Violet asked sniffling slightly.

"Look at me Violet... I made a life, AND a small fortune, out of 'damaged goods'. For the record, yes Violet Hayes, I'll have you if you'll have me and... I'll have you just the way you are."

That was it. Violet was looking for a sign of some kind. She didn't know what but... something. Seeing Talon, bathed in the firelight and being open and honest... that was what she was looking for. Now, Violet made the most trusting, and vulnerable, move of her life.

"Talon, may I have your phone?"

That kind of threw him a bit, but, he gave it to her. Violet brought up the tunes, then, backed it up one song. Once again, the Nevada night would see a third, and final, tango.

"Dance with me?" Violet asked softer than soft.

Talon asked "Are you sure Violet?" knowing full well what she was up to, and what she was offering.

"Talon Grayson... I've fallen in love with you. Yes, my dear... I'm sure."

Talon turned off all the lights, locked the door, walked back and snapped Violet into his arms. She had no idea how to dance like that, but felt she wouldn't have to for long.

The music ramped up and snapped, and she hung onto Talon committing every moment to memory. The music ramped again, he spun her, and when she stopped... she ripped open his shirt. Talon stared at her with, for the first time in years, loving eyes. He bent her backwards, and put his mouth to her firm stomach, and kissed it as he went upward. When Violet was upright again... her shirt was off now too. Talon had love written all over his face. Unlike earlier, he wasn't play acting this time. Talon undid her jeans. In time with the music, he curled his leg around her hip, and slid them down and off.

"Pity... Eileen didn't have to leave tonight after all."

Violet thought that an odd statement but asked "Why's that?" as Talon kissed her neck ferociously.

Talon gave her a grin that made her melt and told her "Because... you won't be needing that bed... not tonight anyway."

Violet was now completely naked. She sweetly looked at Talon as she undid and dropped his jeans, just as he had to her. Now Violet smiled lovingly, and took Talon by the hand.

"You won't be needing yours either," she told him as she led him to the fire. "You might say, I've become rather fond of this spot."

Talon scooped her up, then knelt down and laid her gently on the floor.

"Listen to me very carefully Violet. Here, right here in my arms, I promise you... you will always be safe."

Violet was mush right now. The last thing the firelight saw was Violet arch her back and draw a deep breath, right before she pulled the alpaca blanket over the two of them.

Chapter 14

"Afterglow Sunday... Revelation Monday"

Violet had never known 'serenity', until now. Violet was in the full throes of what the rest of the grownup world refers to as afterglow. She was wanted. By her own choice, she loved. Thinking of the love she got back was still making her smile. She wanted... and was wanted. And this house! Oh the peace of this house, the calm feel of Talon under the blanket, and the knowledge that she finally belonged somewhere, had her on damn near overload... and she wasn't even moving a muscle.

The morning got chilly once the fire had gone down. Talon was out cold and right now, every little bit of him made her smile. From the way his powerful shoulders flared out from sleeping on his stomach, to the slightly boyish grin that never seemed to leave his face. Violet worked the fire then, cold herself, quickly got back under the covers. Violet decided she didn't care what time it would happen but, right here is where she would be when Talon woke up.

"Well... good morning Miss Hayes," Talon grumbled, but sweetly.

Violet giggled and replied "Good morning Mr. Grayson."

Talon told Violet as he propped himself up on his side, "Last night I was very happy. This morning though... not so much."

Violet was nervous on the inside now. Knowing how much Talon hated that, she hid it on the outside.

"Why's that?"

Talon gave her a sexy smile, and said "Because now I'm pissed at myself for inviting everyone over for breakfast!" Talon rolled on his back, snuggled Violet in tight, and said "I could stay here... just like this... all damn day."

Violet chuckled at him and scorned mockingly "Yeah, that was kind of a dumb ass maneuver on your part huh?"

"Why Miss Hayes (tickle)... did you just (tickle) call me (tickle tickle tickle) a dumb ass?" Talon scorned back playfully as Violet shrieked and laughed. Talon rolled on top of her and stared into those amazing eyes and said "Yeah, I guess I kinda was huh?" Talon went back to sexy again as he looked at his watch and stated "Still, I know my family aaaaaand.... I don't think they'll be here for awhile yet."

Talon went back for a second helping of 'Violet'. She was only too happy to give him a banquet.

Talon came out of his bedroom dressed in comfy Sunday clothes. Being the smart girl that Eileen was, she called first to say the crew was on their way. It was around 9 a.m. and Violet was dressed now too, and cooking up a storm.

Talon sat down and got callous saying "Ya know Violet, last night? Yeah, that can't happen again." Then Talon laughed at Violet's response, changed to a jesting tone and said "Why... sleeping with the boss!? Whatever would the neighbors say!?"

Violet made Talon laugh as she gripped the handle to the pan and threatened "They'd say nothing... or 'ghost lady' is gonna kick their ass!"

Talon just laughed, hugged her sweetly, and told her in the kindest of tones "That's my girl."

Violet kissed him sweetly saying "Ya know?... I do like the sound of that."

Just as sweetly, Talon responded "Ya know?... So do I."

"Okay... where's the Doc?" Talon asked seeing only Grant and Eileen.

"He had an emergency call," Eileen replied. "He sends his apologies and says he'll miss breakfast. He did say he would likely make lunch though."

Talon snickered and asked "And you know this how?"

"Why... heh heh... he called me and told me of course."

Talon laughed and proclaimed "Eileen Grayson wastes no time... film at 11!" and he just hugged his sister.

"Yeah... well..." and she just finished with a sly grin.

Violet was nearly beaming all morning. She was also very curious. She had a tune in her head she was humming to herself. What had her curious was that it was a song she never heard before, yet somehow knew it by heart.

Breakfast was a hit, and everyone had a great time. Sunday was going to be a lounge about, do nothing day... so sayeth the master of the house. No one in present company complained about that order whatsoever.

"So, judging by the look on your face, it was a wise idea that I called first, wasn't it?" Eileen asked as she helped Violet clean up.

Violet gave a thankful smile to Eileen and confirmed "A very wise idea indeed... and one that I thank you for."

Eileen now asked "Tell me Violet... and I'm not judging... what do you do for my brother exactly?" Eileen laughed, caught herself, and corrected with "Work wise, I mean."

Violet laughed, but asked "Before I answer that, do you remember last night? More specifically... Thomas?"

Eileen said cautiously "I do... and it's why I'm asking now."

Violet was slightly stunned and said "Aaaaaand... that doesn't freak you out..... becaaaaaaaaaause?"

"Oh it did... still does. Just, not in the way you think. My mother and father, in my opinion, were the perfect couple. Not that others aren't or can't be... just that they definitely were."

"Okay, I'm with ya so far," Violet told her.

Eileen told her "Everyday I saw them look at each other... and each day was as tender as the one before. Let me tell you this... if it hadn't been for your stunt with Thomas... I wouldn't be telling you what I'm about to tell you now."

Eileen checked to make sure the men were occupied.

"Mom and I were very close till I hit my teens. She fancied herself a Wiccan Priestess or something. I used to think she was the coolest thing when I was a little girl. Once I got curves though, I thought she was anything but. Typical teenager shit."

"Sorry, I wouldn't know anything about that. I was anything but typical."

"Ooooh, sorry," Eileen said realizing her goof.

"Oh, you're fine," Violet reassured.

"Anyway, I saw mom do some wild, and nearly unexplainable things. Dad supported her though. Together they were amazing. I think mom was a little let down I wouldn't follow in her footsteps. Talon always teased her about it, I wanted nothing to do with it, and Grant was just a baby. My father was an amazing man. Grant is like him in talent but, Talon is exactly like him in mentality. It's like my father got split between the two of them. Did you know we recently lost mom?"

"I do," Violet said kindly, "And I am truly sorry for your loss."

"Thank you. Anyway, in my mind, my mom was a lot like you. Talon is just like my dad. So you see, when you pulled that stunt with Thomas, I saw them somehow coming back in the form of you and my brother. It's why I backed off."

Violet stared at Eileen, and decided to take a chance.

"Eileen, try this. Ya know how there's thousands of radio waves out there, among others?"

"Uh... yeah?"

"Now," Violet explained, "Imagine if you could hear them... all of them AND... all at once, including the non-radio ones. That would get kinda noisy, wouldn't it?"

Eileen said "Boy, I'll say. That would drive me nuts."

Violet shocked her by saying "It did... once. And, it was the reason for the last known address you found. You wanna know what I do for Talon? I monitor those 'signals' and steer him and the others clear of the bad ones. Would you like to know why I love this house so much?"

"Do tell," Eileen said in near disbelief.

"Aside from the fact that your brother is in it of course, this house has been turned into a shielded bunker from such things. Courtesy of your mother."

Violet decided to let that sink in for a bit. It only took a second.

"Wait... what!?"

"Mm hmm. Also, your mother made it that way for Talon... and me... years before I even knew of any of you."

"Watch it, ghost girl. And, you know this how?"

"She told me so. Grant knows but... Talon doesn't. Now, just between us girls, Talon is trying to protect you from what you used to call the 'creepy house'. Suffice to say, it's gotten a lot more creepy since your last visit, and the very reason I came here. As for your mother, she didn't speak to me as much as 'left a message'. Trust me, anyone who could do what she did, was a tad higher than a priestess in my mind."

Eileen was part stunned, part curious, and part amused.

"Ya know, I am really looking forward to our little shopping date now!"

Violet smiled and told her "As am I."

Over in the living room, the men were having their own conversation while the ladies talked in the kitchen.

Grant told his brother softly "I went up and down the road outside 3 times. I told Eileen I lost a hat the other day and wanted to see if I could find it. If there was anyone out there, I didn't see him."

"Thanks, bro. I re-trained two of the cameras to see farther out as well."

"Still Tal... that guy was hired by someone. Wadda ya gonna do?"

Talon was cold and said "Whatever I have to."

Now Talon threw out some ideas to Grant.

"Listen buddy, I was outside VC and Lucinda still talked to me. Hell, Violet was across the country! Point I'm making is, keeping Eileen away from the mansion to keep her safe, well, I doubt that'll work."

"Yeah, gotta agree with you there. So, what do we do?"

"I was thinking, of bringing her in on this job when she's done training Lashonda. If she's going to be coming out here, well, how much can we really hide from her?"

"Let's not forget how much 'should we' hide," Grant interjected.

"Agreed. I can't say I don't find the Grayson trio working together an unpleasing thought. Still, if Shadow Man wants to try and come after me, fine. IF however, he goes after Eileen... what could either of us really do?"

Grant was getting frustrated.

"Look, everything you just said are good points. I say this. You've been her protector for years. Yet, in all that time, how many times did you actually have to? Jeez Tal, more times than not, you treat her like your baby sister rather than your older one. Look, all I'm saying is, let her decide. Let's show her a small piece, and see how she does. You know damn well she'll either run screaming... ha ha ha... or take over! Either way, I think it's time we let her decide for herself."

Talon smiled and told him kindly "Mom and dad would be proud of you. You grew up well, baby G. With wisdom like that? Yeah, very well indeed."

Grant smiled and said "Thanks, bro. Listen, just remember this. IF she joins us and... IF Shadow Man does indeed go after her... he'll have two Graysons to deal with, not one."

Talon chuckled and added "And from the looks of it... a Holliday too!"

Grant glanced at the ladies, then went back to Talon.

"Tell me true, bro... you okay with that?"

"With what... Doc and Eileen?"

"No... Bert and Ernie."

Talon chuckled but told him "Ya know, lately I got people coming into my life, some quite literally, out of nowhere. At first I was very suspicious. Now though, not so much. When I had the Kansas team check out Violet, I had them do a little digging on Cody too. I told them though if anything odd popped up, they were to stop and call me. So far, he's exactly as he's claimed, and I had them stop digging. Now, before you go barking at me and calling me paranoid and shit, think of this. I got a girl who shows up right on time, seems to have other worldly fine tuning, and a P.I. following her around. I got a Doctor who's straight out of the past, and my own small fortune to protect. Add to that I got ghosts... as in real fucking ghosts. Tell me, would you do any different?"

Grant kindly told him "No I wouldn't."

"So," Talon continued, "People showing up out of the blue but, eh, I dunno bud... it seems more like someone is putting together a team or something. Everything, and everyone, we need... seems to show up or fall into place just as we need them. So far, each new player has been another piece to the puzzle but, yet again, right on time and just what we need. That... not the Doc... is what has me bugged a little. As for him and Eileen, I'm actually finding those two funny."

Grant kind of cocked his head and asked "How so?"

Talon sneered slightly and answered "Look, as brothers, we do the guy thing and protect her right? Do the whole 'check out the new guy' routine. Well, we had already known Cody for a bit so that helped. Still, I find it funny because, as her brothers you'd think we'd be watching out for our sister right? Ha ha ha, well, something tells me... we're gonna have to watch out for him!"

Grant sat back with a laugh and jokingly imitated Althea.

"LAWD! Ain't THAT tha truth!"

Talon's buzzer rang, and it was the very same doctor Grant and Talon were just discussing. Eileen let him in and was sporting a huge smile when she did. Grant and Talon merely got up to greet their new friend.

They were all in the kitchen, and just enjoying the day. Cody told them, though serious, it wasn't as big of an emergency as he was first led to believe. A quick and easy job for him and he was back with the Grayson gang in no time. Talon was mulling over what he and Grant had been talking about. Talon was nowhere near the kind who made friends quickly nor easily. Now he had a new and good friend... and a new love, and all of it... in less than a month. Talon was the most guarded of the three, and was not used to any of this. Still, he was guarded because he had a bit to protect, and felt rushing into things was a baaaad idea. Yet, here he was and for all the quickness of it, he was still sitting pretty. So, in a departure from his normal ways, Talon decided to throw caution to the wind... just to see where it would take him.

"Eileen? I have a proposition for you," Talon said aloud.

"Sure. What's up, Tal?"

"I'd like you to join us on this job. I'm letting Grant show off his work to potential new clients when the job is done. I'll do the same for you and tell anyone I need to that you oversaw the financing of the project, including the budget. This job though, has some serious conditions to it. I insist that you get a small taste then... Grant and I have decided to let you make the call."

"Okay, there's those looks again. What is it about this job you're NOT telling me?" Eileen asked seeing Cody's and Violet's stunned looks.

"Violet? I need you to do me a favor."

Violet asked warily "And what is that exactly."

Talon told her "This mansion, and all that it is, isn't going away anytime soon... if ever. I can't, and won't, hide it from Eileen... so I've chosen not to. If you wouldn't mind, head for your shopping date tomorrow afternoon. After the crews go home for the day though... introduce her to the name you were so not concerned about... please."

Cody was nervous and said "You sure about this?"

Talon was certain and said "Doc? While I appreciate your concern for my sister... she is still just that... MY sister. As long as Violet is there, well, I think if I'm not too concerned, then neither should you be."

Eileen smelled a challenge, and was on it in a flash.

"Okay brother, I'll see your challenge and raise you one of my own."

Talon smirked and said "I'm listening."

"I'll see this little shop of horrors of yours. IF I decline, you can keep all the secrets you want. But... if I don't... then I want in. And I mean in. I wanna know everything you know. Every secret, every concern... all of it."

Talon called her on it easily saying "Deal. Choose the latter however, and I think you'll find wanting and having to be two totally different things. Also, when you're done with Lashonda, I'll need you onsite. Sell by then, or just turn it over to them till they can purchase it. Fuck your lease, I'll pay off any remainder but I want you here... not there."

Violet was still concerned, but just said "Well, candlestick... I'm game if you are."

Full of fire, Eileen told her "Ghost lady? Gear up. I got a challenge to beat!" she looked at Talon and said "Listen, we're all adults here. You and Violet have obviously gotten close. Me staying here? Yeeeaaahhh, not a good idea right now. So brother... mind telling me where I'm gonna stay? Grant's is great and all but, I want a place of my own."

Talon told her "Our old home then. The papers will have gone through by then, and it's yours anyway. I'll admit it's dated but, it's still very functional." Talon laughed slightly and said "Or, if that's not to your liking... I can have a room setup in the mansion."

Eileen got snotty saying "Don't push your luck, gray dude."

Talon laughed and said "Anything you say... 'red'."

While the children and their friends were having a lovely Sunday, two other people's children were using theirs to pack. Each was going on a journey and neither knew of the other. In time though, they would end up being good friends. Just a routine trip, would turn out to be the start of a journey neither could fathom now... but would look back fondly on in the years to come.

"Well Pete, looks like you're going to have to find a new friend. I'll be leaving tomorrow and... well... with any luck I won't be coming back anytime soon. Thanks for being my friend there little buddy, heh heh, my only friend sometimes," Zachariah told the parrot on his fire escape.

Zack figured it must have been someone's pet that got loose. 'Pete' however, sort of bonded with Zack. He showed up everyday right on time for lunch. The slightly brooding brown haired man with the buzz cut, would always have some sort of seed ready for him. He was right though... Pete was his only friend. Zack heard a ding on his laptop and went to check it. It was a reminder that his train left tomorrow at 7am local time.

"With any luck Pete," Zack told the parrot, "This job will hold me for awhile. Maybe one day I'll even come back and visit you but... this town is not my style... and I've had all of it I can take."

Pete nuzzled his neck, then flew out the window to a place or places unknown. Zack looked over a file of papers one last time, then went back to packing his things.

On the complete opposite side of the country, a young woman was packing her things as well.

"HONEY! IT'S FOR YOU!" a woman's voice called from downstairs.

"Thanks mom!" she hollered back. She picked up the phone saying "Hello? Oh hi, Officer Glass, thanks for getting back to me on a Sunday."

"Mind telling me what these numbers are you sent? They look like coordinates or something."

"They are actually. If you bring those up on a computer, you'll see I'm not out in the middle of nowhere." She chuckled saying "I just didn't want the boys in blue freaking out in case this lovely ankle jewelry goes off the radar."

The man on the phone was kind and said "Listen sweetie, you have been one of the best parolees I ever had to work with. You got only a month to go and the monitor likely comes off. Your good behavior is the only reason I signed your travel papers. One month, that's it, and you're done. Do me a favor dear... have fun but... don't do anything stupid okay?"

Kindly she told him "I want this thing off as much as you do. Trust me, I won't. You're a nice man so don't take this the wrong way but, I'll be quite happy to not 'have' to talk to you again."

A sweet voice told her "As will I. Have a safe trip," and Officer Glass hung up the phone.

The pretty, but rather nerdy, girl with the long dirty blond hair went back to packing and checking her things.

Talon was out back with Cody, and showing him his latest idea.

"Okay Doc, here's how I see this," Talon said as he laid out his plan. "I don't use this shed for anything really."

Doc laughed and joked "You call this a shed? It's like what, 25 wide by 35 long? That's some shed!"

"Not anymore it isn't. Say hello to your new lab," Talon said with conviction. "Look, Violet says this place is protected from the ghostly beings. Anything we may find, or rather you will, well... I'll take all the secrecy I can get. When the mansion is done, we'll see about keeping it here, or moving it over there."

Doc was nearly drooling at the possibilities.

"Speaking of, here's that list you asked me for. You may not understand the names but, if they're for sale anywhere, those names should help you find them," Cody told Talon as the latter looked over the list.

He put it away and both men headed back for the house.

The rest of the day was just a blast. Eileen was showing off for Cody in little bits here and there. Talon actually thought her cute, acting like a lovestruck teenager. Still, if she was happy then so was he. She helped Violet cook dinner, but made Cody's favorite dish herself. Childhood stories flowed, and so did the laughter and good times.

Several hours later, and Violet found herself right back where she started this day. Naked, and in Talon's arms. Neither of which displeased her in the least. This time though, it was a fairly warm night so, now she was in Talon's bed. A soft but nice breeze was blowing through the slightly open window, and Violet was in heaven.

"Are you sure you want me going to the mansion tomorrow with Eileen? Alone I mean."

Talon hugged her saying "Grant and I talked about it. No, I'm not sure... which is why we're going to be there. However, we'll be outside. You and her need some time together. That house however damn near took me out, so... we'll be on hand in case something goes awry."

"I like her. I think she likes me. I don't mind the whole shopping thing but, taking her to the mansion alone was making me nervous. I'm glad you'll be there."

Talon told her he wouldn't be anywhere else.

"I'm glad you two are getting along. I don't know what happened in that bathroom but whatever it was... it worked."

Violet snuggled and asked "I'll tell you if you want."

Talon asked "Is it anything I need to know?"

"Not really. Nothing critical anyway. You might say, she got her point across... and so did I."

"Then don't bother. Some things I just don't need to know. As long as you two aren't at each other's throats, then I don't care."

"That's fine. I just want you to know that... OOOH! THIS IS REALLY PISSING ME OFF!!" Violet hollered cutting herself off and sitting upright.

Talon was a little caught off guard and got immediately alert.

"What's wrong!?"

"This damn house won't leave me alone, that's what's wrong. I've had this song in my head all damn day! More like broadcast. I've never heard it before in my life... but it's as if I've heard it a thousand times. It won't go away. All I want to do is lay here with you..." and then Violet yelled at the house itself saying "... but SOMEbody won't change the damn record!!"

Talon chuckled a little seeing a potential crisis not actually be one.

Violet smacked him lightly and whined "It's not funny. It won't go away!" She laid back down and told him "I've never heard it before, but it's like this house is trying to teach it to me. There's another sensation too."

Talon wanted to protect Violet now and stopped teasing.

"Okay, what sensation is that?"

Violet said "It's as if it's telling me you have permission for something. Weird I know but... it's what I sense all the same."

Talon tried to be supportive and said "Okay then... sing it to me. I'm pretty good with the tunes, maybe I can help."

"Sorry, gray guy... no words... just a melody."

"Alright then... hum it."

Violet sighed and said "Don't see why not," and started humming.

The moment she did, Talon went cold.

"Stop it, Violet.... STOP IT!" he hollered in true anger.

It was more like indignant. Talon acted as if Violet had just stolen a precious family heirloom.

"I'm sorry," she quickly said.

Talon checked one last time and asked "Are you SURE you never heard it before. Don't fucking lie to me Violet, cuz I'll know. Now more than ever... you had better tell me the truth."

"I am, ya big bully!" Violet said slightly upset.

Talon got out of bed and just said "Stay here," and left.

He came back a minute later and was holding the picture he showed her when she arrived.

"Violet tell me... I don't know how this ghost thing works but, do you get sensations from objects too?"

"Not usually no. I have but it's rare," she said meekly.

"And you're sure your getting permission. That word, no mistaking?"

"Mm hmm. Mind you, not I am... but you are," Violet said nearly under the covers.

Talon sighed, then calmed himself and said "Sorry I yelled at you. Now, if you wouldn't mind, let me give you what you don't know."

"What would that be?"

Talon said with a faraway look "The words. Hum it again please."

Violet did and, as promised, Talon gave her the words. He also looked odd doing it too. Like, it wasn't his place to, or something.

Violet hummed and Talon sang softly "Sleep myyyy love, and dream as you do....... I will love you, all my life throuuuughhh.... aaaalll my dreams depending on you....... ONLY saaay that you love me tooooooo."

"Oh my God... you know it!?" Violet said with big doe eyes.

Talon had a tone in his voice like he was lost in the past.

"Know it? It's more like seared into my memories. It's an old song. Not well known either. Bunch of different versions but...." and Talon grabbed his phone. "... This is the one he liked the best," and he pushed play.

Violet heard it and seemed to get battered by the house that was supposed to protect her.

"Um... 'he' who?" she asked.

"Papa Joe. My father used to sing this to my mother. It was 'their song'. No matter how old I got, nor what mental phase I was going through at the time, I always thought it pretty, and touching, when he sang it to her."

Talon told her it was called 'Sleep My Love' by Glen Yarbrough.

Violet was cautious, but told Talon "Do you remember when I came here? I told you this house had a definite 'feminine' feel to it?"

Talon wouldn't look at her, and just said "I do."

Violet was loving in her tone and said "This however, is certainly 'male'. I can also tell you this...... 'he'...... is now very happy." Violet smiled caringly and told Talon "Ya know what else?"

"What?" Talon said distantly.

"He's gone, but in a good way. Talon, my love?"

"Mm?"

"I think it's pretty. I'd be honored if you ever felt like singing it to me. I know 'he' would be happy as well."

"I'll be right back," Talon said as he left to hang the photo back up. "So dad... it's my turn now eh?" Talon pet the photo with a kind smile and told it kindly "Dad?.... thanks."

Talon got back in bed. He hugged Violet sweetly.... and sang the song from the beginning. Violet smiled for two reasons. First, because she thought it sweet. Second was... because the song in her head was gone. The last thing she remembered before sleep took over, was Talon finishing the last chorus.

Monday morning came around. Unlike the day before however, it was a flurry of activity. Grant dropped Eileen off on the way to the mansion. Talon gave her the keys to the Cuda so she and Violet could get around. After all, Papa Joe gave her the car first before he got it. Talon told Grant he'd show up later. He already had a line on 3 items on Doc's list, and wanted to monitor the auction. That same doctor had acquired enough basic forensic equipment to start doing some sweeps around the property. Today he was going into the hidden entryway to look for any residual blood, hairs, fibers or if he was lucky... latent prints. He promised however, that for safety, he wouldn't go in unless Grant was on standby.

Violet and Eileen were in the guest room. Eileen was giving Violet some of her dresses and such that she bought but never wore. Violet as promised, started telling Eileen of her life. She flat out told her though, she would not tell her about the night she arrived until they were both at the mansion.

Talon laughed seeing Eileen come out holding a huge pile of clothes, and he asked her "What the hell are you doing?"

"Why, rearranging your closet of course!" Eileen smarted right back.

Violet was behind her with her own pile, and just shrugged her shoulders and giggled. Talon just shook his head, laughed, and went into his office to check on the online auctions.

"Okay ghost lady, I got a surprise for you," Eileen said. "It's clear to me you ain't going anywhere for awhile. As such, and if you're gonna hang out with the Grayson's, then the time has come for you to be a grownup."

Eileen told her this, as they sat in the mall having lunch.

"Okay, candlestick... what did you have in mind?" Violet said holding her ground.

Violet was friendly towards Eileen now, and the same was true in reverse. Violet however had never met a powerhouse like Eileen before. Quite frankly, she just didn't know how to act around her. Violet was sweet by design and was only as forward as Eileen was when she had to be... not by nature. So, not knowing how to act around her, she just mirrored Eileen as a means to fit in.

Eileen stated "Well... here... let's go and you drive," as she handed Violet the keys.

"Sorry Ei, I can't drive. Even if I could, I don't have a license."

Eileen smiled a sneaky smile and told Violet "Exactly." Eileen sipped her coffee and asked "How about an inheritance? You did say you had a grandmother right? You're here so, obviously there was a mother at some point as well," Eileen joked but meaningfully. She got sweet and said "That story you just finished telling me? Yeah... it sucked. Don't get me wrong, I give you a lot of credit for surviving the way you did. My brother may have given you a reason to stay. My gift to you, to you both, is I'm gonna give you some roots.

Running time, Violet... is over."

Violet was actually liking this. She was getting to the age a few years ago that she considered doing just what Eileen said. Now at legal age, even if the teen years returned, she was a grown woman with legal rights. Problem Violet had was she didn't know how to be a grown woman. Well, not a normal one anyway. Now, with Eileen's help, she was ready to take a giant leap into adulthood. The other night at Sterling's was magical to Violet. She loved getting dressed up and playing the grownup. Now, she would have something more concrete to back it up.

"Did any of the guys show you the video of me in the psych ward?" Violet asked.

"Uh... what video?"

Violet smiled knowing they kept their silence.

"Cody had gotten one. It showed me and, well, it wasn't one of my prouder moments. I had no idea either, and was about to leave fearing I might hurt someone. Talon was the one who saw past the horror. Yet another reason I fell in love with him. Your very own Cody discovered that the psychotic episode that followed, was actually drug induced. He discovered the drugs they gave me weren't to suppress such things... but actually create them. THAT, Eileen, is what I have been running from ever since. There are some very powerful people working there. I tell you this because, if they come around one day... I wouldn't mind having some of those roots you mentioned to fight back with."

Violet thought a moment, then continued.

"Also, I was a very young girl when I went in, and still one when I ran away. I know what a will and such are but, I have no clue how to search for one. Can I tell you something?"

"Sure," Eileen said still a tad unsettled from Violet's revelation.

"Your Cody had to put me under his 'watchful eye' as a doctor just for me to stay here. The other night, when Grant and I left for dinner... someone was following us. I didn't say anything to Grant but, life under the radar teaches you to notice these things. I had no idea till later that he crushed his fuel line so he couldn't follow us, but it made me happy knowing he cared that much."

Eileen smiled caringly and said "First off, he's not 'my' Cody. Heh heh, not yet anyway. Secondly, Talon likely tipped Grant off but, had he not, he would have done what he did all the same. For the record, that's the kind of guy baby G is and... I'm damn proud of him for it too."

Violet told her "I highly doubt it was Grant they were following so that means, I'm being watched. Truth is, Eileen, I would have been gone days ago just to get away from them. Truer still... I'm tired of running." Violet was kind and told her "You and your brothers taught me that."

Eileen smiled and said "Thank you. So... ready for a little trip to the

DMV?" Eileen had a thought quick and asked "The whole being watched thing... now?"

Violet sipped her soda on purpose, and told Eileen while she did "Older guy in the corner by the candle shop... your 10 o'clock."

Eileen smirked "Heh heh... c'mon!" and practically pulled Violet to get up and go.

Eileen took them right past where Violet said. Suddenly, she stopped in the middle of the hallway and made a playful boast.

"There's a Hemi under the hood... and a driver who knows how to use it... good luck keeping up."

She never even turned around to look at the man hiding in the corner. Violet giggled and was starting to become a huge fan of the whole 'not running' plan. Once on the road it only took 3 exits for Eileen to lose him.

The first stop was to a spy store of all things. It was run by an old classmate of Eileen's from high school. She asked her if she could do a sweep of Talon's car for any kind of tracker.

Eileen joked to Violet and asked "Paranoid much?"

Coming here was Violet's idea, not Eileen's.

"I saw it on a news show once," Violet told her. "Thieves can buy them from a shop like this, and track you, using an app on a cell phone of all things."

Eileen was laughing. She stopped laughing when, her old classmate reached under the front left wheel well, and pulled out one. Eileen was stunned and Violet just had a 'told you' look on her face.

"Sneaky bastard," she decried menacingly.

There was a lunch shop right next door, and a guy from the cable company was in it having lunch. Eileen smirked, and put the device on his truck instead. She gave her classmate a $20 bill, and a hug, and she and Violet were off once more.

"Violet? Play along," Eileen commanded as they walked up to a counter. She walked up to the lady there and said "Miss? My cousin here was one of them city folk, and never had a car. What will we need to get her a license now that she's living here?"

The lady told them she would need a permit first, but that Violet could get just an ID card rather than a license with what she had. Eileen told the lady that would be fine, and Violet stared at Eileen questioningly.

"And you acquired that how exactly?" she asked Eileen.

"Like my brother said to Al the other night... don't ask," Eileen told her.

It was Violet's birth certificate. Back when Violet was a mystery, she planned to possibly use it against her. Instead, she ended up using it for her.

Eileen had a job once, in Maine. Unknown to her at the time, it was a front for a crime syndicate. Nothing happened to her but that was too close for her comfort. Being a hot sexy natural redhead can have its advantages sometimes. She searched for, then made nice with, a local group of nerds. They were also, collectively, putty in her hands. They were hackers and she used them on every job to dig a little deeper than most would... JUST so she didn't unknowingly run into another Maine situation.

Turns out, once Eileen got Violet's basic info from Grant, she wasn't hard to track prior to a certain point. It also turned out she was born only 90 minutes from where she lived in New York. So... she had the nerds get into the hospital's computer system, and put in an internal request. The document came up, her assistant had it printed in a local office store and overnighted it to her at Grant's house. The assistant made it look legit enough to fool a DMV clerk who sort of didn't care. Eileen used some old bills from Talon's office as proof of residency. A little doctoring on those as well, and Violet walked out with a legitimate ID card and some forms for her learner's permit.

"I don't mind telling you... that was a little scary how easy you did all that," Violet said.

"Technically we didn't lie... well... not much anyway," Eileen joked. "There. Now, wait awhile and then, call the hospital for a legit one," Eileen told her as she handed Violet all of her papers she was holding for her. "Until then, welcome to the big leagues."

Violet hugged Eileen sweetly and just said "Thank you."

Out in the parking lot, Violet looked at her watch and said "We got about 2 hours before the workers leave for the day."

Violet smirked and held out her hand to Eileen.

"Phone please," she chirped with a huge grin.

Eileen asked "Yours broken?" as she handed Violet her phone.

"Nope but," and Violet pulled up a number and called it saying "Yours has a phone number mine does not." She put up a finger to Eileen as if to say 'stay quiet' and said "Yeah hi, Doc? It's Violet. Listen, I sort of snuck Eileen's phone away from her. We're at the stores and... um... what kind of cologne do you like?" Violet smiled and said "Why do I ask? Well, a certain someone is looking for a gift. I thought perhaps I might be able to 'suggest something'... if you get my meaning." Violet finished with "Okay got it. See ya soon but she's coming back so I gotta go," and Violet quickly hung up the phone.

Eileen was laughing at the silent and smiling Violet as she took her phone back and said "You're learn'in kid... ha ha ha... you're learn'in!"

Violet chuckled as they walked to the car and said "Ya know? I could get used to this grownup thing."

A few 'make sure we're not being followed' passes through the DMV parking lot, and the girls were off to the local men's shop.

Two hours later, an old Plymouth drove under an iron sign as it turned right and got off the main road. Eileen and Violet got out to 3 men standing by Talon's truck.

Cody hugged Eileen and coyly asked "Didn't happen to get me anything did ya?"

Eileen cooed and teased right back.

"Mmm... maybe," she said with a sexy wink.

Talon walked over and took Violet's phone. He setup a headset on it, then called himself. Then on his phone he called Grant and Grant called Doc. One big conference call but, all 3 men could hear Violet.

"Okay brothers of mine, I have to say, you've done some nice work as usual." Eileen chuckled and told them "At least it doesn't look aaaaas creepy as it used to."

Talon was serious as he gave Eileen a quick rundown.

"The arch you drove under... said Adair house... that would be Lucinda Adair. Turns out this mansion was a brothel back in the day," Talon said using the preferred term. "Lucinda ran the place. Cajun queen that was murdered in the very room Grant giggled to as a child."

"Yeah THAT figures," Eileen exclaimed. "Still, how does that figure into the house now?"

"If Lucinda is in a good mood.... you're about to meet her."

"Wait... huh!?" Eileen questioned.

Talon said "Yeah, ya see, she sorta never left. We're here because, the guy that killed her? He hasn't left either." Without waiting for a reaction, Talon walked back to Cody and Grant and stated "Your show from here Violet. Me and the boys will be on standby."

Violet let out a deep breath, and held out a hand to Eileen.

"Shall we then?"

Eileen warily followed her in but kept looking at the men as she did.

"Wow, Grant's work is still impressive. From the look of this place I'd swear I just walked back in time!" Eileen stated proudly at seeing the parlor.
Eileen turned to Violet and said "Okay, ghost girl... let's hear that story you promised me."

Violet was slightly nervous, but told Eileen her story. She told of how she woke up across the country in a screaming sweat, and finished where Talon caught her just outside the doors.

"Okaaaaaay, I get it," Eileen snickered. "I mean really... what would a house like this be without a ghost story!" Eileen laughed. Then she looked and smarted "Oh don't THAT figure?! A house full of construction guys... ha ha ha... of COURSE there'd be a picture of some hot chick hanging about!"

She didn't laugh for long.

"Well, would y'all look at this. Tha eldest ginjuh chyld grew intuh a fiiine young woman," the soft Creole whisper said.

The cool breeze that accompanied that whisper made the hairs on the back of Eileen's arms stand on edge. She looked sharply at Violet, but the 'ghost lady' merely waved a hand inward. Next, a real ghost lady made an appearance.

Lucinda walked up to the two of them looking fine as could be for her day. She also did it... by appearing straight out of the fireplace from under where her portrait hung.

"Eileen Grayson? May I present to you the once... and obviously still... lady of the house. Lucinda Adair," Violet said in a tone that was part pride, part 'get ready to run'.

Eileen was open mouthed as Lucinda curtsied to her.

"Last time ah saw you... y'all were but a chyld. The pleashuh is awl mine ah assure ya."

"W..... wha.........what the FUCK!!!!!????" Eileen blurted out.

"Why ginjuh girl, thah's no way faw a lady tuh beehave!" Lucinda admonished slightly. She was sweet to Violet and asked her "Ah cannot stay much lawnguh. Can ah assume that fine gray-haired man of yaws got what he was aftuh?"

Violet play curtsied to Lucinda saying "Thank you ma'am... I'll take it from here."

Lucinda faded away but, walked straight through Eileen when she did.

"Thaht was an amaze'in dance y'all did by tha way. Ah look fawuud ta see'in y'all again soon ginjuh girl," was the last Eileen heard of the lady in the old clothes.

The chill Lucinda left inside Eileen as she walked through her was her way of showing the red haired girl... this was no joke... nor illusion.

"I assume you heard?" Violet asked.

"We did," Talon told her. "Well, at least I did. All good in there?"

Violet saw the look on Eileen's face and told him "Time will tell."

Just then... time ran out. The doors that had been open the whole time suddenly slammed shut.

"VIOLET!!??" Grant hollered out.

She was calm but concerned and told her earpiece "Scare tactic, nothing more. However... you may wanna have a battering ram ready just in case," Violet said half joking and half serious.

Grant walked over to his truck without saying a word. He pulled something out of the back of it. It was an iron beam about 5 feet long. He had welded a square flat plate on each end. Two curved pieces of re-bar were welded on as handles as well.

"Actually," Grant said walking back with the large metal contraption, "I got ya covered."

Eileen was confused. She wanted to curl up into a ball and cry... and kick somebody's ass... and both at the same time.

"Well... the white witch failed, so she sends a devil haired child to do what she couldn't. HA HA HA HA HA!......... Pathetic," the new voice said.

Shadow Man had arrived.

"White witch?" Eileen questioned Violet, and nearly crying.

Violet was soft and told her "Your mother."

Cody got a reaction from Talon and Grant he wasn't expecting. Neither was Violet. The two brothers were laughing.

Cody was a tad pissed and his tone showed it when he asked "And what exactly do you find funny in all of this!?"

Still laughing, Talon told him "Chill Doc. Shadow man just made the biggest mistake he could've made. He's about to experience the full force fury that is Eileen Grayson! Ha ha ha ha ha!"

Violet suppressed a giggle but, Talon was right.

Eileen went from near panic, to the full fury Talon promised Cody.

"Okay, you cowardly shit... SHOW YOURSELF!" Eileen commanded. She marched around the room and exclaimed "Scaring a bunch of women eh!? HAH! And you call ME pathetic!" Eileen kept talking to nothing and said "Got a name, asshole!??"

"Your sad excuse for a family call me Shadow Man," the voice told her in an 'I'm not afraid of you' tone.

"Well, you piece of shit! MY MOTHER was TWELVE times the woman you NEVER were as a man!"

"WATCH YOUR TONE, FREAKISH CHILD!!!" Shadow Man barked.

Now Violet was kicking into gear as Eileen got hurled into the wall behind her. Eileen though did something that slightly stunned Violet. She waved her off and got up on her own.

"HAH! I've known men like you," Eileen barked. "Your ego can't handle a real woman so you slap them around in anger. Wanna know what happened to the last guy that tried that on me?"

"I couldn't care less," Shadow told her.

"HE COULD!! It took a team of surgeons weeks to rebuild his face!" Eileen barked her last order and said "Shadow Man is a fitting name for you. Once a coward always a coward. STAY in the shadows! If you don't, so help me God I will find a way to kill you myself! AGAIN!!!"

Cody was just stunned as he looked at Talon. BOTH brothers were smiling with pride.

"Told you," Talon said affirming his earlier statement.

Soft and slow, Cody declared "Now that..... is my kind of woman!"

Shadow Man snickered "Your little sensitive friend beside you can't protect you for long. Leave!..... And never return."

"I do NOT!... AND NEVER WILL!!... take orders from you. You wouldn't dare harm me. You know it... and I know it!"

"Do I?" Shadow Man again snickered.

"Oh you do alright. Kill me!?? That would be the WORST mistake you EVER made!"

"And why is that?" Shadow now laughed menacingly.

"Because you don't scare me! And I would spend all of eternity KICKING YOUR ASS!!!!!!!" Eileen gave her final warning and said "The white witch as you call her may be gone. I however, will take GREAT delight in showing you... she left three behind. Her legacy will see to it that living OR dead... you won't harm another soul. Now open these doors, before I get medieval on your ass."

Shadow Man didn't open them, but Lucinda did. Only however, because Shadow was out of juice, and Lucinda had been borrowing some of Violet's the whole time. Eileen marched angrily right to Talon... and quoted a line from an old gangster movie.

"I want him DEAD!... I want his family... DEAD!" she calmed herself some and said "Count me in... aaaaallll the way in! I want... mmmmmffff!" Eileen cut short as Cody could take no more and kissed her hard.

"What an amazing woman," Cody said staring into her eyes.

"Doc? Heh heh... stick around... it only gets better from here," Eileen joked as she finally calmed down.

"Lady? I'm not going ANYwhere," Cody proudly claimed.

Talon calmly walked into the house, and proclaimed, "Shadow? I didn't tell you... I showed you. Grant did too. Now it would seem, my sister has as well. She was right you know... the white witch left 3 behind. We're coming for you. We will expose you and finish whatever it is my mother started. Your days... in this realm OR the next... are coming to an end," and he walked out of the house without another word.

Chapter 15

"Patron Saint"

Eileen mumbled "Hello?" as she answered the phone that woke her from a sound sleep.

"Wellllll, g'mornin sleepy head," the voice teased.

"Grant, why are you calling me... and why do you sound like you're on the road?"

"Because I am," Grant smarted.

Eileen lost her haziness and said "Wait... you left without me!?"

"Heh heh... I did."

"Great, how the hell am I gonna go anywhere now? Did you at least leave me the keys to the truck?"

Grant had a mile wide smile on his face as he just said "Nope."

"Ya know, baby G... this brotherly protection thing can be a pain in the ass sometimes," Eileen scowled.

"Aw, don't get mad sis! Let's just say... I uh... arranged an alternative form of transportation for you."

"It had better be classy at least," Eileen warned.

Grant kindly asked "Will a BMW do?"

Now Eileen understood.

She smiled like a schoolgirl and said "Nicely, thank you."

Grant told her in a voice that oozed brotherly love "Eileen look, think of this as my way of saying, I approve as well. Just remember, if he makes you happy... tell him. If he doesn't... tell me."

"Love you too, baby G," Eileen said in an equal tone as Grant's.

"I just passed him. Your chariot should await in 5. See ya there!" and Grant hung up.

Girls talk to each other. They also share things. As such, Violet told Eileen about the whole wearing Talon's shirt thing. Eileen was scrambling now, then just laughed at herself.

"WELL! Good for the goose good for the gander right Violet?" Eileen said to the empty house with a laugh.

She ran into Grant's room and just borrowed one of his. When she opened the door for Cody, she got the reaction she was looking for.

"Sorry Doc, I just woke up. Give me a minute to get changed."

"Take... uh... your time. No... no rush," Doc said with a stammer as he enjoyed the view.

"Hmm, maybe I will then. Coffee?" Eileen said slyly as she stopped walking away.

"Don't mind if I do," Cody said with a smile as he, in full sight of Eileen, threw the cup in his hand in the garbage.

"Must be a guy thing," the barefoot Eileen said softly to herself. She smiled at the results however and said "But who cares!" and made some coffee.

An hour later, a black Beemer pulled into the driveway of Eileen's old stomping grounds. For the 'new guy', Eileen's clothes were a tad tighter than usual these days. This was a jeans and sneakers kind of day. Eileen decided to open the house today. Talon told her, even if the cops said something, she's still part owner. And so, with the water running again, and the power company leaving after having turned the power back on... Eileen's new home was ready for a good airing out.

"Kinda seems silly to get this house up and running again for only 3 more days," Eileen stated. "However, I know me. If this house is up and running, I'll be more willing to return." Eileen cooed and said "Of course, having a doctor around, well... that's just a bonus."

"Who is this healer of which thy speak m'lady? Tell me his name so that I may challenge him for the fire haired maiden's hand," Cody smarted.

Eileen joked "Oooooh THAT would be HOT! Can I watch!??"

Cody and Eileen just laughed at the other, and joined the waiting group in the driveway outside the front porch.

Eileen asked as she and Cody walked up "And you're all out here why?"

Talon told her "No one goes in till we pay our respects. Just waiting on you dear, is all."

"Ah, right," Eileen said realizing.

They all walked down a path through an open meadow area, then into a clump of elm trees. Inside that group of trees, was a small family cemetery. Papa Joe loved his home, and wanted to be buried there and nowhere else. It gave their mom comfort to visit him almost daily. When she passed away, none of the children thought of burying her anywhere else. The ranch Eileen inherited had plenty of acres so... in the elm grove they were.

Violet was concerned when they walked up to the pair of headstone crosses.

"Talon? Know that I reeeeeeeeaaaaallly don't mean any disrespect when I say this but... are you sure mom is 'here'?" she asked pointing to his mother's gravestone.

Talon said "I'm not insulted, and yes I'm sure. Why do you ask?"

Violet seemed confused and said "Let me give you all a bit of 'how things are'. Imagine you're on a boat, and you cross a wake. Now, you can't see the boat that made it but, you do know what the wake is right?"

Grant told her "Of course."

Violet continued with "So, the wake, you could say that was residual energy from the original boat. When 'we' leave this world, we leave something like that. Now, imagine I'm the boat that crossed it."

Cody said "Okay, at least I'm with you so far."

Everyone else nodded and Violet continued her observation.

"Well, this one here," and she pointed to Papa Joe's headstone saying "Has left a wake. The rougher the disturbance, the worse the death. This one is calm and peaceful."

Talon was somehow happy for that but he knew Violet. He was almost dreading what he knew was coming.

"Okay Violet, I won't get mad, so just spit it out."

Violet sighed and said "This one confuses me. This one isn't rough nor peaceful... it's missing. That's why I asked. It's as if... wow... I have never felt this ever... it's as if..."

"As if what? Like she never left or something?" Eileen politely prodded her new friend.

Violet had a 'please don't kill me' look on her face, and told them "It's as if... she never existed."

Talon's tone let everyone know he was being cautious. It also let everyone else know, they should be too.

"Tell me Violet, is this sensation a good thing, or a bad thing?"

"If I had to guess? I'd say neither. Think of it like your car. You take out the engine but yet, it still drives you around like it should. No noise nor vibration that you're used to, but the car still behaves perfectly. You know that isn't possible, yet it's happening all the same. It's kind of like that for me. I'll be honest, I've never felt something like this in my life so I can't tell you what to make of it. Just know I meant no harm by telling you, nor meant to upset any of you. I only mentioned it in case it has some bearing on the other mystery we find ourselves in."

Talon gave Violet a hug to show he wasn't upset, then knelt down at his mother's grave.

"Okay, you hippie priestess... what are you up to now?" Talon said only loud enough for just the gravestone to hear.

If someone was to build a replica of what a house in the 70's would look like... this house would be it. Two story farmhouse with ship lap siding and a covered porch on the outside. On the inside however, it was a shag carpet lover's wet dream. Talon's parents were born in the early 70's and always complained they were 'born too late'. Papa Joe bought the house the way it was... and because of the way it is.

Cody joked "I feel like I should be wearing platform shoes, and watching a black and white TV or something."

Grant pranked Cody slightly saying "Do you even know how to work one of these?" he asked handing him something.

Cody was in slight awe and proclaimed "I've never even seen a real one of these."

It was a princess phone... an original 'rotary' princess phone that is.

Violet was confused and asked "How would you know who was calling?"

All 3 Grayson's chuckled at that and Eileen told her "You didn't." Then she laughed towards her brothers and mocked "I mean... can you imagine? You ACTUALLY had to pick it up and say hello!"

Talon feigned insult and said in a dead pan tone "Truly barbaric."

Grant laughed and chimed in with "Oh the horror!"

Violet and Eileen were busy cleaning now. All 3 men though, put in just as much effort. An hour of that, and Eileen complimented Talon for all the work they didn't have to do... because of the great job he had already done. Now, they were all in the living room, and filling Eileen in on all the goings-on till now.

"Wow... okay... that's a lot to absorb," Eileen said with a sort of blank stare. "And you say... Lincoln? As in not the car, but the actual President!?"

"'Tis what Violet said," Talon confirmed.

"Wow" Eileen said honestly. "This is some mystery!" Eileen looked about at present company, laughed, and stated "All we need is a Great Dane named Scooby!"

Grant asked Talon "So, almighty history guru... how does he fit into all of this?"

Talon stated "Only to let us know just who, and what, Lucinda was... and the kind of clients and power she wielded. I have a theory."

Cody smirked saying "I'm all ears... heh heh... 'Shaggy'."

Talon retorted "Shaggy was a stoner, I'll be Fred. No wait... Fred was gay... okay, I'll stick with Shaggy."

Everyone laughed and Talon got serious.

"Okay so, the guard said July 19th 1864. The Civil war was fought from 1861 to 1865. Lincoln was elected in 1860, then again in '64. By late '64 the

Union was finally winning the war. Now, out here you got high-powered people flush with money. It's well known Abe loved his wife, so I doubt he was coming here for Lucinda's services. If I had to guess, with the south starting to lose now, he was likely coming here to either get these guys to help out the Union's cause... or simply keep them out of the fight entirely."

"Sounds about right so far," Cody told him. "As I'd tell any of my students though... got anything to back it up with?"

Talon said "Just history, Doc. Civil War ends in 1865. However, the Trans-continental Railroad completed in 1869. Its construction was made possible by the US Government under the Railroad Acts. Those just happen to be in 1862, '64 and '67. So, with Civil war starting in '61, and the Railroad acts starting only a year later... I'd have to guess Lincoln was not only looking towards the future, but throwing these guys a serious bone to keep them on the Union's side. They were losing at first, badly, so I can only imagine Abe's dilemma. He needs to convince the guys out here to side with the Union, and keep them on his side... or risk losing them to the South. They're not gonna piss off the boys back in DC by taking the South's side in a war that didn't affect them much, and risk losing their lucrative contracts. Add to that, out here those guys are powerful. Back east, however, they're nobodies. That rail line goes through and they extend their power from coast to coast. If it doesn't, or if the North lost, then they could tell the South 'Hey look what we did... let's close the gap!'. Either way, they get what they want or, have enough rail in place to push farther east and bolster against the expansion they knew would come.

So... stick with the North, or just simply do their bidding, they expand their influence and Lincoln gets a hell of a perk for the country when it's all over. He truly loved and believed in this country. I can only guess that with the prejudices that were certain to follow a war like that... having west coasters who had none, would only heal the country faster. He gets a big feather in his cap, and only further chokes out the South. In the end, it was a mutual gamble with each side needing, and playing, the other."

Cody grinned and said "Well... I'd give you an 'A'."

Violet was proud of her man. She also felt a tad intimidated by the surrounding brainiacs. Still, she decided to speak up all the same.

"But if these guys were already in bed with the North, why come here then? No less beckon a President of all people," Violet asked.

Talon explained "Well, people like them need assurances from time to time. It's well believed that the war lasted as long as it did due to the generals the Union had. They were either cowards, incompetent, or both. Not till Lincoln installed General Grant did things start turning in the North's favor. Abe comes, lets them know the leadership problem has been solved, and finally gives a favorable progress report. Also Lucinda's was safe territory, and discretion was her trademark. The mansion gave them access to get Abe in and out unseen. Get him in and get him out, and no one knows he's doing some back end dealing. The big wigs already feel safe here. With what the mansion did for a living, Lucinda's girls offered the perfect diversion."

Eileen called Talon on it saying "Even I know Abe was a telegraph junkie so, why not just make use of that?"

"Easy," he told her. "Those could've been faked. Not to mention the wires didn't come out this far."

Eileen smiled kindly and said "Well then, I'd give you an 'A' too."

Talon kicked back in with "While it all makes sense, it still leaves us with holes. Uncle Lucian's book said Lucinda was killed in November of 1865. Everyone blamed Doc's great granddad but Lucian thought otherwise. We now know it wasn't Henry but, whoever it is, has a serious issue with Cody. My guess would be a rival. Hey Doc?"

"Yeah?"

"Shadow Man said 'you soil your name by even being here'. That's like he cared about that somehow. Henry have any brothers or assistants maybe?"

"Not sure why?" Cody asked.

"Well, we in the modern world know how mentally sick people can make up love affairs that don't exist. Many act on them given time, and not usually in a good way. That would be possible back then, but definitely unheard of. My question is, who would have fallen in love with Lucinda, seen Henry as a threat, yet still cared enough to not want him ruined?"

"Couldn't say. None of the letters mentioned anything like that," Cody told him.

"Yeah," Talon confirmed, "I didn't see anything in them either. Problem is, they're written about secondhand accounts, and only vague ones at that. What we need is something from Henry himself. Lucian spoke to him but never noted down what he said. He only mentioned he found him forthcoming, and didn't appear to be lying, nor hiding anything."

Talon thought a bit and said "Okay, we're missing something. Nothing of the logical adds up. How about we try this? Suppose we stop focusing on what we know. Just like Violet's video... let's stop looking at what we got, and focus on what we're *not* seeing."

Eileen asked him "Such as?"

Gray guy said "Well, we're all focusing on two people... Henry and Lucinda. What if we take either of them out of the equation?"

Violet told the group "I've done that a few times when certain things didn't make sense. What did you have in mind?"

"Well, we keep focusing on two people madly in love. What if Henry was the object of Shadow's desire?"

Cody chuckled and said "Oh this should be good."

Talon told him "Think about it though, Doc. We keep focusing on what we know, and keep ending up nowhere. Let's say someone was in love with Henry... not Lucinda. Or simply idolized him. The one thing all the letters said was that as a doctor, he was brilliant. What if this guy saw Lucinda taking all that away... including his idol? People have killed for less."

"Indeed they have," Cody said somberly as he spoke from experience.

Eileen threw in her 2 cents worth now.

"Listen Tal, these alternatives you just came up with are all plausible. Problem is... any one of them could be correct."

Talon cut in with "Or all of them, but, just a piece of each."

"That too," Eileen confirmed. "Okay, how about this. We got this house as nice as it can be for now. Let's look for this box you mentioned." Eileen spoke to the group and said "I say let's go with all of Talon's theories. Let's get some more clues... fill in some more holes... and see which one of my brother's guesses take shape. Wadda ya say?"

"Sounds like a plan to me," Grant stated.

Everyone else said pretty much the same.

Talon told them "I got one last thing. If the old Doc was truly that good, then consider a rival who moves up as Henry falls from grace."

Eileen asked "I got a question for ya, Violet. I remember mom teaching me some of that 'white witch' stuff. Basically, if mom was correct, Lucinda trapped herself here with unfinished business. Can't bear to leave either her house or Henry. My question is, why is Shadow Man here?"

Violet told her "Remember that wake I mentioned?"

"Mm hmm."

"Well, it also has a sensation. Lucinda's is profound loss, mixed with a sense of 'I didn't deserve this'. Shadow Man however is anger and justice. Mind you, this is only what I sense."

Eileen didn't get it and said so.

Violet told her "Lucinda created her own sensation. Many who pass on do. Shadow however... only created the anger."

Eileen was nearly dazed at that thought and asked "So like what, some higher power saw fit to keep him here? As what... punishment?"

Violet chuckled "Sorry, candlestick, that's a little above my pay grade. Suffice to say, all wakes have a sensation. Most are created by the ghost themselves. The others... well... I couldn't say. There yes... know who created it?...No."

Eileen extolled "Great. So, Shadow Man kills Lucinda. Mom or some higher power sticks him there as punishment for his crime. Now he's like, what... pissed that he got caught?"

"Pretty much," Violet confirmed.

"Greeeeeaaaaaatttt," Eileen said in an exasperated tone.

"Well gang, if Talon hasn't found this box, then that means mom hid it. No one knew her better than me. Mom had only a few hiding spots and I checked them all... nada." She looked at Talon and told him "You and dad didn't always see eye to eye. Mostly because you were two peas in a pod. Like it or not, you think just like him. Act it too. Now, I know mom. If she thought this box was that important, she would've asked dad to hide it for her. Likely not tell her where either."

Talon was a tad annoyed at the reference, but said "I'll accept that observation to a point. His values yes. His method of going about them no. Dad would find an answer to something and then that was the gospel. He NEVER accepted that there may be more than one, whereas I did. I saw a man, with less than a high school education, do the New York Times crossword puzzle... *in pen*... and in under ten minutes."

Cody whistled low and asked "Ten minutes?"

"In pen," Talon confirmed with a hint of pride in his dad. "He was the most brilliant... and stubborn... man I ever knew. Aside from that, I concede your point. Now, assuming you're right, dad would have put it somewhere clever... yet accessible in case mom asked for it. If mom said it was important, then he would've treated it like a brick of gold. Knowing dad, he'd put it in plain sight and take great delight in you not seeing it, but someplace where he would know if anything was disturbed. Only one place I can think of like that," Talon finished with a smirk.

"THE WORKSHOP!" Eileen and Grant bellowed in unison.

Talon just smiled and said "Mm hmm."

Papa Joe's workshop was his sanctuary. Not a single day went by that he didn't go in there for something. The 5 of them, respectfully, scoured the place.

Nothing. They checked under tables. They checked for drawers with false bottoms, cabinets that weren't as deep as others, but 90 minutes of searching only turned up everyone's aggravation level.

"Damn. And I was so sure it was here somewhere," Grant stated.

"I still am," Talon said with conviction. "Okay, workshop, but it's not here. What am I missing?" Talon closed his eyes and said "Okay, I'm dad. I gotta hide something for mom but always keep an eye on it." He was thinking like his dad as best he could and continued, "We turned everything upside down but came up empty. Grant gave up and that's exactly what dad would've wanted, from anyone. So... it's here... but it's not here. It's in plain sight... but hidden. C'mon Talon, think man think!”

He wasn't having much luck... until Violet came back from going to the bathroom. Then it hit him, and he beamed.

“HA HA! Oh, you slick bastard you!” Talon declared as a compliment to his father. “We can't find it because it's not IN the shop. Tell me, what did dad do everyday?” he queried.

“He came here!” Eileen said in an annoyed tone. “But we looked 'here'... and 'here' is where it ain't!”

“Exactly,” Talon stated. “Okay, you said dad came here. He did. You're problem is you're not thinking basic enough. Come to the shop, and you have to leave. Just like your favorite burger shop, Eileen... if you come in... then ya hafta go out. It's AT the shop... but not IN it. C'mon!”

Talon ran out and scanned the house.

“Okay, mom and dad's bedroom was there,” Talon said pointing to the corner of the house. “Everyone knew dad came in here. Dad was smart enough to know that too. He also knew if someone ever came looking for it, like we did, this would be the first place they'd check. Trust me, it's out here somewhere AND!... In sight of that window.”

Now everyone was looking around where Talon said to.

“Violet, show me with your hands. How big is this thing?”

“I told you, about the size of the ones ya keep fancy silverware in.”

Talon said “Oh yeah that's right. Okay so, about 14 inches wide by 10 deep and 4 high. We're looking for something that would hold a box that big.”

Everyone started looking around with a renewed vigor.

“Violet? Any of your special friends got anything for us?” Grant asked.

“Nope. This house isn't like Talon's. I've already 'reached out to them' being that they can get onto this property. Big fat load of nothing. Sorry.”

Talon was certain he was right, he just had to figure it out.

“Ha ha ha... like I said... slick, dad, real slick.”

Talon believed he just had.

“Hello, Joseph. I promise, I'll be as gentle as I can,” Talon said with a grin as he stared at the statue. “Saint Joseph... patron saint of carpenters and craftsmen. Like I said, my dad was brilliant.”

Cody came over and said “But that statue is too small for a box like that.”

“True,” Talon confirmed. “But the base is big enough. It blew over one day and dad was pissed. He sat it on a concrete base he made. The years have sunk it but trust me, it's under there. Dad changed colors of the outside, and rearranged the inside several times. The one thing that never changed however...

was good ole Joseph here. Dad used to say, besides mom, he was the only other angel looking out for him."

Grant ran off to his truck to get some tools. Eileen just walked up beside Talon with a kind smile.

"Told you you were like him," she said sweetly.

Grant wasn't sure what they'd need, so he just drove his truck over. Talon told him to turn it around. Once he had, Talon hooked a tow strap to it. Grant drove slow, and the statue leaned over. It strained a bit, as if the ground didn't want to give up its secrets. Grant's truck however convinced it otherwise.

Baby G felt the tension on his truck go away, and he put it in park. Behind it, St. Joseph was lying face up. Just as Talon said, there was a square concrete base attached to the bottom. Talon took the tow strap off, and stood it upright. Grant had an D/C to A/C converter in his truck, and fired up an electric hand grinder. He cut carefully around the base till he got the two separated. Talon lifted it up and smiled.

"Well sonuvabitch... nice going guys!" Eileen said with pride in her brothers.

Just like Talon thought, the big square base was hollow. Inside it was a wooden box. Talon took it out carefully, and showed it to Violet.

"Yep, that's it," Violet confirmed.

Everyone but Talon was let down when they saw the contents.

"Aw man, all that work for that!? It's just a bunch of old aluminum sheets. And rusted ones at that!" Grant said in a tone that said out loud what everyone else was feeling. All but Talon. He was smiling from ear to ear.

"Tin... actually."

"Aluminum... tin... who fucking cares! There's nothing in there but those metal plates and an old ceramic doll!"

"Grant? These are photographs. Very, very early ones. Before photos went to paper, the images were burned onto a piece of tin. The conditions in the base ruined them but... heh heh... I'm betting I know someone who can help."

Talon made a call and chuckled at the answer he got. It was a live person talking as if they were a recording.

"Erik the Viking here. Sorry I can't take your call right now. Just leave a message and when the crazy gray-haired guy unlocks the ball and chain, I'll get back to you."

Talon smirked saying "I considered tar and feather but hey, you're a friend so I took it easy on you."

"Ha ha ha, what's up old friend?"

"Erik, how good are you with tin-types?"

"How bad off are they?"

Talon answered "Image gone, each one has about 50% rust on them."

Erik replied "Pfff... about 5 minutes each. Can they wait? I'll be back down in a few days to start on the second floor. I can get them from you then."

Talon put his hand over his phone and told the group "Three days."

Everyone said they didn't care and that it was no big deal to them.

"That'll do fine my friend. See ya then!"

Erik told him "Talon, wait. I have your rendering. I'll be emailing you the color tints and chemical makeups later today. Colors are what you'd expect but the lacquers were some serious high end custom blends. Some you might not be able to replicate but, I thought you should know."

"Thanks, Erik," Talon told him and hung up the phone.

Talon put everything back in the box, walked to his truck, and wrapped it in plastic same as he did Lucinda's portrait. With their new found clues safely locked in the toolbox, Eileen locked up the house, and everyone headed out to the mansion.

They finished up the day over there and for a change, Cody invited them to his place for dinner. He told them with this latest revelation, seeing the house where it all began seemed like a good idea.

Cody winked at Talon and told him "I even got Kona."

Talon and Grant laughed as Eileen said "Oh please... not you too."

Mansion locked up for the night, everyone headed out and followed Doc Holliday. A long day was followed by a very pleasant evening, and Talon was on cloud 9 feeling like he was one step closer to solving this mystery.

When the sun finally set... Papa Joe's protector was right back where they found him.

Chapter 16

"An Ex-Mormon... And A Ghost Made Real"

"Honestly baby G... it's a wonder you're not bankrupt," Eileen reprimanded slightly the way only a big sister can. "Your financials are a mess!"

Eileen was going over Talon's and Grant's business cash flows, just to make sure they were okay. Talon sucked at large scale money management, and so did his brother. Difference between them was, Talon hired a good 'bean counter'... Grant didn't.

"Baby G, look... I'm not gonna yell at you, but if you keep this up much longer, you're gonna be as old as that mansion before you straighten everything out."

"Okay, I admit it, I'm no 'you' when it comes to the large scale dollars. Question though is... can you fix it?"

Eileen was pulling out papers, putting them down and pulling out others, and got more exasperated as she did.

"Honestly? Not in the time I have left. Look, I'm gone day after tomorrow... tell ya what... I'll get what I can sorted so you can last till end of June. That way I, and you, get some breathing room till I get back and can straighten out this quagmire."

Grant hugged his sister with a soft smile and said "Thanks, sis."

Eileen was annoyed her brother would get to this state, but kindly told him "You're lucky I only cranked on ya for the state of your money. (chuckle) DON'T EVEN get me started on this utter mess you call an office!"

"HEY!" Grant barked with a hearty laugh, "At least I know where everything is!"

Eileen snickered at him and joked "Typical man."

Grant bowed to her with a boyish grin and headed out to the mansion.

Cody came and picked up Eileen like he had the other day. He was doing that everyday now. He wanted all the time he could get with her before she left.

Today was his turn to show off. He had patients to see at his office, then at the hospital. He proudly introduced Eileen at each place, and all the nurses and office staff had smiles on their faces as they met her. Most were happy to see the semi-famous 'Doc Holliday' finally find a companion other than his work. The rest had polite smiles but were a tad annoyed it wasn't them. They were also a tad annoyed, as only a girl can get, at the lovely red-haired powerhouse on his arm. Their faces showed forced smiles that said "Nice to meet you," but they were hiding scorns of "How the hell do I compete with that!?" Eileen made nice to all of them however, and pretty much 'wowed' the crowd.

Doc finished up his rounds and he and Eileen made it to the mansion just after lunch.

Abigail was, in a ghostly sense, bugging Grant. Everywhere he turned... there she was holding a baby. Walking across the end of a hallway and into a wall... showing up in the not too far off distance... stuff like that.

A dirty-blond-haired girl, sporting some slightly nerdy glasses, hopped into a taxi from her motel in Reno, and made her way to a destiny she didn't know she had.

"Where to miss?" the driver asked.

"Adair House please," she said kindly.

"Where's that?"

She sighed a little, reached into her purse, and handed him a piece of paper.

"What's this?"

"Coordinates to Adair House," she said in a tone only a techno-geek could have when addressing a techno-dummy.

"Coordinates!? This is a taxi, lady... not the Queen Mary." He caught her attitude and teased her saying "Got something a little more normal... like, say... an address? Ya know... something us 'lesser humans' can actually use."

She got a tad huffy and asked "Don't you have a GPS?" She caught the slight British accent on the man and said "Or perhaps you know it as a SatNav?"

"Like I said lady, got an address?" the driver said in a slightly annoyed tone.

The young lady huffed, and pulled out her own phone. Technically, that was a 'toy' she wasn't supposed to have. She punched in the coordinates and said "Here... just follow this," and she handed him her phone.

The driver got even more annoyed now.

"Oh Jesus Christ! THAT place again!?"

"Problem, driver?"

"Let's just say, I'll take you to the driveway... and that's it," and the man started off. He handed the blond her phone back saying "Thanks, lady, but I got it from here."

Turns out, it was the same driver who took a violet-eyed girl there not so long ago.

"Okay... even with all I know now... yeeeaaahhh, that's still creepy," Eileen told Grant as they took a break on the porch.

Grant was a little confused and asked "What is?"

"Oh... I dunno... perhaps the lady over there holding the baby? You know, the one that walked right out of a mound of dirt... then just happened to walk right INTO the other one?" Eileen smarted.

"You saw that!?" Grant asked happily.

"Of course I did."

"Wow," Grant said low, "She's been appearing only to me mostly. Not even Violet knew she was around most times."

"She hid from Violet!? Yeah okay, that just makes it even more creepy."

Grant, in a rather annoyed tone, just agreed and said "Tell me about it."

Eileen asked "Who is she? No wait... don't tell me... um... Abigail? I get that right?"

Eileen was trying to remember who was who from the stories she had gotten. She figured if she was going to hang around this place... AND avoid Shadow Man... then she was going to be as versed in this place as her brothers and Cody were.

Grant smiled and said "The one and only."

Eileen was kind to Grant and said "Baby G, let me tell ya something. As a woman, I can tell ya... sometimes we like to be sly. Ya know, say one thing... but mean another. Normally not in a nasty way. We just like to be playful sometimes. That said, I can tell ya, even I have no idea what she means by the baby is 'for' you.

Grant replied in the same tone "The other night when Violet stayed with me, we talked about that. Given her kind of 'insights', I thought perhaps we might figure something out."

"End result?" Eileen asked truly wanting to know.

Back in an annoyed tone again, Grant said "Big fat load o'nothin."

Eileen shifted gears now and asked him "Okay baby G, just between you and me. What do you think of her? And... what do you think of her and Tal?"

Grant smiled and decided to give his sister a little insight into the male psyche. Eileen was always doing that. She was never mean or condescending, but many times she had a tone in her voice like Grant or Talon didn't know something, and it was her job to 'enlighten' them to the ways of the world. He and his brother always found it annoying. So, both men just starting doing it right back.

"When Violet came out I thought I was looking at a supermodel. When Talon saw her, heh heh... as we 'guys' say... she really twisted his shorts."

Grant paused a few moments while some workers walked in and out. A lot of the guys play-flirted with Eileen. Seeing her act like a female version of the boss, only endeared her to them. She thought it nice that they found her attractive, and usually gave back what she got. She also thought it cute seeing Cody get all protective when they did. Still, no one got out of line and Eileen just thought it fun, and a nice way to work through the day. Alone once again, Grant continued.

"There's a different feel to him lately though," Grant said.

"Him who... Talon?"

"Mm hmm. When he was with Sarah, he had a certain confidence to him. The kind that only comes with familiarity. With Violet it's different. It's like, he knows how to be him... but not how to be him and her. Honestly? I think that'll pass the longer they're together."

Eileen confirmed "Yeah, like, it'll take him awhile to get his rhythm."

Grant said "I agree. Still, he's my bro. As such and, as much as I like Violet, it was her I kept my eye on. Just so you know... I no longer do. All I ever see, is her truly caring for him... and us by default. I give what I get. As far as I'm concerned, Violet has been nothing but sweet and kind to me too. I've sensed nothing to make me believe it's anything but genuine."

Eileen smiled and said "Good to hear, little brother."

Grant chuckled and said "And what about you and the Doc!?"

Eileen smiled but asked "What about us?"

Grant wasn't letting Eileen off the hook that easy.

"Yep... that's what I asked alright," he said with a smirk that just said 'don't play that game with me'.

Eileen chuckled knowing she was caught.

"Yeah yeah, okay. Honestly though, I was gonna ask you and Tal."

Grant looked a bit confused and asked "Ask us what?"

"Well, I know you haven't known him long but... it's still longer than I have. I've seen enough bad men lately, and had even worse dates, to know a good one when I see one."

Grant stiffened some and queried "Wadda ya mean?"

Eileen saw his posture and said "No no, lil brother, nothing like that. Honestly? He scares me a little. He's everything I've ever wanted in a man. Not rich but not poor either. Good looking yet not arrogant. Talented by his own hand... I mean... it's like he's TOO perfect. Well, for me anyway. I keep feeling like something bad is gonna happen or turn up, but, it never does."

Grant relaxed and asked "Is that why you canceled that date you promised him?"

"Oh please... I was petrified to tell him. I thought he would hit the roof or something. Then I realized that was exactly what I needed. So I did."

Grant asked "And?"

Eileen looked almost confused and said "And... he didn't. To be fair though, I told him how I felt. I also told him when I come back in a few weeks, I'd give him two. I felt like, those few weeks would let us know how we truly felt about each other."

Grant inquired "Okay, sounds reasonable enough. What did Doc say about it when ya told him?"

"He understood," Eileen said still not believing Cody didn't throw a temper tantrum. "He said it was wise and, if that's what I wanted, then he could, and would, easily give it to me. The fact that I promised him two dates he felt was a fair trade off."

Grant chuckled and said "Okay, nothing about that sounds the least bit scary to me."

"Nor me. It's just, shall we say, not what I've become accustomed too. Sometimes I'm afraid I'll lose him. I'm afraid to go too far too fast... and I'm afraid to not go far enough. Honestly, brother of mine, I've never had a guy like him before and quite frankly? I'm not sure what to do most times."

Grant was kind and said "I like your plan. For what it's worth, I think Doc is lucky enough to have you. From what I've dealt with so far from him... I'd say the same is true in reverse. Take the 2 week break, see how you feel, and just get over your nerves. I'll lay odds... that's all it is... nerves."

Eileen hugged Grant and said "Thanks, baby G," and they both headed back inside and back to work.

It was an hour later when a blond girl finally worked up the nerve to go up the driveway. The taxi driver left her right where he said he would. She had been dreaming of this since she was a child. Some nights... literally.

It took her 40 minutes to work up the nerve. When she finally did walk under the arched iron sign, she almost turned around, several times. In her nerdy mind she was making a bold move. She had been researching this for as long as she could remember. Now it was real. She was here... she was really here. She stopped outside the double front doors, and was just about ready to run.

"Sounds like they're busy. I... I... I'll just come back another time," she said aloud to herself.

She was about to do just that, when a handsome, gray-haired man came out and stopped her.

"Oh hi, Abigail," Talon said walking right past her and over to his truck.

A stunned and painfully shy girl just waved with a confused look on her face as he passed by.

"I like the longer hair... that's a good look for you but... what's with the glasses?" Talon asked as he got some stuff from his truck.

"Tal!? Hold on a second... I also need..." and the red-haired lady said sideways as she bolted after the other guy "... Oh hi, Abigail," almost as an afterthought. "What's with the glasses by the way?"

"Uh... I kinda need them to see?" was all she could manage.

Years of dreaming, and wishing, and digging and hoping... and that was her introduction.

Talon stopped what he was doing and asked "You're joking right?"

"Actually... she's not," the woman called out leaning on the pole that held up the porch roof.

The blond girl got even more confused by the lady with the amazing purple eyes.

"Mind cluing us in?" Eileen asked standing beside her brother.

"That's because this one... heh heh... is real," Violet declared.

Violet had been around the dead long enough to know the living. She was standing by the doorway admiring Talon when he wasn't looking. She saw the blond girl and decided to check out the new goings-on.

Talon and Eileen were slowly circling her and it made her quite nervous.

Talon looked at Violet, nearly laughed, and asked "No shit!?"

Violet actually did laugh and confirmed "No shit."

Talon took one quick look at her, then back to Violet.

"Get Grant," Talon commanded.

Violet chuckled, threw a playful salute, and told him "Yes sir, Mr. Grayson, sir!" and still laughing walked back into the mansion.

The blond girl finally uttered "How did you know my name?"

"OH NO SHIT!?" Eileen bellowed with a smile, "Your name is really Abigail as well!!!?"

"That... uh... a problem?" the blond girl said utterly confused.

Talon stood up, composed himself, and said very kindly "Not a problem at all, Abigail. My apologies for our rude behavior but... ya see... we already know someone by that name. She also happens to look like you... a LOT like you. My name is Talon... Talon Grayson... and this is my sister Eileen. I own this mansion."

"Abigail Jensen, Mister Grayson... a pleasure to meet you," Abigail said honestly but meekly. "And you, Ms. Grayson," she said to Eileen.

Violet didn't say a word and had a rather annoyed Grant on her heels.

"Okay, what the hell is........ so........ important that......you...... Abigail?"

Grant stammered as he caught sight of the latest arrival.

Abigail turned and, the moment she laid eyes on Grant, was a story she would tell for the rest of her life. He would tell a similar one for the rest of his.

Call it fate, call it kismet, call it good old fashioned love at first sight. Whatever your choice... Grant and Abigail were it. They were staring at each other like two lost lovers.

Talon broke Grant's stare with a kind hand on his shoulder and said "Well, I guess we now know what she meant by 'for' you, huh buddy?"

Talon knew in an instant the moment he saw Abigail. The real one that is. That's why he asked for his brother. The original Abigail caught Grant's eye. She was off in the distance behind the trucks. She had the most glorious smile on her face. She looked straight at Grant, proper curtsied... and faded away.

"Abigail? I'd like to introduce you to my brother Grant," Talon said still leaning on Grant's shoulder.

"A pleasure to meet you," Abigail said lost in a dream.

"The pleasure is all mine I assure you," Grant said in a similar tone.

Talon walked inside a moment, and walked right up to Lucinda's photo.

"Just what we need, just when we need it, eh Lucinda?" Talon stared a moment then just said "Thanks, lady."

A soft whisper of a voice answered him "Ah looked out faw mah girls then... and ah still do."

Talon looked over his shoulder at Grant. Baby G was still sporting a smiling but glazed look on his face. Talon looked back at the photo once more and said "Miss Adair?... Thank you... we'll take it from here."

He tipped his baseball cap to the photo, turned, and rejoined the group on the porch.

Talon called Abigail up onto the porch. Doc had come down from doing some forensic sweeps on the safe areas of the second floor. He was coming to tell of his latest finds, when he found 'the gang' out on the porch.

"Oh I didn't see you... heh heh... but maybe that was the point. Anyway, hello, Abigail," Cody said in a friendly manner.

"Okay, I don't mind telling you, the fact that you all seem to know me is creeping me out juuuuuuust a little bit."

Doc was about to say something but Talon cut him off with a chuckle and a grin.

"Yo Doc... ha ha ha... before you need your surgical skills to remove your foot from your mouth... this one," and he waved to Abigail and told him "This one is live, not Memorex."

"Oh NO SHIT!" Doc said happily. "The resemblance is remarkable!"

"So I've been told," Abigail said warily.

"My apologies, my dear. Ya just sorta caught me off guard is all. My name is Cody Holliday."

"Abigail Jensen," she said nicely. "Pleased to meet you Doct... wait... doctor......DOC Holliday!?" she said giggling at her own realization.

Jokingly and with a ton of flair, Cody gave her a grandiose, sweeping armed, gentlemanly bow.

"Often imitated, never duplicated. And yes, Doc Holliday I am... at your service," Cody said smiling as he took a seat next to Eileen.

"So Abigail, I hear a New England accent. What brings you all the way out here?" Talon queried.

"New Hampshire actually," she answered.

Talon grinned and said "Last map I looked at... that would qualify as New England."

Abigail giggled and said "Kinda still there too. We thought of moving it once but, well, it got voted down," she said with a chuckle.

She wasn't sure who this guy was but, she did like his sense of humor. Also, as the owner, if she was gonna get any possible answers, then keeping him happy was key.

Talon took his hat off and brushed a hand through his hair. He put it back on but Abigail had caught sight of the silver locks.

"Holy crap! You're the not-so-old old guy!" she rather blurted out when she saw the color of his hair.

"Ha ha ha... I've been called worse," Talon said meaning it.

"Oh I'm so sorry, I didn't mean... I mean............ sorry, Mr. Grayson."

Talon waved a hand "Oh, call me Talon." Then he got serious and said "How about, you tell us why a dilapidated mansion brings a pretty girl like you from lobster country all the way out to tumbleweed territory. Oh... and while you're at it... feel free to include the story of how you acquired that lovely ankle jewelry on your left leg."

Talon was the only one who noticed it too.

Abigail was a little sad, and a little afraid, and said "I will but, I hafta warn ya, it's a tad bizarre."

Violet laughed and said "Oh, I think you'll find... 'bizarre'... is something we do rather well around here."

Abigail was still sad and said "That's a first. Most don't usually laugh till after I tell the story." Abigail took a gamble and asked Talon "I'll give you what you ask for, if you'd be willing to give me something in return?"

Talon didn't know why, but, he liked this new girl. He thought her cute. Grant however was still staring like a little puppy.

"Depends on what you ask for," he said in a rather business-like tone.

"If it's alright with you, I'd like to see the inside please. I would also like you to be my escort. When you hear my story, you'll know why I ask."

Talon smiled "Consider your wish granted. However, many areas are not structurally sound yet. For obvious reasons, those are off limits. Otherwise, I'll be happy to trade you one guided tour for one story."

Abigail went from nerdy nervous, to happy camper, in an instant. "Deal!"

Abigail took a deep breath and prepared to tell her story... when she went almost ADD on Talon. His phone 'binged' him. He took it out, read the text from Erik, and put it away. When he looked back up, he laughed. Abigail was staring straight at his hip from only a foot away.

"WHOA! Is that the new Isis 7!?" she asked now completely sidetracked by the shiny toy.

"Nope... heh heh... it's the 9."

Abigail had a scour face on saying "There isn't a 9. The 7's only came out last month."

Talon smirked and told her "There is a 9... when you're friends with Mister Sakamora," he said slyly.

"Whoa! YOU know the CEO of CelTek!!??" Abigail asked totally enthralled by the tech. "Does it have the optical security lockout!!??" she asked all excited.

"Expandable RAM, and 3D holo display, projector capabilities, and satellite ready," Talon said with a chuckle over her sudden focus shift.

"The holo thing is buggy. I came up with a fix for that like 3 years ago and I could totally clean that up for you and..."

"Abigail?... Story," Talon said as part warning, part friendly reminder.

"Oh yeah... sorry," Abigail said realizing she just 'geeked out'.

Talon just laughed, looked at Grant, and said "Cell phone, one... blatantly staring brother?... Zero."

"Huh? You say something?" Grant said partially coming out of his fog.

The whole crowd, except Abigail, just laughed at him.

A buzz cut, clean looking, brunette left his motel and headed back to the train station. He needed a cab, the station was only 2 blocks away, and at least 10 of them were lined up there. It was a fine day, so he walked to the station and looked the central city over as he went.

He had no idea why but, the closer he got, the more an odd feeling crept over him. It was a feeling like he was being watched. He got to the station and was heading for the first taxi in line, when the feeling got stronger. As such, and not knowing why, he went to the third one instead.

"Sorry, young man," the driver told him, "We go in order. Try the first cab."

"Something tells me, you're the man for the job though," Zack told him.

The driver called out to the one at the front "Hey Louie, mister crew cut here wants a ride... ya mind?"

"Nah, yer good," he called back.

"Thanks, bud!" the taxi driver called out as Zack got in. "Okay pal, where to?"

"Ever hear of a place called 'Adair House'?"

"Oh sonuvabitch!"

"That a problem?" Zack asked him.

"Kid? To answer your original question... I'm likely the only cabbie around here who has!" and he pulled away from the curb.

Zack thought he heard a woman laughing. Not just any woman, but one with a southern accent. He saw nothing so just shrugged it off and took in the view as he rode along. That 'woman' was devilishly playful on the driver for treating Violet so poorly. With her power growing daily, she decided to give the slightly rude cabbie 'what for'.

He took Zack where he wanted to go. It took 20 minutes from town to get there. As he got closer, a blond at his destination was telling her story.

"So, the dreams started when I was around six," Abigail began, "And lasted till I was about nine. There were 2 dreams really, well, more like 2 different versions of the same one."

"Nightmares?" Grant said in a rather protective tone.

Eileen just grimaced at her baby brother and shook her head.

"Sorry," Abigail continued, "Nothing so exciting as that. They seemed more like those boring history videos you watched in high school. Not that I dislike history or anything... or that it's a problem if you do or don't... it's just that if you did, or didn't well then I...."

"Aaaaaaabigaaaaaiiilll," Talon sang kindly correcting her runaway diatribe.

Abigail giggled, but truly meant it when she said "Sorry, I kinda do that sometimes. Mostly when I'm nervous."

Violet was kind and could relate to Abigail somewhat.

"Abigail? Try this. Do you do any public speaking? Even in a small group?"

Abigail imitated her peers as she snidely said "Oh hey look... it's the nerd girl... ha ha ha." She looked at Violet and said "As you can likely guess, not really."

Grant kicked in with "Prettiest 'nerd girl' I ever saw."

That really threw Abigail off, but she meekly said "Thank you."

This crowd was different from the one's back home. She really had no idea how to act around them, but tried her best to come out of her shy little cocoon as best she could.

"I do write a blog though," she answered Violet.

Violet smiled, stood up, and took Abigail by the hand. She walked her off the porch and down onto the driveway.

"Okay Abigail, now, you stay right here. Guys and gal? Can I have an audience please?" Violet asked calling up to the porch.

Everyone swung around, sat on the railing, and stared at Violet.

"There Abigail. Now, just imagine they're your readers!" purple girl said with a kind expression.

Eileen joked aloud "Ooh ooh... can I have one of those cool nickname thingies!?"

"Sure... 'candlestick'," Talon taunted playfully.

"Heh heh... watch it 'not-so-old old guy'," she jibed right back.

Violet said "Actually, that's a good idea. Okay, we already have 2 nicknames. I'll be 'purple haze'."

Cody raised his hand and said "Doc Holliday here!"

Grant said "I'll be 'The Contractor'."

Talon laughed at him saying "Yo dude... ya sound like a hit-man." He looked at Abigail out in the driveway and said "Just call him 'ginjuh chyld'."

Everyone on the porch... but not the driveway... heard a polite, southern drawl-infused, giggle.

Normally, Abigail would be sweating bullets by now. Somehow though, she thought it cool. She also, very much so, noticed how comfortable she seemed to be around these strangers. As such, she told her tale.

Abigail gave a polite and playful curtsy, and said "Welcome to the story of 'me'... by 'Abby Gale'," she told the crowd.

That was actually the nickname she used for her blog, and she said so.

"So, as I was saying, I started having dreams. I would be escorted by a guy with very gray hair. He was nice but odd... because he was young."

"Not-so-old 'old' guy. Got it," Talon interjected.

"Exactly," Abigail confirmed. "To be fair, Talon, that isn't an insult. I was six after all, and it was the only way I could describe him. Sorry but, the name kinda stuck."

"Not to worry," Talon said nicely.

"Anyway, he would take me up the stairs, like some sort of tour guide. Sometimes the house I see, is the wreck that it is now. Sometimes it was in pristine shape. Always the same thing... he would take me up the stairs, then down a hallway. There were lots of rooms but only on the left side. Also, it was always the third room he took me too. He would wave a hand, as if to say I should go in. Inside there was a grown woman but, she looked like me. She was always sitting at a small desk with a mirror on it, and brushing her hair. She would stop when she saw me, give me a hug, and tell me I was special to her. She always smiled at me, told me I was pretty, then just faded away."

Talon smiled and said "Nice story... so far. Now, how about that ankle bracelet?"

Abigail sort of whined and asked "Do I have to stand here? It's really hot."

Eileen laughed at the cuteness of it and said "Nah, you're good."

Abigail went back up onto the porch. Her audience... still sitting on the railing... just turned around.

"Well, now that you know that, understand that was the beginning. I told my mom about the dreams. That's when she told me a secret. She said I was adopted. She told me that might have been my real mother."

"Awful young to tell a child something like that," Cody said with slight concern in his voice.

"I agree. However, in my mom's defense, she and my dad were going over my adoption papers shortly before I told her of my dreams. She thought I saw them and decided to tell me, rather than have me figure it out wrongly as only a 9- year-old likely would."

Cody eased up some saying "Okay, that makes a little more sense."

Abigail said "She and my dad love me... and I them. They promised they wouldn't lie to me and they didn't. I was, to put it mildly, a tad shy back then. I didn't have many friends... still don't. I found my dad's cell phone one day and it fascinated me like nothing else ever did. It had a habit of just shutting off on him randomly, and it kind of pissed him off. I don't know why but, I wanted to know everything about it. How it worked, how it was built, everything! So, I took it apart."

Grant chuckled and said "I'll bet he must have loved that when he saw it."

Abigail said flatly "No, he was furious. He told me I was grounded till I put it back exactly as it was. I went on the family computer and researched soldering. I found a loose wire and figured I'd lock it back down. Turns out it was one of the power wires. Two hours later... my dad was stunned when I handed it back as requested... and I wasn't grounded anymore. Ever since then, computers have sorta been my thing. They make sense to me... they DON'T make fun of me... and I just feel comfortable around them."

Abigail smiled at Talon and told him "I haven't forgotten your request. To know the answer though, you needed that other stuff first."

Talon nodded and said "Abigail? Watch this." Talon looked at Eileen and asked "You in the mood to tease the blond over here?"

Eileen knew what he was doing, smiled, and said "Nah... I'm good."

"Doc? You?"

"Heh heh... nope... I'm good as well."

Talon asked with a smile "Violet?"

She looked at Abigail and said "I give what I receive, Abigail. Fair to say, if you don't tease me... then I won't tease you either."

Talon stated "I know I won't. Grant? How bout you?"

"Helllllllll no."

Talon smiled at Abigail and told her "Well blondie... there ya go then."

Abigail was stunned. Pleasantly so... but stunned all the same.

"I'm sorry, Mister Grayson, but I'm afraid if I tell you the rest, you may not give me my tour you promised. May I?" She asked holding her hand out.

Talon took it and followed her lead. She had him stand in the doorway, then walked off the porch and onto the driveway again. She turned around and stared at Talon.

"This is how it always started. Me here and you there inviting me in."

Talon smiled, held a hand towards the parlor, and asked "Abigail Jensen, won't you come in?"

Abigail was shaking now, but managed "I'd love to, thank you."

She walked past Talon and into the parlor and was absolutely floored. It was her dream.

"How is this possible!? I've never been here in my life... and yet I've seen this room a thousand times!" Abigail stated.

"Oh... I think you'll find this house has quite a few tricks up its sleeve," Violet said kindly from behind Abigail.

The gang let her enter first, then followed her and Talon. Talon held his hand out, and Abigail gently took it. Next, he led her up the stairs. The second floor was unsafe past the fourth room but, Abigail only needed the third one.

Just like in the dream she described moments ago, Talon said nothing... and merely held out his hand and bid her to enter the room she dreamed of so many times. The moment she did, the door slowly closed. Everyone in the hallway heard the lock tumble.

"We'll be downstairs when you're done!" Talon shouted through the door.

Everyone filed back downstairs. The only reason they did though, is because Violet confirmed it wasn't Shadow Man who locked the door.

"HEY! LET ME OUTTA HERE!" Abigail hollered as she banged on the door. "What kind of sick joke is this!?"

"Oh my word... look at you... you're beautiful," was the kind voice behind Abigail.

She turned to see who the voice was. As she did, the room seemed to follow her vision. As she looked, the room changed from the water damaged wreck, to original condition. When she stopped, she nearly had a heart attack. She found herself staring at a room with a bed, a small desk with a mirror just like in her dream... and an occupant that wasn't her. Well, it kinda was.

Abigail was looking at a room that restored itself, on its own, in seconds. The voice belonged to a woman who, was the lady from Abigail's childhood dream. She was staring at a woman who was a few years older, but only a few. Shorter hair and styled differently, and no glasses. Otherwise, Abigail was staring at a mirror image of herself.

"Okay I get it. This is some sort of illusion and..." Abigail stated trying to make sense of what just happened.

"I assure you," ghost Abigail said as she walked right into real Abigail. "This is an illusion... just not the kind you think it is."

Real Abigail heard the woman's voice like it was inside her head. That's because it was. She felt a sense of love so powerful that it was almost overwhelming.

Ghost Abigail stepped out knowing she got her point across, and asked "Does that answer you're question... or offer you the proof you require?"

Real Abigail was in tears.

"You DO exist! I knew IT!" she hollered. "Tell me... I have to know... who are you?"

"Oh I think you know that already, my beautiful child."

"But... but... that's not possible!" real Abigail hollered out.

"And yet... here I am." Ghost Abigail told her guest "I must leave soon. Before I do, know this. I helped you all I can. Now, the rest, is up to you. I saw how Mister Grant looked at you. I also saw how you looked at him. He is a good man and even Miss Lucinda likes him. You've dug into your past haven't you, my dear?"

"I... I... I have. It's why I'm here."

Ghost Abigail was kind and said "Then you've seen what I have seen. I only guided you here, nothing more. Your beauty, and your talents with those fancy machines, are all your own. Get to know Grant. If it's right, then, end our little family curse once and for all."

Ghost Abigail put her hands on real Abigail's shoulders. The latter felt like somebody put ice packs on her.

"You are more beautiful than you believe... and more talented than you give yourself credit for. Remember that always. The parents who love you always will but, here, you will not know the taunts of the bullies of your youth."

Ghost Abigail sat down and brushed her hair. Real Abigail never turned around when she heard the door open behind her.

"No, please, don't leave... there's so much I wanna ask you!"

"You have answers from the past. The good folk downstairs have what you lack. Together, you will get all the answers you will ever need."

Abigail sneezed and closed her eyes for only a moment. When she opened them, the room was back to the way it was when she entered it.

"NO! COME BACK!" Abigail wailed. She stared at an empty room, cried, and said "Goodbye............ grandma Abigail."

She turned and went back down the stairs. The Abigail that went down them however, was not the same one that went up them moments ago. Years of taunting, teasing, and near crippling self doubt and shyness....... gone in a flash.

Abigail was near furious when she went onto the porch. She marched right up to Talon... and slapped him hard.

"Bring her back! And I mean like RIGHT now!" Abigail commanded.

"Or what?" Talon challenged.

Talon didn't know what happened behind that door, none of them did, but he could take a fair guess. It was because of that, that he overlooked her current attitude. He remembered he had a similar one himself.

"OR!... I will go online... and make your life a living hell."

Talon got extremely serious now.

"Abigail, let me tell you something. What you just experienced, we each did in our own way. Also, we all pretty much reacted the way you are now. That's why I'm going to ignore this recent spurt of bravery. IF however, you ever threaten me like that again, or try and make good on that one... I won't have to bring her back... because I'll see to it you join her. Are we clear?"

Abigail was drained and told him "I will trade you my talents, I will cook or clean or hell... I'll help you fix up that floor myself! All I ask in return is... let me stay. Let me come here, let me be close to her.......... please," she nearly pleaded.

"Violet? Tell her," Talon said as he stared at Abigail.

Purple girl was kind and said "Sorry, Abigail, it doesn't work that way. She had a purpose. That purpose it would seem, was to bring you here. She isn't gone yet but, she'll not likely come back. Not for quite some time anyway. Talon can no more 'conjure her up' than you can."

Abigail stared her down, but nicely, and asked Violet "And you know this how?"

Violet told her calmly "Let's just say you have a story to finish... and we have one to tell."

In a bold departure from her usual self, Abigail stared back at Talon. She just felt free now. Utterly, and completely free. As such, she was going to have a little celebratory fun.

"My apologies for my reaction, Mr. Grayson, but in my own defense, you have to admit that was enough to reboot anyone's PC."

"Apology accepted," Talon said flatly.

Abigail gave him a serious look and told him "You're right, I still have a story to finish. Before I do though let me ask you something."

"Hmm?"

Abigail's face changed to a playful smile and she asked "That brother of yours still checking out my ass?"

Talon grinned... slid his view past her ear... then brought it back to stare into her eyes.

"Um... heh heh... yep!"

Abigail beamed and nearly chirped "Good!"

Blondie gave her ass a little wiggle, then sat back down. The crowd just laughed.

Abigail restarted her story. She was feeling a huge dose of confidence and was just running with it. She never felt this way before but was liking it a lot. Violet would later tell her it was a 'residual effect' from contact with her ghostly grandmother. That affect would indeed wear off but, Abigail was addicted to it now and would eventually bring it back but... all on her own.

"So, as I was saying, Mom told me I was adopted. They also said that there was more to the story but, because of my age, they gave me only what they thought a 9-year-old could handle. To this day I still think that wise of them. They told me that, when I reached 16, they would give me all they had on the matter but, not until then. They felt that at that age, I would be able to handle it. They were right... and a bit wrong."

"In what way?" Eileen asked.

"They gave it to me at 14 saying they thought me mature enough. However, I had to promise them something. I had to promise them that, while I was free to research my own past, I wasn't allowed to act on it till I was 21. I also had to keep them involved in anything I did."

Cody told her "Biological or not... they sound like great parents."

Abigail kindly replied "They were... and still are. My dad told me something once I never forgot. He said don't be upset that my biological parents didn't love me... and always remember that 2 who weren't... did."

Grant, with a voice dripping with puppy love, said "I wouldn't mind meeting parents like that."

With a smile and a matching tone, Abigail told him "One day perhaps, I'd like that too."

Abigail saw Talon's expression, and picked up the pace a little.

"Okay so... I'm 14... and feel like I've been given the keys to the city. I started digging into my own past. Like any teenager of that age, I thought myself the smartest girl in the world, and that all the grownups were idiots. I found my birth mother was an 18 year-old girl living in Boston. She planned to marry her boyfriend when he came home from Iraq. He never did. Apparently, she became despondent. One day, as the police reports state, she wasn't paying attention and walked out in front of a truck. The driver was cleared of any wrongdoing but my mom was left in a coma... at 8 ½ months pregnant. I went back further, and found something odd. It seemed my family, had a repeating pattern. All single mothers. One of them was a woman named Jill. Her records were sealed and she was adopted like me."

"I'm guessing this is where the plot thickens?" Talon jested.

"Indeed. I thought, no big deal, I'll just hack the records. I mean... who's gonna care about some random single mother, right? Besides, it's not like these tech-dummies would have a clue anyway. Well, I turned out to be very wrong. They were county records from 1947. I hacked into the county courthouse but, in my ignorance of computers at the time, it turned out I had just enough knowledge to be dangerous. The county records were tied into a military database. Turns out she was a translator for an ambassador. That made her a federal employee and as such, I didn't realize that following the chain, I went into a military database, not a civilian one. Given the state of this country today, and the 9-11 aftermath... alarms went off. I got tracked, and arrested."

The small crowd around Abigail was still quiet. Most importantly, they weren't teasing nor judging. So... she continued. What no one saw however, was the brunette gentleman a short distance away who was listening too.

"My trial was in federal court. I even took the stand in my own defense. I told them, all I was doing, was tracing my lineage. I proved that, and the jury took pity on me. The prosecutor tried to show I was a threat. His case was flimsy but he milked it to try and get a feather in his cap. The judge laughed as I helped my own defense team chew up every 'computer expert' they threw at me. The judge found it amusing, and even chastised the prosecutor saying if the best the government had, got eradicated by a 15-year-old girl... then perhaps they ought to stop trying me... and start hiring me. In the end, the jury found me not guilty of searching for, or trading, any government secrets. They DID find me guilty of hacking them. The judge warned me I'd see jail in a heartbeat if I broke my probation but, he was lenient with me. He put the bracelet on me, and said I'd be in jail instantly if I went anywhere near a large gathering of... and I quote... 'A large gathering of nerds like me'. My home PC was monitored and that was that. I've been the good girl I promised I would be, stayed to public libraries that had blocks in place to prevent me from doing such things, and now I get this thing off in a little under a month."

Talon was nice, and told Abigail "I don't want you wandering about young lady. Many areas are still very unsafe. That said, if you keep to the areas that have been fixed, then I don't mind if you visit."

"Very fair of you and... thank you," she honestly told Talon.

Talon had a thought and asked "Abigail, what do you do for a living?"

Abigail giggled and said "Tell me, how hypocritical is this!? I work with computers and security systems!"

She caught Grant 'checking her out'. He looked away quick but Abigail smiled and told him "Actually Grant, I don't mind. I'm flattered actually."

"Well then," Grant said happily, "Don't mind if I do!"

Demurely, Abigail told him "I won't."

She looked back to Talon and said "I had 300 hours of community service to do. 100 of that was spent teaching seniors how to use their computers."

Talon asked "And the other 200?"

"Yeah... heh heh... that's the hypocritical part. I spent those working on, or upgrading, the local police department's IT including their networks. The judge figured, with a building full of cops watching me, I couldn't get into trouble. I did it with ease and, when I was done with my hours, they liked me and my work so much that they hired me as an independent contractor for the city. I became a tax paying citizen, and they got to keep an eye on me.

One of the lieutenants there though was a prick. One day, he was really mean, so... hah hah... his computer got 'mysteriously' set to Lithuanian. He barked at me but, the captain told him it served him right. I told him however, if he was smarter, he could have fixed it himself. The captain also warned him he shouldn't bully little girls. Point made, and having made him the joke of the station... he left me alone after that."

Talon asked slyly, "Are you required to work for them only? Or can you be hired for other jobs?"

"I don't see why not. They never said I couldn't but, I don't want to ruin my probation. Not when I'm so close. What did you have in mind?"

Talon said "I have a legally acquired thumb drive, that just happens to have files on it that need cracking. I own my own business so, hiring you would be legit. Look, I have no desire to get you into trouble. I'll provide a reference if you can provide me with one to attest to your skills. If anyone asks, I'll tell them

I'm interested in hiring you to perform a cyber security check on my computers to look for any places that need or could use improvement. I will do a full background check on you, same as I would for any new employee. IF you check out, then my offer is firm. Interested?"

"Very," Abigail said with great interest. "I really am sorry for how I acted before. Tell me, you would still do that for me?"

"For you no." Talon chuckled saying "For my brother who seems to have taken leave of his senses?... Yes."

"I've told you a story. Politely put, I believe you owe me one now," Abigail reminded him as politely as she could.

"Fair enough. One clarification though. You've yet to tell us why you are here," Talon told her.

"Indeed. Well, from all the information I could get, the trail ran cold here. I don't remember how many 'greats' she is but, it seems my great grandmother was tied to this house somehow. I think she may have owned it. Regardless, I tried tracing it... and ran into another federal database... so I stopped. This place, Mister Grayson, is a ghost. It literally doesn't exist. That alone made me curious. I found my great grandmother was also named Abigail, and she was somehow tied to this house. Without further information on this house, I couldn't go farther back. All I know is, she had a child out of wedlock, and starting with her, that 'curse' seems to have purveyed all the way to me."

Violet smiled and said "Sorry Abigail, she didn't own the place... but uh... she did work here."

"She did!? I knew she was tied to this house somehow!" Abigail bellowed with a tone of vindication. "Tell me more..." then catching herself, she told the nice lady with the purple eyes "... please?"

Talon asked in a grave tone "This 'house' as you call it... was actually a working mansion back in the day. We will tell you Abigail as we promised. The question is... are you sure you wanna know?"

Abigail was soft in her demeanor and told Talon "Mister Grayson, I have imagined my grandmother to be everything from the owner of this place, to nothing more than a housemaid... and everything in between. Trust me, whatever you know, or suspect, then yes... I surely wanna know."

Talon was about to tell her. Another voice finally came out of the shadows and did it for him.

"Adair House. So called for the lady who owned it... a certain Miss Lucinda Adair. This mansion, oh blond one, was the most reputable 'house of ill repute' anywhere in the country. Abigail Johnson, born to John and Anna-Mae Johnson in Forrest County, Kentucky, was the only daughter of a school teacher, and a butcher. She came to work here in 1860 at the tender age of 19. She was to marry a miner but he died in an accident, leaving her an unwed mother. All accounts I could find, point to her dying during childbirth, leaving a child that was cared for by the ladies of the house. When the mansion was abandoned a few years later, one of the 'working girls' named Linda Tavish, left the life of prostitution, and raised Abigail's daughter as her own. That, as you put it, started the 'curse' that has run all through the generations since... including you."

Doc said nothing and just walked off the porch and down to the brown-haired man.

He gave him a huge friendly hug saying "Good to see you old friend."

The man hugged back saying "Good to see you as well Doc."

Talon walked down and extended his hand.

"Zachariah I assume?"

Cody put his arm around him, smiled, and said "You assume correctly. Talon? Allow me to introduce you to the finest history tracer I have ever known."

Zachariah shook Talon's hand saying "Like I said... call me Zack. So Mister Grayson... like my entrance?"

"I did indeed. Doc and I haven't known each other very long. That said, he has earned my trust, and my respect. If he vouches for you, then that's good enough for me."

Talon heard a whisper just then. He was also the only one who did.

"This one 'Mista G'... is tha last," Lucinda's voice told him.

He wasn't certain what that meant... but he had his suspicions.

All 3 men walked up onto the porch, and Doc introduced him to each one in turn. Zack was as polite and well mannered, as he was smart.

"Well, seeing as how we seem to be telling family histories... would you care for mine?" Zack said with utter confidence. "Not as long and involved as the nice blond lady here, but, interesting enough."

Talon told him cutely, "The porch Mister Zack... is all yours."

Zack half bowed and began his tale.

"I was raised in an ultra orthodox Mormon family. That's the proper name for it. I however, would call it a stifling cult run by a narcissistic despotic wannabe prophet."

Violet teased Talon saying "Sorta sounds like you."

Talon grinned and stuck his tongue out at her. Violet just giggled and gave him a kiss.

Zack grinned at the obvious couple, and said "I grew up under the strict and utter domination of my father. I worked with my grandfather as a means to escape the tyrant. When Grandpa died, I lost my only true friend. He was the ONLY one to make my father see any sort of reason other than his own. Stuck full time with 'dad' now, I didn't feel like I needed to leave... I felt like I needed to escape."

"That bad, eh?" Eileen asked.

"Miss? Yes, it was that bad," Zack confirmed. He continued with "I ran away. I let my family know I was okay via letters and an occasional phone call or two. Mostly it was just to spite and taunt my father. Knowing I was out there... and out of his control... well, it was the only thing that made me smile most days. To me, religion, ANY religion, is a choice. To my father it was a holy duty and only he knew how best to carry it out. Whether it was out of fear, or a lack of caring on their part... the church elders were no help and only told me I should do as father instructed. That's when I knew I had to leave... and so I did."

Talon said "Doc here says you went underground. You're like what, early twenties or so?"

"22 actually."

"Well then, as of a year ago even you could legally tell daddy to go to hell. Going underground is a tad severe even for that story. Care to tell me what I'm missing here?"

Calmly, Zack told him "Not at all. I left at 18. My brother is a sweetheart, but a pussy when it comes to him. I have 2 sisters and they're the same walking talking Stepford women that my mother is. Father wanted me back and saw me as his heir apparent. He left me alone till I was 20 thinking I would see that the 'outside world' was full of the devil's work and return on my own. When he realized I wouldn't, he started trying to force me back. Perhaps out of fear of me telling anyone what he was really like, or perhaps just shear arrogance at me defying him... I truly don't know. When a rather unsavory looking van started following me one day, THEN, parked outside the apartment I was staying at, I knew it was time to change tactics.

So, I ran. The next town I was in, I found a lovely lady working in a local theater as an actress. I paid her to be my 'Jewish bride'. I knew only pissing my father off in such a way would make him leave me alone for good. I needed to make him disown me, plain and simple. It worked too. Then, for some damn reason I still can't fathom, my mother and sisters took up where my father left off. That's when I cut off all ties to them, went underground so no one could find me... and haven't spoke to them since. One day, a neighbor I befriended before she moved out, showed me an ad in the paper. I called the number on it, and the rest you know."

Talon had an inquisition like tone in his voice, and spoke to Zack.

"A couple questions for ya Zack. First, do you believe in ghosts?"

Calm and cool, Zack said "Can't say I've ever seen one. Till I do, my answer is... I believe it possible."

Talon continued.

"And... what about religion? More to the point, someone with a lack of one, an alternate one, or one that's not Mormon?"

"Dad pretty much burned me out on religion. I'm pretty much tolerant of them despite my upbringing. As long as you don't shove it in my face, or use it for your own personal agenda... then I don't care what an individual believes."

"Fair enough," Talon pressed on. "Lastly, how do you feel about being part of a team?"

"Team or solo, I don't care. As long as the people I'm working with are good people, then I can be a team player."

Talon smiled and said "Well then, Zack... welcome to the team. You too, Abigail."

"Wait... huh?... What team?" she blurted having come back to reality from staring at Grant.

"The one that's gonna solve a 150-year-old cold case murder mystery." Talon smirked and knew just how to get to someone like Abigail, and asked "Interested?"

"I have to leave in three days," Abigail said warily. "If you don't mind me working remotely... then yeah... count me in."

Talon chuckled and asked "Want me to call mom and dad for you?"

Abigail joked right back and said "Nah... but Officer Glass would be nice!"

Talon was kind in his response, looked at his brother, then back to Abigail and said "That... I can do."

"Mind telling me where I fit into this little impromptu A-Team of yours?" Zack asked.

Talon said confidently "Not at all. I'm the historian and, as owner and financier of this project... the boss. My sister here manages the money. Grant and I restore and build. Doc is our medical and forensic guru slash scientist. Abigail here, if her boasts hold up, is our resident tech aficionado. You're the guy that gives us the personal history. You follow the chain of real life events, and get us the relevant info we need."

Zack looked lovingly at Violet and asked "And the stunning lady with the dazzling eyes?"

Violet smiled at him, but warningly said "Sorry there, handsome," and she hugged Talon to show her intent and finished with "This lady is taken."

Talon smiled, hugged her back, and said "Ya might say, she's our DJ," Talon said with a wink referring to Violet's explanation she gave him once.

Zack immediately pulled the same trick on Abigail.

"If you can get me the access I need, I'd be happy to give you my requirements... over say... dinner?"

Grant was suddenly jealous. He didn't stay that way for long.

"Sorry, jar head. Tempting as that offer is... I like my men a tad more ginger... and not so much brown."

Zack had stunning looks for a guy. While always a gentleman, he was what any other guy would call a dog. He didn't want 'a' woman... he wanted all of them.

He just laughed at being shot down and joked "Wow... tough crowd."

Cody stood up and said "Zack? Wherever you're staying, you ain't no more. I insist you stay with me as my guest. We've got a lot of catching up to do and THIS time... well, I have one hell of a story to tell." Cody turned to the crowd and asked "Dinner? My place?"

Violet jumped at the chance and said "You buy the groceries, I'll cook."

"M'lady? You got yourself a deal!" Cody turned to Abigail and said "Will you be joining us, my dear?"

Abigail gazed at Grant and asked him "Will you be going?"

"I will if you will," he told her sweetly.

She turned to Cody and said "Then sir, I accept you're kind offer. Do you have cell reception at your home?"

Cody thought that an odd question and said "I do... why do you ask?"

Abigail just smiled at him... and crossed her left leg over her right, and bounced her foot.

"Ah.. yeah... no worries there."

"Well then, allow me to check in, and I will be happy to join you."

The day was almost over, so the new gang of 7, headed out to get all of them well fed... and 2 new members up to speed.

Chapter 17

"The 'Inside' Scoop"

Al pulled into the mansion with Lashonda the following morning. Eileen was packing to go and Cody was with her. Grant and Talon were already hard at work building the patio and gardens out back. Both brothers thought Cody would be a sad puppy with Eileen going away. He was actually the opposite telling both men he was already anticipating her return.

"It may not be a Lamborghini," Cody told her as she locked up the house, "but if you'll find a humble BMW to your liking... well, my dear... then, your chariot awaits."

Eileen told him sweetly "It's German not Italian... and the driver is a lot less monochromatic... but both suit me just fine."

He put her luggage in the trunk and told Eileen "I hope you don't mind but, I kinda stole a page out of your brothers play-book."

"Oh?"

Cody got in, smiled, and said "Mm hmm."

Moments later Eileen laughed as a Beemer took off down the road... to the sounds of CCR.

They pulled into the driveway of the mansion, and Talon and Grant took a break.

"You two take care of yourselves till I come back," Eileen said with a hug to both brothers. She hugged Violet and said sincerely "Keep them safe for me. I'm counting on you. If ANY thing comes up... you call me right away, you got it?"

Violet hugged her back and spoke to her like the friend she had become. "I dreaded your arrival. Now... I look forward to your return."

Eileen chuckled "So do I... heh heh... ghost lady."

Violet winked and said "I'll see ya in a few weeks... 'candlestick'."

Zack wasn't there but Abigail was. Dorky as ever she waved from the parlor and hollered "Have a safe flight! It was nice to have met you!"

Playing with her some, Eileen shouted back in the same dorky manner "And you as well!" and giggled when she didn't get it. Then Eileen looked at Grant and told him flat out, and with a total attitude change, "Violet didn't escape my watchful eye... neither will she."

Grant just laughed and told her "Sounds good to me. Saves me the trouble anyway!"

Eileen looked at Lashonda and asked "So, my little helper... ya ready?"
"As I'll ever be ma'am."
Lashonda had spent the last half hour dealing with a nervous grandma. Warnings of "Mind ya mannahs now, baby girl," and several others were still ringing in her ears.
"Okay first rule," Eileen commanded. "When we're at work, call me Miss Grayson. When we're not, call me Eileen. But don't eeeeeeeever call me 'ma'am' again."
"Yes ma'am."
Talon and Grant just laughed.
"Lashonda," Talon started, "I want you to know I'm investing in you. I don't expect you to become an expert in two weeks. I am however, expecting you to be better than you are right now. Deal?"
Lashonda hugged him and said " I will, sir... promise."
Talon hugged her back with a smile and said "I'm holding you to that. Have a safe flight and bug my sister every chance you get, okay?"
Lashonda giggled, hugged grandma, and got in Cody's car.

Eileen walked into the parlor, and right up to a hanging photo.
"If anything happens to them... I'm holding you personally responsible," she told the photo in no uncertain terms.
A soft whisper of "Safe jernee, young ginjuh girl. Come bahk to us safe now ya hear?"
"Lady? Count on it!" and Eileen marched out without another word.
Waves all around, along with a few honks, and Eileen was gone.

"Mista G, I'll be leav'in mahself shortly. I'm driv'in cross country to get supplies and such for yer next job, then I'll be pick'in up mah baby girl from ya sistuh."
She hugged Grant, then Talon.
"I'll be back ta pick up Big Mack around end of August. Y'all tayk care of yo'selves till then now, ya hear?" Althea leaned past Talon and hollered into the house "And if the hoochie mama's get outta hand... I'll be bahk even soonuh!"
"Ah shall relish tha peace an quiet till then, oh loud one," the Creole voice told her.
Al got into her truck shaking her head.
"A N'awlins ho house in tha middle o'nowhere. And with ghosts no less! I swear tha crazy ass white boy dun lawst his miiind." Al took a moment then

reflectively stated "Lucinda? He's a good man. Tha don't mean tho that he may not get in over his head one day. Tha said, he's become lyke famlee tuh me. Maybe not so much with yaw famlee but, I think even you recawl how we treat 'em back in da bayou."

Lucinda couldn't resist a playful jab.

"Well well, thuh loud manly one has the heart of a woman aftuh awl."

Althea gave her window a 'watch it bitch' stare.

"If you be referr'in to tha kind of woman that consorts with a married man... then no... I'm not."

Lucinda was sad but, couldn't disagree either.

"Point made, loud one"

Al finished with, "Y'all reached out tuh Violet... I'll expect ya tuh do tha same tuh me... iffin he does. We clear?"

"Ahr you ask'in me... or tell'in me?" the familiar accent queried.

Al changed her tone and said "Miss Lucinda? The way folk be back home, ain't much diffrint now then they were back in yaw day. Sumptin happens tuh any of 'em, and I find out you dint call me? Well, I think y'all get my mean'in now dontja?"

It wasn't much but, Al was right... it was how 'their' folk were. Lucinda knew it too. She also knew, however tough she might be, Al was offering her version of an olive branch.

"Well then 'lady Althea', y'all have mah word thah if I feel y'all be needed... I will do whut ah can tuh let y'all know."

"Ha HAAAAAAA! Lady Althea!!?? Oh Lawd ain't thah rich!?"

Even from the ether... Lucinda winced at the ear piercing cackle. Althea waved and within minutes of Eileen, Al was gone now too.

"I know it's my first plane ride and all but... I think I can handle a line," Lashonda told Eileen sweetly.

She wanted to give Eileen and Cody a private goodbye.

"I'll wait for you right on the other side," and Lashonda headed off.

Cody hugged Eileen sweetly, and she did the same right back.

"You are an odd man, Doc. I expected a whole lot less."

Cody was in good spirits and asked "I hope that's a 'good odd'."

Eileen gave him a passionate kiss and told him "Oh, you can bank on that. Remember, I'm 3 hours ahead so watch when you call." She kissed him passionately once more, hugged him tight, and said "I'm gonna miss you."

Cody winked and said "Don't worry, I'll have my house cleaned up and all the hookers out by the time you come back."

Eileen play slapped him and stated "YOU sir... have been hanging out with my brother too much."

Cody smiled softly, hugged her hard, and whispered "Perhaps but... I'm gonna miss you too."

Eileen let go and coyly asked "Promise?"

Doc grinned and said "To quote you... bank on it."

One more kiss and Eileen headed around the corner for the gates and was gone. Doc walked out of the Reno/Tahoe airport, grinned mischievously, and turned his stopwatch function on his wristwatch on. He wouldn't turn it off for another two weeks.

"Ya know... I could get used to this," he told his empty Beemer.

He was referring to the fact that he was still listening to CCR when he left the parking garage.

Everyone had left for the day, and now, standing in the parlor, it was just Talon and Violet.

"Are you SURE about this!?" Violet asked thoroughly not liking this plan.

Talon was sweet to her and said "As long as you're nearby, I'm not worried at all."

"You may not be... but I sure am," Violet said in a clearly unhappy tone.

Talon ignored her and called his plan forth.

"Miss Adair... a moment if you please?"

Her photo swirled. A mist descended from it, and formed to the same rotoscope image he saw once before.

"Ah buhleev y'all called faw me, good sir?"

"Lucinda, I have a favor to ask. A rather personal one."

"Ah am listen'in," she told him as she lightly strolled about.

"I was wondering if you could do something. I was also wondering that if you could... would you?"

"An wut might tha bee?"

Violet was nervous when Talon asked "Can you show me 'you'... on the day you left this world?"

"Why in heavens would you wahnt ta see thaht?" Lucinda asked as nervously as Violet was feeling.

Talon stated calmly "If I could see that, It would help me help you. Perhaps something you didn't notice. Perhaps some small sight or sound you ignored. I don't know but, can't hurt to try right?"

Lucinda emphatically told him "Tha's where yaw wrong. If I show you, yool not only see an heeyuh... but feel too. Ahr you sure about this?" Lucinda said with great sadness "It's as painful faw me ta relive it, as it will be faw you ta experience it."

Talon told her "Violet and I have discussed it all day. I'm aware of the risks. I'm sorry, Lucinda, but... I gotta know."

"Oh go ahead... it may even be fun!" laughed Shadow Man.

Violet went into a major defensive mode, but Shadow Man actually waved her off.

"Have no fear, little girl. I wouldn't daaaaaaaaare interrupt this. Go on, you worthless whore... show him my handiwork!" Shadow taunted.

Lucinda actually stood up for herself saying "I may have been a whore... but I was far from worthless. Remember this. Whatever Henry was ta you, he loved me. NEVUH fawget that."

Shadow Man was glib and told her "And yet... I took that all away didn't I? OH!... Why yes, I believe I did."

Now Talon stepped in saying "You had to. Those who can't compete always have to. And yet, you thought yourself smart by getting away with it in life... only to end up trapped here. The very house you despised, and the only woman you despised more than this house. As they say in our century..." and Talon glared at Shadow and finished with "... payback's a bitch."

"Enjoy your little adventure," Shadow Man seethed as he threw Talon into Lucinda's ether. "Assuming you survive."

Talon was suddenly on a virtual trip like no other. He was seeing history, real live history, through Lucinda's eyes. The view made him a bit nauseous at first but that settled down quick.

It was nighttime and Lucinda was making her rounds through the grand living room. Lucinda AND Violet were right, he could feel everything. Lucinda shut a window by the front door and Talon could feel the breeze. Lucinda walked through the parlor checking this and that as she went. She was also making nice to all the men folk that were tipping or raising their hats to her.

Next, she headed up the stairs and made a sweep of all the rooms. Only a couple were 'in use'. Talon could feel her satisfaction that all was right with the world as she headed up to her room. She was walking down the hallway to her door when she tripped slightly. It took a moment for Talon to realize she didn't trip... she just all of a sudden lost her balance.

"Oh my... perhaps I shouldn't have had that sherry," Lucinda told herself as she regained her balance.

Talon was motionless in the parlor, and seemed to be somewhere far far away. Violet was getting more nervous by the second and grabbed his hand. To her dismay, she felt nothing like she thought she would. She could sense Talon like he was in some far off place, and only picked up sensations. Suddenly, those sensations shifted and... not in a good way. Violet thought quick and looked for a way to get Talon back. To her, he was so far away, she felt like yanking him back too quick would do some serious harm. Now instead of getting him back, she was looking for an alternative.

"Oh this is gonna suck," she said when she realized she had only one option. "Sorry, love. I know you're gonna be pissed at me for this but, at least you'll be alive to yell at me."

Violet was now super focused. She knew she had one shot at this, and had to time it just right. Hell, she wasn't sure she could even do it at all.

Talon suddenly felt a wave of dread come over him. He quickly realized he wasn't feeling it, Lucinda was.

Talon's view spun hard behind him as Lucinda called out "Who dares come up heeyah?"

No one was there however. Lucinda looked a moment or two, then turned back and headed for her door.

Suddenly, running footsteps were heard coming up from behind. Lucinda was brave. She gripped her parasol and got ready to swing it. THAT... was when Talon's view shifted.

"wwwWWWWHAAAAT!?" Shadow Man cried out in anger.

Violet could sense Talon, and he felt like he was in serious danger. Knowing Lucinda was bashed in the head first, she couldn't risk Talon getting hurt by default so... she shifted his focus. She stuck a hand inside Shadow Man and, willed herself to pull Talon from one... and put him in another. To say Shadow Man was a tad upset she did that, was an understatement.

Violet was menacing now and told him "You move so much as an inch... and I'll show you that cattle prod was but a toy compared to what I'll do to you."

Lucinda accepted Talon. More like embraced him. That's why he felt so far away. Shadow Man was a different story however. He wanted out of this situation... badly.

Talon's view suddenly shifted. He was no longer looking out from Lucinda. He knew in an instant he was somehow in somebody else... and he knew exactly who that somebody was. He was watching Lucinda's murderer kill her. Inside Lucinda, he felt what she felt. Right down to her femininity. Shadow Man was different however. He was pulling away from Talon like a foreign intruder. The more he did however, the more Violet got a hold of Talon.

He saw her die. Shadow had some white heavy object in his right hand, and hit Lucinda hard across the left side of her head. Lucinda went down and Talon heard a horrible cracking sound. The only sensation Talon could get from Shadow Man was rage. Pure, unadulterated, rage. By that point Shadow hid all his other feelings away by now. He had survived all this time on one thing...

anonymity. Shadow was heavily concerned that may now be compromised. Talon felt the rage, and the fear of discovery, and that was it.

Shadow man felt pleased with himself and turned to leave. He was almost to the stairs when he was truly shocked. He turned hard to see Lucinda crawling for her door. Now the fear of discovery was back and Shadow Man ran for the door. Lucinda was behind it and couldn't lock it in time. Shadow kicked it hard, and sent Lucinda to the floor even harder. He looked around quick and saw her oil lamp lit on the table by the door. He picked it up, turned up the flame, ignored Lucinda's pleas... and threw it on the ground. It shattered, oil spread, and Lucinda was doomed. He was certain the thumps made to the floor, and the smell of smoke would attract others. Lucinda's hallway, by design, had only one way in or out so... Shadow Man ran. A few of the ladies were coming up to investigate and Shadow literally slammed through them on his way down to the main floor. At the bottom of the stairs, he made a hard right, and headed out into the night. Next thing Talon knew was he was in Violet's arms.

"You'll pay dearly for that, freak!" Shadow Man said as he retreated.

"Empty threat. If I was to pay for that, you would have made me do so by now. Don't you EVER fuck with me again or I will sacrifice my life just to see you burn away into oblivion."

Shadow Man was incensed. He was also breathing heavy and... for the first time ever... treating Violet as a serious adversary.

"Now who's handing out empty threats!?"

"Empty? Go ahead, you piece of shit... TRY ME! You fucking phantoms have controlled me my whole life but NO MORE! I am now stronger, wiser and... sadly for shits like you... no longer afraid." Holding a groggy Talon she stated with confidence "To quote my new friend, get out of here before I get medieval on your ass."

Shadow Man seethed but... did as commanded.

"This isn't over, freak."

Violet stood up confidently and said "You're right, it isn't. However, we'll be back... again... and again... and again! We now have resources Lucian couldn't have dreamed of in a thousand years. Talon was right. Enjoy your taunts, Shadow Man... for they're coming to an end."

Talon was lucid but he was a tad woozy from the ordeal. Violet hung onto him and got him out of the house. She got the truck door open and got him into the driver's seat.

"I'm... I'm okay, Violet. I need a minute or two but, I'll be okay," Talon told her.

Shadow and Lucinda had both gone, but Violet heard a whisper in her ears.

"Ah am prowd of you, purple girl... very, very prowd indeed," Lucinda said with kindness and conviction.

Talon was almost his old self again. He could actually feel his energy coming back in leaps and bounds. Violet went to check on him and he surprised her with strength she didn't think he had. He held her head firm with both hands, and kissed her deeply. Ignoring all around her, Violet relaxed and kissed him back just as hard.

"THAT... was the most dumb-ass thing I've seen you do yet."

Talon gave her a smile that made her melt and just said "Thank you." Talon looked at her and honestly stated "There's a song I'd like to quote you. It goes like this...

... Daddy was a wild one, when he was younger. Everybody told my momma he was too tough to tame. Full of himself, he said sir to nobody... but you oughta see him come a'runnin, when momma called his name."

"Interesting" was all Violet could think of to say.

"That's me, Violet. One day... when you need me for a change... I WILL be there for you."

Violet hugged him and let the tears flow.

"Talon I... I..."

The gray guy hugged her back, pet her hair, and said "Shhh shhhh... I know. And for the record... I've fallen in love with you too, Violet."

Violet just hugged tighter and refused to let go.

Talon would deliver on that promise. He would also do it with a whole lot of metal backing him up... and swinging him forward.

Chapter 18

"Senior Prom"

Violet was quiet, and awash with feelings, on the drive home. She was more amazed at herself than anything else. She told a man she loved him. Even more amazing to her, was that now, he told her the same in return.

One thing that amazed her the most was what she did tonight. More to the point that she did it at all. She had no after effects that she could tell, unlike when she arrived. She was realizing that, with the peace and recharge Talon's house afforded her, and her own confidence brought out by this new group of people, she was starting to realize she was more than she once believed.

When she and Talon finally got home, she marched him straight to bed. She proceeded to practically rape him shortly thereafter. Violet was on a confidence high and decided she wasn't ready to come down just yet.

"Wait... you did what!?... Then, whoa wait a second... you did WHAT!?" Grant extolled in near disbelief at what he just heard.

His usual carefree self, Talon chuckled at his brother's response and said "You heard us."

Talon and Violet had just updated Grant while working on the half finished patio. Talon had an architect design it... but hated it. Then, he called a landscaper Grant recommended, and as the phrase goes... 'voila!' Talon knew of a local company that did something pretty cool. They had a truck with a specialized crane. They would go to a house or job-site and transplant trees whole. Talon put an ad in the local papers for people who had full grown trees they wanted gone. Talon would pay the fee for the crane and now, the back of the house had a semi-circular border of full grown elms and maples that would have taken decades otherwise.

Talon's father planted a vine many years ago. Only 2 years later, it took him over another year to eradicate it. It was a Trumpet Vine. Long yellow flowers by the hundreds the same size and shape of a trumpet... hence the name. It grew well but, Papa Joe planted in the wrong area. He thought it would just fill in a bare spot in the garden. It did... and broke the fence it was trained on... three times. Talon's father had no idea how invasive it was, and found out the hard way. Remembering all that, Talon ran some wires like fencing in between the trees, and planted the vines to fill in the area with a wall of flowers. Now knowing, what his father found out the hard way, he would let them go nuts and give himself... and any guests he rents it out to... a living backdrop for taking photos or holding outdoor events. Not to mention the vines wouldn't bust the wires, and in only two years, Talon would have his desired living wall going 10 feet high and in total, 175 feet wide. He had no idea though, that in only a few short years, that wall would become more photographed than the governor's mansion just 20 minutes away.

"I'm guessing that's why you're not your usual self today?" Grant asked.

Violet joked, but used a serious expression to do it. Talon caught on and played his part right back.

Looking between the two brothers, Violet stated "Well, there was that, and... wadda ya think Talon?... Think the, what, 3 hours of sex may have added to that?"

"I could have sworn it was four?" Talon replied equally as seriously.

Violet countered "Could have been. To be honest, by my third orgasm... and your second... I kinda lost track of time."

"Yeah," Talon mused, "That is pretty likely. Tell me, what do you think Grant? Ya think that was a bit much?" and in perfect sync, Violet and Talon stared at Grant with the same questioning looks on their faces.

Grant just laughed at them and stated "Oh you two are something else!"

Talon and Violet just grinned at Grant.

Talon was indeed lacking in energy today. He was gathering plants and setting them in the walls of the patio. He and Grant had built a patio that looked like many in Florida. Half high walls ringing a concrete floor, with capped columns every 8 feet or so. To give it a little extra class, there were two smaller, and slightly elevated, side patios. One to each side. The walls were covered in concrete and about 12 inches thick. Openings along the top edges held plants, giving the patio a nice botanical effect. The concrete was stained to give it a more aged look, and slate pavers were laid over the concrete floor.

"Yaw tahlunts, Mista G, and yaws, Mista ginjuh chyld, are simply ahmayzin'," the disembodied voice told the two men as they planted.

Grant chuckled at the nickname, and decided to call her on it.

"Ya know Lucinda, last I saw you... you were looking a tad ghostly. With this new patio, perhaps you could come out and tan yourself now. I know 'I' wouldn't mind if you did it like the photo in the parlor," Grant said finishing with a wink.

"I'm shaw you wouldn't (giggle)... 'Mistuh Grant suh'... I'm shaw you wouldn't," Lucinda told him using the more 'preferred' name.

Talon asked Violet "Would you mind giving me and Grant here, a few minutes alone?"

She smiled, kissed Talon, and said "Not at all," and granted his request.

Now alone, Talon looked at Grant and asked "Okay, yesterday you were a cheerful little puppy. And the day before. Hell, EVERY day since Abigail arrived. Now you're practically moping. What's up lil brother?"

Grant eased some and said "That noticeable huh? Well, it's Abigail."

"Do tell," Talon ordered in a brotherly way.

"Well, she's leaving tomorrow. I've spent every moment I could with her. She's everything I could want... and everything I've been looking for."

Talon was kind but cautious when he asked "Does she feel the same?"

"Near as I can tell she does. Honestly bro, if it wasn't for my usual rational demeanor... I'd be married right now."

Talon chuckled and stated "Thank the heavens for rationality." He got serious again and asked "So what's wrong then? Is it that she's leaving?"

Grant thought about it a moment, then answered.

"Nah. She said she was coming back as soon as she gets the ankle bracelet off. With modern technology, I can stay in touch till she does," Grant explained.

"So... what's the issue then?" Talon asked not getting his brother's reasoning, nor demeanor.

"Look bro," Grant began to explain, "The other night at Sterling's was probably THE best one ever. You also can't tell me that that wasn't your's and Violet's first 'grownup' date. As a first one goes... that night was a winner. That's what I want for Abigail. I want to make our first date as magical as Sterling's was. That make sense?"

"Very much so," Talon said kindly. "I do agree that night was magical as you put it. I can also tell you, it was so, all on its own. THAT kind of magic you can't plan nor script."

"I'll say," Grant agreed. "That's what I want though for me and Abigail. I want our own magical, memorable, totally cool first date."

Talon spoke kindly and said "Nothing wrong with that. If you need any help... you just let me know."

Grant checked that the coast was still clear, then leaned in to Talon.

"Look bro, I like Violet. She truly is an amazing woman. But, even you gotta admit, she was a scared little rabbit at first. Eileen is the powerhouse and Violet was the complete opposite. Now though, she seems to have settled somewhere in between. Not quite Eileen, but not her old self either."

"I'll agree with that," Talon confirmed.

"Now, I see Violet as... well... like what we see now is her true self. Kind, confident, mild mannered and just overall sweet. Fair to say?"

Again, Talon totally agreed.

"Well, I'm starting to see... at least I think I am... the real Abigail." Grant laughed some and said "She's cute. One minute she's calm and normal and the next... she's totally geeking out. She reminds me of those computer girls ya see on those TV cop shows. Still, she's everything I could want or hope for."

Talon had an odd look and asked "Still not seeing a problem here bro."

Grant told him "What I'm saying is, I want our first official date to be special. To do that I have to match her personality. I'm getting bummed because I can't come up with a single idea." Grant sighed and added sadly "Not one."

Talon told him "Don't then."

"Huh?"

"You heard me. Don't come up with an idea... just ask her what she wants. Then, put a spin on it to make it your own, and you'll have what you seek."

"Tried that too. So far, nothing," Grant told him.

"Don't worry baby G... just stop trying. Once you do, that first date will find you. Trust me, you'll sort it in time," Talon said in an encouraging tone.

"Feeling better today?" Grant snickered as he asked his brother the next morning when he showed up for work.

"Oh loads, thanks. We decided to keep the sex down to just inside the tolerances of human endurance. Violet was a little sad I took down the monkey bars, but understood it was for the best," Talon joked right back.

Grant laughed, but told Talon "Honestly bro... all jokes aside... it's good to see you like this again."

"Uh, like what?"

"Like this! Laughing... happy... and because of someone being in your life that you're happy with."

Talon gave Grant a friendly pat on the back, smiled at Violet in the distance, and replied "Yeah, ya know what? It kinda is." Talon looked at Grant and asked "Abigail get to her plane okay?"

"Oh yeah." Grant laughed saying "I must have a hundred texts from her and that was before the plane even took off!"

Grant looked around, then spoke to Talon in a hushed tone.

"Listen bro, I wanna ask you something."

"Sure G what's up?"

"Don't help me on this one unless I ask okay?" Grant began to explain, "I know you're this big corporate powerhouse around here... AND on this job... but with Abigail, well, I'd like to be one for a change."

Talon knew where this was going, and was actually happy for it.

"Not a chance 'little brother'. I'm going to stick my nose in where it don't belong, pull hundreds of strings, and..."

"Like HELL you are!" Grant challenged.

Talon just laughed as he sat back in his chair. Grant was confused for a second before he caught onto the joke.

"You dick," Grant said now laughing along with his brother.

Talon told him kindly "Look pal, aside from your office practices being nearly non existent, you are actually in good shape to do what you're asking. You know I won't interfere but..."

"But what?"

Now it was Talon who checked that the coast was clear before leaning in and finishing his thoughts.

"But... you're going to run into snags. When I do a job I am never so egotistical as to think I can do it all by myself. EVERY one needs help now and then. You wanna get Abigail on your own? Fine by me but, for a change, I'm gonna be your wingman. Remember, when you come up on that snag... and you will... I insist you come to me rather than lose it all. Deal?"

"Thanks bro... deal," Grant said with a kind brotherly hug.

Talon sat back with a grand smile and said "So, what's our first move in 'Operation Abigail'?"

Grant chuckled and corrected "MY first move... is I want to meet her parents, and see where she grew up."

"New issue to factor in, oh red dude. She's their baby, their ONLY... and adopted... baby. You won't just meet the parents on that one. You'll be grilled like a terrorist in Guantanamo."

Grant had an expression that was part sadness, part pride.

"Ya know what I say to that? I say... bring it! Look Tal, you and Eileen have never been mean to me. Growing up though, I always felt like I was the third wheel. I know you two didn't do it on purpose, but I guess with how close you two were, it was kind'a inevitable. With Abigail though, none of that matters. My office mess aside, is there anything so wrong with me that I shouldn't or couldn't get a girl like her?"

Talon kindly told him "Not that I can see."

Grant continued, "Nor I. Thanks to mom and dad, I'm far more educated than many of our peers who have college degrees. More self sufficient and more successful too. I like to think I have manners, and I certainly have enough money to provide for her. Last I checked, I seem to be okay looking too. Bottom line, what good was all that upbringing, and all my hard work good for, if I can't show it... and me... off, at a time like this?"

Talon agreed, and in a brotherly tone, said "Eileen keeps spewing about the Grayson women. I say, go show 'mom and dad', what the Grayson men are capable of."

Talon got up to go back to work. He playfully sneered at his brother and said "And when you do... I'll expect a full report on my desk by morning."

Both brothers laughed, and work on the mansion resumed.

It was later that night, and Grant was waiting for his computer to 'ring'. He was waiting on a video call from Abigail. He was stuffing his face with some take-out and was wondering about something. He was curious why all the girls in the restaurants he frequents, all seem to be angry lately.

"No, not angry really... angry *at* me!" he pondered to himself. "Jeez, what did I do?"

Poor Grant had no idea that, as happy as Abigail made him on the inside, it showed just as much on the outside. As such, Grant would learn that girls pick up on things like that. Seeing Grant obviously happy, and knowing full well why, had them a bit unhappy knowing it wasn't them.

"Looks yummy, did Violet make that?" Abigail's computer image asked.
"Nah, it's takeout."
"Ya know..." Abigail cooed, "... that stuff is no good for you. You, uh, you need more good home cooked meals."
"Sounds like a good idea. I've been thinking about getting a woman in here to take care of me. Got anyone you could recommend?" Grant asked toying with her a little.
With a little girl smile, Abigail winked at him saying "Wellllll, I do know of ONE person."
"Well, if YOU recommend her, I guess I could interview her then," Grant teased.

Grant talked to her now in a serious tone.
"Abigail I wanna talk to you."
The dirty blond haired nerd girl now got nervous.
"I was talking to Talon," Grant started.
Now Abigail got even more nervous. Violet was nearly petrified over Eileen, and whether she'd approve of her or not. That was how Abigail felt, except her imaginary demon was the gray haired brother, not the candlestick.
"Um... what did he say?" Abigail asked nervously.
"Nothing major. We were talking about us... as in you and me," Grant told her.
Abigail was nearly squirming now. Her computers didn't judge her. People however were a different story. After her life altering experience at the

mansion, most of those insecurities went away. Talon however, was one she still felt she needed to impress. She also knew how her new love felt about his older brother.

"Anyway," Grant continued, "I decided something. I asked for his opinion and he agreed. Abigail?"

"Yes?" was the near panicked response.

"I don't like hiding. I want to meet mom and dad. More importantly, I want them to meet me."

"Um... you suuuuure about that?" Abigail asked wincing at the thought.

"Positive," Grant told her confidently. He saw her face and complained "Oh no... Abigail!?... You didn't tell them about me did you?"

That made her laugh.

"Just the opposite. (giggle) I haven't *stopped* talking about you!"

"Okay then, mind telling me why you nearly looked sick when I mentioned it?" Grant asked clearly confused.

Abigail relented and told her story.

"Senior Prom. Did you go to yours?" Abigail asked with a heavy dose of sadness in her voice.

"I did. Odd question, what about it?"

"I was supposed to go to mine, but never did."

Grant knew in an instant he wasn't going to like this story.

"And?" he pressed.

"I had no boyfriends growing up. Like... zero... none, nada. When I got asked by a boy to go to prom, I was over the moon. I couldn't stop talking about it for weeks. Mom was happy for me and helped me with the girlie stuff. Dad was happy for me too... until prom night."

Slight tears were starting to form in her eyes as she continued.

"I was waiting for him to show up. He never did."

"HE STOOD YOU UP!!??" Grant bellowed with some serious anger in his voice.

"Sadly. I felt like such a fool, because I called around thinking something bad may have happened to him. Dad called his house and his parents were nice, but clueless. He had asked someone else and never told me. More like... forgot to."

Grant was barely containing the locally famous Grayson anger. The guy Eileen mentioned to Shadow Man, who tried slapping her around, was a senior when she was a junior. He seemed dreamy... until his darker side showed up. Eileen quite literally put him in the hospital. It was the only time Talon didn't defend her. That's because Papa Joe did. When the kid's parents showed up at the police station yelling and screaming, Papa Joe told them he was still alive, and that they should accept their losses and go. He also told them, if anyone came after Eileen or any of the Grayson's, he would see to it they'd be laying next to their son shortly thereafter. He also told them they'd be in worse shape than he was. Momma G also made it known her talents would be applied as well. She told them she would simply smile as all 'conventional treatments' seemingly failed to work. Mom and dad were more than well known in town but, extremely well liked as well.

Now, hearing this story from Abigail, Grant was about ready to destroy her little home town. Talon and Eileen had established themselves 'as a Grayson'. Now, Grant was about to serve up notice and make his own mark.

Abigail finished with "I was sad as you might expect. I didn't cry though, until I saw how hurt mom and dad were. They were truly sad for me. Anyway, since then... well, I think you can figure it out. Mom more so than dad but, I'm afraid you may get a little more 'grilled' than you might expect."

Grant stood tall and proud and made his stand for his own honor.

"Sorry Abigail, but I've got work I need to do so I'm gonna make tonight's call short."

"Awww" Abigail whined.

Grant told her "Tomorrow night, um... tell mom I'd like to talk to her... alone. I'm not scared of them, and I want them to see they have no reason to be scared of me."

The usual blowing of kisses was next, then Grant hit the 'end call' button.

"Hiya Jim, it's me Grant," baby G said as the other end of the phone picked up.

"Yo Grant! Good to hear from you! What can I do for ya?"

Grant told him "Listen Jim, ya know that little organization of yours? You know, the one I just happen to be a major contributor to?"

Jim changed tones in a heartbeat and said "I do. What's up?"

"Well, you might say I need a little something back now," and Grant told him why he called.

"Honestly, I would love to help you locally but, ours is already over. At your destination however, they usually do things later. I may be able to help you out with that. I know the guy that runs that side of things. He's a notorious night owl. Give me a few minutes and I'll call you back okay?"

Grant wanted this done.

"I'll await your call," Grant told him.

It took about ten minutes and Jim was calling back.

"Hey Grant. Okay so I talked to the guy. There's only one way to pull this off but, I think you'll like what I got," and Jim told him of his plan.

Now Grant was smiling... large.

"Tell them they will now. I'll fund it on one condition. I want nothing of the New England lifestyle that hurt my new gal anywhere near that event. If they're willing to make it an old west theme... then I'll take care of the rest."

In an honest tone, Jim told him "Grant? You are truly a good man. I know they'll be thrilled. As for that plan of yours, well, I hope it turns out in your favor in every way possible."

"Jim?... Me too. Thanks for all the help."

The next night, Grant was ready, willing, and able. He placed the call, and smiled at the image that greeted him.

"So... you're the man my daughter hasn't stopped talking about, hmm?"

Grant grinned and said confidently, "Grant Grayson, Mrs. Jensen. A pleasure to meet you. I apologize it couldn't be in person but, until I arrive, I hope you'll accept this technological substitute?"

"Arrive?" Abigail's mother said slightly thrown off.

"Indeed. I plan on coming out there to meet you and your husband properly. I also plan on taking Abigail on a first date, and, not just any first date. I wanna take her on a first date she'll talk about for the rest of her life. That's where you come in. I want to make it special, and make up for past sins as it were. Abigail has warned me you'd be rather critical and judgmental... but in a protective way. Hearing why, I can't say I blame you. So, I invite you to give me the 'grilling' I was told I'd receive." Grant smiled and finished with "I have no doubt that when you're finished... and hear my plan... you'll know you have nothing to fear from me, and why I wanted to talk to you."

Mrs. Jensen was thrown off by the confident but caring young man. From Abigail's rantings, she figured the real version would be far less than she was led to believe. Now seeing, and hearing, the charming red-haired man on her screen... she was almost as enamored with him as her daughter was.

Mrs. Jensen told him "Okay then, how about some rapid fire questions?"

"Name your terms m'lady," Grant jested without a care in the world.

"I ask... you answer in 5 seconds or less."

Grant confidently told her "Fire away."

"Do you love Abigail?"

"Too early to tell but if how I feel stays true, then I would say very likely in time."

That was actually the answer she was looking for.

"Should you two become heavily involved... will it be here or there."

"Here."

"Tell me why."

Grant said "Simple. There, she's locally known. Here she's unknown. With my hair color I've never been much of a beach fan... and I hate fish. There, she has a reputation, and not a good one. Here, we'd be close, and she gets a fresh start based on 'her'... not her past. I also have plans to offer her a job. A proper job, mind you. If I can't my brother can so either way she'd be employed. Also, out here... IF the old taunts and bullies resurfaced... then I'd see to it they knew she had a knight in shining armor waiting in the wings."

Abigail's mom was getting answers she wasn't expecting. She was however, liking the one's she got. She grilled Grant for another 5 minutes or so. He though, never faltered once. Now, she pulled out her trump card.

"She plans on coming back out there. My husband and I however, plan on coming with her this trip. Any problem with that?"

"Yes and no," Grant told her.

"Feel free to enlighten me on each."

"Did Abigail tell you what I'm doing?"

"Heh heh... in lavish detail."

Grant answered "Well then, my brother and I are at a critical phase and really can't stop at this point. Not for about another 3 weeks. Then, I can take no more than a week off before I'm needed back here. I plan to use that window to come to you. When you arrive here, I'll be busy most days and some nights. If you were expecting to be entertained, then know I won't have very much time for you. If not, then I'll have mostly nights free. You're welcome to stay in one of my guest rooms, but I live a bit out of town. If you find those conditions okay, then I don't mind showing you around 'the old west'."

Mrs. Jensen smiled... and ended the grilling.

"Well then young man, I find your offer most gracious."

Grant joked "So... did I pass?"

Abigail's mother smiled and joked right back.

"Let's just say, you didn't fail. Now... heh heh... let's hear about this date idea you have!"

Grant laid out his idea. He gave her every detail he had, and asked if she'd not only play along, but be his 'go to' person for anything in the local area he wasn't familiar with. Mrs. Jensen was liking this idea, but also felt old wounds start to reopen.

"Mind if I call you Grant?"

"Mind if I call you Linda?"

"Not at all."

"Then Grant works for me," he said with a dashing smile.

"Listen Grant, that night was a terrible one in our family. It broke our hearts to see her treated like that. I know what your doing with this plan of yours. While I commend you on 'why' you're doing it, I warn you, we won't go through that twice."

Grant told her kindly "The very tone in your voice is the whole reason I'm doing this. I get to help out a bunch of kids, and give a grownup something she was denied... cruelly... when she was one. Also, I don't want her knowing a thing till that night. That's why I asked for you. I'd like you to help me help her. Get her 'costume' ready, so that when I arrive... she'll be surprised as hell. This time however, in a good way."

"I warn you Grant, if you don't show up, I'll..."

He cut her off saying "I will be there. You have my word that IF for some reason I'm not... then you may want to start checking the hospitals and jails. I'm telling you... THAT... is the only reason I wouldn't be there. So Linda, care to help me with my little plan?"

"Hold up your end of things... and I'll hold up mine. Grant?"

"Yes ma'am?"

"I hope this plan of yours works out."

Grant told her "Linda? So do I."

Polite goodbye's and the video link went dead. Both people at each end were smiling when it did.

Talon told his brother as they worked "See baby G? What did I tell ya? For the record, I think it's a fine idea. Smart, kind, and everything mom and dad taught us to do or be. They'd be proud of you lil brother."

Talon was commenting on Grant's plan. Grant told him what happened, and what he decided to do about it. He and Talon were finally getting the floor beams put in to cover up the hole in the floor just inside and to the right of the entry doors. The 2 brothers were chatting while they got the new floor joists in place, and took out the temporary jacks.

"Yeah well, when I heard that story, I was pissed. Then I realized, that was the idea I was looking for."

"Dude, seriously, it's a great idea. We can easily afford to lose you for a week. I know what you're doing for those kids too, and I think it's grand. How many 'like you' do you have so far?"

"So far, just me and Abigail," Grant told him.

Talon smiled already planning something.

"And how many do you need?"

"At least 6," Grant answered.

"Bro? I got this. Consider this my gift to the two of you but, I'll get you the rest," Talon said smiling at the thought in his head.

Grant just said "Tal? I trust you. We give each other shit like brothers do, but I know you wouldn't do something dumb. And by the way... thanks."

And with that, the last of Grant's plan took shape.

The next 3 weeks was a flurry of activity. The mansion's first floor was 75% complete by the time Talon called a halt to the restoration. All the electric was tied in by now. As a manly joke, all the crews cheered when the first toilet to be installed... flushed without a single leak. The well was operational again, and the back patio became a favorite among the workers. They would all take a break, or take lunch, out there. A few of the trumpet vines even had tiny flowers on them by now.

Talon had never done this much carpentry in his life. He was loving every bit of it though. Thanks to some modern tools, he managed to rebuild many of the corbels. The lathe was going almost nonstop one day. The living room however, had 5 more tables either repaired, rebuilt, or replaced. Seven of the chairs were as well.

Erik had gotten him the chemical makeups for the lacquers that were used. The local store said they couldn't do it as one of the original ingredients was whale oil. Not exactly in large supply around 'these here parts'. Grant laughed at Talon one day, because he actually acquired some. Baby G never asked how either.

The last week saw the grand staircase that went upstairs from the parlor come back to life. Talon managed to save half of the original spindles. Using some of the old teak beams he had delivered, he recreated the other half. He and Grant even managed to re-lay the wood flooring in the living room, just like they said they would. Talon had made a call, and the 'tile guys' he boasted of knowing, would be by in about two weeks.

Several times Shadow Man tried to wreak havoc. Once he turned the electric breakers back on as the electricians tried to work. Lucinda however wasn't having any of it. She was getting stronger by the day. She moved two live wires together and created a hell of a spark but... the electrician got the message. Lucinda stayed in the shadows around the workers. Once or twice, Shadow Man did not. Yet again he was thwarted as Lucinda managed to steer the workers away from danger. Once or twice they knew it too. With no concrete proof, they merely offered their thanks to the portrait downstairs. To them, she started off as a good luck charm. In the last few weeks though, she became more of a patron saint... and was now treated that way. A ritual began too. Every Friday night now, the workers left a glass of sherry... and a bloom of Edelweiss from the garden... on the mantle below her picture. It was a form of thanks for another safe week. Every Monday morning, the flower would be gone and the glass would be empty. Talon promised them it wasn't him doing it. Some didn't believe him, some did, but all thought it nice and treated the empty glass and missing flower as a sign of good luck. This Friday however, they left 2 glasses and two flowers... and told 'The Grand Lady' they'd all see her in 10 days time.

Abigail was nervous as she walked into court. Linda, and dad Jerry, were at her side. It was just them, the original judge who sentenced her, the court clerk, and a representative from the prosecutor's office. Right after she walked in, Officer Glass came in and gave her a smile. What had Abigail nervous was, today was the earliest she could get the bracelet off but, even her parole officer told her that wasn't guaranteed. She was wearing a nice, but proper dress, and was just hoping to impress the judge. A few minutes later, the judge walked in, and everybody stood up. Now more than ever, Abigail tried her best to not 'geek out'.

      "As these proceedings are small to say the least," the judge began, "I'll skip the formalities. IF everyone can behave, then I see no reason to make this the spectacle it was last time." He looked to the side and said "Officer Glass, how have you found the defendant's manner, behavior, and compliance in these last years?"

      Officer Glass was proud to tell him "I have seen no desire to harm anyone, nor to sneak around her restrictions. She has been not only a model citizen, but a model parolee as well. I recently gave her permission to leave the state on personal business. She complied with all the rules I gave her and even checked in with the local parole office in that state as proof of that."

      "Very well officer. In your opinion, do you see any reason to alter, or extend, the punishment set forth by this court?"

      A short, and confident, "No your honor... I do not," was his answer.

      The judge then asked the prosecutor for his opinion. He tried the 'once a threat always a threat' thing but, even he wasn't too enthused about it. Figuring he didn't have much chance, he barely prepared and honestly couldn't care less what the outcome was.

      The judge was kind and asked Abigail to stand up.

      "Well young lady, when first we met, you were a teenager. I am happy and sad for you at the same time. I see, and am happy for, the lovely and responsible young woman that you've become. What makes me sad however, is the empty seats I see behind you. Abigail listen, I know you were just an exuberant teenager when you got in trouble. I also know, you were, as an adopted child, just trying to find out who you were and where you came from. However... knowingly or unknowingly... you still broke the law. Regardless of what I think of you personally, I won't let that interfere with my ruling. Tell me this though Abigail, in all the years since my original ruling... have you found no friends? No solace in the company of others? Not one person who would stand up for your honor?"

Abigail was about to say something. Someone else did it for her.

"My apologies for the intrusion your honor, but, I'm not from around here. Seems we got a little lost finding the place," Grant said nearly blowing through the door.

"I? We? Just who are you young man and what business do you have in this courtroom?"

Grant walked in and Abigail beamed from ear to ear. She was choked up with tears at the others who filed in behind him.

"My name is Grant Grayson your honor. I believe I would be the 'friend' you just asked about."

"As would we, your honor," Talon said walking in behind his brother.

The we he referred to was the fact that Violet was on his arm.

"You can add us to the list as well your honor," was the proud comment from an out of town doctor.

Doc Holliday had arrived with a very lovely red-haired woman on his arm.

"And me as well judge," Zach said bringing up the rear.

Linda and Jerry were stunned. Abigail however, was just over the moon.

"And who would you be?" the judge asked.

"My name is Grant Grayson your honor. Sole proprietor of G-Man Construction Incorporated. My reputation hasn't quite made it out this far across the country... yet. I assure you though, the one you'll find if you researched it would be a good one. I am the defendant's boyfriend."

The judge had a slight smile and said "And you sir?"

"Talon Grayson your honor. CEO and COO of Grayson Industries. This lovely lady here is my girlfriend Miss Violet Hayes."

The judge chuckled and pointed to Cody.

"Your turn."

"Doctor Cody Holliday. This lady with me is not only my girlfriend, but a Grayson as well."

"Doc Holliday eh? Remind me not to play poker with you," the judge politely joked. "And lastly, you young man? Who are you?"

"My name sir, is Zack Jameson. I work for Mr. Talon Grayson, and am a dear friend of the defendant and Mr. Grant Grayson."

Abigail was about to say something. Linda knew her though, and gave a slight kick to her ankle to remind her not to.

The judge looked the new crowd over and asked "And you're all here why exactly?"

"May I?" Grant asked waving a hand to the room.

The judge nodded.

"Your honor, we are here as character references, and to merely support a friend. While you don't know us, and you only have my word on the matter, I can assure you... my family would not be here supporting Abigail if she had not earned it. Not even for me. That said, I'll be happy to answer any questions you may have on the defendant's behalf."

"Alright then, romantic interest aside, what plans do you have for the defendant?"

"As an owner of my own company, my talents more than speak for themselves. However, while I could fix or restore your house for you, I'm not much of an office manager. I have offered the defendant, a position in my company to organize, and run my office including the operational finances. I'm happy to say she's accepted my offer."

"I have?" Abigail blurted softly. Another kick from mom and she said "Uh I mean... I have!"

Talon piped in with "Your honor, my office is well sorted. I also offered her a job, though as my IT specialist. I have put her in charge of network security. Abigail's talents highly impressed me when last she visited, which is why I offered her the position. My brother and I mention this so you would know, she has... on her own merits and talents... secured full time employment for herself. She has agreed to that offer as well. Neither mine, nor my brother's job offer, is enough for full time employment. Both are part time jobs, but put together, add up to full time work. Not to mention, while frowned upon... last I checked, nepotism wasn't illegal. So, my brother was right. While only we have jobs for her, ALL of us are here to support a good friend, nothing more. You'll also find my reputation, and that of my siblings AND our companies... are as sterling as the silver that runs through our hills."

Now the judge was happy.

"I hereby declare a recess of one hour while I verify your claims. Once I have, or have not, I will deliver my ruling when this court resumes."

The judge smacked his gavel and everyone filed out.

Abigail's dad, Jerry, told Grant "So, you're the man who stole my little girl's heart eh?"

Grant politely replied "Grant Grayson... a pleasure to meet you sir. And, to be fair... she stole mine first."

Jerry laughed lightly and said "So, you and your brother are the one's my daughter has been calling the 'G-Men' huh? Heh heh... to be honest... it took me an hour to realize she wasn't talking about some federal agents!"

Grant made nice for around 15 minutes or so as Abigail introduced him to mom and dad. All the others stayed away to give Grant a moment. After that, he called the others over and Abigail introduced them all one by one. She also thanked them for their efforts on her behalf. So did mom and dad.

Talon said "My brother was right. If Abigail hadn't impressed or charmed us too... we wouldn't be here... not even for him."

Linda playfully teased to Violet "You my dear should consider yourself lucky. If I was single, and 20 years younger... welllllll," and she finished with a playful wink to Talon.

"Mmmmmoooooooooommmmmm!!!!!" Abigail whined in embarrassment.

Even Jerry laughed, but both parents honestly thanked Abigail's new friends for their efforts on their daughter's behalf. They also treated them to a quick lunch before going back in.

"Mr. Grant Grayson... you sir check out," the judge said as the proceedings resumed. "You sir... Mr. Talon Grayson, you have a very interesting list of friends. Seems a certain senator called to vouch for you as well!"

Talon nearly sneered and asked "Oh Bob? Yeah... me and him go way back. That wasn't a bit over the top was it?"

"Hmmm," the judge nearly admonished. "Suffice to say, you have all checked out and seem to be all that you have claimed. Abigail? Approach the bench please."

She did and the judge laid it out for her.

"It is the decision of this court, that you have served out your punishment in accordance with the law. I want you to know, had your friends not spoken up for you... AND been the people they claimed to be... I likely would have extended your sentence. My fear was that, without some solid direction, and some good people in your life, I was afraid you'd only end up right back in here. As a person, I am happy for you. As a judge of the state, and the law, I hereby declare your punishment served. Also, because the events that led you here, were done when you were a minor, I'm ordering those records sealed for all times. Congratulations Abigail... you are a free woman," and he banged the gavel saying "THIS court... is adjourned."

Cheers broke out all around. Officer Glass was hoping for this. As such, he had the keys and the shutoff codes. With a kind smile, he knelt down... and Abigail was free of her ankle jewelry. She gave him a friendly hug, then gave her parents a loving one. At only 5ft 6in to Grant's 6ft 1... she jumped and wrapped her arms around him. In full view of everyone she planted a hard kiss on him. She was crying happy thankful tears when she did.

Abigail was sitting on her bed when her phone rang. When she saw Grant's picture on the screen, the high she'd been on since court this afternoon came spewing out at full Abigail force.

"Grant! Oh my God did you see the look on the judge's face when he spoke about the senator!? Your sister looked amazing by the way. I wish I had her fashion sense, hell I wish I had her wardrobe! Officer Glass was so nice wasn't he? Oh and don't get me started on..."

"Hello to you too sunshine," Grant chuckled as he cut her off mid blather.

He had gotten used to it now, and it was his sweet way of letting her know she was rambling.

"Aaaaaah... hi my sweet... sorry."

Grant told her "I'm dropping out of mom's dinner invitation. Let her know I said that please, it's uh... kind of important."

"Awww. I'll see you later though right?"

"Oh, I think you can count on that," Grant told her.

Abigail gave her mother Grant's message. She also thought it a bit odd at how happy it seemed to make her.

"After dinner, dear, I have a present for you," Linda told her while they sat at the table.

"Mom, you didn't have to get me anything."

Abigail braced herself, and gave them some bad news.

"Mom? Dad? I uh... have some news. I want you to know I love you both dearly, I truly do. I loved growing up with you. Sadly, I've never liked it here. And when I say here, I don't mean this house... I mean this town, this state, hell this whole part of the world. I want you to know, I'm moving out west."

Abigail braced for an uproar... that never came.

Jerry calmly ate his dinner and told her "Is that so huh? Well young lady, you know the rules of this table. If you're going to say something like that, you...?"

"Daaaaad," Abigail giggled, "I'm not 12 anymore."

"Hmm, perhaps but... rules are rules my dear," he retorted.

"Fine then," Abigail said in a playful 'I accept your challenge' tone. "If you are angry or happy or sad, you can stay totally silent but people around you would still know. Basically your body language gives you away. I've been thinking a lot lately, ever since I came back from the mansion. I think that may have been why I was bullied so much. My body language gave that away and people just picked up on it."

This was more debate than discussion. Jerry was a lawyer and not only that... he was Abigail's defense attorney. Dinners were often times a mock trial. It was his way of teaching Abigail how to present herself, stand up for herself, or explain herself. Point and counterpoint. Mom was no slouch in that area but, Abigail and Jerry could do this for hours.

"I'm still listening," Jerry told her. "If you're going to present an argument like that Abigail... at this table anyway... you're going to back it up."

"If I could... I would move this entire house... and put it on Grant's block. There's just something about life out there that doesn't just appeal to me... it's as if it's calling me. I feel like, if someone had me design my perfect life, out there would be it. Like I said, I loved growing up in this house... and with both of you. Now that I have... I want to 'grow old' out there."

Abigail was a little confused by how well mom and dad were taking all this.

Dad stopped being judge and jury, and returned to just good old Jerry.

"Abigail listen to me. From the moment you came back, mom and I were actually expecting this. We've always felt sorry for you but only in the sense of how you were treated... and why. Even we can't say you weren't treated unfairly. We love you tons Abby and only want to see you happy, like any parent would. We know how young love, or new love, can be. But you're right, we both saw the sparkle in your eye. Even we saw that beyond Grant, there was a love that was for a place, not a person. Mom and I were planning on telling you soon, that we've been thinking of doing the same thing. Winters here are now for the young, and your mother and I are at the point in our lives where, well, we're ready for a change as well."

Abigail hugged them both and said "Until you do, I'll come and visit whenever I can. I'll expect you to do the same and know wherever I end up, you'll always be welcome."

Mom and dad hugged her back.

"Uh... Abigail my dear... we're running out of time," Linda said as she looked at her watch.

"We are?" Abigail said totally clueless.

"Yeah... we are?" Jerry asked just as clueless.

"Oh yes, we are indeed," mom said with a smile. "Abby, go up to your room and I'll meet you there with that present I promised you."

Abigail put her plate in the sink and did as she was asked. Upstairs, mom walked in with a long box.

"That man you chose is a rather impressive young gentleman. I think it's time we show him... you are a fine young lady."

Linda opened the box and Abigail was confused at the sight.

"Mom, this is one of the dresses from your theater group."

"It is aaaaand... it isn't. This is the dress you always liked but, Martha the seamstress made it all new for you."

"And you got me that why exactly? I mean, it's beautiful and all but... um... a tad out of fashion," Abigail extolled.

"Not tonight it isn't," Linda said with a smile. "Go get undressed and I'll help you get into this one."

Abigail did and had a fun time playing dress up. Linda brushed her long hair then used and old style leather oval and stick to hold her hair in a loose ponytail. She came out and presented herself in the cobalt blue dress... and bustle. It was a dress that was more suited for Virginia City, than New England. Abigail put in her contacts and stood in the mirror and admired herself.

Linda half hugged her and said "You grew up to be very beautiful... never forget that."

Abigail was smiling at that as Linda walked away to get Abigail's ankle boots. Still looking in the mirror, a 'second Abigail' smiled back at her from over her shoulder. Abigail pet the glass lovingly as the image faded away at Linda's return.

"I don't mind telling you I feel pretty in this but, do ya mind telling me why you're dressing me up like a doll?"

Linda pinned a hat to her hair as Abigail laced up her boots.

"Not really," mom said playfully. "There! All done. You look stunning. JERRY!! COME UP HERE PLEASE!!" Linda hollered.

Jerry did and was smiling as only a proud poppa can.

"You look gorgeous Abby," he stated kindly.

Abigail got into the spirit of it, and curtsied.

"Thank you sir," she giggled.

Mom took Abby's phone, brought up a number, and texted it. The reply she got had her beaming. She grabbed Jerry and hustled him downstairs.

"Stay here!" mom shouted to Abigail.

She just chuckled at her parents and said "Uh... ooooooookay."

The doorbell rang, and Linda smiled.

"Jerry? I think you may want to get that," Linda said with a kind smile.

He opened the door and said "Grant! Nice to see you young man. Why are... you... dressed like....... ohhhhh, I get it now," Jerry said seeing his attire. "You're taking Abby to a costume party aren't you?"

"No sir. Good evening Mister Jensen, is Abigail home?" Grant said with extreme manners.

"She is indeed. Won't you come in?" Jerry said all friendly like.

"Mrs. Jensen," Grant said with a tip of his hat. He turned to Jerry and said "Actually no sir, it's not a costume party. I was wondering if I might escort your daughter to the prom?"

This was Grant's idea of a first date. He was going to give Abigail the night of her life, and see to it he righted a wrong done several years before. He even had a corsage.

Before Jerry could respond, Linda stepped in saying "Well young man, look at you looking so spiffy."

"Thank you ma'am," Grant said with a smile.

He was decked out in a similar outfit to his brother when he went to see Lucinda. Right down to the silver chain and pocket watch hidden in a vest pocket. Oh yes ladies and gentlemen, the old west had just arrived in the land of crab and lobster.

Linda grabbed Grant by the arm while Jerry rushed to find a camera. He was hurt probably the most by Abigail's rejection, so she said nothing in case it happened again. If however, the prom date DID show up this time, well, that would be a nice surprise for him too.

"Abigail!? I believe you have a gentleman caller! Would you mind coming down here please!?"

Abigail was still not getting it and said "Like this!?"

"Oh yes dear... EXACTLY like that," mom told her kindly.

Abigail got her walk she was denied. It's the one all girls dream about where they come down the stairs and 'wow' their date. This time at least, he showed up. She rounded the top and came down and caught sight of Grant. Seeing him dressed up like she was, now she smiled.

Grant just stared and said "You look amazing."

She actually blushed and told him "Looking mighty handsome yourself there 'Mista G'," flirting some as she walked down the stairs.

Grant stood tall and proud and said "Miss Jensen, if you would be my escort for the evening, I would be honored to take you to the prom," and he pulled out the corsage.

"I would be... wait... prom!?"

"My idea of a first date. I think you'll like what I came up with."

Abigail was about to cry seeing Grant care for her so much. She held her hand out gingerly, and Grant slipped the corsage on her wrist. She ran and hugged mom.

Pictures all around and, with all the usual posing. Grant didn't mind at all and was determined to give Abigail everything she was denied and more. When it came time to leave, Grant teased her a little.

"Sorry but, I kinda ran out of money and couldn't afford a limo. I sorta had to... um... downgrade a little."

Abigail was mush right now. Grant opened the door to a cool June New England evening. Out in front of Abigail's house... was a horse and carriage.

Now Jerry teased Grant about having his daughter back home safe... and early.

Dad pulled Grant to the side quick and said "Thanks for this."

Grant replied "I don't mean this rudely but, I didn't do this for you. If however, I can please a set of parents too... well... no harm in that right?"

"No young man... none at all."

Grant walked over to Linda and held his arms out with a questioning look on his face. She smiled and gave him a hug.

"Thanks for all your help Mrs. Jensen," he whispered to her.

"Oh... you two just get out of here and go have a good time," she told them fighting back the happy tears.

Abigail looked over her shoulder at them as she walked away. The smile on her face, and the kiss she blew to them, had made their hearts melt.

The carriage rode through town. Everybody smiled and politely waved seeing the decked out couple. Abigail got her own, and unplanned, revenge. This was one of those 'truth is stranger than fiction' kind of moments. She politely waved to a young man and woman walking up the street. Grant had no clue who they were and just followed her lead.

"Holy shit! Is that Abigail Jensen!? Wow, I almost didn't recognize her. Damn, she turned out to be hot!" the man said as he walked with his girlfriend.

With scorn in her voice, she replied "I'm not much for redheads myself, but, if that guy smiled at me like that!? I'd drop you like a hot rock!"

Abigail had a smile on her face that just seemed to say 'nyaa'. That guy was the one who ditched her on her first prom night.

"Who was that? Grant asked.

Abigail sat back and snuggled into Grant's shoulder, and told him "Just some nobody I used to know."

Grant just shrugged it off as the carriage rolled on by.

The carriage came to a stop in front of a one level brick building.

"Okay you... we're at the 'Boys and Girls' club why exactly?" Abigail asked with a chuckle.

Grant helped her down and took her in his arm as he walked her inside.

"I promised you a prom... and that's exactly what you're going to get."

With that, Grant blew open the doors and showed Abigail a portal back in time. It was the gymnasium, but, it was decked out like a street in the old west. There were over 200 kids and all of them were dressed in similar outfits.

"Oh my!" Abigail said nearly in shock. "You did this... all this... for me?"

"Because of you... and yes for you but... for them as well." Grant explained, "My company is a major contributor to this organization. They teach kids who have nowhere else to go valuable skills and lessons, and keep good one's from becoming bad one's. I hate the fact that they don't teach shop classes in schools anymore... so I support an organization that does teach them. They have a formal dance every year but due to budget issues, they couldn't afford one this year. So... I paid for it on two conditions. First, it had to be western... not eastern. Second, we had to have official invitations," and Grant pulled out a pair and showed Abby as he held them in between two fingers. "You got gypped out of your prom. You're a little older now so, we get to be the chaperone's but..." and Grant smiled and finished with a wave of his hand saying "Welcome to the Grant Grayson First Date Extravaganza!"

Abigail was in awe. Awe at what she saw around her... awe at what lengths the G-men would go to... and just plain awe that someone would do ALL that... just for her.

She hugged Grant hard and said "I love it. And I love you even more for doing this for me. Grant? It's perfect."

Grant got a kiss that made a small group of nearby teenagers holler whistle and applaud.

Talon and Violet, Cody and Eileen, and even Zach walked up to Abigail. They were all dressed in period piece clothing to go with the theme of the evening. They were 'the rest' Talon promised Grant.

"So Miss Jensen... enjoying yourself this evening?" Eileen asked with a friendly smile.

"Honestly Eileen... I ... I ... I don't know where to go first! Everything is so amazing."

Talon said "The kids made all the props and scenery themselves. A lot of the girls, I found out, find this type of clothing romantic. So the theme was an easy sell."

The Grayson's were used to this type of dress and knew how to rock it. Eileen went for more of the saloon girl look, and that sat just fine with Cody. Being that the chaperone's were older but, according to the kids, 'not old'... they were getting checked out by more than just their dates. A song came on and several girls pulled Abigail onto the floor with them. She had a blast just being her dorky self, and was nothing more than a big kid. Grant laughed seeing her but thought she was cute all the same. It didn't matter to him but, if Abigail had a wonderful time, well then, that's what this was all about anyway.

The DJ stopped and two kids, a boy and a girl, got up on the little stage and took one microphone each.

"My name is John, and this lovely lady beside me is Judy, and we are the organizers of tonight's event," the boy said as he started his speech. "I'd like to call to the stage Mister Grant Grayson and Miss Abigail Jensen!"

Neither Grant nor Abigail knew of this but made their way to the stage. The boy dropped back and the girl took over.

"We would like to thank you Mister Grayson for making all this possible. I don't mind saying, all of us were quite bummed when we found out we couldn't have a formal this year. For many of us this *is* our prom... and our last year here with the B&G club. So from all of us here, we wanted to thank you for giving us back what we almost didn't have."

A huge round of applause rang out across the room. The boy stepped back in and said "As such, we'd be honored if you'd read this," and he handed Grant a ballot total.

"What is this?" Grant asked.

"Mister Grayson? You hold in your hand... voted on by all present, mind you... the winners of prom king and queen. We would be honored if you would read it."

"I'd be happy to," Grant said kindly as he opened the envelope. "Is this some kind of a joke?" Grant asked though not in a nasty way.

"No sir," the boy told him happily.

Grant read with a chuckle "The winners of Prom King and Queen are.... Grant Grayson and Abigail Jensen!"

"WWWWWWHAT!?" Abigail blurted out in shock.

Judy told them " When we heard what you were doing for Miss Jensen... and why... then what you were doing for us as well... we all just felt it was the right thing to do."

Cheers and applause erupted again as Grant and Abigail were crowned king and queen. Both made nice, hugged John and Judy, and made their way out to a solo slow dance in the middle of the floor. Abigail was in heaven and Grant swore he'd remember the look on Abigail's face right now for all his days. Mission accomplished, he waved everyone onto the floor halfway through the song. The party was a hit, the Grayson's were a hit... and the evening rolled on into history.

Chapter 19

"Kuh-POW!"

It was a sunny morning as the Grayson entourage filed into the airport. Talon made the arrangements for everyone, but hated it.

"If we EVER do this again," he grumbled to Violet, "I am not making the reservations. I'll either let someone else do it... or I'm getting my own damn plane!"

His own comment gave him an idea... and a new item to shop for on the auction sites.

Abigail was teary eyed at leaving mom and dad. They had the usual response any parent would have. Still, they stayed happy for Abigail's sake, and reminded her it would only be a month before they arrived. They packed up a bunch of Abigail's things and shipped out most of it. They also thanked Grant for the wonderful evening their daughter, and nearly all of the town, were still talking about almost nonstop.

The plane taxied and began its runup on the runway. It let off the brakes and rocketed the gang into the morning sky.

"Grant? Look at this... quick!" Eileen said pointing out the window.

The plane reached for the sky and had to go over a bridge to do it. There on the bridge... were over 200 kids... and one parole officer. They hung a huge banner across the bridge that simply read...

> Thanks Again G-MAN!!<

They were all jumping and waving at the plane overhead.

Abigail was smiling as she leaned into Grant and said "I may have let it slip which flight we'd be on."

Grant smiled as the bridge went out of sight.

"Damn. I wish I had known or I would've had my camera ready."

Violet smiled a kind smile and said nothing. She merely handed hers over to the youngest Grayson, and showed him the shot on the rear screen.

"Awwwww," Abigail cooed. "Thanks Violet."

With a short layover in Denver, the whole crew would be back home by dinner, local time.

Somewhere over Kansas, Talon sat down next to Zack.

"Okay paper trail guy... here's what I need. We know Lucinda was born and raised in New Orleans. We also know she left for what we believe was east Texas. I need you to give us all you can find on what she was doing prior to the mansion... and where she was doing it. If she didn't make her way across the gulf, then come out to us by land... then that means she went under South America and came up the Pacific side. Work on those two angles and let me know what you find okay?"

"You got it boss. Not that I won't but, why are you tracking her again?"

"She was murdered."

"NO SHIT!" Zack exclaimed.

"Nope, and Shadow Man did it. We thought we knew who he was, but we later found out we were wrong. The more we can track Lucinda, the more likely we are to find out who Shadow Man is or might be."

"Shadow Man?" Zack queried.

"It's what we call him. He came out of the shadows when he killed Lucinda, and his face is still shadowed today."

"Dude, what are you talking about? Even if he was still alive today, he'd be about 150 years old! Not much of a threat there gray guy," Zack joked.

"That old... definitely dead... sadly though, not gone. Nor is the mansion's Grand Dame."

"Boss, you sure this thin air ain't making you a little squirrelly?"

Talon chuckled saying "Listen 'Mister sea level'... I grew up in that thin air you mentioned. Even growing up in Utah," and Talon teased like a little boy telling Zack "My air was thinner than your air." Talon got serious but friendly and told him "Tell ya what, when we get back to the mansion, I'll see if either of them is in the mood to say hello. Until then though, track Lucinda okay?"

Zack merely said he'd get on it once they returned. They landed safely and on time. It was 5:15pm local time and Violet told them she was cooking dinner. She lightly, and jokingly, asked if anyone was interested. She giggled when everyone put their hand up. They caught a pair of taxi's and all filed out for Talon's home.

An hour after that... a doctor was getting ON a flight back in New York.

"Welcome aboard Doctor Barnes," the stewardess said greeting the only passenger on the rented corporate jet. "And where are we traveling to?" she asked politely.

"The biggest little city in the world," he replied with just a hint of sinister in his tone.

The stewardess hated him. He was an ass and... a creepy one at that. Still, for her salary, she made nice all the same. The doctor used to rent this plane quite a lot, but hardly ever in recent years.

"Oh I've stayed there many times during lay-overs. You'll like it there," she said trying to force some polite conversation.

With a sense of true sadistic glee, he took a glass of champaign, and said "Oh, I'm sure I will," as he strapped into his lounge chair.

Twenty minutes later, a GulfStream twin turbojet was airborne... and heading westbound. He was confident in his plan's outcome. What he didn't know was... if Rod Serling had been there... he would have told him he just crossed into the Twilight Zone.

Talon was as quiet as a mouse as he snuck into his own living room. Violet had told Abigail about sleeping in front of the fireplace. Still feeling like a kid herself, Abigail was looking to change that. Sadly for her she goofed. She did everything Violet said she had done. That was her goof, it was too exact. Grant saw it but kindly didn't say a word. He knew what she was trying to do, so he just played dumb, and gave her one of his shirts.

"Abigail... shhhhhhh," Talon said as he kindly woke her.

She grumbled as she put her glasses on.

"Talon? Something wrong?" she asked.

"Shh, I need you to come with me please," he told her.

She carefully got up, but was still a tad groggy.

"If this is one of those weird brother sharing things... I ain't interested," she mumbled

Talon just hung and shook his head, and motioned her to follow him.

They went into his office and he said "Sorry for the rude wakeup, but I need your talents."

"Now!?" she barked.

Grant stirred a little and Talon quietly closed the door.

"Yes now," he said clearly annoyed with her. "Listen Abigail, I need to know what's on this thumb drive. I can build, but I don't code. Certainly not to your level. Whatever is on here has some seriously damning evidence. I would do it myself but I can't. Now, I don't want anyone to know what's on here, but I have no choice but to involve you. Them..." Talon said hooking his thumb to the door, "... well, the less they know the safer we keep them."

Abigail's mind was starting to clear. Hurt Grant? No way in hell. Hurt the others? Not if she could help it.

"I JUST became a free woman. Is whatever is on here gonna jeopardize that?" Abigail asked seriously.

"Honestly? I don't know. I can say this though," Talon said honestly. "I will tell whoever I need to... WHAT ever I need to... in order to keep you that way. Sorry to scare you Abigail but the less anyone knows the better. Till we find out what's on there, the less that know, the safer we all stay."

Abigail nodded in agreement and opened the contents of the drive. She looked at it for less than a minute before she closed the window.

"Whoa! Okay, gotta say I wasn't expecting that!" Abigail stated with some dread.

"Enlighten me," Talon commanded firmly.

"This is high level encryption... custom job too. We're talking, like, DARPA level stuff. This is dark web shit Mister Grays... uh... I mean Talon."

That same Talon asked "Dark Web? Like, the sites the terrorists and hackers use?"

"Mm hmm. Not all are used for those purposes though. Many are sights for hire. You want some high level skills with no questions asked? You get an untraceable IP address and make contact. Whoever owned these files did not want it unlocked by anyone," Abigail said with a hint of fear in her voice.

Abigail now had another thought, and enlightened her new boss to it.

"There's another problem Talon. I can't do this here. You're rig here is nice but, to do what you're asking requires more than what you got in this office. I need a serious custom rig, possibly several. I'm talking Linux servers, coding programs that don't come cheap... the works. Add to that, these guys and gals take paranoia to a whole new level. If I start ringing any of their alarms, they're gonna wanna know who did it. I try it with this rig of yours, in its current state? It'll be compromised in less than 2 minutes. Trust me, you don't want these people poking around in your stuff."

Talon was honest and said "No... I do not. Thanks for being honest anyway."

Talon thought a moment, then made a decision.

"Abigail, your original prom, would you want video of what happened to you being shown to any stranger?"

"No, I would not," she replied.

"Exactly. Some things are just private. And well they should be. I am about to trust you... and possibly break another's in me," and he brought up Violet's video. "You didn't see this... you NEVER saw this... and if discovered, I will throw you to the wolves. Got it?" Talon said with extreme warning.

"Got it," Abigail said meekly but honestly. "What 'this' are you referring to? she asked warily.

"This is a video of Violet. I hafta warn you... it ain't pretty. I'm showing you this because it came from the same source. My hope is, because this is NOT encrypted, it may help with the other stuff in some way."

Abigail was smiling now at having some sort of edge. She actually wanted to prove to Talon she was all that she claimed. That encryption made her look like a boasting idiot though, and she wasn't happy about it. She hit play, and immediately knew why Talon didn't want to show it to her. She felt like she was somehow spying on Violet.

"No no no no no... what the hell!!??" Abigail said with a bit of confusion. "This is... is a... wow," she claimed thoroughly engrossed in the video.

Not the image it showed mind you... the file itself. She clicked a bunch of keys and suddenly, lines and lines of code spewed up on the screen. Remembering a printed piece of paper, Talon played an inside joke on her.

"A forgery?" he chuckled.

With a confused tone, Abigail said "More like a menagerie. Look here, see these lines at the bottom?" Abigail said as she paused the video.

Talon was impressed and said quietly "You actually saw those? They're on only one frame!"

Abigail joked "Tech dork remember?" She got back on track and told Talon "Listen boss, those lines actually mean something. Each little color bar represents gamma, hue, saturation, frame rate, contrast and white balance. You know how a PC spits out different info during boot up? But it's regarding that machine and THAT boot up?"

"I do," Talon stated.

"This is what, technologically speaking, a camera does when it's first booted up. A digital camera also does something else. It has codes for every frame. Time, date, camera info... stuff like that. Now, notice how these bars show up... BEFORE she rips the camera off?"

Now Talon was getting answers he liked. Abigail just kept going. That made him happy as well.

"Normally, you wouldn't see these at all. Only a new camera would spit out those bars. Looking over info most normal people wouldn't even know was there, I can tell you two things. Sadly, the images on the video are real. The video itself however is another matter. It's not a straight video as you were led to believe. At best, it's a highlight reel... and a seriously out of order one at that."

Talon grinned at yet another revelation coming his way.

"And... at worst?" he asked staring at his screens.

"It's propaganda, plain and simple. Someone wanted you to think this was legit... real badly."

Talon commanded "What else can you tell me?"

"I can sort out the times and such, maybe get a clue or two hidden in the code. Boss? Can I ask ya something first?"

Talon was still staring at the screen, and smiling a 'you're so fucked' smile as he did.

"Anything you'd like," he said with cheerful menace.

"Do ya mind if I put some pants on? It's kinda cold in this office," Abigail whined slightly.

Talon laughed, and ended this little revelation.

He told Abigail as he turned off his computer, "Nah don't bother. Head on back and get some sleep. I don't want my brother thinking I'm trying to take his gal. You can sort this out later."

That statement made Abigail think. She didn't want Violet thinking she was making moves on her man either.

Talon stopped Abigail on her way out and told her "We Grayson's are honorable men and women. Staying with Grant may come in time, but, I think it's a little early for that."

"Mind telling me where I'll stay then?" Abigail said with some consternation.

"Not at all," Talon replied confidently. "I was thinking, perhaps, the third door on the left? I have a feeling 'grandma' wouldn't mind a little company" he told her with a sly grin. "Abby? Get a list together and get it to me asap. I want the mansion rigged with every piece of tech you can imagine. Room 1, I want you to turn into an office for Zack and get him any tech he requires. Room 2, I want as a computer room, that would make even those dark web dorks you mentioned, cream in their pants. Room 3, is yours. Stay at Grant's if you wish but, I want you to have a place all your own... just in case. You go through me for approval and you go through Eileen for the financing. Deal?"

Abigail beamed and softly stated "Deal!"

Talon got serious and said "Shadow Man is still a threat." He lightened some and told her "I think though, that grandma... heh heh, and her boss... can keep you safe enough."

Talon turned off the light as he and Abigail left the office.

"Oh... and one more thing," Talon added.

"Hmm?"

Talon laughed low and whispered "I know my brother. I'd reconsider those pants if I were you." He winked and smiled at her and said "Just say'in."

Abigail giggled, but took his advice, and she scurried back to her G-Man still sound asleep by the fire. Talon laughed slightly and headed back to a sleeping, purple-eyed ghost hunter.

Talon was in the Cuda and getting jerked around... hard. He winced, just as hard, every time he did.

"Uh, Violet? First gear... is the other way."

A meek but honest "Sorry," was her reply.

They were in a strip mall parking lot at sunset. It was 80% empty and now, with official permit in hand, Talon was teaching Violet how to drive. He was teaching, but Violet wasn't exactly learning. Another hard jerk and the car stalled. That, was enough for Talon.

"Okay, maybe this wasn't my best idea," Talon stated putting his hand over hers as she went for the keys. "Let's call this quits. Switch seats Violet, while I still have a transmission left."

Violet wasn't happy at her failure, but teased Talon all the same.

"Yeah, you're right. Let's go back and get the Lambo. I'm sure I'll do much better in that car."

"Ha ha ha. You can't handle 4 on the floor... what makes you think you can handle 6?" Talon joked back as he got in the driver's seat. "Look Violet, just watch me. Get the general idea first, and we'll practice another time. For now, wadda ya say we stick to the truck?"

Violet flirted saying "Watch you? Oh... that I can do." She giggled when Talon smirked at her comment, and told him "Oooohhhhhh, I was supposed to learn something!? Sorry, I was a little distracted by some hot guy in a hot car who told me I should stare at him."

Talon just laughed and shook his head. Just to get Violet back though, he slammed the car into first gear... and Violet back into her seat... as a Hemi headed back for home base.

They stopped for some burgers, and were enjoying a nice quick meal, when Violet's phone rang.

"Hey Abigail, what's up?"

"That guy you're with, I plan on stealing him. Mind if I talk to him so we can make some secret plans?" Abigail jested.

Violet playfully whined saying "Oh no fair. Then you'll have two and I'll have nothing."

With a grin on her face, Abigail joked back saying "Sorry sister, but when you're a hot blond like me... wellllll...." and she just giggled.

Violet chuckled, stared at Talon, and handed him her phone.

"Your newest harem member wants to talk to you," Violet said with playful annoyance.

Talon took it and said "Newest member eh? Did I approve of you, or are you a recommendation from my brother?"

"Yeah well... wait... what?" Abigail stuttered losing her train of thought.

Talon chuckled and asked "What's up sweetie?"

"Huh? Oh yeah. I wanted to let you know I fixed your phone's twitchy interface. I'll have it done in about an hour. That's not why I called though."

"I know it's not," Talon said confidently.

"Wait... you know why I called?"

"Of course. With such a hot and sexy brother, you called to tell me you've finally come to your senses. So, when exactly will you be leaving my brother for me?"

Violet merely stuck her tongue out at him. Abigail was a lot like Violet, in the sense that she matched personalities to who she was with... as a means to fit in.

Abigail giggled and said "Well Mr. 'not so old' old guy... I just wanted to let you know the equipment I ordered will be in by mid week. Figure by Saturday I'll have it set up and locked down. Once I have, you and I actually do have a date... with a thumb drive."

"Sounds like a plan. Thanks dear. Listen, that whole harem thing? Yeah do me a favor... don't mention any of that to Violet okay?" Talon teased.

Violet had an annoyed look on her face as she threw a French fry at his face.

"Yeah, (giggle) not a problem there," Abigail said as she hung up.

Talon just laughed at the look on Violet's face.

While Talon couldn't say teasing Violet wasn't mildly amusing, it was also for a reason. The more he threw her off, the less she knew about what he was doing on her behalf. Two days ago, he had a 'conversation' with Lucinda. She didn't answer... but she heard him.

Since then, the PI they all knew about, was having a tougher and tougher time staying hidden. He had a lens on his camera that was almost 3 feet long. Lucinda took great delight in making all his pictures a bit blurry, and his life miserable in general. Staying part way between the realm of the present, and the ether, the lens picked up nothing but the bottom of her dress. Other times it was blowing dust so bad he had to move. It disturbed him some to see that dust, blowing only where he was... and seemingly follow him wherever he repositioned to... while all the other land around him was perfectly calm. On a few occasions, Lucinda managed to let loose the familiar 'beep boop' of his car alarm. Talon heard that in the distance the other day and just smiled when he did.

"Thanks lady," he whispered low when he heard it.

Today though was the last day he came around. Grant had snuck out and drove his truck past the guy, then turned around and parked right on his rear bumper. The PI was about to take off, when a small tractor with a big bucket parked on his front one. A gray haired man in the front, and a red haired one behind him... just smiled and waved. Talon backed up after a few minutes and let him leave. After that, Lucinda no longer had anyone to torment.

The second floor was far more unstable than either brother realized. So much so that Talon halted work on it completely. Abigail whined a little at that, but understood. Zack whined about it too. Still, both agreed falling 15 feet to the floor below was not exactly something they were looking forward to.

"So 'G-Man', ya mind telling me why you spent 10 grand of my money for some rolls of fabric?" Talon asked not happy at what was spent compared to what was received.

Grant confidently told him "Shark suit stuff."

Talon now grinned and told him "I look forward to seeing your work." He then asked "And the Gunite? I mean I know what it is, but I've never seen it in action. Same project?"

Grant just smiled and joked "Na na na na na na na na BAT CAVE!"

Talon walked away with a smile, and joked back "Still a pussy! Besides, that's more Thunderbird 2 than bat cave."

Grant relented in a friendly tone and said "Yeah okay, I concede your point... hah hah hah."

Talon walked down and called everyone on the first floor together.

"Listen up people! My brother and I just finished inspecting the second floor. Half we can fix on the fly as you work, half we can't. NO one is getting hurt on my work site so, after today... work is halted for at least a week. I want you to know I will be calling all of you back once work is ready to resume. Until then, today is the last work day for a week or two."

They all groaned slightly but thoroughly understood. The only reason they groaned though wasn't because they wouldn't be working for awhile... but because they wouldn't be around Lucinda.

Talon smirked, and played with them a little saying "Aw thanks guys... she says, she'll miss you too."

Talon walked back upstairs and right to Grant.

"We give it a day, then, I wanna see what you got."

"Gladly," was all a smiling little brother said.

It was two days later, and Grant was getting ready to show off. Doc had half of his items now installed in his lab. Yesterday, he was in the secret tunnel gathering hairs, fibers, and prints. The latter he never did before but the kit he got had directions that were easy enough to follow. This kind of 'get your hands dirty' work was really starting to appeal to the Doc. History and science rolled up in one package. Cody was having a blast.

While he searched, he was never far from the drone. Talon thought the camera on it was a pretty good one. Abigail thought it was a joke and replaced it. She also upgraded it's software, and now it had thermal capabilities, and GPS as well. So while Doc searched, Abigail kept the drone near him wherever he went. Still somewhat the little kid, she was having a blast flying it and got more than a little good at it too. Now, today, and with Cody feeling like he got all there was to find... Big Mack was called forth.

Grant explained "Okay so... this tunnel is one long rib cage mounted on a stone walled walkway. We start at the mansion, and work outwards. Big Mack digs sideways between the ribs and opens it up. We expose the beams 2 or 3 at a time. We put the dirt to the side as we'll be putting it back once we're done. When we open up the beams, we wrap them in the carbon fiber I ordered. Once hardened, we screen between the ribs. Once we get the whole thing done, we spray the screens with the Gunite. A few inches of concrete, then, cover it back up! Simple as that. So Tal, wadda ya think!?"

Talon smiled, and held out the keys to the huge machine.

"I think... you're driving."

Grant was pleased but Talon had a thought.

"Yo baby G hold up a second," and Talon climbed atop the hill above the entrance.

He walked away towards the opening, turned around, and stopped.

"Hey bro... I can see Slide AND Mount Rose from here! How about if we put a walkway to nowhere up on top? The construction workers are bound to notice the disturbed earth but, if we put railings up, we can say this is for outdoor vista pictures! Walkway on top... and no one will be the wiser what's under their feet!"

Grant was stoked over this modification.

"Tal! We'll have to get some steel beams to support the weight between the ribs but... I LIKE IT!" he hollered back with joy in his voice.

And just like that, the mansion now would have two favorite places to take pictures from. Grant fired up Big Mack, and Talon was on his phone getting some steel before he even got off the mound.

Grant dug out the first two sections. All hands on deck, and Talon worked the pressure washer. The first two beams got exposed and Grant showed the ladies how to work the fabric. Those same ladies were happy the men gave them meaningful work, but work they could handle, and not treat them like 'girls'. Grant and Talon worked the scaffold and took the wet fabric as it became available. Just like Grant said it would, it wrapped the old oak beams nice and tight. Talon couldn't get any beams from an auction or his own stock. Not in time anyway. So he had those ordered new, and they arrived on time the next afternoon. With 40 feet exposed, the ladies worked the screening into place, while Talon and Grant set the steel beams in, and ran all the electric.

The ladies didn't complain about the work. They did complain about the sun and the heat though. So did the men. Two of Lashonda's tent city area were now empty, so, Talon stacked the pallets even higher on either side of the hidden tunnel. A few tarps linked together to provide some shade, and all involved were far less cranky.

By the end of the week, the tunnel was now ready for the Gunite. That was basically concrete under high pressure, and shot out of a nozzle like a fire hose. The tunnel had angled sides and a flat top, which only made putting in the walkway above that much easier. Now, with a completed metal skeleton, and Grant and Talon switching positions every so often, the 'shot-crete' spewed and spewed. Talon had half the 'crew' inside the tunnel two hours later smoothing out the new walls and ceiling. Grant had the other half on top smoothing out the new walkway. Abigail thought doing that work was cool, and was proud of herself for learning how, and doing well. Violet was happy to help in any capacity, and she too was happy learning, or at least experiencing, new skills.

It was the weekend now. Saturday morning to be exact... and Talon and Grant were onsite. So was the local news crew. They were there to do a piece for the 6 o'clock news on how the old mansion no one knew about, was coming back to life. Talon and Grant made nice, but Talon made sure Grant got just as much limelight as he did. They also didn't care about, nor filmed, the odd concrete walkway to nowhere.

"From what this reporter has seen and heard so far... I can say this project is in just the right hands. I look forward to returning, and reporting on, as a piece of forgotten Nevada history comes back to life. Reporting for KOLO 8 news... I'm Rita James."

A certain senator smiled on Tuesday when a copy of that news piece reached his desk. He smiled because a certain gray haired friend of his kept his word. Public history, not the hidden one, was all that was revealed. He even thought his friend winking at the camera as he mentioned 'the ghost' that resided there, was amusing, and just the sort of thing the locals eat up.

Zack had been busy, till Talon shut down the second floor. This new 'gang' he found himself part of, seemed to be a decent lot. To him though, that only meant they needed checking out even more. Talon and Grant and Eileen turned out to be squeaky clean. The rest of the crew had interesting pasts, but nothing more. Violet was the exception, but, Talon already told him enough so he wouldn't freak out when he found out about her. Violet however was an open book to him. She wasn't proud of her past. Now however, among these new people, she was no longer ashamed of it either.

When Violet was growing up, her talents were primarily focused on. How to, and how not to, use them. What to, and what not to do. Things like that. Grandma however never went into detail about the other things in life. Aunts, uncles, cousins... her biological dad... stuff like that, got put to the wayside. Now, as an adult, Violet decided these things were now important. She was fully committed to putting down roots now. A week ago, she was walking around Talon's back yard. Just that, enjoying a nice sunset walk. She decided to heed Eileen's words, and finally do something she's never done in her life... put down roots. She decided, if she and Talon ever did break up, she would stay right here. She found she had truly fallen in love with this general area, and decided Talon or no... this part of the country would become home.

So she asked Zack if he would find all he could on her and her family. Ever the cautious one, finding family, and contacting them, to her were two different things.

"Ha ha ha ha," she laughed to herself aloud. "I hope there are at least some people I could contact. If not, and Talon and I ever got married... that's gonna be one lopsided guest list!" She smirked as she looked about, and asked aloud "What? No jokes or comments from the peanut gallery!?"

She just chuckled at herself, shook her head, and headed back inside. Seems the ether truly had no comment on the matter.

Now, Zack was 'holding court' in Cody's living room. He had some info Talon asked for. Talon implicitly told him, **not** to be one of those guys that got the whole picture together first. Talon wanted info as... and when... it became available. To ram his point home, he reminded Zack that as the boss, he got what he wanted. Zack promised he would, and that was the reason for tonight's pow-wow.

"Okay, let me start this little get together off by asking you all something," Zack began. "You all know about social media right?"

Everyone nodded and Zack continued.

"Okay then. What makes me so good is this. You get on one of those sites, and you get friends. Those friends have friends, and so on. What I've always been good at, is finding someone 5 or 6 links down the line... but trace them back to you. In your case boss, the reverse is true. This time, I started with you and your family, and worked my way outward. I was trying to see if anything tied you to any of the current players in this little saga." Zack chuckled and added "Both living and otherwise."

Cody sipped his beer and continued.
"To my surprise, I found one."
Talon was stoked and said "Do tell."

"Well," Zack began, "It regards your family actually. Does the name Emily Garrison ring any bells?"

Eileen told him "The last name... but not the first."

Zack told her "Indeed. She was your 7 times great grandmother... on your mom's side. She was a nurse in the south, and had 3 daughters. Her husband was a colonel for the local militia. He died of unknown causes and left her a widow. She died only 1 year later of typhoid. That left 3 orphans... Mary-Jane, Samantha, and Addison. They went into an orphanage at the ages of 10, 7 and 5. Only 7 months later, they were adopted. Anyone care to guess by who?"

None of the 3 siblings had a clue.

"Seems they moved to a little city called New Orleans. Anyone ever hear of it?" Zack joked.

"Let's say, you have my attention," Grant told him.

"The census 4 years later shows them living at 121 State street."

"And?" Talon blurted in a 'get to the point' tone.

"It was the home of Arella Adair."

Zack let that one sink in on all the stunned faces around him.

Talon excused himself, and walked out onto Doc's front porch.

"Ha HAAAAAA! Mista G! Wha can good ole Althea James do for ya?" was the loud response to Talon's call.

"I need a favor Al," he said as he put the phone back to his ear.

"Anything ya need shugah."

"Al? Reach out to the folks back home. Get me myth, legend, or fact. I don't care but... I need any dirt you can get me on Arella. Can do?"

"Faw you Mista G? Will do!" Al changed tones to a cautious one and asked "Them hoochie mamas not giv'in you any grief now... are they?"

"Not at all. It would seem she took in some orphans. Three little girls to be exact. I believe she may have turned them into her apprentices. Focus on that and let me know what you find, okay Al?"

"Ah shaw will Mista G."

"Oh and... Al?"

"Mm?"

"I don't care what time it is here. You find something... you call me."

"Count on it Mista G. Y'all take care now."

"I will Al... and thanks."

Talon hung up and went back in for more chit chat.

Talon sat back down and asked Zack "Is that all you got?"

Zack said "Nope, but not much more. I traced Addison to what would become Long Island, New York. Samantha was in Saint Louis, but Mary-Jane landed in the infamous Tombstone. By the next census, Arella was alone again.

Or so the census said. I saved all I had and can pick back up when my office becomes available again."

Eileen queried "Here's my question. While this info is interesting to say the least, I thought you were supposed to track Lucinda?"

"I was. Trail ran cold, and until I can figure out what alias she used, I came up empty. So with more info on her 'mom', I decided to see if that took me anywhere."

Talon was deep in thought. Eileen called him on it too.

"Okay brother, I know that look. What are you conjuring up?"

"A theory," Talon told her.

"Care to share?" Eileen commanded in that big sister tone.

"Well, 3 different points in the country. Seems to me, like the original white witch may have sent out a search party. Back in those days, St. Louis was THE major hub for all points west. East, central, and west coasts covered. Perhaps Arella wasn't so over her daughter as we once thought." He looked at Zack and said "Follow up on those three. Let me know if you can find anything that said they did a bit of traveling. There's just one catch though. Three daughters would have married in time. As such they would have taken their husband's name. So, how do we get the moniker of Garrison carrying on when there were only girls?"

Zack told him with a smile "You're the one who likes mysteries... you tell me."

Talon politely fired back "That's your job." Talon looked at the small crowd and stated "Look, you're all going to be at the mansion in time. So, the fact that you know about the secret entrance was only prudent. Grant and I will get those beams safe by end of next week. Then the crews come back in. I want you all to tell them, when they see the disturbed soil, it was nothing but a pet project to build the walkway. Good work Zack but, I want you back on it asap. I also don't want anyone but 'us' knowing what you, or any of us, are really doing. Got that everybody?"

"No prob boss. This job is even better than the Doc's trail. Wanna hear my theory on that one?"

"Go for it," Grant told him.

"I firmly believe, that the Doc's history, will either cross paths or better still... merge... with yours."

"A fair assumption," Talon confirmed, "but what makes you think that?"

"Well, I didn't, till a few moments ago. When you mentioned a search party. If someone was to do that, it's a fair bet that even back then, they would have found her eventually. IF they did, and assuming you're correct, then they would have moved in close. Do that, and we may have some pretty solid connections in the near future."

"Zack? If it gets me closer to solving this murder, I won't care if they were neighbors," Talon said with conviction.

Now it was Cody's turn. He had a mini revelation of his own.

"So, I still can't say... yet... who Shadow Man is. I can tell you however what the murder weapon is."

Grant excitedly hollered "That's great Doc! What was it?"

"The white ceramic doll we found. It is highly stained with blood. And yes, it's human. I have no DNA to match it with, but it's seriously old. Given that, I'm gonna say it's Lucinda's. I scanned it, with what I have so far, to see if there was any other DNA. Sadly, there wasn't. Sorry Tal but, I got an even bigger mystery for you."

Talon wasn't happy about that, but asked "Let's hear it Cody."

"Remember when I showed you the picture of Henry and my grandmother? He was wearing a wool coat, remember?"

"Yeah?"

"I found fibers in the tunnel. They were wool and embedded all along the right side of the tunnel. I had the fibers checked. They were dyed wool. Thing is, that kind of wool, and dye, only comes from one place."

Talon had an 'oh great' look on his face now as he asked "Let me guess... the Alps?"

"Bingo."

Eileen was dumbfounded and asked "So... it WAS Henry?"

Cody told her "I still don't think so. Now, either I'm wrong, or..."

"Or what?" Eileen queried.

Talon stated calmly "He was in the house the night Lucinda was killed."

Cody just said "Mm hmm."

Talon now threw out the big picture.

"Okay, wadda we got? Arella takes in some orphans and turns them into her bloodhounds. They go looking for Lucinda, but carry the family name to only a generation back. Shadow Man kills Lucinda, but does it all cloaked up. When I was inside him, I could feel something over my mouth. I think it was a bandanna of sorts. So either Henry trips out, or someone took his coat and such to throw everyone onto his trail. When Lucinda was killed, I felt something heavy in 'my' hand, and caught a glimpse of something white and... OH SHIT!"

Talon pulled out his phone quick, and scanned the photos.

"Well! Looky what we got here," and Talon turned the phone so all could see the picture he brought up.

"I thought there were no pictures of Lucinda?" Eileen said with some confusion.

"So did we. Apparently we were wrong. This is one of the tin types we found. Erik sent this to me this afternoon."

"Pity we can't see who's beside her," Grant extolled.

Talon showed them a picture of Lucinda sitting in a chair. There was a man's arm on her chair, but the rust ruined the image of who it was.

"Yeah. Erik said it was ruined beyond even his capabilities. But that's not the point."

Cody looked and asked "Okay, what am I missing here?"

Talon smirked and said "Same as Violet's video. Get off the main focus... and what do you see?" Cody still missed it, and Talon said "Look on the mantle in the background."

Lucinda was sitting in front of the fireplace in the parlor in the mansion. Cody smiled now as he saw what Talon was talking about. There in the picture, on the mantle, was the ceramic doll.

"Well Helloooo Dolly," Cody joked in song.

Talon showed the others what Cody now saw.

"Okay so, I got two scenarios," Talon said picking back up. "Henry is here. Something happens, and he snaps. Expecting it to be a clean kill, it goes south. Knowing no one would think anything of him being up there, he doesn't bother to hide himself. Now there's a ruckus, and now he's rethinking the whole wardrobe thing."

Zack said aloud "Plausible. And number two?"

"The killer is there already, or follows Henry there. Something snaps him, and he takes Henry's coat and hat to make it look like Henry, in case he was spotted. Cody? What can you tell me about the fibers?"

"All the same."

"No pal, I mean, anything in where or how you found them?"

"Oh! Kind of. Some were embedded deeper than others. If I had to guess, I'd say whoever wore it, was stumbling down the tunnel."

Talon was clinical and asked "Like hurt kind of stumbling? Or more like the realization of what they just did kind."

"I didn't find anything but the fibers. No prints but there were smudges of bloody hand prints. Same blood as the doll too. If I had to guess, I'd say the latter... and the killer wore gloves of some kind."

Talon thought a moment, then recalled "He was."

Cody told Talon "I've only heard her a few times Talon. She seems to like you though."

Zack asked "Heard who?"

"Lucinda," Doc said like it was no big deal.

"Oh not you too?!" Zack chuckled.

Talon smirked and asked Cody "What are you getting at Doc?"

Cody told him "She died. It was covered up. What I wanna know is, who buried her... and where?"

Talon chuckled and asked "Why? What are you gonna do, exhume her?"

Seriously, Cody replied "I had thought about it."

Talon told the small crowd "I have been all over that property. So has Grant. I doubt they would have buried her there but, if they did, we haven't found her grave. Knowing the crowd she hung out with... I doubt we'd ever find that." Talon laughed at an imaginary conversation and shared aloud "Hey Lucinda... by the way..." and Talon just laughed and never finished his sentence.

Now Grant was serious and said "Ya know, that might not be a bad idea. Who knows what Doc will find out now? Modern tech, versus ancient cover up. Hey bro, didn't you say you had a lunch invitation in San Fran?"

"Yeah. So?"

"Sooooo.... maybe you can pull out some of that Talon charm and see if they have any info they'd be willing to share." Grant sported a sly grin and told him "And, bringing a beautiful brunette along might not be such a bad idea either."

Talon mused that idea and said "Hmm, you may be right about that. Hey Zack, care to be my lunch date?" Talon teased.

Zack scorned "Boss? That's not even remotely funny."

Everyone but Zack was laughing now.

Two days later, Grant and Talon had half the support beams done. Talon told his brother he had some late night tech dates with his gal coming up. He also told him it was to help Violet. Grant understood. Talon made him aware they were indeed 'geeking out'... but nothing more. Grant told him he trusted him. Talon offered him to call or video link in at any time just to prove it.

"Okay here's the deal Abigail. This room is safe... barely. Suffice to say, walk out that door? You had better make a right and not a left," Talon said in an 'I'm not kidding' tone.

They were in Abigail's tech room, not her personal one. That was one room over... and in the left direction Talon warned about.

Abigail joked "Right good... left, hang out with grandma... got it."

Talon was still serious and told her "Also, the worst 'occurrences' happened at night. I don't know why that is, and I don't care why. I only know it is, so, you go nowhere alone. And I mean, if you have to go to the bathroom, I'm gonna be outside the door. Got that?"

"Clearly," Abigail confirmed.

"Good. Shadow Man has been pretty much absent of late. That alone makes me nervous."

Abigail asked "Hey boss, just what exactly is on this drive? I mean, do you have **any** idea?"

Talon relented, and told her. If she cracked the drive, she'd know anyway. So, Talon took a chance, and involved Abigail a little more than he would have liked.

"Seems the doctor that had Violet incarcerated, was a sick piece of shit, with some seeeeeeerious mommy issues. I'm guessing this drive has some sort of concrete proof of that. We know he used Violet in some manner but we only think we know how, or to what end. We had a PI hanging around, but he's gone now. He was watching Violet, not us. I don't know why but, I get the feeling like either time is running out, or something really bad is coming. Either way, I promised Violet I would keep her safe, and that's exactly what I'm going to do. I get the feeling, whatever is on that drive, is gonna help me do it. More than that you don't need to know. For Violet's sake... and yours."

"Boss? I ever tell you how you, even knowing some of the stuff you know, is just as creepy?" Talon laughed, and Abigail swung around in her chair saying "Okay, let's help Violet," and she started banging keys.

Two hours later, and Abigail did indeed have to go to the bathroom. True to his word, Talon escorted her there and back. Abigail went back to work while Talon took a break, and sat on the top stair.

"Lucinda? Are you there?" Talon asked kindly.

No answer.

"Meh, no biggie. Listen darl'in, I got a mystery to solve. I got more pieces to the puzzle, but Cody needs something. I have a weird... very personal... and slightly awkward question to ask you."

"If it'll help, I'll ansuh what ah cahyun."

Now Talon smiled.

"Miss Adair... do you know where you're buried?"

"Well... an awkwahd question indeed. Sadly howevuh, no I do not. Those Pinkerton men took what was left of me away. Ah tried tuh tawk to them, and couldn't unduhstahnd why they were ignor'in me so." With extreme sadness, Lucinda finished with "It took me quite a while, tuh figger out whut I had become. Ah am trapped heeyuh, in this house. Ah only reached Violet, and you, beecuz y'all let me. Even then, I reached out to y'all... but remained grounded heeyuh in this house." Lucinda then asked "Why do y'all want tuh know?"

Talon kindly told her "If your real body was found, our science today can tell us things your doctors and scientists never could... and could only have dreamed of."

"Ah can oenlee imajun. See'in those fancy muhsheens of yaws, I'll bet that fine Mista Cody could tell all sawts of things."

Lucinda had a thought, and made a request.

"Y'all asked me an awkward question. Now let me ask you one?"

"Anything you'd like my dear," Talon said kindly.

Lucinda asked "Ah have come tuh recognize, tha this is yaw house now. If you did find me, mah questjun is... would y'all bring me home?"

Talon queried "In what way?"

"This house Mista G, was evreething to me. Ah have come tuh accept whut ah am now. Still, if you woodint mind, ah can think of no other place I'd rahthuh be."

Talon stood up to go back to Abigail. Before he did, he made a promise, proudly, and to the Grand Dame of the house.

"Madam? You have my word as a gentleman that SHOULD I find you, I will do everything possible to honor your request."

"Yaw words sir, give me great comfuhrt... and I thank ya from thuh bottom of mah heart."

With that, Talon went back to work, and Lucinda's voice just faded away.

Talon and Abigail came up empty. She made some progress, but nowhere near as much as either would have liked. The next day, Talon and Grant were back at work on the beams. Talon however had a second project to do today. Around dinner time, he alone worked this project. He took Big Mack, and cut through the hill behind the trees he planted. It took him an hour but, he cut through it. That was enough for today, and Violet brought him and Abigail some dinner. She had gotten some appliances for the kitchen in the mansion. That section was safely supported. It was being setup to feed them, or a whole party of people if need be. It wasn't fancy like Grant's or Talon's kitchens were, but setup halfway between those... and a kitchen you'd expect at any restaurant. Violet laid it out well, and even managed to use the existing chimneys for venting.

Violet and Grant stayed in the kitchen while Talon and Abigail headed back to work. Baby G knew Talon wasn't doing anything with his new girlfriend, but, he didn't like the thought of them being alone. Not with Shadow Man lurking about that is. Violet was also very much in agreement with the younger Grayson. They promised Talon to leave him be, but they refused to leave him or Abigail alone.

"I don't mind telling you Abigail, this is getting more than a little frustrating," Talon extolled after 90 minutes of coming up empty. "How about if I just offer them enough money to crack their own code?" he asked the blond nerd tapping away at the keys.

"Um... not liking that idea boss. This code isn't hard to crack actually. It's the timing sequence that's stumping me."

Talon questioned "Timing sequence? Like on an engine?"

Abigail giggled and said "Not exactly. I figured out there's a pattern. Like a clock sort of. Multiply by 1... then 2... then 3 and so on. Hit 12, and the sequence starts again."

"So there's 12 different encryptions!?" Talon asked.

"More like the same encryption, cycled through different styles. I found nine in all. It could be based on when he entered them, or some random numbers used over and over. 'IF' I could get the pattern, the technological house of cards crumbles."

Talon mused a bit. He thought of a few things, when a memory hit him. It was a recent one at that too. He smiled hoping his idea would pan out, and called Cody.

"Hi Tal, what's up?" Cody answered when his phone rang.

"Doc, I need your help. Remember Violet's video?"

"Indeed I do," Cody told him.

"Now, she said one of the pills had the number 315 on it."

"I remember."

Talon snapped his fingers at Abigail and pointed to the pen and paper she was using for notes. She slid it to him and Talon got ready to write.

"Well, what about the other two? Do they have numbers on them? Or perhaps, associated with them?"

Cody told him "They do in fact. Hold on let me get my books."

Talon wrote what Cody said, and hollered back "Got it! Okay, thanks Doc. Why do I need that information? Trust me... you don't wanna know... and I don't wanna tell you. Thanks again!" and Talon quickly hung up.

"Well Abby... 315, 722, and 525. Try working with those numbers, and see what you come up with, okay?"

Thinking Talon was on to something, and having no luck otherwise, Abigail was stoked at having a possible lead. Thirty minutes later, possible went to probable.

"C'mon... c'mon... I just know you're in there somewhere," Talon muttered as Abigail appeared to be onto something as well.

Another 30 minutes, and probable became definite.

Abigail watched in horror, as Talon watched in disgust.

"Is that the doctor Violet still despises?" Abigail asked as she watched the video alongside Talon.

"His name... is Doctor Jeremy Barnes," Talon declared in a tone that implied he was disgusted to his very soul, by what he saw on the screen.

The drive was essentially a video diary of experiments. He was indeed using Violet... for his own sick purposes. Each video showed a progression of sorts. Doctor Barnes appeared to have promising results at first. Then, the Doc was not getting what he wanted, and was struggling to find the right drug combination. What Talon and Abigail saw, was Violet getting more and more violent as the diary progressed. The more she did, the more Jeremy's prize slipped away.

Abigail may be a techie nerd... but she was a sweet one. She saw Violet and decided to stand up for her new friend. She didn't know why, but she felt it important to let the new boss know where she stood.

"No way... NO fucking way! There is no way you can convince me that's Violet. Not our Violet, nuh uh, no way. Those drugs had to be causing this. I flat out refuse to believe that's her. I mean, yeah it's her and all but... it's not 'her'. Am I making sense?"

Talon turned off the video, and smiled kindly at the upset and blathering blond.

"For a change, you're making perfect sense my dear." Talon then said "I know what annoys Violet. I'm no shrink but if I had to guess, I'd say Doctor Barnes wasn't getting what he wanted because he got the drugs wrong. I'd say, seeing that? He was up against Violet's sub conscious. Far more extreme sure, but that sounds more like Violet to me."

Abigail told him "Good! Cuz there's no way that... hey... what do you mean 'for a change'?"

That was the first thing in hours that made Talon laugh.

He stopped laughing and told her "Okay you, here's what I want. I want that doctor, that place, ANY thing associated with that operation... locked out. As far as I'm concerned... if the NSA wouldn't be scratching their heads if they hacked us... then you failed. If anyone with an IP from that rehab place even tries to get access to our stuff, and I want klaxon horns going off on the very first ping. I want our system monitored 24/7. Sorry Abigail," Talon said as he reached down.

"Sorry for what?" she asked totally clueless.

"This," and Talon pulled out the memory stick.

Next, he waved a big magnet from a speaker over the side of the computer.

"HEY!!!" Abigail shouted as the PC went haywire... then black.

"Sorry blondie but, I have to make sure not even a hint of that is on your drives. Reformat them, then... put those blocks in place that I ordered. Oh and... for the record... great work Abigail."

Talon said nothing as he left a rather angry blond to do a lot of reloading.

Talon was out back digging again. He had gotten a path dug out. Now he was clearing a nice flat area. He made was making it circular. He also placed another ad for more trees. It was a fairly decent sized area, but not too big. He figured a single sprinkler mounted up high, and swinging back and forth, would do the trick. He was just finishing up the far section when Violet flagged him down from the entrance.

"So gray guy, what's the opening for?" Violet queried.

He smiled at her and said "This one is a bit of a personal project for me."

Violet shrugged, and told him "Twenty minutes, then come get some lunch... okay?"

"I will. I'm almost done here anyway. Another ten minutes and I'll pack it up and come in."

Violet kissed him sweetly, and walked back to the mansion as Talon headed back for Big Mack. She wouldn't see Talon, but he'd see her... and a whole lot sooner than twenty minutes.

Violet was making her way to the stairs to get back to the kitchen. She never made it.

"Hello Violet. Have fun with your new friends?"

The voice that stopped her dead in her tracks, was Jeremy Barnes.

"I am. Going to continue to do so too," was her ice cold response.

Jeremy sneered "Oh Violet, when are you going to learn? Your life is mine to do with as I please. I allowed you your little vacation. Now it's time to come with me."

"Try and make me," Violet honestly challenged.

One of the workers snuck up behind her, and stuck a syringe in her neck. He wasn't one of the real workers either.

Violet passed out in his arms, and Jeremy merely replied "Gladly."

They were heading for the doors, when they suddenly slammed shut. Something akin to a mini tornado blew up out of nowhere. Now... the Grand Dame of Adair House... was pissed.

"Y'all are NOT welcome heeyuh! I suggest y'all leave... while I still permit it."

Jeremy, calm as could be, pulled a small orb from his pocket and dropped it on the floor. It gave off strobe light beams in all directions. For whatever reason, that really threw Lucinda off. She lost her grip, and Shadow Man snuck in and opened the doors.

"That... whoever you are... is the general plan," Jeremy said in a cocky tone.

Two of the real workers came in, and tried to stop the guy holding Violet. He dropped the purple eyed girl. Seconds later he dropped the first worker. The second one came in for a swing with a hammer, and stopped mid swing as he stared down the barrel of a quickly drawn pistol. He put his hands up as Jeremy grabbed the out cold Violet. The hired muscle kept the gun pointed as he walked backwards and out the front doors.

The moment Lucinda lost her grip, she went to the only help she could think of.

"Mista G! MAYKE HAYSTE!! Violet is being taken by scoundrels! One of them has the strangest 6 shootuh Iev evuh seen!" was the panicked warning in Talon's ears. He heard 'gun', and opened his little tool box in the cabin of Big Mack. He was about to make his way to the mansion, then changed his mind. For the first time in it's service life, Big Mack became a hot rod.

Talon was making the behemoth move at whatever speed he could get. Going over the hills he was getting bounced pretty good but, he was indeed gaining ground. He was cutting around the back hills alongside the driveway.

Jeremy and his 'prize' were heading down the driveway at top speed. The hired guy was driving, and Jeremy was in the front passenger seat. Violet was out cold across the back seat. The only piece of luck Talon caught, was when the car got to the road, the driver turned right, instead of left. Grant was already doing what Talon was doing, but he was in his truck, and on the other side of the property. Lucinda didn't warn one brother... she warned both.

The driver was on a single lane road and hauling ass. He was almost past the property, when he saw a big pickup truck come into view from the right, and start heading at him. Unfazed, he hit the brakes, slammed it into reverse, and did a rolling 180 degree turn.

Grant was chasing him, and the six cylinder in the rental was starting to lose to the GMC V8 behind him. Just past the driveway he came out of moments before, that same truck jammed on it's brakes hard. He looked back for only a second.

"What the?... SHIT!" was he comment when he turned his view back to the road. Next thing he did was curl in fear, as his car came to a sudden stop as well. Sudden crash would be a more accurate term. What he saw, a nanosecond before the airbags went off... was a big metal something swinging hard. Big Mack's bucket decimated the front end of the car all the way to the windshield.

Jeremy poured himself from the passenger door, and was looking rather piss poor. The driver did the same thing. He got to his feet, but was wobbling rather badly. Wincing at the sunlight, he saw a shadow casually walking towards him, and he pointed his gun as best he could.

"9 millimeter. By the look of it, I'd say it's a Glock. Generally, that thing has a muzzle velocity of around 11-1300 feet per second. From the looks of you, I'd say you'd likely shoot yourself rather than me. At least, that's what I'll insure the police report says. Ya know what your problem is? It's the same problem most of you assholes have really. You pull a gun like that..." and Talon swung out his and finished with "... but the other guy always seems to have a bigger one." Talon saw the look on the guy's face, and told him "Since the P.I. disappeared, I thought keeping this close by, might be a good idea." He smirked at the guy and said "Looks like I was right huh? This is a gambling town... tell ya what... I'll see your 9... and raise you one 45... at your head that is."

The guy wobbled some as Talon got even closer. He tried a swing at Talon. That didn't go as well as he hoped.

"My sister danced. My brother built. Me? I used to sweep the floor with assholes like you," and Talon bent his wrist, took the gun from his hand, and put his right knee to his gut.

He nodded hard to Grant, who got Violet out of the back and put her in his truck.

Talon was beyond pissed, and pointed his gun at the guy's head and said "Make the call."

The hired help was on his back, groaning on the road, and putting up both hands.

"All good here. I ain't being paid enough for this shit."

Talon picked up his gun, and tossed it to Grant. That same Grant kept it trained on it's former owner.

Jeremy was in better shape... and laughing.

"You have NO idea who I am, or who my friends are, Talon."

"Oh, you sick piece of shit, I know FAR more than I care to know about you... 'Jeremy'."

Talon kept his gun handy and walked over to the other side of the car. That same Jeremy was still a little wobbly as well.

"Let me tell you something asswipe. You are a sad little boy, who's only playing at being a man. You're mother ran your life. She was a sick piece of work and used you like a tool. You, Jeremy, put a whole new meaning to the term 'mamma's boy'. Breast feeding till you were 17? Diapers till you were 12!? Being mommie's good lil puppy, even now, huh Jeremy?"

Talon was so disgusted by Jeremy, he refused to even touch him at first. He did however pull his phone out.

"This one, is my particular favorite," Talon joked as he showed him a video. "This one should win you the sick fuck award of the year!"

It was a video of Jeremy, naked, and cowering on his knees. Violet was sitting in a chair, but he was talking to her as if she was someone else.

The audio could be heard, and Jeremy's voice nearly cried saying

"Mommy, I was a good boy. I will bring you back I promise! This girl is the perfect vessel for you to return to me. I will fix her, and break her willpower I swear it! And when I have, you can come back to your little boy... okay mommie?"

Talon put his phone away and pulled Jeremy up to his face.

"You come anywhere near me, Violet, or ANY one I'm close to... and I will bury you so fucking deep even 'mommie' wont be able to find you," and Talon threw him to the ground. "Get out of here... both of you... and don't let me catch even a whisper of your return."

Jeremy was exposed... but still cocky.

"I will see you burn Talon. I don't take orders from you! I WILL REMEMBER THIS!!"

"No you won't," was the last thing he heard before he slipped into semi-consciousness.

That voice was Doc Holliday. He shot him the same way as his hired gun did to Violet.

"It's a sedative. It has a nasty side effect of wiping short term memories though," Doc proudly told Talon. He smirked, and told Grant "I told you there'd be something nasty for you to find," and he winked at the redhead.

By now the whole crowd was at the road. Talon was a great boss, and just a great guy in general. Everyone loved Violet as well. So now, they were showing their support as well.

Talon looked at the hired gun, and told him "You're alive. Don't make me regret that. Take the asshole... and go."

He half carried the sluggish Jeremy, and started walking down the road.

"You have the heart of a warrior. One, to another, he has plans ya know. He won't quit... and he will return."

Talon called after him asking "Ranger or SEAL?"

"Neither!... Ex Marine!" he called back as he made some distance.

"Well then... Semper Fi."

The guy threw a soft salute... and headed off. Talon had his eyes on him, and his back to the crowd, and picked up his phone.

"Mr. Smith? Clean up won't be necessary. I have left the final blow for you however. See to it that he rots in hell for the rest of his life. That lifespan however, I leave to your discretion. The drive has been opened, and you can expect a courier from me shortly. Use it to any full advantage you can. IF, you fail at that task, I shall stop by to collect my fee for services *not* rendered. And when I say 'stop by'... I mean that unassuming split ranch in TeaNeck. As the saying goes Mr. Smith, two can play the 'I found your house' game."

The voice on the other end just laughed.

"Mister Grayson? It has been a pleasure doing business with you."

All Talon heard next was the click of the call cutting off. The next thing he did, was look up.

"See to it blondie, that when she's lucid again... Violet sees everything you recorded."

Talon, was speaking to the drone, and he knew damn well who was controlling it. With that, the crowd at the road broke out into applause and cheers. Once they did, the drone peeled off and headed back to the open window on the second floor.

"Huh? What the... SHIT! WHERE IS HE! TALON! HE'S HERE!" Violet said as Doc Holiday gave her a shot to counteract the first.

She was waking up but, Talon kept his word. He was the first person she saw. He was holding her and just smiled at her.

"Shh. It's okay now Violet," Talon told her as she woke up in Grant's truck. With love, Talon told her "In my arms Violet... and safe like I promised. This time sweetie, I had your back."

"And Doctor Barnes!??" her still foggy brain inquired.

"No longer here... and no longer a threat."

Talon scooped her up, and carried her back to the house once he had.

"Talon? I love you."

"Violet? I love me too," he teased. He smiled at her lovingly as she slapped him playfully, and told her "But there's more than enough love for you too."

Violet melted in his arms. A voice from the ether came next.

"It does mah harht good to know the new owner of Adair House is such a brave man."

"Thanks for the warning Miss Adair," Talon said kindly.

"Ah looked aftuh mah girls. Faw as lawng as Iem heeyuh, I shall look aftuh y'all just as much. Mista G?"

"Yes?"

The voice faded, and said as it did "Iem glad she is awlrite."

"Lady!?... So am I," and Talon just walked to the house.

Chapter 20

"Lunch in San Francisco"

Talon took in the whole of it, then asked each team to report in. He was more than pleased so far at what had been done. Some projects amazed him at how quickly they were sorted and finished. Others... not so much. Still, on a rehab of this size and magnitude, he was truly pleased with the overall level of progress.

Talon promised his brother he would do whatever he had to, to keep Violet safe. In his mind, that's all he did. The slight level of hero worship that surrounded him now had him polite on the outside, but a tad annoyed on the inside. Still, Violet was safe for the moment, and that's all he cared about.

Today, all the equipment in Abigail's PC room got removed. She setup a few pieces to keep Zack working, but all the rest got stored away. All the second floor beams were in now. With that floor safe to work on, and now Erik and crew working on the 3rd floor, the brothers Grayson went to work on Abigail's computer haven. Her job, for now, was done and with nothing new on the horizon, her room got done first.

"And... you guys do this for a living!? Well, better you than me," a nervous Abigail said said to the workers as she climbed up on the roof.

The roofers were almost finished, and they rigged her in the same harness and protection gear they used. She was getting the layout to know where to put satellite dishes, and more importantly... security cameras. Talon ordered them hard wired with wifi as a backup, not a primary connection. Talon gave her 3 orders for those.

"Hide them... make them invisible... and did I mention hide them?" Talon smarted to her yesterday when he told her what he wanted.

He also mentioned 'security' was now a top priority. A psychopath who just drives up in a rental car... and no one noticed!?... That wouldn't happen again. So, while the men worked in her room, Abigail got to work on her latest mission. She felt bad about what happened, or that it even happened at all, and how the bad guys almost got away with it.

"If that was me in that car, would you have done any different?" Abigail asked her G-Man coquettishly.

That was last night as they finished dinner in Grant's house.

With pride, Grant told her "I sure would have."

Abigail got annoyed and asked "Oh, you would have let them take me!?"

Grant told her "Talon let them go." Then, in an ice cold tone, Grant finished his sentence with "I would have fired."

Abigail smiled softly on the outside, but on the inside she was beaming.

"Hey! I was eating that!" Grant complained as Abigail took his fork from him and set it down.

She made a decision right there... and took him by the hand.

"I... uh... had a different sort of dessert in mind," she said as she led him away.

Grant stared at her a moment. Abigail nodded kindly... and the kitchen didn't get cleaned up till morning.

All 3 ladies were in the kitchen and chatting. Everyone was still asking Violet if she was okay. Eileen was beaming like a Cheshire cat. Violet was too, and so was Abigail. All 3 of them, also... were beaming for the exact same reason.

"Ooooookay," Talon said as he walked in to get a drink, and the chatter stopped on a dime.

He figured it out though, and got playful on the way out.

Talon gave Violet a sweet kiss on the cheek and exclaimed "Just leave out the part about the axle grease, okay?"

Matching his dry humor, Violet playfully whined "Aw, but that was the best part!"

Talon smirked, said "Enjoy your chat ladies," and went back to work.

After 30 minutes of intimate details all around, Abigail made a slightly sad statement.

"I wish I had this growing up."

Eileen joked "What, a falling down mansion? Oh yes Abigail... EVERY girl should have one of those growing up."

That made Abigail chuckle.

"No silly... I mean you two. Hell, I'd have been happy with just one of you! No insult Eileen but, compared to me and Violet... you have no idea how lucky you were," Abigail stated kindly but with conviction.

Eileen said "Thank you, I guess you're right to a degree."

"To a degree?" Abigail questioned.

"Yeah. Abigail, look at you now. Now, consider how you were a year ago. Painfully timid, compared to now. Abigail, the point I'm making is... you have a computer AND the knowledge of how to use it. If the locals were assholes, well, you have the talent to pong anyone in the world. Even a long distant friend would have been better than none at all."

Abigail giggled and said "That's 'ping'... not 'pong'."

Eileen joked back "Hey Missy! No making fun of your elders!"

Abigail still giggled, popped a mock curtsy, and said "No ma'am... of course not ma'am... won't happen again ma'am."

Eileen feigned arrogance and said "Well now! That's better."

Now all 3 women giggled some.

"Anyway," Eileen continued kindly, "As I was saying, to some degree it's your own fault. You had what you needed all along, you just didn't believe in yourself, that's all. Because of that, and be honest Abigail, to some degree you have to admit it was your own fault. I'm not being mean Abigail, I'm only pointing out that... now that you have come out of your shell... you may want to consider never going back in... ever."

Abigail affirmed in a kind manner "Trust me, I won't."

Eileen gave her a friendly hug and told her "I'm gonna hold you to that."

While the ladies chatted, Abigail's phone pinged her an alert. As the new head of IT security, she had her phone set to alert her to any news feed, or internet traffic, based on key words. In a heartbeat, she ignored the other two women... and called out for a man.

"TALLLLLLOOOOONNNNN!!!" She wailed down the hall.

The requested gentleman was there in a flash. Still a tad spooked by the events of the other day... his brother was right on his heels. Abigail beamed from ear to ear, and showed Talon her phone.

Talon went from a concerned expression... to a sinister smile.

"Violet?" he said kindly. "Remind me to do something when we get home later, please."

"Certainly. And what would that be exactly?"

Talon smiled caringly and showed her Abigail's phone.

"Remind me to give away your backpack. You won't be needing it anymore," he told her in the most loving of tones.

Violet looked at the phone, and began to cry happy tears.

"Well!? Someone wanna clue in the candlestick!??" Eileen scorned.

Violet put her hand over her mouth. Sweetly, Abigail took her phone back and began to read. It was a news article that popped up that caused her so much delight.

"Channel 4 news has just learned that famed doctor Jeremy Barnes, chief doctor and administrator of the Rock Ridge Rehabilitation Hospital, has become a temporary member of his own facility. Damning evidence has surfaced showing the doctor abused patients, and technically should be one himself. This reporter has gained access to leaked videos of the doctors indiscretions. I don't mind telling the good readers that... I wish I hadn't. Doctor Barnes was arrested by FBI agents this morning in what this reporter found out was an ongoing investigation. The AMA has suspended his license, and he is now under the watchful eye of Federal agents. A team of psychologists have been called in to assess every patient, and the facility is officially closed pending the outcome of the investigation. Based on what I've seen, it is this reporter's opinion that Dr. Barnes should become a patient in the very facility he so mismanaged... and rot there for all eternity. More to come as this shocking story unfolds."

Everyone was happy at that news. Talon was so much so, he made a phone call.

"Well Mister Grayson... I'll assume you've seen the news. We decided to heed your suggestion. Like what we came up with?"

Talon was all business when he replied.

"Mr. Smith... you know what I do for a living, yes?"

"I do," was the polite but abrupt reply.

"That house in Teaneck, I noticed it had a floor to rafters front parlor. In one of my jobs, we discovered a solid silver chandelier. It also had real lead crystal as well. I had it appraised for well over a hundred thousand dollars. I'll be shipping it to you in a day or so. Enjoy the 'illumination' it will provide you. Also, if you ever have need of a reference... have them call me... first."

"Your generosity is most appreciated. I don't mean this rudely but, I hope to never need to speak with you again. If I should however, I offer you your own words... call me first."

"I will call no other. An extreme pleasure doing business with you," and that bit of business was done.

Violet was a ball of happy tears as Eileen and Abigail hugged her.

"You'll pay dearly for this you miserable witch!" was the ghostly voice in Violet's ears.

Looking to the distance, Jeremy's crazy mom was in the doorway.

"Try it... and I'll fry your ass."

Everyone was looking at Violet wondering who she was talking to. She just dried her tears, and pointed to the doorway.

"It's 'mommy dearest'," she said in an annoyed tone.

Lucinda, to men anyway, was a tad submissive. To women? Just the reverse. She wasn't mean to them but... she didn't take any shit either.

"Y'all will do nothing of the sort. Not while Iem heeyuh anyway. In THIS howse... y'all take orders from ME you wretch!" and Lucinda flung her arm in disgust and anger.

Jeremy's mother turned and put two outstretched arms to Lucinda. She only got halfway to her when she wailed in pain... and simply vanished.

Lucinda's image was gone but her meaningful voice told Violet "Ah doent care who's howse this is now... I'll have none of her sort bother'in anyone inside these walls. Least of awl you dahlin."

No one but Violet saw it. Violet sure felt it though. Mommy Dearest was truly gone. Now for the first time in her life, Violet, felt free. The happy tears returned once more.

"Thank you, dear lady," she told the ether.

"Maw than welcome, sweet chyld," the voice said as it faded away.

Violet just ran and hugged Talon. That night, when everyone had gone, it was Violet who left a flower and a glass of sherry on the mantle.

It was 3 days later, and a rather sporty Italian car was heading westbound over the infamous 'Donner Pass'. Talon had a lunch date with the descendants of one of Lucinda's close friends. A rather exquisite looking brunette was with him.

"You okay over there? It's not that uncomfortable is it?" Talon queried to a fidgeting Violet.

"Comfortable!?" Violet said slightly concerned, "I could fall asleep for a week in this seat!"

"So what's with all the shifting around then?"

Violet told him meekly "I'm afraid if I so much as fart, the cleaning bill would cost me a month's pay!"

Talon just laughed... and slammed the gas just for fun.

Talon pulled the silver and black Lamborghini into the grounds of a mansion he could only describe as 'palatial'. It was outside the city proper. It also looked as old as his mansion.

Talon turned to Violet as he shut the car off, and said "Listen, I want to talk to you."

"Mm?"

"Look Violet, normally I just bitch at you for the scared little rabbit thing. These people? They will eat you alive if they see you act that way. I know this is way out of your element. It was for me too at first, but I learned how to deal with them out of necessity. Tell me Violet, ever been inside a house like that?" Talon asked pointing out the window.

"Not even on a guided tour," Violet replied.

"Didn't think so. Thing is, I need to impress these people. Inside that house however, the 'rules of etiquette' are drastically different. I'm only warning you Violet so you won't do a faux pas without realizing it. Try this, if you get nervous, channel Lucinda, and you'll do fine." Talon laughed at his words and said "I meant that metaphorically... heh heh... you know that right?"

Violet beamed and joked "Touch everything, and act like a spoiled 4 year old... got it!"

Talon laughed and quipped "Oh, I see you've met these types of people then huh?"

Violet laughed, but said "Yeah, well, thanks for the heads up," and exited the car as the doorman opened it for her.

"Park it for you sir?" the clean dressed man asked.

"Son? Ever drive a Silver Ghost?" Talon inquired sharply.

Confidently, the man replied "Several times a week actually."

Talon huffed, but tossed him the keys.

"This car is actually worth more. That thing is low-jacked. If it leaves the premises, I'll fire up an app on my phone, and hit the ejector seat button."

The man smiled and winked at Talon with an understanding look.

"Have no fear Mister Grayson. Harold the butler will show you in. He's waiting for you at the doors." He nodded to both of them saying "Sir... ma'am... enjoy your lunch," and he drove off and parked the car.

Talon, with Violet on his arm, walked into the huge old house. Mansion would be a better word for it. It also looked like, with a few minor changes in décor, as if he and Violet had stepped back in time as well.

"So, this is what 'old money' looks like eh?" Violet said softly to Talon.

"If you think this is impressive, you should see the study Miss Hayes," was the kind but assertive reply from the man who walked up them. "Thank you Harold, I'll take it from here," he told the butler.

"Certainly sir," and Harold headed off. He stopped and asked "Will you be taking lunch in the dining room sir?"

"Oh, I think we'd be more comfortable in the lounge, Harold."

"As you wish sir," and Harold was gone.

The man stuck his hand out to Talon saying "Apologies for my manners. Collis P. Huntington the seventh. A pleasure to meet you Mr. Grayson. And you Miss Hayes, as lovely in person as your photos showed."

"Photo's?" Violet queried as the man stood up from kissing her hand.

"Indeed. Seems a certain private investigator found himself without a paycheck recently. He found my offer, only too reasonable."

Talon chuckled, looked at Violet, and hooked his thumb at Collis.

"I like this guy already," Talon joked.

Collis smiled saying "That's the spirit Mister Grayson! Your phone call some time back caused a bit of a stir, to say the least. Still, I see no reason to be all stiff and close ranks and such. Not till at least I've had a chance to hear you out, and assess you for myself." As a small show of clout, Collis told him "Oh, and, Robert asked me to say hello for him."

Talon caught it, and replied confidently "Bob? He always was the friendly sort. Send him my regards in return next time you see him."

"I shall!" Collis said happily. "We're scheduled for golf next week."

Talon knew this type of showing off clout, and replied "I'm happy to see Bob was able to fill the slot I had to suddenly back out of."

He smirked at Collis's reaction and asked "So, the seventh grandson of one of the 'Big 4' is backing the senator now are we?"

Collis said with a bit of pomp "The Huntington family has always been concerned with the welfare of the common man... and seeing to it the right people are elected to serve that greater good." He smiled, ended the pecker contest, and asked "You know of the Big 4 eh? It would seem, 'Bob' as you call him, was right about you. Quite the historian, aren't you Mister Grayson?"

"Oh... call me Talon." To show off in return, Talon pointed down the hallway they were standing in and said "Study is that way. Library is to the side of that. That room right there is, what was called back in the day, the parlor or sitting room. Stables below that have likely been converted to garages by now."

Collis laughed and asked "We'll be having lunch shortly. Would you like me to guide you there... or would you rather do it?"

Talon smirked "The internet can be a wonderful tool."

Collis probed further.

"And my great grandfather?" he queried Talon.

"Collis P. Huntington... the original that is... was an east coaster actually. Got into railroads at 40, and pretty much built the Southern Pacific Railroad. Locally referred to as the west coast Vanderbilt. Those rail lines are still major arteries to this day. The Big 4 was actually 5... but the other 4 bought out Theodore Judah. Collis came out here with his brother, during the gold rush of 1849, and never left. He became a driving force in the creation of the Trans-continental Railroad," then to throw Collis off a bit, Talon finished with "... and a regular patron of the fine 'boarding house', of which I now own."

Collis smiled to Violet, and told her "While he may not be the 'old money' you referenced earlier, if you don't mind some friendly advice, I say you may want to hang onto this one my dear." Collis waved his hand inward and asked politely "Shall we then?"

Three people went deeper into the house, and off to the start of a rather interesting lunch.

Lunch was fine. As a show of his wealth, and to honor Talon's Nevada heritage, it was served on silver trays. When Harold came to take the plates away, Collis gave him an order.

"Harold, please close the doors on your way out. I have some business to discuss with Miss Hayes and Mister Grayson."

"Certainly sir," and the fine study type room they were in was sealed from prying ears behind two massive oak doors.

"Well... are we alone?" Collis asked.

"Don't know. Your house Collis, you tell me," Talon told him.

In a dry tone, he said "I was talking to Miss Hayes."

She picked up real quick on the polite but sly behavior. She recalled Talon's advice, and answered Collis's question.

"Know about that do you?" She smiled at Talon with an 'I got this' look, and told Collis "No... we are not. Suffice to say though, it isn't anyone you would know."

Collis smiled, got out of his high back chair, and opened a box on a table.

"Cuban, Mister Grayson?"

"Don't mind if I do."

Violet looked hard at Collis.

"Yes my dear?" he asked seeing her expression.

"I would have expected better manners."

Collis laughed saying "Indeed! Forgive me my dear. Would you care for one as well?"

"Thank you," she said with a sly smile.

Collis smiled to Talon and raised an eyebrow. Talon just shrugged in return as Collis offered her a light.

"Well Mister Grayson, as the modern vernacular goes... wadda ya say we cut through the bullshit and get down to business?"

Talon sat back down, casually popped the ashes in an ashtray, and replied "Fine by me. Violet?"

"Suits me as well," she replied as she puffed away.

Collis told him "I wasn't kidding about your call Talon. I'm sure you can appreciate a family like mine, not having it's skeletons exposed, nor it's dirty laundry aired out in public. So Talon... what exactly do you want from me and mine?"

"You asked me to tell you some history. What can you tell me of what I've inherited?"

"History was never my best subject. Why don't you enlighten me?" Collis deferred.

"Fine. You obviously know about Violet. You hold that as your trump card, and your unsaid way of telling me to watch what I say or do. Great grandpa was a good friend of Lucinda. A lady, and a house, that I'm just betting you know more about than you let on. I know how friendly granddad was with Lucinda. What your paranoia is telling you however, is completely wrong. Truth is Collis, I know about families like yours. More truth is, like I already told you,

I'm not out to hurt you. I truly only need the tracks replaced like I said. I would also like history that I know you have. A lot or a little, I don't care. Whatever great grandpa did back then, it's ancient history. Bringing that up now, can only hurt both of us. Also, making you and your family into an enemy is not on my agenda. I want the switch put back in, and the tracks repaired and made functional. I give your family some good press, and everyone is happy."

Collis queried "And then?"

"I intend to rent the mansion out to formal affairs. Like the grand lady of old, I intend to keep it neutral ground. Democrat or Republican. New money or... the 'older' kind. The train will come once more to Adair House and only be more of an attraction. The house, and what it did, will be public knowledge. The 'guest list' however... will die with me. 'IF' however, you decide to make an enemy of me, those skeletons will get exposed. If not, then I like you actually Collis. As a person of your stature, I'm sure you can appreciate a true friend of any stature. You have my promise that I will honor the same discretions, as the lady I'm certain grandpa called 'dear friend'."

Collis looked Talon over. Talon didn't care and let him.

"And you Miss Hayes?"

"I have no desire to harm anyone. As I'm sure you already know, my life and talents, are interesting to say the least. Like Talon said, if you don't harm me or mine, then I won't ask my 'friends' to make your life a living nightmare."

Collis looked them both over one last time, then smiled, and called the butler back in.

"Interesting terms you have there Mister Grayson," Collis told the two. Harold walked in, and Collis told him "Harold, would you ask grandmother to join us please?"

"Right away sir."

"Oh, and Harold? Tell her they have gained my trust... for now."

"Certainly," and Harold left to his task.

Talon called him on it saying "I had a feeling you were the front line defense." Violet looked at him questioningly, and Talon told her "Matriarch or Patriarch my dear. Collis may be important, but the real power almost always lies higher up."

"And you sir, would be correct," came an aged voice.

Harold was wheeling in a frail old woman in a wheelchair. She had an annoyed look on her face that belied she was angry that her body had given out on her still feisty personality. Collis got up to get her, but Talon put a kind hand on his shoulder, and stopped him.

"Call it a show of my intentions... and manners," Talon told Collis.

Collis smiled and waved a hand.

"I'll take it from here. Thanks Harold."

The butler nodded kindly, and closed the doors once more, as Talon wheeled her into the room.

"Well Mister Grayson, seems my grandson approves of you. Whether I do or not, remains to be seen." She looked at her grandson, and politely commanded "Collis, how about if you take Miss Hayes on a walk of the gardens? I'd like to discuss business with Mister Grayson on my own."

"Of course grandmother."

He held a hand to Violet, and she politely accepted it.

On the way out, he stopped and told Talon "I'll take good care of her Talon. Mind a piece of advice?"

"Always," Talon replied confidently.

"Left alone? With grandmother? Well... now would be a good time for that 'stiff backbone' I was told you possess," Collis snickered.

He kissed his grandmother, and said "Try not to be too hard on our guests my dear. After all, it is their first time here." He stopped by the door and said "Oh, and Talon? The doctors take a dim view of grandmother indulging in the Cubans. Just so you know."

He laughed lightly at his grandmother's annoyed look, and took Violet out of the room.

The old lady asked "Mind if I call you Talon?"

"Not at all," Talon said with ease. "And I should call you...?"

The feisty old lady told him "Don't screw with me Talon. You know damn well who I am. A man like you wouldn't dare come here and not do his research. Well, not a real man anyway."

Talon smiled and said "Adelaide Huntington. A pleasure to meet you."

"Call me Addie. I never did like that name. I caution you though Mister Grayson, anger me, and I'll have you call me something else."

Talon liked this lady, and asked "And that would be?"

She smiled and asked "Would it surprise you, that I had some of the most powerful men in recent history, cowering at my feet... and saying things like 'yes mistress'?"

Talon laughed hard at that one.

"Now I understand your grandson's warning," he stated calming back down. "No Addie, I would not. However, I've known women like you. Shall we say, politely put, I am not one of those men?"

"Hmmf," she snorted. "If I had a dime for every time I've heard that!"

Talon thought this old lady was, as his parents used to say, 'a trip'. He also called her on it.

"Sorry to disappoint you, but I think you'll find... I'm all out of dimes."

"THAT sir..." Addie decried, "... would be refreshing indeed." Addie shifted attitudes, and told him "While I enjoyed toying with men like them, I didn't respect a single one of them. Tell you what Mister Grayson?"

"Hmm?"

Addie sneered and told Talon "Prove me wrong, and I'll give you more than you bargained for."

Talon just chuckled at the surrealism of his current situation, and asked "And if I don't?"

"If you don't... then my offer remains the same... just not in a way you might have hoped for."

Talon just grinned, hung, and shook his head.

He stared the old lady down and told her "Tell ya what... 'Adelaide'... how about this? How about if you stop yanking my chain... hmm?"

"And if I did anyway?" Addie challenged confidently.

"Then, you feisty old broad, I will treat you like a clueless submissive arm piece... eeeeeevery time you do."

Addie smiled, and said "Fine then. Shall we seal the deal? With say, a Cuban?"

Talon sat back in his chair, smiled, and blew a huge puff of smoke at her.

"Sorry. I sort of promised I wouldn't," Talon told her with a wink.

Addie waved the smoke towards her, and gave a smiling nod of approval to her guest.

Violet was enjoying a lovely garden, with a charming host, while Talon was inside going toe to toe with grandma Addie. Collis tried flirting with her. Each and every time though, he was shot down. All of them politely, but shot down all the same.

Collis just laughed, admitted defeat, and exclaimed "Mister Grayson is a lucky man indeed!"

"I'd like to think so," Violet said with a sly smile. "However Collis, I am flattered you would even try." She walked on some, then called over her shoulder "You're a dog with a wagging tail... but at least you're a polite one."

Collis smiled, laughed a little, and went back to being a fine host.

"You are far more than I expected Miss Hayes. For that much at least, thank you."

Violet smiled, and held out her hand.

"Shall we then?" she queried.

Collis smiled kindly, bowed slightly and took her hand.

"I'd be delighted."

A lovely stroll, only mildly interrupted by a snide power play, resumed once more.

Violet was walking and talking with Collis, when she came to a polite but an abrupt stop.

"Something wrong?" Collis asked.

"Honestly? I'm not sure." She looked firmly at Collis and asked "How much do you really know about what I can do?"

Violet had gone from hiding, to a desire to show off discreetly. Now that doctor Barnes is right where he should be... and mommie dearest left a wake Violet swore even the non sensitive could feel... she truly felt like a new woman. She decided, here and now, was a small but good place to test those new feelings of confidence, and see where it took her.

Collis stared at her curiously and asked "I guess a better question is, how much do I *want* to know?"

"Also a fair question. Only you can decide but... do it quickly," Violet countered.

Collis stared questioningly for a moment. Then, a little boy smile emerged, and he held out his hand.

"Now what kind of a host would I be if I let such a beautiful woman come to any harm on her first visit, hmm?" Collis meaningfully joked.

Violet stared ahead and told him "Time to keep an open mind then Collis," and she walked towards something only she could see.

Violet explained as she walked "Collis? Not everyone who dies becomes a spirit. Those who are, often lack what they need to get their desired effect." She followed the specter and continued with "Collis, if you needed a carpenter, but had no talent at it, you'd hire one correct?"

"I suppose," he said trying to absorb all around him.

"Many spirits are like that. They can't get a message across, so they find someone who can."

Collis was trying to understand, and thought he had.

"So, like a courier? I wish to send a message, but the person I send the message to sees only a stranger. Only the message he or she delivers is what makes sense. Like that?"

Violet smiled kindly and told him "Exactly like that. Tell me Mister Huntington... do you know any Indians? Or perhaps have one in your family history?"

"Real or native American?"

Violet smiled slightly and told him "As in turban wearing real live... heh heh, whoops, I mean 'real dead'... Indian. Could be a Turk possibly. My talents at history is not exactly on par with that of my boyfriend's."

"I neither know of one, nor know of any in our history."

Violet said "Well Collis, if that's the case, I'd say we have a courier to follow." Violet grinned politely and asked him "I like that analogy actually. Mind if I use it?"

"Not at all," Collis said back just as nicely.

Collis looked about as if he would see what Violet saw at any moment. "So... what now?"

Violet was staring forward again and said "He wants us to follow him," she answered as she led Collis along the garden pathway.

The man in the turban ahead of them was stone faced, and just kept beckoning Violet to follow him. The walk path they were on was a well maintained slate stone path. Suddenly, turban guy stopped, and pointed down a barely noticeable dirt path. Violet looked down it, then put her arm behind her bent leg and took off her left high heeled shoe. Next came off the right one.

"Coming?" Violet asked in a dead pan tone.

"You're serious aren't you?" Collis asked in true surprise.

"Dead serious," Violet quipped. Then Violet almost giggled at Collis's raised eyebrow. "What!? (chuckle) They're Italian!" referring to her shoes.

Unlike Nevada, which was mostly sand and brush, this part of California was loaded with trees. Violet was heading into a small but dense wooded area alongside the main path. Collis relented, and got down on one knee, and undid the laces on his shoe. He switched balance, and untied the other. He took his socks off, tossed them inside the shoes, and walked into the woods. Violet teasingly raised an eyebrow back at him.

"These are Italian too... and about 3 times what yours cost," was his proud response to her unasked question.

Violet chuckled, waved a branch away, and followed behind him.

While Violet was on her little adventure, Talon was holding ground indoors.

"So Talon, what exactly do you want from us Huntington's? And don't give me any of this bullshit about wanting to restore some old tracks," Addie barked a little too snottily.

Talon fired right back saying "That's all I truly want. I would give you the details but, I wouldn't want to bore you with things like that. Best leave that to us men, now wouldn't you agree?"

Addie caught his snide tone and realized Talon was only honoring his promise. She actually admired him for it.

"My apologies for my tone. To say 'its been awhile' since I've talked to a man with a backbone, would be an understatement. Now, bad attitudes aside, wadda ya want gray guy?"

Talon puffed some smoke her way, as a means of a peace offering, and told her the truth.

"I want to make Adair house a quiet little gem. One of those places that only the west can provide. I have access to a lot of antiques, but train tracks isn't on my list of inventory. The train will come once a week, and we make nice for the tourists. Other times it can be rented for things like weddings. Even if I had the tracks, I wouldn't know how to lay them. Of course, if you honored my request... your 'gift' would be honored with a plaque or something... and the Huntington family would certainly get some good press."

"And it's history?" Addie queried seriously.

"Like I told Collis. Enough real to give the locals some charm... and let rumor and folklore do the rest. I told your grandson that dredging up ancient history, good or bad, does neither of us any good. It's obvious you're a force to be reckoned with Addie. So am I. You can make an enemy or a friend of me. The former serves no purpose but that's never stopped folk like you before. The latter serves us both."

Addie smiled, and asked him "Who is CQ?"

Talon responded "I don't know. While I uncover more seemingly daily, I've yet to run across that name or reference. Actually Addie, I know you have history of back then. Maybe a lot maybe a little, but either way I'm betting it's more than what I got."

"And you'd be right Talon," she said as she put her left hand to her thigh.

Addie pulled out an old book she had stowed under the blanket that covered her legs. She touched it gingerly, then handed it equally so, to Talon.

"I would appreciate it if you would only read the pages I marked, please."

Talon gave a nod of thanks, and gently took the book from her.

He read aloud from the first marker "My sister CQ surprised me with a visit today. I was elated and we shared a wonderful afternoon together." Talon stopped a moment and asked Addie happily "Is this who I think it is?"

Addie proudly proclaimed "Mister Grayson? I was born on June 19th, 1924. As of a few days ago, I turned 91. You hold in your hand, the journal of a man I never met... but used to call 'great grampy'. My father, his son, gave me that book on my 16th birthday. Even at my age I can recite most pages by heart. He thought it just a unique gift to give his only daughter. I thought it a revelation. Great grampy was a visionary, and I followed in every footstep of his I could. Now Talon, I need something from you."

Talon joked with a sweeping one arm bow saying "And what can I do for the great Addie Huntington?"

"Tell me who CQ was. I always believed it was 'her'... but I never had any proof. Get me that proof... and you'll get your tracks... and a lot more of that history you so desperately want. "

Talon honestly asked "Not that I think you incorrect but, what makes you think that?"

Addie sneered "Keep reading."

Talon gave Addie her wish.

"April 3rd, 1863. CQ concerns me gravely. She has finally found love. While the man she has chosen is a good one, he is however the wrong one. I have started spending more time on vacation than perhaps I should. CQ and I have talked about this extensively. Still, as much as she trusts me, my sister will not heed my warnings. I disdain our arguments. Though friendly, I would much rather bask in her fine company, and her charming smile. I fear that my sister will find nothing but heartache in this endeavor," Talon said reading aloud from the next marked page. He then asked Addie "Did it ever occur to you she may just be his sister?"

Addie told him calmly "He had two, Marylin and Jeanine. Great grampy mentioned several times that, aside from the brother he came out west with, he was a bit estranged from his family. At no other place in that book does he talk of them in such a tone as he does that sister."

Talon nodded and read the third, and last, marked page.

"December 15th, 1865. Business proceeds at record pace. And yet, I find myself with such melancholy that I can hardly bear to put my thoughts to paper as I have done since my teens. My beloved CQ has left us for what I can only hope is bigger and grander things. I have spared no expense to find, and remedy, the cause of her departure. My partners have lent their kindnesses to my endeavor, and have joined me wholeheartedly in my new found purpose. I saw to it personally, that her funeral, had those who loved her most in life... beside her as we laid her to her final slumber. I can only hope that when the Lord finally calls me to my eternal sleep, that he sends my beloved CQ as my guiding angel... to take me home to his divine bosom."

Addie concluded with "Suffice to say, the man he was in the beginning of the book, was a far different one from the one he was towards the end."

Talon was now on fire.

"I want to read this book... the WHOLE book... and I want my tracks." He stared Addie down, and in a no nonsense tone commanded "Name your price."

She was about to, when his phone rang.

"Violet? You okay? Kind of bad timing sweetie."

"Come out to the gardens. I'll meet you on the path. I'm alright but... get here now."

Addie cocked her head slightly, as Talon said "I'm on my way."

Talon was brisk paced, and talking to Collis who was guiding him to where they were. He was using Violet's phone, and Talon got there as quickly as requested. Violet was standing there and holding her shoes. She hugged him sweetly when he arrived. Collis saw the genuine affection, and silently mused to himself how he would like to find a non ghostly Violet of his own one day.

"You're not gonna believe this," Violet said with happy anticipation.

Collis was a tad stunned and added "I'm not sure I believe it."

[15 minutes ago]

Violet walked through the woods with Collis. It was clear to both of them that there once was a small path here, but it had since become overgrown. What neither knew was, they were heading for a small and private spot that was for the original Collis only. The ghost with the turban appeared again as Violet reached the end of the partially covered path. She and Collis the seventh emerged to a small clearing. It was evident, this had overgrown as well.

"And you didn't know this was here why?" Violet asked.

"Miss Hayes, the grounds cover twenty acres in total. 'Camping out' wasn't exactly something I did as a child, so I never explored much."

"No camping!?" Violet chuckled, "Jesus Collis, just what kind of childhood did you have exactly?"

Slyly, Collis replied "One I'd be happy to tell you about over dinner."

"Ya know, I am a pretty good cook. I'll see if 'Talon' and I are free some time next week. I'm sure he'd be interested to hear your story as well," Violet said just as slyly, and letting Collis know she caught him yet again.

"Hahahahaha! Touche Miss Hayes. Sorry but, I'm not exactly used to being rejected. Consider it a bit of a knee jerk reaction." Now he joked in a grand manner, feigned insult, and boasted in a grandiose tone "Why Miss Hayes, am I to understand that you are ACTUALLY rejecting the one and only Collis P. Huntington the seventh!??"

Violet winked at him and said "The ramifications are indeed mind boggling, don't you think?"

Collis relented, and honestly told her "I can only hope Mister Grayson truly understands just how lucky he is."

Violet gave him a soft peck on the cheek and told him "Tell ya what, if he ever forgets, I'll call you so you can remind him."

Collis gave her a soft bow and stated "See that you do."

The clearing had a low corral type fence around it. Half of if was busted and Violet and Collis just walked in through one of them and looked around. The moment Violet crossed the small perimeter, her senses were buzzing.

"So Miss Hayes, what do you..."

"Call me Violet."

Collis nodded politely and resumed with "So Violet... what is this place? Aside from the obvious of course."

"I wish I knew," Violet said as she looked around.

Suddenly, Collis grabbed her and pulled her away.

"Sorry Violet, but you were about to step on some Oleander. It's rather toxic. I don't know much about plants, but I did have a rather nasty run-in with that one when I was a boy. Needless to say grandmother had a fit. She also had the gardeners rip out all they could find. It's usually a vine however. I've never seen it grow on the ground like that before though."

"Huh?"

Collis pointed to the white flowers on the ground.

"Grandmother would have a fit if she knew these were here. Jesus, they're everywhere!"

Violet looked around and saw that Collis was right.

She told him "Unlike you, I have spent a great deal of time camping. While I appreciate your concern, I can tell you it's not Oleander. True it looks similar but... oh my God... COLLIS! Look around! I'm betting there's a gravestone here somewhere! Start in the middle and work outward!"

Violet was right, and it only took mere moments to find it under some brush.

"Well then Violet, if it's not Oleander... care to tell me what it is then!?"

Violet smiled as they revealed the small but ornate headstone. She answered with only one word.

"Edelweiss."

Collis read aloud from over Violet's shoulder.

"My dearest CQ. Beloved sister of... OH NO WAY!... Collis P. Huntington!??"

Violet touched the stone with kind reverence. The response she got nearly spooked her.

"Violet dah'lin, are y'all alright? Ah sensed a great urgen... Violet dear, where are we?" Lucinda said as she got a grip on what reality she could.

Violet smiled, and believed she figured it out. To test that theory, she took her hand off the headstone. Lucinda was mid sentence when she suddenly vanished. Violet grinned, almost sinisterly, and touched the stone again.

"Ah did naht expect you Violet, of awl peepul, ta be so rude," Lucinda scorned at being cut off.

"Lady? I wasn't being rude... but I was testing a theory." She smiled at something only she could see, and said "Stay here as long as you can my friend. If you can't, then just know that this time, I'm helping you for a change," and she immediately went for her cell phone. "Shit... no service."

Collis said "I spend many hours among the gardens making or receiving calls. Mostly to stay out of grandmother's prying ears. I know it will work on the path we were on. By the way... who were you talking to?"

"C'mon Collis!" Violet beamed, and nearly dragged her host back to where they were. "I'll tell you on the way!" and back to the path they went.

Now, with Talon updated, he was beaming as well.

He looked at Collis and said "Ya may wanna get Addie out here. I sort of promised her something, and this will help me deliver on that promise."

"Are you insane!?" Collis barked. "Grandmother is very ill! Seriously Mister Grayson... you have way overstepped your bounds on this one!"

He was about to berate Talon, when a rather elderly voice stopped him.

"Oh hush Collis. I may be old, but I'm far from feeble!" Addie barked.

Walter the butler was wheeling her up to the 3 of them. With Talon taking off so urgently, she wanted to know why.

"One day grandmother, you'll realize the error of that statement," Collis said in a tone that clearly belied he didn't like being corrected.

"So Miss Hayes... discover something?" Addie asked.

"You could say that," she said looking at Collis as if to get some sort of direction from him.

"If you're going to talk to me Violet... I would appreciate it if you would do just that. My grandson is a good man, but he tends to worry too much when it comes to me."

Collis was clearly unhappy, and snorted "Give the old lady what she wants. She usually gets it anyway."

Talon pulled out his phone, switched it to satellite mode, and called Violet's phone on a video call.

He took hers, and gave it to Addie, and showed her a live video of herself.

"I'm going in there. If there's no objections of course. You asked for proof Addie? I'm willing to bet it's in where Violet said it was."

Violet called to him as he walked into the woods.

"You can't! Another few feet and you lose all bars!"

Talon smiled over his shoulder and said "Time for me to show you why Abigail was so enamored with my phone. Trust me... I don't need bars," and Talon disappeared from sight.

Now, everyone gathered over Addie's shoulders to watch the video.

The video bounced like one would expect from a walking videographer. Addie was the most attentive of all of them. Nine plus decades, and the proof she's always wanted, was right under her nose the whole time.

"You were right Violet... it is Edelweiss. I'm surprised to see it at all. From everything I've read about them, they're an alpine flower only."

"So?" Addie queried.

Talon's voice replied "So my dear... they need thin air and altitude... not sea level and humidity. These also don't look the same as the one's back home. If I had to guess, I'd say Collis was right too. Someone with great gardening skills likely hybridized them with Oleander."

"To what end Talon?" Collis asked the phone.

Talon's voice replied "Assuming Violet is correct, then I'd bet they were made for her. For any of 'us' however, well, get too close... or wander where you weren't welcome... and the plants would serve as silent body guards." Talon continued as he stepped over some plants and such, "Also, people back then knew of poisonous plants, but almost no one knew which ones were. Animals munch and learn fast where to stay away from. Pretty white flowers that look like roses? Why... who wouldn't want to pick some of those!? They get sick, the place develops a 'stay away' reputation, and only serves Collis's purposes." Talon was truly impressed at the slyness of it and added "I'll say this much... 'great grampy' was one slick fellow."

With pride, Addie told the phone confidently "He was indeed."

Talon reached the old clearing. Then he walked to the stone in the middle, knelt down, and touched it.

"Y'all mien tell'in me why we are in thuh middle of tha fawrest Mista G?" Lucinda's voice cackled in a clearly unhappy tone.

Modern ghost hunters use a slew of electronics to capture even a slight voice or image. Addie put a trembling hand to her mouth. It was faint, very faint but, she heard what only Talon and Violet could hear.

"Oh great grampy," Addie said in a clearly trembling voice.

Seeing Addie, Collis immediately barked for Walter to return her to the house at once.

"You so much as move me an inch!... And I will rip off BOTH of your nut sacks with my bare hands!" Addie commanded.

Walter cautiously removed his hands from her wheelchair. Talon just laughed hearing Addie being Addie.

"Whyyy Mista G, do you fien it nessuhserry, ta associate with such hahrd women?" Lucinda queried hearing the woman on Talon's machine.

Talon only laughed harder.

Addie had always respected 'great grampy'. She treated that journal, from the moment she got it, like most people treat the Bible. When she herself would sit in his company, she would find out it was the original Collis, who lent her what little power he had so that she would finally hear... and have her proof.

"Lucinda? Do you recall a moniker of 'CQ'?" Talon asked a presence he could hear but not see.

"Ah doo indeed suh. No fine-uh man walked tha earth in mah opinion. He was like a brothuh ta me... and I a sistuh in return ta him."

Addie was in tears. Happy tears... but tears all the same.

"What did it mean!?" Addie queried into the phone a bit abruptly.

An unhappy Lucinda asked Talon "Are y'all somehow spy'in on me with that muhsheen of yaws?"

"A little yes, and a little no," Talon answered. "How she's hearing you is unknown to me. I'd be willing to bet though, aside from me and Violet, she's the only other one who can." Talon looked around, spoke kindly, and asked the clearing "Fair to assume... it stood for Cajun Queen?"

A voice answered him "Naht ownlee would you be correct suh... but in life... he was thee ownlee one who could call me thaht. How evuh did you learn of thaht?" Lucinda's voice was sounding irritated and asked "Now, ah have ansuhd yaw questions. I buhleev y'all were about tuh ansuh mine?"

"Lucinda? Trust in me now and just know, I'm going to do my best to honor a request you gave me."

"And that would be?"

"I'm gonna do what I can... to bring you home."

Lucinda's voice was smiling now and she faded out saying "Then guud suh... ah will leave you to thaht fine piece of bizniss."

Violet's voice came over the vid link "You're good now... she's gone."

"See you in a few."

Talon shut off the call and headed back to the path.

Addie smiled at Violet as she handed her the phone.

"I must say, this has been the most interesting visit from guests that I can ever remember." Talon emerged from the woods and Addie nearly barked "You sir, and I... have business to attend to."

Talon nodded politely, and the group returned to the house.

Back in the parlor, Addie was like a general directing a battle.

"You and you... stay..." Addie commanded to Talon and Violet. "...the rest of you... leave us."

Collis barked but Addie barked right back.

Collis was clearly unhappy, and snidely said "You know I love you grandmother. I would love you a whole lot more if you weren't such a witch sometimes." He had his hands on both door knobs, looked straight at Talon, and stated "Best of luck Mister Grayson. Miss Hayes? It truly was a pleasure."

Violet smiled softly at him as he closed the doors.

Addie looked at Talon and proclaimed sarcastically "Meanwhile, back to that 'let's cut through the bullshit' part of our earlier conversation."

Talon nodded and said "I knew nothing of this till Violet called me. I think you know that to be true. My request remains the same. Now however, I have an addition."

Addie studied him calmly and asked "What did you mean by bringing her home?"

Talon got firm and told her "You wanna cut through the bullshit? Fine by me. I want her home where she belongs. I promised her that much. I will be as discreet as you need and this little incident... well... it won't exactly become public record. That said... I want her home with me."

Addie was intrigued and commanded "Tell me more." She saw the look on Talon's face at that one, and politely added "Please."

Talon eased up and said "She never belonged here. From what little I gathered of the original Collis, he brought her here to keep her safe. That 'safety' is no longer required. I have, among my friends, a surgeon... and some ground penetrating radar that can see China all the way from here. We come in, secretly of course, verify our findings... hide her, and get out." Talon now got into 'don't fuck with me' mode and said "My original question remains... name your price."

Addie smirked and asked "You'd wait me out wouldn't you?"

Confidently, Talon exclaimed "I'd be here with a deal for your grandson... and a backhoe... one day after they put you in the ground. So, fair to say, you're damn right I would. Mind you, I'd rather not, but I would all the same."

Addie just laughed hard.

"Mr. Grayson? Ya got balls I'll give ya that much. Refreshing to say the least."

Then Addie said something Talon almost didn't believe.

"Take her, I don't care. I got the proof you promised. I will of course hold you to your promise of discretion however." Addie softened in her demeanor and said "You're right, she never did belong here. I further believe you're right again when you said it was great grampy's way of keeping her safe from the rabble of the day. IF it is truly her, then I won't stop you."

Talon was waiting for the other shoe to drop.

"And in return?"

Addie smiled, got coy, and replied "Well Talon, I've invited you to my home. Don't you think, that as new friends of the Huntington family, it would only be polite to invite me to yours?"

Violet chimed in with "I'm sure that wouldn't be a problem. I'm a fine cook and..." and Talon stopped her by putting his arm across her chest.

He was staring straight at Addie when he did.

"I told you not to yank my chain you old broad. What exactly do you want?" Talon asked defensively.

Addie smiled, and said "I'm sure you are my dear but... that wasn't the home I had in mind."

Violet was a tad confused and asked "You want to come to the mansion?"

"Why not?" Addie asked with glee. "My dear, I have known of its existence for some time. Life, as it were, has seen fit to show me in real life what I've only imagined many times." She stared Talon down and told him "I want out of this wheelchair. I want to stand on my own two feet, and walk where he walked. I want to see what he held so dear. You want to know my price? That's it. And of course, as 'dear friends' of the family, I'm sure you would understand that a woman of my stature would only arrive in the finest of styles."

Talon smirked and said "I think the driveway can accommodate a Silver Ghost or two... hehehe... or five."

Addie sneered "The Rolls is a fine machine of course, but, I had something a little more Italian in mind."

Talon roared.

"HA HA HA HA HA! DEAL!" He sported a huge grin, and slid a Cuban cigar from his sleeve... and handed it to Addie.

"Shall we seal the deal then?" Talon said with a laugh.

"Mister Grayson?" Addie said, puffing the cigar as Talon lit it, "It's been a pleasure doing business with you." She sat back, sported a sly grin, blew some smoke into the air and concluded with "A real pleasure indeed."

Chapter 21

"My Dearest Sisters..."

{February 10, 1857}

– My dearest sisters. I hope these letters find you healthy and happy. Lucian is doing well, and I swear the boy grows like a weed almost daily. He is a very noble young man of 15 years now, and has just completed his schooling. No finer human specimens of depravity and evil dwell in this town. And yet, for all the wickedness that abounds here, there are just as many good folk who wish to see it come to an end. Lucian had one more year of schooling, but the completion I mentioned was at my insistence. I have begun to teach him in our home and find him not only learning better, but I believe I will instill in him a desire to do so for his own children. Sadly, I find him far more learned... and far more eager to learn... under my tutelage, than at the school he once attended.

And why have I taken this path you ask? Well, your nephew was caught fighting after school one day. I was called in to discuss the matter. No one here has questioned why Lucian has no father (per our plan). All believe as I have told them, that his father was killed some years ago and that I am here to start a new life for us both. That has only endeared us more to the better folk of the town. So I showed up to discuss the matter. The teacher asked me what punishment I felt was fair. When I asked her why he was fighting, she proudly proclaimed it mattered not, and only asked about his punishment. She was more than shocked when I calmly asked Lucian why he was. He admitted he was indeed fighting. When I asked him why, he admitted there were 2 strong boys, taunting a single one who was less so. Lucian, noble as he is, stood up to both of them in defense of the younger boy who could not defend himself.

Dear sisters, you may find this amusing... the two taunting young men were displaying bruises for weeks... whereas your nephew barely had a scratch on him. I thanked the teacher for alerting me to this deed, and promptly asked if Lucian was merely being noble, why was he to be punished too? I was told noble or no, fighting was fighting and it simply wouldn't be tolerated. I thanked her again for giving me insight to the ways of thinking about town, told her Lucian would no longer be any trouble for her, and promptly removed him from the school.

To say the teacher was shocked by my actions, would not do the look on her face justice. I mention this because, in this foul town, I am considered a strong woman. A commodity that is in zero supply around these parts, save me. And yet, as momma lady taught us all, I harm none, I am kind to the land that feeds me, and help those in need where and when I find them. While I can tell I am considered 'different' around here, I am however well respected for it. Lucian's grace, charm, and nobility... only strengthen that impression upon me and himself.

Per our plan, I have been traveling since our arrival some years ago. Foul as it has been at times, I honestly believe both Lucian and I are somehow better off for it. The pottery shop I opened as a means to support ourselves is doing very well. Many traveling miners seeking their fortunes west, or returning from, provide both valuable information and a source of income. I have made that income doing useful items, such as plates and cups and the like. I am now at a point where I can start making finer things and have even cleared a spot for them in my shop. I am most interested in the molds for some figurines I have recently purchased. One of them is of a lady in a hoop dress, like the one's we would see in our youth. Sadly, glazes are in short supply here. Rather, certain colors are... so I will be making most of them in only white.

I have recently met a fine man. He has courted me proper, and I have accepted for now. He treats Lucian as well as any father would a son, and for that I am more than pleased. There is a large security firm in these parts called the Pinkerton Security Agency, of which my new beau, Jonathan, is employed. He has (I believe as a means to bond with Lucian) begun teaching him how to be a 'Pinkerton Man'. While I am not always pleased with what he teaches him, I cannot lie and say they are not valuable skills... especially in this town. Also, as I have been both father and mother to him, I cannot deny that a good male presence in his life has been good for him as well. Lucian approves of him also, and Jonathan has said if he stays to his studies for another year, he will see about gaining him employment, and an early admission, to the same company he works for. He has also brought up the topic of marriage. I have told him I am not opposed to the idea, as long as he is willing to wait. Jonathan graciously has. Oh sisters, he truly is a fine man indeed and I find myself flush at times, as if I was still a little girl. He makes my heart sing with joy and has even told me that my 'independence' is what he finds most attractive. When I told him I may move, he told me any place on earth would be paradise, as long as I was in it and by his side. I cannot say I do not feel the same in return.

And now dear sisters, with family news out of the way, on to the real reason I write you this day. Momma lady would be proud... as I believe I have found 'her'. Some miners came into town some days ago, telling tales of a point north and west of me, and of a fine house being built. It is said a woman of some darker complexion, with the strangest of accents, is in charge. The latter I mention seemed to really surprise them. As I am the only woman here of a similar disposition, I laughed some when they felt the need to tell me this. I however, politely thanked them and wished them a good day. Oh dearest sisters, I only hope this news to be true, and for it to be the one we have sought for lo these past 7 years. While we may be a continent apart, and with myself perhaps going even further towards the sunset, it makes my heart smile to know the name of Garrison will live on in Lucian... and in your son Michael dearest Addison. Rejoice dear sisters, for I wholly believe we will soon find her... become the women we were meant to be, and the one's momma lady hoped we'd be... and finally grant her last request.

I have taken her teachings, and used them where I could. Local doctors take a rather dim view of me as many folk would rather come to see me for cures to ailments, than them. They further disdain me as my rate of success is higher than there's. In public, just like momma lady, I am well respected but, they keep to a polite distance. In private however, I am sometimes the only one they seek out. A rather small and hateful woman in town called me a witch one day. All around her gasped. I merely smiled and calmly stated there are no such things. I told her if there were however, I would be a white one, not a black one. The term 'white witch', seems to have stuck. I can only imagine how that term would have made momma lady smile.

I will write more soon I promise. For now, that is all the news I have. Blessed be to you both and know, that all my love, travels with you both daily.

Loving regards...

Mary Jane
(the newly appointed white witch)

{March 15th, 1857}
--My dearest sisters...

I have just returned from my travels. It is with great joy that I contact you so soon after my last letters. I have found 'her'. Jonathan has accepted a position in Carson City, which is in the western territories of Utah. Oh I could scarcely believe my luck! I traveled with him to secure lodgings. There was nothing suitable, so Jonathan bought a small parcel of land and has promised to build a home for all of us, including Lucian. One thing I have learned of him is that he is the tradesman he claims himself to be. Lucian became gravely ill on the journey. Even my skills could not cure him. I worried night and day, and Jonathan remained at my side all that he could. Upon arrival in this nondescript town, the local doctor came by. This man's talents amazed even me. He even thanked me for doing a wonderful job of caring, and not panicking as he claimed most women would do. He said, had I not, Lucian would have likely perished along the way. He is now fully recovered thanks to that wonderful man, and is slowly putting back on the weight he lost.

 The doctor's nurse was also his wife. While her beauty left much to be desired, her kindness and charm did not. I took a small amount of pity on her. She seemed like a lost soul. She is a foreigner, and appears to have no friends except that of her husband. She invited Jonathan and myself for lunch one day, and her hospitality left nothing to be desired. I sensed she had little or no friends in this small but growing town. She confided in me she despised it. I told her if she knew where I lived, she would know the meaning of the phrase momma lady taught us, about how the grass is always greener on the other side of the fence. While I could tell she truly grasped the meaning of it, I sensed she cared little. Her husband seemed her only concern, but she said she would be happier if those concerns were in a larger city.

 I have told you these things so you will know my plan. I have made friends, for now, with the doctor's wife. While Jonathan was away on business, I traveled to the hills outside of town. Just as the miners in Tombstone decried, the house they spoke of is being built at a record pace. Calling it a house would be an understatement. This place is larger than any hotel I have ever seen. I was caught one day... by the owner herself! I claimed it to be a beautiful building, and was soon to build one of my own. I also told her I was there to see about possible ideas for the house Jonathan will be building.

 I was almost shaking. The woman however, was kind to me, and had beauty beyond compare. I swear, it was like looking at a younger version of momma lady. I never saw such a fine, and refined, woman... act like a man... in all my life. She was confident, commanding yet not in a mean spirited way. Everyone doing the construction knew exactly who the boss was when she was around. She offered me to stay and look around, but excused herself and went back to tending to the construction.

 Rejoice my dearest sisters, for we can now repay our beloved momma lady, for caring for 3 young orphans. Samantha, please keep the article entrusted to you safe but, I have no doubt, I shall be calling for it soon. I am sending these letters to you from my new home town. We leave tomorrow to return to Tombstone. Even the very name appalls me, and I can find no better name suited to the town I shall leave with all due haste. I plan on closing my shop, and Jonathan has promised to help me in that task. I plan on setting it up anew here, and continue observing from a distance all that I can. Unless something comes up to the contrary, I will not write you again until I am here for good.

All my love my dearest siblings...

Mary Jane.

{January 5ᵗʰ, 1858}

--- My dearest sisters Mary Jane and Samantha,

     As you have both done to me in the past, so I am doing the same to you now in writing these letters, one to each of you. Mary Jane, my heart sang with joy at the news of your nuptials in your last letter. I have received your invitation and I shall be nowhere else but at your side on that happy day. I prepare even now to travel to Samantha. The three of us shall then travel together, and we expect to arrive in early June with approximately 10 days to spare. Michael has talked of nothing else since I told him of our plans to travel west. Oh dearest Mary Jane, it seems odd, yet pleasing, to think of you as a married woman. True that is not for some time, but it makes me smile all the same. I also believe... that Mary Jane Grayson... is a fine and proper name for a woman such as you. I look forward to meeting this mysterious new beau of yours that you have so irritatingly told so little of.

     In regards to telling Lucian of momma lady, and of our self imposed quest, I leave that decision to you. You have always been wise Mary Jane so whatever decision you come to, I will gladly abide by it. I am thrilled to find out he has been accepted by the fine security firm you mentioned. If I may advise however, then know this. If you choose to tell him, I feel it would be best to do so when all 3 of us are together. Knowing your fine fiancé has been told and not only understands, but accepts, is truly a relief. Should this Mister Grayson of yours be all that you claim, then perhaps I should inquire about a brother or a cousin maybe?

     It has been many years since we have all been together and I look to the future with much anticipation. Know that, while necessary, I have not enjoyed these years we 3 have spent apart. I have nothing to hold me here now that you have found her, and perhaps we can discuss my moving closer once I arrive. The talk of war is in every paper, as is a draft. If it does come, Michael will be of age by then and that thought pains me to no end.

     I will be posting these letters, then promptly looking for a suitable dress in the local shops. I can hardly wait, and hope both of these letters find you each happy and well. Blessed be to you both until we meet again.

With Love...

Addison.

{September 19th, 1858}
--- My dearest sisters,

  Having you both here for my wedding still makes me smile. The tin type, as its called, that you both had done for us hangs proudly in my new sitting room. I can't thank you both enough for getting that for us, and shudder at what this must have cost you both. It amazes me to this day what mankind can invent.

  I also wish to thank you for helping me tell Lucian of what we have been doing all these long years. Jonathan and I discussed it heavily, but decided in the end it was best to tell him. Having you agree as well made it that much easier. I feared greatly how he would take it, and if he would even understand. To my great surprise, he has decided to keep our secret and even help where he can. Oh my dear sisters, I am so filled with joy these days I feel as if I will burst.

  Jonathan has built 3 rooms so far. The sitting room I mentioned, a kitchen of such modern conveniences I feel I may never leave, and our bedroom of course. The rest remains but he works at it every chance he can and I have no doubt he will finish it soon.

  I want you both to know some things. First, I am happy you both approve of my new husband. He also has taken a fancy to both of you as well. Next, it saddens me Samantha that you will not be as close as Addison will be. Still, your choice is a valid one and I shall abide by it. Jonathan oversees the security on the work on the train tracks that are laid in miles each day. He tells me that in only a few years, this train will take either of us only 2 days of travel, rather than the weeks by coach it currently does. To you my dearest Addison, I will help you all I can to establish yourself in San Francisco. While not as close as I had hoped, we will only be separated by hours with these new tracks being seemingly laid everywhere. Oh my dear sisters, did you ever once imagine we would live in an age where we could travel from coast to coast... and do so in only a week!? Sometimes this modern age we find ourselves living in truly boggles even me.

  Samantha? Don't forget now... we promised no more lonely years with only our letters for company. You will come to visit every even year, and I shall do the same on the odd one's. Jonathan has promised our guest room will be finished by then, so there'll be no hotels or boarding houses for you. On that I insist.

Also, the new shop is finally open and business is doing well. Having a woman earn her own wage with a husband like Jonathan, has certainly raised some eyebrows. When a local woman snidely remarked about it, Jonathan made me laugh. He told her how sorry he was for her that her husband was not secure enough in his own mentality to allow her to do the same. It also seems that, like in Tombstone prior, the 'white witch' has resurfaced once again. Still, the town folk treat us well enough and our little family is well respected by all.

The sound of gunfire has ceased so I imagine Lucian's and Jonathan's target practice to be over. I must get supper ready. I have always enjoyed the life of an independent woman. I am finding now, the role of wife, to be just as pleasing.

All my love to you both...

Mrs. Mary Jane Grayson.

p.s.- Addison? Jonathan has mentioned a cousin of worth and about your age. He also lives in San Francisco. Jonathan has said if you wish, he will arrange for you to meet.

{November 15th, 1865}
--- My dearest Samantha,

I write you today with the most tragic of news. My heart is full of sorrow and I am weeping even as I write this. A foul scoundrel has murdered 'her'. That which momma lady entrusted to us was, for a short time, lost. Addison and I had decided to finally come out of the shadows, and tell her who we really are, but this murderous fiend has now made that opportunity lost to us forever. As you know, she wielded great power and influence. That same influence has hired the very agency Lucian now works for. He pulled in every favor he had to be put on this case of foul treachery. Still, it does my heart some good to know my sweet boy is taking care of this sad bit of business. He was even made the lead investigator!

I stopped in to the mansion a week after 'she' was gone... and was in a near panic shortly thereafter. The gift momma lady gave us to give to her... the one I so cleverly hid... was nowhere to be found. I searched at a near fever pitch. I am happy to say I found it, discarded on the grounds some distance away. When I saw how much blood was on it, I wept knowing I had found what killed our beloved 'her'. I cleaned it, and returned it to it's rightful place. I told only Lucian, who thanked me for giving him a secret he might use against the foul criminal who did this awful deed.

Lucian tells me this is being 'covered up' at the highest levels. It makes me sad to see the local town folk, who she so kindly assisted on many occasion, turn their backs to the whole affair. It is even speculated that the good Doctor Henry Holliday is thought to be the culprit. I swear I cannot fathom the reasoning in this. I have known that man since before I moved here, and can see no truth in these allegations. I have even shared my views with Lucian.

My dear sister, I feel as if I have failed in some way. I could not bear to take momma lady from that house, even now. I can only hope that it gives 'her' some comfort, and pray her soul finds peace.

Blessed be dearest sister...

Mary Jane Grayson.

Zack sat in solemn quiet next to Talon as he read the last letter.

"I swear boss, I have been doing this for years, and it still amazes me what people will either share... or put on social media," Zack told him kindly.

Talon was having a hard time getting his head back in the present. He also, in a flash, thought of a way to get Lucinda home, and payback some new employees, in one felled swoop.

"Abigail! Get in here please!" Talon commanded.

He was still staring at Zack's screens when she came in.

"You bellowed?" she joked.

"You were the one that cleaned up these original letters?" Talon asked the blond girl in the doorway.

"Mm hmm."

"Both of you... you're off for the next week. No arguments. Abigail? I'm buying you a plane ticket home. Tell mom and dad we said hello. Zack? I wouldn't dare send you home. So, pick a place, any place, and you got a plane ticket on me. This was some really excellent work you two."

Talon got up and walked out, but stopped a moment alongside Abigail.

"Oh and uh... if when you come back, there just happened to be a lobster or five in your suitcase... hehehe, I won't tell TSA if you won't."

Abigail giggled as Talon walked out, and fired up a plan as he did.

Chapter 22

"The 4ᵗʰ Of July"

"So, ya mind telling me why you kicked my girlfriend out for a week?" Grant politely scorned to his brother.

They were in Grant's truck. He, Talon, Violet, Doc and Eileen were riding over the pass. Grant also had the trailer hooked on the back and was towing one of the smaller tractors.

"We believe we found Lucinda. The radar in the back is to verify before we dig up a stranger. If it is her, we have to get her out unknown and unseen. In order for me to get even this much, I had to promise total secrecy. Zack and Abigail did a fantastic job and deserved their vacations. In turn, they're out of the way and we claim we just found her on the property somewhere," Talon told the group in the truck.

"Holy Shit!" Eileen barked. "And you were going to tell us this WHEN exactly?"

"I believe I just did."

Talon then told the group in the truck about Collis and Addie.

Eileen gave Violet a friendly hug saying "Atta girl" when she heard how she held her own without any of Talon's help.

When Talon finished, Grant had a different purpose to his tone.

"Tell the old battle axe she won't even know we were there," Grant proudly proclaimed.

Two hours later, Grant's truck pulled into the huge semi-circular driveway. An old lady in a wheelchair wheeled herself up to the passenger side.

"Oh good, you must be the gardeners my grandson hired. Look, there's some white roses in the back I want destroyed. Every last damn one of them. You'll also find a tree stump back there I want dug up as well. Break any of the paver stones on the pathways however, and I'll have your heads!"

"Yes ma'am!" Talon acknowledged.

Addie winked at Talon, and rolled herself back inside as Grant pulled around back.

The first thing down was the GPR. Violet and Eileen had metal rakes and were clearing the hybrid Edelweiss off to the perimeter. Doc saw the image on the screen and smiled.

"Those hips are definitely female. Can you get up a little higher?"

Talon rolled it where Doc asked. Cody just kept on smiling.

"That is a skull that has had a significant trauma to the left side of her head. Grant? Fire it up and lets bring our grand gal home."

"You got it pal," Grant said happily.

Moments later, Grant rolled into the small clearing with the requested machine. First, he used the bucket to get rid of the hybrids, and strip the clearing all around the headstone. Next was the headstone itself. Grant dug a trench on either side, and Talon worked it loose. All 5 of them were surprised to see it had sunk by a full 3 feet.

"Sit Deo manus solandus," Talon read curiously as the stone got cleaned.

He was pulling out his phone to translate it but Cody stopped him.

"It says-- 'May you find solace in the hands of God'."

Talon smirked over his shoulder "Let me guess... you were an alter boy weren't you?"

Cody sported a stupid smile and proudly proclaimed "5 years running!"

Talon just shook his head and chuckled, and put the straps under the gravestone. Using the front bucket, Grant lifted it up and set it carefully in the truck.

"Okay, I should'a thought of this. We don't have the room for the stone AND her," Talon admitted aloud.

"OH MISTER GARDENER MAN!! Can I speak with you a moment!?"

That voice was Addie. Talon left the clearing and went to her on the path. Harold had wheeled her out, but then retreated to a polite distance.

"So, have you figured out your mistake yet?" Addie asked with a touch of glee.

"Should'a brought two trucks," Talon admitted in a 'you idiot' type tone.

"Mm hmm. Leave the tractor. You can come back for it another time."

Talon asked her "We can do that, thank you Addie. We brought enough tarps so no one will know what we got."

Addie sweetly told him "Oh you'll have no need of those. I recently purchased 12 rather large Gardenia bushes. I 'read in a book' somewhere that, well, it was a very popular scent of 'certain ladies' back in the old west days. I thought of planting them here and there but I, um, have since changed my mind. I bought them on a special and cant return them. Perhaps you might, oh say, find some use for them? I have no doubt if you centered what you haul out, those bushes should fit nicely around the perimeter."

Talon caught it in an instant. He also called Addie on it.

"You did that on purpose didn't you?"

Addie smiled slyly, played dumb and said "Perhaps, perhaps not."

Talon looked at her questioningly, and asked "Is that true kindness I hear coming from the one and only Addie Huntington?"

"Well, I may be that cantankerous old broad you once called me, but I do have a heart you know. Besides, I know it's what great grampy would have wanted. So, it is her then?"

"It appears so."

Addie began to roll away, and told Talon "Well then, I'll leave you to your work." Harold began to wheel her away but she suddenly stopped him.

"Oh and... one more thing. That bit of kindness you mentioned? I would become rather cross with you young man if I found out such a rumor was spread around regarding me in such a manner."

Talon sported a kind grin, and gave Addie a one armed sweeping bow.

"Why m'lady... I wouldn't dreeeeeeam of purveying such untruths about the great Adelaide Huntington," Talon jested sincerely.

A much happier Addie than Talon last met, actually smiled, and said "I'm holding you to that young man," and Harold wheeled her off to the house.

Talon just smiled, shook his head, and rejoined the others.

Grant asked "What was that all about?" as Talon came into the clearing.

"Okay folks... new plan!" and Talon happily laid it out for them.

Five days later, and Doc told Talon that it was likely Lucinda. He also told him there was little new to report. He told him the blood on the doll matched the DNA of the exhumed corpse. He also said the man that struck her did so from a higher angle.

"How high we talking here Cody?" Talon asked.

"Around 6ft 2 to 6ft 3. There is one odd thing though."

"Tell me," Talon commanded nicely.

"Well, here... catch. That's a replica of the doll from a 3D printer. Now, say I'm Lucinda," and Doc crouched down a little. "Okay so, with a slight heel Lucinda was about 5ft 8, or right about how high I am now. Okay then, your Shadow Man. Now, strike me like you wanted to kill me."

Talon did and went in slow motion.

"Ya see, that's what bugs me," Doc told him. "Look at your position. Two things right now. First, you struck me like a pitcher throws a ball. Now I said strike me but I didn't say how. The way you just did is consistent with how just about any man of your size would. Also, look at how your gripping the doll."

"Yeah, so?"

"So, again that's normal. The thing that bugs me is this. Let's switch roles and I'll show you."

Talon crouched down some and Cody demonstrated.

"Now, like I said, you held the doll and swung in a manner consistent with a man of your size. This however is how Lucinda was struck," and Cody showed him.

Cody had more of an over arm swing.

"And I can say for certain, the doll was held in this fashion."

Cody was holding it by its head. Talon grabbed the whole thing in his hand, but Cody was holding it more like a baton.

"Okay Doc, I see what you mean," Talon affirmed. Then he changed tones and said "Sorry Doc but I gotta ask... how tall was Henry?"

"It wasn't him. For the day, Henry was considered a tad short. He was about 5ft 7. He often wore platform type shoes or boots. His letters never mentioned it directly, but I could sense from reading them that it was a source of insecurity for him. IF he had done it, the angle of the blow would have been slightly lower... or perfectly level."

Talon asked cautiously "And great grandma?"

"Same thing. She was 2 inches taller, around 5ft 9. If it had been her, again the angle is wrong."

Talon mused a moment at this new intel.

"Hehehehe, Doc? I think I got it. Okay, tall man but 'swinging' the doll not slamming it. You said it was held like a baton right?"

"Right," Cody said with anticipation knowing Talon was onto something.

"How about not a baton... but a pick?" Talon smiled and continued "Think about it. Who would, by muscle memory, swing like that? Only someone who was busting rock for a living Doc, that's who."

"A miner!" Cody answered as he now got it too.

"Mm hmm. Now, a regular miner wouldn't likely afford Lucinda's place. Even if he did it would be a one time splurge. Certainly not enough to kill her for, yet still have affections for your family name. No Doc, my gut tells me we're looking for a regular."

"So like what, a Comstock man?"

Talon said gravely, "More like a Comstock owner. Listen Doc, you do the medical, I do the historical. Those mine owners would have been robbed blind if they didn't know what was going on in those shafts. They often had enforcers disguised as surveyors. They knew every inch of those mines, and knew every swing of a hammer... and were often miners themselves at one point. It was the only way they would know what was really going on. Trust me, if we're right, that man wouldn't be some clueless desk jockey... he would've certainly known how to swing a pick."

Talon looked at the slightly darkened skeleton on Doc's table in his new shop. She was wearing the same blue dress when he first met Lucinda. Now,

Talon was nothing but kind.

"And that's all you got Doc?"

"Sadly. There were no new additional fibers, nor trace residue. Nothing new to aid us except that which I've already told you."

"Well then Doc, there's only one sad bit of work left to do. Sunrise Doc," Talon told him flatly.

"All will be ready."

The next morning, a small group of family and friends, all dressed in black, gathered in the parlor. Abigail had returned with mom and dad in tow. To show their support to those who once showed it to them... they were there too. Eileen lit two candles on the mantle. Abigail and her parents made a sign of the cross, and all but Talon left for the backyard patio.

"Stay out of this," Talon said coldly and commandingly.

"Hahahaha... or you'll what?" Shadow Man asked glibly.

Talon said nothing, he merely waited for the entity to get a little closer. Once Shadow Man had, Talon sparked up the cattle prod.

"Or that," he said as a wail let loose through the ether and was gone.

Talon slipped it back up his sleeve, and walked out to join the others.

The coffin was still intact for the most part. No one saw any reason to change it. Talon and Grant at the front, Cody and Zack at the rear, they lovingly carried her to the clearing Talon made just beyond the trees. Abigail told Linda and Jerry all about how Talon and Grant 'found her' just past the old tracks. Having been told that story from Grant, she was convincing enough when she told it to her parents.

"Dear family and friends... you now know why I made this clearing. I commit once more to the Earth the body, and spirit, of Lucinda Adair. Finally found after all these years, and laid to rest properly. I chose this time of sunset to mark the rising of the sun, and hopefully, the rising of her spirit to the great beyond."

Grant whispered to Eileen "The great beyond? Laying it on a bit thick don't ya think?"

Eileen elbowed him and just said "Hush."

Talon continued "While none of us knew her personally, we have all come to know her in our own way and..." and Talon stopped abruptly.

He did so because thirty men had just come through the clearing.

"Apologies for the interruption Mister Grayson, and for being a tad late. The men and I were wondering, with respect, if we might join you?"

Talon sported a caring smile, and leaned his ear to her coffin.

"What was that? Oh, okay... I'll tell them." Talon stood up proudly and told them "She said she would be honored."

Sporting respectful smiles, the workers who so kindly took to her in the present, filed in and stood behind the Grayson clan to honor the past.

Talon nodded to them, they nodded back, and he said "See that Lucinda? Even now you still have throngs of men seeking you out."

It took a moment for the polite laughter to die down.

Talon picked back up, but Abigail felt a sudden sense of love wash over her. Love... and sadness. Now standing beside her, dressed in mourning clothes, very old mourning clothes, was grandma Abigail. She was also crying. Abigail looked around slyly and quickly, then put her right hand to her side. She felt something ice cold grasp it... but she never let go. Both Abigail's were now smiling slightly.

"Gardenia was a prized scent back in the day. I have since learned, through historical records of course, that it was her favorite. As such, I have seen to it that she shall forevermore, sleep in peace among their smell. Lucinda Adair?... I am honored to say, properly this time..." and Talon looked down and said "... promise delivered... welcome home. Sit Deo manus solandus." He looked at the crowd in the morning light and told them "I invite you all to pick one of the Gardenias, and send our grand lady home upon their sweet fragrance."

Thirty grown men in the rear, and nine men and women to the front, all had tears in their eyes. When it came time to pick a flower, Abigail picked two, and covered the other one with hers so no one would see she wasn't actually holding it. Once hers, and the 'other one' hit the casket... Abigail's hand was warm once more. A sweet smile was on her face as she headed back to the house. Talon went last.

"I wasn't sure I would get to fulfill that promise. I'm mighty glad I was able to though," Talon said sweetly as he dropped his Gardenia.

He, Grant, Cody and Zack all picked up shovels and began to fill in the grave. The head of the construction crew put a kind hand on his shoulder to stop him.

"If you wouldn't mind Mister Grayson, me and the boys... well... we got this. Consider it our gift to our grand mascot. Go now, be with your family and friends."

Talon smiled and told them "You're all a great bunch of men. The kind of men Grayson Industries, and G-Man Construction, won't forget in days to come. Thank you gentlemen, thank you all."

Talon tipped his hat to them, and left the men to their self appointed task.

Back in the house, Talon was mixing with all the others, when he got a request only he had heard.

Talon stepped away, pointed to his phone, and told them "Excuse me a moment but... sadly, duty calls."

Talon walked to the side and pretended to talk into his phone. To his surprise, with no call engaged, it answered him.

In his ear he heard "Mista G suh, Ah wuud like ta ask y'all a question Ah have ownlee asked one othuh man."

Talon was impressed, and looked at his phone for a moment. He put it back to his ear and spoke into it.

"And that would be?"

"Wuud y'all mind come'in ta see mee... in mah room?"

"Um... why sure 'Erik'... uh yeah, I can check on that for you," Talon said for all to hear. He put his hand over the mouthpiece and said "I gotta go check on something upstairs. I'll only be a moment." He walked off and all could hear him say "Yeah sure 'Erik', I'll be there in a moment," and Talon headed upstairs.

He walked down the hall and as he did, Lucinda's door creaked open. Upon walking through it, he heard it close behind him.

"Mista Grayson suh?" came a voice from his right.

Talon spooked a bit because, this voice was normal, and not the reverb infused voice he had gotten used to. Standing off to his right, was a woman who once only appeared as an out of focus blur. Now, she seemed as real as he did. Oh yes, Violet was right... fixing up the house gave Lucinda a power boost indeed. She picked up her dress, and walked straight towards him. Inches away, she placed her hands on his cheeks, and gave him a loving kiss on the lips.

She pulled back softly, and told him in a teary voice "Tha white witch has rayzd a fine young man indeed. Ah thank ya guud suh, from tha bottom of mah harht, faw be'in tha fine man y'all promised me ya were... and faw keep'in yaw word. Evun now Ah cannot leave this hows, but Ah entrust awl tha she will be in the days tuh come... ta you. May she be as guud ta you as she was ta me."

Lucinda stepped back, lowered her gaze, and curtsied properly.

"Faw as lawng as Ah am heeyuh, if y'all evuh need me... Iel only be a whisper away."

Talon blinked hard as Lucinda just suddenly stopped being there.

He was sweet when he told the now empty room "Lady? It may not be much, but know that it's truly sincere when I say... your most welcome."

The only response Talon got, was the creaking of a door opening. He walked out touching his lips, and was truly stunned at the thought that Lucinda's touch... was warm... not cold.

Two weeks later, and at the crack of dawn, an antique Italian sports car was westbound through The Pass once more. That same car also cut a three hour ride in half. It was early on a Saturday morning when Talon did something in that car he never did before. Two things actually. First, he made Violet damn near piss herself with fear. Second, for the first time since he had it delivered... he hit sixth gear. Violet had never done triple digit speeds in a car before, no less that first digit being a 2 and not a 1. Talon only did it for a short run once the highway straightened out coming out of The Pass... but he had a little boy smile on his face for an hour because of it.

"Well, good morning Mister Grayson. Happy 4th of July!" Addie said cheerily as Harold wheeled her over to him. "A bit old fashioned I must say, but, you look quite dashing in that outfit."

She said that because Talon was wearing his Virginia City getup.

"Oh, when we arrive at our destination, I think it will become apparent why," Talon told her with not a care in the world.

The Rolls Royce pulled up behind Talon and Collis got out.

With a brisk and friendly handshake, Collis told him "Happy holiday Talon, wonderful to see you again."

Gray guy returned it and said "Same to you Collis."

Collis looked down and said "Well grandmother, much as I'm opposed to this little jaunt of yours... shall we be off?"

Addie smiled, and put her hands up... to Talon.

"I believe we shall Collis," Addie said happily as Talon cradled her, picked her up, and gently laid her in the passenger seat.

Talon shrugged at Collis, and told him "Sorry, it was part of the deal."

Addie just chuckled like a little girl as Talon folded her wheelchair up, and put it in the forward trunk.

"Oh REALLY grandmother! For ONCE would you just act your age!?"

"Oh Collis really, how about for once... you act yours."

Collis just huffed and walked behind Talon's car.

"At least YOUR company my dear... will be far more pleasurable to what I'm used to," Collis told Violet loud enough for Addie to hear.

"Ya know, for once Collis... I have to agree!" Addie hollered as Talon closed the passenger door.

Talon just shrugged again, put his hands wide with a 'Sorry Collis' look on his face, then closed his door as well.

Collis was a gentleman, and got Violet's door for her. She was dressed in one of Eileen's black and purple saloon girl outfits. Collis found that attire most pleasing indeed.

He spoke to the driver and told him "I know grandmother. Lose that car... and I will dock you a week's pay!"

"Yes sir Mr. Huntington!" was his slightly scared reply.

An Italian 12 cylinder motor fired up in the crisp morning air. So did a

British one. Talon circled the driveway, Collis followed, and both parties were off to breakfast.

Up in the beautiful Sierra Mountain range, Addie asked slyly, "So Mister Grayson... is this car truly as fast as it looks?"

Talon said flatly "Nope," and playfully slammed it into third gear. He smiled slyly at Addie and told her "It's faster."

"WOOOO HOOO HOOOOOOooooo" Addie wailed in shear delight.

"Son of a BITCH!!" Collis wailed at the silver car disappearing from view. "I knew it!" He rapped hard on the window between him and the driver and scorned "And we're still back here WHY exactly!?" He looked at Violet with clear annoyance on his face and exclaimed "One day grandmother will realize she's 91... not 21!"

Violet merely stated "Looks like today is not that day."

The look Collis shot her had Violet saying nothing more.

Talon only meant to give Addie a thrill, and slowed down after a mile or so, to let Collis catch up.

Seeing the Silver Ghost coming up in the rear view, Addie said "Aw... party pooper."

Talon just chuckled. He then smirked as the Rolls pulled up alongside him... not behind him. Seeing the driver's side passenger window on the Rolls go down, Talon put down Addie's window.

"Well grandmother, if THAT'S how you wish to be... I'll see you there!" Collis challenged in an 'I've had enough of your shit' tone.

Next thing Talon saw was the Rolls take off down the highway.

"Well!? Are you just gonna sit there with your tail between your legs, or are you gonna go after that pipsqueak!?" Addie asked Talon as half challenge, half admonishment.

"Yeah but I..."

"Well for the love of God man... GO!"

Talon could not believe the situation he was in. However, with one check of his rear view mirrors... Talon granted her wish. Seconds later he was laughing so hard he almost couldn't breathe. He was laughing because this 91 year old passenger of his... actually quoted Star Wars.

"Now THIS is what I call POD RACING!" Addie wailed with pure delight and even purer joy at feeling young again.

Talon would tell this story, and smile every time he did... for a long long time to come.

The Silver Ghost did well, but coming out of The Pass on the Nevada side, was nothing but twists and turns. This is what the Lambo excelled at. It's also what the Rolls did not excel at. Still, both Collis and Addie felt like the victor, and it ended with Violet's phone ringing.

"Hey sweetie, put me on speaker-phone please." She did and Talon's voice called out "Collis? That wasn't my idea. Let Violet bring you in, I have a surprise for Addie... and a far less speedy one at that. I won't be long but we'll be making a slight detour."

"Anything happens to her and..."

"Yeah yeah, I know. Trust me, this is a little present even you would agree on. See ya there!" and Talon hung up.

Shortly after, a Rolls went left when a Lambo went right.

"And we're here why?" Addie queried.

If ever there was a stranger sight, it was Talon's car in the middle of Virginia City. Talon pulled right up to the train station. He put the car in park, but left it running. He got out, popped the hood, and got out the wheelchair. Once he set it up, he got Addie out of the car.

"I have to say Talon, I like your seat better than mine," Addie said with a sly grin.

"Ms. Huntington? I'd like you to meet Jim, an old and dear friend of mine. He'll make sure you get to where you need to be."

"What are you up to gray guy?" Addie asked suspiciously.

"You said you wanted to see what he saw, go where he went... and walk where he walked. Well Addie, I intend to give you that wish... and it all starts here."

Jim hollered back as he helped Talon get Addie on the train "I'll take good care of her Mister Grayson, don't you worry."

Talon waved as the train puffed smoke, and started chugging away. He got back in the car, called Violet to say he was on his way, and took off for the mansion. Never one to ruin history, he took the back roads out of town.

Addie actually enjoyed the ride. Right up to the point when it stopped behind a hill, and out of sight of the mansion. Seeing it come out of nowhere, as she rounded the bend coming in, truly thrilled her. Now, she was the old Addie again.

"Put me down you imbecile! Do you have any idea who I am!!?? And you would leave an old woman out here in the middle of nowhere!? Ooh I swear when I get home I... wait... where are you?... HEY! Don't you DARE leave me here, you maggot!"

Jim never said a word, he merely set her on the ground as he was instructed to do. The train took off with Addie still yelling epithets at the departing train. Suddenly, Addie stopped yelling.

"Ha ha ha, you know Talon, I must admit, you were right. THAT!... Was hilarious," Collis said as a clump of sagebrush parted to reveal her grandson, and the new owner of the mansion.

"Collis? You can be a real ass sometimes ya know that?" Addie said in a highly rebuking tone.

"Dearest grandmother," Collis mocked, "You brought that one on yourself."

"Yep... still an ass," Addie said as Talon wheeled her in.

"Addie," Talon started.

"For THAT stunt, you can call me Ms Huntington!" Addie barked.

"Right, okay Addie, As I was about to say," and Collis laughed as Addie just huffed.

He actually liked Talon for being bold enough to give grandma the 'what for' she has so freely given to so many others.

"Great grampy used this. The crew you sent had the tracks laid and aligned in a day. The next day the switch went in. You were actually the first person to ride those rails in over 150 years. Seeing as how it was you, I thought it only fitting."

"Well... I'll grant you that much," Addie said calming back down.

Talon continued "This was how he and the others came and went. This tunnel was recently rebuilt, and made a tad higher. Other than the new concrete, and the wrappings on the timbers... it's all original."

Talon stopped midway and got deadly serious.

"Collis, I know you don't believe, but Addie? I know you do. The lady known as CQ, was murdered here in the mansion all those years ago. Believe me or not but, the murderer is still here too. Violet and I, and yes... even CQ... will protect you all we can. That said, the choice to proceed any further, I leave entirely up to you."

Collis laughed saying "My god man you are good. Ghost story and all! Let's stop fooling around now though hmm?"

Talon looked at Addie. She had a look of steel on her face.

"I did not come all this way to be run off by some man... alive OR dead." She looked up at Talon, winked, and said "Shall we?"

Talon tipped his hat to her, and wheeled her down the last half of the entrance.

"My God, it's exquisite!" Addie declared seeing the basement meeting room below the stairs.

"Being down here, and unknown to any trespassers who entered, it was nearly as they left it all those years ago. All we really did here was spruce it up and add some candles. We added electricity to the house but, we all decided, this room should be left as they left it."

Addie was trembling a little. She rolled to the end of the long table, and immediately freaked out Collis.

"Grandmother!" he bellowed as he ran for her.

She was trying to get out of her wheelchair, and into one of the chairs at the table.

"Help me Collis... please."

That alone threw Collis off as Addie was actually being nice. She sat in the chair, and pet it lovingly.

"He sat here... right here."

Talon stated "Could be, but we really don't know for sure."

"Oh, I do Mister Talon. Great grampy had a thing for blue velvet. It's all over the room he used back at the house. Much of the upstairs as well. Look Talon, only this one is... the rest are all leather! No dear man... trust me... this was his."

Collis saw his grandmother, and was truly pleased for her. He did love her. Her behavior annoyed him most times but, he truly loved and respected her. As such, he nodded to Talon to give her a moment. Talon smiled softly, and nodded back.

"Enjoy yourself grandmother," Collis said with a soft kiss. "We'll be down the hall by the stairs. Call us when your ready."

"Yeah yeah... okay," Addie said barely acknowledging with a wave of her hand.

Talon and Collis merely honored his promise, and left her be for a few minutes. Addie just beamed, and touched gingerly, and reveled at what she had been shown, and where she was.

Addie finally called for the men, and they carried her up the narrow stairway. Talon in front, Addie in the middle, and Collis below. Talon opened the secret door in the wall paneling beneath the stairs, and Addie gasped.

"Oh... my..." was all she could say. "Your brother's talents are truly remarkable indeed!"

Talon blocked her left side view, and rolled her to the double doors.

"Ms. Addie Huntington?" and Talon spun her to see the room, then said with a grand smile "Say hello... to CQ."

Now Addie commanded.

"Get me out of this chair. You promised me I would walk where he walked. I expect you to honor that promise... now."

Talon and Collis flanked her, and gave her her request. Her legs were weak and could no longer support her weight for long. Long, wasn't something she needed though. She walked with as much pride as she could... straight to Lucinda's picture above the fireplace.

"Thank you my dear, for being all that you were to the one true man I have ever known..." She looked at Collis then Talon, and concluded with "...until today."

Talon and Collis walked her around the room and Addie was on cloud nine. Then, she got quite a shock.

"Wait! THAT wasn't there a moment ago!"

Addie was looking at a flower under the portrait and sitting on the mantle. She was also correct, it wasn't there a moment ago. It was a Gardenia. The two men sat her back in her wheelchair, as Addie was suddenly feeling flush. Addie got her second shock, when she looked down to her lap. There was the white Gardenia that was on the mantle only moments ago. Addie smiled at the portrait, and carefully handed Talon the book she promised.

"A deal is a deal Mister Grayson," she said with tears in her eyes as she sniffed the flower, and just stared at the portrait.

Talon bowed gracefully, took it, and said "To quote you, it's been a pleasure doing business with you Addie."

He took the book, and nearly bolted up the stairs.

While Abigail was busy scanning every page of the book upstairs, Talon was busy showing Addie the refurbished living room downstairs. Abigail had some high powered scanners going. She scanned each page with several different wavelengths, including infra-red. She finished the same time Talon finished giving Addie her tour. She was also wearing the same outfit her mother had made for her 'prom'. It would seem, everyone of the Grayson's were, and so were all their partners. Abigail came down the stairs, and gingerly handed the book back to Addie with a smile. Also, to send an unsaid message, Abigail was wearing white gloves.

"Don't you want to read it Talon?" Addie asked.

"I do, and I will. The book isn't the gold I wanted, only the writings in it. Seeing as how you treasure it so, I thought it only fair you should keep it," Talon replied nicely. "Addie? Collis? May I present to you Miss Abigail Jensen. You might say, she's our resident tech guru around here."

Abigail was having fun in her outfit today, and played her part with a slight curtsy.

"I... I don't understand," Addie said all confused.

"Siiiiimple," Talon joked to Abigail.

She stuck her tongue out at him playfully, and explained.

"I used a device to scan every page into the computer. Sort of like putting it on a copy machine... but far less destructive and with far greater resolution. Like Mister Grayson said, it was the writing that was important, not the book itself. Now, he can read them anytime he wants," and Talon's phone dinged. "That would be the files boss. I sent copies to your phone."

Addie looked at Talon with wonder and asked "You can do that!??"

Ms. Huntington may be young at heart, but had no clue about tech. Talon smiled nicely, brought up the pages on his phone, and showed her. Addie was blown away when Talon took her finger and 'swiped' it sideways and the page on the screen turned.

"Impressive!" Addie said in shear delight. "Still Talon, all these new fangled gadgets aside, those pages are for you alone."

"And I shall honor that request. So, Violet will be coming along with breakfast soon. I have invited the workers of this project, a few local dignitaries and such, for an old fashioned 4th of July barbecue. They will arrive after lunch but, I thought, someone like yourself deserved a more 'private' viewing. Shall we return to the living room slash dining hall?"

"One last bit of business first, Talon," Addie commanded politely.

"Oh?"

"Indeed. What have you done with... well... these?" and Addie held up her Gardenia.

"Installed... as requested," Talon said slyly.

"Show me?" Addie asked kindly.

"It might be a tad bumpy, but I think we can get you there."

"Let's then," and Addie was wheeled out back.

"Thank you gentlemen," Addie said as she was wheeled up to Lucinda's gravestone. "If you wouldn't mind, could you both give me a moment?"

Collis and Talon nodded to her, and backed away to a polite distance. Addie took in the whole of it, then stared at the gravestone. She never said a word, not aloud anyway. She sat there staring a few minutes more, then called the men back.

"Talon? Thank you for this... all of this. Now, shall we go see if that lovely woman of yours is the cook she claims herself to be?" Addie jested happily.

Collis and Talon wheeled her back in to do just that. The 'Scooby Gang' as Eileen calls them were all there. Even Collis's driver was with them. Breakfast wasn't too fancy, but it was delicious and plentiful. It made Lucinda smile from the beyond to hear such banter and good times in the mansion once more.

"Mister Grayson, may I speak to you in private?" Addie asked politely. "And you as well Collis."

The latter joined them. He was amazed how his normally cranky grandmother, was suddenly a sweet old lady, and all because of this house.

"I have a new business deal for you Mister Grayson, albeit a macabre one. If your interested of course."

"I'm listening."

"Look Talon, truth is, I truly thank you for today. In my day I would have been the first one here, and the last to leave. Even now I feel myself growing tired. Collis knows but, no one else does. Mister Grayson? I'm dying. Doctors have given me 3 months, 5 at most. Collis doesn't like to talk about it but I'm a practical woman. I am also not afraid... well... not anymore thanks to you. I have gotten my affairs in order, all but one. Mister Grayson, Collis, I would if physically possible... like to die here... not at home. Great Grampy used his house as a show of wealth, but as you'll read, lived here more than at home. I want you to know I'm very serious about this, and offer your same words back at you... name your price."

Talon looked at her, and hid his small amount of shock.

"There is no price."

"Oh come now, there is always a price," Addie said sweetly.

Collis was slightly aghast, but held it together like his breeding taught him to.

"Grandmother, while I can understand your desire... that request is far more than even you have the right to ask."

"Perhaps... but I'm asking it anyway."

Talon still flatly said "There is no price." He looked at Collis and spoke kindly saying "She's right, it is a tad macabre. Still, when the time comes... and IF it's even possible... just know I won't ignore your call." Talon sweetly kissed Addie's hand, and honestly told her "I only wish I met you 20 years ago. You have my sympathies for your condition... and my respect for your bravery."

He stood up and without a word, offered his hand to Collis.

A shocked but grateful grandson, shook it in earnest.

"Thank you Talon. Your attitude is greatly appreciated. It also won't be soon forgotten. We Huntington's know who our friends are. We know who owes us favors... and who we owe. Again, thank you."

Talon smiled at them both, tipped his hat, and said "Allow me at least to see you to the Rolls."

Addie smiled and kindly said "I'd like that. You're an impressive man Talon, with an even more impressive house. Mind a piece of advice from someone who's been around the block a time or two?"

"Always," Talon said nicely as he wheeled her onto the front porch.

"Do big things with it. Make them good things but... make them big."

"Words I shall remember always," and Talon helped Collis get her into the back of the Rolls Royce.

"Mister Grayson? I wish to thank you for the most interesting last few days I can ever remember. Happy 4th to you sir... and thanks again."

Addie and Collis said goodbye to their hosts, and the Rolls headed for Interstate 80... and home. An old lady in the back seat was smiling the whole way there.

It was around noon when the local news crew setup their gear. It took them 30 minutes to do an update piece, and Talon invited them to stay for lunch. A barbecue was setup and at 1pm, the first guests were arriving. The local mayor and sheriff, and their families, were on hand as were all the tradesmen and theirs. Talon decided to treat them to an authentic period party, and it's why he and the gang were in period clothing. It was just a little special way to celebrate. Those who could make it on time, were treated to a steam train ride to the mansion, courtesy of Talon and Grant. People milled about all day. The mayor was impressed, as was the sheriff. The latter gave Grant and Talon his card, and said if ever he was needed, to call him personally.

The workers families ooh'd and aah'd at the work dad or mom helped create. A few of the wives, seeing Lucinda's portrait, even thought of replicating that pose for their husbands. Not one single worker however, did not... at some point... stop and pay their respects to Lucinda. There was a new flower on her grave every time one of them left.

Now, with nighttime in full effect, Talon brought out the big guns. More like big tubes really. At sunset, he and grant were out back with fire hoses and soaking the place down. Fire... in these here parts... was taken very seriously. Now, with blow torches in hand, Grant and Talon were like little kids in the backyard, while everyone enjoyed the show in the front yard. Just like the big shows would do, both men let off a barrage at the end. When the last shell faded, they could hear cheers and applause from the crowd. The train returned promptly at 10:30pm, and this party was history. All thanked their hosts as they boarded the train. They all remarked how even unfinished, the work done so far, and the mansion as a whole, was simply amazing. Talon and Grant thanked them all for coming. The train blew it's whistle... and carried it's passengers off into the dark of night.

"Y'all are a cruel cruel man Mista G," Lucinda's voice giggled. "Why... y'all didn't save a single one of them sausages faw lil ole me!"

Talon chuckled, but looked at the lit up house and smiled.

"Yeah well, hot dog deprivation aside... it was a good day, wasn't it?"

Talon headed back to help clean up, and call it a night.

"Oh and... one last thing. Lucinda? Happy Birthday. I hope it was a good one at least," Talon said kindly.

"It waz indeed guud suh... it waz indeed."

Chapter 23

"A Parent's Revelation"

With her and Doc Holliday an official couple now, Eileen was looking to improve her cooking skills. She neither liked nor hated cooking. What she did like however, was cooking for Cody. Abigail was much the same way. Now, with her and Grant discussing 'future plans', she was enjoying caring for her man as well. So, Violet showed them how to do what they knew, and just make it better. Linda helped also, and threw in some 'family recipe's' to add to the dinner menu. Violet and Linda also promised them more to come but, thought this was a good place to start.

It was Sunday, and everyone was still talking about the party. They all howled with laughter when Violet and Talon told them of the impromptu drag race through the mountains. Violet proudly proclaimed that, having had enough of what she called 'ground bound supersonic speeds', they came in the truck this evening. She even drove... and said so. Eileen gave her a wink and a small bit of applause.

They were all in Grant's house today, but at Abigail's request. Violet had taken short videos and pictures yesterday. Early this morning, Abigail made a presentation and set it to music.

"I'd like to replicate something if you all wouldn't mind," Abigail told the crowd happily.

"That's y'all... shugah... not you all," Talon teased.

Abigail frowned saying "Do I look like a smok'in hot Creole woman?"

Everyone chuckled but Abigail arranged all her guests in a semi circle.

She giggled, popped a quick curtsy, and said "I call this... 'Yesterday'... by Abby Gale."

All the Grayson gang laughed as they knew Abigail recreated her arrival at the mansion. Still, Violet's excellent photographic eye, mixed with some new accessories Talon got her, made for an amazing 10 minute show. Abigail did a great job putting it all together, and the small applause she got when it was over made her smile knowing she did well.

"So, Linda and Jerry," Talon queried. "Find anything you like out here?"

Linda answered "Not really. It's been ages since Jerry and I took a vacation. Right now, we're just enjoying your brother's fine hospitality. We leave in two days. I have a cousin in Tuscon we're going to stay with for a few days before heading back home."

Jerry interjected "I've reduced my workload back home. It would be our luck we find the perfect place... when we're not looking for it. As such, with less to do back home, I could leave on short notice if I had to."

"Don't forget," Grant hollered over, "If you don't see anything you like, just get some land and I'll build it for you."

"We won't" Linda answered sweetly.

Jerry looked over and said "So Talon, that was the infamous mansion we've heard so much of?"

Grant joked from the counter "And heard... and heard... and heard..."

"Hey!" Abigail whined as she slapped his arm. "Who's side are you on anyway!?"

Everyone chuckled, and Abigail just huffed and went into the kitchen.

"Yeah yeah... laugh it up red... see how much 'dessert' YOU get tonight!"

To save his brother, Talon got the conversation back on track.

"It is. Hey Jerry?"

"Yeah?"

Talon smirked and told him "It's haunted ya know."

Jerry ran with it and said "Oh cool! Wouldn't happen to be that smok'in hot lady Abigail mentioned would it!? The one over the fireplace?"

Talon smiled saying "Mm hmm, Miss Lucinda Adair herself."

Jerry crossed his arms over his chest and huffed like a little boy.

"Aw man... she didn't appear to me or noth'in!!"

Linda gave her husband a sweet kiss on the cheek saying "I'm sure there's plenty of room on this couch for Grant AND you this evening... 'dear'."

Abigail just high five'd mom. Mom smiled and returned it right back.

Jerry got serious and asked "All jokes aside, Abigail tells us your solving a murder?"

"More of a cold case really. Lucinda was murdered in that mansion. As we rebuild, we're putting together what pieces we can... and what pieces we come across."

Talon didn't want to tell Jerry the whole truth. He however, saw no harm in just enough truth.

"I've always been fascinated by those," Jerry said with some excitement.

"Lord I'll say," Linda scorned. "It's the only TV he watches nowadays."

"Guilty as charged," Jerry proudly stated. "She's right though. I find them to be like the ultimate puzzle. If I can be of any help, just let me know."

"Well Jerry, we have a pow-wow every so often to go over what we already know, and add the new pieces in that we get, and see where it takes us.

We were going to have one today. Care to sit in?"

"Why, I believe I would good sir... yes, yes... quite," Jerry teased as he imitated an upper crust New England accent.

Talon gave the gang a look that said 'It's okay, but not too much'. They all got it and everyone pitched in getting Jerry and Linda up to speed.

"Sonuvabitch!" Jerry bellowed in delight. "This is better than ANY of those TV shows. Seriously Talon, you should write a book about this. I would buy it in a heartbeat!"

Talon snickered and said "I would but I'm kinda missing a little something."

"Like?" Jerry queried.

"Oh nothing much, just an ending is all," Talon joked.

"Yeah, that could be a problem," Jerry joked right back.

"Hey!" Abigail cutely barked. "Listen here now mister... no corrupting my dad with your evil humorous ways," Abigail teased seeing dad being just like Talon. "His humor is drier than the dust at the mansion already without any of your help, thank you very much."

Talon put the back of his hand to his forehead and said "Why blond one, your words wound me so. Truly, I must protest!"

"Yeah yeah, zip it gray guy," Abigail giggled.

"Do you hear this Jerry? Insults! INSULTS I SAY! And From Abigail of all people!" Talon looked at Grant and said "That's it, I'm mad now. I'm going to ruin your wedding... you know... when you have one that is."

Grant laughed and said "Do it... and I'll kick your ass and bury you next to your girlfriend. The dead one that is I mean."

Talon smiled and turned to his sister.

"Really Eileen, you're the oldest... I INSIST you talk some sense into that boy!"

"Talon? Bite me," Eileen told him.

Talon smiled and nudged Jerry.

"See that Jerry? I get no love, I swear."

Everyone roared when Violet stated "Keep picking on your employees, and you're right... you won't get no love."

Talon just smiled and blew her a kiss.

"Okay, all jokes aside," Talon said getting serious again. He looked at Cody and said "Give them the new pieces."

Cody nodded in a friendly manner, and told them what he told Talon. Jerry, having heard the latest piece, stopped being Abigail's 'dad'... and went back to being lawyer Jerry.

"Talon, did Abigail ever tell you of our dinner conversations?" Jerry asked while still deep in thought.

"More like mock trials the way I hear tell. Why?"

Jerry said "Well, that's a fair assessment too. Most days I consider it a victory if I can send a text without screwing it up. Abigail was into those machines on a level I just couldn't compete with. Law, or tech, requires a more clinical way of thought. It was my way of imparting a lesson on her, and my way of having some sort of bond with my own daughter."

"Aw... I love you too daddy," Abigail said as she hugged her father. Now, with a sense of pride in her dad, Abigail told them "I think I know where he's going with this. Daddy taught me, sometimes, life is like a trial. You can't have one of those, unless you gather your facts and evidence together first. You also can't be biased in any way. Often, he would have me rip apart his case or his arguments, just to see if I could, or if they truly had holes in them he didn't notice. Point is, if you go in believing one thing, but the evidence points to something else and you refuse to see it, you're gonna get torn to shreds by the truth."

Talon smiled, raised his Kona to Jerry, and said "That's one smart dad you got there Abigail."

The crowd raised their drinks affirming "HERE HERE!"

Abigail hugged him from behind the couch, smiled, and said sweetly "I always thought so."

Talon asked "Okay Jerry, let's do it your way for a change. A fresh point of view never hurts."

Jerry told him "First, you have a lot of emotion in your assumptions."

Talon defended with "Sometimes, that's all we got. Even you Jerry deal in 'motive' do you not?"

"True, but, I've always found... when emotions come first, and facts come second... once exposed, the latter usually changes the former."

Talon actually liked this change of perspective, and challenged "Okay Jerry, let's hear it... wadda ya got?"

"Well, you believe it a mine owner. While 'possibly' correct, did you ever think he might have hired someone? A person like him would likely never get his hands dirty, and would likely be downstairs in the crowd as an alibi."

"Good point," Talon mused. "Jerry? I can't tell you how I know this, and you wouldn't believe me if I told you. Suffice to say, Shadow Man hated Lucinda. He didn't hate women... he hated 'her'. So a hired hand wouldn't have had such a personal interest. True it could have been a hired hit. Truer still he could'a had a beef with Lucinda and someone used Shadow Man like a tool, but I highly doubt it."

"Care to back that up with some evidence?" Jerry queried.

"Like I said, you wouldn't believe me... and no I wouldn't. You'll have to take my word for it that what I've told you is fact. We didn't plan on telling you any of this, so, needless to say... now that we have... for your protection and ours, some 'extra details' were left out."

Jerry jested with a slight laugh and asked "What, are you some sort of medium or something?"

Before Talon could utter a word, Jerry heard "Nope!... That would be me!" Violet stated from the kitchen with a raised hand.

"Huh!?" Jerry said slightly caught off guard.

Talon decided to give Jerry a little more than he bargained for, just to see how he'd react.

"Grayson gang? How about we give good ole Jerry and Linda here, a Mickey Mouse roll call... shall we?"

Grant smirked and called out "Historian and financial backer?"

Talon raised his hand and smirked back saying "Present." Talon then took over and said "Builder and chief engineer?"

"Here," Grant said.

"Financial whiz?"

"That would be me," Eileen smarted raising her hand.

"One man M.E. and chief science officer?"

"Yo!" Doc called out.

Jerry and Linda just kept looking at each person in turn.

"Medium and head documentarian?"

"Cooking!" Violet answered with a laugh.

"Chief of IT operations?"

"I'm here," Abigail stated with pride.

"And last, but not least, Chief records officer?"

"Present and accounted for!" Zack cried out.

Talon stared at a stunned set of parents and told them "I'm paying for this, so I get to be the boss. I'm the overall historian, but Zack follows the paper trail of real life. My sister sees to the budget, while Doc over there does all the science work. Abby gets us any IT intel we need, and Grant sees to any structures, and how they might fit in, or what role they played, if any. Violet documents it all but, well, ya might say she's a bit 'sensitive' to certain things.

Now Jerry laughed a bit and said "You're pulling my leg now, I can tell."

"Uh... dad?" Abigail winced. "Ya remember that news story you were telling me about the other day? The one with the doctor in New York?"

"That guy was a sick sonuvabitch. What of it sweetie?"

"Weeellllll..." and Abigail looked to Talon.

"Ya know what?... Yeah... go ahead," Talon told the remote control holding blond."

Abigail was still unsure, and just said "Uh... daaaadd?" and she pointed the remote at the TV.

She showed mom and dad the footage from Talon's drone. This wasn't the highlight reel either... this was the raw footage.

"JESUS!" Linda hollered as she jumped back on the couch when the bucket of Big Mack smashed the car.

Linda was stunned. So was Jerry. The video stopped and Abigail turned it off.

"Mom? Dad? Um, ya know that footage they showed of him? The one where he's cowering at Violet's feet?"

"THAT'S where I recognize you from! You're the girl on the news!" Linda bellowed at Violet.

"Younger but... yeah... that was me," Violet said a bit sadly.

Both parents looked straight at Abigail.

"Heh heh, I um... well? Oh okay fine! I was the one who unlocked that video for Talon. Trust me, sick as that was... that was one of the tamer one's. Talon did what he had to do and before you say anything, I want you to know I'm damn proud of him for what he did! We all are! He gave the video to some, shall we say, 'special men'. They leaked it and brought down that sick sonuvabitch as you called him. If it wasn't for Talon, that bastard would STILL be running loose!"

Talon kindly added "And if Abigail hadn't been as talented as she is, I'd still be in the dark about that guy... and Violet would be stuck in that hell hole right about now."

Jerry asked Abigail, still in disbelief "You did that!?"

"We all did dad. I'm finally doing good work, and with some damn good people! I couldn't let that prick get away with it. I'm proud of what I did and I don't care if you're mad at me or not."

Jerry stood up, walked around the couch, and just hugged his little girl.

"I'm proud of you my dearest Abigail. Very proud indeed."

Abigail thought she needed to defend herself, and didn't realize a parent's love made it all unnecessary.

Linda slapped Jerry's chest as he sat back down and scowled "You and your damn cold cases... are ya happy now!?" Still stunned, Linda just shook her head saying "Jesus Christ, that's gonna be some book!"

Chapter 24

"Luci Adir"

Jerry knew he had to get back on track, or risk being freaked out for weeks. He managed to do just that.

"Okay, I'm the judge and you all are the prosecutors. My first question would be this. You've told me about the murder. What you haven't told me is what led up to it. Where is that motive you mentioned Talon? I heard you... I heard you all, I truly did. What bugs me is, you all focus on one moment in time. Why? Go backwards. Get out of the moment, and go back to what led to it... and see where it takes you."

"We're trying," Zack told him.

"How so?"

Talon answered "We're trying to track Lucinda prior to coming here. My mansion got built on a whim, and in only a few short years. She had some super powerful men backing her too. Someone like Lucinda doesn't just get that way for no reason. She may have charmed her way to the top, or whored herself there... maybe even both! Either way, it would take time to put herself in a position of such power and influence. That's what we're doing now."

Jerry asked "So, what do you have so far?"

"Bupkis," Zack said with some annoyance.

Jerry now went out on a limb. Well, for him anyway.

"Talon, you know my family is Irish Catholic, yes?"

"I do now," he said with a slight laugh. He got serious and asked "Your point?"

"Well, try this one on for size. Let's for a moment, say that you were Jewish. Now, I wouldn't believe what you believe, but I'd respect that you do. So, with that said... have you ever thought of just asking her?"

"Ask who what?" Talon queried.

"Lucinda! If you're trying to track her, and you believe you can talk to her, either by yourself or with Violet's help, why not just ask her?"

Talon was about to say something, but Violet cut him off.

"I have actually."

"And?" Jerry asked truly wanting to know.

Violet was sweet and asked "Have you ever done something for so long that you lose track of time?"

Jerry answered "Of course, who hasn't?"

Violet then asked "Ever truly believe, without a doubt, that it was Friday... when it was only Wednesday?"

"At times... so?"

"So, you're cognizant of life around you. While you may have made that error with the days, sooner or later something corrects you. Lucinda, and those like her, don't have that type of internal clock like we do. She is the most cognizant of any I have ever encountered, bar none. That said though, even that has its limits. It's like talking to an elderly person who has dementia. The past is a blur most times, with only glimpses coming into focus now and then. She's been dead for over 150 years. To her however, it seems like only yesterday... literally. Now, believe me or not but, it is however the truth."

Talon said "Uh, yeah... what she said."

Now Jerry switched to detective. Linda was still bugging out, albeit quietly, and was more than happy to let Jerry talk.

"Well then... what DO you know?"

Talon told him what Althea told him, and what they surmised.

"Hmm, okay try this," Jerry mused aloud. "As a lawyer, I often have to put myself in the moment, not to mention the mentality. Lucinda leaves thinking her mother a joke. That promise however comes true, even if it is coincidence. Now, say you're Lucinda, what are you gonna think?"

Zack leaned forward and said "Okay, I see where you're going with this. If that ship did indeed sink, it's obvious Lucinda survived."

Jerry had a soft smile form at his lips, and said "Exactly. Now, put yourself in that moment. You're either defiant at what you feel mommy did, and tell her how she won't stop you... or?"

Zack laughed and said "Ha ha ha... or you shit your pants and won't go anywhere near momma again."

Jerry smiled at Talon and said "Nice crew you formed here. Wouldn't have room for one more, now would you?"

Talon chuckled and said "Sorry Jerry, but, I'm good."

"Hmm, pity," he replied slyly.

Jerry then told Talon "With my years in the court, I can tell you Talon, a lot of women turn to prostitution not because they have to, or out of desperation, but desire. I've seen enough shrinks in court testify that many girls find it as an affirmation of their beauty, and a way to make big money. Based on what you've told me, I'd say this Lucinda of yours is the latter."

Talon was smiling as 'dad' just kept going, but in all the right directions. He was also getting some new line of thought going, just based on Jerry's point of view.

"I like your line of thinking Jerry. I'll do you one better. Let's say Lucinda believes momma really did put a curse on her. If I were her, I'd put as much distance between me and mom as I could. Either to keep me out of mommie's reach, or to buy time and regroup, then come back swinging."

"Now yer talk'in," Jerry said with a sense of actually getting pumped up.

Jerry's words, gave Talon the thought he needed.

"Zack?"

"Yeah boss?"

"Can I assume, you've checked ship manifests of the day?"

"Twice. Noth'in," Zack said unhappy at his defeat.

"Okay then, good ole Jerry here has got me thinking. Check them again, but this time... track back every damn passenger. Start with the men only, and see who traveled with a wife... but was never married. Or perhaps, an only child in real life, but traveling with a sister."

"Fucking BRILLIANT! Shit, I should have thought of that. Okay, I'll get on it first thing tomorrow. Also, try this."

Talon only said "Hmm?"

"You're on the lam," Zack started, "You need to stay hidden, and can't afford to blow your cover. Most people I found stick as close to the truth as they can, just so they won't trip themselves up."

Everyone just watched silently, as Zack and Talon fed off each other, and took off like greyhounds.

"Boss? What was legal age back then?"

Talon told him "Most areas, same as now, 18."

Zack countered "Well, I'll dig into the ship. Once I find the anomaly, we'll have a birth date, roughly. IF I can get that, that will make it faaaaaaaaar easier to track her. Almost no one who goes underground uses a fake birth date. You get tripped up too easily. Trust me, I would know. I swear, if I can get one, JUST one point of origin, I'll be on her like white on rice!" Zack turned to Abigail still standing behind her dad, and asked "That's gonna be a huge list to track though. You got anything in that bag of technical tricks of yours to help me narrow it down?"

Abigail beamed at the chance to show off in front of mom and dad.

"I have some algorithms I've been dying to try out that just may do the trick! I'll get them to you in the morning, okay?"

"That, will do nicely," Zack said kindly.

"Jerry?" Talon asked.

"Yes?"

"Heh heh... thanks."

Jerry smiled, nodded a little, and said "Glad I could help. I do have one request though."

"What's that?" Talon asked.

"When this book of yours gets made into a movie, see what you can do about having Brad Pitt play the part of the suave father," and Jerry winked.

"HA HA HA! No promises Jerry!" Talon told him with a hardy laugh.

Linda finally spoke up.

"Oh great... juuuusssst great," she extolled.

"What's wrong dear?" Jerry asked.

"What's wrong? I'LL TELL YA what's wrong! I've gone, in the space of a single evening, from ordinary mom, to ghost hunter, to the wife of Brad Pitt!"

Everyone just laughed, and Talon and Zack and Abigail were looking forward to morning.

Talon walked into Zack's office, and laughed. It was just after sunrise, and he was holding 3 coffee's. What made him laugh was... Zack was already there, and had brought coffee as well.

"Yeah, I couldn't sleep either," Zack snickered.

"I hope the one with my name on it is at least Kona," Talon joked.

"Sorry... is there some other kind?" Zack teased nicely.

"Nope," Talon joked back.

Zack had two different computers in his 'lair'. Talon sat at the other one and started helping out.

Abigail giggled and said "Good thing I brought donuts huh?" seeing the coffees, and the two men already working.

She arrived only minutes after Talon did.

"Yeah," Talon started.

"We couldn't sleep either," Zack finished.

Abigail asked "Hey boss? Mom and dad are downstairs. Do you have a minute for them?"

"Sure," Talon said cheerily as he got up to go downstairs.

"Thanks for coming down to see us off Talon. I can't remember a better vacation ever," Jerry said shaking Talon's hand briskly.

"See you off? I thought you were staying another day or two?" Talon asked as he shook back.

Linda said "We were, but my cousin's plans changed suddenly, so we're going a few days early." She said "Jerry I'll be right back. I'm going to hit the bathroom before we hit the road."

Jerry smirked saying "Make sure if you see any ghosts, you introduce them to me too!"

"I think I'll leave the ghost hunting to you dear. I could live quite easily never having seen even one."

Linda headed off and both men just chuckled.

"It's been a pleasure having you around Jerry," Talon said kindly and honestly. "Stop back and see us anytime."

"Just promise me one thing, take good care of my little girl for me?"

Talon smiled slightly and said "As much as I can... and as much as I need to,"

"Coming from you sir, I'll accept that. Pity though."

"Mm?"

Jerry winked saying "My wife may not care for them, heh heh, but I wouldn't have minded one or two."

Talon gave an understanding nod... shook his hand again, and headed back upstairs.

"I'll be outside at the car dear!" Jerry hollered.

"Okay! Be there in a minute!" Linda's voice called back from the distance.

Jerry went outside, stared at the mansion, sighed, and got into the car. He flipped the ignition, and it fired and fired... but wouldn't start.

"Oh great... JUST great!" Jerry extolled.

He was about to get out, when the radio came on, all by itself.

"I want to thank you sir, for seeing to my legacy. She grew up mighty fine, mighty fine indeed."

Next, the car started this time... and all by itself. The voice sounded a little like Abigail, and nothing like her at the same time. He adjusted the rear view mirror as he stared at the radio in disbelief. He thought it may have been one of Abigail's technological tricks, till he saw her in his mirror.

He turned to the backseat and asked "Honey, what are you ... WHAT THE!!???" and he slammed his view back to the mirror, when he saw the backseat was empty.

The blond in it smiled softly, nodded, and just faded away. Jerry was beaming, and got out of the car.

He faced the mansion, and gave an honest bow, and only said "Thank you," as he stood back up.

"Jeez, I wasn't gone THAT long," Linda smarted as she came out of the front doors.

Jerry smiled at the house, then to his wife, and only said "No dear... you weren't"

Jerry winked to the mansion, as he drove off for the airport. Linda had no idea what had him smiling like a little boy, and figured it might be better if she didn't know.

Talon was helping on the second floor, but Violet showed up some time later, and started helping out on the third floor.

"Lucinda? Do you have time for me?"

"Why uv cawz Violet dear,"

"I'd like to visit with you, for a little while. Is that okay?"

"Maw than fien sweet chyld. Ah so rarely get vizituhs these days."

Violet saw nothing, but she heard all she needed to hear.

"What shall we tawk about then, hmm?"

Violet remembered her own explanation to Jerry, about how 'ghosts' appear to have something akin to dementia, and took a chance.

"I was hoping to talk about you my dear?" Violet asked sweetly.

"Naht much tuh tell Iem uhfrade," was Lucinda's response.

"You remember the day you died. I was wondering, what about the days before? Anything you care to tell me?"

Now Lucinda was agitated.

"Ah would be delighted... if I could."

"Tell me about it," Violet said sweetly.

"Ah remember mah Henry... barely. Uhsied from that horrid day you menshund, mah memories appear jumbled. Sometimes, they come in clear as a bell. What annoys me, is thah they fade shortly thereafter."

Violet knew what she meant. She was also expecting an answer like that. As such, she came prepared.

"What can you tell me about this then?" and Violet held up the ceramic doll towards the room.

Said room was awash in wind and Lucinda cried out "How DARE you bring thah wretched thing heeyuh! Remove it... AT ONCE!"

Violet just waited out the tantrum as she lowered her hands.

"Lucinda, let me tell you something. Do you know the meaning of the word 'dementia'?"

"No, Ah doo not" was her curt answer.

"You might know that word as 'senile'."

Now Lucinda was cross again.

"Aruh you tell'in me ah have lawst mah mind!??"

Violet was sweet and said "In a way, yes. Lucinda, what happens on Fridays?"

Lucinda was sweet and said "Those wonderful men leave me offer'ins. I think thah is thuh sweetest thang."

"Lucinda? Yesterday, when you had lunch with Collis... what did you have?"

"It was dinner mah dear, and thah was two dayz ahgo."

"Lucinda... that was over 150 years ago. Collis died in 1900. You died, in 1865. You lived during the 19th century. Collis barely made it to the 20th. You may be interested to know... it's currently the 21st."

"Haz it reeely been thah lawng?" Lucinda said with slight sadness.

"It has," Violet told her calmly. "Lucinda, most, um, 'like you', don't even know they're dead. In all my years, you Lucinda, are unique. You are far more aware of yourself than any I have ever met. Only Shadow comes close to you in that regard. Now, try again... focus on the doll... and don't think of what it did. Focus on it and tell me, how did you get it?"

"Ah got it as a gift from Henry about a yeer ago. A lady in town owns a shop, and he said she was a friend of his. He got two, one faw his home, and one faw mien. Collis became so busy Ah hahrdlee saw him, so Ah gave him mien as a muhmento."

Now Violet smiled.

"See Lucinda? When you focus on something, your memory becomes clear... even if only briefly. Still, it was more than a year ago. Now, Talon is downstairs as we speak trying to track you down."

"Why wuud he doo thah?"

Violet told her "If we can, we can find out how you became the most powerful lady of the day. The more we find out about you, the closer we get to finding out who Shadow Man is."

"THAT... I'm afraid... I can't allow," Shadow Man taunted as Lucinda's door flung open.

Violet felt someone pulling on her hair, and yanking her out of the room. He was in the doorway, but the wind Violet felt before was back, and twice as strong.

"In awl theez yee'uhz, YOU ya foul creechuh, have NEVUH entered these wawlz... and y'all shant now!!!" and the door slammed shut.

"Thank you Lucinda," Violet said kindly.

"Maw than welcum mah deeyuh."

Violet returned to her queries.

"Lucinda, (giggle) I think it's cute how your accent thickens when you get upset."

"It does? Why, I hadunt noticed."

"Anyway, as I was saying. If we can track you, we can 'discover' you. That will tell us what you did, where you went, that sort of thing. The more we know about you, the more we know about those around you. We're hoping, that, will lead us to Shadow Man," Violet explained kindly.

"OOOooooh, this is so frustrate'in!!" Lucinda bellowed. "Ah wuud be happy tuh help but, I jus cannot seem tuh remembuh!"

Violet knew she'd have to push Lucinda's buttons. Now, she was just hoping to hit the right one's.

"Lucinda, how about if I... well... gently prod that memory of yours, and see what happens?"

"If y'all think it will help," Lucinda said.

Violet blurted out "121 State Street."

"Now THAH is a locayshun Ah shall NEVUH reeturn to!" Then Lucinda was ecstatic and cried out "Violet... it worked! Ah remembuh now!"

"Tell me about it," Violet said still remaining calm.

"Ah grew up there. Momma was awlways blather'in on about 'do good' and 'do right' by folk. Say'in stuff like 'Do guud or do hahrm, and it will come back to ya three fold', whut nonsense! Ah was a lady of thah day! Ah cuudint be bothered with momma's antiquated ways." Lucinda sighed lovingly and said "Aaah, Michael Stanton was mah true love at thah time. We planned tuh marry but momma refused tuh give me her bless'in. She was furious with me, and Ah her! She jes didunt want me tah leeve her all alone is awl! I toeld her Ah was leav'in with aw without her bless'in! She toeld me if Ah did, she would curse me tuh nevuh return! HAH! Return tah whut!? Her sad little life!? Ah had men dripp'in off me most days. I had maw than momma EVUH wuud have liv'in her sad little life. Ah had thah fienest ov clothes, an much to thah gentlemen's deelite, I was not afraid tah show off mah fine curves," Lucinda stated with pride in herself.

"And then?" Violet nicely prodded.

"On mah 18th birthday, Michael said he would take me far away, and we wuud stahrt a new life tuhgethuh. He said then, Ah wuudint need momma's blessin as Ah cuud decide on mah own."

"Then what?"

"Ah remembuh momma caught me leav'in. Ah stood up tuh her though, an momma was furious. She told me ah wuud nevuh see mah wedd'in day till Ah returned home an mend'ed mah ways. Ah nevuh seen mah momma thah angry in awl mah life."

Lucinda's memories were starting to blur again. Thankfully for Violet, she knew it, and tried to get out all she could before they did.

"Ah remembuh we boarded uh ship. It had a tremendous set of wheels on eithuh side, right in thah middle. Michael woke me up in thah dead of night. Ah recawl wawtuh be'in on thah flaw in our room. He got me to a small rowing boat. It wasn't till I got outside thah I noticed thah stawm. The little boat swayed horribly. There was no maw room in mine and Michael took another. It was tha most terrify'in night o'mah life. Come thah morn'in, thah stawm was gone, but thah day was still as gray as Mista G's hair. I recawl 5 boats... or was it six?

Well, come morn'in, we made it to shaw." Lucinda was sadder than sad and said "Ownlee two boats made it... an Ah lawst mah Michael." Sadness got replaced by anger and Lucinda said "Ah was furious with mah momma an swore she wuud nevuh beat me like thah ahgin. Ah swore ah wuud become maw powerful than she EVUH beeleevd she was... an thah she wuud nevuh hurt me agin."

Lucinda's voice was all Violet ever heard, but even that sounded drained now.

Violet was sweet and asked "Is there anything else you can remember?"

"Ah recawl a lot of travel'in. Ah... Ah think I remembuh someth'in ahbout travel'in towards thah sett'in sun. Oh Ah am sawry dah'lin... its awl a blur now."

Violet stood up and was kinder than kind.

"Lucinda? Rest now and when you do... do so with my thanks."

"Violet dah'lin... Ah... Ah, think Ah will."

Lucinda's voice faded away. The sense of energy that accompanied her, faded away too. Violet walked out, and closed Lucinda's door as she did. She never got to turn around when she heard heavy footsteps run up behind her.

"HOLD IT!" Violet barked still staring at the door. The footsteps stopped and she declared "I was utterly exhausted the night I arrived... and I still managed to kick your ass." Violet had a menacing tone in her voice and said "I am no longer exhausted... and you had BEST not be there when I turn around."

Violet did turn around. When she did she walked calmly down the hall then down the stairs.

As she started her descent, she called back "Smartest move you made all week."

Shadow Man just laughed at the taunt, but only to himself.

"Stay without a clue freakish one. You will only make it that much easier for me."

Now, a second ghost retreated back to the ether.

"Are you sure?" Zachariah said in a pumped up tone.

"That's what she said," Violet told him.

Zack looked at Talon and asked "And what about that steamer?"

Talon replied "Don't know much off the top of my head. A twin wheeler though was built for speed. Most of those back in the day were confiscated and used by the South to run supplies past the blockades. Also, a lot of those were converted cargo ships. Likely, that thing was carrying a bit more than usual cargo for a cruise ship. They sacrificed some room for passengers. Problem was, they were notorious for sinking as most didn't know about engineering back then... or cared. Money was all that mattered. Reduce cargo to carry passengers, on a ship built for cargo only, and they became unstable in rough seas."

While Talon, was explaining, Zack was using the new info to narrow down his search. Next, Zack rolled his chair with him on it, and ripped a piece of paper out of the printer.

"Like... the Santa Inez!?" he said beaming. "Passenger manifest shows a one 'Michael Stanton' traveling with his fiancé... heh heh... a certain Miss 'Luci Adir'. Slick dude even booked the honeymoon suite." He stared at the monitor and said "Lady!? Ha ha ha... I got you."

Talon got up, gave Violet a big hug, and said "C'mon... today I'm making you lunch! Zack?"

Zack never looked up, and just waved a hand saying "Go, I'm good. Give me until dinner and I should have more than you could imagine."

Talon joked "Let's go dear... and leave the Mormon to his work."

Zack just laughed saying "Boss? Fuck off! And my air was JUST as thin as yours!"

"Was not," Talon laughed back... and he and Violet were gone.

It wasn't elaborate, but, Talon kept his promise. He made a simple but nice lunch, but sat quietly with Violet.

"Penny for your thoughts?" she asked him sweetly.

"Huh? Oh... sorry. I was just thinking is all."

"About?"

"Shadow Man," Talon answered with some concern.

"I'm totally fine sweetie, nothing I couldn't handle," Violet told him kindly.

"Oh I know you can. I'm not worried about that."

"What then?" Violet asked.

Talon took out a pen and grabbed a napkin. He looked around quick then wrote Violet a note on it. When he finished, he slid it to her. It read...

>Lucinda stronger... Shadow should be too. Not seen in awhile. Sense a trap or more like lying in wait... Making me nervous<

Violet smiled. Talon got her an old wood burning stove. As in, a real cooking stove that used wood. It was brand new but looked like it was a 150 years old. Violet took her paper plate, and crumpled up the napkin, and dumped both in the fire box.

"I know what you mean. I feel the same," she said as she kissed him on her way out.

"And where are you going?" Talon asked.

Violet smiled, winked, and said "Napkin patrol," and she headed out.

Talon just chuckled and finished his lunch.

Long shadows were now everywhere in Zack's office. He was almost done and, per his prediction, coming up fast on dinnertime. When he finally set his computer to sleep, he had several sheets of paper in his hand.

"Boss? Where are you?" Zack asked into his phone.

"I'm home. Just got out of the shower. What's up?" Talon's voice asked.

"You might say, mission accomplished. I got her like you asked. I have a feeling though, you might want this hidden."

Talon curiously asked "In what way?"

"As in, you might want to be, shall we say, 'shielded', when I tell you what I got."

"Know about that do you?" Talon queried cautiously.

"Yeah well, like I told you. I neither believe nor disbelieve. I know you and Violet do though, and right now? I'll take all the edge I can get."

"Fair enough. She's still there. Catch a ride with her and bring everything you got. If it's as 'hot' as you believe, then I'll ride that edge with you."

"See you in a little while. Shall I let the others know?"

"Nah, we'll get them on video conference. See you when you get here."

Zack hung up the phone, and went to find Violet.

"And where's Cody?" Talon asked Eileen.

"He's got a late shift at the hospital tonight. I told him about this and I told him I'd update him later," Eileen answered her brother.

"Fair enough. Abigail? You sure we're secure?" Talon asked the other box on his screen.

"Pfff... totally," she said without a care in the world.

"Alright then people... welcome to history class. My name is Zack, and I'll be your host for this evening," Zachariah joked.

Everyone geared up for a good story, and Zack took center stage.

"Alright, here's what I found out. Lucinda went by several alias's but Luci Adir was her main one. She survived a shipwreck and ended up on the east coast of Texas. Back in the day, there was still a heavy Spanish influence. With her skin tone, I'm sure she either played herself off as one, or was just taken for one and she played dumb. She was nursed back to health by some missionaries. Apparently her injuries were minor, and she didn't stay long."

"Got some dates for me?" Talon asked.

"Yeah but, that wasn't easy. Seems this Althea you mentioned was right. Arella moved around a bit and was taken in by the locals at times. Those same locals sort of hid her."

"Hid her?" Grant asked curiously.

Talon answered "Makes sense. Those people were highly superstitious back then. A 'black witch' was a real concern of theirs. Having a white witch in your midst, well, you're gonna take care of that one. It also showed intent. Help out Arella, and it shows her you're on her side, and possibly procure a favor or two. That alone would've been worth more than gold back in the day."

"I'll take your word for it but it sounds about right," Grant concluded.

"So," Zack started again. "Lucinda turned 18 on July 4th, 1854. She was rescued a day later on the 5th. That at least explains why the house was built to open on the day it did... it was a birthday present to herself."

"Some birthday!" Talon declared. "That means she got into town in only 2 years, 3 tops. That is one tight time-line."

"Hey boss?" Abigail asked sweetly.

"Yeah Abby?"

"I'm a lot like your brother when it comes to history. Wasn't exactly my thing in school. How about that big picture thing you do so well?"

"Heh heh, thanks Abby. Let's get a little more from Zack first, and see if I even need to."

Zack nodded to Talon, and continued.

"Now, we all know a person can't conjure up a storm, but Arella believed in her powers. Apparently Lucinda didn't, till shitty timing made mom look far more powerful than she actually was. Back then, crossing the continent by wagon train was the only way but Lucinda was smart. She crossed Texas, then caught another ship up the coast and over to the Baja Peninsula. A certain Luci Adir got on the ship, but... get this... a certain Arella Adair got off ha ha ha! Like I said boss, stick to what you know. The Arella that got off that ship was only JUST 18 years old, so we know it wasn't really momma. A ship by the name of 'The Virgin Queen' docked on August 10th of that same summer. Looks like our girl was moving fast."

Talon was forming a travel plan in his head and asked "Okay, what then?"

"Records then are spotty, but it appears she headed straight for the gold rush scene, showing up just after Christmas of that same year. Our girl was focused I'll give her that. This is where, as the old novels say, the plot thickens. Nothing on her directly till around April of the next year. Seems Abigail's dad was right. There was an article about how a certain merchant was accused of murder. Turns out it was Collis's brother. Collis left the shipping business to be by his brother's side. Seems a certain madam of what the paper called, a Spanish complexion, told how she was in the store that day. The paper said she observed the man trying to get out of paying his bill. Seems his credit was no longer any good. The store owner refused him any more and he got mad. Lucinda's testimony turned it from murder, to self defense. Collis's brother closed up shop and moved, but Collis went into railroads about that time. He was quite prominent back then so the social columns would follow who went where, and with who. He was listed with a lady, who the paper's would list as a most stunning woman of obvious southern charm and breeding. Collis would only identify her as his dear sister, and by the initials 'CQ'."

Zack checked his papers for anything he missed.

"After that, she becomes the mystery we know of today."

Talon was deep in thought, then complimented Zack.

"A tad sketchy for our purposes. However, real nice work Zack."

"Thanks boss."

Abigail had a sly look on her face.

"Now can I get the big picture?" she asked like a little girl asking for a doll for her birthday.

Talon laughed as he saw everyone else have the same exact look.

"Okay okay!" Talon relented with a laugh. "So, part truth, part guessing... here goes. Lucinda thinks mom cursed her. Thing is, so did Arella. Arella believes harm comes back to you 3 fold. So, without an heir... and bad mojo looming, she looks to correct both by taking in 3 orphans. Lucinda on the other hand is likely near destitute, and knows she can't go home. Either that or pride forces her not to. Either way, with little hope, she heads for the gold rush. Now, it appears our girl is really smart. She takes the overland route across Texas only but, at that time, it's a bit of a hot bed, so she's not wasting any time. Using her money or her charms, or both, she makes her way to California. She doesn't strike me as the miner type, but servicing all those men, is quick money. She takes that money and parlays it into investments. She's shrewd but knows momma is a force to be reckoned with. So, with that as motivation, she's looking to become her own powerhouse so momma can't ever fuck her over again. Or, if she tries, she'll be in a better position to take her on."

"Sounds about right so far," Grant agreed.

"Does to me too," Zack chimed in with.

Talon kept going and said "Now, I'm guessing Arella felt bad. Likely even tried to make amends, but had no idea how or where. Zack said Arella died roughly 5 years later, but now we got 3 wannabe white witches scouring the country looking to make right what went wrong. Yet again, in that world anyway, comes the power of 3. Mom used to talk about that being either a good thing or a bad thing, depending on the event. The letters said it was a self appointed task so I'm guessing they saw it as payback on Arella's behalf."

Zack told the group "Here's some more facts for ya. Samantha didn't stay in St. Louis. She moved a few years later back to New Orleans, where she lived until her death. She had no children of her own but, get this, she adopted 3 girls. I stopped looking when they were about 20 each. I pulled what little train records I could find. Looks like her and Mary-Jane kept their promise to each other. That's about all I got on them as nothing new really showed up there, and that wasn't the trail I needed to follow."

Talon was a tad pissed and said "While this was some excellent work Zack, it tells us about her and Collis... but we still come up short on Henry."

"Perhaps not," Zack said with a glint in his eye. "I agree Henry's side of things is a little light. So I looked into him as well. Seems he had a colleague of sorts. Henry went to medical school in New York before moving out west. He had a friend by the name of Michael Dupree. By all accounts, they were the best of friends. I contacted some living relatives, and actually told them the truth. I said I was hired to look into Doc's family, and found little or nothing. So I was looking into old associates for any kind of letters or diaries or whatever. Turns out, Michael kept a journal."

"You never mentioned this to me," Cody slightly scorned.

"Nice of you to join us Doc. Thought you were working?" Zack asked the vid link.

"I was but managed to get off early."

Zack nodded and said "Sorry Doc, but with dad over my shoulder most the time, I was kind of splitting my focus when I did my earlier work. Suffice to say, I found a lady who is a direct descendant, and she had the journal. Lucky for us she is an artist, so she knew how to scan pages and such. Michael told of how he never lost touch and how he constantly wrote or sent telegrams. Seems Michael got concerned when he found out about his love for Lucinda. Being already married, Michael was adamant Henry should break it off. Seems Henry was a bit too unorthodox for Michael who, by all accounts, was a by the book sorta guy."

Talon was smiling huge now and said "Okay I'll buy that. This other doctor sees his best friend ruining himself. He sees what he feels is a brilliant man heading for self destruction. Get Lucinda out of the way, Henry sulks some but then comes back to being the friend and prominent physician he once was. Now that's the thought leading to her murder, but he has no idea Henry will never recover... so his plan seems like a solid one at the time. Question is, did he care for Henry enough to kill for?"

"Possible, but seems a bit of a stretch to me," Violet said.

"Perhaps but, people thought differently back then. Plus, a by the book sorta guy would likely have the kind of cold and pragmatic mentality to do something like that. Black and white world... with Lucinda being an unwanted gray bit. Also, a whore wasn't worth much in those days and likely wouldn't be missed much either. Plus, she wasn't the 'right type' for a fine upstanding doctor like Henry. Not in his mind anyway."

"I have to agree with Violet," Cody told the group. "Possible yes. But in my mind, not likely."

Violet was feeling off. Not bad, but definitely off. She also noticed there was a sort of rainbow effect on the video every time Cody spoke up. It took her a second, then her eyes went wide.

"Uh... guys? I'll be right back," and she headed out.

She was texting on her phone as she did.

"Hey gang... hold that thought a moment. I uh, gotta use the little girls room. I'll be back in a minute or three," Eileen told the crowd, then disappeared herself.

Everyone held up for a few minutes till the ladies returned. They also did return... at the same time.

"Cody? I forgot to tell you, I changed the oil in your Cuda today. I also topped off your halogen light fluid," Violet told him when she returned.

"Thank you so much dear, that was very kind of you," Cody told her.

Now Eileen was brandishing a rather large kitchen knife, and pointing it right at Cody.

"You have a Beemer... my brother has the Cuda. And halogen lights don't get filled at all. Okay... who the fuck are you!?" Eileen commanded all fired up.

Cody beamed and said "Well played purple eyed one." He looked directly at Talon, completely ignoring Eileen, and told him "You have done amazingly well Mister Grayson. Suffice to say, while your argument sounds plausible in theory, I can tell you it would hold no basis in reality. Michael took the oath of 'do no harm' to the extreme."

"And you would know this how?" Talon challenged calmly.

"Know this Mister Grayson, you have done some amazing detective work. How do I know this you ask? I know because Michael loved writing everything down. You've found so little on me because... I did not. Might I ask a favor before I go?"

"Depends on the favor," Talon said confidently.

"You'll find me in the back of the church in Virgina City... in the paupers section. If you could find the kindness in your heart, I would very much appreciate it if you would put me next to my beloved Lucinda. My apologies everyone but... it's time for me to go."

"WHO THE HELL ARE YOU!?" Eileen said brandishing the knife still.

Cody's imposter stood, turned to face her, and kindly said "I'm sure your brother will tell you."

He was about to go when he heard Talon call out his name.

"HENRY... wait!" Talon was nice and asked "Will I see you again?"

"Perhaps... perhaps not. I only wished to steer you down a proper path... not an erroneous one." He looked at Eileen, smiled and said "Apologies if I frightened you my dear."

With that, what looked like Eileen's solid boyfriend, turned and walked into the fireplace... and was gone.

"Sis? Say the word and I'll be there in less than 10 minutes!" Talon hollered as he headed for the keys in his office safe.

Eileen was curled into a fetal ball and rocking a bit.

Zack was stunned and cried out "FUCK ME! Did you see that! The sonuvabitch walked right into a brick wall!"

"I was here Zack. Yeah, I saw. Talon?"

"I got keys in hand sis... call it."

"You wouldn't let those bastards run you out of your house... I will not let these bastards run me out mine. I'm good but... thanks. Love ya bro."

"You sure?" Talon said still wanting to fly out of the house.

"Yeah, I'm good. A little freaked out but, I'll be fine in a few."

Grant was stunned, and not listening to his sister.

"You may be good but I'm not. Abigail and I are coming over... and I don't wanna hear shit. At least till the REAL Cody gets there... you ain't gonna be alone tonight!"

Eileen was still curled up but stopped rocking now.

"Love you too baby G. I'll leave the porch light on."

"How did you know?" Abigail asked.

"Violet texted me. She sensed something was 'off'. I called Cody at the hospital... and he answered."

Talon gave Violet a huge hug.

"Thanks Vi."

Violet cocked her head and smiled.

"Anytime. Besides, I can't let anything happen to my future sister-in-law now can I?"

Talon laughed and asked "Future sister-in-law eh?"

Violet smirked at him slyly.

"Well, a girl can dream can't she?"

Zack stammered "He... he... he walked through the wall! I mean, right through the fucking wall!!"

Talon told him kindly "If it helps... it only gets easier from here."

Grant was back on the vid link again, and everyone could hear the engine of his Charger revving up loudly as he drove.

"Tal? This is getting fucked up, you know that right?" Grant said with extreme annoyance in his voice.

With an equal annoyance level, Talon said "No need to remind me. Okay folks, gimme a minute to piece this all together. Eileen?"

"Yeah?"

"Step out of sight... and I'll show you just how fast that Lambo really is."

Eileen threw a playful salute, but for a change, did as she was told. Talon also had the Lamborghini keys in his pocket.

"Someone mind telling me why you're all not freaked out by some guy walking INTO A BRICK WALL!?" Zack exclaimed still clearly freaked out.

That actually made the crowd laugh a little, even Eileen.

"Speaking of, why did he show up now?" Grant asked in general.

"Soon as I figure that one out I'll let you know. Of course, if anyone but me has an idea... I'm all ears," Talon told everyone.

Talon was the big picture guy. No one else had a clue, and their collective silences pretty much said so.

"Okay so, Doc's lineage not withstanding, Zack? Go through everything we got on Mr. Dupree. Henry may not believe in his guilt, but I'm not taking any chances in ruling him out either. So far, he's the only piece of the puzzle that fits. I don't mind telling you all, while we now know more about Lucinda, it still doesn't help us with finding who hated her enough to kill, and still care for Henry. Shit! I thought for sure we'd get a better insight, knowing what happened to her. It's a nice history tale, and would make a hell of a movie I'm sure, but it still leaves us no closer to Shadow Man."

Violet leaned in and told everyone "Talon is concerned about him. It seems that with Lucinda getting stronger, he's getting weaker. Tal believes it's a ruse, and I tend to agree. So, if you go to the mansion, be extra careful."

"Oh this just gets better and better," Grant extolled angrily. "Ten minutes to your door sis... like Talon said... stay where I can see you."

"Grant? You don't hang up till I see our sister in your phone."

"Count on it!" Grant stated with macho determination.

Grant kept his promise. His phone went off 8 minutes later, when Eileen opened the door.

Grant, Abigail and Eileen were on the same screen now. Zack was finally calming down, and Grant had one final question.

"So then, tell me this. Shadow is one pissed off dude. If he loved Henry like a brother, why's he so angry?"

Talon chuckled and said "What are ya all looking at me for!?"

"That is a rhetorical question, right?" Eileen half teased.

"I have no clue," Talon told the group. "Assuming it is him, I can only guess that this guy went way over the line, and broke every rule he ever knew, or believed in. Seeing as how his ultimate prize was Henry 'coming back to the fold', I can only further guess that seeing Henry's downward spiral only pissed him off. He does a lot of stuff for Henry, only to find he did all that for someone who, in his mind, became unworthy of all of it."

Violet started yawning. So did Talon.

"Alright gang. I think we've had enough fun for one evening. If no one has anything else, get some rest and I'll see you all at the mansion tomorrow."

"Love ya bro," Eileen said sweetly. "G'nite Violet... you too Zack."

Grant and Abigail waved and now it was just the 3 in Talon's home.

"Zack? You can stay in the guest room tonight if you want. There's a night light in there and I think I may even have one of my old Teddy Bears around somewhere if you'd like."

"Boss? Not funny. Noooot funny at all."

Violet gave him a small kiss on the cheek.

She was giggling when she did and said "Actually? I thought it was."

Violet and Talon just laughed some, and headed for bed.

Chapter 25

"Sugar Dump"

"I came in the Jeep next. It's fire engine red, and it doesn't even have halogen lights," Cody answered Talon. "Would you like me to tell you what a fire engine is?" Cody playfully sneered.

Talon chuckled saying "Okay, it's you."

"Honestly though, you should have called me... I would have come straight away," Doc lovingly told Eileen.

She was back to her old self and told him "I was good. I had company, and I wasn't in danger. Besides, freaky as it was, those sick or hurt people needed you more... and I was neither."

That was why Cody admired, and loved, Eileen so.

"Thanks for looking after her though," Cody told Grant sincerely.

Grant laughed some, looked at Talon, and said "You wanna remind the Doc who her brothers are? Or should I?"

Cody laughed with the rest, but said "True, however, I think you know what I meant."

Grant hoisted his coffee, and nicely said "Indeed I do."

They were all in the kitchen of the mansion having breakfast during this conversation. That very same conversation, got rudely interrupted by Zack.

"Okay you guys... NOT funny!" Zack said rather irritated.

Everyone laughed seeing him holding a teddy bear nearly the size of him. He sat it in a chair and huffed as everyone just laughed. It was actually Eileen and Abigail who left it on his chair in his 2nd floor office.

"Aw... but he's soooooo cute!" Violet playfully chided. "Wadda ya gonna name him?" she added nearly chuckling.

"Oh fuck off the lot of ya!" Zack said in a huff as he marched back to his office, leaving the bear in the chair.

Talon joked and told Violet "I think he should name it Zack Junior. He does have his eyes ya know."

Everyone just laughed and went about their day.

A few hours later, a Jeep and a truck pulled into Virginia City.

"This is your idea of lunch?" Grant asked.

"Why not!?" Cody answered merrily. "It's one of your favorite places is it not? Consider this my way of thanking you for last night. Besides, it's always your house Talon, or yours Grant. This time... lunch is on me."

With a friendly smile, Talon said "Ya know what? I am all sorts of okay with this idea."

Equally as friendly, Violet grabbed his arm and said "So am I."

And so, 3 couples went into one of the old saloons to have a nice lunch. Zack was still a tad pissed and, not wanting to be teased anymore than he already was, declined the Doc's offer.

Eileen had a silly face on, and kept poking Cody playfully.

"Still me my dear," he said with a chuckle.

"Aaaahkay.... jes check'in!" she teased like a 4 year-old.

Abigail stated "This place is amazing! You three were lucky to have grown up here." She looked around a little and asked "And this is all real?"

Grant proudly told her "Yep, all of it. There was a fire that burned most of it down like 100 years ago or so... but this is all the rebuilt stuff from that time. So yeah, it's as authentic as it gets."

Talon teased his brother with a smile, but said nothing. He leaned back in his chair, and gave him some light applause, but in a circular fashion.

"Ha ha ha, bro? Go fuck yourself, and take your 'round of applause' with you. I admit history isn't my thing. I never said I didn't know any though."

Talon jokingly stuck his tongue out at him.

"If I have to pull this table over, you two are gonna be in trouble!" Eileen playfully admonished like a mother would.

Grant told her "He started it," and everyone just laughed.

They were all out on the covered walkway outside the saloon now. Lunch was fun, but the girls wanted to shop.

"Grant, how about if you stay with them while Doc and I go do a little 'family business'?"

Grant joked and said "A chance to steal your girlfriend away from the almighty Talon? Why... I'd love to!"

Violet and Eileen giggled as an annoyed Abigail asked "You really don't like 'dessert' do ya G-man?"

Grant cooed "Oh now honey you know I only have eyes for you... but... pass up a chance to tease my brother!? Hehe... not gonna happen!"

Abigail just huffed and walked into the shop. Grant tipped his hat to his brother, and followed the ladies in. Talon and Cody tipped theirs back, and headed off to a grave.

Talon and Cody looked around, but came up empty.

"And you're sure he said behind the church?" Cody asked Talon.

"That's what he said... in the pauper's section."

"Well then Mister history professor, how come he isn't here?" Cody asked in a tone that belied he was clearly unhappy at coming up empty.

"Hey, why pick on me!?" Talon asked.

"Sorry Tal. I'm just a little bummed is all. I've been chasing him all my life, and when he actually 'appears'... I'm not around. Oh I would have given anything to have just 5 minutes with him."

"I'm sure my sister would be happy to trade you," Talon said with a laugh.

Now Cody snapped out of his funk, and kicked into gear.

"Okay, between you and me, we are the best historians anywhere around. Now, what do we know? He said a paupers grave, and behind the church. Any possibility this church was somewhere else?"

"Nope," Talon confirmed. "I know what you're getting at but... this church has been in this same spot since it was built."

Cody acquiesced and said "Alright then, that's out. Still, if I recall, a pauper's grave would be at the farthest point from the actual church. That means we're in the right section."

Talon chuckled saying "Real Christian like huh Doc?" Talon mocked "We like you... but we'd like you a whole lot better if youuu were over theeere."

Cody scorned "Don't even get me started. While I can't say I've lost my faith in 'The Almighty'... his church, for me anyway, is a whole other matter."

"I never went. I neither believe nor disbelieve. I can tell you this though... the believe and disbelieve... have gotten rather shaken up of late."

"Of that I have no doubt. Okay, so, if we're in the right section, what are we missing?"

Talon now said "If he was a pauper, or simply insulted and buried as one, it's possible he may not have a stone at all."

Cody beamed and said "He would have had a wood marker! Likely rotted over time! Genius my friend."

Talon mock bowed and stated "Yaw flattery suh doth overwhelms me."

Cody and Talon searched again, and found 3 wooden markers. Just like Cody said, they were rotted and broken off just above the ground.

"Tal, as family, I can have him exhumed on that alone. Because I, um, 'wasn't involved' in the last one... no one will question a second exhumation."

Talon toyed right back with "Because... as we all cleeeearly know... you can't have a second one without a first one... ain't that right Doc?"

"Quite right young man... quite right," Cody said with a smirk. He got serious again and said "Okay, that leaves us with 3. There's no way I can exhume them all. So my friend, how about putting that analytical mind of yours to work then... hmm?"

Talon merely said "Challenge accepted."

Cody just chuckled lightly to himself as Talon gave him his request.

Talon looked up and said "Okay, see the trees?"

"Uh... yeah?" Cody said having no clue what Talon was up to.

"That one is a sycamore," he said pointing to one on the corner of the graveyard. "It's not native to here so the priests likely planted it. The rest though, are cedars and redwoods. They're known for 'not' rotting and being bug resistant. Now, 150 years will break any wood. Around here Doc, winds kick up out of the west around 4pm everyday. The worst storms come from that way too. That means, we follow the wind."

Cody was surprisingly getting pumped, and knew he made the right choice in challenging Talon.

"In what way!?"

Talon said "Well, wood breaks... then follows the wind. That means, these 2 graves here," and Talon pointed, "Are our best hope. The marker blows back, then gets buried over time. We dig here... BEHIND the busted markers... and we should find the broken off tops."

Cody smiled kindly and said "And now you know why they all look to you," referring to the big picture thing. Just as kindly, he finished with "Myself included."

Talon and Cody looked around, and Cody found a storage shed.

"Fuck... it's locked!" Cody exclaimed.

Talon looked around, and picked up a big rock. Taking it in two hands, he raised it over his head, and bringing it down hard, smashed it open.

"Lock? Hmm... I didn't see a lock... did you?" Talon taunted.

"Nope... can't say I did!" Cody said in total collusion.

Inside was exactly what they were hoping for... a pair of shovels. Both men started digging. Cody was stoked to see Talon was right. Problem was, the one behind the grave he was working at, was all splintered.

"Hey Doc!? You may wanna come see this!" Talon declared happily.

His was splintered too but, not as badly.

"Lousy bastards," Cody exclaimed seeing the carved splinters being assembled side by side.

He said that as he saw what was originally written on the wood marker.

"Him? They couldn't even give him a name for God's sake!?"

Cody was insulted as he read the marker. It read <Him... 1835-1868>

Talon asked "How do you even know it's Henry?"

"Look at the bottom. Even back then, the staff and serpent was the symbol of doctors," Cody said barely containing his anger.

"I can barely even make that out it's so rotted."

Cody was walking away and said "Trust me, even battered like that... I'd recognize that symbol anywhere."

Talon marked the spot with GPS using his phone, then put both shovels back in the shed. He put the lock back as best as he could, then ran after Cody.

The church was downtown, and the men were struggling slightly walking back up the steep hill. They were also talking as they went.

"Sad though," Talon said, "Henry was only 33 and Lucinda was only 29!" Talon was truly sad for them and stated "That's far too young in my book."

"I blame Henry for his own death. He above all should have known better. Lucinda however didn't have much of a choice."

"True," Talon agreed. He stopped, then stopped Cody, and told him "Look Doc, all I wanted to do was rebuild for a change, rather than destroy. I didn't plan on ANY of this shit. Now, that said... I want you to know... I have no issue in granting Henry's request... none."

Cody put a kind hand on Talon's shoulder and said "Thank you. I wasn't going to ask but... it means a lot to me."

"Anytime Doc. You've earned that much at least," Talon said truthfully. Then his phone rang and he answered saying "Yo bro... did they max out your credit card?"

"Pretty damn near it. Where you at?" Grant's voice said.

"Just coming up to main street. Where are you?"

Grant answered "Outside the 'Bucket O'Blood'."

"Okay we're a block away... see you in a few."

"We'll be waiting," and Grant hung up.

Talon and Cody got up onto Main Street, got under the covered walkway, and started heading for Grant. A girl coming out of the bar diverted them. She came out of the bar all giddy, then suddenly dropped to the ground. Instinctively, Cody ran to her, and the small crowd that gathered.

"I'm a doctor... let me through!" he told the small crowd.

They parted for him and Cody knelt down beside the girl.

"Easy there young lady. My name is Cody and I'm a doctor. Tell me what happened."

The girl was coming to and told him "I dunno. I only had a single drink. It hit me like ten though. I came out and felt the world spin, then, my legs gave out. Thanks Doc but, I'm okay now."

Cody had his fingers to her neck and was looking at his watch and said

"You just let me be the judge of that. How old are you?"

"22."

"Any history of diabetes?" Cody asked.

"No... no wait... yes. My mother had it when she was pregnant with me."

Cody let go of her neck then helped her up with a smile.

"You'll be okay, but I wouldn't drive for at least a half hour if I were you."

The girl smiled and walked off saying "Thanks for the help Doc."

Cody gave a mock but friendly bow to the applause the small crowd that had gathered gave him.

Talon was deep in thought and asked "What was that about?"

Cody chuckled and said "Someone is gonna get a surprise in a week or two. I believe you would call it a 'sugar dump'."

Now Talon was on fire.

"A what!?"

Flippantly, Cody answered "Yeah. Some women in the first few weeks of pregnancy have a severe reaction to sugar. Those with a history of diabetes have it even worse. She's gonna get a plus sign on her stick in a week, two tops... and likely doesn't even know it yet."

Talon nearly burst with joy, when good timing came his way, via his phone. It was a text from Erik.

> Re-scanned rusted image. Tech kid managed to get the resolution way up. Pic too large to text so sent to your email. Hope it helps.<

Talon's hands were moving at lightning speed, and brought up his email. Sure enough there was the email with the attachment. Also true... it was huge, and it took the phone a while to download it.

"C'mon c'mon ya piece of shit... move!" Talon commanded the inanimate, and slowly moving, download bar.

It finally obeyed Talon... and it made him feel happy but weird at the serendipitous timing of it. The picture just made him smile from ear to ear.

Talon put both hands on Cody's shoulders, beamed, and kissed his forehead hard.

"Mmmmmwwwwaaaaa! Ha ha ha ha!" Talon let go then ran up the walkway screaming "VIOLET!!! WE GOTTA GO!"

Talon ran up to the girls and Grant, and practically skidded to a stop.

"I don't have to charm Abigail do I?" he asked puffing a bit.

"No you don't. What's up with you?" Grant curiously asked.

Abigail teased "You could try... I ... I wouldn't mind!"

"HEY!?" Grant bellowed.

Abigail huffed coyly, put her arms across her chest, and said "That'll teach you to ruin dessert."

"What's gotten into... WHOOOAAAAA!" Violet said sharply as Talon yanked her away beaming.

"CODY! Take them back in your Jeep! Oh and... wait for my call!"

Doc Holliday called after him "What's gotten into you!?"

"With any luck!? The answers!!!" and Talon, with a protesting Violet in tow, went out of sight.

Talon drove like a madman to get home. Once he arrived, he dropped Violet off... outside the gates."

"Okay crazy man... what the fuck!?" Violet asked in an unhappy voice.

"Reach out. Do it as only you can. Tell Lucinda I'm coming. I don't care how you do it... just do it... then meet me in the house," and Talon sped up the driveway hard, and left the truck out of the garage.

Violet saw him run into the house and disappear. She shrugged, and attempted what Talon asked.

"Ahr yue awlright Violet dear?" the voice in her head answered.

"Lady? I have no idea. Something lit a SERIOUS fire under Talon's ass. All I know is... he said to expect our arrival."

"Ah shall due as yue ask young one. Fair warn'in though, Shadow Man is up tuh some'thin devious... Ah kin feel it."

"Duly noted," Violet said as she head into the house.

The moment she crossed the gates... Lucinda was gone.

Talon was like a madman, pouring over all the notes and such in his office. When Violet arrived, she noticed he appeared to be looking for something specific. She wasn't there long when Talon seemed to have found it, then put it all away, and grabbed her once more.

"Oh shit... here we go again," Violet said as she got yanked along with Talon once more.

'Mista G' was driving as fast as possible to the mansion. Violet was getting nervous as hell.

"If you don't slow down, you'll be JOINING Lucinda!" she barked in protest at the current speeds.

"Don't be a baby," was all he said but, never took his focus off the road.

The truck plowed up the driveway and actually skidded to a stop.

"C'mon c'mon c'mon!" Talon barked in annoyance as he opened her door.

"TALON!" Violet screamed going no further. "What the hell is wrong with you!?"

Talon just beamed and only told her "I need your help... now c'mon!" and he dragged her into the parlor.

"Miss Lucinda! Grand Dame of Adair House! Might I request your presence!??" Talon hollered joyfully.

"Ah see whut yue mean dah'lin," her apparition said to Violet. "Whut in tarnation has got yue so fired up Mista G?"

Puffing, Talon said "Lucinda, I need you to take me inside again... please."

Lucinda adamantly told him "Naht eevuhn faw you will I doo thaht again!"

Puffing still, but slowing down, Talon joyfully told her "We found Henry. Doc and I agreed we'll be putting him next to you. As for my request... I don't need to see 'that'."

"Ah am as befuddled as yaw fine lady friend then. What ahr yue ask'in me suh?"

Talon smiled, and said "Lucinda? I need you to show me that day. Just that... the day... not the moment in your hallway."

Lucinda was cautious and asked "Whut faw?"

Talon stood up straight, and said "Just..." and he walked willingly right into Lucinda, and finished with "...show me."

Lucinda's blurry apparition faded away... and Talon was once again worlds away... yet only a few steps from Violet.

That same medium was angry and merely exclaimed "Crazy ass white boy!" and took his hand for insurance.

Unlike last time this happened, Talon seemed calm, even peaceful. Violet was happy for that and just kept watch over him as best as she could. Suddenly, she felt the presence of Shadow Man. Also unlike the last time... he seemed to be hovering on the outskirts. Violet figured he didn't want a repeat and was only watching this time 'from a distance'.

Just like the last time Talon did this, he saw and felt everything. He tried to talk to Lucinda but, inside this virtual trip, he was a mere spectator.

She was walking through the mansion. It was morning, and she was gathering all the girls for some form of meeting.

"Now y'all remembuh... yue are fine ladies, and Iel expeckt y'all tuh behave as such!" she commanded.

"Yes ma'am," were the multiple replies.

"See thaht yue doo," and Lucinda opened the front doors.

"So... you're Henry eh?" Talon mused to himself as he saw the driveway of old.

It had a coach in it, and Henry was helping a rather Amazonian woman down from it. He clearly looked agitated at having her near. Now Talon remembered what Cody said sometime back... his wife was also his nurse. To Talon, Henry looked like Cody's older brother. That kind of 'very similar' look, but not a clone copy either. He had a well trimmed beard and mustache. It was the kind that just went around his mouth... the type Tony Stark sported in all those Iron Man movies.

Talon smirked and said to himself "Ya know, that's actually a good look for you Cody... hehehe... I'll have to remember to mention it to ya."

Henry walked in and tipped his hat to Lucinda, who curtsied back. You could tell the tension between these two was thick. No one cared however, to notice Henry's wife... but Talon did. The look on her face was not a happy one.

"Doctor, as always, I would like to thank ya on beehahff of mah girls faw insure'in their good health," Lucinda said with a smile.

Being... technically... inside Lucinda, Talon felt what she felt. The rush of desire Lucinda felt had Talon feeling a tad uncomfortable. He was also feeling a tad ill as, doing this, was from that first person shooter viewpoint he so despised. Still, he managed to focus as only he could.

They all lined up in the parlor in a sort of circle. Doc, and his nurse, checked the vitals and other basics, one by one. Henry singled one girl out in particular.

"Julia, have you been eating your spinach like I told you?" Henry queried like a school principle.

"I have," she said weakly. Henry stared her down and she confessed "Maybe not as much as you said though." Lucinda looked straight at her and Julia protested "It's just so damn awful!"

"MANNERS! And y'all will watch yaw language young lady."

She shrank back and said "Yes ma'am... sorry ma'am."

Henry chastised her, but kindly, and told her "If your iron levels drop any lower... you'll like the sickness you get from it even less."

"Doctor, isn't there any other way?" Julia pleaded.

"I know of no other food that's as rich in that vitamin. Tell you what, I'll do some research, and see if I can find an alternative. Until then, 2 bowls a day for a week... and you're off duty for the same amount of time."

"A WEEK!?" Julia protested.

Henry held firm and asked "Would you like me to make it two?"

"No sir... thank you sir."

Lucinda was not happy with her downtime. She was also not happy with the thought of her being sick either. Lucinda took care of business, but, true to her boast, she looked after her girls too.

"Thank you doctor... Ah shall see to her rehkoveree personally," Lucinda said with a glare.

Julia just shrank back and didn't say another word.

Henry took them upstairs one at a time for the more personal checkup. Each girl took no more than 10 or 15 minutes, and he came and got the next one. Each time Henry showed up, Lucinda felt flush at just the mere sight of him. Talon felt a tad awkward each time she did, but he ignored it, as he was after something.

"C'mon c'mon... I know it's here somewhere," he said to himself.

Suddenly, as if by Talon's command, he got what he was after. Henry was upstairs with one of the girls when Lucinda just lost it. Fainted was the word of the day, but Talon could feel it. THIS is what he was searching for.

"Oh my, perhaps Ah shouldn't hahv skipped breakfast this mawnin," she exclaimed as several of her girls came to her aid. Talon did everything he could now to separate himself from Lucinda, yet still stay with her. He tried everything Violet ever told him about this stuff. Finally, he managed to move his gaze from seeing it through Lucinda's eyes. Now he beamed large, and sensed to the extreme he had had enough. Seconds later, he was holding Violet's hand and back in the parlor... and in the present.

He was a tad weak, but nothing more, as he bowed and told Lucinda "My dear? Thank you... I got what I came for."

Violet was still annoyed and asked "And that would be?"

Talon smiled huge and said "A sugar dump. Vi? Where is he?"

"Who? Shadow?"

"Mm hmm."

"Here... but on the fringes... why?"

Talon yelled out "You have one hour before I return! Enjoy it... for it's your last hour of freedom. I got you you sonuvabitch. I warned you not to fuck with me... and now I'm gonna show you why!"

Shadow's dark apparition appeared in the doorway to the living room, and said in a glib manner "I'm not afraid of you..." then he taunted with "... not so old old guy," and Shadow laughed.

Talon was dead serious, and stated "In an hour... you will be."

"Save your empty threats gray freak."

Talon fired back "Enjoy your last hour on this or any other plain of existence."

"We'll see..." and Shadow Man disappeared.

Talon spoke to the now empty spot and stated "We will indeed."

He left without another word. The moment he got to his truck, Talon was calling in 'the gang'.

Cody was the last one he called. That was out of friendship.

"I've told everybody else just to come here. Cody? You are the only one I'm telling why."

"Okay... why then?"

"Doc?... I know who Shadow Man is."

A very serious "I'm on my way," was Talon's answer.

"May wanna bring your pipe."

"It's in my hand. See you in 15."

"Ah await yaw arrivuhl good suh," Talon teased as he hung up.

Chapter 26

"Nowhere To Hide... And Nowhere To Run"

Everyone was assembled in the parlor now, as Talon requested.

"So, you may be wondering why I asked you all here. Let me first state, this was part so you could say you were here when it all happened... and part joke. Eileen? I believe you once called us the Scooby gang. Zack calls us the Grayson Gang, and Abby here calls us the G-men. "

"Well... only sometimes," she said meekly.

Eileen was fired up and asked sharply "What 'it' are you referring to?"

Grant added "And what joke?"

Talon smiled and said "The 'it' will become evident in a moment. The joke is, with all those group names I mentioned... what do they all do at the end?"

Violet was still annoyed and answered "How about you enlighten us?"

"Why Violet my dear... heh heh... they have the big reveal! You all look to me for the big picture stuff. This is more like the last pieces to the jigsaw puzzle." Talon began the event by asking "Cody?"

"Yeah?"

"That pipe... let me guess... it was Henry's wasn't it?"

Cody said "Not sure. I know it's a family heirloom, but it's origins got a little lost. Could be though."

Talon smirked and replied "Trust me... it was his."

"And you know that how?" Doc asked curiously.

"I saw it in a pouch... on his hip."

"And just how did you see that? Did he return?" Cody asked excitedly.

"Something like that," Violet answered still a tad annoyed.

Talon told him "Doc Holliday? Not yet but... get it ready."

Cody nodded and did as requested.

Talon took out his phone, and showed everyone a picture.

"I got this today from Erik. In layman's terms, he managed to get a better scan of the tin type. Everybody? Say hello... to Henry," and Talon waved the phone slowly.

"Holy shit!" Cody blurted.

"Indeed Doc, but... you're missing something. Henry and Lucinda but, look... the background is the fireplace right over there!" and Talon pointed into the parlor. "Notice what's on it?"

Eileen stated "The ceramic doll. So what, we already know she had one."

"Correct," Talon said in agreement. "BUT, she had given hers to Collis by then. So... where'd the one on the mantle come from?"

"Henry..." Cody said almost dreamlike.

"Exactly," Talon confirmed.

"Dearest Lucinda! I wish to invite you to a meeting!" Talon called out joyously. "I seriously 'suggest' you attend."

Lucinda's image appeared from her photo on the wall. It was like a mist that slowly fell to the floor, and coalesced into a human shape as it did. She walked a few steps towards them all, and for the first time to a large group, since Talon and Grant decided to rebuild the place, the Grand Dame of Adair House... seemed as solid as any of them.

"Now how can Ah reefuse a reequest from a mahn such as you Mista G?" Lucinda teased nicely.

Talon tipped his cap to her, and said "You're looking rather well these days my dear."

"Thanks tuh yue suh, and yaw brother... I am feel'in better as well." She chuckled at the staring and stunned Zack, and leaned into Talon saying "Is yaw friend going tuh be ill? I'd hayt tuh have tuh clean up such a finely repaired flawuh."

Zack was just speechless and dumbfounded.

Talon laughed a little as Lucinda turned to Zack, and softly and kindly, just said "Boo."

Everyone laughed a little as Zack actually jumped back.

Now Talon took over, and told everyone why he called them there.

"So, when I first met Cody here... a puff of smoke grew arms, and tossed us like a couple of drunks from a bar. Later, he did it again, and yet again, Shadow Man appeared. I always wondered about that but, I wonder no more. Grant knows but, aside from Violet who was my guardian angel, none of the rest of you were told. I actually merged somehow with Lucinda, and saw the night she was murdered. I'm still not sure how but suffice to say, I did."

"Holy shit!" Abigail blurted out.

Talon kept going.

"Violet sensed I was in trouble. Even she isn't sure how she did it but, she managed to switch me from Lucinda, to Shadow Man. Had she not, I would have felt what she felt... and been dead myself. Shadow was beyond pissed at Lucinda, and then Violet. He did a fine job of pulling away from me, and that allowed Violet to yank me back to the present.”

Eileen was now pissed at her reckless brother, and told him “Yep, Althea was right... crazy ass white boy.” Then she yelled at him and said “What the hell were you thinking!!?”

Before Talon could answer her, his oratory was interrupted by the chime of a clock. It was the kind under a glass dome with the 4 gold balls that rocked back and forth.

Talon smiled sadistically, and changed his answer.

“You're about to find out. Doc? Now I'll take that sparkage please.”

Cody said nothing, and merely gave Talon his puff of smoke.

“Oh look... you brought an audience to your execution,” Shadow Man taunted as he appeared.

“Two things,” Talon said staring him down. “First, the mere fact that Cody's pipe brought you here, only confirms my suspicions.”

Shadow just laughed and taunted “And second?”

“Your hour is up,” Talon said with pure confidence.

Talon paced back and forth. Half the gang wanted to kick Shadow's ass... while the other half were looking for an exit.

“I'll admit, you had me fooled,” he told Shadow as he paced. “You were good, I'll give you that. A century plus of perfect anonymity, and you blew it all with just one sentence. 'Not your Henry' you said... and it doomed you.”

Shadow Man just laughed “Oh do continue,” his gruff voice said, “Even I want to hear this.”

Talon told him “No you don't. That one sentence let us know it truly wasn't Henry. That alone set us upon a path of finding out who you really are. Today, I got my answer... and all because you tripped up once again.”

The whole gang was riveted on Talon.

“Miss Lucinda? You truly have my sympathies... for the loss of your life...” Talon said.

Before he could finish, Lucinda interjected “Much appreciated guud suh.”

Talon finished with “... and that of your unborn child.”

“WHAT!?” Grant bellowed.

Lucinda was sweet and said “Mista G... Ah ashure you, Ah was not with chyld. Ah think Ah wuud hahv known if Ah was.”

“No you wouldn't have... and it's the very reason you were killed.” Talon turned to Shadow and said coldly “Isn't it?”

Shadow was getting nervous. Had this gray haired guy figured it out? He was nervous now, but merely smiled and waved a smoky hand as if to tell Talon to keep going.

“Mista G... Ah insist y'all explain yawself!” Lucinda said in a highly aggitated tone.

"Lucinda, you were only a few weeks pregnant... 2 or 3 tops. Those dizzy spells were what we call sugar dumps. You had something sweet, but your body reacted poorly to it due to your 'condition'. That's what those dizzy spells were you had. You were only a week or two away from finding out. Problem you had was... Shadow here noticed it."

Now Shadow was getting pissed, and let Talon know it.

"Silence gray freak," he said angrily.

"Or what... you'll illusion me again?" Talon taunted.

Violet however warned "Watch it Tal."

She was sensing some seriously bad mojo. The kind that said she, and the others, were walking into a trap.

"Ya see everyone, seeing Lucinda's murder wasn't the only time I 'stepped into the past'. I did it again today. Henry came the day she was killed to check all the girls. Lucinda had one of her spells while he was upstairs checking one of the girls. Only thing was... someone downstairs saw it... and knew exactly what it was. Someone with some medical knowledge... like say..."

"SILENCE!" Shadow bellowed.

Without a care, Talon said "Like say... a nurse?"

"Mista G! Explain yawself suh!" Lucinda commanded.

Abigail now called out saying "Wait wait wait... Shadow Man... is actually a WOMAN!?"

"Sure is," Talon said with pride.

He turned to Shadow and did something he never could do before. He reached up and pulled 'his' bandanna down... revealing the true face of Shadow Man.

"Isn't that right... Hildegarde?" Talon said with pride, and a bit of amazement at his feat.

"You vill pay dearly for this gray freak!" Shadow seethed, only now with a slight German accent in her voice.

"Mind if I call you Hilde?" Talon asked flippantly. "Hildegarde rolls off the tongue about as hard as that face of yours."

"Awl these yeeyuhs... and it was YOU!" Lucinda said barely containing her anger.

Hilde sneered "Silence Hure... no one is talking to you." She turned back to Talon menacingly and commanded "Go ahead... finish your story."

"This time 'Hilde'... that's an order I'll be happy to take, even from you."

Talon told all of them "Doc came in twice a week like clockwork. The real Doc that is. That's how he and Lucinda met. Now I'm guessing Hilde here didn't care for that too much but, while Henry lost interest in his own wife, I'm betting he was the world to you... wasn't he?" Talon just laid it out and said "A woman of charm and beauty you couldn't compete with. Tell me Hilde... how long did Henry look in on those girls hmm?"

She seethed "Three long und miserable years."

"Well then," Talon continued, "You wouldn't let Henry down so, rather than tell him you didn't want to go there... you went because it was Henry's wish to do so. You had a son who was about two at the time. It must have been humiliating for you to have to get your own husband drunk, or drugged, just to get him to make love to you. Don't bother lying I saw the look on his face."

"You are skating a really dangerous edge there Talon," Violet warned to no avail.

"Even having a child STILL could not keep him out of Lucinda's arms... nor her bed." Talon still paced and said "So you did your best to run interference. Then, one day, you see Lucinda drop in a way that left you horrified. YOU knew what it was, being medically trained yourself. Now, much as you hated Lucinda, you knew her to not be a loose woman. Rumors of the day ran rampant about how the only woman who didn't sleep with the customers, was good ole Lucinda. That meant only one thing... it was Henry's."

Hilde seethed "Dummkopf ruined EVRYting! Vee had famlee, OUR famlee! And he goes und gets Hure pregnant!"

Talon stated "Not your kid, he would have left you for her AND his child. He had power and influence. You knew he would have taken your son away eventually, leaving you with nothing. A strange manly woman in a strange land, who nobody liked except the pottery lady."

"Yue say NUTHINK about Mary-Jane! She vas ONLEE good person in this wretched place."

"Faw yaw sake Mista G, Ah am contain'in mah anguh... barelee. What does tha pottuh lady have ta doo with it?"

Talon stared at Hilde and said "She would have killed you on the spot if she knew who you were... or what you'd done." Talon told Lucinda "Your mother felt bad about the storm, and believed she caused it. A white witch would never do harm lest it come back on you 3 fold. Mom taught me that. Arella died without being able to tell you how sorry she was. As such, she adopted 3 orphan girls, as a means to make amends and ward off an evil she felt was coming. Those 3 girls scoured the country looking, for you. Mary-Jane was the eldest, and knew who you were, and was about to tell you who she was... but you were killed before she could. Now, Hilde here goes into a jealous rage, and my family on BOTH sides, managed to form an alliance to look after you, and solve your murder... that's lasted throughout the generations, right down to the three Grayson's you know today. 150 years Lucinda and all of it... just so Arella could tell you she was sorry. She did love you Lucinda, and only wanted to tell you that."

Lucinda was lost. Tears streamed down her face. She was sad, furious, feeling redeemed, and awash in feelings of what might have been.

"Oh momma... Ah was so angree but... Ah always loved yue." She turned to Talon and told him "Henry planned on marry'in me. Said so many times. Once we had, Ah planned on go'in back ta see momma, jes ta show her how rawng she was. Ah wahn ya tuh know thaht, had we married, Ah would have carried owt thaht plan."

Lucinda wept for a mother's love lost, and didn't care who saw it.

Hilde was furious and said "Oh spare me your pitiful tears. Vonce a Hure, alvays a Hure. You took vat vasnt yuers!. I did NUTHINK tue yue! Yue got vaht yue deserved."

Now, Violet's warning was about to be heeded whether Talon wanted to or not. Hilde was furious and retreated back to ghostly form... and went absolutely berserk with rage.

Violet sensed it and was about to run right into Hilde. Like Talon did the night he 'met' Lucinda, she got flung hard against the wall. Talon went wild and swung at Hilde, but got nothing but smoke and empty swings for his effort. Cody tried to grab her and got pretty much the same response. Hilde flung the doors closed, pinned Zack, Abby, Eileen and Grant against them... and began to unload secret after secret.

"Silly man came here dat night. Mehbee I not pretty like Hure, but he vas mine! I gave him evree'ting, and all he did vas break my heart. I gave him SON!... STILL he not love me!... only Hure!" Hilde got cocky now and told them "Vun night Henry tell me he go to sleep. I figger vith Hure gone, vee be a famlee again. No... silly man veep like baby for poor Hure. He sez vee stay here, in dis wretched place. No one talk tue me behfor, NOW tankz to stupid man... people treat me eevun VORSE! So, he says he go to sleep? I help him... stay dat vay!"

Talon went to help Violet, but Hilde swung him back hard as well. Inches from a back breaking crash, Talon just stopped. The wind that seemed to circle Violet when she arrived, built up behind him and cushioned him to a stop.

"A 150 yeeyahs Violet tells me! Know this yue wretched woman... Ah hahv had MAW than enuf of you and yaw interference!"Lucinda barked in a pure fury.

Now she was flinging her arms, and bouncing Hilde all around the parlor.

"Rehgahrdless... you killed MAH CHYLD!!" Lucinda seethed and told her "Ah will see yue buuuuuurn faw thaht!"

While Lucinda was whacking Hilde all around, Eileen and crew got released. Talon ran right for Violet, who was conscious but groggy.

"I tried to tell you," Violet grumbled, "She's too strong."

Talon was at a loss, and slightly afraid. Not so much for himself but, now, he was wishing he wasn't so stupid in bringing the rest of the gang here.

"What can I do!?"

With loving eyes that had lost all hope, Violet looked up at him and honestly said "I... I... I wish I knew."

And at that very moment, is when Lucinda got flung past them... and history repeated itself.

"Theh onlee vun who vill burn... is YOU Hure!"

Talon saw Cody trying to get everyone outside, and tried to run some interference in order to let him. He started to taunt Hilde, but the plaster came off the walls again.

"TALON!!" Violet wailed.

Talon took a few small hits and said "Yeah... not a reflection this time!" as he realized it too.

Now he did the only thing he could do. He took off his Kevlar vest, and gave Violet whatever shielding he had.

"You'll be killed!" she barked at him for the vest swap.

"Come say hello to me... when you can. Violet? I love you," and Talon went into the fray.

He had resigned himself to joining Lucinda... and was hell bent that if anyone was going to this night... it would be him and him alone.

"Oh look, the ugly hag is throwing a temper tantrum. Boo hoo I got revealed. Hure this and Hure that. It's whore you ugly piece of shit... not Hure. Do these mountains look like the fucking alps to you!? Stupid bitch. THAT'S why the natives here never took to you... you never let go of 'the old country'. That was your real problem Hildegarde, your attitude was as ugly as your face," Talon challenged.

He was prepared to die, and almost welcomed it. He felt, now, it was the only way he could fight back.

"You took Henry's coat and hat... and even his shoes! With your build, hell, it would be easy to mistake you for a man. He left for the mansion, but you followed him didn't you? The one man you loved, and you were gonna see him go down for it. You were done with even him!"

That got Talon flung against the wall again. Hilde yanked the departing humans back inside and re-closed the doors. Violet pulled the trick she tried on Shadow when she arrived, but it did nothing but make Hilde laugh. Violet got thrown yet again. Now she was with the gang groaning on the floor as bit after bit of plaster pelted them like some sort of freak hail storm. Now, she switched from attack, to defense. She used what energy and talent she had, to keep them shielded as best she could.

"B... BOSS!!" Abigail wailed. "PHONE! DISCO APP!!!" and that was all she could shout.

Thankfully, it was enough. Talon struggled to get his arm free, and took several painful shots doing it. He almost had it when Hilde, sent his phone flying. Lucinda kept fighting her, but was losing. She was furious but felt herself draining, and knew, that was exactly what Hilde wanted.

"Mista G! Whut kahn Ah dooo?" she pleaded looking for anything that would help.

"Muhsheen! Pick it up!..."

"What... what do Ah doo with it?"

Hilde went to snap it from her hands saying "Oh no yue don't Hure!"

Talon was getting pummeled and going down, So Lucinda did to him what Violet was doing to the others.

"Ah don't THINK SO!" Lucinda hollered pulling the phone away.

She was losing power, but had enough to keep the phone.

"Lucinda! See the pictures!?"

"Ah doo Ah doo, oooh Mista G how do ya work this new fangled thang!?"

"The one that looks like a ball of mirrors... (cough cough)... PRESS IT!"

Lucinda tried but put her hand through it. She couldn't go solid anymore without a 'full charge'. Slow down a solid however, that she could do. She waved at a few small chunks of plaster and sure enough, they came at her in slow motion. She put the phone up, and one of the chunks hit it just right and turned on the app."

"Mista G! Ah diid it!" Lucinda said all excited.

"Good now... GO!"

"But you'll be..."

"GO!!!!!!"

Lucinda didn't want to, but had a feeling Talon was up to something. She headed for the ether, and made it there only a second before the light show.

No less than 8 modified strobe balls lit up at once. It was the same type of light show Jeremy did when he dropped the orb. Abigail took it, figured it out, then built even more powerful ones. She didn't know why they worked on things like Lucinda, but figuring out how they worked was a breeze. So, she modified some standard dance lights one could get anywhere, tied them into the parlor, then made an app for Talon. She yelled to him because she noticed... he'd forgotten.

Hilde lost her grip, and was now struggling.

"vvvVVVVAHT IZZ THIS!?" she wailed.

Grant got up and he was hurting, but not as bad as his brother. One quick look to him was all he needed. Talon waved him off, and pointed to the rest. With Hilde frazzled now, he pushed the twin doors open with all he had.

"ZACK! (mmmff) GET 'EM OUTTA HERE!" and he kept the twin doors from closing.

Hilde was getting pissed, and now even more so at her party guests leaving. She tried to focus but couldn't. She was also, randomly, switching from solid to ghostly. Talon swung hard at just the right time and landed one punch to her gut, and it sent her tumbling back. Grant was getting crushed somewhat holding the doors open, but an expensive scuba suit saw to it it wasn't too badly.

Zack stumbled to his feet, and heard Eileen say "Get her outta here!" referring to Abigail. "I'm in far better shape than (cough) she is... now GO!!"

He did, and just as he got clear, Abigail wailed in terror.

"GRANT! NOOOOOOOOOOO!!!!!!!" as she saw him lose the battle with the door and get sucked back in.

She hobbled to a standing position... and 'told off' the night in no uncertain terms.

"I spent my whole life chasing you, or helping you! Now it's your turn! Dammit woman... GET ME BACK IN THERE!!!" Abigail hollered.

"I am not as strong as Miss Lucinda, dear one. I did what I could."

"Fat lot of good THAT did! You didn't even show up!" Abigail scorned at her great grandmother.

With kindness, the voice only said "Who do you think helped your love hold the doors open?" and granny Abigail was gone.

Now it was just the original team. Talon couldn't get to Violet, but, he was making sure Hilde didn't either. It was then, that he had a crazy thought, one he wasn't even sure would work. But, given current circumstances, he was willing to try anything. He made it to the stairs, got halfway up, and hollered at Hildegarde.

"HEY BITCH! Don't like the light show!? Well then... you've hated me perhaps most of all. Tell ya what... COME AND GET ME!!" and he ran up the stairs.

Talon half ran, half stumbled down the hallway. Hilde indeed followed him, and was throwing her arms side to side as she calmly walked behind him. Every time she did, pieces of the wall came out at Talon like timed explosions. One more swing up the half round staircase and he used the last of his speed to get him down the hallway.

"Lucinda!... (puff puff puff)... Keep the door open!" Talon commanded.

Hilde got to the door and tried crossing it. Some form of energy Talon couldn't see repelled her back every time she tried.

"Lucinda? I wanna try something. I'm asking you now to trust me." Talon stared at ghostly Hildegarde and said "I thought as much. Tell you what bitch, you want me? Fine by me. I, Talon Grayson, invite you Hildegarde Holliday, in for a one time chat."

"Are yue insane Mista G!!??" Lucinda bellowed.

Hilde sneered and walked through. Talon sneered right back.

"Thought as much," Talon said with delight that his plan worked.

"Vaht is dis!?" Hilde barked.

A 'solid' Hilde that is.

Talon told her with venom in his voice "I invited Hildegarde Holliday in... NOT Shadow Man. You, ya horrid bitch, are now as solid as I am."

Talon finished that sentence with a roundhouse kick and Hilde went flying across the barren room.

"MISTA G! You BRILLIANT MAHN you!" Lucinda hollered in sheer and utter delight.

"Time for a taste of your own medicine," Talon said as Hilde charged.

He was hurting and a tad sluggish, but he was on fire. He let her choke him, then popped his arms inside hers and threw hers away. He finished that maneuver with an elbow to her face and Hilde went stumbling back yet again.

She realized now she was the one in trouble, and bolted for the door. Talon however dove on her and tackled her.

"Leaving so soon?" Talon taunted as he dragged her back into the room. "Ya know? I don't think so," and he snapped her ankle.

It didn't break like he'd wanted it to, but it had her screaming in pain all the same. Talon came in for another strike but she played lame. Just as Talon got within reach, she hurled some ashes in his face from Lucinda's fireplace. Now Hilde crawled for the door but Lucinda shut it hard. Using strength Lucinda didn't anticipate, she managed to pull it open just enough to squeeze out... a mere two seconds before Talon reached her.

While Talon was going rounds with the bad lady upstairs, Cody was tending to the wounded.

"I'm good! See to Eileen!" Grant commanded.

He was on the floor and holding his side. Bad off as he was, he was in far better shape than his sister. Eileen was out cold. She had a concussion and a fractured shoulder blade.

Violet was on all fours and called over "Stay with (cough) her... I'm going after Talon!"

She tried getting up, but only made it back to all fours again. She felt the room spin just from that try alone. Thanks to the recharge of Talon's house, she wasn't as exhausted as the night she arrived. She was however, fast approaching it. That's when, a little intervention came her way.

"Violet... I need you to help me help them. NOW Violet... Smash the doll!" came a sweet voice from the ether that only she heard.

"Who... who are you?"

"No time for that now Violet... Shadow Man will return shortly. Break the doll Violet... SMASH IT NOW!"

Violet struggled to her feet. She was woozy as hell, but utterly defiant. "Who... are... you. I won't ask again."

Grant called out "Who... mmmff... who are you talking to Vi?"

"Soon as I find that out, I'll let you know."

The voice was exasperated and finally said "Did you enjoy the peace I left you my dear?"

Violet was stunned and said softly and lovingly "Diane!?"

"I need your help Violet. I wasn't strong enough on my own. I could keep them safe but not here. Without you all hope is lost. I need you Violet to help me now... so I may help them."

Violet was now not happy and said "Oh no no no no... I can't do that."

Mom was near frantic and said "Yes you can, I'll help you, but you must do it now Violet. Smash the damn doll!"

"I can't!" Violet protested through her tears.

"WHY!?"

She just let go and hollered out "BECAUSE I'M AFRAID!!"

Now mom was frantic, but kept a loving tone and told her "I can't do it alone Violet. It's why I summoned you. You're grandmother was wrong, you won't lose control. I promise you... I'll see to that."

Violet felt Shadow Man disappear. Now, she was feeling him return, and in a hurry. With no other option, and Talon in God only knew what form of danger... she did the one thing she was told never to do. Hildegarde returned in the form of Shadow Man and popped all the strobe lights one by one. The last thing Hildegarde saw before all hell broke loose on her, was Talon rushing in behind her... and Violet throwing something on the floor.

"Now... vere vehr we?" she taunted.

That was the last moment she would have any form of control.

A mist swirled around Violet from the ground to slightly over her head. Next, 3 children would get the shock of their lives. Violet appeared to have walked into a ghost... literally. There was something akin to a superimposed image surrounding her. It was an image none of the 3 remaining Grayson's thought they'd ever see again. Technically, in the room now, were 4 Grayson's...

not 3.

"I believe we were at the part where I tell you to leave my children alone!" the ghostly voice from Violet said.

Violet was feeling supercharged like never before. She could feel this other entity but, as promised, it was assisting her, not taking over.

"Oh look... zeh little freaks called for help... how touching." Hilde snorted at Violet and asked "Care to tell me who yuu are?"

Violet flung her arm and sent Hilde flying hard into the fireplace.

"Say hello... to the white witch!" and the ghostly apparition surrounding Violet came into focus.

"HAH! Eef dat iz deh best dey can do... you are all DEAD!" and Hilde headed straight for Violet.

Calm as could be, Violet let her come.

"vvvVVAHT! Dis iz not possibuhl!" Hilde barked as she got to Violet, and simply passed right through her.

"YOU! You cowardly wretch, have no idea what's possible." Violet turned to her and said "But... you're about to find out."

Grant was in disbelief. So was Talon.

"Mom!?" Talon asked in near shock.

Sweetly, the partial apparition said "Yes my darling Talon, it's me."

Now, mom went to work.

Mom swirled her hand at the fireplace. Suddenly, from a hearth that had no fire in it, a torrent of flame came pouring out into the room and formed a circle of fire.

Mom looked at Hilde and chanted "Blessed be... by the power of 3... I call forth justice for thee," and the flames shot across the floor and circled around Hilde.

She tried to get out of it, but hard as she tried, Hilde was trapped. Talon and the gang were hugging the walls and staying to the sidelines all that they could. The flame circled Hilde faster and faster and lifted her off the floor. Inside the ring, Hildegarde saw beings made of the fire, come out of the ring off and on... and they were chanting.

"NOOOOOooooo... BE GONE!" she wailed in shear pain as her apparition flailed wildly.

Those 3 beings of fire, were once... in life... 3 orphaned sisters.

"The power of Arella Adair is one we've hidden throughout the ages till it was needed. Tonight, is that time. Powerful as you are, you are no match for the original white witch. Momma Lady, will seal your fate, and for all times!" Violet's 'dual voice' hollered over the loud windy noise.

Suddenly, Hildegarde dropped to the floor, and rather ungracefully at that. She looked at herself however, in horror. She was solid again. This time however, the safety of the ether was no longer an option. Three powerful sisters saw to it that this time, she was stuck in Talon's realm for good.

"Talon my son, she no longer has the other realm to protect her. Feel free to show the murderess... just how good you are."

Talon sneered, and picked up Hilde by her collar. The power of the original white witch... made her solid once more.

"Love to," Talon sneered as he began to do in life, what Hilde had done to him from the ether.

He tossed her like a rag doll. Now solid, she was doomed, and it wasn't even Talon who would seal it. She fought back and Talon caught a few shots, but, since this night started, he was winning for a change. As he did, 'mom' seemed to go into a trance. Violet stood with her arms out as mom's ghost just chanted low and slow. What Talon didn't notice, was the black swirl forming at the bottom of the stairs. Hilde was a little busy to notice it too.

She managed to choke Talon with both hands again. He however, was defiant and grabbed her throat too. Then, with power Hilde couldn't match, Talon ran her into the fireplace. He pounded her into the stone bricks until she could no longer keep her grip. She crumpled to the floor and started to cry.

"I dint deezerv enny of dis," she said with true sadness.

"You murdered three people!" Violet chastised. "Then, you tormented for nearly TWO centuries more!" Mom's ghost told her "Even if Lucinda is partly to blame... you murdered an innocent AND unborn child! KNOWINGLY AND WILLINGLY!!"

Hilde looked to Cody with sad eyes and pleaded "You are my famlee... help me please my dear boy."

Cody looked on her in disgust and proudly stated "I am utterly ashamed to know that you truly are family. Grandmother Hildegarde?... I, Cody Holliday, hereby disown you."

Now Hilde had nothing left but her rage. Talon was closer but, for his words, she ran screaming with outstretched hands straight for Cody. He stood there and never moved, just to show her his true intentions.

"I VILL KILL YOU... I VILL KILL YOU ALL!!" she screamed. Inches from Cody however, she stopped hard and bellowed "Vat izz dis!? NO! LET GO OF ME! NOOOOOOOO!!!!!"

She screamed because, just shy of her great grandson... her wrists were now covered in handcuffs. Very old handcuffs. It would seem, Mom called forth Hilde's final justice. Three Pinkerton men... the same Pinkerton men who were once on a mural... had finally gotten their man. In this case a woman but, as they dragged Hilde screaming into the black swirling portal, one man tipped his hat to Talon with the kindest of smiles.

"Uncle Lucian wait!" Talon screamed.

The man stopped and looked at his spitting image.

"Thanks," Talon said honestly and solemnly. Then, in a term only Lucian would understand, Talon said "By the way, '...no hiding place'."

Another smile and a tip of his hat, Talon's own voice could be heard in another.

"No young man... thank you."

Lucian smiled, and was the last one into the vortex before it just faded away.

"Why don't we let your friends back in now shall we?" 'mom' said sweetly as she flung open the doors.

Abigail ran in and hugged Grant. Zack was just stunned.

"What the!? Violet!!" Abigail ran and tried to grab Violet.

"Whoa whoa whoa... it's okay Abigail," Grant said kindly as he pulled her back.

"But... but... who is she?"

"A pleasure to meet you my dear. My name is Diane. Grant will tell you more but... later."

Violet, still encased in Diane's ghost, walked over to the smashed doll, and picked up a small lock of hair. That was what many Garrison and Grayson women have protected throughout the years. It was Arella's and, she infused all her power into it before she died. Now, Diane began to explain.

"Talon my son, you grew up well," she said sweetly. "No one ever existed like Violet. Once I had found her, I did all I could to bring you together. Arella left all her power to us women, for the one time it would be needed." She turned sweetly to the picture over the fireplace, waved her hand inward, and nearly commanded "Why don't you join us my dear?"

Lucinda had arrived now. She was still weak but, she didn't show up on her own. She was truly summoned this time.

"Justice has been served. But even that is not complete. Arella has a message for you," and mom walked right out of Violet.

Still in ghostly form, she hugged each of her children. Eileen had woken by now and was quite groggy. One touch from mom, and a smile, and her head was clear.

"There. Now, you won't be needing the nice doctor's services this evening," Diane told her sweetly.

"Mom!?" Eileen said with tears in her eyes.

"Shh, my time here is short, and I must finish before I go," and she stood up and went back to explaining.

"Arella had the three orphans search for Lucinda. Once that fateful night occurred, the mansion was bought out by the Garrison's. It changed hands many times between them or the Grayson's. All of us tried to right what went wrong, but none were strong enough. Not until you three. Your father mentioned to me, with all the failures to date, perhaps it was time to try something new. He saw the potential in you three. It's also why I took you from this house. I couldn't let Shadow Man learn of our new plan."

Talon was awash in feelings, but managed to ask "So, I was right? There was a hidden agenda to your teaching us wasn't there?"

"Indeed there was my darling boy." She turned to Violet and said "Throughout the bloodline, we became the 'white witches' as we were called, in order to guide and protect those who came after us. That is why you my dear, felt me missing. Now... you know why. Shadow Man was strong... TOO strong. So with each passing woman, our powers were added to hers, in the hope that one day... it would become strong enough. I must leave now, so come quickly and give me a hug while there's still time."

All 3 without hesitation did just that.

They all felt the most intense feeling of love wash over them, and individually, each one said goodbye.

"Violet my dear... thank you. My husband was right," Diane said getting back up. "You were key to it all. The peace I left you will remain as long as there's a Grayson alive to live in it." She looked at them all and said "I was the one who helped put this little team together. Believe me when I say, even 'we' didn't know Shadow Man's true identity till this evening. By exposing her, you weakened her just enough to give us the edge we needed all these long years. You did beyond anything I could have hoped for... and I am more than proud of you all."

Now, she turned to Lucinda.

"Your mother has passed on. I managed to 'stay behind' but only long enough to help my children help you. The debt 3 orphaned girls owed to a unique lady has now been paid in full. Arella wanted you to know she loved you, in spite of what you did. She never meant to cause you any harm, and was truly sorrowful she did. You however, have a debt to pay of your own."

Lucinda was in tears, and asked "And whut wuud thaht be?"

"You consorted with a married man and knowingly committed adultery. Had you not, none of this would have likely happened. You loved this mansion and as such... you Lucinda... will guard over it until it is no more. You will also see to the safety of any innocent that comes inside it."

"Ah shall do as you ask. May Ah ask one smawl favuh?"

"What?"

"If you should see mah momma... tell her I said thank yue... and thaht Ah nevuh stopped lov'in her in return."

Kindly, Diane's entity said "She already knows my dear. She has one final gift for you," and Diane waved up the stairs.

Down came the shock of Cody's life... and the shock of Lucinda's afterlife. A gentleman in old clothes walked right up to Cody.

"I believe, that..." and he pointed to the pipe in Cody's hand "... is mine."

"H...He.... Henry!?" Lucinda asked not believing her eyes.

"You sir, caused more trouble than you were worth," Diane said admonishing him. "I said justice will be done. For you it has been. You will help Lucinda in her task, and help your great grandson in his. You will become the healer you were meant to be, and you shall never leave until Lucinda does. Then and only then... will your penance be served." She warned him "That sir, comes from a power far higher than me. Had you not lusted after Lucinda, none of this would have ever come to pass. Still, you were murdered too and some would say a fitting justice for your adultery. That decision however, also does not lie with me."

Henry bowed to her and told her "I will do as you have said."

"Do no harm, doctor... isn't that what the oath states?" Diane queried.

"It does indeed."

"See to it doctor... that THIS time... you don't."

Diane hugged her children individually, then, gave one each to the others. All except Violet.

"This my dear, will keep you safe for all your days," Diane's ghost said in the most loving of terms.

She touched Violet's forehead and all saw a faint glow for only a second.

"Cody? I leave my daughter in your hands. Abigail? I know the love in your heart... and the love in Grant's. I have no doubt that one day, you Abigail, will break your family curse." She turned back to Violet and said "The gift I gave you will be to always have control. For all your days, no evil of any kind, or realm, shall ever control you against your will. Thank you my dear." She looked at Talon and said "And you my son, know this. When you look into Violet's eyes, know that for all your remaining days, that look is genuine and given freely... and not because of me. Mind a piece of advice?"

Talon didn't want mom to go, but only said "From you? Always."

Diane smiled kindly as she started to fade away, and told him "See to it that she sees the same look in your eyes."

"You have my word on that... you marvelous 'hippie priestess' you."

Diane smiled once more, and said "Ya know? (giggle) I always did like that name."

Now, mom was truly gone and... finally at peace.

Violet was bawling, and staring at a now empty spot in the room.

"Do you remember when I told you all about the boat and the wake?"

Talon hugged her softly and asked "What about it?"

"That glorious woman just left one like I have never EVER felt in my life," and Violet just broke down in Talon's arms.

"Mista G suh?" Lucinda asked in the kindest of tones.

"Mm?" he asked looking up.

"There is an emptiness in this house now thaht Ah have nevuh known." She was sweeter than sweet and told him "It's a guud emptiness though. There haz awlways been a sense of malevolence in this house since thaht day. Now, theeruh is a sense of calm like Ah hahv nevuh felt. Y'all aruh a lucky mahn to hahv had such a mothuh. I jes wanted yue tuh know that."

Lucinda nodded to all the gang. Henry tipped his hat to them, and the two of them had love in their eyes as they started walking up the stairs.

"Lucinda?"

"Yes Mista G?"

"I hafta say... I'm looking forward to the coming days," Talon said with a grateful tone, and an equally grateful smile backing it up.

"As am I guud suh... as am I," and she and Henry faded away as they walked up the stairs.

The last thing all of them heard as they all started to file out... was the sound of an upstairs door slowly creaking closed.

Chapter 27

"Making I.C.E"

Talon called all the crews and told them there'd be no work on the mansion for at least a week. To cover his tracks, Talon told them a water line broke in the walls downstairs and up, and that he and Grant would be fixing it themselves. The plumbers were adamant it wasn't due to shoddy work, and were thankful when Talon totally agreed with them.

"There were some weak points in 2 of the pipes I had brought in. Nothing any of us could do and I don't blame you OR your crew. Any of us could have easily missed that," Talon told the lead plumber. "Suffice to say though, the damage has been done so, Grant and I will fix the walls, then, I will gladly pay for a full inspection if need be, once we have made repairs. We'll call you back in once we're ready to proceed. Trust me, this was bad luck... but no one's fault. I will certainly be calling you back to finish your work."

The plumber told Talon he was sorry for the accident, and was happy no one was hurt.

Also on Talon's orders... the mansion was off limits for 3 whole days. This job, and all it entailed, consumed him like no other. It also consumed everyone else... or nearly did. So it was nothing but 3 days of coming to terms with what happened, sort it out in each one's own way, and just recharge in general. Violet thought it touching how, for the 1st day, Talon wouldn't let her out of his sight.

Now, it was day 4, and all 3 siblings had the same idea. Everyone showed up at Eileen's house... and went to the group of elm trees.

"Violet?" Talon asked cautiously.

She smiled lovingly to them all, and stated "Now... all is as it should be."

Violet, and Talon, were referring to his previously 'never existed' mother.

Everyone took a turn thanking the hippie lady. Zack in particular.

Softly he spoke "I don't mind telling you, I'm sure glad you were there. Well, sort of anyway. I also don't mind saying, I'm still sorting that part out. Ya know Mrs. Grayson... my dad used to spew on and on about the great hereafter, and how one should live their life in the here and now so as to prepare for it. I never gave it much thought, till the other day. As I said, I'm still sorting some things out, and coming to terms with others. One thing... no, TWO things... I can tell you though. First, I will never be that spooked again. Second? Well, second is, I would have been proud to call you and your husband mom and dad... and not the one's I got. Your children were very lucky indeed."

Zack made an honest sign of the cross for the first time in years, then gave another a turn.

All had gone now, and headed back to the house. With kind and understanding looks, they left Talon alone to go last. Now all alone, he knelt down, and spoke in the most reverent and kindest of tones.

"Well lady... I almost don't know what to say. I will say this though. When I have my own children one day... I can only hope to be half the parent you were. You should have trusted me though. I don't blame you for not doing it, I'm just saying you should have. Still, in the end, I'm pretty sure it all worked out the way it was meant to."

He stood up, and gave the stone an update.

"I don't come here much. I want you to know, I'm changing that habit. Yesterday, Violet and I went and donated her backpack to a nice charitable organization. It was a symbolic thing I know but, it meant the world to us. I don't know where our relationship will go from here but... I truly look forward to finding out." He kissed his fingertips, then pet the stone lovingly, and finished with "All my thanks, and all my love... for all my days... you beautiful hippie priestess you."

Talon turned and walked away but, unknown to him, he wasn't quite finished yet. A huge breeze blew up just then, and a voice made him turn around.

A soft and kind whisper merely said "Missssssttaaaaa GGGGggggg."

Talon turned and saw, behind his mother's gravestone... a bush spring up into full bloom. It was a Gardenia bush.

"Awll our love, faw awll of ours as well," was the kind whisper.

Just as the breeze came... it went away just as quick. Talon smiled, tipped his hat to the sky, and walked back to his childhood home.

"Jeez, hehehe, look at us!" Abigail laughed slightly. "Aren't we a sorry looking bunch!?"

She said that because, everyone was sporting bruises, bandages, and walking around almost as badly as Addie did.

Talon truly felt bad, and sadly said "Yeah well, if it wasn't for my own stupidity... none of you would be as bad off as we are."

Eileen kindly told him "Don't beat yourself up over it Tal. You had no way of knowing what would happen."

"But I should have. I was the one who told all of you Shadow was getting stronger. My apologies to you all for that one. I will say this though, it won't happen again. Consider the other night... lesson learned."

Zack was reflective, and said "I for one, am gonna miss it."

Grant chuckled, but even that had a slight grimace to it.

"Ha ha ha, miss what... getting your ass kicked!? Tell ya what, once we're 100% again, I'll ask my brother to take you to the mat for a few rounds."

Even Zack laughed at that one.

"No seriously though, I mean, I won't miss 'that'. Trust me, I'm still coming to terms with the other night. Don't lie cuz I can see it on all your faces, so are all of you."

Cody told him "I won't say I disagree with you old friend, but, what exactly are you gonna miss?"

"This... all this," Zack said slowly waving about. "In all my years of doing what I do, and as good as I got, I almost gave it up. Usually it's some sleazy guy or gal looking for an inheritance. Or some crazy cat lady obsessing over 'who she was'. It was actually getting boring, or just downright annoying."

Violet smiled softly and told him "I sense a 'but' coming."

"Indeed," Zack confirmed. "The 'but' is, working with all of you has been the best time of my life. You all support each other, and act like a family... not just blindly follow some deranged tyrant. Working with all of you, was like being in the family I never had. Plus... there was a noble purpose to my work. I felt like, I dunno, like there was an urgency to it or something. Hard to describe but, I think you get my point."

"I'll say..." Abigail chirped in with, "... I know we're all coping with what happened in our own way. Me? I spent a day in my grandmother's room. Now, I'm not like Violet is but, all I could feel was a sense of emptiness. I reconfigured the security cameras, optimized the sat-link feeds... and was bored out of my mind. Like Zack said, I felt like I had a purpose as well. Like, what I did really mattered and had truly mind blowing consequences if I failed."

Talon said nothing, and just watched as the conversation took on a life of it's own. It made him smirk seeing the gang get all 'fired up' just like they described they had been.

Violet finally spoke up saying "I know how you all feel. What you're all describing, is two things... family... and purpose. I never knew any sort of family except for my grandmother." She looked at the 3 Grayson's and said "Aside from Talon, none of you have really known 'true love' till just recently. So I guess what I'm saying is, we're all feeling down because, we all finally had what we've all sought for so long. You all know damn well, that mansion's mystery was the glue that held it all together. Now, ALL of us are like... now what?" She sat next to Talon and gingerly hugged him saying "At least, that's how I see it."

Abigail had a look on her face akin to an epiphany.

"Oh my God Violet... that's it! I mean, I knew that and agree with you, but, I just couldn't put it into words."

Talon still had said nothing. He'd had his fill of being boss for awhile, and was just being Talon now. Finally, he interjected his own 2 cents. It made him laugh inwardly however, as everyone stopped and focused on him.

"Sorry computer girl but... heh heh heh... I'm all out of cold cases."

Now Abigail had another epiphany. She beamed, practically ripped out her phone, and went diving into some sort of search. Talon had a questioning smile on his face as he stared at his brother.

"Don't ask," Grant laughed, "I've learned to ignore it and just wait."

Zack honestly told Talon "Well... if you did... you could count me in."

Before Talon could quip some smart answer, Cody chimed in just as seriously saying "And me as well."

Now, the proverbial snowball started rolling downhill.

Eileen said "Odd as this sounds coming from me... I'd join you."

Talon chuckled and said "Oh now THIS is something I want to hear!"

Eileen had faraway eyes and said "Until the other night, I was okay with my relationship with mom. Call it survivors guilt, or whatever. Bottom line is, I can't help but think how much she, and all the others, put into this endeavor. While I can't say she sacrificed her own children to this family project, and to right a major wrong, I also can't up with a better word for it."

Talon knew better and asked "And?"

Eileen told him "If you had... another case I mean... well, can you think of any better way to honor a woman like her?"

"I can't" Violet stated kindly and honestly.

"Nor I," Cody said wholeheartedly.

"Ya won't hear me disagree," Zack stated truthfully.

Talon and Grant just smiled at each other... and raised a hand each.

"I CAN!!" Abigail beamed with joy as she finally pulled her face out of her phone. "Look!!!" and she showed her phone... to Talon.

"Um... oookay?" gray guy asked having no clue.

"Jeez boss... look! They're all cold cases!"

"Heh heh heh... I can see that. Your point?" Talon queried.

Abigail just laid out her thoughts.

"Look around you. Yes this was your house once but it was HER house first! I can't think of any better place to have come up with this," Abigail said with pride. "Think about it boss. I mean, I look good in that old style dress but, being a hostess isn't exactly something I wanna do for the rest of my life. Why not use the mansion for what you originally intended!? Except, now, and... to honor her... we can help others. Charge a reasonable fee but, look at us!? If we could solve this one... we could solve ANY one!" Abigail said in her usual perky and dorky way.

Now, the conversation took off yet again.

"I know you spent a lot of money on my lab Talon," Doc confirmed. "And, it would seem, a certain 'elderly' doctor has some sins to atone for. I for one think it would be a shame to just let it all go to waste."

Eileen totally agreed with Abigail "I could setup my new company a little earlier than planned but, you could be my first client!" Eileen stated as uncharacteristically pumped up as the others.

Still laughing slightly at this odd turn of events, Talon asked "Well 'Ginjuh Chyld'... what say you?"

Grant was calm but determined.

"Talon look, when you setup your company, you know you made some mistakes that you learned from. We all did. Well... that said... I'd say this one had a few. Even if not mistakes, there were definitely lessons learned in how not to do something, or how to do it better. Odd as this might sound coming from me... I kind'a miss it too. I don't know how much help I'll be but, count me in for anything that you need." Grant was soft and said "If it wasn't for mom... I'd be attending your funeral right now or worse, joining you. What did Addie tell you? Do big things? I can't think of anything bigger than that... and no better way to honor our heritage... and mom."

While Talon almost didn't believe what he was hearing, he also wasn't disagreeing with any of it. He was perhaps the most 'busted up' of all of them. Still, he understood in a way the others didn't about the new hole in his life. Still, one more person needed to weigh in.

"Well Miss Hayes... you out of all of us were the most reluctant to join in our little adventure. I also can't say it wasn't without good reason. What do you say to all of this?"

Violet was sweet and kind and told them "I had nothing but a lousy life on the run. No one to hold, and no one to hold me. Some stranger I never met pulls me into the biggest whirlwind of my life, but... I wouldn't have missed it for the world. I have a love I couldn't have imagined, powers I'm still not sure of, and even though it's an 'adopted' one... I finally have a family and a place where I belong. Anywhere... and anytime... the ether returns? I'll be wherever you need me to be, lending whatever help or support I can give." Violet finished in the kindest of tones with, "I owe 'her' that much at least."

Talon mused at how, hurting as he was, he was liking the idea too. He wouldn't tell anyone, not even Violet, but... he'd felt a sudden hole in his life too. Talon however, went back to being Talon again.

"Alright how about this then? We do one... maybe two the most... then see how we feel. Even if we did only one of those, it would still honor mom. Maybe we don't fix the world, but, we'll certainly give some deserving people some peace they may not have gotten otherwise. Also, we don't advertise this on the main mansion. A small sign perhaps but, I want that to be not only our 'base of operations', but our haven as well... got it? Under the radar, or your little ghost club can find another home."

"Got it!" were the multiple happy responses.

Talon just grinned, hung, and shook his head.

"Like I once said at the beginning of this little saga... ha ha ha … good Lord what have I gotten myself into!?"

Talon would indeed find out. What he thought would only be a few jobs at best... would turn into a lifelong passion.

Talon laughed and said "You're all doing that staring thing again," referring to everyone looking to him.

"Well?" Abigail nearly chirped.

"Well what? Heh heh... 'Abby Gale'."

Abby actually smiled, and proudly stood up and addressed the group.

"As the new member of this cold case team , I saaaaaaay," and she playfully giggled, and stared straight at Talon and said "We need a name!"

Everyone else was still staring, and smiling, and nodding... at Talon.

"Ha ha ha ha ha... ow... why do I get to choose!?" he replied.

"You're the boss that's why," Grant teased.

Talon joked back "Ooh ooh... I know... we'll call it... 'You're All Out Of Your Fucking Minds Incorporated'," and he laughed as everyones expressions just soured on a dime.

Grant joked and hollered out "Hey I know... how about 'The G-Team'!?"

Eileen chuckled, waved about the outdated living room they were all in, and said "Oh... that would be groovy man."

Grant teased back "I see you're feel'in my vibe babe."

Talon laughed and, before the suggestions got even worse, he said "I thank you for the honor. I'll come up with some ideas, then we all vote on it. How does that sound?"

Violet smiled and said "That sounds groooooovy man, I totally dig it," and everyone laughed.

Zack now got serious and said "Violet?"

"Mm?"

He told her "One way I found to cope the last few days, was to dive into some work. I guess it was because, of all the illogical and irrational of the last few days... I needed something 'less so' to balance it out."

"Well, while that makes sense, why tell me?" Violet questioned.

"For trying to keep us safe, I uh... have a present for you," Zack told her as he handed her a folder that was nearly overflowing. "It's just preliminary but, that's you."

"You call this preliminary!?" Violet laughed seeing the huge pile. "Thank you though... uh … I think. What is it?"

"You Violet. That's your dad, mom, and even your grandmother. I'll follow any trail in there you want but, I thought that would at least get you started. I truly hope it helps," Zack said with true friendship in his voice.

Violet was pleasantly stunned, and gave him a loving hug. He saw Talon for a second. That man had a kind smile on his face and gave him a nod that just seemed to say 'thanks'.

It was the following day, and Talon got serious now, and pulled out Lucian's book. They were all back in Virgina City... and behind the church.

"And you dragged us here why exactly?" Eileen scorned slightly.

"I want each of you to read this, then, sign your name at the bottom please," and he handed it to Cody first. "I made a small box from the carbon fiber scraps we had left. I want you to know... I'll be burying that book with him," Talon told the entire assembled group.

Abigail told him sweetly, "I think it's a fine idea."

Cody read it, smiled kindly and asked Talon "Wouldn't happen to have a pen, now would you?"

Talon just pulled one out and clicked it. Cody signed his name with pride, and passed it to Eileen. Each one read it in turn, and passed it on to the next till it came back to Talon. To honor Lucian... he signed it last. Something happened after he finished, and it just made him smile. All 3 Grayson's then picked up a shovel, and dug a small but deep hole in front of the gravestone.

Talon told them all as he dug "My way of dealing with the last few days, was this stone behind me. Lucian had a simple marker and, well, I wasn't going to stand for it. If it wasn't for him giving us the help he did, we would still be scratching our heads, and Violet would be hitching on some highway somewhere right about now. I've developed a huge respect for the man, and felt he deserved nothing less. For all he did for me, and later 'us', I felt it was the least I could do. So... I had this one put in to replace the old one."

Talon was right, the original one was just as plain as he said. The new one now had a cross on top, and a huge plaque area below for his name, the date, and a little something else. The whole stone stood almost as tall as he did.

"And the rock cried out no hiding place?" Eileen asked as she read the inscription. "Mind telling me why you had that put there?" she asked truly curious, but not in an admonishing way.

"Don't mind at all," Talon said nicely. "Lucian's book had one last line in it. It was only a piece of one really. Took me a bit to figure it out too. All he wrote was the first half... 'And the rock cried out...'. It's actually a line from a hymn. Zack found his name on a lot of the church's records, so it's a fair bet he was a religious man. That's why I had the cross put on top."

Zack interjected "He stayed here in Virginia City till he died. Back then there was no pension or anything like that. So, to help him, and keep him close, they made him a Deputy Marshall. He held that post till he passed away."

Talon picked back up with "The full line is there on the stone. It's a song about ultimate justice where even the rock itself told the bad guy there was no hiding place, even here. It was Lucian's way of saying he was a Pinkerton man even in death and that one day, somehow, he'd see justice done. Basically... it was a warning from the grave."

Eileen chuckled in a nice way and declared "Do we have some bad-ass people in our family or what!?"

Talon looked over the small but tight-knit group and answered kindly, "Candlestick? You'll get no argument from me."

Eileen was referring to the historical... while Talon chose the present.

Talon put the book in the box, pulled out a small bicycle pump, and closed the lid.

"There's no lock or hinge," Eileen slightly protested, "How are you gonna keep that from getting ruined?"

"Simple science my dear sister," Talon said confidently.

He hooked the pump to a small valve he buried in the side, and started pumping till he could pump no more.

"I rigged this pump to suck air out, not blow air in. Go ahead..." and Talon tossed it to her saying "... try and open it."

Eileen really tried, but couldn't. Now pleased at her rather clever brother, she handed it back with a kind smile.

"That, dear brother, will do nicely."

Talon placed it in the hole, then all 3 covered it up. They all made some sort of sign of respect, and filed away one by one.

Sealed for all times, with the man who wrote it, was the book he treasured throughout his life. There was one final page... a new page... and it was written in Talon's handwriting. It read...

[We the undersigned, do hereby declare, that on the 15th of July, 2015... we can now say to you, Lucian Garrison... 'mission accomplished'. We could not have done it without your help, and thank you ever so much for the same. Rest in peace dear uncle and friend, and know that when you do, you're one and only failure has been turned into a resounding triumph.]

There were 9 names written below... not 7. What caused Talon to smile when he finished signing his name, was he saw 2 new one's appear. They were Henry Holliday, and Lucinda Adair. As Talon walked away with Violet and the rest, they all heard the faint sound of a team of horses pulling a coach, and what sounded like Talon's voice hollering 'heeyah'.

A few days later, and the mansion was a flurry of activity once more. It was only the cold case gang, but everyone was pitching in. Eileen and Abigail were putting plaster on the walls, just like Grant showed them. He and Zack were putting up new lath boards and smoothing out the walls. Talon was outside planting some evergreens, and Cody was using Zack's office to make arrangements for Henry's exhumation. Violet was busy mopping and cleaning the wood floors, and straightening up the living room. It was coming along nicely, when the FedEx truck pulled up the driveway.

"I'm looking for a Mister, uh," and he checked his clipboard, "A mister Talon Grayson?"

"That would be me. What can I do for you?"

"Special delivery for you sir... I need your signature here, here, aaaand here please."

Talon saw a box, and immediately knew who it was from, just by its size and shape.

"There ya go pal," Talon said as he switched the clipboard for the box the delivery guy was holding.

"This is some place ya got here Mr. Grayson. Oh wait, now I know this place... this was that mansion the news channel did a piece on isn't it?"

"One and the same," Talon answered with pride.

"You're a lucky man to have such a place." The guy laughed slightly and said "I know I wouldn't mind if someone left me a place like this."

Talon nicely told him "If you knew what I've been through since I got it, you might just change your mind." Talon looked up for a moment, at a third floor window, smiled softly, and said "Ya know what? Maybe you wouldn't."

"Is it okay if I look inside?" the man asked. "The news article said you would eventually rent it out. My grandparents 50th wedding anniversary is next year and all of the family is pitching in for it. If it's affordable, I'd love to rent the place out."

Talon realized, now would be a good time to imitate Phil, and did just that. He took him in and showed him a little bit, but told him other areas were under construction still and just not safe yet. The driver totally understood. He thanked Talon for the tour, said he'd talk to his family, and be back with a deposit and a date later in the week if they agreed.

Talon was digging a hole to put in a fencepost with a sign on it. It was to be temporary, and it was laying on the ground.

"Here, let me give you a hand with that," the driver said kindly as he gave Talon a hand putting it in the hole. He read the sign aloud and said "Adair House, opening soon... and the new home of I.C.E." He asked jokingly "What's that, some sort of new fraternity?"

Talon chuckled with him and said "Hardly."

"So then... what's it stand for?"

"It stands for Investigative Civilian Enterprise... I.C.E for short."

"Sounds cool!" the man quipped nicely.

"Ha ha ha... son? You have noooooo idea!" Talon laughed.

The driver headed out. Just before the end of the driveway, he rung out his ears. He could have sworn he heard a woman tell him, softly, "Y'all come back now ya hear?"

He turned onto the road, shook his head, and stated to no one "Oh this is gonna be some party indeed!"

Talon walked into the house with box in tow. He walked right to the fireplace, looked up, and asked the photo above it a question.

"Miss Adair? Would you like this to be hung here? Or back where I found it?" he asked in a very gentlemanly manner.

Everyone stopped working for a moment and focused on Talon.

"Why Mista G... whut is it?" the voice all could hear asked.

Talon said nothing, he merely sported a huge grin... and pulled out the contents in the box.

"While Ah cunsidduh mahself a modest woman... Ah think ryte theyuh, will doo jus fine. One might say, I hahv beecum uhkuustumd to tha response it seems ta get," Lucinda told him sweetly.

Talon smiled and asked "Grant? Would ya mind?"

"On it," and Grant put a concrete bit into a drill.

He and Talon drilled into the mortar and put in two concrete screws. The photo, with a small and playful ceremony, came down.

"Lucinda? Henry?" and Talon looked kindly to his sides saying "Latest members of I.C.E?" then back up to above the hearth and finished with "Let me be the first to say... welcome back... and welcome home."

When he finished, the Grand Dame, and the finally and fully restored painting, frame and all... went up for all to see.

It would hang there, in that very spot, for many years...
and many adventures to come.

The End?

{See Talon and all the I.C.E gang in the next book
titled "Modder - Dancer - Tower – I.C.E"}